DAVID *the* KING

GLADYS SCHMITT

DAVID *the* KING

ENGRAVINGS BY CATHAL O'TOOLE

DIAL PRESS · *NEW YORK* · 1946

Printed in the U.S.A. at
The Country Life Press, Garden City, N. Y.

TO MY
MOTHER
AND
FATHER

BOOK ONE

BOOK ONE

BOOK ONE

❧ I ❧

ALL DAY the sheep had been skittish with mating, but now it was night and the last of the stragglers had been dragged back under the first of the stars. Two fires had been kindled against the lions. One burned near the three shepherds who slept with their cloaks over their faces. The other snapped and smoked near the spring, in the little niche of rock and vine and glimmering water where David, the youngest son of Jesse, spent his nights.

He lay on his back with his lute across his belly, and now and then, simply to spend a little of the restlessness left over from the excitement of the day, he reached down and pulled at one of the strings. The instrument vibrated subtly against him and roused a kind of delicious creeping in his skin. The tones—sweetly inconsequential, rich in possibilities that did not imply the responsibility of pursuit—burst against the quietness. If he wished to make a song, here was a rich combination that he could build upon; but he was too exhilarated for songs tonight. He would lie idle in the niche with the everlasting water trickling near by. He would lie remote, above dull sheep and the dull keepers of sheep, a poet with his lute, contemplating the vast pageantry of the firmament.

He closed his eyes and called up an image of himself: David, the son of Jesse, in his seventeenth year, stretched out on a cloak alone in the night, slender, young, and fair. Long limbs to chase the errant ram—no matter, someday they would be swift in battle. A pale skin—the sun, loving it, had touched it with the mild gold of honey. Wide eyes—what dreams, what knowledge withheld from the common run of men had deepened those wide gray eyes? He saw his own thick hair spread out around his face. Now, with the firelight moving upon it, it looked red indeed. He saw the whole fine, long length of him, including the lute. Then it struck him that the lute was ridiculous there across his belly, and he laid it on his chest. True, he had to strain to reach it there, but the picture was good: David the poet, lying between earth and heaven with his lute against his heart.

The next three tones linked themselves together into a mournful progression, and he made up his mind not to forget them; they would be very useful if there was ever need for an elegy. Elegy on the death of King Saul . . . No, Jahveh forbid, may the King of Israel live for a thousand years! Elegy for a great bowman . . . The music, growing in spite of him, took on a poignant air. "A mighty bow, a bow of oak, anointed with the sweat of your hand, O my brother Eliab. I have touched your fingers, and they are dry in death. . . ." He started and flushed. To pack his own brother off to Sheol for the sake of a song! He was fond of his brother, and it was comforting to think that Saul's armies were not in the field, were celebrating the Feast of the New Moon in the ancient city of Gilgal. It was the second day of the festival, and Eliab would be sitting at a table heaped with the burnt meat of the sacrifice. There would be talk of war and high deeds, and the sound of the holy Jordan, flowing near the city, would wash continually above their speech. To eat at the table of the great, to hear the women of Gilgal sing an antiphonal song in praise of the brave . . .

He was roused out of his dream by a stirring in the brush—the immemorial call to fear that had roused all herdsmen from the days of Abraham. A lion? He was on his feet. Below him, beyond the sleeping shepherds and the huddled flock, he could see the outline of tangled brush and thorn. It moved, but there were no twin yellow fires there. A patch of white, the skirt of a tunic, caught the light of the stars.

"May your bowels wither!" he said under his breath. And then, in the dignified tones of a false calm, he asked aloud: "Who is it? Who is there?" There was only a gurgling, familiar laugh such as can be heard after an evil jest when shepherds talk of women at the gates and knowing boys stand by. "Joab?" he said.

The twelve-year-old boy leaped out of the thicket, bounding, and roaring deep in his throat. He held two long blades of grass in his mouth; they stuck out on either side of his face, farther than his ears. He pointed at the grass. "Whiskers. I am a lion," he said.

"You are an ass and the son of an ass."

"The son of your sister," he said, grinning, and settled himself cross-legged at David's feet.

These sudden visits of Joab's took place two or three times a year. They began pleasantly enough, but if they lasted for more than a day or two they left a bad taste, like the end of the wine. Joab was not used to towns and houses. His father, an Ishmaelite, had spoiled him by dragging him for months on end across the desert routes. He was forever yearning after open vistas, distant cities, and jingling caravans. Tonight he looked the desert rat that he was, with a golden crescent dangling against his brown cheek, with his hair twisted into outlandish ringlets, and with God knows what monstrous lies ready to tumble from his lips.

"Why have you come up to the hills in the middle of the night?" David said.

4

"Could I sleep in the house of Jesse without a sight of David? I have bruised my soles and scratched my shins on thorns to behold your face, O Star of Bethlehem."

David kicked at the fire. One broad yellow band of flame unfurled and lighted the dusky, exotic face. "See, I have brought a gift for my uncle." The eyes of the little Ishmaelite were lustrous and tender.

David surrendered himself to the nimble fingers, which laid some light and slender thing in his hand. It was a statuette of a woman carved from pale stone—a woman with a thin body and young, high breasts. A serpent was coiled around her legs, and she suckled two doves. Longing burst in him like tone in the body of a lute.

"What is her name?" he said.

There was no answer except the knowing laugh. Joab was rocking back and forth in obscene merriment, clasping his knees against his chest. What David held in his hand was a heathen image, the likeness of an abomination, the body of the Canaanitish passion goddess whose name was Astarte. David said that name aloud and flung the lust-provoking thing into the fire.

"No matter," said Joab. "I will pull her out when you are gone."

"I do not mean to go."

"Oh, you will go." Joab lay on his back and clasped his arms beneath his head. "There is a thing I was sent to tell my uncle."

"What were you sent to tell me, you son of a desert dog?"

"Son of my uncle's eldest sister. I came to say that Eagle-Nose is abiding this night in your house."

"Who?"

"Eagle-Nose. Samuel."

"Samuel?" The name was a thunderous reprimand. For Samuel was God's man, a man of frequent prophecy in an age when Jahveh was tight-fisted with His visions, a strong destroyer of heathen groves, an uprooter of trees sacred to the Baals and Astartes. His face had risen, white and holy as the new moon, on every town in Judah, Ephraim, and Benjamin. His eyes saw beyond the hour and the year; unborn generations revealed themselves to his sight. Many times he had been thrown down in the high places of the cities by the force of his visions, and the foam of prophecy was often upon his lips. If the house of Jesse was more blessed than other houses in Bethlehem, it was because Samuel sat often in the common room. . . . David stared at the hand that had held the Astarte and wiped it upon his tunic; but the creeping would not leave his flesh, and he was afraid.

"Samuel. None other. If only my uncle could have seen him! He had fallen into a fit on the way, and it was said that he prophesied. O my uncle, if you could have seen him! There was spittle on his beard and dust on his face. Well, no matter, I see that you are angry. They have cleaned him and dressed him, and he has sacrificed a three-year-old heifer, and you are to go home, and I am to look after the sheep tonight."

David turned aside from the evil little face that grinned in the firelight and stared at the remote, moon-washed edges of the hills.

"Let my uncle forgive me," said Joab. "If I brought an abomination, it was only to give my uncle a dream of delight."

"Let us speak of it no further."

"Kiss me farewell."

"Tomorrow, not tonight."

He turned from Joab then and walked past the huddled flock, past the thicket, and onto the road that showed white in the wan light. He stopped on a little hillock and looked over his shoulder. Joab, with a shepherd's crook in his hand, was fishing about among the flames—no doubt in search of the little Astarte.

⋞ II ⋟

HE CAME to the town through shrubbery and shale, up the side of a lime-stone crest. He could measure the lateness of the hour by the silence. The dull, earthy buildings, washed pale in the light of the moon, stared at him with lightless windows. The watchman at the gate nodded wordlessly as he passed. The streets were unpeopled and still. Only here and there, near some walled garden or on some doorstep, the pariah dogs, dun-colored like the wilderness from which they had come, dug in the day's waste or chewed upon bones. It had been a feast day, and in many houses there had been sacrificial meat.

The house of Jesse was more commodious than most. There was a walled garden before it, and two trees stood near the garden gate, a fig and a pomegranate, both in bloom. David had thought to find his father and the seer in earnest conversation on the bench beneath the fig, but the garden was empty. No light shone from any of the windows, and for a moment it seemed to him that the whole household slept. Then he heard voices—Samuel and Jesse talking solemnly, eagerly, on the roof, above the sleeping town. He broke a bit of blossom from a low bough, thrust it behind his ear, and mounted the ladder which led to the roof.

All round the roof, save where the ladder touched, there was a parapet of sun-baked brick as high as a man's waist; but the center of the roof was open to all the light in heaven. There in the brightness the seer and his father sat, with a black goat's-hair rug at their feet and a bowl of curds and a loaf between them. Their heads were close to each other, and their beards and hair were a flowing whiteness under the moon.

"But in this matter of Agag I could no longer deceive myself. I have seen at last where the King's heart lies," Samuel said, and then broke off, seeing that David was standing beside the parapet.

"David?" said Jesse in a voice which told all who cared to listen that "David" meant "darling" and that he who bore the name was truly the beloved.

6

"Yes, my father."

"Come, David, and let us see your face," said the prophet.

He came forward, looking down discreetly, knelt, and waited to be blessed. The scent of the old man's body was faint, holy, and desolate, like a sanctuary long closed. The dry lips set a kiss upon his brow. "May Jahveh walk beside you and above you and below you," Samuel said. David looked up then and saw the face of the seer—the jutting nose, the hollow cheeks, the skin cracked like sun-dried clay into minute and delicate crevices.

"Have you eaten, David?" said Jesse. "There is meat below."

"At sunset, my father, I ate bread and cheese and wine. Let me tarry with my father and my lord."

They nodded and turned from him, the two old men, and began their eager talk again. They spoke softly, in secretive voices; but he could not rid himself of the thought that whatever they said was meant for his ears. Now and then he could see beneath their half-closed eyelids that their glances were turned in his direction.

"We were in the midst of this matter concerning Agag, the King of the Amalekites," Jesse said.

But that was not called for, David thought. Even a shepherd boy in the wilds of ignorant Judah knows that Agag is King of the Amalekites. It was like drawing a lesson in the sand for a child. . . . He remembered his brother Eliab saying, "Behold, Israel has two enemies, and one lies to the south, and its name is Amalek, and the other lies to the west, between us and the sea, and its name is Philistia. And therefore Israel has no peace."

"I was not at the battle, Jesse," Samuel said. "Saul would not have me there. He spoke to me of the number of my years, he reminded me of the long march and the harshness of the camp, he said it was best for my sake and for Israel's that I should tarry at home."

The boy closed his eyes and saw the day of the setting-forth for battle. The pearly light of sunrise whitened the mist that floated over the assembled host. From the springtime fields in the valley below Ramah, the faces of the warriors were uplifted toward the hill and the town, waiting in charged silence for the benediction. And among them were all the faces of the mighty, dream faces that obsessed a shepherd in the mean and peaceful hills of Judah—blunt face of Abner, captain of the host; ardent face of the young Prince Jonathan; legendary face of Saul, black-bearded face bent to comfort a prophet whose battle days were over long ago.

"And you?" said Jesse.

"I? What can an old man say to those in their prime who pity his infirmity? Am I to run after a departing army? *He* willed that I should stay in Ramah, and in Ramah I stayed, to the belittling of Jahveh and the everlasting shame of Israel."

"But it is said in Judah that Israel and Jahveh had a victory . . ."

7

"A victory?" Some of the brazen clang of earlier years sounded in the prophet's voice. "Saul had a victory. The city of Amalek fell and was burned with fire, and the fields round about it are cinder and ash, it is true. But Jahveh? Jahveh was despised in Amalek, and the heathen King Agag was preferred above Him."

"But it was said that Agag was slain."

"Yes, but by whom was Agag slain? By Saul? No, now, why should Saul slay him? There is a business between kings, a nudging of elbows, a winking of eyes. For if a hair is plucked from one kingly head, what king under the firmament can sleep without a bodyguard around him? Saul strike Agag? No, not with a feather. In a lordly house he housed him, nor was he displeased in the least when the heathen made it known that he wished to pay court to the only daughter of the King of Israel."

"Then," said Jesse in wonderment, "he was not slain?"

The wrinkled face was strained by the coming of a smile. "He is slain. I slew him. On the black altar stone at Gilgal I slew him with a sword, and he is as a burnt bullock at the feet of our God."

It was said softly, yet it was as a battle cry in the ears of the listening boy. He heard, with closed eyes, the whispered manner of it. He saw Saul and Samuel waiting inside the ancient circle of black monoliths that the host of Joshua had raised beside the river Jordan—Saul in the black robes of a penitent, with ashes on his beard and hair, and Samuel in the white robes of the invulnerable, the beloved of the Lord. He saw Agag summoned from the presence of the King's daughter, guessing the reason for the summons, his cheeks gray against the gold earrings, his jeweled fingers faltering at his lips. What was it he had said when his eyes found the sacrificial blade? Strange words of obscure meaning, question without an answer: "Surely the bitterness of death is past." In the scarlet of his kingliness, he laid his head upon the stone and accepted the falling sword.

"And what of Saul?" said Jesse timidly, peering under frosty brows at the other's rapt face. The boy's mouth tightened. How commonplace, he thought, is my father's voice.

"I have departed utterly from Saul," the prophet said.

Try as he would, David could not keep a discreet face. His lips parted in astonishment. If Samuel had gone out from Saul, then Jahveh also had departed. The Lord of Hosts no longer reigned in Israel. . . . Upon all three of them, huddled there on the roof in the white square of light, the terror and the strangeness of it fell. The minute was wordless and desolate.

"Woe!" said Jesse in a voice too feeble for the occasion. He looked uneasily toward the mountains of Moab, visible through a cleft in the far hills. "Who knows what will be?"

"I know what will be," the prophet said.

They waited, and the waiting was drawn out in utter stillness. "There will be another king in Israel and Judah," Samuel said, and turned slowly, almost imperceptibly, toward David, without veiling his deep, shadowless eyes. "Jahveh has had His fill of strong men and warriors. He has known the insolence of the lion, and He has asked for a lamb." The ash-dry hand of the prophet moved through moonlight. Groping like the hand of the blind, it came upon David's hair. "I have seen it. The lion will claw at the rocks of Gilboa, and the gazelle will perish by a spear, and the hour of the lamb will come, yet the lamb will weep." The brittle finger found the boy's cheek and drew upon it a strange tracery, the course of an un-shed tear. "A lamb, a lamb, Jahveh will have a lamb," the prophet said.

David saw that the foam of prophecy was upon Samuel's lips. Jesse had risen, and Samuel had fallen forward like a sick child, his face against Jesse's knees.

"No, now, my brother, no, now, my heart's beloved," Jesse chanted, crouching to embrace the seer and rocking back and forth like an old woman. "It is enough. You have been with Jahveh all this day. Come now, and sleep."

Without a glance for David, they rose together and crossed the roof, shaking and leaning against each other. In the band of shadow near the parapet, against the vast night, they looked very small, very old. The voice of Jesse went on crooning senseless, soothing things, speaking of sleep and a soft bed. But for David that night there was no sleep.

⌘ III ⌘

For the first time in his life, David was glad to see the end of the Feast of the New Moon. With Samuel's departure toward Ramah at dawning, high purpose had gone from the occasion. With Joab's return from the hills, a sense of chaos broke in. There were too many people in Jesse's house; Zeruiah, the fat mother of Joab, was in every conversation and in every room, and David's whole body was tensed against her per-vasiveness. As for her son, from him there was no deliverance and with him there was no peace. He was a dog of the wilderness who could not be put off by subtleties, but so subtle a dog that nobody but Cain could kick him. "My uncle has not kissed me." And the brown fingers held over the wounded heart, and between the wounded heart and the tunic, a certain bulge which could be nothing except the accursed little Astarte. "By sun-set I will be gone; so wheresoever my uncle goes this day, let me go also." But a man must have at least an hour's privacy, he thought. There are high thoughts which I may not even name to myself while you are in the room —you and your mother jabbering about the wonders of Shechem, you and she and half a dozen neighbor women come in to celebrate a sacred feast but far more concerned with stuffing their disgusting mouths with cakes and the best of last year's wine. . . .

In the midst of the confusion the wife of Jesse, mild and wizened, was making a batch of new bread. She sat on the floor in the corner, near the clay oven. Under her thin white brows her eyes kept darting from side to side, anticipating the next cause for confusion. She had not had time for ten words with her youngest son, her beloved. He had eaten nothing, and now he stood solitary in the crowded room, like a lost lamb that has blundered into the wrong fold.

"What is it that troubles my darling?" she said.

"Nothing. I did not sleep last night." The remembrance of the moonlit roof came upon him, and he shivered.

"Are you cold?"

"No, it is nothing. I tell you I did not sleep last night."

"Then go, my child, and enjoy a little sleep."

"Let me lie on the bed beside my uncle," Joab said.

"No, now, stay where you are!" Zeruiah shouted from the crowd of gabbling women.

"Let him rest, Joab," said the wife of Jesse. "He will be a better companion after he has slept."

High laughter exploded among the women.

"And what is the jest?" the mother said.

"Zeruiah has said it is not sleep that he needs."

"What else?"

"What else? A bride!"

He walked haughtily away from their laughter. But the other rooms were not empty. In one of them Jesse was mending a saddle. In another two of his brothers were quarreling over who should have the questionable pleasure of escorting Joab and Zeruiah home. There was no place to which he could escape. . . .

All through the turbulent morning and afternoon, he sustained himself with a dream of peace. He imagined how he would sit on a bench near the lamp and think; but when he considered what he would think, he felt such a quaking within him that the very sight of food made him ill. Between himself and the ultimate thought he put a number of trivial things: he worked intently, wordlessly, with Jesse over the saddle; he became disproportionately involved in unraveling some linen thread that had been tangled on his mother's spinning whorl; he insisted on picking up, to the last wisp of chaff, a bowlful of parched corn which one of his brothers had spilled on the floor. In the desperation of his weariness, in the turmoil of the disordered house, he would look up from the task at hand and close his eyes. He could see the unborn evening, the floor new-swept and empty of going feet, the sky paling beyond the window, his mother's hand carrying a burning twig from the hearth to the lamp. Quietness for thought at last—but what disintegrating thought would advance upon him with the light of the returning moon? He started out of his dream then, blushing to the temples because Jesse had been staring at him gravely under downy white brows.

By dusk he was almost drunken with the sweet closeness of the end of confusion. He found it possible even to be tender with Joab, and he went to the door with the departing visitors to give them an appropriate farewell. From the gate of the walled garden, Zeruiah advised him, for the ears of all the neighbors, to find a strapping virgin and go to bed. He made a feeble jest about being too sleepy to think of such matters tonight. He found a skin of wine and a few cakes for his brothers to take with them on the journey. All four of them were going. They would be gone for hours; they would stop on the way home to talk with the group that always gathered at the gate. He remained in the garden while his mother gathered up the scraps and drippings left at the end of a festival and his father moved the benches about and strewed fresh reeds on the floor. Then he saw by the wan glow at the window that the lamp was lighted, and he sighed and returned to the house. He had a transitory sense of fulfillment; the house was blessedly empty, blessedly still. The burning wick, floating in the saucer of oil, was steady and yellow. Over everything was the pale, cool rind of light separating the serene life of the house from the amorphous darkness around it. Jesse and the wife of Jesse sat on a bench near the hearth, their backs to the dying fire, their shoulders touching, their hands idle and close to each other on the wood.

Old lovers, he thought, leaning against the window sill and staring westward toward the hills. The love that had burned between them now flickered thin. Gold gone, blood gone, and nothing left but a trembling and a whispering. Old love, a moon fire, a silver fire. Tonight they would talk together when the rest of the household slept. Sometimes he and his brothers would waken and wonder at the laughter that came, long after midnight, from their father's room. It was always brief, dry, and sweet, like the sudden smoke that rises from sun-dried brush. Old lovers, he said to himself, beyond desire, laughing in the core of the dark, at the edge of the grave. And will I ever know such laughter, such quiet and silvery love? Kings do not know it. Kings have wives and secondary wives and concubines. Kings . . . The moon came up like a summons, like the blast of a golden horn, out of the dark mass of a cloud. What was it that the prophet said?

He walked from the vastness beyond the window to the table, to the circle of lamplight. He sat on a bench and laid his head within that brightness and encompassed his face in his arms. Oh, he had deceived himself when he believed he had put the matter from his thoughts! He had risen a king; he had been the King of Israel all day long. How much he had possessed, and how dubious was the possession, founded on a few words spoken on a roof in moonlight—evasive symbols, equivocal rhapsodies! Empty them of the day's imaginings, and what is left?

"David," said Jesse from the bench on the hearth.

"Hush, my husband, let him sleep."

Samuel did not say it, thought the boy. My ears cannot remember his voice saying, "David will be king over Judah and Israel." It was such a dream as men in the desert know when they see floating palm trees. . . .

"How blessed it is to have an empty room," the mother whispered. "There was no peaceful corner in the whole house."

"Little wonder it should be so when Zeruiah is in the place. She has grown as fat as——"

"As fat as the pet pig of a heathen child."

There it was again, their smoky laughter. The more the night deepened, the more convivial and intimate they grew. No doubt by this time their fingers were intertwined. Without lifting his head from the circle of darkness, he knew that Jesse's beard was brushing her cheek. They were glad to believe that he slept. They kissed and did not care that he was solitary, crownless, and a fool.

"I have not told you the worst of it as yet, Jesse. Within the three days of the festival, they emptied five skins of wine."

"Do not let it lie heavy in your thoughts. There is enough left for present needs. Shall I pour a little cup for the wife of my heart?"

"No, save it for the children."

"Come, drink, it will deepen your sleep."

Then pour for me, my father, so that my sleep may be as deep as the cistern of death, deep to drown the ache of returning to the tawdry world and the shame of this childish wish to weep. Wait! What was it that the prophet said? "The hour of the lamb will come, and yet the lamb will weep." And it was on my cheek that he traced the passage of a tear. . . .

He started up from the table. "Father——"

"We thought you slept."

"I could not sleep. Not since last night when we talked with Samuel on the roof."

"Come, drink a cup of wine."

"I want no wine!" His voice was more urgent than he had meant it to be. "Father, last night when there was speech between the two of you concerning Saul and the kingdom and another king that is to reign over Judah and Israel, what was it that Samuel said?"

It seemed to him that a look and a smile passed between the two old lovers. He knew in his heart that they had spoken of this matter before and would speak of it again tonight in their bed. But whether they smiled because they pitied him or because they fancied that the vision of a crown had revealed itself to their eyes alone, it was impossible to tell.

"We spoke mostly concerning this matter of Agag the King of the Amalekites," Jesse said.

"Did Samuel prophesy?"

The old man's glance shifted toward the hearth. "No, now, David. To say that he prophesied is to say too much."

"I saw the froth upon his lips."

"In Israel one does not chatter of such things. They are very holy. They are of the Lord."

It was said so mildly that it could scarcely be called a reproach, yet it smote against the rawness of his heart. But even on the verge of weeping he felt a desire to smile, for he had seen a blurred image of his father's face and had recognized there the tenderness that had granted many a minor indulgence to his tears.

"To Samuel," Jesse said, "you were as a little brook in a barren land. Samuel's burden is large, and last night his weariness was great even unto death."

It was not enough. He permitted the tears to rise. They clung to his eyelashes, and he saw how they would be glimmering there.

"Perhaps," said Jesse, bending to pick at a bit of chaff on his robe, "perhaps there was some such thought in Samuel's mind . . ."

"What thought?" His voice was exactly as it should be—musical, piteous.

"Some comparison between Saul's stiff-necked worldliness and your innocence. . . ."

He stood in the loveliness of his innocence, the lamplight making a golden edge around the honey-paleness of his cheeks. He stood like a lamb, and thought how nobody could dream that he had laid a lustful hand upon an Astarte.

"A thought that if such a one as you were king in Judah and Israel, it would be a delight to Samuel . . ."

It was not yet enough. He blinked, and the great, hoarded tears spilled down his face.

"A delight to Samuel, and to the Lord."

The triumph of it was too great. He could not master his lips. They curved upward in a brief smile. He knew at once that his pleasure in his power had betrayed him into bad strategy. The old eyes suddenly widened and cast a hawk's glance at him. Jesse's smile disappeared and left his face cold as a stone, and David's own grew blank and afraid.

"You dream too much," the old man said in a chill voice. "You kill the cub of a lion with a dagger, and on your journey home your delight in yourself is a headiness upon you, like the headiness of wine, and lo, the event grows, and you grow, and before the door is opened to you, the cub has become a he-lion, lord of the thickets, and the dagger is fallen away, and with your bare hands you have slain the terror of Judah."

He could only stare at the reeds on the floor. There was no answer; it was so.

"You make a song, perhaps a good song. I am a plain old man, a shepherd, not versed in tones and half-tones. Still, I will say that it is a good song, since you say as much and I do not know. You make a good song, and three old men who sit at the gate hear it and are stirred, and one of them weeps. But in your heart, is it enough? Is it an elder of the city who weeps? No, you must make another song to glorify the first, a song in which the seraphim themselves look down from heaven and weep."

The mother rose and threw a bit of brush on the fire. "No, now, Jesse, it is enough," she said.

"It is not enough. A prophet honored this house with the living flesh of his holiness last night. In his weariness he rejoiced in the youth and the loveliness of David, and in the morning he remembered it no more. But for this one here, nothing is small and nothing goes. He thinks himself a king."

"My father, I have not said this thing."

"You are no king. You are David, the son of Jesse, a shepherd in Judah. You are that and no more."

"My father is right," he said. "I am nothing and less than nothing. Let me tend sheep. I will dream and play the lute no more."

"See, now, Jesse," said the mother. "See what you have done."

"It was always so with him," said Jesse. "Either he is a king or he is a wretch. There is no middle way." He knelt and tilted the heavy wine jar. The wine gurgled slowly into the little cup. "When I was a shepherd in my father's house," he said, "a dream visited me also. We did not speak of kings in the days of my foolishness. We spoke of prophets then. And my heart was big with the dream and swelled to bursting and could not find room among these hills, and it seemed to me that unless the fullness within me were taken unto the Lord, I would die. That was fifty years ago, and I am still here, I am not yet dead. The fullness within me flowed out to lesser things, to a wife and the fruit of her womb, to the walls of this house, to the earth under the hoe, to these songs of yours, to this table and this lamp and this fire. The Lord wished me to die a shepherd. There is wisdom and also mercy in the Lord. I knew how much I had been spared—last night I knew it when I looked upon Samuel's face."

He rose and carried the cup across the room and set it in his wife's withered hand. "When Saul is finished with his feasting in Gilgal," he said, "he will come to encamp at Ephes-Dammim with the host. Your brothers will be there. Go to Ephes-Dammim and carry a present to your brothers and be merry. But see to it that you find time to look upon Saul's face."

"Yes, my father," David said.

There was no sound in the room save the slight sipping sound that his mother made above the wine. Now and then she would lift the cup to Jesse's mouth and he would drink a little. It was plain that they wanted no more talk. And at last they rose together and went wordlessly out of the room.

But David went to the window to watch night come upon the insignificant village of Bethlehem. One after another the lights went out in the windows of the neighboring houses. Known hands pulled curtains between themselves and the dark; known feet hurried toward familiar doors; a child cried out and was soothed by a lullaby; and in every house husband turned to wife, wife turned to husband, and they kissed and slept. A nameless uneasiness was upon him. For a long time he stood before the fire, watching the last of the brush turn to gray ash. What does Saul dream? he kept wondering. How is his sleep?

৵§ IV §৵

WHO COULD look at the camp of God without exultation? The heart went up like a bird at the sight of it. There it lay, martial with heaped arms, festive with supper fires. The red cleft of the watercourse went down in one sharp declivity below it, and the willows trailed above it—a flowing, yellow-green effulgence in the last light of the sun. He stood on a hillock, clasping his lute against his chest and gazing at the vision with rapt eyes. The little donkey that had followed him down from Bethlehem— a mild young beast, laden with two baskets of bread, five skins of wine, and ten fat cheeses that Jesse and the mother had prepared for their warrior sons—the little donkey nuzzled at his back, but he did not stir. He counted the shaggy black tents, visible below the tender green of the willows. There were only a few. One for Saul, and one for the women of the royal house—Queen, Princess, and concubine. One for Abner, the captain of the host, one for Jonathan, and one to house the remembrance of the ark of God, lost to the Philistines at Shiloh a generation ago. There were no tents for the warriors. The host of Israel slept on the ground, under the stars. And while they slept, *He* walked among them, cloudy and terrible. Jahveh's breath blew upon the red embers of their courage by night, and their terror was as the melted frost.

It was the best time of the day, the hour before the evening meal, the hour of the wind's return. Silence was upon the Israelite camp, and the Philistines also were quiet in their sprawling encampment on the other side of the red-clay cleft. David went forward in this stillness, walking along the bank under the dark leaves and unripe fruit of the mulberry trees. About half a mile from the camp, he came upon a solitary sentry leaning against a willow and staring at the life in the watercourse below him—a glimmering network of darting lizards and dragonflies. He was a veteran, scarred in earlier battles, and too long in the service to make much of a sentry's duties. He had seen the boy and the donkey advancing for the last quarter of an hour along the bank, and he turned slowly, his eyes still fixed upon the lizards.

"Jahveh be with you. What is your name?" he said.

"David, the son of Jesse, the brother of Eliab."

The last name should have been a trumpet call to bestir the sentry from his dreaming. But he only went on staring into the gorge. "Eliab?" he said. It was plain that the name of the mighty bowman was not yet a watchword on every sentry's tongue.

"He is with the host," David said.

Apparently the sentry did not consider this fact worthy of comment. "Are you pure in the eyes of Jahveh? Is there any uncleanness upon you? Have you lain with a woman these last three days?" The sentry sang it all out rapidly and without inflection, meanwhile watching, with regret, the desertion of a whole cloud of dragonflies.

"I am pure. There is no uncleanness upon me. I have not been with a woman. Not in these last three days."

"Not in these last three days?" said the sentry. "Not truly? But no doubt earlier in the month you lay with twenty virgins and twenty wives and twenty prostitutes, and could scarcely drag yourself hither for sheer weariness." It was a tried man's mockery of virginity, but there was no malice in it. Now that the dragonflies were gone, he watched the boy and spent no more, no less, upon him than he had spent upon the dragonflies.

And this was galling. "Is it necessary," said David, "to be ashamed of chastity?"

The sentry laid his arm around the boy's shoulder. "No, now, treasure your chastity, that you may have honor among the daughters of Judah. Take your precious virginity and go to your Eliab, or whatever his name may be. You are fortunate. One called Elhanan slew a giant of the Philistines this morning, and Saul has sacrificed heifers in thanksgiving. There will be roast meat for all tonight."

He had no more glances to waste upon the son of Jesse. He lay down on his belly and became completely absorbed in the minute and glittering life that darted and quivered over the red clay. David, looking over his shoulder, saw him bring up a lizard on a bit of willow twig. To him, he thought, a lizard is more than I. He sees my Judahite meanness—the prudishness of Judah in my mouth and the ignorance of Judah in my eyes. He walked more slowly toward the yellow supper fires, and turned now and again to pat the donkey's moist and friendly nose.

⁓ V ⁓

IT WAS SAID in Israel that if a man wanted orderliness and discretion, let him not marry, let him dwell in the camp of God. Whenever the host of Jahveh settled down, Jahveh Himself came up from Sinai and drew a circle around the encampment with His fiery spear. From that moment until the last baggage wagon had taken to the road again, all that was within the circle was holy; and no man built a fire, laid down a spear, or ate a fig without asking himself, "Will it please the Lord?" All that was inharmonious with God's design had to be borne beyond the circle. There was no place for love—Saul kept apart from Ahinoam, his wife, and from Rizpah, his concubine. Michal, Saul's daughter, lived like a boy among boys, and nobody could have distinguished her from a young armor-bearer if it had not been for the length of her hair. There was no room in the encampment for the dying or the fallen. The surgeons remained on the field of battle to do what they could; blood and the cries of the mortally wounded were not for the ears of God. Old veterans stayed without to dig the shallow furrows for the slain; and afterward it was necessary for them to exile themselves from the host for seven days, until their hands were cleansed of the dank contamination of the dead.

So all around him the son of Jesse saw only orderliness and a seemly merriment. He was told with courtesy that he must leave the donkey with the other pack beasts near the edge of the watercourse; the soldier who instructed him was very patient and considerate. In fact, every warrior whom he encountered—the one who directed him to Eliab's battalion, the one who pointed out Saul's tent, the one who begged him by no means to spit, when he had not the slightest intention of spitting—every warrior was kind. Yet there was no balm for him in their graciousness. He knew that they were courteous not for his sake, but for Jahveh's sake.

He tried to bear himself well, to walk gracefully between the golden fires, to leap lightly over the piles of spears and the dishes set out for the evening feast. But he was awkward with a profound self-consciousness. Once he struck his ankle hard against a tent peg. The ache, hot and disintegrating, rose within him, melted his frail discipline, and threatened him with tears. All around him were the unknown faces of bearded men. At this hour in Bethlehem, his mother was setting the meal upon the table. At this hour . . . Well, here was Eliab.

But he could take no pleasure in the first glimpse of his brother. Was this the mighty bowman of whom he had sung in the hills above the town? Eliab had changed, Eliab had thickened; he had the big, coarse muscles of an ox; his neck was heavy; the sun had dried and frizzled his hair. For some moments the two of them stood staring at each other.

"So you have come up from Bethlehem, my brother?" Eliab said at last. "How is it with our father and our mother?"

"They are well." His voice was cold. He had expected a more ardent welcome than this.

"And our brothers?"

"Well also."

"And you? But it is plain that you are tired and hungry. The food is on the fire. Come." He walked a few steps in the direction of the campfire and then turned again. "We have not yet embraced," he said, and folded his great arms around David's neck and kissed his cheek. The strong scent of the warrior was upon him. "I am very lonely these days," he said. "You could not have come at a better hour. And because of Elhanan who killed the giant, I have meat to offer you tonight. We will feast together, we two."

David answered with a tentative, shy pride that he could better the feast—there were delicacies from home.

"But today we have an abundance. Tomorrow will be a lean day. Let us eat your gifts tomorrow."

Suddenly he saw plainly how it was with Eliab. There would be something shameful in it—to trek across the camp to the grazing field, to come back in the stare of the whole army, followed by a green brother and burdened with home cheese and home wine. Bethlehem was not wanted in the camp of God. To send food had been a piece of foolishness. He saw Jesse's hand pulling the cord of a wineskin tight; he saw his mother's fingers patting the cheese. Suddenly the cheeses became ridiculously and unbearably pathetic. He longed to eat of them and knew that all desire for food had left him.

"Still," said Eliab, "now that I consider the matter, my tongue yearns after the cheese of my mother and the wine of Bethlehem. Come, let us go to the donkey. No, leave the lute." He laid a heavy arm across his brother's shoulder and shoved him into a melee of moving men. "You have grown taller since I saw you last. Yes, and even more fair."

As they walked among the warriors, many of whom by this time were sitting in little crowds with their suppers before them, David felt the bruise of pity still upon his heart. He was troubled also for the lute—suppose a sword were to be dropped upon it; suppose the kettle boiled over; suppose some heedless foot were to tread upon the frame. . . .

Eliab was talking with forced energy about some Philistine giant of the city of Gath. He had begun when they were halfway across the encampment, and he was still harping on the same theme when they found their donkey grazing among the sand-colored herd. "This beast I do not know," he said. "He was born after I departed from home. It is five years now that I have been with the host. As I was saying, this giant, this Philistine—Goliath was his name—God bear witness to the fact that our father is a very generous man—there is enough cheese here to feed me for half a year, and I shall have to invite comrades to help me consume the wine —— This Goliath was a thorn in Saul's side. He had the voice and the insolence of a bull, and dawn and twilight he stood on the other side of the watercourse and bellowed that one of us should come over and meet him in single combat for the glory of God and the honor of Israel. Saul would have gone up, but Abner would have none of it. As for Abner himself, how could he go, he that has been ailing these many years with the splinter of a Philistine spear in his thigh? Then Jonathan spoke of going up, but that roused the host. He is the jewel of their hearts, and they would not risk one hair of his head. Therefore there was no man to answer the Philistine."

David, balancing three cheeses and two wineskins, thought, Would God I had been there! . . .

"So Elhanan spoke up—he is old, past his best days, of no consequence in the host, a slinger, yes, and a bastard into the bargain. 'Why should I not go up?' he said, 'inasmuch as I have neither wife nor child nor father nor mother, and am despised, and despise myself.' And lo, this morning when we wakened he had gone up and slain the giant of Gath. Who will say what man may be chosen to be the vessel of God's wrath? Goliath is dead, and Elhanan is made captain over a thousand. And I who have often flung a breastplate at him and said, 'Polish it'—I rejoice for him with all my heart. There, then, that is the last of the wineskins. No, come, I did not mean to make a pack mule of my brother. Give them to me."

The sun had gone down while he spoke. The willows had grown black against the wan green sky. Their faces were strangely luminous in the withdrawing light. They stood looking uncomfortably at each other. The question that David did not dare to utter flared up in his look. Where was Eliab, the mighty bowman, when Goliath bellowed on the ridge? It would have been otherwise with Jesse's house had David been there.

"Perhaps it is easier for the old to have courage," Eliab said. "The old and the young—they can throw their lives away. With the young, death is a glorious business. And the old—they have had enough, and what is it to them, a little more, a little less, of what has already become savorless? But the time between—Jahveh knows what it is to have no courage, to be caught with loose knees and a melting heart in the time between." He turned away and pushed the donkey's side, hard with the flat of his hand. "Come, we will go back before some clown takes it upon himself to play your lute," he said.

✥ VI ✥

Now that the meal was laid upon the ground before him, he could not eat. The ache in his ankle was so intense that his stomach lurched whenever he moved. While the others ate—Eliab and the two unkempt Judahites who had come to stick their snouts into his wineskins—David held his peace. He had worn away the ungratified wish to weep. Now rage—foolish, stifled, and impotent—rose in him at the two sweaty and condescending Judahites who troubled themselves to explain the most obvious things for his benefit. "The Philistines are encamped on the other side of the watercourse. You will notice, brother of Eliab, that they sulk in their defeat. Observe how there is not one fire in all the Philistine encampment this night."

He did not see that it was necessary for him to stand up and look at firelessness on the other side of the cleft, but it was "Rise and see for yourself, Bethlehemite," and "I beg you, look upon it," until, simply to rid himself of their touching fingers and their fixed, animated glances, he stood and stared at the faint line of the crest. The sight of the landscape filled him with a baffled mournfulness. On that ridge, David the Bethlehemite might have walked up the first terrace to greatness. A golden filament of music spun itself out of his wretchedness. "On the ridge of Ephes-Dammim, the heathen giant stood like a monolith. Over the holy watercourse was the shadow of a black stone. And the Lord said unto the son of Jesse, 'Will you go up, my beautiful, my dove?'" But the music could not anchor its frail arc upon that blank hill. He sank back, a Judahite among Judahites, nursing his throbbing foot in his hands.

"There will be other battles," Eliab said. "Tomorrow they may come down upon us, and the flame of God may descend upon the meanest of our hearts."

His lips are slobbered, David thought. He drinks too much.

It was as if Eliab had felt his censure. He lay down on his stomach in the red light of the embers and covered his cheeks with his arms.

"Have a little wine to warm your bowels, brother of Eliab," said one of the Judahites.

He wanted neither wine nor talk with these ignorant farmers. He shook his head.

"Drink," Eliab said without moving, speaking against earth.

"Wherefore?"

"Wherefore? Why, to comfort yourself for my shortcomings. To ease your heart of the wrong I did you this morning when I did not go up for the honor of the House of Jesse to give my body to the giant of Gath."

David looked down at Eliab and saw that his buttocks jutted ridiculously and that the back of his hair whorled in all directions, like trampled hay. "I thought of no such matter," David said.

"No? My little brother, would you know what you are? A liar. A fair and ingratiating liar. Drink, nevertheless. If not to drown my misfortunes, then to cover your own. How pitiful a thing it is that you did not go up. Think—this night your head might have had the honor of hanging on the tent of the Seren of Gath. So drink. If not for these reasons, then to be charitable to me in my besottedness. For it is no delight, my brother, to sprawl in drunkenness before a prude who will not wet his holy lips."

"Truly, it is not," said one of the Judahites, taking the wineskin from his own mouth and setting it on David's knee. In withdrawing, the drunken warrior lost his balance, stumbled forward, and came down with full force upon David's bruised ankle. The pain was so amazing that he could not even cry out. Tears stood in his eyes. He caught the toppling wineskin and drank deep, to hide his face.

For a long time he sat with his head resting against his knees, mourning over the loss of the dream that he had carried with him from Bethlehem. How magnificently the watch fires had flared in his imaginings, what sonorous names had sounded in his ears; what regal cloaks and buoyant banners had unfurled for him; what visions of high meetings in renowned places. And this was the end of the dreamer—that he should sit, a wretch among wretches, a Judahite among Judahites, enduring a dull hour between food and sleep, easing a fool's ill-gotten bruise. The area of the encampment allotted to Judah was in no mean place; it was close to the King's tent and opposite the aloof and haughty tribe of Ephraim. But, like all Judahites, he knew why he was suffered to tarry there. To flatter a new tribe whose allegiance was tentative; to let it nourish itself upon a sight of the King's face. A thousand times he had heard how Judah was the least in Israel and how the sons of Judah reeked with the dung of their oxen and sheep. And he—how had he found the insolence to dream of kingly courtesy? "Truly, the son of Jesse is a peerless lutist and very fair," his dream of Saul had said. Truly, the son of Jesse will be presented to the servant of the servant of the armor-bearer of a captain; among hillsmen and farmers, among the slow-witted and the despised, he will spend his days.

He raised his head and drank again. The three around the fire had fallen silent. They lay on their bellies, and their contempt for themselves was plain in their sprawling aimlessness. Beyond them, in the red islands of light floating on the blackness, there were other more radiant worlds. The sons of Benjamin, all scions of a royal house, were singing a song beloved of Saul. The sons of Ephraim were sitting in dignified quietness. Some young lutist, inept with his instrument but doubtless highborn and with good connections, strummed for the entertainment of the sons of Dan. Only here was vulgarity and obscurity. He took up the wineskin and drank yet again. What golden fantasies would have sprung up before him if he had dreamed in the hills of sitting near Saul's tent! And here was Saul's tent not two hundred feet away, yet more removed from him, less real to him, than it had been when he tarried in Judah and saw it in his dreams.

"They are growing weary earlier than usual," said one of the Judahites.

He looked about him and saw with aching regret that the merriment was waning. Most of the supper fires had subsided into small areas of glow; fewer men wandered from group to group, and more lay on the ground with their cloaks pulled over their eyes. He drank of the lees at the bottom of the wineskin. As he laid it by, it seemed to him that the world was melting, that fires, faces, and stars were all dissolving in one pale blur. But it was still there, like the red disk of the sun in the morning mist—the pain in his ankle would not be gone.

"Tomorrow I will go back to Bethlehem." He did not know why he had said it.

"Let my brother do what best pleases him," Eliab said.

The ache intensified, and now he could not tell what was the seat of the ache—his ankle, his head, his breast.

"Is the lutist already weary of the wars?" asked one of the Judahites.

The other said, "Is the shepherd homesick for the sheep?"

A hot answer sprang up in him. He opened his lips and choked upon it.

"No, now," said Eliab in the voice of one who struggles against sleep. "Let him be. He is a child. Let him be."

"We meant him no harm." The voice was conciliatory. "Let him at least see a little before he departs, so that he may beget wonder among his brethren. Let us at least take him to look upon the head of Goliath. Let us at least——" The Judahite fell silent, and David knew with amazement that a hush had come down upon the whole camp. There was only the stir of thousands turning in darkness toward the ridge of Ephes-Dammim. Out of the utter stillness on the other side of the watercourse rose a thin trumpet call.

"They have sounded the retreat," Eliab said.

David lifted his eyes again to the crest. In the faint starlight, he could discern a subtle motion upon it. "Where will they go?" he said.

"I am not in the confidence of their captain of the host. I do not know."

A strange sound floated to them across the cleft of the watercourse. The Philistines were singing some wild, unhappy song. It was said that they had come to Israel over the western sea from an island named Caphtor—an island where the waves washed the steps of the palaces and the gardens were paved with sea shells and watered by the tide. There was in their chant of defeat and resignation something of the remembrance of great waters. He listened, and a nameless yearning arose in him, expanding like the legendary flowers which were said to grow in the cool greenness of their sea. It seemed to him that he was borne out on the prow of a vessel. Foam broke against his sandals; the white, glistening wings of sea birds darted past his face. On the eastern shore, among crocuses and irises, some being waited—male or female, god or human?—with closed eyes and parted lips.

"Truly, they are retreating," one of the Judahites said. "We have heard that song before."

A great shout went up from the ranks of Israel. David sat in the midst of the cheering, holding his pulsating foot in one hand and guarding his lute with the other. The host milled about, hands gestured, heads moved. The yellow glare of torches was suddenly before Saul's tent, and in that area of light figures paced about, shadowy, elongated, stirred with the same excitement that moved the host. He could not tell whether he saw or dreamed that he saw the anointed of Israel among them—a long lean warrior in a somber cloak, with broad shoulders, a nervous hand, a beard of dull black.

The two Judahites had risen on unsteady feet and were making their farewells. The clusters of men around the fires were falling apart. Such bits of food as might offend Jahveh's eyes were being hastily thrown into the fire. Sparks and an acrid odor went up; smoke floated above their heads on the still air. The host settled itself for sleep.

It was not so easy for David to lie down. However he disposed his body, the pain in his ankle became intolerable within a few minutes. After a while he was so wearied with it that his eyes must close, and then he would immediately find himself in the midst of some fever dream. Now he was lying on the ridge of Ephes-Dammim, and Goliath was crouching above him to cut off his head with a sword. Now he had been summoned to play the lute before Saul. But the King was mad and would hear no song unless the lutist stood up to his ankles in a brazier of hot coals. . . . So it went on until the stars sickened before the false dawn. And it was an offense to him that Eliab slept soundly and snored against the earth all that night.

⇜§ VII §⇝

THE ARMY slept the late, deep sleep of victory. Only the sentries and the youngest son of Jesse did not sleep. With the paling of the last star, David had resigned himself to wakefulness. When the light evoked the cloud of yellow from the stark branches of the willows, he knew that he could not lie here any longer, shuddering with the hurt and the cold.

He stood up. The pain stabbed upward as high as his thigh. His belly was swollen with wine and food, he was unholy with the necessities of the flesh, and he must find for himself a patch of unholiness.

He entered the tangle of brush with a full body and a throbbing head. He came out on the other side of it empty and still, but so weak that he could barely walk. The sun had come up while he tarried. The whole gray, pearly world that stretched before him in undulating swells was brightened by patches of the faint, dry yellowness of hay. There was yellowness upon the branches of the little clump of willows before him, upon the ancient circle of stones round the cistern, upon the edges of the massed clouds on the eastern horizon, upon the tall wet grass at his feet. He limped into the dappled grove, panting against pain and blinking against light. He reached the cistern and lay down beside it, pressing his cheek against the damp stone.

Years afterward he tried to remember how long he lay there in the strengthening light. In later days, when he looked back upon that moment by the cistern, he saw it in the glimmer of a high tenderness which he could not yet have known. The hour was subtly, tremulously bright with wind-shaken leaves and early sun, musical with the tentative pipings of the first birds, with the rustle of footsteps in the grass. And into that music—more magical than any sound he had ever known—came the voice.

"Friend," it said, "is there a sickness upon you, or do you sleep?"

He raised his head and saw a young man standing above him, with shadows of willow leaves moving upon him, with sunlight effulgent in the pale-brown cloud of his hair. He wore a white tunic fastened with a broad girdle, white also but richly embroidered with bright-blue thread. Body and face were at once austere and delicate. His skin, as smooth and tan as the surface of an almond, was stretched tight over his high cheekbones. His hair came down like a wing over his round, still brow.

To do honor to this gracious stranger, David tried to rise. But the pain was so intense that he sat back on the edge of the cistern, and winced and pointed to his foot and smiled. His gestures were far more unrestrained and expressive, his face was far more naked, than would have been possible in the presence of Jesse or Eliab or his mother. How is it, he asked himself, that when strangers look upon strangers, there is no veil, no decorum, between their eyes? . . .

The young man drew closer and looked intently at the bruised ankle. In the patch of sun into which he had come, his beauty was even more plain. It was told how Jahveh had found common dust in Eden, how He had pressed it with His hands and mixed with it a few drops of His spittle, and made thereby a living soul. Yet, in the case of this stranger, the hand of Jahveh must have worked upon the roseate dust of broken shells, the fine, pale sand washed by a century of tides. The hands were particularly beautiful; every tendon, every bone was exquisitely articulated. The stranger knelt on the grass before David and laid these hands upon the bruise; and the pain that they begot was a melting pain, like the pain of love.

"How did my cousin come by this?" the young man said.

The "cousin" was something beyond courtesy, some affirmation of the intimacy that was between them. Now that the face was close, there was in it a certain tension, a melancholy and an urgency that had not been visible before. The corners of the mouth were strongly marked and turned downward. There were blue veins in the temples, and dark marks, like the stains at the bases of iris petals, around the eyes. The eyes themselves were small and dark and had the flat earnestness of the eyes of a gazelle. They shattered the first impulse to ornament the truth. One could only say: "I stumbled against a tent peg. As my cousin sees, an awkward, unheroic wound, the wound of a fool."

"Were you then also walking in darkness?" the young man said. Something in his voice bestowed pity upon all who walked at night alone. "Perhaps we passed each other." That thought was strangely moving. David thought how, among the sleeping thousands, they might have passed and touched. "I also found it impossible to sleep." What nameless grief was embodied in those words and deprecated by the uneasy smile? "It is a bitter thing, is it not, my cousin, for one man to lie down on another man's victory? My father——" He stopped and spread his hands as if he wished to make it known that what he had to say was too mournful for the saying. Upon the almond-colored wrist, where two veins branched out, David saw the mark of the tribe of Benjamin. The gazelle eyes were veiled. The head was bent. The hands came down upon the bruised foot, waking again that strange hurt that could not be distinguished from delight.

"Why should my cousin wait upon me?" David said.

"Ask it of Jahveh, who knows. In my thoughts I do not know the reason." He flushed, and David waited, feeling his own pulse hasten with the waiting. "Let us say that it is a matter of the heart."

This is indeed a dream, David thought, shuddering with the mingled pleasure and torment of the touch. And out of a dream's earnestness and nakedness and intimacy, I can say to him, "For me also it is of Jahveh and of the heart." . . .

"Do you speak to me or to my girdle?" the stranger said.

David looked in wonder at this girdle and saw that it was embroidered with a curious design. The horns of the gazelle were worked upon it in pairs, and between pair and pair was the letter J. It was rich and intricate; he had not seen its like before.

"Is it possible that you do not know this girdle, Judahite?" The beginnings of a smile indented the corners of the chaste mouth. The glance moved again beneath the half-shut lids.

"My cousin will pardon my ignorance. I have not seen the girdle of my cousin, or any girdle that is its peer, before this hour."

"And it is not known to you of what house I am, and who is my father?"

"I am a new man in the host. My ears have not yet been delighted with the music of my cousin's name."

Suddenly the stranger was no longer kneeling before him. He had sprung up and stepped backward. His head was tilted back. He swayed on the balls of his feet and laughed aloud. Then all at once his fingers were at the girdle, unwinding the rich length of cloth, tearing the whole bright white-and-blue of it to shreds with a rasping sound. This also had in it the abandon and the incredibility of events in a dream. And if I dream, thought the son of Jesse, may Jahveh let me never wake, inasmuch as there is so much wild tenderness in his face. . . .

"It is to bind your wound, my cousin," the young man said. He took the foot between his hands, this time with force, and bound it hard and tight. David saw that his flat brown eyes were not upon the work wrought by his hands. The eyes were closed. The head leaned backward. The lips were parted to make way for hurrying breath. So prophets look when the fit of Jahveh is about to descend upon them. So the faces of nameless women look, moving toward a sleeper in a dream. So David looked— he knew it with gladness and wonder, feeling the parting of his own lips, the hastening of his own breath.

Long after the foot was bound, the stranger continued to kneel in the tall grass, his hands clasped around David's foot, his head lowered, his cloudy hair just touching David's knee. He will arise and go and be gone from me, David thought, and the thought was as blank as death.

The young man started, rose, and sighed. "My father will have sent after me, I must not stay," he said, flushing and moving stiffly, like a chidden child, toward the clump of willows.

He will not turn again, thought David. He is a Benjamite and returns to the Benjamites, and the son of Judah will know the touch of his hand no more.

But under the boughs he turned and said: "See that you wear my girdle three days, both for the healing of your bruise and for my love."

Eᴌɪᴀʙ was slow to awaken. Always at the morning meal he was watery-eyed and remote. So it was no great wonder that he did not see the wrappings upon his brother's foot until the last of the bread had been eaten and the scraps had been thrown into the fire.

"What ails my brother?" he asked. Concern struggled to the surface of his big, moist eyes.

David turned aside uneasily. The wound had become strangely significant to him. It was private and dear, and he had no wish to discuss it. "It is nothing," he said. "I stumbled against a tent peg yesterday. I had no wish to trouble my brother with it, seeing it was such a little thing. I——"

He stopped and stared. Eliab was pointing at the bandage. His mouth hung open. Had he seen a ghost, there could not have been greater astonishment in his face. "Where in God's name did you come by that?" he said.

"A young man came to me by the cistern——" Leave me alone with the wonder of it, he said within himself.

"What young man?"

What is it to you and to these other herdsmen and fools? thought David. "His name is unknown to me. He is of the tribe of Benjamin." Clear, clear until the day I die, the mark and the veins beneath the mark upon the wrist. . . . "He was young." And, since you drive me to it, let me proclaim it, let me shout it to the host. . . . "He was delicately made, and very fair——" He could not continue, for Eliab had grasped his foot and pulled it forward, and he gulped with the pain.

"Where did *he* get such stuff?"

"He tore a girdle."

"Where did he find this girdle?"

"Around his own waist," he said coldly. "Are you finished then with your questioning?"

"From his own waist? Delicately made? Fair? Of the tribe of Benjamin?"

"As you have said." He stared angrily at the rough and hairy hand that lay upon the loved cloth.

Eliab withdrew his fingers. "Does my brother David know the name of this young man?"

"No. Who is he?"

"The Gazelle, the son of Saul, the heir to Israel. It is Jonathan's girdle that was torn for your sake," Eliab said.

BOOK TWO

BOOK TWO

❦ I ❧

During the three days that followed the retreat of the Philistines, Saul did not show his face to the host. It was plain to the army that some heavy distress had settled upon him. The warriors told each other how the concubine Rizpah had not been sent for; how Abner, captain of the host, had not stepped out of his quarters all day long; how the Princess Michal had not carried cakes of her own making to her father's table; how neither Jonathan nor the little Ishbaal had gone in to sit at the King's feet. They indulged also in more self-centered speculations: The army was not going back to Gilgal, where the temple women were beautiful. Nor were they to be disbanded, to travel to their own towns in time for the Feast of the First Fruits. Would they stay forever by this accursed watercourse, polishing armor that had never been bloodied, drinking the dregs of the wine?

Toward noon on the third day they heard the voice of their King call out, loudly and urgently, a name which they had forgotten these many moons. "Ahinoam!" he said. There was a stir within the tent of the legal wife. She came forth alone, without veils or amulets, looking like one of the dead in her loose white gown. She had never borne herself royally, and now her head was bent until her chin almost touched her chest. They saw with wonder that her brown hair was streaked with white, that her breasts had sagged and flattened, that her unrouged cheeks were hollow and wan.

There were some who remembered the days of her bloom. Kish, the father of Saul, had brought the colorless girl from an unknown house to make of her a king's bride. Had she been fair? They could not remember; they knew only that she had been different from the rest. The pure-bred women of Israel were dark and ardent; and she was not pure-bred. She was brown and white, gray and yellow, like a pebble found close to the sea. It was said that an ancestress of hers had come with the hordes washed in from Caphtor, that legendary island from which Philistia had also journeyed into Jahveh's land. An Israelite had taken this

29

ancestress to wife and brought upon his house forever the alien magic—
the thin, pale skin, the cloudy, honey-colored hair, the white temples with
the blue veins showing through. She was said to have been wise, but
who remembered the words of her wisdom? What was she even in the
days of her ascendancy save a living silence, a slow and gentle smile?

That, and the mother whose belly cradled princes. Saul had begotten
five children upon her, a princess and four princes, the eldest a young
man and the darling of the host, the youngest a forgotten child. It was
as if the first and the last of these were not Saul's children but hers alone.
She had carried Jonathan in loneliness. Abinadab, Malchishua, and Michal
had been born in better years, when the King came often to her bed.
But while she was heavy with her final burden, he had turned from her,
and had taken in the place of her pallor the aromatic loveliness of Rizpah
the concubine. Saul had other children, but Ahinoam bore no more.
And Israel was resigned to this. Abraham had gone in unto Hagar; Jacob
had known Billah; it was always so. But Israel was disturbed that its king
should cry out for a forgotten woman in a loud voice. It was like calling
up the dead.

Through the noonday meal the host questioned and wondered, sending
out a dozen conjectures that wandered like tropical vines from one group
to another. Then, while the last of the food was being eaten, their thoughts
fled utterly from the King and the King's women to another matter. A
new song had risen in the host. Judah had sung it first, and now it was
spreading to Ephraim and Benjamin. It came like a burnishing cloth to
take the tarnish from their victory. Elhanan had been old, but the song
was young. The event had been mean, but the words were glorious:
"On the ridge of Ephes-Dammim, the heathen giant stood like a monolith. Over the holy watercourse was the shadow of a black stone. And
the Lord said unto the hero, 'Will you go up, my beautiful, my dove?'
Behold, the dove has fluttered up. . . ." By dusk the Benjamites were wishing Ahinoam back in her own tent, so that they might sing the song to Saul.

In the purple of the evening, their eyes were drawn again toward
the royal tent. Bright embers on a brazier glimmered through the opalescent mist, and a certain savory, familiar odor issued from the entrance,
healing and consoling. So Ahinoam had been called out of her silence for
this little thing—to brew him a pot of herbs. They snickered at this end
to their fantasies.

And while they smiled, she came out of the King's tent as she had
entered it, alone. Her face was lifted. The wind of God blew her garments
against her unbeautiful body and lifted her colorless hair. But those in
the first ranks observed that her lips were parted, that a muted rapture
was in her eyes. "It is enough for Ahinoam," they said, "that she should
be the servant of her lord."

Jonathan came out of his tent to meet her. He wore a girdle which
they had never seen, dyed in blue and green. He knelt in sight of all
the camp and kissed Ahinoam's hands. It was as if he had cried out to the

host, "Behold the mother of the Gazelle, look upon the source, remember the womb!"

As the two of them moved into the shadowy abyss of her tent, many in the ranks of Israel ceased to smile. "Truly, the hope of our children was suckled at her breast," they said.

✑ II ✎

In saul's tent, the heat of the day had not yet begun to dissolve. Without, the air was cooled by the evening wind, yet the King of Israel sat in the shut warmth, close to the glowing embers on the brazier, breathing the scent of brewed herbs. He was drenched with sweat, and the folds of his robe lay heavy upon him, as though they had been carved from stone. In the pungent smell of the brew there was a nameless remembrance that he must identify before he could sleep. Whenever the black spell was upon him, he turned to the gone days—only through remembrance was it possible for him to find his way back into the world.

His illness no longer amazed and terrified him; he could name it and measure it; he had described it twice, once to Rizpah and once to Jonathan. It had to be spoken of in terms of water, but no man on earth could understand the quality of the water of which he spoke—the leaden grayness, the heaviness, the cold. It began with a gurgling sound, as if some hidden wellspring bubbled in his brain. It begot nausea and a shuddering disgust. Light, sound, and motion were intolerable to him then. He muffled his eyes in his cloak; he pressed his fists against his ears; he cursed the jarring beat of his own heart. In that shut silence the water rose inexorably. The water rose and covered everything—one vast, chill, gray expanse of sea. And when it receded, it left a bleak, blanched beach behind it, a waste of sand in which he wandered, witless and childish, stooping to examine the flotsam and jetsam of his life—the old songs, the odors, the sound of lost voices.

So in the dank, darkening tent he sat above the brazier, inhaling the savory steam and conjuring up remembrance. He bent closer to the pot of herbs, so that the moisture of the steam was upon his face. The pain was no longer boiling in his head, but it had left its aftermath: his forehead ached under his own touch. He breathed slowly, deeply, parting his lips. Marjoram, steam, hyssop—when had he breathed them before, in what departed year, in what forgotten place?

Suddenly he knew. He saw the sunlight in the upper room in Kish's house in Gibeah. Ahinoam lay upon the bed, her damp hair hanging down on either side, her face quiet in sleep. The pot of herbs stood on the floor beside her. A cloth soaked in the pungent stuff was folded across her brow. The midwife pulled the squalling red child out of the water and said with a sourness that belittled the whole race, "Behold my lord's firstborn." The arms and legs were pitiable as the wings of a new-hatched bird. But there, in line with the bleeding navel, was the bud of power, the manhood that all Israel yearned to beget and bear, the promise of a race of kings. . . . He saw her waken and turn her head slowly over her shoulder; he saw her subtle, knowing smile. "My lord need not labor to hang the jewels of his words upon me. I am already bedecked enough, in that I am the mother of my lord's son." He could not remember whether he had kissed her, either in that long-gone year or in this recent hour when she had knelt before him with the scent of herbs in her hair.

Yet he had remembered enough. The heat of the tent was suddenly intolerable. He rose slowly, fearful of jarring his body, and pushed back his hair, and sighed. He wished to go at once, out of the tent, out of his sickness, into the world of cool wind and singing warriors, where he would spend the evening sitting under a clump of willows with Jonathan.

He saw with wonder that night had come while he brooded. There was no light in the tent except the small glow of the embers. In the dark, he pulled off the drenched tunic and stood for a long time, feeling the moisture drying upon his nakedness. The Benjamites were singing a new song, ardent and strange. The words—what he could hear of them—were also fresh and moving. ". . . Will you go up, my beautiful, my dove? The dove has fluttered up out of the sullen host." He went to the carved chest, lifted the lid, and pulled out soft shoes of antelope skin, a girdle embroidered in scarlet, a new-washed tunic still fragrant with wind and sun. He dressed slowly, listening to the blurred cadences. He combed his beard, but did not dare to drag at his wet and matted hair—the very thought threatened to revive the pain. ". . . He has gone up, in the whiteness of his age, in the milky whiteness of his many years." Of whom did they sing? And whence came the song, out of what tribe? And what was the songmaker's name?

As he came out, he saw the tent of Jonathan, yellow with lamplight. His son's armor-bearer was entering with a wineskin flung over his shoulder. Two servants followed, carrying fruit. Then I will go and sit at meat with him, he thought. But the Benjamites raised their voices, urging him to stay and hear. "My lord," shouted a captain over a thousand. "Does my lord find pleasure in our song?"

They wished him to be hearty and brusque. Bracing himself against the certainty of pain, he raised his shoulders in a manly shrug and shook his head.

"A good song," he shouted, laughing, "but wretchedly sung."

They agreed in high good humor, spreading their hands and making excuses: It was not their song; they had heard it for the first time only a few hours ago; it was a song of the Judahites.

"Well, then," he said in the ringing voice that they loved, "in future days have the grace to permit the Judahites to sing their own songs."

Laughter and cheering rose in the ranks of Judah. Striding as they wished to see him stride, and wincing every time his heel struck against earth, he walked out of their sight. They were content now that he was with Jonathan.

❧ III ❧

JONATHAN'S tent was orderly and festive, but for Saul's aching eyes there was too much light. Seven wicks burned yellow in their saucers of oil. A square of linen was spread upon the ground, and a servant was setting the dishes of bread, fruit, and curds upon it. There were two places, and Saul knew with immoderate regret that the Gazelle expected a guest. The young man himself was lying upon a clothes chest, his arms beneath his head, his look fixed upon the patch of darkening sky that showed through the vent, his lips curved upward in a secretive smile. The smile was provocative, like the mysterious phrases that a sleeper says aloud in a dream. The servant coughed uneasily and rattled a bowl against a plate. "The King is with us, my lord," he said. The youth leaped up then, flushing to the temples. With the vagueness of his dream still obscuring his glance, he crossed the tent and knelt and bent his head. He wore a fantastic garland. The common yellow bloom of the mustard flower, the white tassels of the grass, showed through his silky skeins of hair.

Well, Saul thought, let him kneel awhile. I have come to him naked and vulnerable out of my pain, and he is gone from me into the impenetrable tower of his own dreams, his own desires. I crossed his threshold yearning after peace, and what peace will there be in this tent tonight? "Well, then, stand up," he said.

The young man rose with constraint and awkwardness. "I am blessed in the knowledge that health has come again to my father. Let my food be the first food to pass his lips this night."

Dignity lay in refusal. Yet before he took his leave, he meant to learn who would partake of Jonathan's curds and wine. "What other guest have you also bidden to this supper?" he said.

"No other guest, if my father so wishes. Let me send to the tent of my guest to tell her to come to me some other night."

"Is it your mother, then?" He wanted none of Ahinoam; her hair would smell of herbs; the afternoon would be embodied in her—the heat, the sweat, the pain.

"No. My mother is weary in my father's service." The flat eyes cast one audacious glance at him for Ahinoam's sake and then were hidden behind the discreet eyelids. "It is my sister Michal whom I have bidden for a little talk over cheese and bread. She need not come . . ."

Wild whelp that she was, willful and troubling—he could look at her with pleasure; she was dusky, long, and comely. He could listen to her with delight; her wit was sharp; her talk was sour-sweet.

"My father, let me tell her to come tomorrow."

"Let her come," he said.

33

"My father is gracious." There was a shade too much of pleasure in the young man's smile.

"Is it for her that you wear that madman's chaplet?" the King said.

Jonathan flushed again. "I wear it to please myself."

"And if it so happens that it pleases me not?"

"Then I will lay it off tonight—" he raised his slender fingers toward the wreath— "and wear it again tomorrow."

"Oh, wear it, wear it, what is it to me?" The ache was growing behind his eyes. He had stood too much, he had talked too long. He went to the clothes chest, sat upon it, leaned against the curve of the tent, and closed his eyes.

"My lord, what sweet shall I bring up?" the servant said.

"No sweet. The Princess will bring the sweet. She has made it with her own hands."

Saul winced at the blithe voice, the buoyant rustle of garments, the light step going about the tent to see that every wick was trimmed and every dish in place. Not since the day when Agag last broke bread with me, he thought, have I delighted in preparing for a festival. . . . Jonathan sat down on the rug at his feet.

"Indeed, my father," he said, "it was chiefly because of the sweet that I rejoiced when you said, 'Let her come.' If she had stayed in her tent, her sweet would have stayed with her. And all day I have dreamed of her honey cake. Once in Gilgal when she was not with us, I had such a longing for her cake that I ate it twice in my dreams."

"Well, let her teach your servant this great art," he said in bitterness.

"No, my father." The answer was given in all good faith. "I have asked her, and she will teach no one. But she has made this covenant with me: On the day before I marry, she will instruct my bride."

"And when will you take a bride?" He was disquieted to find his own voice so earnest. He had asked the same question many times before, but always with a secret desire that his son would interpret it as a jest. Courtly as the boy was in the company of women, he had always, when the matter of marriage was broached, grown cool. And Saul knew that in the tabernacle of his heart he had not been overeager to find a daughter-in-law forever at his son's elbow. But of late he had a nagging necessity to set his house to rights. If there was a quaking confusion within him, let there be order at least in the outer world. Let the children of Rizpah be provided for; let Ahinoam receive the delayed word; let Jonathan take a bride.

Suddenly he knew that his son had not answered him. "Well, when?" he said.

"I do not know, my father. Perhaps next spring."

"And if I desire to see a marriage feast?"

"If my father truly so desires, let there be a husband for Michal. She is ripe for it. As for me, there are other matters that lie closer to my heart."

34

The question "What matters?" rose in Saul's thoughts. But the moment for the question was past. The host murmured as it always murmured at the sight of a fair woman. Michal stood at the entrance of the tent, carrying the famous honey cake.

She had come to the tent through darkness, and now the light of many lamps dazzled her. She stood at the threshold, blinking and biting at her lower lip. "Who is with my brother?" she asked in no cordial tone. It was plain that for her also any second visitor was an intruder.

Jonathan was on his feet too soon. It was as if he feared her next word. "The King our father—it is he who does us this honor. I have entreated him to break the fast of his sickness with my bread."

"Truly?" Her dark, plucked eyebrows, thin and almost straight like the antennae of a moth, went up and descended again. She laid her cake in the servant's hands with elaborate care. Then, none too swiftly, she came and knelt at the King's feet.

Saul bent and kissed the top of her head. With her it was not as it was with Jonathan—having no mystery, she had no sting; he was proof against her sullen ways. It pleased him to bend long above her. Her hair and his beard were the same dull, curling black; her skin was dusky, like his own. Clusters of big, coarse ringlets grew from her rounded forehead, over her narrow nape, around her small, pointed ears. He laid a forefinger under her chin and lifted it. He felt a perverse delight in claiming her unwilling glance. But she was out of his reach, she was on the other side of the tent before he had finished telling her to rise. And, seeing her at a distance, without her amulets and in the short tunic she had borrowed from Jonathan, he knew the best of her loveliness. Like certain young trees, she was most comely when seen from afar. All minor flaws receded then and the long, supple lines of her body were made plain.

"When will my brother serve up the meal?" she said. "The food that I ate today would have brought sickness upon a dog."

Jonathan turned to the servant, who was still hovering over the food. "We will eat now," he said. The servant went soundlessly through the entrance of the tent to sit cross-legged before the flap, to turn away unwanted guests, and to stare at the sky.

It was Jonathan who broke the hush. In the court of Saul, he was considered the soul of tact, and now he chose a subject at once innocuous and interesting. He spoke above his bread and curds of the song that the Benjamites had been singing before the royal tent. He pointed out that the tune could not be an old one. There were certain ardent, halting, haunting passages that seemed almost too personal, too poignant—such passages had not been heard among the tribes before. Plainly, it had risen in the ranks; it dealt with the slaying of Goliath; it had been composed quickly, but in a masterly fashion. What lutist was there in the host who, like Elhanan, had hidden himself only to appear in full bloom all in a single day?

35

Michal's glance had begun to wander, following the restless stir of the shadows, moving to the mottled girdle around Jonathan's waist. Suddenly her eyes narrowed. She broke rudely in.

"I see that my brother has very soon grown weary of the girdle I embroidered for him," she said.

Saul saw for the first time that Jonathan had laid off the fine girdle—stitched in blue with a pattern of gazelle horns—that was the admiration of the host. All the color had receded from the boy's face.

"I have valued the girdle that came from the hand of my sister above any other girdle," he said.

"By laying it aside when it is not yet three months old?"

"By giving it to a friend."

"What friend?"

"A friend to whom I would gladly have given my heart."

It was not only the ardor of his answer that silenced her. The King, glancing over the rim of his tilted bowl, saw the brother and sister exchange a swift look. It was as if Jonathan had said aloud, "It was of this friend that I would have spoken to you if a third had not come to destroy our privacy." It was as if Michal had replied, "Forgive my indiscretion." Saul closed his eyes. Let the two of them conspire, he thought. In small matters or in great—it makes no difference—who wishes me out of his tent for the fraction of an hour is not truly mine; he also wishes me into my grave. . . .

Now it was Michal who took up the burden of the conversation, turning it to the niece of Rizpah, who was to be given to Elhanan. A little fat girl with raisin eyes, she said, no prize even for a bastard, but kindly, with a good heart. Such a girl as could leave the court without too many regrets—for who had even known she was there?—to spend the rest of her days with an aging man and a few bedraggled sheep. . . .

Jahveh have pity on her husband, Saul thought. He had known only one man who could have put a bridle upon her, and that man was dead. Agag, King of the Amalekites. . . . He closed his eyes. With that peculiar vividness which had sharpened all his memories since the day when his illness first came upon him, he saw the burning of the city of Amalek. He felt the furnace heat of the pyre flowing his way with a change in the wind, singeing his beard. He and Abner had stood together, looking down upon the holocaust. The whole city was to be a burnt offering unto Jahveh—so Samuel had decreed; every son of Amalek, every pariah dog that roamed the streets, every snake in the house walls, every tree and vine, were to be transmuted into savory smoke to delight the nostrils of the Lord. In those far upper regions, he thought, the smoke might be savory; but he felt that he could no longer breathe it. He turned aside and saw his own sickness mirrored in Abner's gray face. "There is one siege too many for every warrior," Abner said. "We are growing squeamish, my lord, we are growing old."

It was then that the robust captain over a hundred and the raw young armor-bearer scrambled up the crumbling heap, bringing with them, as hunters bring back a lion from the chase, Agag, the King of the Amalekites. Crownless, rumpled, with his beard scorched and his tunic pulled awry, the King of Amalek in defeat looked upon the King of Israel in victory. Long silence was between them, and in the silence it was as if they had said, each to the other, "Behold, we are men." And as a man knocks a scorpion from the arm of his companion, so Saul thrust the hand of the armor-bearer from the courtly heathen's wrist.

"Is this then the hour of my death?" Agag said. A gravity, a mild regret, was in his voice, and nothing more.

How was it possible to put him to the sword? Standing in the hot blast, with the screams of a thousand dying men sounding in his ears, the King of Israel knew what died with a single man—the dreams, the lusts, the tenderness, the wisdom and the foolishness, the hopes and the remembrances, the subtle, changing, incandescent fire. . . . He bent and kissed the heathen on the brow. And since that hour—even in the face of Samuel's rage, even now, with the marks of his punishing sickness upon him, even in this tent when it was as Jahveh wished it to be, his sons and daughters falling from him as the fruit falls from the rotted bough—even now he could not find it in his heart to regret that kiss.

Michal was complaining over the fact that Ishbaal, the youngest of the royal house, had been left on her hands all day long. Not only had he plagued her while she made the honey cake by sticking his dirty fingers in the dough. Being something of a fool, he had also fallen on his belly, with his fists in his face, and had blackened both his eyes. Then all at once she ceased to chatter. In a tone that was sincere and urgent she said, "Jonathan, tell me, am I fair?"

The young man teased her. "Not hideous certainly, fair within reason," he said.

Agag, Saul thought, had found her more than reasonably fair. With the charm of a scholarly worldling who pays compliments in a language not his own, he had likened her curls to clusters of grapes, her downy skin to the wing of a moth. A man delicate like Jonathan, but darker, more resilient, tempered in the southern desert by keen wind and violent sun. A man with a voice like a jewel, hard and clear, with small glints of fire. The long nights of talk in the upper room in Gilgal. The laughter of Agag rising like living water in that dead priests' town, that place of long faces and stubborn silences. . . . Well, Agag would laugh no more. Agag wandered in the Sheol of the Amalekites as Saul would wander in the Sheol of Israel, and the ghost of Samuel would stand, forever watchful and militant, between the circumcised and the uncircumcised.

"My father, is it well with you?" Jonathan said. "Let me pour for my lord a little of this excellent wine."

"Where is this much-heralded honey cake? Let her who made it serve it up," Saul said.

Michal rose then, a little unsteadily, for she had tipped the wine cruse many times, and brought the honey cake. . . .

They returned to the subject of the new song. "There is a rumor," Jonathan said, "that it is the work of a Judahite."

Michal lurched forward to gather a handful of raisins. Her eyes were moist and bright. "How long is it," she said, "since you have reviewed the ranks of Judah?"

Jonathan blushed. And what was it that sent the blood surging to his temples?

"Why do you ask?" he said.

"There is a new man among the Judahites. The maidservant of Rizpah saw him. She wearied my ears with talking of him all morning. She is like a fly in honey. She wallows in delight."

"Truly?" The young man stared at her coldly, and she stared back, insolent, flushed, and fair.

"They say that he is very comely." Her voice put a bloom upon the words. "They say he is better to look upon even than the Gazelle, taller by the height of a hand, and very white. The maidservant of Rizpah has said fifty times that his eyes are of a strange color, gray like the eyes of our mother. His hair also is not like the hair of other men. The maidservant of Rizpah says there is a redness in it. It shines like polished wood."

Jonathan shoved his dish from him. He was plainly distressed.

"The maidservant of Rizpah saw him bringing water up from the cistern, and he was beautiful."

"Does the maidservant of Rizpah go often to the cistern?" he said in a chill and bitter voice. "Is she a pursuer of men?"

The girl was untouched by the reproof. She laughed and stretched luxuriously, and her little breasts showed firm beneath the folds of cloth.

"The maidservant of Rizpah told me not," she said. "I was at the cistern. I saw this Star of Judah with my own eyes." She stared her brother full in the face; and the King knew that she had come to the tent to speak of this stranger and could not hold her peace even in his presence, since she had drowned her prudence in wine.

But Jonathan turned from her and looked at his father. For the fraction of a second, their glances met; and Saul saw confusion, pain, and something close to fright in the flat, brown eyes.

"Let her be married, my father," Jonathan said.

"Wherefore?" His surprise sounded in his voice.

"She is a wild mare. She will couple with whatever pleases her in the host."

She stiffened with the righteous anger of the betrayed. "He calls me a wanton without cause," she said. "He knows nothing with which he can debase me before my father, even though wine has loosened his blabbing lips." Her wet eyes sought Saul's face.

"No, now," he said, stroking her coarse black curls, "it is your own lips that are loosened, my girl. Only, I would rather you did not go down to watch young men at the cistern. Do not walk without an attendant in any of the ranks save the ranks of the Benjamites." He kissed the dusky cheek. "As to your marriage—do not trouble your heart needlessly," he said, rising and shaking the crumbs from his robe. "To whom should I give you, seeing that the man I chose for you is dead?"

They were all then that he wished them to be. They knelt on either side of him, forgetting their quarrel for his sake. Michal drew close and leaned her warm head on his thigh. Jonathan's eyes, grave and pitying, fixed themselves upon his face. "I will go now and leave you to yourselves," the King said.

ᨒ IV ᨒ

JAHVEH has withdrawn his evil spirit, and my sickness is fallen from me, the King of Israel told himself. . . . He spent the morning sitting on a rug before his tent, eager that the host should see his vigor and industry, talking more brusquely than ever, discharging a number of petty matters that had long troubled his conscience. He called Elhanan to him and gave to the hero a magnificent breastplate of hammered bronze from his own collection of armor. He forced himself to see Doeg the Edomite, the keeper of his herds, who had recently come up from Gibeah—a sycophantic, soft-voiced man whom he abhorred. The overseer gave a commendable and perfectly honest account of affairs in Gibeah, but gave it in so sickly-smiling a manner that he seemed to be protesting constantly against a general conviction that he was the living embodiment of dishonesty. I cannot endure his presence; he is like an intolerable stench in the nostrils, Saul thought. . . . So he sent him off to take a token of victory to the priesthood at Nob. It was a stroke of inspiration. At the same time, he had rid himself of both Doeg and the putrid head of Goliath. The keeper of the herds departed, flattered and flustered by the importance of his mission, carrying the monstrous sword of the giant of Gath upon his shoulders, and followed by an armor-bearer who bore the head and was in his turn followed by a swarm of flies.

At the noonday meal, in the shadowy and silent tent, the King arraigned himself over his bread and curds. What have I accomplished? he asked himself. . . . And he knew in his heart that he had avoided the chief question. He had not yet sent for Abner, to discuss the business of strategy, to decide whether the army should pursue the Philistines to the sea, or disband, or return to Gilgal for rest. He rose from his meal and began to walk about in the tent. It was humid, umbral, with a band of harsh light showing beneath the goat's-hair and the ground, with hard blueness glaring through the vent. It was then that he knew for the first time that his sickness had not utterly departed. All morning he had been sensing it beneath the cheerful confusion, as a man tastes under the tang of herbs and spices the faint bitterness of tainted meat. Certainly, he told himself, it would not be wise to sit down to strategy in the heat of the day. Later, in the cool of the evening, when the wind of God had come again, when this last remnant of his wretchedness was gone, he would send for Abner. Meanwhile, he would talk to the scribe who kept the accounts.

The young man who came to him with the accounts had not been long in his service. He was not fit to bear arms with the host, being sickly and very shortsighted, but he had served with scrupulous care among the baggage wagons. His name was Ahitophel. He had a certain gentleness, a kind of quiet grace. His little eyes peered into the shadow as if they did not expect to see.

Ahitophel began at once to read the list of remaining supplies: three hundred cheeses, a hundred cakes of dates or thereabouts, three wagon loads of barley, scarcely a trace of wine. . . . As his voice droned mildly on it became plain to Saul that the crisis in supplies was acute. Four days more, five days more, and the army would be destitute. Either the host of Jahveh must be moved or the baggage wagons must be sent into the eastern plateau for foraging. Well, had he not already decided to settle the matter of strategy with Abner that very night?

"Concerning this matter of the flock of goats," Ahitophel said, "my lord will remember that they were pastured in the valley two moons ago. I would bring to the mind of my lord the fact that they have eaten all the grass in the place, that nothing but a little scrub is left, and that the she-goats are ceasing to give milk. Does my lord wish them to be led to some other pasture, so that they may eat and the host may drink?"

A rasping annoyance rose in Saul. "What else could I wish? Could I wish them to starve?"

"No, my lord."

"What then?"

"Nothing, save that it seemed to us foolish to move the flock when every morning the captain of the host has thought, 'Today we depart.'"

It was just, it was humbly said, but Saul could not let the matter be. "Has it entered the tabernacle of your all-seeing mind that a little fodder might be brought down to the goats? Should they starve and the host thirst because some lout does not care to weary his shoulders with fetching and carrying?"

"No, my lord."

"What then?"

"Only that there is so little fodder left. We have scarcely enough for the oxen that pull the baggage train. Even the donkeys have been without fodder this day. My lord knows that the hour for going is long past, and we——"

The King walked more swiftly round the tent. With each step, he felt a vibration at his nape and behind his brow. "Well, leave it, leave the whole matter!" he shouted. "Take a little fodder from the oxen, and tomorrow this and all other questions concerning the host will be clarified."

"Certainly, my lord," Ahitophel said.

40

The walking had become intolerable. Saul sat down upon the clothes chest and shut his eyes.

"Does the King wish his servant to depart?"

Even this small question was a burden. He did not reply. If the young man went out of the tent, how then would the afternoon be filled? The sin of brooding and dallying would then be plain, to himself and to the host. To sit dreaming in one tent while Abner waited in another, to be motionless while the host fretted, to lie on the rug and sleep . . .

"Shall the servant of my lord——"

"Yes, go, it is enough." He rose and stopped the young man at the entrance of the tent and laid a conciliatory hand upon his arm. "But go first to the tent of Abner and tell him that I will be with Rizpah at the hour of the wind of God. And after that, go to the tent of Rizpah and tell her that I will come to break bread with her after I have refreshed myself with a little sleep."

✥ V ✥

In the tent of Rizpah, more than in any other part of the encampment, the King could take his ease. All the comforts he would have scorned to ask for himself, she bespoke for him. She had prevailed upon Ahitophel to find room for a chair of hers in the baggage train—a particularly deep and comfortable chair with a curved back. Whenever Saul came to her, she contrived to have some piece of soft stuff draped over the wood—a mantle, an embroidered skirt, the lambskin on which she pillowed her head at night. And in the end, he would find himself seated in such luxury as he would never have claimed, a bowl of rare wine at his elbow, and the lamps set behind him so that his eyes would not be afflicted with their light.

Her devotion was such that she knew his most subtle need and filled it before he had named it, implying always that she was guilty of doting and he completely free of any cause for shame. Her passion was tempered to his passion; her strength extended to the degree of his needs, was never less and never more. And in the aching passivity that came upon him in these latter years, she would kneel beside his bed and rub his worn body, renewing him with her touch. "Not for my lord's ease, but for my own pleasure," she would say.

It was this subtlety and devotion that bound him to her, rather than her beauty. He had seen many fairer women, and yet it had never entered his thoughts that he might take another concubine. She was no longer young. She had been with him ten years and had borne him seven sons. A few gray threads showed in the black abundance of her hair, and the slight down above her upper lip, so delightful in her girlhood, had grown more pronounced. But to him these were minor flaws; they evoked pity and tenderness and enhanced her real charms—the long body that bore its splendid bosom proudly, the peak of hair that grew down into her round, smooth brow, the slow smile and quiet eyes. If the lutists of Israel had ceased to sing of her beauty, it was no matter; they were boys or impotent dreamers; they could not value the midsummer ripeness, the practiced and seasoned loveliness.

She had made herself beautiful for him tonight; her robe was of fine linen; her girdle was a broad strip of greenish blue; her amulets—little glimmering moons of gold—shone at her ears, her throat, and her slender wrists. But her hands, which usually lay open and serene upon her knees, were not quiet. They dragged at a bracelet, pulled at a chain, put back a wisp of hair.

"Peace be with my lord," she said, bowing to the ground.

But there was no peace, even with Rizpah. He sank into the chair and sighed.

"You have been long away." There was no reproach in that, only a confession of loneliness.

"I have been sick, both in the flesh and in the spirit. Otherwise I would have come to you long since."

"I know. The sickness of my lord is my own sickness."

"It has passed," he said.

"Then truly I have a new heart."

In that case, he thought, why should you pull your rings from your fingers one by one, and put them back again? He said, far too loudly, "What ails you tonight?"

She gasped and grew still as a stone. "Nothing, my lord. I am not well."

"Not well? What is your sickness?"

"Nothing—a small thing—the manner of women is upon me."

Swiftly, craftily, behind closed eyes, he counted the weeks. She had lied to him, and he was profoundly shaken to know as much. It was not that she had never lied before; she preferred a kind falsehood to a harsh truth. But tonight she had lied poorly, using any shabby tale in utter desperation, not asking to be believed, but only to be given a little time.

In the days of his victories at Michmash and Jabesh-Gilead, he had never feinted at suspicions. As a lion leaps upon his prey at the lightest stirring in the brush, so he had lunged at the vaguest shadow and borne it forth and shaken it to death. Rising from the chair, he strode toward her, meaning to demand the name of the ominous thing that lay behind the lie. But when he stood above her, looking down upon her bent head, he was unmanned by tenderness. He, also, was in need of time—a few hours of quiet, a few calm words, a little food, a little rest. He laid his hand upon the dry, familiar softness of her hair.

"Come, then," he said, "I have kept you long from the evening meal. Before we have broken bread, Abner will be upon us. Let us eat at least a few bites together in peace."

She would not let him sit beside her on the rug. With a persistence that told him how shaken he looked, she urged him to return to his chair.

42

She crouched on her knees and handed up to him the choicest portions of the food, bit by bit, so that overabundance might not rouse his disgust. This brief respite had made her gentle and almost merry.

"Would we were in Gilgal, and the ban of Jahveh lifted. Then I would sleep against my lord's side," she said.

He made no reply. He could not reconcile the two of them—love and the black city. How could he embrace her in rooms still blank with the remembrance of Samuel's departure? How could he kiss and sleep among stones that had been washed in Agag's blood? He would march after the Philistines, he would drive them into the sea in spite of Samuel's displeasure and Jahveh's displeasure, in spite of the resurgence of the cold madness and the pain. But the streets of Gilgal he could not and would not walk again.

"Surely we will lie together, but not in Gilgal," he said.

"Where, then, my lord?" Her hand, holding his hand now, began to tug at his rings, pulling them over his knuckles.

"Askelon, Gaza, Gath—whichever of the cities of the Philistines best pleases my beloved. They say that the palace of the Seren of Gath looks out upon the sea . . ."

"But, my lord," she said, dropping his ring in fright, "my lord knows . . ."

Then she fell silent, seeing that they were no longer alone. Abner stood at the entrance—an aging man of mighty frame, a sick man with melancholy eyes.

"Forgive me," he said, "I have come too early. I thought that you would long since have risen from the evening bread."

Saul stared at the red-rimmed eyes and saw in them a mingling of trouble and sorrow. The pale hand fumbled in the iron-gray beard, the iron-gray hair. "Then it is well with you at last?" Abner said.

"It is well with me." He could not add the words "at last." Abner had spoken them so hollowly, so wearily, that it was as if he had said, "Then it is well with you too late."

Rizpah's eyes darted from one to the other. "Even though the captain of the host has already broken bread," she said in a voice shaken by her hastening breath, "let him sit and eat a little fruit with us. The King has barely tasted what I have prepared for him. Let us all eat."

It seemed to Saul that she was pleading for him. Abner's purpose melted before her warm eagerness. He laid aside his cloak and his spear, and sat with her on the rug at the King's feet. He went further still in his desire to see her soothed and satisfied: he began a courtly conversation to grace the respite. He spoke of the worthlessness of the young lutist whom he had sent to Saul out of the tribe of Dan. "And truly," he said, "I would have done better had I sent you an ass, for if an ass brays, at least his breath is sweet."

"Can nothing better be found?" Rizpah said.

"There is an accomplished singer among the Judahites, a shepherd come out of Bethlehem. I have not seen him, but those who have set eyes

43

upon him say that he is comely beyond any man in the host. It was he who wrote the song of Elhanan and Goliath. If the occasion should arise, and if my lord should so desire . . ."

The bread was as ashes in the King's mouth. They prepare for the return of my sickness, he told himself. They wait for the spell to come upon me again. Have they also found a chorus of antiphonal singers to go before me when I am carried to my grave?

The noises outside, the chatter of the host, became very distinct in the ensuing stillness. Did the King dream it, or was there truly something more than the usual murmur beyond the goat's-hair walls? He thought he heard a noise as of a gathering storm upon water—a long, receding roar. Rizpah was the first to move. She went to the entrance and called upon the maidservant who sat before the tent. The girl rose and came in to clear the cloth. Her presence was a diversion, and in some measure her activity restored seemliness.

When the last plate had been put aside, when the rumpled cloth had been shaken into the night, when the wicks had been trimmed and the maidservant had gone forth, Rizpah said, "Shall I depart and leave my tent for the captain and my lord?"

He could not let her go. He motioned her to the rug, close to his knees. He wanted her within the line of his vision, so that he might stare at her warm cheek without turning his aching head. He wished that Abner would sit on the rug also, but the captain of the host had gone to the other side of the tent, to sit on the clothes chest and to lose himself in shadow.

"My lord," said Abner, "this night must not pass before we are of one mind concerning the disposition of the host."

In the old days, Saul had not waited for such a word. When the cloth was half-cleared, he had been already upon his knees, drawing his battle plans upon the ground with a twig, pursuing the enemy over rugs, driving him past the goat's-hair walls into the night, into the sea. . . . Now he sat on the chair, pressing both hands against his temples, waiting for the next sentence that Abner would send in his direction. But when the captain of the host spoke at last, it was to Rizpah that he turned.

"Does the King know what has come to pass in these last two days?" Abner said.

"He does not know."

"But I bade you tell him, and I had your promise . . ."

"My lord came hungry and weary into my tent. I wished him to eat and rest."

Saul clenched his fists against his temples. "God of hosts!" he shouted, "They bicker in my presence as to who shall tell. Do my concubine and my captain plot together while I sleep? Am I a third in council? Shall the King wait to be told what two already know?"

The woman bowed her head almost to her knees. The weary man who sat in the darkness drew his hand across his face. "Let my King hear, then," Abner said.

44

He heard, above the first sickening gurgle of that well of pain which rose behind his brow, how yesterday, while he sat above the pot of steaming herbs, three hundred of the men of Jahveh had risen and departed to their homes—all the fierce-hearted desert rats whose names were written in the ranks of the Calebites.

It was a loss, to be sure, but so small a loss beside the amorphous and monstrous tragedies in his imaginings that the faint nausea which had been rising in his stomach began to subside. "The men of Caleb," he said, "were never so close to my heart that their doings could take the savor from my food. Had you spoken earlier, I would have laughed and eaten three times what I have eaten this night. Instead, I ached much over nothing and dreamed a thousand horrors that were not so."

He rose and pushed the rug aside and knelt upon the ground. With his forefinger he drew the westward slopes, the plains of Sharon, the cities of the Philistines that bordered on the sea. "Let us go to gather the fruits of Elhanan's victory. Let us move against the city of Gath," he said.

"My lord," said Abner, "last night the Kenites also departed."

Truly? Had these zealots for Jahveh, these fire-worshipers of the southern deserts, these smiths and cattle-breeders, followed the banners of their foolish Calebite brethren and gone forth? It was to be expected and to be borne with resignation. . . .

"How many?"

"Two hundred."

"It is nothing. Let them depart." But it would have been wiser to name Caleb and the Kenites in the same breath—one blow instead of two upon his throbbing head. His hand, drawing the walls of Gath, trembled. Let the matter be settled soon. He needed darkness and peace. "Come, how shall the rest of us move westward?" he said.

Abner had risen and was moving slowly out of the shadow. "My cousin, my dear cousin and my beloved lord, only listen a little, inasmuch as we cannot march against any city . . ." He fell silent. He clutched at his beard and bowed his head.

Saul sprang from his knees and stood glaring into the gray face. The woman behind him gasped; perhaps she wept. In the charged silence, the noise of the host rose again—an unwonted noise, as of spears and breastplates taken from their stacks, as of many going feet. But louder than these was the sickening gurgle of that spring of cold black water within his skull.

"Dog and son of a dead dog," he shouted at Abner, "what else have you taken it upon yourself to hide from me? Is Ephraim also gone, and Judah, and Benjamin?"

"No, my lord," said Abner. "No. Only the tribe of Dan is gone forth—is going forth even now, this night. Only Dan."

"How many?"

"A thousand—all."

"Wherefore?"

"In anger that my lord—that Israel—that we have tarried in our tents and lost the fruit of Elhanan's victory. Because it seems to them manifest that the anger of God is upon us—so it seems to their ignorance. They are poor tribes, unlettered men—they cannot tell what they dream and what is so."

Saul reeled and leaned against the chair. "When did it come upon you," he asked, "this knowledge that Dan would depart?"

"This afternoon, my lord."

"This afternoon? God of Sinai, how was it that you told me not?"

"My lord slept."

"Could I not be wakened? Did I sleep the sleep of the dead?"

"Truly, my King, I came to your tent only an hour after Ahitophel went from you. I called upon you with a loud voice, and I laid my hands upon you, and a priest was at my side and conjured the spirit of sleep from you and sprinkled holy oil upon your face."

He saw how it had been, how they had bent above his senseless body, how he had lain with the secret wounds of his spirit unveiled to them in his sleeping face. The thought was like a lashing tongue of fire.

"And when you would not awaken, the priest bade me withhold my hand. It was plain, the priest said in his ignorance . . ."

"What?" He bellowed like a bull under the knife. "What was plain?"

"That Jahveh desired that the men of Dan should depart—and that my lord should sleep."

He knew now how he had been publicly called accursed, how the priest-hood and three of the tribes had come to the belief that Israel was to be shamed before Philistia for Samuel's sake. It was a bitterness not to be borne. Violently, with the flat of his hand, he struck the bearer of such tidings full in the face.

Even as he withdrew his hand, he was unmanned by a great remorse. The captain was sick and no longer young; his body bore the scars of Jabesh-Gilead, Michmash, and Amalek; for seven years a spear wound had remained blue and galling on his thigh. And Saul, remembering these things and seeing the welt of the blow on that sober and honorable face, felt a wild longing to strike his own chest and weep.

"Let my cousin forgive me. Saul was not Saul when he lifted his hand against his captain," he said.

"My lord is the King. He may strike whomsoever he chooses. He may throw to the dogs whatsoever outworn thing no longer gives him satisfaction."

"Not so, Abner, not so . . ."

"Let my lord find himself another captain. Let my lord . . ."

He was terrified. Samuel had departed; it was possible that Abner also might depart. "It was not I that struck my cousin, it was not I, but the accursed spirit which Jahveh has sent upon me. My right hand goes forth against the command of my heart."

Rizpah called out his name behind him. He stepped backward, groped for the chair, sank into it, and laid his hand upon her head.

46

"My lord," said Abner, and came and knelt before him, and took his free hand and kissed it. "What has the King to do with the ignorant babbling of the dullards of the north and the savages of the south? Shall the lion trouble himself with the braying of a pack of asses? Come, let us talk at long last of this matter of the host, for the hour is late."

"Well, then, Abner, what is your counsel?" Saul said.

Quietly, without veiling one harsh detail, Abner brought forth to him the nakedness of the calamity. The host had lost fifteen hundred men in two days and could not turn its ranks toward the west.

Well, Saul could endure that. He knew as much.

Then two possibilities remained.

Only two, after the score that had sprung from Goliath's blood? Well, he would bear it. What were they?

The army might disband and assemble again after the Feast of the First Fruits.

Unthinkable! Imagine the cries of delight that would go up in the streets of Askelon and Gath. Consider the time that would be given to the Philistines.

Yes, truly, what the King said was so. There was another way, a better way. Let the host proceed undivided to some eastern city, for rest. Then, when the ranks had been augmented, when Dan at least had been won back by diplomacy, when Philistia was drunken with confidence—then let Israel fare forth out of Gilgal . . .

Gilgal? The King shouted the abhorred name at the top of his voice. Were there no other cities in Israel? Let the host proceed to Hebron, Shechem—any other place. But those who marched to Gilgal would march without a king. He had vowed before Jahveh, and he vowed it again, that the city of priests and blood would never see his living face.

"My lord," said Abner, "I beg you, shout it not to the host."

He shouted it more loudly still.

"The hearts of the men of Jahveh are turned toward Gilgal," the captain said. "They will proceed to Gilgal and to no other place. Forbid them the city, and the host will fall apart."

"Wherefore?"

"What does the reason matter to my lord the King? That they so desire —is not that enough?"

"Have they turned womanish while I slept? Is it for the soft beds of Gilgal and the thick wines of Gilgal that my will is to be laid aside and my honor sacrificed?"

"No, my lord, no."

"What then?"

"Since my lord asks it, and since he who withholds ill news in mercy becomes to my lord a dog and the son of a dead dog, let it be said. The host is ignorant and given to superstition. The host believes that since in Gilgal my lord sinned against God through disobedience to Samuel, there and there only can the evil spirit be conjured forth from him, there and there only can he be purified."

What passed after that Saul saw darkly. All shapes, all movements around him were aqueous and blurred. The world turned gray and green with his sickness. As the face of one swimmer rises to another, vague, undulating, transformed by the moving water between, so Rizpah's face moved toward him, saying some intolerable sentence, insisting that he must go to Gilgal, that there was no other way. . . . And, God of Sinai, what had he done? He had meant only to turn her aside, but his hand had again gone out in spite of his heart. He had thrust at her with such violence that she had toppled backward and had struck her head against the corner of the clothes chest. Through the dim, multitudinous waters of his torment, he saw her hand go up slowly to the back of her head. She stared at him in wonder. Her fingertips were marked with blood.

It was then that his captain turned upon him with a cold stare of loathing. Through the increasing blur he saw Abner bending above Rizpah and Rizpah looking up into Abner's face. They were together in that glance. "See what I suffer," the dark eyes of the woman said. And Abner's eyes answered that he saw and wept silently for what he beheld.

A torrent of insult surged into the King's thoughts. He opened his mouth to spew out the bitter words: how they might make their bed together in Gilgal, how Abner was doubtless beyond the getting of sons, how she who consented to be a concubine might also consent to be a whore. But the words were never uttered. They were lost like all things in the onrushing madness, the all-immersing torrent, the all-consuming roar. With the last of his strength he strove against the fit, buffeted it back until he was out of their presence, out of the light. In the outer darkness, a pair of arms caught him and bore him up. Whose arms he did not ask, nor did he see the face. He reeled past the sleeping ranks, past the tent of Jonathan, past the tent of Michal and Ahinoam, past the black and empty tent of the captain of the host. At his own threshold, he shouted aloud to his armor-bearer that all the tormenting lamps should be extinguished. Then he fell upon his face. The waters closed over him utterly. It was as it had been in the time of the Deluge. The world became one blank, motionless sheet of waters, gray as iron, cold as death.

✤ VI ✤

IN THE FIRST pearly light of the morning, the captain of the host started out of a deep sleep, sitting bolt upright and pulling the coverlet over his nakedness. He felt, rather than saw, a presence within his tent. In the misty triangle of day which showed beyond the threshold, the red light of a torch shone, making the fog around it radiant and effulgent with its glow. He remembered Saul's departure from Rizpah's tent; the King had left him in madness and fury; he should have wakened with a heavy and troubled heart. But for some incomprehensible reason he wakened joyous and light. It was as if Jahveh had bent above him while he slept, renewing the blood in his veins, placing under his ribs a new heart. The air seemed charged, holy, tremulous with the promise of high events. He waited and knew not what he waited for—the voice of the presence within the tent, the clearing of the mist, the rising of the sun.

"Is the captain of the host awake?" It was a voice that he knew well, the voice of the King's armor-bearer. He had come in haste, half-dressed, from the royal tent. It was his torch, thrust into the earth, that spread the rosy radiance through the fog outside.

Abner stood up, dragging the coverlet with him. Remembrance had broken upon him, increasing his exaltation a hundredfold. Last night, *she* had turned to him for pity. A rose had grown upon the barren stalk of his years of waiting. She had crept toward him out of her distress. Her cheek had lain against his hand, her head against his knee.

"I come to Abner from my lord the King."

"Bearing what message?" He did not greatly care. He raised the hand where her cheek had lain and pressed it to his lips.

"My lord the King has been sick even unto death."

He had forgotten it. "How is it with him now?" he said.

"Only a little while since, his sight was restored to him. His voice also is restored, but for the most part he sits like one hewn out of stone. He bade me ask Abner to summon to the royal tent the lutist whom he knows, the Bethlehemite."

Abner felt again the strange blitheness. The thought of seeking at dawning for a comely boy with a lute filled him with a disproportionate delight. He knew the same joyful excitement that he had known in his childhood when, in the hills that lay around Gibeah, he had gone searching before sunrise for the feathers of a fabled bird that was said to soar on wings as long as a man's arms to the very doors of Paradise. He smiled at his own childishness. "Say to my lord the King that I will go, and gladly," he said.

The armor-bearer bowed and went out and laid his hand upon the torch.

"But leave the torch for me." He cared nothing that there was no longer need for it, that soon the whole flat plain would be washed in long and silvery rays of light. He would bear it out of season, for its useless beauty, even as he carried his love.

⤳ VII ⤳

ABNER had come with his paling torch into the ranks of Judah. All around him, in groups of twos and threes, hand touching hand, knee grazing against knee, the embattled shepherds and farmers slept. It was as if he were the last living man in the world, going forth to call a dear brother back to life out of the ranks of the dead.

The lad he sought would be lying among the bowmen. As he had hoped in the days of his childhood that the legendary bird of heaven would be big enough to shadow the whole town of Gibeah, so he hoped that the lutist would be dazzling in his comeliness, not for Saul's sake, but for his own. After the tenderness of Rizpah, after the holy glow that had been upon him when he awakened, only a miracle could suffice.

The first oblique rays of morning were streaming over the encampment when he saw the lute. The hand of the lutist lay upon it—long, supple, white, and young. The sleeper was wrapped from head to foot in a cloak of goat's-hair. Those around him had huddled close to each other for warmth, but he lay proudly apart. The captain of the host planted the torch in the earth near the shrouded one and knelt on the ground and touched the cloak. Dew rolled about on it like beads of glass. Warily, skillfully, he folded back a corner and saw the brightness of the hair, the pale and dreaming face, younger than he had thought to find it, graver, and far more fair.

And even as the chill of the morning struck the face of the sleeper, Abner felt a poignant regret. Why should a beardless boy be dragged into the tent of a mad King? Why should his visions of magnificence be shrunken and confined to the tawdriness of realities? In Bethlehem, as in Gibeah, the legendary bird still soars; in Bethlehem, as in Gibeah, the young are nourished upon dreams; and what is a king beside a dream of a king?

The flame of the torch blew about in the fitful wind. The light quivered upon the parting lips, the opening eyes. The boy sat up and stared wildly about him, first at the torch, then at the captain.

"Do my eyes behold the captain of the host?" he said.

"Yes," said Abner, thinking how the dream of a mighty warrior must have dwindled to fit his own shape. "I am he."

"What does my lord desire?" Now the lad was on his knees, shaking back his hair, fastening his tunic over the naked whiteness of his chest.

"That you arise and come with me."

"I?" The gray eyes grew large and still with wonder. "Whither, my lord?"

"To the tent of Saul."

The boy sprang to his feet. "To the King? Wherefore?"

"To sing before my lord."

"Truly?"

"Yes, truly, and even now, even within this hour. Take up your lute and come softly. It would be better if we did not rouse the host."

"Yes, my lord."

"Come, let us go first to the grove of the cistern, so that you may drink and refresh yourself."

"My lord is kind."

50

They moved through the shaking tangle of brush and thorn into the grove. The air was cool. Sun lay in brightening patches upon the grass and the mustard flower. The worn stones of the cistern reflected the early light, and the surface of the water shone. The boy went about his ablutions awkwardly; all in a moment he had been transformed into a lank and angular child.

"My son," said Abner, staring at the shifting patterns of sun on the water, "what is your name?"

"David, the son of Jesse, of Bethlehem."

"Well, then, David, let us talk a little of this matter of your going to the King."

The boy stood rigidly at attention. He had not yet dried his face. Water trickled over his brow and into his eyes.

"No, now, there is no need to stand before me. Finish what you have begun. I have talked with those whose hands were busy before."

"I am grateful to my lord." He wiped his face quickly on the skirt of his tunic, bending his head very low so that he need not show his thighs.

"The King is ill. The King is very ill. There are those who say that an evil spirit is upon him. There are some who might think in their ignorance that the King is mad."

The lutist knelt and tied a second knot in the thongs of his sandals. But Abner knew that he had bowed down to hide a look of fright.

"The King will be sitting alone in his tent in darkness."

"Alone? Will none be there save he?"

"None."

"Not even Jonathan?"

The name of the King's eldest son was lovely to speak and to hear, but the captain of the host had never before savored the fullness of its beauty. The syllables fell from the young man's lips as reverently as the names of the heroic dead.

"The King sits alone in his tent," the captain said. "He will not speak, nor will he stir. Trouble him with no greetings. Walk ten paces beyond the entrance and kneel on the rug and lay your hand upon your lute and delight him with your voice."

Suddenly the young man turned very pale. He leaned forward and laid his hand upon Abner's knee. "Will my lord go with me?" he said.

"No, David," he said, gently, so that the name meant "darling" in his mouth. "Jahveh will go with you, but none save He." The gray eyes pleaded with him still; the supple hand still lay upon him. "I will go to the threshold, but I can go no farther."

"My lord is very gracious to my frailty."

The captain smiled. "Those unto whom the Lord is gracious, they can afford graciousness," he said.

As he walked toward the royal tent, with the young man coming up deferentially behind him, Abner asked himself wherein he had seen any sign of Jahveh's graciousness. The mark of the King's blow was still upon his cheek; his old wound had begun to fester again; the host was seething with rebellion; the matter of Gilgal was not yet settled; the King his lord, the Lion of Israel, was sick in body and spirit. And yet his heart glowed like a torch, transforming his whole body into a roseate effulgence. He was as light, as radiant as a morning mist. Wherefore? Ah, yes, let him remember it—how she had crept toward him, how her cheek had lain against his old, unlovely hand last night.

✺§ VIII §✺

Light seeped slowly into the black tent of the King of Israel. A faint line of it crept through the gap between the goat's-hair and the earth. A pale patch of it shone above the vent. A breastplate, a spear, the polished side of the clothes chest on which the King sat, had taken on edges of light. But the King saw them not. He saw only the bald beach from which the waters had withdrawn, the blank sky, the infinite stretch of sand.

Sounds of awakening spread through the camp—the age-old murmuring of the host. Breastplate clanked against breastplate, spear against spear. Priests chanted their incantations, and captains harangued their battalions. But the King did not hear. He heard only the sound of the wind upon the beach—the wild, continuous, penetrating whine.

It was then that another sound, borne upon the chill mourning of the wind, made itself heard. The boy had lifted his voice again in the ranks of Judah. He was singing under the stars. While Rizpah bent in the lamplight to pour the wine, while Abner sat in the shadow, he sang. And let him sing forever, since in the silence after his song comes the red welt upon the captain's face, the blood upon the fingers of the concubine. . . . No, that was finished and immutable. That had happened yesterday. The wan sunlight crept into the cup of darkness which he had made with his hands. He knew the place, the hour, and the bitterness of the hour. They had brought the singer out of the host to exorcise the evil spirit and to soothe the pain.

"They brought you to me that you might sing, did they not? Well, then, sing, my son," he said.

The tones of the lute fell into the stillness slowly. The measure was solemn, elegiac. Elegy for a dead bowman. . . . "A mighty bow, a bow of oak, anointed to goldenness with the sweat of your hand, O my cousin. . . ." How detached, how childishly remote was the melody! Only the very old who had long since forgotten the blood, or the very young who had not yet looked upon it, could mourn so lyrically over the mighty gone down in battle. "I have touched your fingers, and they were dry in death. . . ." In the darkness behind his hands, Saul smiled. No, he thought, you have never touched a dead man's fingers, my dear son; your voice is the voice of those who wandered innocent in the first garden, before the Lord withdrew the veil from the face of death. . . . "Your bow is my bow.

On the strong string is my slight hand. . . ." Slight indeed, the King thought. Keep to the lute, my lad, and let the bow alone. For Jahveh has given you a golden way with words and tones, and even your young dream of grief is more poignant than the elegy that bleeds out of another man's torn heart. . . . "Hear me in Sheol, my unavenged, my cousin. . . . " The melody sprang forth, marvelous in its complexity. "May it be done so to me and more also if I do not find the hand that sent the arrow into your chest. The hand that smote my cousin shall be as the hand of my cousin. . . ." A wild descent of tones, such as had never been heard in Israel, was pulled from the cavern of the lute. The voice sank almost to a whisper. "Dry as a stone."

The King could wait no longer. He withdrew his hands, and dimly, through the curtain of his own damp, matted hair, he saw the maker of songs. Sun streamed through the entrance of the tent and edged the slender body with an aura of light. There was a gleam as of polished wood upon the opulent, flowing hair. This, then, was the Judahite of whom Michal had spoken in the unguardedness of an amorous mood and too much wine. And he was fair, fairer than even her nimble tongue could tell, fair in form, fair in face. Weary with kneeling, he had sunk back upon his heels; his head was tilted to one side. With a diffidence that only heightened his grace, he raised and quickly lowered his large gray eyes.

"Shall the servant of the King go forth out of the King's presence?" he said. His speech was no less lyric than his song.

"Wherefore?"

"Lest my lord be wearied with my poor singing."

It was plain that the lad thought nothing but good of his own singing, and knew well that he put no burden upon any listener's heart. Yet he uttered the words so naïvely that the King could not refrain from smiling. "I think the lutist knows I am not weary," he said. "Unless he himself is weary, let him sing another song."

"A song of my lord's choosing? A song out of the past?"

"No. Another song of your own."

The boy knelt again, pulling his body erect, bending his head to listen to the plucked strings. Yet only part of his attention was given to the tuning of the instrument. Through the long lashes, the gray eyes kept darting upward, eagerly, covertly examining Saul's face. Nor was his glance the mere stare of the curious who wish to carry back to their gaping neighbors the story of the mole on the royal cheek. The lutist out of Bethlehem looked as though he thought to find in the man before him the reply to some easeless question that had long destroyed his rest.

"Would my lord find a love song burdensome?" the youth said.

Again Saul found it impossible to suppress·a smile. The question had implied that love and the King had nothing to do with each other, that the King was either too regal or too old for ardor.

"Believe me, I can yet find pleasure in a song of love."

The boy bent his head then and veiled his eyes and gave himself up utterly to the lute. The tones that he plucked forth were morbid tones; they embodied the brooding ache of the virgin who has not yet confined love to a single act, an isolated hour. They spoke of love uncongealed, the yearning that washes sky and earth in one sick tide. And, listening, the King was borne back to a forgotten time in his own youth, when he had stood in the fields around Gibeah, looking at the furrows that his plow had made, feeling his eyes grow dim and his heart dilate with the same sick desire. Who, then, had been the beloved? The face was lost; he could not remember even an occasion or a name. Yet the dark furrows existed in his remembrance—the turned sods black in the light of the declining sun, the yellow mist of foliage upon the brush, the fronds of the fig tree in feathery bloom. . . .

> The beloved of my heart I saw once only,
> In the morning, by the willows at the cistern.
> He is my cousin,
> He is my love.

> For the binding of my wounds he tore his princely girdle.
> He has touched me, and the coolness of his fingers is upon me.
> Fair is my cousin,
> Fair is my love.

> I have worn a path among the tender grasses,
> I have bruised the mustard flower by the cistern,
> Seeking my cousin,
> Seeking my love.

> How shall I find him? Where shall I seek him?
> The wound he healed is nothing to the wound he put upon me.
> Where is my cousin?
> Where is my love?

The young man sank back upon his heels again, spent with ardor. The King looked down at him and smiled and pondered over the song. Had the boy praised himself through a woman's mouth? It was possible. The young are all drunken, and justly so, upon their own fair persons. The vision of themselves, transfigured and glorified—that is what they seek when they stare into each other's eyes.

The lutist, quieted and refreshed, raised himself again to his knees. He had shaken his dream from him. His eyes were discreet and clear. "Will my lord hear another song?" he said.

"What other song, my son?"

"That which I made to the glory of Elhanan because he slew the giant of Gath and made of Ephes-Dammim a holy place."

All radiance was withdrawn from the occasion. The mist of poesy dissolved and left the grim reality: the embittered tribes, the lean provisions, the welt on Abner's cheek, the blood on Rizpah's fingertips, the accursed necessity of turning toward Gilgal—all the harsh exigencies of the hour.

"No, not that song," he said.

He turned his head slowly from side to side and knew that his pain was gone. The singer had restored him, but to what? To the knowledge that he had let slip from his fingers the fruits of Elhanan's victory. He knew that the gray stare of the boy was upon him. He encountered it and saw what he expected to see: pity for the great King in his sickness, pity for the lion that lies gasping at the river's edge but remains a lion nevertheless.

"My lord's victories—they are the victories for Israel to remember," the Bethlehemite said. "Amalek and Michmash and Jabesh-Gilead. The servant of my lord could make such songs as were never heard in Israel if he could hear the story of those battles from the lips of the King his lord."

What a strange mingling, Saul thought, of policy and tenderness! With one sentence he pours balm upon my sores and assures himself of a place at my side.

"What victory, then, would the lutist wish to raise from the dead?"

A delicate glow spread upon the white cheeks. Was it pleasure in the thought of a place at court half-won? Was it a boy's delight in the legends of old battles, told since his childhood around watch fires in the Judean hills, strewn with all the garlands that the old heap upon a lost event lest the young should guess that it is dead beneath the banners and the flowers?

"Jabesh-Gilead," the lutist said.

How was it? thought Saul. Let me strip it of all the dreams in which I have draped it, let me lay bare the small but honorable core. A little town of no consequence, besieged by a band of Ammonites and an implacable general—a little outpost town. . . . "They were very few, the men of Jabesh-Gilead within the walls. They were few and poor—farmers and farmers' sons. They had wrested their land out of stony earth. They had few plowshares and no swords, and they were lean because their harvests were meager and their flocks were scrawny and small. Who was to care that Nahash the Ammonite rode down upon them, to shout for a tribute that they could not pay, to roar in the tents with a mighty voice, to talk of the cutting-off of hands and the gouging-out of eyes? And yet in their hour of stress, they warmed themselves at a little ember of hope. 'We also are of Israel,' they said, 'Jahveh's men and circumcised. And if we send messengers west and north and south—who can say?—perhaps one man yet remains in Israel who will hear and pity and rise from the shadow of his fig tree and put aside the banter and the wine.' "

It was the time of the planting, he remembered, in a year when I was not yet King even in Benjamin. I and the oxen before me were drenched with the day's sweat, and my heart was high with the sowing of seed. It was the hour for resting, but there was in me a fervor that would not let me rest. . . .

"The men of Gibeah were gathered in the field when I returned from the plowing. They stood grieving around the messenger from Jabesh-Gilead, making the little whimpering sounds of the impotent, free with their tears but very sparing with their blood. And it came upon me as I listened that all Israel was unmanned, that the hand which was strong in the desert had grown lax beneath the tree and the vine, that there was weeping in Jephtha's grave and in Barak's grave. . . ."

This came upon me, he said to himself, and also some wild mood for which words are too frail—an understanding of the need to wreak violence, the desire to hack and kill, the heritage of desert vengeance that will have its blood. . . .

"And the spirit of Jahveh came upon me, came in a whirlwind out of the south, and I took up an ax that lay by a fallen tree, and I laid my hand upon the yoke of oxen, and I cut them in pieces so that the garments of the fearful and the faces of the effeminate were spattered with red. And the pieces of the oxen I sent throughout all the borders of Israel by the hand of the messengers, save only the thigh bone, which I kept in Gibeah that we also might remember our shame. And I said, 'Whosoever comes not after Saul and after Samuel to the succor of the men of Jabesh-Gilead, so shall it be done unto his oxen.' And it was as a trumpet call in the ears of the dreamers; they were roused in the shadow of their vines; they girded their loins and came forth to war. Three hundred thousand came to me out of Israel, and thirty thousand out of Judah. And Jephtha and Barak ceased to weep, and the song of Deborah was heard again through the length and breadth of the land. And we came in the midst of the morning watch and smote the Ammonites until the heat of the day. And it came to pass that those of the uncircumcised that remained were scattered, until there were not two of them together. And it was as it had been in the days of Gideon—we were men before the Lord."

But how shall I tell of the evening at the high place in Jabesh-Gilead, he thought, of the thanksgiving which was too much and begot shame, of the thin lambs slaughtered and the sour wine poured into the poor bowls, of the lean brown faces and the wet and ardent eyes? In the streets of Jabesh-Gilead the Lion is not forgotten. Were I shamed in Israel, defeated and dismembered and cast east and west and north and south, yet would they find me. The men of Jabesh-Gilead would gather my bones and bury them with honor, and come in the morning and in the evening unto the third and fourth generation to pour wine upon my grave. . . .

Noise beyond the tent—shouts of a battalion going out to practice archery—dissolved the remembrance. He saw the shepherd's face, attentive, humble, staring up at him with wondering eyes.

"There, shepherd, make a song of that," he said, half ruefully, half kindly. "Dream a little, pluck a few strings, play with words a little in an idle hour. Weave me some small piece concerning Jabesh-Gilead, and bring it to me that I may have it with my supper some night."

The boy flushed and bent his head. "My lord knows that what he asks cannot be."

"Wherefore?"

"Because the matter is too great for the art of my lord's poor servant. The King—he is the poet of Jabesh-Gilead. He speaks, and it is a song."

"They teach their lads an apt and courtly language in the hills of Judah."

The gray glance, hurt at the affront, sought him and would not leave him. "What I have said to my King was not taught to me in Judah. My lord the King should know by the poverty of my words that they came without thought out of my heart."

And while he looked upon the shepherd, while he saw that the boy had spoken in guileless fervor and in something close to love, the world—even the bitter world with its burden of shame and defeat—became acceptable to the King of Israel. He would go up to Gilgal, yes, and suffer there. But afterward he would journey on to his house in Gibeah. He would sit beneath the ripening figs, with the warm shoulder of Rizpah under his cheek. He would walk through the arbors with Michal and count the firstlings of the flock with Jonathan. He would make his armor-bearer captain over a hundred and take this comely shepherd in his stead, and there would be laughter in the mornings and music in the evenings. There were yet left to him a few years of well-earned peace. . . .

"Shall the servant of my lord go forth from the King's presence?"

"Not yet. What is your name, my son?"

"David, the son of Jesse, out of Bethlehem."

"David?" The voice laid a bloom of tenderness upon the name.

The boy blushed again. "It was my father's choice," he said. "I am the son of his latter years."

"So? Well, go to Abner, David out of Bethlehem, and say to him that I am more than satisfied with what he has sent to me. Say that I will make you my armor-bearer when I have raised him that I now have to some other honor. Say also that the ranks are to turn toward Gilgal within the hour, if that is what my captain desires. As for you, send back to Bethlehem the word that David is from this day the body servant of the King." He paused to enjoy the amazement and delight in the shepherd's eyes.

"My lord the King is more than kind." He rose, plainly eager to go forth, to exult in his good fortune without constraint. For the first time Saul saw the slender length of him. Jahveh had made him unbelievably fair. The King wondered at his own tenderness, and mocked at it in his heart. Why should he regret the departure of a singer out of Judah, a beardless shepherd, a lad with a white, unscarred hand? And yet he did regret it. The lad had turned too eagerly to the bright world beyond the tent.

"Well, go, then, babble your glories to the host," Saul said.

BOOK THREE

BOOK THREE

SAUL and the host of Jahveh moved on toward Gilgal, over the burning highway, between the sun-baked villages and the yellowing swells of grain, in the first strength of the summer weather. But those whom the King loved he turned from him at a fork in the road; he wished to spare them the crass pageantry of his disgrace.

Since God and the army wanted a spectacle, let there be a spectacle for the army and God. His friends need not look upon it. Let Abner lead Rizpah to her father's house, where she might rest for a little in her rightful place between the generations—her old mother chattering women's matters beside her, her children at her knee. Nor need his own family choke upon the gall of it. Let Ahinoam, Michal, Jonathan, and Ishbaal return to Gibeah and await him there. It troubled him little that two of his sons, Malchishua and Abinadab, were already in Gilgal and would be witnesses to his shame. They were the children of his body only; he had begotten them casually and seen them little; there were times when he could not even bring to mind a clear vision of their faces. He remembered their deeds and asked himself how they fared, but never what they desired.

So, at the fork in the road, under leaves dried by heat and rattling in the capricious summer gusts, he made his farewells. He allowed himself no embraces, since, kissing one, he would have to bestow his lips upon all, and there was in him a hard conscience that would not let him touch Rizpah and Ahinoam within the same hour. He was sorry to forfeit Michal's warm cheek. He could not resist laying his hand briefly upon Jonathan's brown hair. David he called to him last of all. Until the final minute, he had been unable to decide whether this lad was a servant to be taken to Gilgal without shame or something more than a servant, a being before whom a king might blush when the burnt offering was laid in remission of sin upon that black altar where Agag had died. It would have been sweet to have the music close at hand. And yet, and yet . . . He could no longer hide it from himself: He, who had longed above all else to detach his too-fond heart from the world, had loved again. He could not bring himself to stand as a suppliant under this gray gaze.

"Go rest your peerless voice in Gibeah," he said, and his own voice mocked lest it should betray the depth of his affection.

The boy wilted, as he always wilted at mockery. His lute dangled from his fingertips; his eyelids were lowered; his head hung to one side. "What poor magic my lord finds in my voice will be gone from it with the going of my lord. The glory of my voice is that it is a delight in the King's ears. What then is my voice when the King listens to many singers in Gilgal and forgets his servant? What am I to the temple chorus, to the cymbals and the pipes and all the antiphonal songs?"

Saul smiled. "Let your heart rest. Fifty bad voices do not make a good voice."

The Bethlehemite believed it too readily. A delight in himself, an easy complacency that would have been distasteful had he been one shade less comely, animated his face.

It would have been well, Saul thought, returning to his donkey, it would have been well to reprimand him, to send him off to Gibeah with a wholesome thorn in his heart. But, try as he would, the King could find no words. He mounted and watched the little band turn down the road and disappear behind a silvery screen of olive trees. Then, still smiling, he laid his hand upon the donkey's neck and urged the beast forward, speaking to it with unwonted gentleness.

Ahitophel rode up beside him. "That is a fair lutist that my lord the King has found for himself."

And the heart of the King was suddenly warm toward the meek and shortsighted young man.

"Yes, very fair," he said.

❧ II ❧

LONG AFTERWARD, when David looked back upon his arrival in the city of Gibeah, he saw the event as through a mist. All sounds were muted, all colors grayed. The city, seen at sunset from a far hill, had the solemnity and the unreality of a dream. Massed behind it were great somber clouds, with long rays athwart their gigantic curved crests and level bases. A sense of eternity lay over the fortress, the stone houses, the streets trodden hard by generation after generation of going feet. All that was living seemed poignantly transitory against this stony ancientness. The fronds of the trees, the clumps of grass that grew at the edges of the paths, the vines that shimmered against the general grayness like a green haze, the small figures of men and beasts—all were touched with mortality. Whatever lived carried within itself the burden of its own death.

Only one sound existed in his recollection of the journey—the clanging as of a monstrous brass cymbal within his own heart. My God, I also will die and be dust, he thought, and they will exist after me, these stones. . . . Wordless, terrified, with the reverberations of the clash still trembling within him, he moved across the last meadows—too green, unreal in the oblique light—a mortal among mortals, humbled before his first conviction of his own death.

And what next, what came after that? he would ask himself, trying to evoke a clearer remembrance of that first day. Nothing—a dim succession of streets, a snake held forever static in its progress across a moldering wall, a flight of pigeons held forever in space, with the faint gold of sunlight upon their wings. Saul's house—old, sprawling down the side of the hill. Saul's garden, filled with motionless trees, where a long table was spread, where they sat down together before tasteless food, to stare at the receding chains of hills, to watch the quenching of the sun.

At least a score of faces must have floated upon that solemn twilight. His remembrance preserved only one. Across from him and at the far end of the table, with a line of featureless beings between, sat Jonathan. He had never been less comely. The dust of the long journey had streaked his cheeks and dimmed the cloudy sheen of his hair. The flesh of his face seemed to have shrunken with weariness. It was as if he bore his death closer to the surface than the rest. The King's son had never been less kingly; but, to the shepherd out of Bethlehem, he had never been so dear.

In this declining light, David thought, across this nameless assembly, look upon me, let your eyes embrace me, my friend. Holier than the flesh of incorruptible angels is your flesh with your mortal sweat upon it. Let us share our deaths with each other, beloved. . . .

And as though these thoughts had been spoken aloud in the dream stillness, the King's son turned his head and looked into David's eyes. Stared until another inward sound broke upon the dazed quiet—sound of a single pipe, one tone, high and wild and shrill, shatteringly sweet. Then Jonathan laid his hand deprecatingly upon his smeared cheek and put aside a strand of his dulled hair. He smiled, and remembrance dissolved upon that smile.

Later, much later, when David had sat long beneath a tree, nursing the thought of that glance, Ahinoam came to him and led him to his bed. She went before him, a grave, aging figure with a torch, past clumps of trees, past a few lingering beings still lounging upon the lawns, past lighted windows, to the great door. In future days, when he came to know every corner of that house as he had known the house in Bethlehem, he wondered at the dream of limitless space which it had conjured up in him on this first night. It seemed to him then that her white robe streamed before him down endless corridors, up imperial flights of stairs, past cavernous chambers, into aerial towers. He fancied that the room in which he slept soared into the province of the eagle, that from an eastward window he might look upon the Jordan, that from a westward window he might watch the blue, changing surface of the sea.

He did not remember her going, or the blowing-out of the lamp, or the business of stripping off his clothes. He could recall only one more moment, when he lay in darkness, staring at a square of moonlight on the wall. Jonathan sleeps under this roof, he thought. . . . And it seemed to him that the solemn stones also had become mortal, that the sweet liquid of life had flowed into them, that they rose and fell to the coming and going of Jonathan's breath.

⤷ III ⤶

For seven days, while the necessities of penance hung over Saul in Gilgal, a respectful air of gloom lay upon all who lived in his house. Ahinoam managed the affairs of the household with a blank, unsmiling mien. Michal sulked in an upper chamber. Jonathan wandered without companions into an outlying field and practiced there with the bow. He could be seen from the eastern windows, wearing himself out with constant shooting and running; and when he paused it was only to attack the field itself, to pull up weeds and stones.

There was little chance for companionship in those days. The meals were ample and excellent, but the eating was desultory. The long table stood beneath the trees in the garden, laden with great, soft cheeses, fresh figs from the orchard, skins of milk, new-baked bread. But all the signs of conviviality—honey, pastry, meat, and wine—were absent from the spread. It was as if they ate for the sake of nourishment alone.

But on the evening of the seventh day the table gave evidence that the time of constraint was ended. The board was washed and strewn with grass and sweet herbs; two roasted kids were carried smoking into the cool summer dusk; and between them, in place of the skins of milk, were set great jars of wine. Michal, dressed in yellow as for a feast, glittering with amulets and girdled with a wide band of blue, came forth with a honey cake. The warriors, sprawling on the lawn, suddenly remembered a dozen jests that they had not shared with one another. The captain of the guard withdrew to trim his beard. Jonathan tasted the honey cake and told all who cared to listen that his sister had outdone herself. And David, looking down upon a garden suddenly come to life under the stars, turned from the window, admired his own face in a basin of water, and went with a high heart to walk upon the festal lawn.

There had been rain late in the afternoon. Beads of it still lay among the herbs and rolled from the leaves of the fig trees. The scents of the garden—thyme and hyssop and marjoram, bruised grass and turned earth —were drawn out by the moisture. .The ground was soft, yielded gently under his feet. A feeling of high events waiting to come to pass, a sense of multitudinous possibilities, made his journey across the garden a triumphal advance. But when he reached the table, his ardor was baffled; a dozen warriors and overseers stood between him and the King's son, who was carving the meat at the head of the table.

A soft, ingratiating voice assailed him from behind. A pudgy body pressed against him. It smelled of sweat and heavy spice.

"The armor-bearer of my lord the King will do well to wait for the carving of the second kid," the stranger said. "It is the fatter of the two. Permit me to make myself known unto David of Bethlehem. I am the overseer of the herds, Doeg the Edomite."

David thought how a week ago, sprawling with his brother among the rude Judahites in the camp of God, he would have considered himself fortunate to come into contact with a person of such consequence; but the remembrance did not lessen his annoyance. He turned to the overseer with dignity. He heard his own voice, too cold, saying that one kid was as good as another to him, since he had never had much taste for meat. It was a lie, and he felt that the Edomite knew him for a liar. The flesh around the raisin eyes wrinkled; the soft, womanish mouth struggled to suppress a smile. Then suddenly the face accommodated itself to the occasion. It turned gravely toward the sky. "A goodly night for a feast, is it not?" Doeg said.

"Truly, a goodly night." His voice was cordial, but his heart said, When will this toad depart? . . . Many had been served and had wandered off to eat at the other end of the long table or to sit down beneath the trees with their portions. Only four or five soldiers, including the captain with the newly trimmed beard, stood between him and Jonathan.

"It will be merrier here when our lord the King returns," said the sickly-sweet lips. "He will be eager for music when he is finished with his troublesome business in Gilgal."

God of battles, David thought, looking nervously about him, has this idiot no mind at all? . . . In all the seven days of constraint no member of the company had been so gross as to mention the King's name, and now this fool had blatantly alluded to the King's disgrace. Anyone standing within earshot might think that the Bethlehemite himself had provoked this conversation. Fortunately, Jonathan at least had not heard.

And, while he stared at the King's son, David knew vaguely that by his silence he had offended the Edomite. I have made an enemy, he thought, and then forgot the matter, because Jonathan had bestowed the long-awaited look upon him.

The King's son raised his chin and addressed the first word not to David but to the Edomite. "Which tempts the tongue of the overseer of my father's herds—the fat or the lean?" he said. He had broken a rule of precedence and broken it in Doeg's favor. The King's armor-bearer stood higher than the overseer and was to be greeted first. Yet Jonathan had exalted this sycophant above him. Wherefore?

"Whatever the favorite son of my lord has by him," the Edomite said, clasping his fat fingers in a confusion of ecstasy and embarrassment.

"A little of each?"

"My lord is gracious."

"A little of each, then," Jonathan said.

He bent to cut the slice from the joint. His face was veiled by the soft fall of his hair. Through the shining curtain, David saw a signal, a brief and merry look meant only for his eyes. And he knew that Jonathan had served the Edomite before him for only one reason: that Doeg might have no cause to tarry at the table, that they might eat the meal together and alone. Doeg and Jonathan were talking softly together, but he scarcely heard them. He knew that the King's son was striving to make amends for the deception with kindly questions. He knew that Doeg could barely wait to hurry to some secluded spot where he could fondle his triumph in peace.

But when the intruder was gone, neither of them could carry the weight of the anticipated minute. Shyness and uncertainty were upon them both. Jonathan stared at the meat, and David stared at the sky. When at last the King's son found words with which to address the lutist, they were the stale and dishonored words that he had spoken earlier to the Edomite.

"What tempts the tongue of the armor-bearer of my father—the fat or the lean?"

He could not forgo the pleasure of saying the beloved name. "Whatever you have by you, Jonathan," he said.

"I have laid by a piece of the shoulder for you, David." The bloom was upon the name.

"Jonathan is gracious."

While the exquisite hands sought among the herbs for the hidden slice, silence came between the two young men. David groped wildly among his thoughts for some radiant phrase, but he could find nothing, and he blushed at his own emptiness.

"Now that I have found it, it does not seem so fine a cut as I had thought," said Jonathan, laying the meat in David's dish.

"A beautiful cut, such a cut as I have never . . ."

In uneasy stillness, with awkward hands, they took their portions of the rest of the food. Every movement was a crisis. A toppling tower could not have dismayed them more than a falling cake of bread. The quiet was unbearable and must be broken. Jonathan was dipping his bread into the honey jar.

"Are you fond of honey?" David said.

"Honey," said Jonathan with fervor, "is for me the food of angels."

"Truly?" They had turned from the table and were walking carefully with their laden dishes toward a bench beneath a fig tree.

"Truly." They were beside the bench and stood staring at each other with tense, nervous blitheness. "Were all other food gone from the earth and only honey left . . ." They sank in utter weariness upon the bench, set their dishes upon their unsteady knees, looked earnestly at each other, and sighed.

And now the reality, which had been as nothing beside the dream, began to fold itself in the dream's sorcery. The scent of the wet earth rose around them. The foliage of the fig, only a little darker than the sky, trembled overhead. The big warm drops spilled upon their lifted faces. Lights had been kindled without and within the house. Torches flared at the far end of the garden, and the lighted windows cast wan squares of yellow upon the grass. But no light touched them. They were alone in an island of dark.

"There was a time, my cousin," said Jonathan, "when honey was my undoing. Because of a little honey, I stood on the edge of my grave. . . ."

Slowly and with many pauses, he told the tale of the battle of Michmash, of the great black stone in the forest where he had knelt for an hour, waiting for his own death. All day the Philistines had been in flight from Michmash even to Aijalon, with Saul's victorious army in pursuit. The afternoon was golden with the sense of a battle won. When Jonathan came with his fellows into the shade of a forest, none of the enemy was by, the clash of the battle had subsided, and the birds had resumed their song. And there on the ground before him—he had not eaten since morning, and it was as if his valor had been rewarded with food by a messenger of God—there among the fallen leaves was a great, clotted pool of honey, dripped to the earth from a broken hive. He thrust his rod into it and bore it upon the end of the rod to his lips.

But in the evening, when he and his companions rejoined the host, a shadowy possibility too monstrous to be believed at once was there to mar the victory. A great stone had been thrown up unto Jahveh at the edge of the forest; the warriors were bringing their oxen and their sheep to be blessed and slaughtered there; and the King's son heard that his father had sworn at dawn to sacrifice to the God of battles any Israelite whose lips should take food before the coming of the night.

The matter might have passed without question if Saul in his lusty appetite for combat had not decided that the Israelites should fall upon the encamped remnant of the Philistines and decimate and plunder them that same night. The warriors were eager enough, but the priests hung back. It would not be well, they said, to set out on such a venture without an oracle from the Lord. So they called upon Jahveh, called repeatedly as dusk thickened over the smoking altar, called and received no answer. "Wherefore?" the King asked, wild with impatience to continue to chase. Because, the priests said, there was a sinner hiding in the host. Some warrior had broken the vow of abstinence and had permitted food to pass his lips.

And why, Jonathan asked, bending toward the listener in the hushed garden, laying his hand on David's wrist, why had he, a King's son and nurtured in honor, unafraid before the hurtling spear—why had he remained silent in the ranks, a coward evading death?

He paused a little then. His hand lay over David's, and their fingers intertwined. Their heads, leaning against the back of the bench, bent toward each other, and the tale went on, more serenely now. He told how Saul, eager to find the sinner and continue the pursuit, offered to cast lots. On one side the host was to stand and on the other Saul and

Jonathan. The judgment of the lot fell upon the royal two, and still he did not speak. Then—when the lot had been cast between him and his father and the wrath of Jahveh had broken upon his head—only then did he raise his voice. He complained aloud that he had eaten only a mouthful of honey. He made public wail over the fact that for this small transgression he must die. But the people would not have it so. While he knelt, sick and shaking, with his head upon the stone, they shouted the names of his victories. For an hour, while the feverish moon ascended with terrible speed out of the hills, they contended for him with Saul and God. Jonathan was the hope of their children; he had courted death many times for them; now let some other man die in his stead. And a young weaver out of Beth-shemesh came to the altar and lifted up the King's son and knelt in his place and died.

"It is this," Jonathan said, withdrawing his hand and bending forward so that his face was hidden in his hair, "it is this that is the bitterness— that they call me valiant because I went out to meet the easy death for Israel in battles, and he died the death of which I was mortally afraid. We carried his bones with us back to Gibeah. On the other side of the garden, on the slope of the hill, there is a cave where he is buried. Always on the days of mourning for the dead I laid the oil and the fat above him. Always until this year. And this year, because the evil spirit from Jahveh had come upon my father, there was confusion, and his grave went bare of sacrifice. They call me courageous, and he died that death for me— they call me loyal, and I forgot."

How should this be answered, David asked himself, and why, of all the glorious incidents in his heroic history, had he chosen to tell the sole tale that discredited and shamed him? Suddenly David's heart knocked wildly, knowing the reason. Not in renown, not in concealing robes of legends, had the King's son come to him, but naked and vulnerable, saying, "Behold me as I am and love me as such, for I would not deceive you with appearances." And this ultimate incorruptibility was the more touching to the hearer because he knew that he could never be capable of such candor. A dozen damning events rose in his own recollection. He longed to hear his own voice matching shame for shame, but a full minute passed, and he did not open his lips. He sighed, knowing that confession was a virtue beyond his power.

"Will my cousin eat?" Jonathan said.

"I think upon the hour when my cousin knelt at the stone, and I have no taste for food."

"It is nothing. It is past."

"Of all the men of Israel," David said loudly, "it seems to me that Moses was the greatest."

Jonathan looked at him in distress and wonderment and asked, "Wherefore?"

"Because it is said that in an evil hour he broke the tablets of the law and cursed the people and offended the Lord. That he broke the tablets and cursed the people—others might have told these things concerning him. But his quarrel with Jahveh was a matter between him and God. None could have told it—none save he. That he had the greatness to tell his own shame—therein his glory lies."

Jonathan took his hand then and raised it to his cheek. For the space of many heartbeats they remained so, seeing in the darkness the earnest shining of each other's eyes. Then the ancient admonition, the old, unalterable law came between them. Aching and baffled, they drew apart.

For a while there was only the ache, the hush, the dark, and a few warm drops still falling. Sorrowfully, with chastened hearts, they turned to speech; in words at least they might come together. Little by little, they were comforted, knowing what vast domains of remembrance there were to wander in together.

"When I was in my seventh year," Jonathan said, "my father took me into the hill country of Ephraim, and we walked upon those stones and ashes where once the holy city of Shiloh stood. Has my cousin ever visited that place?"

"No. Only Ramah I have seen, and now Gibeah, and the mean hills around Bethlehem where I spent my days."

"May those hills in which my cousin made music by day and slept by night stand forever in fertility and peace! We came to Shiloh in the grayness of the dawn. There are no streets, only fallen walls. Toads and serpents move among the bricks, and the moss is green on the stones. My father led me up the steps, onto the high place where the house of Jahveh once stood. The shell of that house still stands, and the doors on both sides are open, and the wind carries the dust of the bricks in and out through the open doors. I saw the altar and the two horns thereof, blunted by the swords of the Philistines and marked with the filthy symbols of the uncircumcised. My eyes had never looked upon the ark of God. Long before my birth, the heathen had borne it away to make a trophy of it in their cities by the sea. But when I beheld in Shiloh the place where it had stood, my heart opened up within me. That was long ago, but the emptiness has not gone from me. When will a race of heroes arise in Israel and Judah, to march into Philistia and carry back the ark of God?"

Suddenly David found a channel for that fervor which had been locked within him when they drew apart. As he loved Jonathan, so he loved the land and the ark. Israel, which had been before this hour a fair woman for him to possess, was transmuted into something elusive, holy, magical, and beyond possession. As he might mourn over wounds upon the slight body beside him, so he mourned over the ravished temple at Shiloh, over the bleeding Philistine gash along the coast, over the almost mortal laceration where Jerusalem lay in the hands of the Jebusites. This Israel was to be courted forever without consummation, with tears and battles— a fair shape, unattainable, retreating forever, and forever followed down the years. And through the smoke of sacrificed cities, through rainstorm and sandstorm, over the peaks of inaccessible mountains, one banner to follow, and that a cloud of glimmering hair.

"When you next go out against the Philistines, let me go with you, Jonathan," he said in an urgent tone.

"I have dreamed of it, my cousin. Unless my father forbids it, we will surely go together. Let it be soon."

The uneasy silence was again upon them. The thought of Saul had come with strange force into their world of dripping, whispering trees. Like courtiers caught in an equivocal conversation, they flushed and began to pick diligently at their food.

"How many times has my cousin sung before my father?" Jonathan said.

"Only once. Only that one morning, before we went forth out of Ephes-Dammim. I was afraid in the beginning—there was fear in my voice."

He could no longer see the King's son in the darkness, but he knew that Jonathan had turned earnestly toward him. "Do you fear Saul?" Jonathan said.

He could not answer at once. He did not know. Once he had asked himself whether he feared Jesse, and had come to the conclusion that he feared Jesse more than any other living being because Jesse knew a lie for a lie. Now it seemed to him that Saul also had a keen eye to pierce the veils of equivocation.

"The King my lord is like a lion and humbles the heart," he said.

"Do you fear him when his sickness is upon him?"

He remembered the King's face as he had first seen it, loose and vague, emptied of thought. "No. Then least of all."

"There are some who say—I do not know how truly—that in his sickness my father has been known to raise his hand in violence against those whom he loves. If it should so be—Jahveh forbid it!—but if it should so be that my father should strike my cousin, let David remember that it is not Saul. For in our childhood he lifted us when we fell, and he carried us when we were sick, and he held us upon his knees and fed us with his own hand. And if God strikes him, it is not that he sinned through cruelty, but that he could not be cruel even for Jahveh's sake."

"My heart has already told me that what my cousin says concerning Saul is so."

Far off, at the other end of the garden, a torch was uprooted and borne forward. The flame lashed wildly about in the wind. Boughs, bits of ground, and clustered foliage came into being on its passing light. The torch and its unseen bearer moved in their direction. Once more, with a sweet sense of shared guilt, they bent above their honey and bread.

"Jonathan! Jonathan!" A girl's voice, husky and imperious, bade the night yield up to her the person of the beloved.

"It is my sister Michal," Jonathan said.

70

After the long darkness, the yellow glare was feverish and intense. It opened up a sulphurous cavern edged by black leaves. At the core of this painful brightness was such a woman as he had never seen. As when a falling star trails across the sky, he looked, and was less delighted than afraid.

He had seen her three or four times before, on the road to Gibeah and in the camp of God, but always at a great distance. Then she had worn a boy's tunic and moved like a man among men. Now veils floated about her; crescents shone in her ears and between her breasts; her mouth and her eyebrows were touched with dyes; her hair, piled high and held by golden pins, escaped to make serpentine curls upon her brow.

"David of Bethlehem?" she said. "Was he in the garden all this while?"

Jonathan laughed. David turned then and saw his face. It was haggard and harassed; it wore a chill and bitter smile.

The flame ceased to veer and sway. The young woman had composed herself. "Had I but known," she said, "I would have borne word of it to our mother. All evening our mother has yearned after a song."

The cold and pettish voice said, "He will sing another night."

It was plain to David now that some quarrel divided brother and sister. Whatever the quarrel, she had no mind to pursue it. She laughed, and put a curl back from her forehead. "Nevertheless, you must both arise now and come to the house with me. For our mother is uneasy for Jonathan, and the lights in the garden have been quenched, all save this, and there is no guest save only the armor-bearer of my father that has not found his bed."

Jonathan rose and wrenched the torch from her hand. "I will carry it," he said.

In the shifting light and shadow, a sudden dismay came upon David. He yearned passionately over the gone hour and hated the torch that had rent their darkness and driven them apart. Jonathan walked between him and the young woman, looking at neither, staring at the few bright windows that still cast wan squares upon the grass. At the door, Jonathan quenched the torch.

"Jahveh be with you while you sleep," David said.

"And with you," said the Princess.

"With you," said Jonathan. Nor did any other word or look or touch pass between David and the King's son that night.

❧ IV ☙

Next morning when David wakened the sun was already high. For more than an hour it had been streaming through the window of the tower room, begetting within his body a melting sense of generation. As light penetrates to the depths of the sea, so the warmth had descended into his dreams. He could recall nothing—no image, no voice—yet he knew that what he had dreamed had been at once shameful and sweet. Suddenly he started up. Someone was there—a child was there—a slight, unearthly child whose head was covered with silky brown curls, whose forehead bulged and was marked by blue veins.

"Jahveh give you a good day," David said.

The child merely stared at him. By the golden amulet that hung between the knobby collarbones, he knew that this was Jonathan's brother Ishbaal, the youngest of the royal line. The mellowness of the waking hour went out to the small visitor in a wave of tenderness.

"That is a fine amulet," David said.

The child continued to stand on the threshold, mute and staring.

"I know your name. It is Ishbaal."

The child said nothing.

The unwavering look disturbed David. He grew ashamed of his own nakedness. He rose and covered himself with his tunic and stepped into his sandals. The glance of the child never faltered.

"I have a lute here in the room," David said. "Will Ishbaal come and touch the strings?"

The child stared.

Surely he can speak, David thought. He is at least four years old, and none has ever said that he is of halting speech. "Come pluck the lute," he said. He was amazed to know that his own voice had grown peremptory, that he was contending with a child.

Slowly, solemnly, without averting the fixed stare, the boy walked into the room, bent down, and plucked a single string. Then, wiping his hand upon his tunic, he walked into the hall and was gone.

While David stood pondering this strange encounter, a voice sounded in the corridor. It was the same arrogant voice that had torn the intimate stillness of the garden, but now it called upon Ishbaal and added that the anniversary of his birth should be a day of national mourning and that he would have only himself to blame if he broke his neck on the stairs. Then the voice ceased, and the speaker stopped, suddenly meek, upon the threshold of David's room.

"May the sun of Jahveh shine mildly upon the delight of my father," she said. "Have his eyes beheld Ishbaal my brother?"

He could not answer at once. He had dreamed of her, and he remembered it now. Her body had shed its yellow veils and floated toward him through the warm, sensuous water of his sleep. Now, in the light of a summer morning, half those veils were truly gone; she was clothed in a boy's tunic; her arms and shoulders were bare. Her flesh was dark, and her hands were like the hands of Saul—tawny, long-fingered, hard. There was a sting in her, a harsh brown sweetness, like the sting of coarse honey upon the tongue. She looked at him squarely and smiled.

"Where has he hidden himself?" she said.

"He was within this room not a moment since."

"Did he rouse the maker of peerless music out of sleep?"

"No, I lay here upon my bed, awake but still dreaming when he . . ."

By some change in her face, some almost imperceptible movement of her lips, he knew that she was seeing an image of him stretched in morning desire upon the sun-warmed bed. Modesty should have made her turn her head aside, but her look did not leave his face.

"He wanders through this house like a spirit in Sheol, and it is I that must be forever going after him. He could break every bone in his body— the stairs are very steep." Yet she did not move.

He knew that she waited for him to speak, and the tension of the occasion drew from him words that he did not intend to say. "Does the Moon of Benjamin wish me to come with her to look for the child?"

Her eyes brightened and moved with quick conjecture. "No, wait. I will find him. I hear him. He is playing in a heap of old armor at the end of the hall. Only wait for us, and we will break bread together."

"The Princess is gracious."

She bowed to him in mockery, as if to say, "Let there be no more of this courtliness between you and me." She went then, shouting mightily in the echoing hall, "Ishbaal, you wild ass, you apple of Sodom, let that helmet alone!"

While she pulled the child away from the pile of old armor and half dragged, half coaxed him through the hall, David stood at the eastward window and looked out upon the bleak field where during the period of Saul's penance Jonathan had wrestled with roots and stones. He could not understand the ache that was in him. He stared at the parched, uneven surface of the field, empty except for a few disconsolate-looking crows, and he felt as vacant and as desolate as the scene he looked upon. Wherefore?

She was at the door again, smiling upon him above that other small, unsmiling face. "Put a blessing upon the morning of the armor-bearer of our father, my little donkey." Her brown hand lay upon the soft, pale curls.

The child stared.

"It is useless," said David. "He hates me." He was ashamed that his voice should reveal so plainly that he was aggrieved.

"How so?"

"When he was with me earlier, he would not speak," he said, laughing uneasily and coming to the door.

She took her hand from Ishbaal's head and laid it upon David's wrist. "He is not worthy of the concern of the sweet singer. He is a little fool."

Her fingers were light and warm upon him; her face, lifted toward him, was gentle and cordial. He should have experienced pleasure, and indeed her touch called up the beginnings of pleasure. But suddenly he wished her out of the room, out of his world. Why? Perhaps because she comforted him for a pain that he could not feel without humiliation. Perhaps because her body was tainted with some half-remembered flavor of distaste that he had sensed in his dreams.

On the way downstairs they exchanged no words. They walked between the walls of great, uneven stones, now in deep shadow, now in almost blinding squares of light cast by the tall windows. A scent of dried spice, heavy and troubling, clung to her coarse clusters of curls. It did not altogether please him, and he was glad when they came into the common room, where the scent was lost in the wholesome fragrance of baking bread.

Ahinoam knelt before the oven, and a maidservant stood above her, taking the new cakes of bread from her veined white hands. Sunlight lay upon a table spread with cheese, milk, and fruit. But to David the room was desolate, and he knew in his heart that the glory of the day was gone because the room was empty of Jonathan.

During breakfast, a long argument ensued between Michal and Ahinoam concerning Ishbaal. Michal had set her heart upon cleaning and brushing a certain flock of long-haired goats that were her father's pride. She needed a man to help her, yes, but let none suppose that she could manage both a flock of goats and a bothersome child. Where was the nurse who had been brought out of Gilgal for the express purpose of tending Ishbaal? The woman was pregnant again, no doubt. Well, pregnant or not, let her see to him. She, Michal, had already followed him up and down for two hours.

Ahinoam suggested compromises. Let Michal take the boy with her for the morning, and the poor woman would take him away at noon. Furthermore, could the goats not wait? Tomorrow . . .

No, they could not wait. Tomorrow Saul might come. Then he would see his long-haired darlings matted and covered with burrs and dust. She could not, as she had said before, tend the whole flock alone. But surely some guest in the house would offer. . . . Indeed, did not a shepherd sit here at table among them?

And what could David do? "Let me come with the Moon of Benjamin to look to the goats of my lord the King," he said.

After that, she was less violent in her arguments, but still determined to rid herself of her small brother. There was a strange, vague smile upon Ahinoam's mouth, a look of remembering in her eyes. "I will take him, then," she said. "Go with the young man and tend the goats in peace."

He realized then for the first time that he would be absent from the house all day, walking in some far meadow with this brown girl, beyond a sight of Jonathan's face. The day's exile seemed endless, and filled him with baffled anger and bitterness. They have tricked me, he thought; they have disposed of me as they please, these two. . . . And when Michal, laying fruit upon his dish, brushed him with her arm, he said to himself that members of the royal house were very free with their hands, and could afford to be so, since no man would dare to push a regal hand aside.

He glanced up brightly, fearing that some sign of his bitterness showed in his face. The little Ishbaal sat opposite him, slowly eating dates. But he did not look at the dates or at his hand passing between the dish and his lips. He stared into the Bethlehemite's face, and David imagined that he saw an ancient scorn in the child's big, solemn eyes.

᭥ V ᭥

THE TENDING of the goats was not the tedious business that he had expected. The sun had scarcely passed its zenith when the whole task was done. While Michal gathered up the scraps of their noonday meal, he lay on his back in the shadow of a mulberry tree. He was pleasantly tired with so much running, and a little dizzy with the heat of the high summer sun. He watched her as she put the leavings of the food away, and he thought how it had been a blithe enough morning after all; nor was he altogether glad to see it at an end.

On the way to the meadow he had been taciturn and sullen. He felt that she had commanded him forth for the day like any hired shepherd, and because of her he was to be parted from Jonathan. Once or twice on the road she had attempted to draw him into talk, but he had vouch-safed her scarcely a word. She had walked too close to him, so that her swinging hand often knocked against his thigh. God of hosts, he had asked himself, what does she want of me? Does she touch me out of desire, or simply because I am so insignificant that she barely knows I am near by? . . .

But as soon as the flock closed round him, as soon as he smelled the familiar odor of wool and felt the silky goat's-hair rippling past his shins, a wild and merry mood possessed him. He shouted and whistled. He moved among the goats as a temple dancer moves before a god—graceful, intoxicated, catching the curved horns, vaulting over the bony backs, slapping the soft white sides. It was as if the spirit of the herd had leaped from the hairy, incontinent bodies of the goats and fastened upon him. "David," she had said a dozen times that morning, "is the Baal in your flesh? Are you possessed?" But if there was censure in her voice, her face was the face of one in league with the spirit. Her mouth was parted, and the moist white edges of her teeth shone. Her tongue kept passing, swift as a serpent's, over her lower lip. Nor could he imagine any longer that her freedom with him was a matter of sheer indifference. Whenever she could manage it, she brushed against him; and the tension of his mood kept heightening under her touch. What manner of girl is it, he asked himself, who leans forward so that her tunic falls away from her breasts? Who has taught her to leap over goats so that her thighs are plain and also the down upon her thighs? It had been a wild and chaotic morning. He had been hard put to keep the Baal of the goats at bay.

Try as he would, he could not understand her. She should have despised the shepherd in him; instead she never ceased to show her wonder at his skills. "How is it, son of Jesse," she would say—and her voice would lay a veil of honor and consequence upon his father's name—

"how is it that you know without question that this kid will surely die?" And he would become the wise male instructing the childish female in obvious things. "Behold his hoofs. How old is he? Then under what moon was he born? And who would expect a kid dropped under a summer moon to last longer than seventy days?" As the morning waned, she began to contend with him over minor matters, but it was plain to him that she argued for the joy of submitting. In the end she would lean back, breathless and happy to surrender. "The Star of Judah," she would say "—it is with him in herding as in singing. His word is the last and the best."

All through the meal he had been silent, but his thoughts were driven by the Baal of the goats. What lovers had spoken for her? Had she ever been possessed? Or was she, like himself, a virgin wishing to seem wise? What scent was on her flesh, under the perfume? Did she fear Saul? Did she wage an everlasting war against Jonathan? Were the dark curls in her armpits softer than his own? What would she do if he reached across the spread cloth and held her across his knees and kissed her full on the lips? Would she cry out at once? Or would she melt first and lie quiet long enough for his hands to know . . . How would he kiss her? More in hate than in love, he thought, until her mouth was flattened out of shape, until . . . What thoughts to think concerning a King's daughter!

She too had kept her peace. And when she had risen to clear the food away, she had the air of one who had wrestled long with a tormenting spirit. Her shoulders sagged and her face looked tired.

It was no great wonder that both of them were exhausted. In the wildness of their mood they had done a full day's work in half a day. On a far hillock behind them, Saul's favorite herd grazed, their flowing coats as white as milk. David lay perfectly still, staring up through the leaves of the mulberry. They looked solid and almost black against the burning blue of the sky. As he stared, a strange unhappiness came upon him. The day was crass, brazen, striding like a prostitute across the earth, with legs apart. He thought with longing of the subtle, tremulous night.

She came and sat down beside him under the mulberry tree, clasping her arms round her knees. The weariness had apparently left her, and she looked firm and slim and fair. Her flesh glowed softly from so much running about in the sun. The scent of spice was almost gone, and her body had the wholesome odor of sun-dried sweat.

"How tall is the armor-bearer of my father!" she said, letting her glance move slowly over the length of him. "Being the daughter of Saul, I am of a good height. And yet were I to lie down beside David, the top of my head would reach his shoulder only."

He felt curiously remote. His desire had ebbed from him. It is strange, he thought, how much likeness there is between any wench and a King's daughter. Thrice in his life women had sat down beside him after the herding and made the same observation: "How tall . . . Were I to lie down . . ." In Bethlehem he had answered the daughters of herdsmen with a comment that vaunted his own manliness and drove them away at the same time. "Well, then, lie down," he had said in the hills of Judah, "lie down and see." Now the old taunt formed in his thoughts, but it did not pass his lips. Her level look told him that she would not run giggling and squealing out of his reach. She might very well lie down and see.

And then? That desire which he had ceased to guard against, believing it weakened, sprang upon him again. He stared at the fierce blue sky that glared between the black leaves of the mulberry, he stared until his eyes ached, trying to stare down the thought of what might happen then. His body throbbed and changed in the heat of his yearning. The old images, the dreams that he had dreamed of women whom he had met on the road or at the shearing, were not enough. It seemed to him that the daily shape of love could never serve the fervor which she had roused in him. Love must be cruelly twisted and changed, love must take unto itself some of her brown, sweet, stinging violence. Desire must be wreaked upon her as a kind of vengeance—vengeance upon the King's daughter who kept her shy and virginal airs for some lordly bed and turned wench among the goats with a Judahite. . . .

In the midst of these thoughts, he sensed her look upon him. He raised his eyes to her face, expecting a coy glance. He encountered instead a pair of grave, wide-open eyes. There was something admirably unwomanish, something of clean, boyish honor in the frankness with which she saw and accepted his desire. A strangely familiar smile, at once mocking and tender, indented the corners of her lips. Where had he seen that smile before? On Saul's face, and it was Saul's daughter whom his thoughts had put to shame. The remembrance of her somber father stood suddenly there behind her, and David was reproved, and ashamed of the violence and crassness of his longing. He turned upon his face. She leaned against the trunk of the mulberry tree and sighed.

In the complete quiet of the summer afternoon he could hear his heart beating more and more slowly against the earth. It was almost as if he had actually possessed her. The Baal of the goats, subdued and peaceable, re-entered the hairy bodies and grazed calmly upon the hill. He saw that she also had grown quieter. A look of dreaming had come upon her face. For the first time he asked himself what thoughts passed through her mind here in this sun-drenched meadow and in the darkness of her room by night, when she stood at the window, pulling the golden pins from her hair. It is possible, he thought, that she thinks of me. . . .

After long silence she spoke, letting a detached thought float into the hush. "I was betrothed to Agag," she said.

He was slighted, shoved without ceremony out of her thoughts to make way for the mincing heathen from the south. Then he let his own pique be swallowed up by a larger and more high-minded anger. He was wroth for Jahveh and for Israel. The man of Judah, the stern man of God in him, was affronted to hear it. "To an *Amalekite?*"

"No, now," she said, stretching against the trunk and smiling, "had

Samuel not given him up to God, he would have become as one of us. He had consented to be circumcised."

Another woman's tongue would have avoided the word. She said it as smoothly and casually as his mother or sister might have said "bread." He knew with amazement that she needed neither womanly terror nor womanly wonderment in her dealings with men. Honor—a boy's honor—would dictate her ways in love.

"The Star of Judah never looked upon Agag," she said in the same dreamer's voice.

"No."

"He was a sorrowful man. . . ."

And did you comfort his sorrows? he asked within himself. Did you rest his sorrowing face between your small brown breasts?

"He had seen much and known much and suffered much before my father brought him home. . . ."

Yes, thought David, more than I have seen and known and suffered—far more than I.

"Three moons passed after his death before I took the ring that he gave me from my finger, and my hand felt lonely without it."

"Do you still mourn for him then?" he said.

"How long is it that the living can mourn for the dead? Furthermore, I never knew him. Between him and me, it was nothing but words and looks. Saul has mourned longer than I."

He turned on his side and saw her lean brown hand lying open beside him on the withered grass. It was there for the taking; to leave it trailing loose and empty would be an unforgivable piece of coldness. He took it and drew it toward him and turned his cheek against it. It was like the hand of a boy—warm, spare, redolent of earth and heat.

"I saw you in Ephes-Dammim," she said.

"When I sang in the tent of the King my lord?"

"No, earlier. Much earlier."

"When?"

She smiled. "I will not tell. Only tell me this—what Baal was it that you worshiped in Ephes-Dammim by the cistern in the grove of willows? It was said by the maidservant of Rizpah that you worshiped some Baal."

"I?" He started up in consternation.

"Do not fear to tell me," she said. "I am no carrier of tales. It is only that I would leave a gift by night for the Baal that is the Baal of David."

He withdrew his hand from hers and spread it southward, asking the Lord to bear witness. "But I have no God save Jahveh who is the only God in Israel," he said.

She smiled and looked at him with pert, unbelieving eyes. "Think of it no more. I will find him for myself. I already know his nature and his dwelling. He lives in a cistern, and he is a god of pain."

"You speak a mystery, and I cannot understand it."

"No, then," she said softly, "do not tell me. A time will come when you will tell me, and meanwhile I can wait. Only, I wish from my heart that I might have communication with this spirit, because for many moons I have had need of a Baal of pain."

He stared at her in wonder. What was it in Saul's household that made them carry the wounds of their spirits like banners, so that all men might see? And he, who had exhibited his hurts only when there was profit to be pulled out of pity, he, who had always kept silence about his own shortcomings—he wished that he could find the gallantry to say: "I also have need of such a god. In Ephes-Dammim I was despised, and in the grove by the cistern I sought your brother and found him not and wept."

She moved a little closer to him and drew his hair away from his face. "Why is the sweet singer of Bethlehem so grave?" she said.

He laughed uneasily. "I was thinking how all of us must sometimes feel the need of such a god as the maidservant of Rizpah fancied that I worshiped by the cistern."

"You also?" she asked.

"I? How am I different from the rest?"

"What could trouble you, and what would be denied you? All that you yearn after is at your hand even before the yearning, seeing that you are so fair."

"Then Michal my lady also would need no such god. She is as the moon."

"Truly?" She looked him squarely in the face.

"Yes, truly."

"Then," she said without lowering her eyelids, "let the son of Jesse kiss me on the lips."

He bent and surrendered his mouth with hidden unwillingness. He could find no cause for the faint tinge of disgust; her lips were moist and tender, her breath was sweet. He kissed long out of courtesy, and put her from him with a gallant sigh. I have kissed the mouth of the daughter of the King, he thought, smiling and resting his head against the bark. But the glory of it was far less than he had dreamed. The day with all its works was a heaviness upon him.

"Are you thirsty?" she said.

"No. Wherefore?"

"Because your mouth is dry."

He remembered an old wives' saying that a dry mouth never holds the wine of love. He put his hand uneasily to his lips.

She rose and smoothed the skirt of her tunic. Her eyes were no longer frank and wide. It was as if she had been tainted by the duplicity of his kiss. "I am thirsty," she said, "and the milk must be soured with lying so long in the sun. I will shake down some of these mulberries." She shook the little tree with all her might. Suddenly, loosened all at once, the ripe black fruits came tumbling down.

They fell upon his head, upon his shoulders, upon his upturned palms.

They fell gently, as cool and moist as great drops of water. He closed his eyes and relinquished himself to the night. There was no sun-scorched meadow now, no burning sky; there was Saul's garden after rain, aromatic with the smell of herbs, lyric with a voice that spoke of fallen Shiloh and the ark of God. Friend, cousin, beloved of my spirit, he thought, behold, I have been whoring among the lecherous goats when I might have been seeking after a sight of your face. What is she to me? A woman and a stranger. How shall I come to you again with her mark upon me? . . .

"Your lap is full. Will you eat?" she said.

He started up, rolling the berries upon the earth.

"No, now, see what you have done. Do not rise. You will trample them, and they are so big and fair."

He gathered a handful and stuffed them into his mouth, but he could not taste them. His palate was salt with tears. She picked the berries from the ground, dusted them against her brown arm, and ate them one by one. A small purple stain showed at the corners of her lips.

"Let us return now to your father's house," he said.

"Now? In the heat of the sun?" Her face was puckered like the face of a disappointed child.

"But if we wait for the sunset, the evening meal will be over before we have returned. It is best that we arise and go without delay."

"Let it be as the son of Jesse wishes," she said "Only, I had thought that it might be pleasant to walk back to Gibeah in the wind of God, and to eat the evening bread as we ate the morning bread, without the whole world standing by."

He saw that she regretted her speech before it was finished. She rose and stamped upon the mulberries. Some of the juice spattered upon his tunic, and she looked at the stain with a malicious smile.

He felt the same fear that he had felt in her father's presence. She knows more than the surface of things, he thought. She is subtle and strong, and she would make a relentless enemy. . . . He remembered with uneasiness the raisin eyes in the face of Doeg the Edomite. A man must walk warily, walking on the edge of power. . . . He leaned toward her and encircled her legs with his arm, and laid his head against her side. "To speak truly," he murmured into the folds of her tunic, "I am very weary."

"With brushing the hides of a few goats?"

"With struggling all day against longing after the King's daughter, whose lips are the first I have ever touched in love. It is with me as though I had drunk all day of a powerful wine, and my heart turns faint within me, and I have a great need for sleep."

He could feel her body grow vital and resilient as joy tore through it. "Truly?" she said. But she wanted no answer. She believed out of her need for belief. And he knew with mingled fright and triumph that the King's daughter loved him, not for an afternoon of ardor in a distant meadow, but everlastingly. And before the world? Before Saul? Before all the proud

Benjamites who looked coldly upon Judah? He could not leave such questions unanswered. He must know his worth and his destiny.

"No, now," he said in a sorrowful voice, pressing his forehead against her thigh, "what profit is there in it? He who betrothed you to Amalek may give you to Moab, or to Philistia, or to one in Phoenicia who owns forest land in Lebanon."

Her body stiffened again, this time with pride. "My father loves me," she said. "He will not sell me for the price of a forest, nor even for ten years of peace in Israel. Agag had ashes for his marriage portion, but Saul loved him. Saul will give me to him whom Saul loves."

He knew that this was so. Such knowledge should have been to him as the clashing of many cymbals. Fair she was, and a king's daughter, and half-wild with longing for him. Even so, a man might turn his back upon a day of passion with her. But who could walk away from all the glories that lie in a royal bed? Son-in-law of Saul, captain over a thousand, lord of such-and-such an estate with arbors and fields and orchards, owner of such-and-such flocks and herds. . . . Dear son of Ahinoam, friend of Abner, brother to Jonathan. . . . And yet an ache stirred within him; and yet a few mulberries kept falling, moist and cool into the magical night. . . .

"Come, then, beloved. We will go that you may sleep," she said.

He rose slowly. Hand in hand, like lovers, they walked toward the roofs and towers of Gibeah. To those who passed them along the way, they had the air of sleepwalkers, each intent upon some vision within his own heart.

◄§ VI §►

THREE DAYS passed between the time when Saul's goats were made clean for his sight and the hour when the King beheld them. For David they were miserable days, dull backwash after the foamy tide of glory. Both Michal and Jonathan had gone forth from the King's house—Michal to visit a young woman who lived on a neighboring farm, Jonathan to search for certain strayed oxen among the hills. David lolled in the common room and watched the poor remnants of royalty that had remained at home—the faded Ahinoam and the gaping Ishbaal. The talk was just such talk as he had heard with contempt when visitors infested Jesse's house. And the great house itself had dwindled with familiarity; his mind no longer paused in wonder at the mystery of every closed door.

On one of his somber and solitary pilgrimages around Saul's garden, he came upon the cleft in the rock where the young weaver was buried, he who had died in Jonathan's place. Someone, Ahinoam perhaps, had laid a fresh loaf upon the sloping stone and had topped it with a few small withered flowers. It was evening, and the wheat field that rolled downward between the rocks and the arbor made a mournful, silky rustle in the wind of God. He stood for a long time looking at the rock, thinking what lay within, but his thoughts crept persistently away from the dead and moved, as they always moved at last, toward Jonathan.

Since that hour when they had spoken under the wet trees, he had seen little of the beloved, and that little had been bitter. Once they had met in a corridor, once on a stair, and on both occasions the King's son had spoken only the courtly speech of the house. Jonathan was estranged from him, but how and wherefore? David had not been invited forth to seek the missing oxen; and the King's son had set out without saying farewell.

He turned from the burial cave and looked in the direction of Saul's house. Every window in the common room was yellow with light, and he knew that some event of consequence was taking place within. As he drew near to the entrance, he became aware of a noisy bustle, an air of homecoming and family gaiety. Which, then, of the three who could nourish the flat, exhausted soil of his days—which had come back home? A slender figure rose from the table. The head was like a cluster of grapes, one dark bunch of curls. So it was she. . . . Perhaps *he* stood in some shadowy corner or knelt by the hearth with his head below the sill. But as soon as he had crossed the threshold he knew that Jonathan had not returned. Ahinoam sat at the table with Ishbaal on her knee; Michal leaned against the wall; another young woman whom he did not know sat near Ahinoam and stared into a dish of curds. Save for a maidservant, and a courier who was washing his hands in a basin near the door, that was all.

Michal straightened and moved one step toward him. Long absence had made her indiscreet; her greeting failed in her throat; delight at the sight of him parted her mouth. She was dressed in a robe of filmy blue stuff; the little moon that hung from her neck rose and fell with the motion of her breasts.

"The Star of Judah is with us," she said at last.

"The Moon of Benjamin has come again," he answered, kissing her brown hand and finding upon it the old troubling scent, the thick and spicy perfume.

"Then," said the courier, stepping over the threshold, "all is clear to the lily of the King's garden? She knows that the King my lord will come tomorrow evening, and sends his love before him, as I have said?"

"Give it to me," said Ishbaal, moving from Ahinoam's knee to the lap of the unknown young woman and closing his hand upon an earring that dangled below the lusterless loops of her hair.

"No, now, let her alone. Yes, it is utterly clear. Doeg will find a place where you may sleep. Come, truly he will hurt your ear."

"Not with such little fingers," the young woman said.

What a rare voice, David thought, and turned to look at her who possessed it. It had the muted mournfulness of pigeon calls. The woman who spoke with such a voice should have been ample and yielding and fair. But she was meager and plain, with a long face, an arched and narrow nose, and colorless lips.

Michal drew David to the table and made him known to this young woman. Her name was Mara, and she lived on the great farm that lay between Saul's land and the town. She was learned in the ancient lore of Israel, acquainted with forgotten incantations and songs. Her virtues and accomplishments spilled one after the other from Michal's lips. It was as though the King's daughter, troubled to see her dear friend husbandless, sang her praise by rote on every possible occasion. "And I have brought her back, seeing that it was painful to be parted from her," she said, a little breathless from the haste and the vigor of her praise. The young woman kept stroking Ishbaal's hair. Her wan mouth was sweetened by a sad and knowing smile.

Ahinoam bade the maidservant set food before David, but Michal would not have it so. Permit her to serve the meal of the peerless singer whose voice delighted her father? Oh, did he know that her father was departing from Gilgal and would sit at meat with them tomorrow night? Had he a new song for the occasion? Jahveh grant that there be no rain to spoil the whiteness of the goats that they had washed together. What a merry day they had spent with these same goats, Mother, what a merry day!

Mara flushed and worked diligently at the task of fastening the earring in the soft, small lobe of Ishbaal's ear, and David knew that she had heard a full account of that merry day. So they had whispered concerning him—a princess and her confidante—behind the curtains of some massive bed. . . .

His mind turned suddenly alert and vivacious. It ran in half a dozen directions at once: to the brown hand that set his meal before him, to the mild pigeon-voice that addressed the child, to the curds and bread that had regained their savor, to the song that must be made, and made speedily, against Saul's return. "Take back your earring," Michal said. "He will lose it, and whosoever finds it will not wear it with your grace. Yours, more than mine, is a face for earrings." Were the girl a shade less undesirable, David thought, Michal would pay her fewer compliments. It is her plainness that makes her dear. "We will feast, then, tomorrow night," Ahinoam said. "Three kids, a cake of raisins . . . Michal, will you provide us with a honey cake?" Yes, he thought, biting upon a tender green leek, by all means, a new song. A simile would be best. As the rain returns to the parched field, so Saul returns—No, it was trite and would not do at all. As the new moon rises upon the first night, dissolving the thick dark, lighting again the sad cheeks of waiting men . . . "Take the earring out of your mouth, you brat. Mother, make him take it out of his mouth. He is perverse enough to swallow it." He would use the moon. He saw infinite possibilities. An hour of solitary walking, and the song would be finished.

"I will walk a little in the garden," he said.

"And I also," said Michal, "to cool myself before I sleep."

"Come, Mara, give me my troublesome child and walk in peace with these other two."

But Mara smiled and shook her head. She would far rather rest. As for the child, let him come with her. It was seldom enough that she had the delight of holding a child upon her knee. Her mother had died in giving her birth, and she had neither brothers nor sisters. So let her take this little one to her room, where he might play with her amulets and bracelets as long as he pleased. Ahinoam rose and took a lamp to light the visitor up the stairs. The servants, too, departed.

There was no help for it, then. He was imperiously summoned and skillfully maneuvered into an hour of love. He continued to sit at the table, making it plain, at least, that he would show no undue eagerness. He ate the leek slowly to its roots, chewed stolidly at the last bit of bread, cleansed his mouth with a long draught of milk, sauntered to the basin, and dabbled his fingers in the tepid water.

"The Star of Judah is in no great haste," Michal said.

He dried his hands meticulously. "I am a shepherd, and a Judahite, new in the King's house, and as yet not firmly rooted in the King's love. To run into a thicket with the King's daughter before all the world would not be wise."

Her face was sullen. She walked apart from him and a little before him over the moon-washed lawn, past the herb garden, down the slope between tall trees to the arbor—a place alive with shaken leaves and creeping tendrils, spotted with uneven flecks of moonlight, and smelling sharply of wine.

There among the twisted vines she turned upon him abruptly. He had forgotten the potency of her beauty. She seemed to grow out of the vine she leaned against; a cluster hung over her shoulder, leaves sprang from her cheeks and hair. She looked like some dark Canaanitish Astarte borne in a vintage festival among the farmers' offerings. He yearned after her with the stinging yearning of one who delights in what is evil as well as sweet. He longed for her as in his childhood he had longed to run into the temples of Canaan where, in the opulent heat of autumn, drunken with the new wine, men and women sang and danced and coupled in strange ways to provoke the fertility of the Baals and Astartes.

He laid a hard and cruel hand upon her. He pulled the filmy blue stuff from her shoulder. He caught her round the waist and held her until she uttered little gasping cries. A Canaanitish fury possessed him. He set his teeth into her ripe, provoking lower lip.

She was afraid, and began to struggle under his tyranny. "Let me go. I will cry out," she said.

"You will not cry out."

"No, but I will."

He believed her and withdrew from her. Her robe had fallen from her shoulder. One breast was bare.

"Now you have hurt me," she said, putting her hand to her lip.

He did not answer. An unreasonable rage had sprung up in him. It would have been a mad business, possessing her here in the arbor; yet he was bitter against her that she had prevented it. As she had smiled in malice at the stain of mulberries on his tunic, so he smiled at the mark of his violence upon her lip.

"Is it so with all men," she said, "that they kiss to devour and embrace to destroy?"

"No." The anger, like the longing, sagged within him. He felt only a nausea of the spirit.

"Then why did David fall like an eagle upon me?"

"Forgive it," he said. "These three days I have thought only of my lady, and my bowels yearned within me. And when she raised her face to me, I could not subdue my longing—so beautiful was she among the vines."

"Truly?"

No, not truly, he thought, now that she looked at him with eyes as direct and level as her father's eyes. Yet it was not utterly a lie. "Truly," he said.

"Then kiss in kindness the wound which is on my mouth."

He laughed indulgently, and bent and brushed his lips across hers.

"Then will you never kiss me in tenderness?" she said.

"But I have kissed you."

"Not as I desired."

"Perhaps, then, on some other occasion when we are more serene, Michal will teach me how to kiss."

She walked disconsolately before him out of the arbor, smoothing the wrinkles from her robe and picking bits of dried leaves from her hair. "One is happier," she said, stepping onto the lawn, "one is much happier dreaming of David than being at his side."

This at least he could share with her. To sing in the King's tent at dawning, to be the King's armor-bearer, to eat the King's bread, to kiss the King's daughter on the lips—not one of these had been more than the muddied reflection of its dream. And what in all his life had risen to the stature that he had marked for it? The night beneath the dripping trees, the night with Jonathan.

He took her loose and spiritless hand and pressed it against his lips. "I am grieved in my heart," he said, "that I have soiled and broken Michal's dream. Perhaps on another night I will give it back to her clean and whole."

She was sorrowful and filled with pity for herself, and he wished that she were merrier. All the silver magic that he had wanted for his song had gone from him and from the night.

"Did my friend Mara please you?"

"Yes, truly," he said with too much vivacity. "She has a strange and subtle face and a very ingratiating voice."

"Poor Mara!" She sighed.

He stopped, tired and irritated, at a bench close to the herb patch. What grievous tune was she about to whistle for him now? He settled himself upon the bench, rested his chin upon his fists, and waited with ill grace for a long and maudlin tale. "Wherefore is she poor?" he said.

Michal paced back and forth like a restless cat between the bench and the herbs. "It is not only that she lives a solitary life," she said, "though that is wretched enough. . . ."

"Well, what is it, then?"

"It is the love that she has borne these many years for my brother Jonathan."

And now it was Michal who sat upon the bench and he who wandered up and down, treading upon the gleaming leaves in his confusion and his pain. God of Sinai, what was this that had come upon him? When she had linked Mara's name with the name of the beloved, it was if she had struck the quivering surface of his heart.

"It is plain that they should marry. Together, our houses would own the fairest stretch of land in Benjamin—all that lies between this garden and the town. Like Kish, her father's father numbered his sheep and goats in the thousands. They pasture in neighboring meadows, and already our sheep are pregnant with the seed of their rams."

Let her for God's sake hold her tongue! Whatever she did, whatever she said, ended in lechery.

"It is true that she has a sweet face rather than a fair one. Nevertheless . . ."

And this poor student, who had seemed to him gentle and harmless an hour ago, filled him with loathing. He could no more have touched her than he could have touched the noisome owl that flies up at dusk from Sheol and eats the offerings left for the dead.

"Saul and Ahinoam would call themselves blessed if he would lead her to the marriage bed."

No, my friend! he said to himself. Let me be gone from the earth before that day. . . .

"Why are you silent?" she said.

"What is there to say?"

"What indeed? If he will not have her, he will not have her."

He stopped in his pacing and drew a sharp breath.

"Ahinoam has thrice spoken for her, but he has refused to listen."

He sat down upon the bench in utter weariness.

"Poor Mara! It is a sad thing to love and be unloved."

"Yes, very sad," he said.

He was grateful for the quiet that settled upon them now. They sat side by side on the bench, listening to the toads making throaty mating sounds in the marsh beyond the garden. He laid his arm around her and held her against his side. He stroked her shoulder and brushed his mouth back and forth across her brow. But he scarcely knew whom he held or what he did. Jahveh had delivered him, and he was grateful, and his gratefulness was transmuted into tenderness for her and all the glimmering world.

As the new moon rises upon the first night, dissolving the thick dark, lighting again the sad cheeks of waiting men . . . The frogs spoke

86

rhythmically through the hush. Had they made their throaty calls that other night when he had sat with Jonathan? And if Mara's love for Jonathan is a dagger thrust into David's flesh, he asked himself, what then is David's love for Michal to Jonathan? I have betrayed him. For a stale kiss in the meadow, for a moment of Canaanitish frenzy in the arbor, I have betrayed my cousin and given him pain. . . .

"Michal," he said, "have you spoken of what is between us to Jonathan?"

"Not wholly," she said, yawning. "Before we left Ephes-Dammim, one night when I was warm with wine, I said before him that I had never seen so goodly a man as the Judahite."

"And the morning we went forth to tend the goats—he knew of that?"

A slow, malicious smile lifted the corners of her mouth and narrowed her eyes. "He knew," she said.

"Why is it that you smile?"

"Because he liked it not—my going. But I went nevertheless."

"He liked it not? Wherefore?"

"He has set his heart against love. His stomach is the stomach of a little breastless girl. Saul sickens him with Rizpah. I sicken him. Once there was one among the captains who grew thin with longing after Ahinoam, and that sickened him more than the rest—that sickened him unto death. . . . Listen to the frogs calling each other. Would we might sit here forever under this same moon. David, promise me we will sleep together in the grass, some summer night when you are the King's son-in-law and we have a fair garden of our own."

How could he answer? "Yes, surely, if such a day should come," he said.

"It will come." She rose quickly, as though she sensed some danger to her dream. "Now I must return to Mara. Will you also sleep?"

"No. I will walk here in the garden and use what little time is left for the making of a song."

"Do so, and Jahveh walk with you," she said. She departed without raising her face for another kiss.

He walked long in the garden, wearing the parched grass away with his tread. He walked until moonset, but he begot neither words nor music, and in the thin light of the false dawn he fell asleep under the sky, upon that bench where he had sat with Jonathan.

⋅§ VII §⋅

If he had flattered himself that he would waken refreshed, with a song full-formed and ready to be delivered, he was mistaken. He had never wakened so weary, with such blunted senses, with so heavy a heart. The very fact that he had a full day for song-writing was a hindrance to him. Why should he trouble in the morning, while his body still ached from lying against the stubborn wood? And why work at noon in the glare of a coppery sun? Wait a little longer, and yet a little longer. Lie in the shadow of a tree, eat, talk to the captain of the guard, tune the lute, make a sick beginning and wait again. . . . Later . . . But later the strength even to make a beginning was gone. All through the somber, thickening afternoon, he did a thing that he had never done before: he lay on his bed in daylight. A monotonous gray pageantry of clouds moved past his window; it might have been morning or evening; the clouds had completely muffled the sun. Am I sick, then? he thought. Is there some evil spirit within me? . . . He would raise his hand and lay the back of it against his brow. There was no fever there, and the pulse in his wrist was regular and slow. Then I will rise up, he thought, and write a song for the homecoming of the King my lord. . . . But before he had put his feet upon the rug beside his bed, he had lost the desire, even the power, to rise.

He kept up a feeble striving. At intervals whose length he could not measure, he repeated to himself the first lines of his song. Further than this he could not go. Some other thought, nagging and persistent, would take the song's place. Why had his own heart failed to strain joyously toward the hour of the King's return? Was it possible that he feared his lord? Because of Michal and the Canaanitish fury among the vines? He ached to remember the wild, evil sweetness of it—he wanted it and he wanted it not—she was at once a poison and a delight. "As the new moon rises upon the first night . . ." Where were they now, she and the lank and hateful one? On the roof, chattering. "Behold the mark of his love bite. . . ." Those who gloat over conquests are blinded by their gloating and are likely to fall into the pit; so it was with Joseph of old. All the glory gathered at Ephes-Dammim can be scattered at Gibeah for lack of a song. "Lighting again the sad cheeks of waiting men . . ." Was that lightning flickering against the moving masses of the clouds? Where are you, Jonathan, now that the wind is up? In what unknown hills do you seek your father's strayed beasts? . . .

But the threatened storm that might have refreshed him passed on to pour its wholesome violence upon some other hill and gave place to thin sun. He knew now by the slanting rays and the noises which rose to him from the lower rooms that the hour for the evening meal was drawing on. Then there was no time left. Only a miraculous flow of strength from some outer power—only the intervention of Jahveh Himself—could take this sickness and shape it into song. If the Lord would possess him, if the Lord would come upon him . . . But what came upon him was a profound sleep. . . .

How long he slept or what it was that wakened him he did not know. A hot and steady wind moved across his body. Evening or a second storm had brought a glaring grayness upon the room. Sounds assailed him—the rumble of approaching thunder, a confusion of talk in the courtyard below. One sharp streak of lightning tore across the piece of sky beyond his window. Suddenly the realization of his predicament flashed upon him. The sounds of the house were the sounds of arrival. The King was coming home. He saw the furrowed brow, the cheeks and lips moving in the mocking, tender smile, the all-seeing, all-loving, all-disparaging eyes. Jahveh bear me up, he thought. Jahveh hide me with his pinions from the just wrath of the King my lord. . . .

And all at once, standing between the bed and the window with the long, hot streams of air breaking against him, he knew that he had indeed been at fault, and that Saul's anger, should it dart out against him, would indeed be just. He had sinned against his benefactor. Not only in the matter of the unfinished song—that was a minor transgression, one that he had brooded upon chiefly in order to keep his thoughts from the other, more monstrous flaws. In the matter of Michal, he had sinned plainly and grievously; and he had sinned more obscurely, but none the less shamefully, in the matter of Jonathan.

Then Jahveh be merciful, he thought again, watching the white spear of God plunge through the heaped clouds, hearing God's angry mutter sound and resound in the hollow caverns of the earth. But why should He be merciful? Simply because He was not bounded by the small, human limits of reason and justice; He loved whomsoever it pleased Him to love. As Jesse played favorites in the house in Bethlehem, so Jahveh played favorites in Paradise. David, whose name meant "darling," had often appealed from the just rage of Eliab to his father, and had always been supported and forgiven. And David might hope for just such doting should he run from Saul to the lap of God.

"Jahveh have mercy!" he said aloud, moving toward the window, thrusting his head into the wind, feeling his hair lifted upward upon the gust.

The lightning lashed downward and tore the clouds and released the big, consoling rain. Through the downpour, he looked at the field where he had watched Jonathan wrestling with roots and stones. And what miracle was this? It was not Saul whom they were welcoming. The newcomer crossed the field slowly, rain-spattered, weary, followed by a lean little herd. So God showed favor to His minion, sending the beloved to him in place of the feared, withholding Saul in some shelter along the way and bringing Jonathan home.

Now it was as if the Lord had piled the great clouds one upon the other and rent them with lightning for David's sake. The deluge beyond the window was a magical invocation to release the storm within him. His body was shaken with a long, shuddering sigh. As the thirsty field below him drank of the water, so he drank of the sight of the beloved. Above the roar of the rain, above the thunder and the babble of the welcoming voices, winged and sure in its flight, soared the song:

> My beloved, I knew not my barrenness
> Until they said to me, "He is come."
> I knew not the dryness of my heart
> Until they said, "He is at the gate."
> I was as a cistern without rain.

What was in me save a little foul water?
Whosoever tasted me tasted bitterness.
But they have said of my beloved,
"Behold, he is below, he is at the gate."
And I am filled, I am cleansed,
My spirit overflows.
Touch me, I am pure.
Drink of me, I am sweet,
Because he has come again, my beloved.

Even while the lofty cadences formed in his thoughts, even while he
stared at the slight body of the beloved advancing through the rain, even
as he was rapt and transported, he knew that he would be able to give Saul
an excellent song. A few changes—the word "lord" in place of the word
"beloved," the inclusion of some kingly compliment—and the song of
homecoming would be finished. He felt his own face changing at the
thought; the childish, tremulous smile of utter happiness hardened on his
lips and was transformed into a clever, self-sufficient smile. He knew that
this consideration was marring his happiness, and he pushed all consideration aside for the time being, and gave himself up to the white face lifted
toward his window, the hand thrown up toward him in welcome and forgiveness. He ceased to be a courtier counting opportunities. He became,
briefly, a Judahite shepherd thanking God. He thrust his arms outward in
greeting, and stood so until Jonathan had entered the house. Then he
turned to the clothes chest and took up a clean tunic.

My lord, he thought, I knew not my barrenness until they said to me,
"The King is come."

~§ VIII §~

Who would have thought that the King of Israel—who might have
spent a stormy night in the fairest house in any Benjamite town—would
creep home like a sick dog through the rain, wanting his own hearth and
refusing all others? Yet, long after the hour of the evening meal, when
the food was spoiled with waiting, when the company had ceased to
look for him and only Ahinoam continued to stare through the black
windows, the torch flared up in the murky dark and the cry of arrival
rose beyond the barren field.

"Is it truly Saul?" they said, wishing in their hearts that it was not he.
"The milk is curdled with the thunder, the meat is overdone, he could
have found far better fare in the town." They hurried into the common
room, readjusting their wilted finery. "It is strange," they said, "that he did
not sleep in Gilgal another night." They were disturbed, they were affronted by the excessive longing that had brought him through such a
storm. They had not the wherewithal to answer that longing; his welcome

had grown cold. Only Ahinoam was prepared. Since she had not bedecked herself for the occasion, she was not faded. The look of waiting could not leave her face; she had worn it through the latter half of her years.

Saul crossed the threshold, his spear in his hand. His look passed slowly over the room. It was plain that so much sudden light was painful to his eyes. The silence was charged and oppressive. He broke it for them, tossing his spear into a corner, where it clanged ominously against stone.

"Is Abner with us?" he said.

Ahinoam answered the spoken question, and that other question concerning the concubine which he had not permitted to pass his lips.

"Not yet, my lord. Neither Abner nor any other has yet returned."

"So?" he said, and drew her to him, and kissed her long and tenderly upon the brow.

The young lutist out of Bethlehem, who stood on the hearth between the captain of the guard and Doeg the Edomite, was in no state to be acutely aware of the King's affliction. He had griefs enough of his own. All through the futile, lagging evening, the questionable nature of his position had been forced upon him. He had found no moment when Jonathan and Michal were apart. He had sat on the hearth and played at a game of chance with them and the melancholy Mara; he had played stupidly; and whatever responsive looks he had been able to kindle in the equally melancholy Jonathan had been quenched by Michal's familiar gestures, Michal's suggestive smiles. So when Saul entered, David had no heart to greet him. Well, he is come, then, he thought, and what is it to me? What do I . . . But the thought broke against the dark, tormented glance. He knew at last what Jesse had meant when he had admonished him to look upon the King's face.

"The King's armor-bearer," said Doeg in his soft voice, turning and nodding in the direction of Saul's spear, "the King's armor-bearer is to look to the King's arms. Will the son of Jesse——"

He ran forward, colliding with other guests, and for the first time took up the great, regal shaft. He heard the murmur of kindly amusement around him; he saw Ahinoam smile; he caught the little yellow glint of enjoyment in the porcine eyes of the Edomite. But the pain of these things was small beside the pain that issued from Saul's face, transfixing him like a thrown spear.

What had they done to his lord in Gilgal? He had seen such a look of suffering on a man's face only once before. Years ago, in the hills around Bethlehem, one of his father's herdsmen had come home with a mangled arm; he had met and killed a lion among the flock, but only after a terrible struggle. It was plain that, with the torn arm, the herdsman could not live. It was necessary to lop the arm away. Fascinated and feverish, he had watched the operation from a shadowy corner, his manliness proof against the screams and the blood. But in the end he had vomited like a girl. Not because of the arm—because of the herdsman's face, with its look of amazement and loss. Just such a face he saw now in the silent common room. They had committed a sickening butchery at the black altar. In Gilgal they had lopped away Saul's pride.

Jonathan had come forward and was kneeling at his father's feet. He kept his head bent, but his exquisite hands groped upward, found the King's fingers, pressed them against cheek and lips. He is not as I am, David thought. From the beginning, I knew him to be made of finer, more precious dust. He was not unmindful of Saul's agony in Gilgal. He pursued the strayed oxen while I turned lecher among the goats. Saul's suffering was his suffering. Some night beneath the dripping trees we will sit together again, Jonathan and I, and I will tell him that it was with me in Gibeah as it was with him after Michmash—I forgot.

He was startled by a general movement around him and by Doeg's moist voice saying: "The son of Jesse need not hold the spear throughout the evening. Let him set it against the wall." The ceremonies of arrival were concluded, and the company was going with the King toward the long board where the delayed and wilted feast was spread. Ahinoam delivered him from the Edomite. "Come," she said, "hold the drinking cup for the King my lord." As he passed Michal in the crowd, she reached out and touched his bare arm. She had no prudence, none. Must she make a public spectacle of her love?

But no one heeded her, and no one noticed him as he stood for the first time at the pinnacle of his newly attained eminence, with the wine cup in his hand. The warmth of the grape had come upon them. They deceived themselves; they said in their hearts, We needed a little time to accustom ourselves to his coming, and behold how we glow in his presence, now that the little time is past. . . .

Saul did what he could to nourish the illusion. He summoned up a semblance of his old heartiness; he urged more wine upon them all; he raised his wine cup oftener than he drank, and loudly commended the burned meat. Still, whenever he grew silent, his look fell like a frost upon the frail bloom of the festival; it was better to smile into other faces and let him alone. And he was grateful that they left him in peace. He turned from the table, motioned his son and his armor-bearer to follow him, and eased himself slowly into a great chair, with his back to the lamp and his shoulder turned against his guests.

"So, then," he said, sighing and laying an arm on the shoulder of each young man, "sit and be at ease. Wherefore the ceremony? A farmer of Gibeah has visited God in Gilgal, and, being finished with the rites and the city, has come home."

Jonathan's face quivered like a rabbit's. "The crops are large," he said. "The yield of the olives will be richer even than last year."

"Good," said Saul, but it was plain that his thoughts were with some other matter. "Very good indeed."

As mariners on some barren island hear, when the wind blows from another water-bound patch of earth, the songs and laughter of a people far away, so they heard the chatter of those around the table. A vision of the great black altar at Gilgal stood in the stillness that descended upon them; and David saw Samuel exulting over Saul's disgrace, saw the desiccated lips of the prophet stirring in a holy and malevolent smile.

"At least a little work was done in my father's absence," said Jonathan. "I rid the uncultivated field of some of the roots and stones. Also, I traveled even as far as upper Ephraim in search of a few strayed oxen."

"And did you find them?" the King said, suddenly vital, leaning far forward in his chair.

"Yes, I found all that were lost and brought them safely home."

"And did you find Jahveh also?"

"What was it that my father said?"

Then, thought David, is it true that the King is mad? . . .

"I inquired whether you found Jahveh also, along with the beasts. There was a day when I set forth out of Kish's house to search after oxen, and I found Jahveh on the way. But then, it is an old story and of no consequence." He turned a lively, cunning face upon David. "And you?" he said, laying his finger under David's chin and tilting the boy's head backward until there was no way save to stare eye to eye. "How was it with you while I tarried with Samuel's darlings in Gilgal? Has the House of Kish accepted you with the proper tenderness?"

Neither the stiff finger nor the wild, dark glance would release him. A long, vibrating chill ran through his body. Was this madness or the ultimate wisdom of the unearthly wise? "How could I prosper," he said, "with my lord in Gilgal? What is a plant without the sun?"

"Or a courtier without a king," said Saul softly, meditatively, "or a raven without carrion, or a fly without dung. . . ." Then the eyes changed; the bitterness behind them melted away; the hand dropped limp upon David's shoulder. "Tell me," he said in an amiable and casual voice, "not for my own sake, but for the sake of those who must make an occasion of everything, so that quantities of meat must be eaten before a corpse can be decently buried—tell me, will you delight their ears, have you made me a song?"

He saw his own head tilt gracefully backward. He saw himself smiling with charming complacency—a candid, confiding smile.

"I have made such a song as will please even the weary ears of the King my lord," said David.

As Saul might have poked at a troublesome calf, so he poked his fist playfully against his armor-bearer's cheek, too lightly to hurt, yet heavily enough to send him reeling two steps backward. "Go then and sing it," he said. "I would not keep you one breathing-space longer from the pleasure of hearing your own voice."

"But where shall I stand when I sing?" There was a whimpering undertone to the question, and he was ashamed of it.

"Wherever it pleases you to stand."

"No, now, my father," Jonathan said. The eyes of the King's son sought

David. "Kneel even here on this rug before the King my lord. Such is the custom."

But he had no sooner found his station than another and more ridiculous problem confronted him. He had left his lute in his room.

"Well, then," said Saul kindly, "what ails the lutist? Has he lost his lute?"

"May the King my lord forgive my stupidity. I have left it in my chamber."

"Send another to bring it. What breath you lose in running on the stairs will be lacking in the song."

"But whom shall I send?"

"Whomsoever you will."

Jonathan rose. "The armor-bearer of the King has not yet been given a body servant," he said. "Therefore, if it please my father, let me bring the lute."

For a moment, Saul closed his eyes. His nostrils grew narrower; a cunning smile twitched his mouth. When he looked up again, his lively glance was for Jonathan. "So you have taken a friend?" he said. "So you have taken unto yourself a beautiful Judahite? And does this friend also fancy a madman's garland made of weeds and grass? No, now, if three of us divide his heart, each will have only an insignificant piece of it. That is, unless he has a mighty heart."

"My lord!" said Jonathan, flushing to the roots of his hair.

"But these matters are delicate," said the King, stroking the pale hand with his hard brown fingers. "Speak of them, and they lose their bloom. Therefore go, Jonathan, and bring David's lute. As for me, I will find my wife that she may sit beside me when we hear this remarkable song."

Bewildered and apart from the rest of the company, David knelt upon the rug and waited for his lute. A dozen questions pressed upon him, but his mind could travel only one pathway—the pathway marked by Jonathan's feet through the dim corridors, up the long flights of stairs. Where is he now, he that has worn a garland for my sake, the King's son who goes like a servant to fetch and carry, because he loves? How did the lute lie? In the middle of the coverlet. To reach it, he must lean upon my bed. And tonight, when every torch and lamp is quenched, I will bring a little vessel of light and hold it over my couch and find the print of his fingers upon the cloth. . . .

He looked up and saw that the company was gathering in a broad crescent around him, sitting cross-legged, as their forefathers had sat upon sand to listen to the sweet singers of old. Mara and Michal sat in the first bright row and smiled upon him. There were whispers. It was plain that the company had mistaken his ardor for that ecstasy which, in the most illustrious of the minstrels, was said to precede song. To please them, he prolonged the fervent look upon his face; he stared steadily at the ceiling, and sighed. And so it was that Jonathan found him. The pantomime of rapture had been carried too far; for its sake he had to forgo the look which he had meant to bestow upon the beloved.

He took it as another and singular mark of Jahveh's favor that he sang with power and skill that night. So serene, so uninvolved was he in the passage of his own music that he observed half a dozen insignificant details: the white part down the middle of Doeg's fuzzy head, the swollen veins in Ahinoam's hand, the mole on Mara's neck, the curious design wrought in scarlet thread on Michal's little kidskin shoes. He noted coolly how earnestly the assembly listened, and counseled himself not to be overly elated. He reminded himself that they would have been quite as intent had he brayed like a donkey, if only Saul had kept a rapt and solemn face. Yet as one after another bent forward and fixed ardent and amazed eyes upon him, he grew convinced that he had gained something more than a formal success. He heard his own voice ringing down the length of the lamplit room with surprising strength. He heard his own words and wondered at them. When had another flung such words, like handfuls of living sparks, into the darkness of men's minds? "Whoever tasted me tasted bitterness," he sang, and Michal thrust out her red, sour lip. "But they have said of my lord, Behold, he is below, he is at the gate." Mara smiled and looked at the door through which Jonathan had entered his house. "And I am filled, I am cleansed. My spirit overflows." Ahinoam shed slow, easy, habitual tears. "Touch me, I am pure." The hand of Saul stirred subtly on the arm of the chair. "Drink of me, I am sweet." What wonder in the lifted face of the beloved, what thirst upon the parted lips! "Because he has come again, my lord." No, but it was for you, my cousin. The necessities of this life have twisted and marred it. It was to have ended "Because he has come again, my beloved." . . .

They gave him that prize most coveted by all sweet singers—the moment of absolute quiet. It was Ahinoam who dispelled the stillness before it became oppressive. She rose and walked through the crowd of listeners. With a queen's dignity, she took a golden chain from her neck, passed it over his head, and arranged it carefully among the folds of his tunic. "Live forever," she said, "and sing everlastingly." Saul repeated the sentence in his vibrant voice, and the others took it up as a happy convenience. They rose and sounded it from every corner of the room—behind him, before him, to his right, to his left. Then they ventured upon little compliments of their own. "Would I could hear the peerless lutist sing a few of the ancient incantations," Mara said. "What a voice, what a voice!" said the captain of the guard, clapping the singer roundly upon the shoulder. "May the King never grow weary," said Doeg the Edomite. "All night," said Michal, "the voice of David will be in my ears. How shall I sleep?" Jonathan came to him last and said nothing, merely laid his hand upon the lute.

In Bethlehem they had surely loved but sorely neglected him. It was strange that a voice fit to delight a king should have been spent so long with so little reward upon the ears of shepherds. Suddenly, among the faces of the flatterers, he saw a vision of Jesse's little, wizened face. It bore a strange smile, both contemptuous and tender, and this remembrance was as water mixed with the wine of his glory. With every minute, his delight ran thinner. The voices around him betrayed their weariness. He knew that the occasion had been sick from the beginning, had died with the last note of his lute, and should be buried without further delay. When will they go to their sleep? he thought. When will I be alone in the tower room? When can I close the door and seek the print of *his* fingers upon my bed? . . .

IX

BUT HE was not to enter the tower room until the gray light of morning had washed all magic from the walls. After the King and the rest of the company had departed, Doeg lingered and called him aside. "Not that I dream for one moment that the King's armor-bearer has forgotten the obligations of his position," the Edomite said. But the armor-bearer had indeed forgotten, had remembered only the glory of his new rank, and was surprised to learn that now he must fetch and follow.

He went about the empty room, gathering up the bracelet dropped upon the hearth, the spear left in the corner, the cloak of scarlet cloth. Apprehension came upon him as he mounted the stairs. I will see my lord the King alone and in his nakedness, he thought. And he was afraid, and stood long without before knocking at the royal door.

Voices came to him from within—Saul's voice, weary and halting, and another voice, clear and beloved. "He will not come," Saul said, "he has forgotten." "Then it is upon my head, for I should have called it to his mind," said Jonathan. David coughed discreetly, opened the great door, and stood on the threshold, staring into the room.

Only one lamp burned in the whole chamber, and this stood on the sill, so that most of its brightness was diffused upon the summer night. Saul sat upright on the edge of the bed, and Jonathan lounged in a chair. An embroidered hanging covered one wall and rippled in the breeze. A household image stood upon a pedestal opposite the bed—Jahveh in the shape of an angry bull rearing in rage against a host of unseen enemies, hewn roughly and in visionary fury from porous reddish stone. He gazed in wonderment at the image. Such things were forbidden in Judah, nor was it considered any excuse for them that they were beautiful or reverend with age.

"Well, then, David," said the King, "put down your burdens and close the door."

He set the spear in the corner against a gleaming shield; he opened the clothes chest and laid the cloak within; he sought long for the whereabouts of the jewel box, and found it only with the help of a subtle gesture from Jonathan. Then he came and stood at the foot of the royal bed.

Saul had lain down, not serenely for sleep, but desperately, in utter exhaustion. Naked except for his loincloth, long and dark, he lay athwart the white goat's-hair coverlet with one arm crooked beneath his head. This first glimpse of the King in his nakedness was an affront to the lutist's delicacy. He was troubled that Saul's head should be attached to this raw length of humanity. The known head and the unknown body were disjointed in his thoughts, and this sense of division was the more marked because of the difference in their colors; the face was brown, and the body was very pale. The hair showed black against this pallor—the dark tangle in the armpits and upon the chest, the animal shagginess that covered the legs.

"Shall I wash the King my lord?"

"No, David. I have washed myself." There was reproof for his loitering in the words, but the voice was mild. "Rub me a little with the oil that is in the bowl by the side of the bed, and then I will sleep."

David dipped his hand in the fragrant oil. Again he was at a loss, not knowing how or where to begin, and again the fair presence in the chair informed him, raising his hands to the back of his own neck, passing them lightly downward over shoulders and chest, making a curving movement above the abdomen, soundlessly beating palms against thighs. The occasion had made conspirators of the King's armor-bearer and the King's son. And, pondering the bond between them, David did not think of the holy flesh he touched. He thought only of the comely face, softly lighted on one side by the wavering flame.

The hairy chest under the boy's fingertips rose and sagged with a sigh. "Well, David," he said.

The lutist was afraid—suddenly he feared that his lord would speak of the song. The lying trappings—the inserted phrases and too frequent references to royalty—had seemed authentic enough in the confusion of the great hall below; but here in this hush and intimacy they could no longer be relied upon.

"They have told me that you have no body servant," Saul said. "Whom will you call to be with you out of Bethlehem?"

He had to remind himself that he must go on rubbing the oil into the King's flesh. He saw a dozen faces crowding round the table in Jesse's house. Which should he choose?

"It is in David's hands to confer an honor," Saul said.

Eliab was the most deserving, that was plain. And Eliab would gain most from this opportunity. Once in Saul's sight, the kindly and honorable brother would not remain the servant of the King's servant for long. Saul had an eye for plain, uncouth merit. Yes, Eliab was the man, and yet . . . Eliab was unteachable; his beard would be forever frizzled and unkempt; the accents of Judah would never leave his tongue. Stubborn and narrow, he would understand little and scoff at everything he did not understand. How would it be possible to be a polished courtier, an in-spired poet, a heroic warrior, a masterful lover, before such a one as Eliab? The pampered child of a Judahite herdsman—such and only such could David be before his elder brother. No, not Eliab. . . .

"Be wiser than I, and choose a young man, my cousin," Jonathan said. "I chose an old one, and now I cannot decently send him from me. His hands shake, his poor bones are stiff and weary, and it is more often I than he who fetches and carries."

Now David felt no desire save to find a servant who would please the beloved. Whomsoever he called up out of Bethlehem must be a stripling, one whose grace could bring an additional charm to a message carried into Jonathan's tent. Suddenly he knew, and knew so surely that his fingers ceased to move and pressed hard against Saul's sides. Joab, whose manners were exotic and urban and therefore beyond judgment even in the court of a king. Joab, subtle and silky and elusive as a serpent—he who loved his dear uncle and looked at his dear uncle with luminous, lovely eyes. . . .

"Have you chosen?" Saul said.

"If it please the King my lord, I will bring my nephew. It is true that he has lived a strange life among desert folk and in far cities. He has not the courage of my brothers, nor the grace of my sisters. But I will bring him, since he is unfortunate and close to my heart."

Saul turned his face aside. It was possible that he did not believe the offspring of Jesse as magnificent as they had been painted—all the sons brave and all the daughters fair. The words hung in the still air for all to ponder, and the longer they hung there, the more ridiculous they seemed. I should have answered with more simplicity, David thought; and he was glad when the whole surface of Saul's belly shone yellow with the oil, when he could kneel and set his hands to the King's legs, when he could bend his head and hide his face.

Perhaps to break the embarrassing silence, Saul had begun to hum the first phrase of David's song.

"My lord," said David, hoping to turn his mind to some less threaten-ing matter, "shall I use this oil to anoint the soles of your feet? It is said among desert folk that after a long journey the soles require a heavier oil."

"That which you have by you will do well enough," said Saul, and continued to hum. Suddenly he fell silent. "Which came first, David?" he said. "The music or the poem?"

David had finished his task of anointing. He rose and wiped his hands on his tunic. He set the bowl of oil on the clothes chest and turned back to the King's bed. "To speak the truth, my lord, I must search my mind before I answer. They come separately, and yet they come together. A little of this calls up a little of that, and so it goes."

Saul lay very still. His eyes were closed. The black hairs closest to his lips were stirred by the coming and going of his breath. Is he answered then? David asked himself. Will he release me from my fright and let me retreat in peace to my sleep? . . .

"A little of this calls up a little of that," said the man on the bed. "So that is the manner of it? From the days of my childhood the making of a song has been to me a wonder and a mystery, like the unfolding of a seed in the earth, like the growth of a child in the womb." The veined, sun-withered eyelids continued to seal up the King's eyes. His big, lean hand withdrew from the coverlet and came down upon the edge of the bed. "Sit here then, sweet singer out of Judah, and enlighten my ignorance concerning this mystery."

The boy sat, his knees pressed together, his cold hands clasped in his lap. Suddenly he was forlorn, knowing that his source of help had been cut off: the King had placed him with his back toward Jonathan.

"My lord the King will understand," he said, "that it is a difficult matter to make plain——"

"Truly?" The black brows went up, but the eyelids did not open. "Have you never given an account of it before?"

David smiled and spread his hands in self-deprecation, then blushed for the gesture, knowing that neither the King nor the beloved could see. "None cared to know before this hour. In Bethlehem I sang to shepherds and to sheep."

"And now you are raised up. Now you sing to Doeg the Edomite."

"But also to my lord and to Jonathan and to my lady Ahinoam."

"And also to the Princess Michal. She has been smitten with a sudden passion for music. And this is gratifying, but very strange. She never cared for the lute."

A new danger, green and cold as an incoming wave, curved above him. "It is not that she cares for the music," he said. "It is that she takes pity upon the poor lutist who knows not where he should kneel and cannot find his lute. She has a liberal heart, like her father, and will praise the music of a shepherd the more, simply because his accent is the accent of a Judahite."

"Do not deceive yourself," said Saul. "The soil of Judah lies but lightly upon your feet. Now, concerning the genesis of this song——"

The boy felt the sweat starting from his clasped palms. He had fancied that he might satisfy Saul and appease God with the story of some less dangerous equivocation. He had meant to tell, earnestly and without sparing himself, how he had begun an elegy for his living brother. But the still face asked for *this* song and no other.

"My lord, the first line came into my thoughts when I——"

"Begin before that. Begin at a time before the dream became incarnate."

"But these matters are elusive and obscure. I would gladly tell my lord if I knew, but I do not know."

"Then learn to know, David, learn to know."

"How shall I learn, my lord?"

"Remember the time and the occasion. Remember the place."

He remembered. He saw the downward thrust of the lightning. He saw the field through the diagonal lines of rain. He saw the advancing shape walking between angry heaven and barren earth. And, seeing these things, he was miraculously strong. Look upon me, Jahveh, he thought, feeling the mass of the stone bull rising behind him. Look upon me while this spirit is in me, while I cannot lie. . . .

The King lifted his eyelids. For one glaring white minute, in which he saw nothing but the gleaming surfaces of Saul's eyes, it seemed to David that he might tell the truth. He heard how his own voice would say the honorable words. Forgive me, my lord, he thought, the song was for Jonathan. His love is better to me than the love of women. His love is more to me than the King's love. I am grieved that I deceived my lord, but my lord was not deceived. In his soul he knew from the beginning that the song was for Jonathan. . . . The King's eyes remained fixed, drawing him with the power of a magnet. "If the King will forgive this miserable wretch——" he said. And suddenly the power that held him was gone. In the flaccid second that followed, David knew that it was not he who had retreated. Saul's glance—the kingly strength of Saul—these had failed. The eyes still stared, but they stared obliquely. Lie to me, David, they said. I have been to Gilgal, and I am exceedingly weary. Love whom you will, but love me also. Love me enough to tell me a kindly lie. . . .

"If the King will forgive this miserable wretch, I cannot remember the exact hour when I conceived this song. I know only that it came to me after a kind of unwholesome sleep. I rose from such a sleep and went to the window and looked upon the uncultivated field and wondered whether my lord would come to his house that way. I believe it was then that I——"

"Yes, yes," Saul said, turning on his side and drawing the coverlet to his chin. "It is a poor answer to a foolish question. I have asked before and been given worse answers. I will ask again and hope to receive a better one, but not tonight. Tomorrow I will send to Bethlehem for this nephew who has lived an unfortunate life and is dear to your heart. We will fetch him here and make him as fortunate as we are able. Surely, now, all three of us are weary. Let us sleep."

The King's son and the King's armor-bearer spoke at once, the same words in the same tone: "Let me remain with my lord tonight." Each of them had made the request with the same aching sense of irrevocable wrong, the same remorse. And David knew that Jonathan understood the genesis of the song, knew the moment of its conception and who had fathered it, and rose to take upon himself his share of the sin.

"No, my cousin Jonathan, let me stay," he said.

The King raised himself upon his elbow and looked at them both and smiled. "Neither shall stay," he said. "Take the lamp and get hence together. Or take two lamps and get hence separately, so that I need not hear your jabber in the hall through the poor remainder of this night."

✦ X ✦

JOAB came with the end of summer. An autumnal somnolence had settled upon the court at Gibeah. Under trees heavy with fruit, in the shadow of wine-scented vineyards, in the great rooms lighted by a more mellow sun, they spent their hours of idleness. They stirred as little as possible, and each was forever asking the other to fetch him this or hand him that. When Ahinoam, yielding her place to Rizpah the concubine, went forth to Gilgal with Michal and Ishbaal to visit her two dark, undistinguished sons, they were scarcely missed. Saul was happy, and the court drowsed more securely in his happiness. The days were endless and golden. The wine presses creaked; the fat olives dropped with a rustle through the dried leaves and thudded softly upon the ground; the figs lay in pale-green pyramids, waiting to turn yellow in the sun. And over this static, dreaming world—light, evanescent, like the smoke that rose from the autumn fires— floated the songs of the lutist of Bethlehem.

He sang the majesty of Saul and the charms of Rizpah. He sang the strength of Gibean wine and the delights of threshing in the evening under the moon. He sang of his pleasure in watching a gazelle drink at a stream on a gray morning, and everyone knew it for a subtle compliment to Jonathan. He sang the fall of Amalek in honor of the return of Abner, and the stern old soldier was so moved that he found it necessary to point out an error in fact in the third line. He had never before been so fertile. Every evening he had another song.

The evening of Joab's coming was like all the others. The company had wandered into the orchard. Rizpah sat upon a bench with her back against the silvery bark of an olive tree, and Saul lay at full length with his head upon her knees. Jonathan and David sprawled upon the dry grass. Now and then one would prop himself upon his elbow and pluck away a brown leaf that had drifted down upon the other. Both of them were close to sleep when the servant came from the house to say that a certain Joab out of Bethlehem was waiting within.

As David walked across the broad lawns on his way to the house, a sudden mournfulness beset him. It seemed to him that the best of his life had passed, that he and the garden were alike falling into decay. The enchanted summer is over, he thought, and I shall not sing again or love again as I have sung and loved this year. . . . And the thought of coping with Joab made him even more disconsolate.

The dimness within—the sun had almost set and the lamps had not yet been lighted—made him uneasy. He could not make certain at once that he and Joab were the only persons in the room. It was Joab who sat behind the table in a long shaft of shadow—that at least was plain. The golden crescents hung from his ears, and his gleaming teeth and eyes were visible even in this dark. He rose from the bench behind the table, toppling the bowl of curds set before him. No servant came to sop up the spilled stuff; it was evident that, save for the two of them, the room was empty. "My uncle! Do my eyes truly behold my dear uncle?" he said.

David asked sourly, without advancing, whom else Joab could take him to be.

"But it is so long since I have looked upon you. And you have changed, you are more lordly! How can I signify my gratitude? If it were not for my uncle, I would have tarried all through the autumn in Mar Saba, which is destitute of everything save lice and dogs. What shall I say to convince David of my gratefulness?"

"For God's sake," his uncle said, crossing the room and sitting heavily upon the bench on the other side of the table, "say nothing at all."

"Is my uncle sick?" said Joab, looking discreetly at the toppled bowl before him.

"Yes, sick for home."

"Truly? In the midst of all this?"

"Is it well with Jesse?" asked David. "How is it with my mother and my brothers?"

"They are as they were when my uncle left them, all cheerful and in good health. The glory of my uncle shines like the sun upon the old age of his father and his mother. As for my mother," Joab said, "she is fatter than ever. No chair in the house is wide enough to support her hind-quarters."

The lutist frowned.

"I have offended David. He was offended when he first set eyes upon my face. He no longer loves me."

"That is nonsense. Have you had enough to eat? Let us go up to my room in the tower."

During the happy summer he had thought many times of this moment when he would reveal the wonders of the King's house to the little Ishmaelite. Now he saw that this, too, would fall far short of his dreams. It was a melancholy procedure; by Joab's delight he measured how much his own pleasure had dwindled since the evening when he had first ascended these long, imperial stairs. I have seen the King's wounds and the Queen's tears, he thought. I have kissed the King's daughter on the mouth, and I have put aside the folds of her tunic from her breast. And what is it to me? Wherein have I profited? I have profited in nothing, save only in Jonathan.

Jonathan? He stopped on a landing beneath a window, in a long red ray of light. He stood utterly still, unmindful of the puzzled boy at his elbow, and stared at the slit of sky which showed between the hard and lifeless stones. The stones no longer breathed, and he knew with smiting grief that he had come even to this—that he could question his delight in Jonathan. But wherefore? he asked himself. Because in this summer of dreaming and dallying the love between us has sickened and changed. The love between us has been marked and softened, like an apricot that should have been eaten long ago. It is too late, the bloom is gone. Too late for what? For the consummation that should have been between us. What consummation? A battle—there should have been a battle, and I between him and a Philistine sword. I should have died for him last spring. Between him and me there is no consummation save death. . . .

"My uncle, I know it is fitting that you should dwell with the eagles. But I am very weary. Are there still more stairs?"

"Only one flight more."

They mounted it in silence and in silence entered the dusky tower room. But at the sight of the window, Joab could no longer restrain himself. He ran to the paling square of height and blueness, and leaned far out over the window sill. "How vast! How magnificent and exalted is the tower where my uncle sleeps!" he said. "On clear nights it must be possible to see all Israel from this window, even the waves of the western sea."

"No," said David, lying across the bed, "it is not possible. When I first came into Saul's house, I also believed that I could see the waters. But it is a dream. Everything is a dream. What dreams of me do they dream these days in Bethlehem?"

"Glorious, my uncle!" Joab said.

"What is glorious?"

"The tales—the histories—the wonders that they tell concerning the son of Jesse in Bethlehem!"

"What tales?"

He asked because he had planned to ask. He was not interested in the answer. He lay on his back and stared up at the airy emptiness, the remote and watery blue beyond the window. The prattling voice went on and on. . . .

"But if my uncle would know what pleases them most, what makes the hands of the mother shake for sheer delight, what brings tears of pride into Jesse's eyes—it is when they remember how David slew the giant Goliath at Ephes-Dammim, with the help of God and a pebble from the brook."

"I?"

He sat up. The Ishmaelite was rocking back and forth upon the bed. Through his parted lips issued the first phrase of the song: " 'On the ridge of Ephes-Dammim, the heathen giant stood like a monolith. . . .' "

"It was not I who slew Goliath."

" 'Over the holy watercourse was the shadow of a great stone.' "

"Elhanan slew him. I slew him not."

"But the song is plainly a song of my uncle's."

"The song is a song of your uncle's. But the deed was the deed of Elhanan. Is that not known in Bethlehem?"

"The Judahites have given the deed to David together with the song."

"God," he said, striking the bed in rage and bafflement, "what fools—what babbling fools they are!" Oh, they had robbed him of his glory now. They had preferred the spurious stuff of their own imaginings above his accomplishments. And when the legend fell away, how small he would seem, how dull and petty in their eyes—the lad who was said to have killed a giant and who had merely played a mad king into sanity. No, he would never look on Jesse's face again. Now he could never go home.

"But is it an evil thing, my uncle, to be called a hero and the slayer of a monstrous Philistine?"

"Evil or good—what is the difference? It is not true."

"But what is true on this questionable earth? It is said in all Israel that the giant's height was six cubits and a span. None will gainsay it. Yet is it true?"

"I tell you that I killed him not, nor ever saw him. His head I saw, and by his head, I—— But what is his height to me?"

"Nothing, my uncle. His height is nothing to you. I used it merely as an instance, to point out how difficult it is for the feeble wits of men to know what is true and what is not true. And it puzzles me greatly that the armor-bearer of the King should take offense at a good report. Now, had they said of my uncle in Bethlehem that he had raped the King's daughter or had made off with a sackful of coins from the King's treasury—— But when it is said of a brave man that he is brave and of a glorious man that he is glorious——"

"Be still," said David. He would have said more, but his voice betrayed the fact that he was weeping. He went to the darkening window and lifted his shamed and tormented face to the sky.

"What can I do to comfort my dear uncle?"

"Go back to Bethlehem and proclaim it at the gates, how it was Elhanan who slew Goliath, how David of Bethlehem slew him not."

"No, now, my uncle jests. He says it, but he means it not."

"I mean it. I——"

"But will he send me back to break the old, proud heart in his father's breast? Will he send me back to cause his mother to blush and to turn all his sisters-in-law into objects for mockery at the well?"

David could not reply.

"I know that my uncle meant it not. It was said in an excess of nobility. This story of David and Goliath is beneath my uncle's notice. Now, as I pointed out to you earlier, were it a tale of ill repute, were my uncle accused of going in unto the King's daughter, or——"

"She runs much in your mind, the King's daughter."

"It is nothing. It is an instance, like the height of Goliath."

"Then find another instance."

"I had not thought it would offend my uncle."

"It did not offend me. Leave it and talk of some other business," he said.

In the strained silence that followed, he saw that the room had darkened, and knew that his face was hidden at last from the vagabond's lustrous eyes. In this shadow he could afford to think of the King's daughter. "Going in unto the King's daughter . . ." The phrase was crude, but the phrase was somehow consoling for its very crudity. All other longings hung baffled and unanswerable in his unhappy thoughts and feverish dreams. This, and this alone, might be accepted and assuaged; for this single desire Jahveh and the world had offered a consummation. Whosoever loved Saul must stand on the margins of madness, incapable of following him into that barren and fantastic land where the possessed walk alone. And what fruition other than death waited for him who loved Jonathan? But Michal possessed a vessel to quench the thirst that she created. Desire Michal. Learn to want Michal—study it like the art of the spear and the bow. For the end is in the beginning and is sure. Go in unto Michal and be spent and be at rest.

A step sounded in the corridor, and a servant's voice asked discreetly, "Will you have me light the lamps, my lord?"

He started from his dream. "Yes, we would be the merrier for a little light," he said.

The door creaked inward, and the servant entered bearing a lamp. The yellow glow cast a mild radiance upon the lanky wanderer who now sprawled across the bed, revealing his pained and disappointed face. I must make amends, David thought. . . . "Move a little," he said after the servant had gone forth, "and I will sit upon the bed. If you are not too weary, tell me a few more tales of Bethlehem."

"If it were not that my uncle had sealed up my mouth with interdictions and prohibitions, I could truly tell him a tale——"

"What tale?"

"But David has made it plain that if I mention the name of the King's daughter, I am cast out to the dogs."

"What has Michal to do with Bethlehem?"

"She is named at the cistern a score of times an evening."

"Wherefore?"

"It is said that my uncle will marry the King's daughter. It is said that Samuel has prophesied, vaguely, to be sure, in his usual manner. It is said that David will be Saul's son-in-law before the brooks are swollen with this winter's snow."

"I?"

"Why is it that my uncle is forever saying 'I'? Surely my uncle knows that Jahveh has written his destiny in gold."

"I would not have it so," he said.

"What? Not be married to the King's daughter? But it is said that she is young and blindingly fair."

He opened his lips, but the ingratiating babbler would give him no time to make his meaning plain.

"How could my uncle better profit than by being the husband of the King's daughter? There is no more exalted station open to him now, not, certainly, in Israel. True, if he were a Canaanite or a man of Caphtor, he might do as well if he were the beloved of the King's son——"

The sound that issued from David's mouth was no word. It was a wild, tormented cry.

"My uncle!" Joab said.

David was gone from him, was at the window, was bruising his own hand, grinding it against the rough stone of the sill. But I knew long ago, he told himself. I have always known. Since the hour at the cistern, the foreknowledge was with me. This truth has pursued me like a great hawk, and the shadow of its wings has never departed from my face. And tonight he has called it by its name, and it has descended, and its feathery strength is upon me, and its claws have torn at my flesh, its beak is in my heart. . . .

"My uncle, I assure you it was a jest, such a jest as I have heard a thousand times among the Canaanites."

Among the Canaanites and in the pale island of Caphtor, where the steps of the palaces descend into the sea, in the far places where Jahveh is not, there I might have been the beloved of the King's son. There we might have ruled hand in hand upon a double throne, and worn twin diadems, and gone down at last into the same grave. Since it is not so done in Israel, since in the land of God one of us dies and one of us reigns, give me the burial cave and take the crown. Make a place for me in the garden of Saul's house where the weaver of Beth–shemesh lies—that other one who also loved you unto death. Come, beloved, on feast days and pour the oil upon me and comfort me with wine. But do not forget, do not forget. . . .

"Believe me, my uncle, there was no hidden meaning in my talk. May my bowels wither if I meant to cast any slur upon the noble friendship that is between you and the hero Jonathan."

He turned from the window and glared at the boy upon the bed. "Never take his name into your unclean mouth again," he said.

"I am my uncle's servant. My uncle has only to indicate the slightest displeasure, and I will——"

"Very well, then. Only be still."

In the miserable stillness that followed, he knew that he could no longer endure Joab's company. He pleaded certain vague duties that awaited him in the mysterious royal world below; and for more than an hour he wandered solitary up and down the dark halls.

❧ XI ☙

THERE WAS a saying among the warriors of Jahveh that the Philistines returned to Israel with the frost. All summer long they had cooled themselves upon the westward porticoes of their palaces in Gath, Gaza, and Askelon. They had lain in luxury upon their unassailable beaches; they had roasted the unclean creatures of the sea upon hot stones in the evenings, assailing the ears of God's chosen with taunts concerning the weakness of Saul, who had dreamed only last year of driving them into the sea. There were harvest festivals in the temples of Dagon and Astarte, and there was drunken boasting after the festivals. What men were there in the assembly who would dare to venture as far as the fields around Hebron to kill a few of the circumcised dogs and bring a fine head of cattle back home? Who would go up to Nob to take the dishonored sword of Goliath from the temple wall? Who was for the environs of Gibeah itself? Before the Serens of the Philistine cities had lighted the bonfires that summoned the brave to the winter campaigns, some were already gone. The time of marauding had come again. Like spray that goes before a wave, the small, devoted bands went forth into Israel in advance of the Philistine host.

Abner brought the first news of them to Saul's house in Gibeah. He had gone up to Gilgal to review the troops; he had communicated Saul's winter battle plans to the captains over thousands; he had spent an evening with Ahinoam and had confided to her a certain rumor which was passing from mouth to mouth at the court—a tale that Saul meant to give Michal in marriage to the lutist out of Bethlehem. The Princess Michal had seemed sullen and ill, and Ahinoam had looked like a corpse—her lips were blue and in the light of the lamp every bone and tendon in her hand had been visible. Nor had she seemed in the least surprised at the information about her daughter and the Judahite. "Truly?" she had said, and her thin face had been molded by a vague smile.

On the return journey, Abner lay awake in unfamiliar beds, cursing his old wound, which ached afresh with every recurrence of the autumn cold. And at every town where he stopped for rest, it was the same story: "They came again out of Philistia as they came last year; our sheep are stolen; our daughters are carried away; the oil was taken; the wheat field was set afire." Even in the hills around Gibeah itself there were signs that a few of the most intrepid of the uncircumcised had ventured within sight of the King's dwelling-place. A slave had been stolen, and two travelers had been robbed and murdered near the gates of the town. In some far thicket, in the dead of night, the invaders warmed themselves against the frost. The screen of barren branches could not hide their fires.

He came late into Saul's house by design. The prospect of a courtly evening had seemed intolerable to him; and yet when he entered and found an almost empty common room and a banked fire, he felt a profound regret. Where was the King? he asked the drowsy servant who set the bread and wine before him. The King slept. And Jonathan? He also slept; he had spent the day in the uncultivated field, ridding it of stones. And, he asked with a faint surge of hope, where was my lady Rizpah—did she also sleep? Yes, said the servant, with her lord. The single lamp on the table seemed colder, sicklier, than before. What, then, had come over the court that they went like children so early to their beds? Was there none in the whole house awake at this hour of the night? Yes, one, said the servant, and smiled. David of Bethlehem—he was certain to be awake. He walked the halls like a ghost, and was to be seen sitting on piles of armor even after the setting of the moon. Should Abner wish the company of the sweet singer, no doubt he could be found. . . . Abner saw the fair face as he had first seen it when he found the lutist among the sleeping host. "Yes, bring him to me," he said. "He will bear me company while I finish the wine."

But in this also the captain was destined to be disappointed. The youth who walked into the faint redness cast by the dying fire was not the dreamer whom he had wakened on the morning of his brief felicity. The boy was as comely as his remembered image—pale and flawless skin, gray eyes, and reddish hair—but the perfection, the serenity, had wholly departed. The young man was plainly as tired, as tormented, as assailed by unanswerable questions as himself.

"Well, David," he said. But the name would not mean "darling" on his lips. The youngest son of Jesse was no longer a child.

"How can I serve my lord the captain of the host?"

Abner was embarrassed. A young lutist would consider a draught of wine with the captain an occasion, but a troubled courtier could find it only an intrusion. "It is nothing," he said. "I found it wearisome to break bread alone, and the servant said that you had not yet gone to your bed."

"I am exalted above my merit by my lord." He moved forward into the faint circle of light cast by the lamp. He sat on the other side of the table and asked the appropriate questions concerning Gilgal and the homeward journey, and he embellished his remarks with the proper compliments. But it was as if he spoke in a dream.

"Would I had been with my lord the captain of the host in Gilgal. I have never sojourned in any city larger than Gibeah. Since my childhood I——"

But Abner could not listen. Why, he thought, should I sit up late after such a journey to hear these elaborate inanities? Come, then, show me what wound it is that they have put upon your heart.

The young hand, fashioned less for the spear than for the lute, tore nervously at a bit of bread. "My eyes are hungry to behold the wonders of the temple at Gilgal."

"Truly? I would have thought by the unhappy face of the son of Jesse that his eyes were hungry to behold the streets of Bethlehem."

It was an arrow shot into darkness. He was amazed that it had found its mark, had frozen the slight fingers above the bread.

"Go home, then," he said. "Saul will give you a little time."

"No, my lord." The gray eyes which stared into his were the eyes of a stricken child. "I can never go home."

"But that is a foolish thought. Wherefore?"

"Because of the tales they tell of me—the monstrous and ridiculous tales."

"What tales?"

"Is it possible that my lord the captain of the host knows nothing of these tales? Has my lord not heard how it was I, and not Elhanan, who slew the giant at Ephes-Dammim? Oh, they have exalted me in Bethlehem until I cannot enter my father's house unless I become a disgrace to the womb of my mother, or a miserable liar."

To be glorified out of one's own village—that was amusing. Yet Abner could not deny that the situation was painful, nor could he think of any answer save a superficial piece of optimism. "Consider it no more," he said in a hearty voice. "Come with us to the winter campaigns and there slay a giant and go home next spring."

"But I am not such a one as slays giants."

"No?" To that there was no answer either. He was reduced to a jest. "Then, look, I will slay a giant and give you his helmet that you may carry it back to Bethlehem to gladden Jesse's heart."

The boy smiled a feeble smile. "My lord is kind. If that were the only legend they tell concerning me, then I might wait for the hour of my glory—if Jahveh sees fit that such an hour should come. As it is, there is another tale——"

Now it was Abner who plucked uneasily at the bread. Too many legends were gathering around this stripling's head. As a fair flower draws bees, so David had drawn legends—legend of the slaying of Goliath, legend of marriage with Saul's daughter, yes, and a more ominous legend, a priestly legend of the destruction of Saul's house and a lamb out of Judah raised to the lion's throne. . . . The captain had taken no account of the last of these tales. He had laid it to Samuel's malice, and hoped to God that it would never come buzzing into Saul's ears. Saul already carried far more than he had strength to bear.

"What other tale do they tell?" he said.

"I am ashamed even to name it before my lord."

The captain was not sure that he wished to hear it named. Of late, whenever he found himself in a disturbing situation, he felt the persistent ache in his leg. I am sick, he told himself, I am exhausted, I should not be forced to deal with this. . . . He winced and bent forward and rubbed his thigh.

For a few seconds there was silence between them. Then the lutist's voice, vibrant and tender, broke into the quiet. "My lord," he said, "are you in pain?"

Was it the voice, or the comely and wretched face, or the strength of the last draught, that so disarmed the captain? True, none had asked him such a question in all the years that he had carried his sore about with him. Yet it was strange that so small a kindness should bring him almost to the verge of tears.

"It is nothing," he said. "It is an old wound. The ache, like the Philistines, comes back with the frost."

"Then surely my captain should not burden himself with my little grievances. Let my lord go up to his chamber and sleep."

An hour more, an hour less, Abner thought, what did it matter? His weariness was beyond curing with a little rest. "Is it this business of Michal?" he said.

"Then my lord has heard of it—my lord, like all Israel. But believe me, I never thought to raise my unworthy eyes to the Moon of Benjamin——"

Nor I to Rizpah, Abner thought, and yet . . .

"Who am I that I should dream to be the son-in-law of a king? I am nothing, I am a piece of clay out of Judah, without a name. And yet they have spoken of it to Saul, all of them, the captain of the guard, and Rizpah the concubine, and Doeg the Edomite. Look how it is with me, my captain, how I cannot dwell in Bethlehem since I am the slayer of Goliath, nor in Gibeah because I am the betrothed of the Princess——"

Nor in Gilgal, thought Abner, because you are the King of Israel? . . .

"And Saul is forever making jests concerning it in my presence. He has said he will ask no marriage portion, nothing save the foreskins of two hundred Philistines slain in battle. This he has said to mock me, because I have never slain a man, and my lord the King knows as much."

Yet it is strange, Abner thought, it is very strange that the King should find it a reason for jest. Why should he revive by talk a matter that had best be forgotten? Why had Ahinoam said nothing save "Truly"? The Princess lay sick in Gilgal. Was it possible that Michal was sick for love?

He could not understand either Saul or Ahinoam, nor could he, for that matter, understand himself. An excitement, a positive ardor had suddenly been born within him. As he was pleased by the shape of a cloud or a mountain, so he was pleased at the thought that this young man might go in unto the Princess Michal, might pour his propitious seed into the dark vigor of Saul's line. He saw the torch go out above their marriage bed, he saw them embrace; and as Ahinoam had smiled, so he smiled.

"My lord the captain sees to what a wretched state I have fallen. I am covered with shame—it would be better for me if I were dead."

"No, now, that is childish. Nothing is beyond mending. This also will pass."

Suddenly the lutist lifted his head. His gray eyes, larger and deeper than the captain had remembered them, stared nakedly into Abner's face. He had forgotten how the young could suffer. He said, knowing that nothing truly passes, "Truly, David, it will pass."

"My lord the captain is kind. But he does not know what ails me. What ails me cannot be mended and will never pass."

"But if the son of Jesse cannot live without the daughter of Saul, and if the daughter of Saul cannot live without the son of Jesse, then Saul, who is a man of reason, will certainly see how it is with Michal and her lover. He would not jest if the matter were utterly abhorrent to him. Think a little of that and be comforted."

He had held out an ointment that he had no right to bestow, and yet the gray eyes continued to fix upon him the same austere, inconsolable look. He sensed that to withdraw and be silent was the wiser course. But he could not be silent. He had seen the marriage torch go out above their bed, he was their partisan, he would have them together. "Leave it in God's lap," he said, putting all discretion aside. "I have some credit with my lord, and I will plead for you. Believe me, there is no cause for this hopelessness. I have already spoken of this business to Ahinoam, and she also may yet raise her voice——" He stopped, chagrined and wounded. David was not listening, and he was left babbling foolishly. The gray eyes were fixed upon the doorway. Out of the blackness of the corridor into the faint redness of the fire walked Jonathan.

The captain could not see why this chance meeting should cause such consternation, why David's hand should tremble, why the King's son should stand wordless and uneasy before the hearth.

"My captain," said the King's son at last, "I had not heard of your return. Otherwise I would not have gone up to my room this night. I am distressed that Abner should find on the table only the worst of the wine and half a loaf of yesterday's bread."

"It is no great matter," the captain said. But in spite of himself there was an aggrieved note in his voice. It was plain to him that the hour which he had spent with the Judahite, burdening himself with the boy's burden, aching with the boy's pain, committing himself to serve a cause which he had no right to touch, was forgotten. The comely face that had turned upon him a moment since was turned now, more ardently, more tenderly, upon Jonathan.

Nor was there anything in Jonathan's manner to lessen his pain. A specious courtesy, a flustered graciousness, were all that the young man could summon up. "No, now," he said to Abner, "what sort of welcome is this? What sort of wine? What sort of bread? Should Ahinoam hear of it, she would be sick with shame." . . . It was plain that he meant to talk of nothing save the wretchedness of the welcome, would cling desperately to this bread and wine until he had killed the possibility of fertile speech and had talked the captain straight to his bed. And then, Abner asked himself, what then, when the old man is gone and the room is given over to the young? . . . But he had a word that would shatter their absorption in each other.

"The Philistines are with us," he said.

"So soon?" said David. The two words were like a dirge for the long, sweet summer.

"But it is always later than we wish to know," the King's son said. "How far inland have they come, my lord?"

"Even to the gates of Gibeah. Two travelers were slain there yesterday, toward dawn. They have burned and forayed in many places between here and Gilgal. This very night I saw their campfires in the hills."

If the captain had thought to draw their attention upon himself with these harsh tidings, he was mistaken. David rose and stared at the King's son; the King's son leaned heavily upon the table and stared at David; and the captain sat gazing at the crumbs upon the board and knew himself to be utterly alone.

"Let my father hear no word of it," Jonathan said.

"No?" said the captain. "Then shall we all sit drinking and dreaming? It may so happen, if we drink and dream long enough, we will dream the Philistines back into the sea."

"Not so, my captain. Let me see to this battle. I have need of such an occasion. I yearn after the hour of danger, and the sword, and——"

The last, unspoken word clashed in Abner's mind like a spear against a brazen shield, and the word was "death." The captain raised his eyes slowly until the face of the King's son was within the range of his vision, a white and solemn face—the face of a devoted victim yearning to be slain. Yet his look, which should have turned southward to Sinai and God, was earthbound, was fixed upon David of Bethlehem.

And he was answered with the same ardor and with equal devotion. "Let me go forth with my cousin," David said.

"No, now," said the King's son, "stay in Gibeah and pray for me tomorrow night when I am among the hills."

"Wherefore?"

"My cousin is young. My cousin is too young for——"

Again the unspoken word clanged through the hush.

"No, Jonathan," said David, "for I also have need of such an occasion. My cousin has not seen my heart if he believes that his need is greater than mine."

"Even if it should come to pass that tomorrow I would go down into Sheol, I would be comforted remembering that David was still fair and uncorrupted, thinking how David still moved and breathed upon the earth."

"Without Jonathan, what is the earth? In Sheol, as in Caphtor and among the Canaanites—in the burial cave also there is no longer any barrier between dust and dust."

"Stay in Gibeah, nevertheless."

"Jonathan made a covenant with me——"

"What covenant, my cousin? Between me and David there were many covenants, some spoken and some beyond speech. All that could be fulfilled with honor upon the world, they are fulfilled. All that are not yet fulfilled will be accomplished."

"Under the dripping tree, when we first broke bread together, Jonathan swore to me that I would go with him when he went forth against the Philistines."

"It was a rash promise and lightly given."

"Say not to me that it was lightly given."

"No, then, David, I gave it earnestly, but gave it in an evil hour."

"Say not to me that it was an evil hour. Behold, all my hours were evil, save only that hour. What am I? Jonathan knows and Saul his father knows that I am as bad fruit, on one side fair and sweet, and on the other dark and foul. Thus I have been through all my days, save only in that one hour. Then I was perfect, I was whole, I was such a one as might be acceptable to God. Take not my hour from me, Jonathan. Give me my hour, and I will gladly pay for it with any price, yes, even though I should go down to death."

Now that the word had actually been spoken, an unworldly serenity descended upon the room. The captain raised his eyes again, turned slowly from one face to the other face, and saw with wonder that they were alike, that their eyes were closed, that their cheeks and lips were molded in the same smile.

"Then, if it is so with David," said Jonathan without raising his eyelids, "let us go out tomorrow after the evening meal, at the hour of the setting of the sun."

Suddenly the captain started out of his dream. That which had seemed no more of the earth nor of the hour than some ancient tale was about to come to pass in the hills around Gibeah tomorrow night. These two young men actually meant to rise from the supper table and walk into the hills alone.

"God of Sinai, are you mad?" Abner said.

There was silence while they realized and accepted his presence. They turned courteously toward him. Their exaltation embraced all men, even the aging captain of the host.

"No, now, my captain, why should we not go forth?" Jonathan said. "Would you send Saul? Save him for the hour when they come up against us in one array. Would my captain himself go out to a skirmish? Then is Israel truly lost, for Abner is the mind of Israel in those hours when the King is sick and darkness closes upon him. Would you wait until a battalion is summoned out of Gilgal? Then, indeed, the enemy will be established within the town."

The young man's voice was so temperate that the captain wondered whether all that had passed in the dim room had not been distorted by his own dazed and weary mind.

"Let the matter rest with the two of us, my captain," David said.

"Are the two of you such fools as to think of going forth against the marauders alone?"

In one swift glance they agreed to compromise. No, they said, in conciliatory voices. They would take their armor-bearers and five good men; it would be imprudent to go forth alone. And he saw plainly that the affair was closed, that he had no reasonable cause to contend with them further, and that he had neither their permission nor enough strength and understanding to impute to them a purpose which they had left unexpressed. Jonathan bent over the table, feeling the loaf and shaking his head over the quality of the bread.

"How my mother would be grieved to behold this table. . . ."

"Well, think no more of it. She is not here. She is in Gilgal, sleeping, and would to God the same might be said of me," the captain said.

They came to him then and bent over him and kissed him respectfully upon the brow and wished him a peaceful night. He waited to learn whether they would pause to whisper in the corridor; but each went wordlessly upon his own way. Whatever needed saying between them had already been said. But the captain remained long at the table. Why had they smiled? The whole house had grown oppressively still. There was no sound in the halls above. They walked softly; they did not wish to disturb the sleepers; no footfall would startle the ear of Rizpah, who lay in Saul's arms that night. Why had they smiled? He lifted the lamp and walked slowly to the door. Her hair, her wonderful black hair, streaked a little now with gray, but rich and heavy still, was spread, even now, across Saul's shoulders, over Saul's face. He paused in the doorway, leaned his head against the frame, and smiled, thinking of his own death.

❧ XII ❧

THE SUN went down gigantic and red above the far purple hills. All the earth had a brownish, depleted look; everything was faded except the terebinths, which showed tall and unseasonably green against the rest. The forest lands were dwarfed by the moving pageantry above them. The sky looked unbelievably vast and solid; it was a closed dome, red at the rim, hyacinthine at the top, so huge as to seem almost empty even though piled masses of cloud moved solemnly around it, constantly changing in color and shape, showing now violet, now gray, now rose, transforming themselves into scaly dragons, huge wings, monumental faces. Under this dome, across this little world, small and solitary and followed at a distance by a negligible train, the son of Jesse and the son of Saul walked side by side in silence, in search of their deaths.

All that could be spoken, and far more than ever should have been spoken by two honorable sons of Jahveh, had been said in the common room last night. Fleeting touches, half-uttered phrases, eyes hidden in descending eyelids before the meaning of the glance could be known, the print of hands upon coverlets, the mark of feet upon bent grass —these were the things they pondered in their silence.

Now and then the wind, blowing through the rustling dryness of the forest, would carry to their ears the voices of the little troop of warriors who came up behind them. They were a nervous and disgruntled crowd; Abner had bidden them in no uncertain terms to follow at the very heels of the King's lutist and the King's son. But the young men themselves saw the matter otherwise; it was obvious that they meant to walk alone. The complaints of the stragglers were intended to be heard. What ailed the son of Saul? He had always been noted for his circumspection. Since when had it become a custom in Israel to walk to a skirmish in nothing but a tunic, to leave the shield and the breastplate and the sword thirty paces behind in some poor armor-bearer's hands? Behold also the sword and the breastplate of my dear uncle, who is the rose of his father's withered garden. If one hair on his head be touched, it will bring the old man straightway to his grave. No, now, what are they seeking? Philistines or their own deaths?

Then they fell silent, for the sky was filled with a great and sudden light. All the colors that had shone and changed and faded returned to it again in one final conflagration, hiding the pale feather of the crescent moon, quenching the stars. The brown earth turned metallic in the glare; the hills shone like beaten corselets; the leaves were bronze and gold. "How fair," said Jonathan; and David said, "How fair," and thought, How fair was my life, and how lovely was the world. . . .

They moved on without further words until the moon and the stars showed cold against a remote and chilly blue. Then Jonathan said, "If my cousin David wishes to turn back to Gibeah——"

He wished it wildly. He thought of the hearth and the red embers. He thought of the lute lying upon the coverlet and of the consoling and dissolving warmth of his bed. Yet even as they formed themselves in his thoughts, these images and all remembrances of the delights of the earth faded and gave place to Jonathan. The cloudy hair, driven against his cheek by a sudden gust, the naked and earnest eyes, the hand that moved tentatively toward him—he turned to these without reason and without choice, as a plant turns toward the sun. Over the clanging of his heart, louder than that terrible beat, shatteringly high and shrill, sounded the unearthly note that must be followed, even though it should lead over the rim of the world.

"Then I will follow it," he said.

"What will my cousin follow?"

"The high music that has sounded in my ears ever since the hour when I first beheld Jonathan."

"Is it a song, beloved?"

"Higher than a song, beyond all songs. There is no melody that can contain it and no instrument upon which it can be played. It is one high note——"

"Is it of Jahveh? What is the meaning of it?"

"That I should go with my cousin into any country, even the country of the dead."

He went with his cousin; he followed the beckoning sound over knolls and through whispering thickets. And now the fear was gone from him, now he wished only that he might not be forced to follow too far or wait too long. Jonathan's hand lay lightly around his own. As the shadow deepened, they drew closer to each other until they walked shoulder to shoulder. A delicate vibration, as subtle as the trembling of a plucked string, kept David's body in continual agitation. Let death come, he thought, let me see the plumed helmet and the sword rise from behind the next rock. . . .

They did not rise. The night deepened, the stars shone separate and swollen against intense blue, the feathery moon took on the solid sharpness of a sickle, and still they did not rise. And slowly it was borne in upon his unwilling thoughts that the minute of annihilation must be postponed. The vibrant, holy, moonlit death that he had sought could not be found. There must be another death—stark death in the gray morning, death with the fog of sleep still in the throat, death without love. Night had come down completely. Only a faint and watery glimmer, evoked by starlight upon pale, moving flesh, was left to him—the ghostly semblance of Jonathan's arms and Jonathan's face.

"I cannot see my cousin," he said, in the voice of a child who stands in a room where the last lamp has been extinguished.

"I also would look upon the face of David. But they will not permit us to light a torch, lest it be a signal to invite the marauders. They are a burden to us. Now they will force us to put off this business until morning. Now they are whining after sleep."

The words were valiant, but the voice was weary. In the darkness beside him, David could hear the hurried breath. The King's son was worn with seeking. He also, thought David, yearns after the moonlit death; but his spirit has outrun his flesh; Jahveh has fashioned his flesh from frailer, finer stuff than mine. . . .

"My cousin is very tired. The journey has been too long," he said.

"Would it had been longer. Would there had been an end to it."

He also is resigned, David thought. He also would lie down and sleep. . . . "Then seeing that we are both weary, Jonathan, let us rest."

"David is not weary."

"Believe me, I am very weary, Jonathan."

"David will lie down because he knows that I am spent. And I would have it so."

They walked slowly until the others came up behind them. There was an exasperating discussion over the proper place for the encampment. Ten paces back there was an excellent glade surrounded by trees. Twenty paces behind that there was a fine hollow sheltered on one side by a thicket and on the other by a ridge of stone. Which would offer more protection against the Philistines and the frost? When at last they had decided upon the hollow, they settled themselves upon the summer-dried grass, between the crackling thicket and the solemn ridge of stone. The King's lutist and the King's son lay side by side, each wrapped in his mantle, close to the ridge and a little apart from the rest. Each lay with his hand upon his sword and his shield across his breast. But Jonathan held his sword with his left hand, and David with his right, so that their fingers might touch, even in sleep, upon the frosty grass.

For the frost was upon them before they closed their eyes. It congealed upon the harsh blades; it gathered upon the crevices in the rock; they felt the chill of it upon their faces. The earth seemed to grow perceptibly harder beneath their heads. Even the figure of Joab, crouching through the first watch upon the rocks, touched by the starlight, seemed to be encased in glimmering rime. Each fixed his gaze upon the other's ghostly face. So they lay, staring at each other through the blackness until sight gave way to the images of dreams and both of them slept.

This was the dream that David dreamed in the hills near Gibeah: The Lord of Hosts was wroth with the frailties of Israel, and, even as in the time of Noah, He sent a calamity upon the earth. But since men were not the heroes that they had been in ancient days, He said unto Himself, "They are not worthy of great waters; I will destroy them with a small plague of frost." So He quenched His sun and stilled His wind and scattered the frost upon the faces of those who slept. Nor did He say to the frost, "Cease," nor to the night, "Be gone and give place to day." The frost came down everlastingly and turned to ice; it sealed the lips of those who slept and held the eyelids of the sleepers fast upon their eyes. The hosts of the Philistines lay encased in ice upon their white beaches, and the warriors of Jahveh slept a cold sleep in Gilgal, and the King of Israel lay sheathed in ice beside his lifeless concubine, and the King's son and the King's armor-bearer slept among the dead men who had followed them into the hills. Thus it was for a night and a thousand nights. Yet one man still breathed in Israel, even the prophet Samuel, because he was of the race of ancient heroes, and his heart remained as firm as a stone. The Lord of Hosts, seeing the blood of Agag upon his white fingers, said, "Let him live."

So, living, he walked out of Ramah unto Gibeah, and out of Gibeah across the rimy knolls and the whispering thickets, until he came to a hollow between a row of bushes and a ridge of rock. There he found the sweet singer, fair and whole beneath his icy cerements, his hand locked in Jonathan's hand. Thereupon Samuel bent over him and wept, and said, "It is not yet too late. Arise." But the son of Jesse could not leave off cleaving unto the son of Saul, and he did not arise. Then the prophet out of Ramah bent close to the sweet singer and spoke in praise of the goodness of life. He spoke mildly and reasonably and tenderly, with such sweetness that the eyelids of the sleeper were unsealed by tears. Large, warm tears spilled over his cheeks, melting the frost. And he stirred as though to rise, but could not lift his body, seeing that his hand was locked in Jonathan's hand. "But arise, then," said Samuel. "He is of a foredoomed house. It is already written that he shall not reign in Israel. Therefore put him by and arise." Yet David clung to his cousin and wept. Then the prophet leaned above the son of Jesse and laid his fingertip upon the boy's cheek. "Behold," he said, "these are no common tears upon David's face. These are tears unto the deliverance of all Israel. These are a king's tears." Thereupon the lips of all the dead were unlocked, and they uttered a great shout.

"Arise!" they said. "The Philistines are upon us. Arise!" And David wakened from his sleep and saw that the heathen had come into the camp. The hollow was red with the torches of the Philistines. A look of blank wonderment was upon their faces. He knew that they had stumbled upon the dreamers unknowingly, and that they were reaching for their swords.

He saw a bright blade and a feathery crest bearing down upon Jonathan. Even as he watched, he rose in utter calmness to one knee, tilted his sword upward at a precise angle, and received the oncoming body upon the point. He knew with surprise that he need not even thrust. The soft flesh tore and gave way. He pushed the sword and the inert body upon it backward until it toppled upon the grass, clear of the fair, wakening body that it had meant to rob of breath. Jonathan was up at once and at the throat of the next comer. Two guardsmen were charging upon a crested giant whose torch had fallen from his hand. Joab was standing on the stone ridge, screaming at the top of his voice that the Philistines had come. All around, from the frost-sprinkled rocks to the thicket, twos and threes were locked in combat. How many had come upon them? He had no time to think of that. He pulled his sword out of the soft, yielding stuff and brought it bloody to the succor of Jonathan. This time it was necessary for him to thrust. He drove the blade into a white, unprotected neck, and the dying man made a terrible gurgling sound. A third advanced and threw a spear past Jonathan's leg, grazing the flesh, bringing blood and a shrill cry. This third went down under Jonathan's sword. Then there was stillness and less light. Two of the torches were out. The third lay sputtering upon the rime-covered ground. Joab leaped down from his rocky perch and held it up; and in its light they counted nine Philistines dead.

During the counting of the bodies and the division of the spoil, David was wildly, raucously merry. But afterward, when the noise and movement had subsided and the sky had grown wan with the first signs of day, he was assailed by a sickening cold. He could not control the trembling of his knees. He climbed the ridge of rock and sat down upon a flat projection of stone. He clasped his legs with his arms and laid his forehead upon his knees. Now that he was solitary, he fell to shuddering and retching. His stomach was empty, and nothing would come out to relieve him except a little sour slime. Between the fits of gagging he heard from the hollow below him Joab's voice praising the heroic uncle who had slain two Philistines within a single breathing space. "Truly," said Jonathan in the ensuing silence, "your uncle has earned the name of hero this night." But the voice was flat and spiritless, and the sound of it made him shudder and retch the more. He struck his forehead against his knees. "Would I had died for you, would I had died for you, my cousin Jonathan!" he said.

Then there was the sound of footfalls beside him, and he raised his head and saw the face of the betrayed beloved. Jonathan had come up to him from the rest. He too sank down upon the flat stone. The brown eyes looked blankly at David. And he knew that these eyes would forever remain closed to him. The hour when he could look behind their surfaces was gone.

"My cousin came between me and the sword of a Philistine," Jonathan said. "It is to him that I henceforth owe my breath."

"Would I had never wakened out of that sleep!"

"It is an impious wish," said Jonathan lightly. "If it were gratified, the son of Saul your lord would lie even now among the slain."

They continued to stare at each other, and David, remembering his dream, thought that a casing of ice sealed up their eyes.

The King's son was the first to stir. He sighed and looked ruefully down at his own thigh. "I have a wound that is not yet bound up," he said.

"God of Sinai, I saw your wound and forgot it! In my remorse, I would have left my cousin to bleed to death."

"It bled only a little. It is a long wound, but not deep."

They looked down together at the gash, clotted with dark blood, that lay across Jonathan's thigh.

"I waited for my cousin, that he might bind it up for me," said Jonathan. "As it was in the beginning at the cistern in Ephes-Dammim, so let it be in the hills of Benjamin at the end. I have said to myself that as Jonathan bound the wound of David, so shall David bind the wound of Jonathan. So shall that which has no end return to its beginning. So shall the circle be complete. So shall we both have peace."

With numb and awkward fingers, David unwound his girdle and tore it into shreds and knelt before the King's son. He laid his shaking hands upon the thigh and bound it up and pulled the cloth tight, so that, as there had been pain in the beginning, there would be pain in the end. But as he fastened the knot, such sorrow as he had never known came upon him; he could not master himself; he laid his head against his cousin's shoulder and wept.

"No, now," said Jonathan, with a shadowy semblance of the old tenderness. "Do not weep."

"Would I had died!"

"Jahveh saw fit that you should live. Live then and slay ten thousand Philistines. Israel has need of heroes. Come now, be comforted. My cousin must show a decent face to his armor-bearer, who is coming up to us from below."

David raised his head and saw that Joab was clambering up the ledge, clinging to the rocks with one hand and holding two small, bloody trophies in the other. "Behold what my uncle has forgotten," he said.

He was not sure—he did not wish to be sure—what it was that his nephew carried. "Get them out of my sight," he said.

"But these are the foreskins of the two heathen whom my uncle has so gloriously slain——"

"What do I want with them?" he shrieked. "Throw them into the thicket, dog and son of a dog!"

"But I saved them for my uncle, so that he might carry them to the King his lord."

"Wherefore?"

"Wherefore? But my uncle surely knows the reason——"

"Whelp of a lecherous bitch," he shouted, crouching and ready to strike, "do not speak as if there were between us secrets and mysteries."

It was Jonathan who settled the matter. He rose and sighed. "Let him carry them to Saul for you if it pleases him," he said. "He speaks no mystery, but only what is known now in all Israel, how Saul has asked as a marriage present for my sister Michal the foreskins of two hundred Philistines. Saul is a reasonable man, and Michal is sick with love. Saul will be content with two instead of two hundred." He turned and started down the ledge. "Truly, Saul will give my sister to my cousin. And let my cousin take my sister, for such is plainly the intention of the Lord," he said.

◆§ XIII §◆

FOR THREE DAYS after the return of David and Jonathan, the court at Gibeah was uneasy and depressed. The King, angered that they had gone forth against the Philistine marauders without his consent, kept sullenly to his own chamber. While he sat solitary in the shadow of the great stone bull, the sounds of the house rose to him, shattering his waking dreams or penetrating his light sleep. There were sounds of preparation for battle. As soon as the winter rains had ceased, they would march out again to meet the unvanquished and hereditary enemy. Armor clanked under sorting hands; blades sang against the sharpening stone. Milder sounds also—talk and footfalls and the clinking of pottery—floated to him. Sometimes the voice of David wandered like the wretched ghost of itself through the house, chanting a miserable monody—the most desolate song, Saul thought, that had ever been fashioned in Israel.

On the second day, he knew by the cries from the garden and the voices on the stairs that Ahinoam and Michal had come home. Why they had chosen this dreary season for their journey he could not tell. The rains had begun to fall, cold, torrential, out of a sky that looked as solid as a slab of stone. It was plain to him that his wife had lost no time in setting her hand to the duties of the house. He felt the ache-begetting dampness leave the air and knew that the braziers had been filled and lighted in the lower rooms. His own brazen bowl of fire, red, and sweet with herbs, was brought to him by a servant. Another day, he told himself, and I will go down to them. It will be pleasant to sit among them and break bread.

Through the closed door on the following morning, he listened to Michal calling after the little Ishbaal. She cursed by rote now; her voice was spiritless. Abner had brought sorry news of her out of Gilgal. Like a molting bird, he had said, sick in the flesh perhaps, but more likely sick in the heart. The King sat staring at the everlasting rain, pondering the source of her sickness. How long had he known that she yearned after

David? Why had he always laid that matter aside for later consideration? In the secret tabernacle of his desires, he had left her grieving over Agag. She had ceased grieving, yes, but he would not have it so. And had she set out to choose the one lover who would most trouble her father, she could not have chosen more accurately. He could not give her to the young armor-bearer with any conviction that he would ensure her happiness. He could have sworn before Jahveh that the boy did not love her, that he loved Saul more than her, loved Jonathan more than Saul, loved himself above Jonathan. So the King looked at the matter, turning it this way and that, never coming to a solution, coming always to the same futile regret: If she had married Agag, if Agag had not been slain. . . .

On the evening of the third day he sent for Rizpah and Abner. He talked long with the captain and bade him go up and assemble the host of Jahveh on the plains before Gilgal. He commended the concubine to the care of the captain; let her go up with him and look to such matters as the furnishing of the tent; within a week he would join her there. Both Rizpah and Abner made bold to raise their voices in the cause of David and Jonathan. Let the King forgive that which was done for his sake, they said. The lads were grievously troubled; the day of their victory had been as gloomy as the day of a funeral. Abner was particularly ardent for David's sake. "Would I had a daughter to give to such a youth," he said. "Truly, the House of Saul owes him much. Had it not been for him, Jonathan would now be counted among the dead." When they were gone, he shrugged and smiled. Who was proof against David? Certainly not the veteran. Certainly not the concubine. He settled himself comfortably in his chair, ate a cut of roast meat, and warmed his feet before his little fire. A mood of peace, a mood of happy expectancy, came upon him.

But when, in the early afternoon, he descended the stairs and found them in the common room, his dream of household felicity was shattered. Never had he seen such an assembly of sad, tormented faces. Ahinoam and Michal, the one in a tall chair and the other on the floor at her feet, were mending garments before a fire. Even though their backs were turned to him, the droop of their shoulders, the slow and aimless movements of their hands, told him the measure of their wretchedness. Jonathan stood at the window, staring at the never-ceasing rain. David sat by the table, plucking desultorily at his lute. The very servants seemed despondent, going listlessly about the business of covering the floor with fresh reeds.

"No, now," he said in his heartiest voice, "what ails us here? I was angry, it is true, but I never thought to be the cause of such heaviness." He laughed uneasily. "It is as though I had arrived in time to attend a burial."

The words had no sooner been spoken than he wished to God he might take them back. His wife had risen and advanced slowly toward him until the cold light from the window struck across her lifted face. He was hard put to it to stifle a cry. She was a bloodless thing, a walking ghost.

A web of shadows lay in the hollows around her eyes. The purple mark of death was upon her lips.

"How is it with my lord?" she said. And then, with the audacity of one who is beyond the reach of shame, "How is it with my love?"

She swayed a little, and he caught her and held her close to him, her head against his chest. His hands knew, with wonder and with a strange access of tenderness, the frailty of her body. So she had felt in his arms on the first day when Kish had brought her to him. And it seemed to him that he held not the old and dying woman who had borne him five children and lain beside him through innumerable nights, but the enigmatic stranger through whose veil he had seen the shine of pale and alien hair, the gleam of sea-gray eyes. It was this stranger whom he embraced with the ardor that he had been unable to summon up in the beginning. It was on the yielding mouth of this stranger that he pressed a passionate and remorseful kiss. She laid her arms around his neck and smiled like a satisfied bride.

Almost at once they found reasons for going their separate ways. Ahinoam shivered, and Jonathan went to draw the heavy curtain across the window. David walked to the table to pour a bowl of water and wine for his lord. Michal knelt and folded the mended garments and rose and turned toward the door with a heap of them in her arms.

"Where are you going?" Saul said.

"To carry them to the clothes chest, so that they may be ready for my father to take with him when he goes out against the Philistines."

"There is no great need for haste. I will be here seven days."

"Nevertheless," she said sullenly, "inasmuch as they have been washed and mended, it would be better not to leave them lying on the floor."

He shrugged and let her go. Before she left him she gave him one look of mingled anger and pain.

"Forgive her. She is sick and wretched," Ahinoam said.

David came back with the wine; Jonathan brought a chair for the King and placed it close to the fire; but neither of the young men lingered near him for long. As his armor-bearer returned to the table and the lute, as his son took up his former station at the curtained window, Saul had a sudden conviction that some unalterable breach had come between them in his absence. On some other occasion he might have secretly rejoiced at it, but today it roused in him only a vague regret. He turned from this thought to Ahinoam. He took her hand and held it between his own. The skin lay loose upon the tendons and the swollen veins. The flesh was moist and deathly cold.

"If she is lacking in respect toward her father, it is not that she is lacking in love," Ahinoam said.

A moment passed before he recalled that they had been speaking of Michal. He nodded and pressed the damp fingers. "She is a good girl," he said. The servants, having finished with their strewing, took their baskets and went soundlessly from the room. Their going made the place seem empty. Jonathan was far away, beyond the voices of those who sat near the fire. David was hunched over his instrument, drawing from it, note by note, the rueful melody that had sounded these three days through the house. "Yes, truly, she is a good girl," Saul said again, not having anything more meaningful to say.

Ahinoam turned to answer, but stopped on a sharp intake of breath. Her look was a look that he had seen a thousand times upon the battle-field—amazement at the actuality of pain.

"What ails my beloved?" he said.

"Nothing. I do not suffer much. My husband has had many wounds in his time and has borne them all lightly. Beside such wounds, this is not worth a thought. My husband has graciously said of the fruit of my womb that she is good. If there is anything that breaks my sleep, it is my apprehension that we give her so much reason to be otherwise."

"How so?"

"I was younger than she, I was younger than she by a full year, when Kish brought me to Saul's bed."

"It had been better," he said, "it had been far better for Ahinoam if her father and her mother had sent Kish empty-handed from their door."

She smiled and shook her head. "What love my lord gave me was enough for me. I am satisfied."

He could not answer. His throat was tight with tears.

"Furthermore," she continued in a whisper, "it has seemed to me that, at the end, my husband unlocked the last closed chamber of his heart and drew me in. If this were so——"

He said, weeping, that it was so.

"If this is so, then a crown is set upon my love, then is my life well spent. Only this business of Michal remains now," she said.

He knew that whatever she desired would be fulfilled. He had not the will to gainsay her. She wove around him, with words and glances, a web which he could not wish to tear. She had loved a hero in the days of her youth. Michal also had chosen one not easily gained. There were those who, ignorant of the subtleties of the heart, might say that the Queen of Israel had been unloved. Yet there are souls whose capacity for loving is very great—so great that one may be fully nourished on a small portion of their devotion. Saul was such a one. David also might well be such a one. Why should she ask for her daughter more than that abundance which she herself had been given? Let Saul put the hand of his daughter in the hand of his good and faithful servant. This being done, she would go in peace to her grave. . . .

If he thought that later, when she was no longer beside him, he might regret his acquiescence, he put that wounding thought aside. If some inner voice persisted in telling him that Michal was no Ahinoam and David no Saul, he silenced it at last.

"It is enough," he said, smiling. "Let them have each other then. When will it be?"

"Soon. Within the week, before my lord departs. They have waited long enough. I would not have them waiting three more moons."

He knew that she spoke of the three moons of mourning that would pass after her burial. "Let the day be the day that Ahinoam chooses. My will is her will." He strove to conceal his misgiving in a jest. "Well, David," he said, "I hear that you have slain two hundred Philistines at a blow."

"No, my lord," said the boy, raising his gray, candid eyes. "Two at two blows."

"Well, two is enough. The tribe of Judah will no doubt swell the count to two hundred by tomorrow night."

"My lord reproaches me with boasting of my poor accomplishments. May my lord believe me, I have not spoken of my hour of battle to any man. I did not consider it glorious. It was a bitter hour."

Jonathan turned from the window and opened his mouth as though to speak, but said nothing.

"And have you their foreskins upon you?"

"No, my lord. They are with my armor-bearer, Joab the Ishmaelite."

"Wherefore? Because the hands of David are dainty and do not dabble in flesh and blood?"

"That is a poor jest," said Jonathan from the window, "to make at the expense of him whose untried sword killed two for my sake. That which David did for Jonathan deserves more than mockery from my lord."

Saul shrugged and turned back to the lutist. "David knows that I am grateful," he said. "As for the foreskins, have them brought to me by the Ishmaelite."

"Now, my lord?"

"No. Tonight, tomorrow, some other time. I am not one to bicker over marriage portions. I——" He could find nothing further to say.

The voice of Ahinoam filled the embarrassing silence. "After his own strange manner, David, my husband is striving to make it plain to you that if you so desire, you may take the Princess Michal to be your bride."

The armor-bearer rose and laid his lute upon the table. "What am I," he asked, "to be freely given the Rose of Benjamin? Who am I that I should be Saul's son-in-law? I know that my lady is too kind to mock even me, even a shepherd out of Bethlehem. Otherwise, surely, I would say in my heart that this also is a jest."

The King would have been glad to reduce the event to its barest necessities, to summon the bride and accomplish with a few words that which he had no heart to do at all. Yet this was Ahinoam's festival. Let it be glorious, seeing that it was her last. One could be generous with gifts at least, even if one were niggardly with love.

"Let me give you a house," he said. "There is a fine house, big and built for the most part of stone, not seven miles from here, on the other side of the town. That flock of long-haired goats which you and Michal made fair for me when you were wooing—that also will be your own. As for lands, I will give you a portion in Benjamin, and my wife will no doubt see fit to endow you with a few fields in Ephraim. Next spring, after the calving, we will divide the herds. Next spring——" He paused, thinking how she would not be among them to divide the herds next spring.

"My lord rewards me far beyond my merit. I am not worthy of a hundredth of that which is bestowed upon me by my lord."

"As for vineyards, we must find suitable vineyards——"

"Give him the vineyard this side of Gibeah," said Jonathan flatly, staring at the floor.

"No, now, that will not be needful. That vineyard is the vineyard of my son Jonathan."

"I need it not. Give me in its stead that field in which I labored in my father's absence."

The request was fantastic and aggravating. "I would not give that field to a dog," Saul said testily. "It is a wilderness of stones. There is, however, a fine vineyard in——"

"Nevertheless," said Jonathan persistently, "give me that field, since my heart is set upon it."

Suddenly all Saul's suppressed anger turned upon his son. What ailed the fool? God of Sinai, surely he saw how his father struggled to kindle a convivial fire, surely he knew that his mother was dying, surely he also wished this matter well settled for his mother's sake! Why, when this miserable occasion had been coaxed and fanned at last into a little blaze, must he blow upon it the chill blast of his unseasonable grief? Could he not keep a manly face before the dying? Could he not save his tears to shed upon the dead?

"What evil spirit has entered into Jonathan?"

"No evil spirit, my lord." The voice was cold and proud.

"Then why does Jonathan strive to mar this occasion?"

"I? If I strove, I knew it not."

"Then study to choose those words and maintain that countenance which are best suited to a betrothal."

"I do so study, insofar as it is in my power, my lord. If I am not so merry as I am required to be, I regret it. Had my lord given me an hour's warning, I might have made myself merrier with wine."

"Let Jonathan guard his mouth, lest he offend his father and trouble the peace of his mother——"

"*I* trouble her peace?" The clear, brown, insolent eyes of his son reproached him with his concubine. The glance was like a blow across the face. It left him wordless.

Yet again the voice of Ahinoam flowed into the hush. "So it is on all high occasions," she said, turning in her chair and moving her head slowly, so that each of them shared in her serene smile. "Then the heart is charged with many remembrances, and, before we know what we do, some of us have raised our voices and some of us have begun to weep. Those amongst us who have the fewest years and the least to remember—they can reproach the most freely, having for the time being the purest hearts. Yet even in the spring it is well to remember that there is no autumn, nor any harvest, without decay. Abraham and Moses and Barak are the glory of Israel, but not one of these went without reproach to his grave. So let us bear with each other, as man has borne with man from the beginning; otherwise there had been no people to give life to the dead face of the wilderness, nor anything but the perfection of lifeless stones."

While she spoke, she looked long and earnestly at each of them. Her glance lighted last and remained the longest upon the Bethlehemite. "Come, David," she said, holding out her hand to him. "I have not yet embraced you." She kissed him upon each cheek and raised his hand and held it between her breasts. "The son of Jesse will surely think he has bound himself to a quarrelsome family. But these are brief storms that blow up amongst us. They will be forgotten before night. Even now they are forgotten, and we are all at peace."

It seemed to Saul that she spoke truly, that calmness had indeed settled upon the room. The group was drawing together now; only his son remained at the window in the shadow of the drapery. He turned to the young man and spoke with the old brusqueness, the old heartiness. "We have kept the bridegroom waiting far too long. Go, now, Jonathan, and fetch your sister. It is time that David set eyes upon his bride."

"I?"

He had answered this simple request as a man might answer one who bade him walk through a curtain of flame. A strange pity came upon Saul. Whatever was the cause of the grieving, there was no gainsaying the extent of the grief. "Surely not if the going is a burden to you," he said. "Some other will go and bring her, if you see fit to remain."

"No, I will go. I will go gladly, my lord."

When Michal returned with Jonathan, it was plain that she knew what had passed amongst them. She stopped on the threshold and turned her dark glance upon her father, and his heart dilated at the gratefulness in her look. "Well," he said, smiling, "your mother has chosen your bridegroom, and your mother's will is mine. Will you have David of the house of Jesse to be your wedded husband?"

She turned her face from the King to David. "If he will have me for his wife," she said.

Saul laughed. "But that is a settled matter."

"Then surely I will have him."

"Go then and embrace him, for before seven days have passed, you will be his bride."

While Michal and David advanced toward each other and met and embraced near Ahinoam's chair, Saul deliberately turned aside. He could not bring himself to watch them kiss. He stared steadily at the top of the door, and saw, with wonder, that the door had been opened. Someone had gone forth soundlessly into the rain. He looked about and knew that it was his son who had fled from the room. Where? Why? He crossed

126

the reed-strewn floor and stepped into the glaring gray twilight and closed the door behind him. The rain fell heavily upon his head. Not ten paces away, under a drenched tree, stood Jonathan.

The boy was sick; he had been vomiting. He leaned now, in exhaustion, against the trunk of the tree. His feet had sunk ankle-deep into the mud. His whole thin body was shivering, and his face had the grayish whiteness of a stone. Saul stood staring at him, and as he stared, pity fell again like an annihilating blow upon his heart.

"What ails Jonathan? What ails my son?" he said, stepping toward him through the yielding mud.

The boy swallowed and wiped his lips. "Nothing. My stomach would not hold my food," he said.

"But there was no need for this." He drew the limp body toward him and pulled the wan face to his shoulder. "There was no need for my son to carry his sickness out of my house into such a rain."

"But would my father have me retching in their presence, at the moment when they——"

"Come in, come in out of the cold."

"No, I cannot come. Not yet. Let my father go in to be with the others, and later I will come. This will pass."

But Saul could not move. He could not draw apart from this poor body that leaned against him. Touching it, he seemed to touch the dying one who had borne it. He said again, "What ails my son?"

There was long silence then. He waited, for it seemed to him that now some secret would be revealed to him, some mystery would be made plain. But whatever words formed themselves behind the cold brow that lay against his shoulder were never uttered. The others had come to seek them. The others were calling to them from the door.

"What ails my son?" he said once more, knowing that he would receive only a shadowy reply.

"I do not know, my father. It is an inward sickness, a sickness of the spirit, it is a—— It often comes upon me after a day of battle. I cannot understand then how men should care to marry and beget children. I cannot understand. . . . It is a great desire to be solitary. At such times it seems to me that there is nothing in the world—nothing but death and the certainty of death."

⋅§ XIV §⋅

THE WEDDING FEAST was over. The common room, cleansed of the last fig skin and the last crust, was empty and austere. The most meticulous servant had assured himself of its complete orderliness, had quenched the last lamp and gone to his bed. A few lights still burned in Saul's house, behind the curtains drawn against the unabating rain. The little Ishbaal had come suddenly to the realization that his sister would no longer sleep in the room next to his own, and he lay awake, whimpering. A lamp burned in Jonathan's room, on the window sill. An hour since, he had gone into the hall, had found an ancient sword among the heaped helmets and corselets, had borne it back with him, and had diligently set about removing the patina from the blade. Now the sword lay motionless across his lap. He had fallen asleep in the chair next the window. His head lay sidewise against the sill, and the flame wavered above his white face and cloudy hair. There was no lamp in Saul's chamber. When the latest guest had taken himself into the downpour, the King lifted his wife and carried her up the stairs. He bore her into her room, and had not come forth again. One of his servants still waited for him, sleeping against the door. In that room which he had seldom entered within the last five years, the King sat upon the edge of his wife's bed and held her head upon his knees. She lay sleeping in her rumpled finery, her cheek turned against his thigh, her hand under his hand. For the most part, he sat looking steadily down upon her; but now and then he turned aside lest his tears should fall upon her face and break her sleep.

Any Philistine marauder who had ventured out of the shelter of his cave could have seen that there had been some carnival in the town. Sputtering torches illuminated the black canyons of the streets; warriors and women kissed in the doorways, drunken with the wedding wine. Many convinced themselves that they had some errand near the bridegroom's house. They walked slowly past the door where a bough of the fruitful olive hung, gleaming in the rain. They raised their eyes to the blank windows and thought with excitement of what passed within.

Had some curious watcher remained near the window of the back chamber until the hour before the rising of the sun, he would have been rewarded for his pains. A light shone through the curtain and glimmered upon the pools in the street. The bridegroom had risen from his bed, had found and kindled a lamp in the unfamiliar house, and had returned with the little saucer of burning oil to the foot of the marriage bed. Now he stood naked and smiling, holding the lamp above the bed and looking down upon his bride.

She lay on her back among the tossed coverlets. In this light her flesh was not brown, but golden, and her hair had the silky darkness of charred wood. One arm hung over the side of the bed, the hand trailing against the carpet. Here and there some jewel still gleamed upon her—an anklet, a bracelet that had been forgotten in the haste of his desire. It is almost morning, he thought, hearing the first twitter of the birds on the drenched roofs. How long, how full, how ardent was the night! He looked back upon it, and his heart was big with pride.

Three times he had known her—once considerately, because she was a virgin and Saul's daughter; once achingly, to be comforted for all that she had taken from him; once in Canaanitish violence, to know at last in her the mysteries of Astarte. Each time she had sensed the shape and color of his passion; each time she had been whatever he wished her to be.

Oh, he was blessed, Jahveh had showered much upon him—this fair body whose veins held the precious blood of the anointed, this house sweet with herbs and cleft cedar, these draperies and carpets and carved chests, fields in Benjamin, fields in Ephraim, flocks and herds, orchards and arbors, his and his children's unto the tenth generation, and it was no fault of his if she rose barren out of his bed after this night. And yet, and yet—— Some stubborn core in him remained aloof and lonely. Some fortress of his spirit had not yet been taken. He could not lie down again beside her. He set the lamp upon the clothes chest, settled himself beside it, and waited for the dawn.

How long it was before the darkness lessened, he did not know: but it seemed very long, longer than all the crowded, ardent night. Then gradually the pearly grayness seeped through the drapery. The birds sang so loudly that he feared they might wake the sleeper. Footfalls sounded in the quiet street. Voices floated on the stillness and drew close and passed, leaving behind them the monotonous whisper of the rain. He pulled the curtain aside a little then and looked upon the wet and silvery world outside. A ray of sunlight, feeble and striving, broke through a cleft in the clouds and lay upon the age-worn city of stones. He stared at the street, and it was no street, but a grove near Ephes-Dammim, cloudy with willows, dappled with shadow and sun, magical with the lost magic of an irretrievable spring. Once more he saw the slight shape, graceful and buoyant as a temple dancer's, against the blossoming grass and mustard flower. Still clear, but distant now, as from another world, the high and shattering note of love sounded in the morning hush. He leaned against the sill and wept, saying, "Jonathan, Jonathan."

BOOK FOUR

BOOK FOUR

◈ I ◈

ONE SPRING long afterward—the rains of five winters had fallen upon Ahinoam's burial cave, and the Philistines had come up five times from their beaches and been driven back to their temples and palaces beside the sea—one spring long afterward, Michal the wife of David and Mara the wife of Jonathan sat in David's garden in the dusk. They had been embroidering, but they could no longer clearly see the design on the piece of fine linen across their knees. The needles had been thrust into the cloth; the balls of colored thread lay among the blossoming grass at their feet. All afternoon they had been talking rapidly of small matters: the preparations for the Feast of the First Fruits, certain lengths of purple cloth that had come in from Phoenicia, all the vases and dishes that had been broken by their maidservants. Their tongues had run on in rhythm with their hands, sketching an idle pattern over the stuff of their thoughts. But now the light was gone. Only a faint redness lay upon the garden, touching the worn stones of the wall, showing the blooms among the iris blades, putting a pinkish cast upon the front of the house, and reddening the purple, inner darkness that lay beyond the open door. Silence had come upon them and upon many of the women of Gibeah. Women sat silent in a score of towns and cities, waiting for news of the movements of far armies and watching the going-down of the sun. Michal and Mara moved closer to each other. Their knees touched under the embroidery, and each of them turned her eyes discreetly from the other's face and sighed.

Somewhere in the fair corn country called the plains of Sharon, somewhere in those rolling fields between the Israelite valleys and the Philistine coast, it was taking place or it was over—the last battle of the winter campaign. Whenever Michal thought of it, she preferred to think that it was over. It was better to tell oneself that it was out of one's hands and in the hands of Jahveh, that neither praying nor picking up lucky pebbles would be of any use. Certainly she could not make the subject a matter for conversation among a crowd of women. In these five years she had come to consider herself the enemy of all women save her dead mother and her plain companion. It was said in Gibeah that Saul's daughter had grown too haughty to chat at the cistern. Well, let them say what they would. She had tried to mingle with them, and she would try no more. In time of peace, when her husband was with her, she felt their glances constantly converging upon her unfruitful belly. They shook their heads behind her back—a pitiful business, Saul's house without a sprout, Michal married five years and still barren, and Jonathan's wife as flat as unleavened bread. And in time of war, she found them even more detestable. They wore their fears for their men as though those fears had been jewels; they were exalted and adorned according to the degree of their dread. Ill news was always worse in their mouths. They seemed to be forever invoking wounds and conjuring death.

Silence in the garden was better than babble at the cistern. Yet tonight she was weary of silence and the guarded talk that is a guise of silence. In the old days, Mara, she thought, when we were virgins, you lay in my bed, and the night wind bore the curtain into our dark room, and it was like the sail of a great ship, flapping against stars. We talked of high matters then—of Jonathan and Agag and my father's madness, of how it must be to grow old and yield place to a concubine, of charms and incantations, blood and maidenheads, childbirth and the love bite on my lip. Where are these high matters now? How is it that we dare not say to each other what every woman in Israel says of us both—that we are barren? How would you answer me if I took your face between my hands and said: "Mara, my sister, I am wretched. The measure of my lord's love is nothing to the measure of mine. And how is it with you and Jonathan? Are you content?" . . .

Now she could not bear the quiet of the garden. She lifted the embroidery and folded it into a small square, and bent and took up the balls of thread. The young woman beside her barely moved. Her plain, grave face was turned toward the clump of iris. The fixed stare of one who looks upon a dream shape had widened her eyes. What do you dream? What do you see? Have you forgotten that there was a time when my dreams were yours and yours were mine? . . .

"Are we so changed, Mara?" Michal said.

"My sister Michal has changed a little. How could it be otherwise, when she puts her hand to every task and leaves nothing to the maidservants and weeps for her mother and distresses herself for her husband and her father and prays for her brothers and will not rest? My sister is a little thinner, and there is a line or two on her face. But Michal will bloom like the Sharon rose when David is in Gibeah again."

Only more silence in the guise of talk, Michal thought. Surely she knows I cannot rest. When the last loaf is taken from the hearth, then I see the sword crashing down upon his head. When the loom is filled up and the pattern is finished, then the arrow twangs into his chest. When the latest guest departs and the last lamp is extinguished, then he lies on the field—white hand, cruel, unpossessable hand trampled into the earth by file after file of retreating feet. How can I rest? . . .

The red glow was withdrawing from the garden. A pale, cool blueness was settling around them. Soon the lamps within the house would be lighted and a serving-woman would walk out to tell them that the evening meal had been spread. There, over the curds and fruit, they would take up the afternoon's talk again: "And my sister would not believe it unless she saw it with her own eyes, how the fools have ruined the fine scarf, laying it in the same water with a scarlet girdle, so that it has turned a sickening pink. . . ." She could not and would not endure it.

"What were you thinking, Mara?" she said.

"I? When?"

"A moment since, when you stared at the irises and I asked you if it seemed to you that we had changed."

The sad, unbeautiful face turned back to the clump of blade and bloom. "I was thinking," she said, flushing, "that this evening is very like the evening when your brother first came to me and said it was his wish that we should marry."

So long ago, sister? said Michal within herself. Must we journey back through these two long years to come to a spot in time where the silence will be lifted? Well, choose your road and I will follow. Lead me down any path you will, so long as at the end of it we may find a memorial stone and embrace it together and weep. . . .

"How was it, Mara? You never told me how he came or what he said."

The girl's voice, murmurous and tender as the throaty sound of pigeons, told the tale of her own wooing as it might have told some old tribal tale. "It is strange," she said, "that it was the happiest hour I have known in this world, and yet I can never remember it without sorrow. I was sitting by the window on such an evening as this. I was working at something, but to this day I cannot remember what it was that lay in my hands. I think I was dreaming of him at the time. Michal remembers how I was always dreaming of him, so there is little wonder in that. I think I was asking myself how it would be with me when they brought me news that he had taken some other woman. And as I thought of this, my father's steward came to tell me that he was at the door. I knew then how foolish it would be for me to run to my room and make myself fair, seeing that I am ugly and nothing can make me fair. So I sat with my hands crossed in my lap and waited, and wondered whether any misfortune had fallen upon Michal to make her send him after me. He came in the redness of the sunlight through the door. 'Mara,' he said, 'let us not exchange the usual greetings and compliments, since all greetings and compliments have grown dishonorable in the mouths of lying men. If I ask you a question, will you answer me truly, before Jahveh and from your heart?' And I said, 'Surely, Jonathan.' Then he said to me that it was told in Gibeah that I loved him, and that my love for him was beyond curing and had brought me much grief. 'Is this the truth before Jahveh?' he said. My shame was such that I could not have answered him had it not been for his eyes. It was as if his look and mine drew us upward through the red sunlight, and held us above the world and the shame of the world. 'Yes,' I said, 'before Jahveh, such is the truth.' He came then to the window where I sat, and leaned against the sill, and his hand moved along the sill and lay upon my hand. 'There is too much mourning on the earth,' he said. 'Let Mara cease mourning, for it is my desire that she should be my wife, so long as it is her desire also. Only let us not marry in falsehood and beget lies and liars. Let Mara see no exalted one in me, who will bring oil and wine and spices into her marriage bed. For I come to her not in riches, but in poverty. I come with nothing except goodwill and tenderness. Would Mara might be Queen of Israel, for Israel would be happy in such a queen, but I have had many omens that tell me this will never be. Let Mara see me as I am. I come to her in bitterness and wounded almost unto death, to take a healing balm of her, and to be comforted. If she will see me as such and accept me nevertheless, then am I blessed.' So he said, and raised my hand to his lips. And even while he waited for my answer, the red of the evening faded as it faded a moment ago upon the iris. And as it faded, it seemed to me that Jonathan also changed. He that had been as an angel of God to me became mortal, and I saw that he had a wound and did not ask him to name it. He became as a child to me, a child that is sick, to be soothed all night against my breasts. So I gave him my pledge, and he swore to me that I would have no cause to regret it. Nor shall I regret it to the end of my days."

Michal unwound a little of the thread and wrapped it on her finger. "Then you are content," she said, smiling, but speaking in a brittle voice. You fool, she thought, how can you be satisfied, seeing that I have been given far more than this and yet am not content? Either you lie to me or you do not know a lie for a lie, having lied so long to yourself for Jonathan's sake. . . .

"Not wholly, Michal, no. So long as there are wars in Israel, how is it possible for either of us to be content?"

And if there were no wars in Israel, what then? Truce may be called between Jahveh and the gods of the Philistines, but David and Michal will never lie down in peace. We wrestle together forever, and what I strive for is always the same prize—to have his heart, to seize and possess his living heart. I lie with him to own him, and he lies with me to rid himself of his desire for me. At the hour before he comes to me, when we rise from the table and he draws me into the garden, then he is almost mine. But later, among the vines or on the grass or on the shadowy bed, I lose him. Upon our battlefield, I am always the defeated; he goes forth from me and takes his heart with him, nourished and secure and whole. He saunters to the roof and stands alone in the grayness of the morning, and though I have never seen him there, I know the proud tilt of his head and the cold, complacent smile. . . .

"The war between Israel and Philistia will end before the war between David and Michal is finished," she said.

Mara merely smiled. She was remembering certain quarrels that had taken place in her presence, taunts and gibes over an unkept appointment or a forgotten promise, mildly regrettable since they spoiled the pleasure of an evening's visit, but minor troubles such as one would expect to find between a spirited husband and a willful wife. She would have been glad to dismiss the subject with smiling. But Michal would have an answer, Michal kept tugging at the thread which she had wound around her finger, Michal kept staring persistently into her face.

"There will be less to quarrel over as the years go by," Mara said. "You two have already grown weary of quarreling over certain matters, and it may be that soon there will be no new questions left for either of you to seize upon."

"Does my sister truly believe that we quarrel over such things as a lost trinket? Then surely my sister knows me less than she knew me in the old days. We quarrel over love."

"It is true that love is the source of all quarrels. On those occasions when we have quarreled, Jonathan and I, it has always been because I was driven by love to ask too much of him. But afterward, when he goes forth with the host, I remember what hard words have passed between us, and the pain of the remembering is greater than any other pain. So, whenever my heart turns hot against him, I think of the hour when he will depart, and I hold my peace."

The listener kept pulling the thread tighter and tighter. Her finger had grown white with the pressure; the tip of it was numb. When they are about to go out to battle, she thought, all our wants are chided by the specter of their deaths. Let there be peace in Israel, and let Michal be great with child. Let there be a time when I may pour my bitterness freely into his insolent face. Let there be an hour when *he* is the one to tremble at the war between us two, thinking how *I* may die. . . .

"Is it with you as it is with me, Mara? Do all the wives in Israel see their husbands dead a hundred times within a single day?"

"I often think how it would be with me if Jonathan were dead."

"How would it be with my sister?" She leaned forward, tugging at the thread. The turbulence within her was so great that she thought it must call forth an answer. But the large, mild eyes that stared upon her through the gathering dark were moist with the usual easy tears. The common grief—the grief of women gathered around the well—that only was to be seen in the unbeautiful face.

"As it would be with Michal," Mara said. "With Michal and with all the wives in Israel."

Fool, she thought, feeling the pain of the cord cutting into her finger. Lie to yourself if it pleases you. But if they were to come to me tomorrow with David's bloody garment, if they were to say to me, "Behold, he is buried in the plains of Sharon along with the husbands of ten thousand others," there would not be another woman in Israel who would know such grief as mine. It is one thing to mourn over what we have owned and lost; it is another thing to ache over what we will never own on earth. If they were to come tomorrow with evil news, naming the names of the fallen, many would weep together; but none would weep with me —I would weep alone. They would ease themselves by tearing rents in their garments. I would snatch a knife from the wall and tear a rent in my heart. Not out of love, Mara. Not out of your soft and whining love. Out of rage, because I will not have him escape. My dust would find his haughty dust in Sharon. My dust would conquer and compound with his at last, to end his insolence and my desire. . . ."

A big, pale moth sailed past them through the blue evening on its way to the lighted door. Mara shuddered, taking it for an evil omen.

"It is childish," said Michal, "to concern ourselves with signs. The battle is surely over. Whatever was to come to pass has already come to pass." Her voice was harsh and urgent. It is because of the pain, she thought. Now I have hurt my finger. . . . She began to unwind the cord and saw that it was spotted with a little blood.

Mara looked down in tender concern. She lifted the finger, wiped the broken skin upon the end of her veil, and raised Michal's hand to her lips. "Let my sister's mind be at peace in regard to David," she said, laying her arm around Michal's shoulders. "It is written in heaven that no harm will come to him. He is the chosen of the Lord. He has met a hundred in battle and has slain a hundred. His hand is as cunning with the sword as it is cunning with the lute. Yet another moon of waiting, and he will come again. Let Michal be comforted."

Comforted, comforted, thought Michal. How shall I be comforted? On the day we returned to Gibeah out of Gilgal, after Agag was slain, then I crept miserably into your bed and lay against your shoulder, and the curtain billowed and the stars shone, and I wept and was comforted. Why have you changed? The scent of your flesh is as it always was, a sad and lonely scent, as of clay tablets that have lain long in a broken temple, gathering dust. Jonathan has not nourished you nor made you fertile. But he has drawn you from me, he that stole the first place in my father's heart, he that charmed the stare of my dying mother away from my face, he that worshiped the Baal of pain with David at Ephes-Dammim beside the well. And he is beside us here in the dark. He has laid his hand upon your lips. What have I to do with you, accomplice of my enemy, handmaiden of Jonathan? . . .

Another moth sailed past them. She drew aside from Mara and watched its shadowy flight. It had gone to join its fellows. A score of them whirled in the square of strengthening light from the door.

"It is a bad year for moths," she said in such a voice as is suitable for conversation at the cistern. "Last night the house was alive with them. I must ask my brothers to send me some camphor out of Gilgal."

The serving-woman came and called to them from the threshold.

"Yes, yes, we are coming." We will talk of dyes and amulets and fabrics over the curds and the wine. . . . "Be careful, my sister, there is a loose stone in the path. Last night I bruised my foot upon it, and the pain was so great I could have wept." But what is it to you if I weep? What is it to any in Israel, save Ahinoam who is dead? . . . "Wait a moment. Smell. Can you smell it? They have burned it again. The fools, the idiots, one cannot leave them alone in the house for a moment. For the third time in a single week, they have burned the bread."

❧ II ❧

FOR TWO DAYS the weapons of war had clanged on the sloping plains of Sharon, twenty miles to the east of Askelon. Now the battle was over. So much silence was almost intolerable after so much sound. The red sun went down on a stretch of trampled wheat strewn with the angular bodies of the slain.

The Philistines were moving back to their beaches. They would man the walls of their strongholds, but not with too much urgency; the seasoned warriors among them knew that Israel was doomed to have no more than a sight of the sea. For ten years now—they said it on the westward march, counting the campaigns on their fingers—for ten years Israel had come up as far as Sharon and clashed with them among the wheat and the roses, had triumphed over them and robbed them of their bravest and their best, had stood for a little while looking upon the scene of battle, and then unaccountably turned their faces toward home. The ways of the Hebrews were dark and impenetrable. Theirs was a capricious God, given to unwarranted advances and senseless retreats. Fortunately for Philistia, the men of Israel lived too long. Dagon and Astarte were willing to throw away their darlings: the Seren of Ashdod lay dead on the field; the brother of the Seren of Askelon was wounded unto death. But Jahveh wore a long beard and was partial to the old. Saul lived, and Abner lived —which was, in the long view, a fortunate thing for Israel's enemies. Let them live for a thousand years to bring their armies up to Sharon, to pause and waver there, to retire with old men's cautiousness, old men's niggardly strategy.

So they said among themselves when they retreated in shortened but orderly lines toward their cities. Sometimes, tired of talking, they broke into song. Their songs were all ancient; some said that they had been sung in Caphtor, hundreds of years ago, before their ancestors shoved their flat-bottomed boats into the sea. They sang dirges for the fallen, songs to console the bereaved, strong hymns to Dagon, languorous hymns to Astarte. Long after the last plumed crest had melted into the horizon, the Israelites heard this poignant singing. It put a certain gentleness into the victorious hands that took the booty from the dead.

Abner sat on a knoll and looked at the field of battle to the left of him.

Four thousand, he thought. He had seen so many battlefields that he could tell at a glance the approximate number of the slain. The looters still strolled about in search of booty; the surgeons still looked for the living; Joab went back and forth with a clay tablet, making a mark upon it for every thirty dead Israelites. Well, four thousand, Abner told himself, the usual number, the usual victory.

To the right of him and farther down the slope, Saul had pitched his tent in a grove of blossoming almond trees. The boughs looked startlingly white against the black cloth. Beyond the tent, where the slope broke into a smooth and grassy plain, the captains over hundreds were directing the setting-up of the encampment; the priests were drawing the magic circle; the tribes were assembling to be fed. Perhaps before the evening meal was well over, there would be an order to break camp and move again; that would depend on how things went with Jonathan. It was for Jonathan's sake that Saul had set up his tent beyond the sacred boundaries. For Jonathan was wounded, and was therefore an offense in Jahveh's eyes. Saul had carried him from the field and had refused to leave him. Saul was with him now, Saul and a surgeon and David of Bethlehem, who could be seen from the knoll, standing at the opening of the tent. Well, Abner thought, God pity them all. . . . But he was glad that he had a reason for remaining outside. The air within the tent would be charged with pain and rivalry and unnamable desires. He was weary with the sufferings of Saul's house. For twenty-five years he had watched all of them suffering; they suffered too often, too deeply, and too long; he could not understand their reasons, and he was tired of their pain. Joab was coming up the slope with his clay tablet. He was sick of the House of Jesse also; whatsoever was given into their hands, they did too quickly and too well, and they took an inordinate pleasure in their own accomplishments.

"What, are you finished?" he called to the lanky young man. "I would have thought——"

But what he would have thought made no difference. Joab was plainly puffed up over his haste. "I have numbered them all twice over. Our losses are nine hundred and sixty-seven. Two of these are captains over thousands, and seven died among the captains over hundreds. That is the tally, and you can trust it, my lord."

"Joab is always trustworthy," he said absently.

The young man stood before him, courteous, indulgent, holding out the tablet.

"Well, well," said Abner, "lay it on the grass. I will take it to Saul in a little while."

"But, my lord——"

The captain of the host sighed. He must not be impatient with the young man, who was a good young man, and to whom, in fact, he owed a debt of gratitude. Twice today, when the tide of battle was high, this Joab had pointed out to him a gap in the Philistine lines, an opening for attack. The fellow had a talent for tactics, a captain's eye. "See now, I had almost forgotten, in my weariness, that I owe you a captaincy," he said. "But we will talk more of that tomorrow. Now I will sit here a while and rest."

"But my lord the King charged me before he left the field that I should take the tally quickly so that my captain might carry it to him in his tent without delay. The King made it plain that he would have the tally, no matter at what hour."

Abner glanced over his shoulder at the black tent and saw that a lamp had been lighted within. That is for the surgeon, he thought. Then I shall be delivered from none of it; then it has only begun. . . .

"Give me the tally, then, and I will take it to him," he said.

✤ III ✤

AT THE threshold of the tent he paused. Before he could walk in, he must ask David of Bethlehem to step out of the way. The young hero was so absorbed in what passed within that he had not heard the captain's footfalls behind him. He stood motionless in the triangle of thin light, his head thrust forward, the muscles of his back showing tight through his sweaty tunic, his right hand clenched around the goat's-hair cloth. Abner was afraid to touch him. "My son," he said, and the lutist could not have started more wildly if he had been stricken with a spear. He turned, trying to compose his face.

Why does he have the countenance of a poor suitor who loves in vain? Abner thought. He has slain a hundred; it is said of him that Jahveh guides his hand when he throws a spear or thrusts a sword. He is captain over a thousand; this day he laid low the Seren of Ashdod, and Saul has put a precious collar about his neck, a collar of turquoise and gold. He knows the measure of his own glory; he has not hushed the mouths of Judah that babble his praise. Then why does he stand at the door of the tent, like some camel-driver who knows that the stench of his trade is upon him and fears to carry it inside? . . .

"Why should David stand on the threshold?"

"He will not have me within."

"So? Wherefore? When did Saul wish to be divided from David?"

The young man flushed to the roots of his hair. "Not Saul," he said. "I spoke of Jonathan."

They both fell silent, for a harsh, gasping sound had been uttered within the tent.

"He is gravely wounded," David said.

"How?"

"There is an arrow under the lowest rib——"

"That can be grave or otherwise. Wait and see."

"But I have seen. When he fell, the shaft was broken close to the flesh. They must dig it out—there is nothing to grasp."

Abner wished to show a quiet countenance to the young man's distress, but in spite of himself he winced. "Well, it is in the hands of Jahveh," he said.

The harsh gasp tore through the still evening again. Let the House of Jesse take care of its own agonies, he thought. I am committed to the sufferings of the House of Saul. . . . He bowed and went inside.

There were not many within—only Saul, the shortsighted Ahitophel, the lean surgeon, and Jonathan. Ahitophel was kneeling in the shadow among piles of clay tablets, which he kept arranging and rearranging, plainly because this task excused him from looking at the others. Jonathan, naked except for his loincloth, lay on a clothes chest which had been shoved to the middle of the tent. A cloak had been rolled up and put under the small of his back. The tension spread the wound and simplified the surgeon's task. He looked thin and surprisingly tall; his head hung back over the edge of the clothes chest. He raised himself a little, hearing Abner enter. His face was white, but almost merry. "God be with Abner!" he said in an excited voice, and smiled. "What is the tally? How is it with Israel?"

Abner, seeing that he waited for an answer, and that the surgeon also withheld his hand, said that the dead were nine hundred and sixty-seven.

The surgeon set to his task again, pressing the flesh around the wound.

"Before God," said Jonathan softly, "my friend here will make me the nine hundred and sixty-eighth."

"Not if my lord will lie quiet," the surgeon said. He was not a robust man; he had passed his fortieth year; his spare and pitying face was ravaged with the day's butchery; his hands were stiff with doing; he was fathomlessly tired. And whenever it seemed to him that he was touching the arrowhead, at that moment the young man would gasp and try to raise himself. Then Saul would start, and the lamp would waver in his hand. Certainly the wound was grave, certainly the young man suffered, certainly the King was distressed. But if they could not see to the small matter of providing him with a steady light, how could he deal with this much more difficult business? "If my lord the King will hold the lamp perfectly still——" He parted the flesh again, and again Jonathan gasped, and the lamp shook. "Truly, it is necessary that the lamp should be steady. Will the captain of the host take the light?"

"No, now, I can hold it," the King said. Abner saw Saul's face in the wavering yellowness. There were certain ominous signs upon it. He will go mad, Abner thought. The sound of the sea is in his ears, and the waters will break upon him, perhaps tomorrow, perhaps tonight. . . . He laid the tally upon the ground and took the lamp from Saul's hand.

"How long must I lie with this accursed cloak beneath me?"

"Surely my lord knows I will make what haste I can. It will go better now. It would go better still if my lord would raise his hands above his head."

"Certainly, friend." He flung them up lightly. But he gasped again, amazed at the pain.

Saul knelt behind Jonathan, at the head of the clothes chest, and clasped the young man's hands. The faces of father and son were close together; the leathery cheek almost touched the white brow. And now it seemed to the captain that Jonathan's touch and look had suspended the oncoming tide of madness. Perhaps the waters will recede, Abner thought. . . . And it seemed to him that if the young man cleaved to Saul through the worst of this and turned to no other, then the King would come forth whole.

"Now, in the name of Jahveh," said the surgeon, taking up his knife and sending a look half peremptory, half pleading in the captain's direction, "let my lord keep a steady hand. I cannot work in a shaking light."

Now the gasps came often and regularly. It was as if the agony surged upon Jonathan like waves upon a beach. But between wave and wave, there was a trough of peace in which he rested, opened his eyes, and tried to smile. The surgeon had found the arrowhead. The click of it against the point of his knife had dispelled his weariness. He talked as he always talked when he dealt with the wounded—king's son, Ephraimite captain, poor slinger out of Caleb, water boy from Dan—they were all alike to him. Under his knife he felt each of them changing into the same vulnerable child. "Now we have found it. Now it will be quicker. Cry out if it eases you. See, see, it is better to cry out, one bears it better so. Come, now, this is the worst of it. Surely it is painful. Only lie still a little longer, so, so, only a little longer, my dear boy, my brave heart. . . ." The words fell rhythmically, like a chant, uninterrupted by the gasping and the cries.

He is lying out of pity, Abner thought. We have not yet come to the worst of it, and Saul is already shattered by these cries. . . . Still, between cry and cry there was the blessed space of peace, when the tormented face turned against the black beard, when Saul saw that Jonathan cleaved to him alone.

What passed had begun to be a very bloody business. The white slope below the arc of the ribs was stained with red runnels, and it came suddenly into Abner's mind that these were Jonathan's ribs, this was Jonathan's side. He felt the sweat breaking from his body, running from his armpits in great drops. He turned his head a little and looked toward the opening of the tent. But there stood the King's armor-bearer—rather, he seemed to hang there—clutching the dark cloth of the tent on either side.

"A little longer now, a little longer, my poor fellow. . . ."

"No, no, no!"

"Keep the light steady, my captain. In God's name, look to the light."

"Oh, do not touch me, let it be!" And suddenly, descending into one of the troughs of respite, much less frequent now, the young man said in such a voice as he might use at the council table, reasonable and serene: "My friend, you give yourself too much trouble. It is written in the mind of Jahveh that I am to die young. Very likely I am to die of this, so let it be."

"It is not so written," Saul said quietly. "What is written in the mind of Samuel is not necessarily written in the mind of the Lord." Naked and shadowless, they stared at each other—the King's eyes and Jonathan's flat, animal eyes.

"Ah. . . ." said the surgeon, pulling out the bloody arrowhead and hurling it to the ground.

Jonathan started up. He thrust his father from him and sat up on the clothes chest, with blood running from his side.

"Lie down, lie down, my brave heart, my dear child. . . ."

But he pushed them all away and turned and held out his hands toward the triangle of darkness, toward the shape that swayed between the folds of goat's-hair. "David," he said and shuddered and fell back against his father's shoulder.

The name hung suspended in the stillness of the tent, and the name meant "darling." It continued to brood above them until Ahitophel's clay tablets fell again, making them all start except the King's son, who had fainted at last. And it is like the House of Saul, thought Abner, to be stedfast through the worst of it, to look into the right eyes until the conclusion, and then to waver and cry out for what is wrong and renounced and sweet. . . .

The King had risen. The surgeon had covered the wound with herbs and linen. The tender familiarity had fallen from him. As he raised the young man's body to take the rolled cloak away, he was again a Danite in the tent of Benjamin, an artisan touching the holy flesh of the King's son. He was weary, and ashamed of his inability to hold his tongue.

"Let my lord the King be of good heart," he said. "It is a clean wound, the clots are forming well. Unless it festers, he will live."

Without taking his eyes from Jonathan's still face, the King pulled a bracelet from his own arm and laid it in the surgeon's hands. "Would it were a better gift," he said, "but I am stripped of jewels by the number of heroes who have fought this day beside me." There was more silence, and in the silence they thought of the massy collar of gold and turquoise which Saul had given to David of Bethlehem.

Jonathan stirred, and Saul and the surgeon bent above him, holding a cup of wine to his lips. Then he will live, Abner told himself, setting the lamp upon the ground. . . . He repeated this reassurance over and over. But there was no peace in the thought. Now that the light was on the ground, the King's countenance showed clear, and it bore the signs that the captain knew too well. Tonight, he thought, or tomorrow, or day after to-morrow. . . . Well, I must be strong for it, I must have a breathing space. . . .

"If Saul will permit it, I will purify myself and go back to the camp of God, seeing I must rise early and am very tired."

"Surely. I am grateful to Abner for many things this day, and not the least of these is that he held the lamp."

"It is nothing. I am my lord's."

"Saul also is Abner's. Go, my good friend, and rest."

He had left the tent and was crossing the stretch of wheat in the almond-scented dark before it occurred to him that the King's armor-bearer had not been there to bar his passage through the door. He stopped and looked about him. No living presence marred the utter serenity of the place. The plains of Sharon stretched around him, unpeopled and very fair. The soft curves of the grain were broken here and there by clumps of blossoming trees. After the glare of the day and the long staring in the King's tent, the fall and swell of the land, the cloudy branches of the figs and olives, the watery radiance of the stars, were like a balm upon his eyes. Suddenly he became aware of a shape lying at a distance, face downward, half-hidden in the wheat. It is strange, he thought, that one of the host should have come so far from the battlefield to die. And even as he looked, the shape stirred and rose and stood among the grain, and was David of Beth-lehem. As the King's son had turned in his moment of exigency, holding out his hands to the shape at the door, so the King's armor-bearer turned toward the royal tent and fixed his eyes upon the triangle of light.

To take another road, to steal away unnoticed, was cruelty. David waited and needed news; he suffered and needed comforting. And yet the captain of the host could not go to him. The starlight, shining on the massy collar around the young man's neck, showed the gleam of gold, and this sight begot a strange anger in the watcher. Let him look to him-self, the captain thought. Let him hear such news as there is from the surgeon, or from Ahitophel. I am committed to the House of Saul. Let the House of Jesse find another servant. . . .

And he stopped, amazed, knowing that he had come to believe the jab-berings of Samuel and the Judahites—that no man could serve the House of Saul and the House of Jesse at once; that, in the eyes of Jahveh, these two were everlasting enemies.

⇜ IV ⇝

On the seventh day after the battle, the host of Jahveh left the plains of Sharon and moved eastward into the pleasant valleys at the foot of the hills of Benjamin. Progress was leisurely because of the loot and the wounded. There was no reason for haste. The army would disband be-fore Gibeah, and after that there would be plenty of time for those who wished to reach their own towns before the Feast of the First Fruits. A jovial laxity broke the ranks and kept the companies singing. They were giddy with gratefulness to find themselves alive after so great a battle and in so green a spring.

They were troubled only when they turned and looked upon their lord. He did not ride in his usual station, at the head of the host. Mounted on a mild little donkey, he rode beside Jonathan's litter; and whoever glanced in his direction saw plainly that he was heavy of heart. Nevertheless, their affection for him was articulate and strong. What if he had slain few upon the field in this campaign? He was an aging man; in his day he had slain multitudes, and now let Jahveh strike down anyone who was so mean-spirited as to count how many he had slain. In those black days when Jonathan had lain close to death, then they had questioned. Then they had asked themselves whether the evil spirit would visit their lord again, whether the wrath of God would indeed cut off the gallant sprout of the royal house, whether the Lord was truly weary of the Lion of Benjamin. Some of them had even turned toward the spot where the tent of the Lamb of Judah stood, pondering the mysterious ways of the Lord. But now they blushed to remember it. Saul had been heavy in spirit, but had not gone mad. Jonathan had been sick unto death, but had not died. The precious blood of the anointed had not been spilled from the wound; it was still sealed up in that body which they knew and loved; it glowed in the exquisite hands; it colored the gracious and eloquent lips. So, on the long march from Sharon into Benjamin, the army renewed its loyalty. Veterans recounted the old, high incidents, embellished now with years of remembering; and green young warriors were sometimes moved to tears.

The King of Israel had accustomed himself to the slow gait of his donkey. If he sat perfectly still, the sense of pressure behind his forehead became so slight that he had to move in order to make certain that it was there at all. But he took no pleasure in the sight of the countryside around him. The sickness which the Israelites called an evil spirit, and which he knew as a wall of waters, hung between him and any possible delight. The new grass looked painfully green and hard; speckled sun and shadow called up a churning dizziness, and the blossoming trees surged like foam against the intolerable blueness of the sky.

Try as he would, he could not keep his hand from the curtain of Jonathan's litter. He must be forever plucking it aside and looking at the young man who lay within. It was unwise to look, unwise and unkind. The surgeon had ridden up from his place among those who were most gravely wounded to say that sleep was good for the young man, that a sudden burst of light would trouble his rest. Furthermore, there was no longer any reason for anxiety. The wound was healing; let the King lay his hand upon his son's face and feel the coolness of it, the restoring sweat, the pulse beating in the throat, even and slow. Yet the King was not satisfied. It had come to the point now where he made covenants with himself, saying in his thoughts, I will not look until we have passed over the next ridge, or, I will not look unless we come upon a terebinth tree. . . . It was not that he did not trust the surgeon. One looked at certain men and knew them to be trustworthy. He could no more doubt the surgeon than he could doubt Abner. If the man's hand had slipped, he would not have blamed him. He would merely have known that Jahveh stood with Judah; the God of Israel, not the surgeon, would have cut off the seed of the Lion to make room for the Lamb. Nor was there anything to prevent this same

God from destroying what was half-healed. It might delight Him to make the heart high with joy before He smote it with the black hammer of death. Before the train reached the next terebinth, the sleeper might start up at the clash of terrible wings, the wholesome coolness might turn to endless cold. . . .

With the thought that to lift the curtain after such meditations was to tempt the Lord, Saul turned his face from the litter and looked down the ranks through the afternoon glare until his glance focused upon David. The image of the lutist, like all the shimmering world, was blurred. The rich reddish hair, the pale arms, and the white tunic seemed to be changing subtly, as a mountain crest melts and quivers in intense heat. The gleam of the sun upon the collar of turquoise and gold was particularly painful to Saul's eyes. The young man rode alone, at the head of his thousand. His bearing was gallant and fraternal; he had learned his easy, comradely manners from his lord, and he had learned them well. Yet there was no pleasure in looking at him. Wherefore?

Is it, Saul asked himself, because it is said that Jahveh has chosen him? Because it is babbled in the ranks of Judah that he is the Lamb? But if such is my belief, then I believe in magic and sorcery, and all the laws I have spread about the land concerning the punishment of sorcerers—all my sane and reasonable laws are lies. Shall Benjamin be taught by Judah? Judah is ignorance; Judah is the little farm and the little herd and the little mind; Judah perverts what has been by remembering it too long, and cannot understand what is, to say nothing of prophesying what will be. I do not believe in these herders' fantasies of lambs and lions. I do not believe that they issued from the wise mouth of Samuel. And if they truly issued from his mouth, I do not believe them, nevertheless. Samuel was once the Lord's vessel. But the vessel is not, as it once was, whole and sweet. It is tainted with holding the waters of bitterness. Samuel is a dour man, jealous and old. Can it be that I, judging David, am also dour and jealous and old? None counted how many fell beneath my hand on the plains of Sharon. None said, "My lord the King is glorious." Many said, "My lord the King is tired." And while I fainted in the heat of the day, and knew the ache of my old wounds with every thrust of the spear, he made the motions of war as though he performed a dance, using his weapons with ease and skill, as he plays upon the lute. For when he makes death, it is as if he made music. It is his craftsmanship that slays, and not his power. He finds a man's liver as he finds a perfect tone, and his face is untroubled and satisfied; a vague pleasure is always upon it, an engaging and boyish smile. The Lord has said that we shall not covet. Let the Lord believe me that I strive with all my spirit to teach my hardhandedness not to covet his soft skill, to teach my age not to covet his youth. I gave him that collar which he wears about his neck because it tore my heart to give it; Ahinoam brought it to me out of her father's house, and I have held it often and fancied that the jewels stayed warm from her touch. Yet the most secret places of the heart are plain to God's eye: He is not deceived by turquoise and gold; no, nor is He appeased because the living have given away a token from the departed. Envy is a sin to be punished, and, even now, before we come to the next hill, Jonathan may be dead. . . .

Teach me not to covet, O my God. Or teach me to love again, since it is impossible for a man to covet when he loves. Make the son of Jesse as lovable in my eyes as he was in that first hour at Ephes-Dammim, when the tide of my sickness withdrew from me and I saw him kneeling in the sun with his hand upon the lute. Tell me that it is my fear and my sick imaginings which have made him unlovely in my sight. Restore him to me in his innocence. Speak reasonably to my evil heart. Say unto me, "Fool, he never sought to steal the eyes of your son away from your face, he never brought the sins of Canaan into the tent of Israel, he never wished to see you among the slain, or thought to wear your crown." Say to me, "Fool, I have blown away your foolishness as if it were an unwholesome mist. Behold your lutist now, your armor-bearer and friend. Behold the companion of your son and the husband of your daughter, your beloved and faithful child. . . ."

It seemed to him when he opened his eyes that Jahveh had heard him. The young man who rode in the ranks before him glimmered less balefully upon his sight; the white of his arms and tunic was shadowed by a bluish cast; the collar had ceased to shine. It was as if a seraph hovered between the earth and the dwelling-place of the heavenly hosts. The green of the fields, the sparkle of the streams, the brightness of the grass and the mustard flower were mercifully muted as by the shadow of a great wing. They had come by the road known as the Way of the Seacoast from Sharon into the country of Manasseh. Saul looked up and saw that there were two towering mountainsides before him—the verdant slope of Mount Gerazim and the sandy, shale-splintered side of Mount Ebal. A mist, the mist of many fountains and streams, lay over the fertile valley between the mountains. Purpled by that mist, pale and holy and opalescent, shadowed by the two slopes and mildly golden in the afternoon sun, lay the ancient city of Shechem. It was a city of sacred stones and trees, a city of covenants and oracles. Many pilgrims had adorned it with their gifts. Many merchants had built their high stone houses here; grain, oil, figs, wool, and flax flowed bountifully through it into Phoenicia; and the high houses were rich with the northern barter—scarlet cloth from the Phoenician coast, sea-colored bowls painted over with the pink creatures of the sea, panels and pillars carved from the fragrant cedarwood of Lebanon.

A shout went up from the ranks at the sight of Shechem. Five moons had come and gone since they had slept in a city. Saul thought of their expectations and smiled an indulgent smile. They would spend the long afternoon eating and drinking and searching for bedfellows among the temple women. They would drive Ahitophel to distraction by asking to have their booty dragged out of the baggage wagons. They would convert it into coins and spend it in brothels and bazaars. Some of the graver ones would go up to ask oracles of the whispering oak in the high place. He had gone there once, in his youth, to be told that he would be mighty in battle and wretched in love; like most priestly pronouncements, neither statement had been utterly false or utterly true. . . .

As the first of the marchers moved onto the fair stretch of meadow that lay before the city, he found himself wondering whether David would go up to the talking tree and whether Samuel's tales could have traveled so far north as this. He saw a brief and painful image of the young man looking up at the wind-turned leaves, his ear attuned to the priest who told how this rustle meant the Lion and that rustle meant the Lamb. . . . No, he thought, David will not go up to the speaking oak. I will ask him to sit at my table this night, in the seat that is reserved for Jonathan. And afterward we will go to another sanctuary, to the stone of the covenant where God made a treaty with Abraham. We will go up together, in the cool of the evening, with such light hearts as men feel in their breasts when they walk by moonlight in a strange town. We will pour wine upon the stone and make a covenant in God's sight, speaking not with our lips, but only with our light hearts. I will say in my thoughts, "I make a covenant before God utterly to put out of my spirit any dark dreams and imaginings concerning David of Bethlehem. Let the frail limb of the House of Saul lean upon the strong limb of the House of Jesse henceforth forever; and if I raise my hand against the seed of Jesse, let my blood be spilled even as this wine." And as we go down from the sacrifice, I will lay my arm across his shoulders, as in the old days, saying in my heart, "This is my beloved child. . . ."

Someone had turned from the side of the road and was riding silently beside him. It was Ahitophel. He wore a wreath of pomegranate leaves upon his brow to shield his weak eyes from the sun.

"How is it with Ahitophel?" Saul said, feeling a sudden tenderness toward this young man who also sought the shadows and yearned after the night.

"It is well with me. How is it with my lord?"

"Well," he said, thinking how the peace of Jahveh was indeed upon him.

"And with Jonathan?"

"With Jonathan also it is well. He sleeps."

"Will my lord the King leave him in my charge for a little? The captain of the host has asked me to say that it is plain from the van that they are making preparations to greet us before the gates. Virgins are gathered there with pipes and cymbals. They will come forth from the city to praise the King with an antiphonal song. If my lord will ride a little in advance of the ranks——"

Saul sighed. "Abner might have gone forth in my place," he said, dreading the jolting and the haste.

"But if Saul is not at the head of the host, it may seem to the people of Shechem that some evil has befallen the King."

What evil? he asked himself. That I am mad? That the captains have hidden me among the baggage wagons? . . . He turned and glared at the young man, who looked meek and ridiculous under his leafy crown. "Well, stay by the litter, and I will go," he said.

The going was much more painful than he had thought. The little beast beneath him, lulled into apathy by the ambling pace, balked at the touch of his heels. The peaceful shadow of the mountain no longer lay across the host. The helmets, the breastplates, and the shields shone in the afternoon glare; the separate spots of brightness came together as he passed them, were merged into one long, tormenting streak. In the blur and brightness that was the host he saw certain floating faces, and he closed his eyes against them because they were loathsome. Here, under a coronet of leaves and mustard bloom, was the long, stupid face of a sheep; here the face of a dead fish rose from the watery obscurity to gape at him; here a jackal licked its chops with a sharp red tongue; here was a frog with bloated jowls and popping eyes. He turned to the right and stared at the meadow grass; it rose and fell in waves, it was as unstable as the sea. Come, then, he said to himself, I will be better soon. When I stop at the front of the ranks, this will pass. . . . But suddenly it came into his mind that he must ride back again. He had forgotten to summon up the men who had distinguished themselves in the campaign. For the first time in his life, he had ridden forward to take the glory of the battle unto himself alone. He turned and rode past the troubling multitude once more, smiling and calling heartily after the chosen—Abner and Joab, Paltiel, Moriah, David of Bethlehem.

Sound—the blare of ram's-horns, the shriek of pipes, the clang of cymbals—shattered the quiet of the afternoon. He drew in the reins and paused at the forefront of the ranks. A little behind him, in a crescent, stood the chosen. Before him lay the meadow—green, violently green—and the harsh yellow towers at the gate of the town. He swayed in the saddle and closed his hand around the reins until the nails went deep into his palm. White, terribly white, the virgins of Shechem came in two lines out of the town, some shrilling the pipes and clashing the cymbals, others moving in the wild and intricate steps of the dance. Each dancer held in her hand the long white veil of the dancer who moved before her. It was as if a glimmering serpent twisted and turned. The army, divided from women these five moons, sent up a great shout at the sight. The sound nauseated him; the taste of the morning's wine rose sour in his mouth. It was so with Jonathan, he thought. It was so with Jonathan when he retched in the rain and said that man and woman were a foulness, that there was nothing in the world for him, nothing save death. . . .

Now the dancers were upon him. The serpent reared from the grassy ocean and spattered him and his heroes with a foam of flowers. Solemn, self-conscious, and disturbing in their womanliness, their flesh showing rosy through their fine garments, the dancers leaped before the King and uttered a piercing cry. Then they moved to either side to make room for the singers. Three hundred women advanced from the city in six choral groups of fifty. Six islands of glaring white upon the grass, and the first group breaking into high, ecstatic song, and that song the more terrible, since he knew it would be multiplied sixfold.

At first he did not hear the words they sang. It was, he supposed, the usual paean of victory—"Glory to the King and to his heroes." He seldom troubled to listen—it had been said in so many different ways at the end of so many campaigns. Perhaps he would never have known the words if it had not been for a gasp of consternation from the ranks. All three hundred voices were shouting together at the thunderous crest of the song:

> Saul has slain his thousands,
> And David his ten thousands.

He reared up in his saddle, distraught and unbelieving. Surely it was not possible that they had exalted the lutist above him, that three hundred voices should shout his shame before the gates of Shechem, in the presence of the assembled host.

> Saul has slain his thousands,
> And David his ten thousands.

Fifty high voices, sharp and clear, flung the words into his face. He knew that he must not turn, and yet he turned. He knew that he must not look, and yet he looked at David of Bethlehem.

The wall of waters had risen behind the young man. It was as if he and he alone were visible now. He sat utterly still upon a dappled donkey. His face was a white oval, as blank as an egg. There was nothing upon it, not fear, not pity, not shame, not delight. It looked terrible and featureless—an unformed thing waiting for the shaping hand of God. So Samuel had looked in the old days when Jahveh hovered above him, begetting prophecies and mysteries.

The singing had ceased. Saul knew that stark silence had settled upon the plain.

"My lord," said Abner, motioning toward the waiting Shechemites, "will you ride in with them, my lord?"

"No. David of Bethlehem, *he* will ride in with them," he said. "I will pitch my tent and Jonathan's in the shadow of the mountain, this side of the town."

"Let me also pitch my tent in the shadow of the mountain beside the tent of my lord," said Abner.

"If you will. Not for my sake, but for Jonathan's. It is not a good thing that the sick should be left alone with the mad."

So the host went into Shechem, slowly and looking backward often, sick at heart but too hungry and weary and ardent to renounce the food and the beds and the bedfellows within. And some went up to ask oracles of the speaking oak which stood in the high place, but there was not one among them who visited the stone of the covenant that night.

❦ V ❧

A BRIEF spring storm had drenched the streets of Gibeah. Now the massed clouds were breaking apart and rolling toward the east. The gardens were bright with wet foliage and strewn petals. The fronts of the houses were dappled with shadow and sun. Children had run out to wade in the puddles; mourning doves shook their feathers; women drew back the curtains so that the thirsty rooms might drink the sweet, damp air. Everyone breathed deeply and smiled. A fragrance permeated the whole town—smell of rain water drying in sun.

The women of Gibeah set up a cheerful babble—told each other the stories that their sons and brothers and husbands had brought back from Sharon, showed and admired the amulets which their men had carried home from the Shechemite bazaars. It was well with Israel—there had been a victory. It was well with the women of Gibeah—the empty wombs were filled again with living seed, and there were more things to talk about in the street and at the cistern, now that the men had come home.

It was the sound of their chatter that wakened David. A pleasant sound, yet he wakened wildly, as though he had been summoned up from his dreams by the blast of a ram's-horn warning a drowsy army that an enemy was marching across the plain. He groped after his spear and found nothing but the smoothness of the sheet. The confines of the room, the walls paneled in cedarwood, the sun-spattered ceiling, closed in upon him. The presents he had brought back from Shechem lay upon the clothes chest—the purple veil, the blue cloak edged in scarlet, the necklace and bracelets of shells. He saw the teraphim, the tall image of God carved out of pomegranate wood and crowned with a wreath of peacock feathers. Michal had come by it in his absence and had set it at the foot of the bed. He turned his head and saw the woman. She was sleeping the deep sleep of satisfaction and exhaustion. Her hands—long and dark like her father's hands—lay open at her sides. He rose a little on his elbows, scenting the rain and thinking that he would put on his tunic and stand awhile at the door to refresh himself. But even as he set his foot upon the carpet, the fear that had wakened him came upon him again. Some angel of God, he thought, has been with me while I slept. Some seraph has whispered in my ear that I must not go forth from this bed and from Saul's daughter. Today it is she who must be the first to rise. And when she rises I must draw her back and plead with her to remain. I have gratified her flesh, but her spirit is hungry. In the evil day that flickers like lightning behind a few tomorrows, she will not stand with me. She will stand with Saul unless her spirit also is satisfied. . . .

He lay back on the goat's-hair pillow. He felt weak and vulnerable, partly because love always depleted and never renewed him, partly because the amorphous fear that had followed him since the hour of the antiphonal song before Shechem had taken shape at last. In the twenty days which had passed between that hour and this, he had been given little time for thinking. There had been marching and strange cities; there had been alien women taken briefly in unknown rooms; there had been a constant inward ache, an inward bleeding, as though he carried Jonathan's wound in his vitals; there had been a blank look, as of judgment suspended, in the King's eyes. Whenever, in an empty minute, the virgins of Shechem shouted the glorious and terrible song in his thoughts, he said to himself that the outcome of it lay not with him, but in the lap of the Lord. And Jahveh had let him rest. He had lain in a roseate and enervating mist of dreams and expectations. But now the time of repose was over. The angel had told him as much while he slept. In the great house on the hill above Gibeah, the Lion of Benjamin was shaking himself out of the apathy that followed his madness. The trumpets had already sounded in heaven, and the ranks must be formed on earth. Who would stand with the Lion, and who with the Lamb?

The young woman stirred beside him, flung her brown arm across the whiteness of his body, and sighed. He laid his cheek against her dark, coarse ringlets; they smelled of warmth and sweat—for his sake she had laid aside her spices and perfumes long ago. He turned against her, trying to kindle his tired ardor; he assured himself that she was desirable; he compared her with the others whom he had known on the homeward journey; and his longing took fire from the remembrance of those adventures and from the thought that she was more free and passionate than the rest. She kissed him and opened her eyes. In her glance also he saw the look of judgment suspended, and he was afraid. She withdrew from him and smiled a mocking, sour-sweet smile.

"The wars have left you very weary. It is not your habit to lie in bed so long," she said.

He kissed her until his desire was equal to his will to desire. For the fourth time since they had lain down together after the noonday meal, he was with her. He had always possessed her in silence. This time he spoke, wildly, like a distraught and foolish lover, of his yearning for her through blank nights in distant cities. He called her such names as a lovesick servant might call an unpossessable princess—flower of the pomegranate, fountain of waters in the noonday heat, moon over my wilderness, my dove. . . . For a while her grave and honorable eyes stared into his, arraigning and questioning him still. Then she lowered her eyelids and gave herself up to the sweet lie. "Mine," he thought as he lay back upon the pillow. "Mine, utterly mine."

He lay very still, holding her hand against his lips. The fresh smell of the rain water filled the room. The voices of women, talking of battles and amulets, came and went with the speakers past the window. A smith called in a ringing voice that he would mend braziers, corselets, spears, and swords. A donkey made a clattering sound upon the cobblestones.

"David," she said.

"Yes, my beloved?"

"Give me my shells which you brought for me out of Shechem."

It seemed to him that the talk of the women in the street had brought the notion into her head. As he sat up and reached for the trinkets, an overwhelming sense of pity closed like a hand around his heart. She is like a solitary child, he thought, who hears the other children at their games. She is alone, and she tries to console herself in her loneliness with toys. . . .

She held up her hands for the necklace and the bracelets. He had fancied that she would put them on to adorn her nakedness, but she only made a little heap of them and laid it between her breasts. This also seemed childish and pitiable. He was weak with loving and weary with battles; since the hour when he had stood at the door of the King's tent, watching the work of the surgeon, unexpected tears had come too often to his eyes; had she lain so a little longer, fondling these small tokens of his small affection, he would have wept.

But she sat up and laid the shells upon the pillow. "My lord is tired," she said, "and will rest more freely if I arise."

"Do not arise."

She bent above him, and a sour-sweet smile indented the corners of her lips. But now there was no mockery in it, nothing but resignation and tenderness. "No, I will go and bathe now. Sleep a little, and I will waken you in good time. If it please my lord, we are to go up to eat the evening meal with Mara and Jonathan."

He strove with himself lest some sign of the tumult within him should appear upon his face. Since the morning when they had fought side by side for a while on a knoll in Sharon, he had not spoken with the King's son. Saul, still shaken by the evil spirit which had come upon him before Shechem, had given Jonathan freely into the hands of Mara and the surgeon, and the young man had lain these many days within his own house, behind curtained windows that looked sorrowful and blind. Now, after many evenings of walking on feigned errands through the moonlight, now, after long and futile staring at those solemn windows, the door of the tabernacle was to be opened. Again it was as if a hand were closing round his heart. The brown face which bent above him was blurred and distorted by his rising tears.

"Truly?" he said in a casual voice. "Then is the wound healed at last?"

"Not wholly, no. But he is restless and in need of company. Mara sent her servant down to me this morning. Will we go up tonight?"

"Yes, if it please Michal. But it is not yet sunset. Stay with me a little, and afterward we will bathe together. It would be comforting to have you by me while I sleep."

She rose and stood at the side of the bed. Her eyes sought his, and now it was very difficult to meet her look. "Come, now, stay a little," he said.

She shook her head. "No. It is as my mother said to me before we two were married. . . ."

He saw the mild gray glance of Ahinoam fixed upon him at his wedding feast. She had known much and foreseen much. She had not gone down with a quiet heart into her grave. "What was it that my lady said to my beloved?"

"That it is a foolish and wretched woman who whines after more than her just portion. That when a woman is satisfied, she should feel no anger in her heart if her husband should choose to be alone."

"But I do not choose to be alone."

She lifted the purple veil from the clothes chest, muffled her tawny nakedness in it, and walked toward the door. "It is enough that my lord has asked me to remain beside him. It is not necessary that he should also believe the words that he has spoken. He has spoken, and that is enough. I am content," she said.

◄§ VI §►

NOT SINCE the days of his childhood, when his mother and father had led him up to the House of God in Ramah, had he felt such holy thanksgiving as he felt in Jonathan's house that night. The house itself, made orderly and beautiful for the first visitors who had entered it in many days, had the air of a sacred place. New wicks floated in replenished saucers of oil; the draperies were drawn back to let in the moist freshness of the summer night; fine new dishes from Phoenicia and wet flowers from the garden were set in seemly patterns upon the table; and Mara bore herself like a priestess, going in quiet happiness back and forth between the guests around the table and the couch where her husband lay. It seemed to David that he had never before known the beauty of Jonathan's dwelling. Every object shone forth in all the radiance of the reclaimed. The brazier, polished to a subtle brightness, the austere fold of the curtains, the white goat's-hair carpets that floated like islands upon the shadowy floor—each of these was in itself a reason to rejoice. He sat at the table and felt the warmth of food nourishing his body. Yet it seemed to him that he had no body, that his flesh, emptied by the afternoon's long ardor, was incandescent and free. Aerial, disembodied, his spirit moved toward the couch and brooded above the white face, the exquisite hands made soft and translucent by sickness, the flat and dreaming eyes, the cloudy hair. Now and again in the course of the meal Jonathan had looked gravely at him, and each time he had been, as a plucked lute string, tremulous with high music, shaken with a sacred joy.

The three at the table were bound together in a tender conspiracy to soothe and entertain the one who lay on the couch near the window. They were never certain that he was listening; sometimes he seemed to be thinking only of the murmurous noises of the night. When they addressed him directly, he answered in a cheerful voice. Once he asked Mara to illustrate a point with an ancient parable; once he laughed at Michal, who had drawn a brilliant caricature of Doeg the Edomite; once he commended the food, which he ate from a plate set on a low table beside him. They wove their talk from delicate stuff; they made a web of it, a gleaming and fragile tissue stretched across the black, unmentionable chasm of war and wounds, madness and sedition and death. Once, and once only, that web was broken.

It was Jonathan who tore it, turning toward David. "If my brother is ever in need of a surgeon," he said, "let him send for the Danite that he saw with me in Sharon. There are those who butcher the flesh and the spirit, and there are those who affront the spirit while they make the flesh whole. But this Danite neither butchers nor affronts; pity has made flesh and the spirit one in his eyes. Therefore, let David send for the Danite, should he so much as bruise his knee." The speech asked and received no other answer than a nod. The ready tears stood again in the lutist's eyes, blurring the attentive faces. It was Mara who dealt with the subject, making an embroidery of trifles upon it: the surgeon, his afternoon visits, the brew of herbs which he had recommended, the savory stew which she had made from the joints of the lamb by adding a little thyme. . . .

They sat long at the table, so long that Mara took pity on the sleepy servants, and told them to leave the table as it was and go to their beds. They went, and Jonathan called "Good night" after them as they mounted the stairs. Would I were a bondsman, David thought, would I were a servant in this house, to take the cup that has been warmed by his fingers, to turn the pillow beneath his head. . . .

"Is my brother weary?" Michal said.

"No, how should I be weary? I sleep at all hours, and therefore there is no hour in which I feel a need of sleep. Is Michal weary? No? Then stay with us a little longer. I am thirsty. I will have what the surgeon permits me—a small cup of wine."

Mara poured it out, reached across the table, and set the cup in David's hand. "Take the wine to my lord," she said. "Michal and I will wash these dishes and have our women's talk together. Meanwhile my brother and my husband may talk of such matters as concern them. Only let them call up no armies and fight no old battles. Let David see to it that my lord rests."

The room, empty of servants and cleared of the remains of the feast, seemed very long and still. At one end of it, the women chattered softly and made splashing sounds in the basin. At the other end, David and Jonathan were together and said nothing at all. The King's son moved closer to the window to make a place for the lutist. The cup passed from hand to hand; their fingertips touched briefly; they lowered their eyelids and sighed. They had not been so close to each other since the frost night in the hills around Gibeah. They remembered that hour and strove to forget it. They reached back to the evening of rain when they had sat side by side under the dripping tree. They found that evening in each other's faces and turned to look at the summer darkness beyond the window and smiled.

But the smile did not lie upon David's lips for long. Somewhere in that outer dark, the fear took shape and advanced upon him. The ram's-horn of danger sounded in his thoughts; his cheek turned cold under the breath of the angel of the Lord. Up, up, the trumpets have already sounded in heaven. The ranks are forming upon earth, and Michal stands beneath the banner of the Lamb. But where stands Jonathan? He who wandered with Saul in the broken temple of Shiloh, he who stood at Saul's side before Amalek and Michmash, he who was borne forth in the King's arms from the battle lines in Sharon—where is he? Is he with the Lion or with the Lamb? . . .

He turned from the window and stared at the beloved. He did not dare to tell himself what it was that he sought in the young man's face. He knew only that he searched breathlessly for some change. The change was there; he saw it with agitation, regret, and delight. It was not that the face before him was bloodless and thin; there was something else— a subtle softening, a remoteness, and a dreaminess. It was not that the hands were so emaciated that every vein showed clear; it was that they no longer were the hands of one who has the power to grasp and hold. The Jonathan of Michmash and Amalek would have stood with the Lion. But this Jonathan, changed and lessened by the agony in Sharon, might value honor less than love, might well be led into the ranks of the Lamb.

Jonathan drank the wine and set the empty cup upon the table. The movement pained him. He frowned and bit the corner of his lip. "I have got me a fine wound," he said, "one that will rival Abner's. Now he and I can contend together for Rizpah's pity through all the dull summer evenings to the end of our days."

"No, now, it will heal, it will pass."

Jonathan laughed and shrugged his shoulders. "It is an easy thing for those who have it not, to say that it will pass."

"What is Jonathan's is mine also. If my brother bleeds, I bleed."

"Then cease to bleed," he said lightly. "I would not keep you bleeding overlong. I have not bled since that first night in Sharon when my brother stood at the entrance of the tent, when I was as a beast and knew not what I said and said my brother's name." He turned toward the other end of the room and nodded pleasantly at Mara's listening, warning face. "My wife is a hard captain. She will not let me eat the fat of the kid or talk of wounds, and she is very niggardly with my wine. Yet one word, and we will leave this matter. Let David know that I would not have so cried out if it had seemed to me that I would live to blush for it. When they drew out the arrowhead, it seemed to me that they drew out my vitals with it. Well, then, I thought, I will turn yet once to my brother, seeing that there is no harm in it and nothing after it save death."

Though it was said casually, it should have been enough. And yet the angel stood at David's shoulder saying that it was not enough, bidding him to lay hard hands upon this vulnerable one, to grasp for more.

157

"Then is it only upon the brink of Sheol that my brother Jonathan will turn to me?" he said. "Has he renounced me utterly upon this earth?"

"What would you have of me? God has created the world in such-and-such a manner. It is created, it is finished, I cannot change the world."

"Yet in the world I have loved my brother. That I loved him too greatly was no reason that I should wholly shut my heart against him. His friends were my friends, and his enemies my enemies. His pain was my pain, and his cause was my cause. . . ."

The dazed and depleted face turned away from pain and causes toward the vacancy of the night.

Yet the cruel angel would not pause for pity. "Let my brother hear one more word from me," David said, "and then I will let him rest. Since the hour when I stood at the door of the tent, I have asked myself whether, if I had been in Jonathan's place, Jonathan would have come to me. If there were a day when the shadow of death lay upon me, would my brother stand with me then? Would he rise up and put aside all the world and say: 'I am David's and David is mine'?"

There was nothing but stillness and the rushing sound of stillness. It seemed to him that the very flames had ceased to flicker now. Jonathan continued to stare at the window. What thoughts came and went behind his bloodless face it was impossible to know. There was a clatter at the end of the room. The women were setting the last of the plates and cups in their proper places. Soon they would bring their light talk with them, muffling the unanswered question in the silvery web of peace, leaving the inflexible angel still unsatisfied.

He dared not wait. "Then if my brother Jonathan no longer loves me, I will become resigned to it," he said.

Jonathan lifted his hand a little and let it fall upon the couch, turned upward and open, close to David's knee. He moved his head slowly from side to side upon the pillow, as a sick child moves in protest against pain.

"I will be resigned to it, and remember what has been, and ask no more save that Jonathan also remember me. . . ." He paused in blank wonder at his own pitilessness. It is not I, he thought, who tear out his honor with inexorable fingers. It is not I. It is destiny. It is the angel of the Lord. . . . It was the angel also who laid David's hand upon Jonathan's hand. He felt the old, remembered magic flow from palm to palm. The room was filled with the recollection of shy talk in a wet garden, with moist leaves turned in the rain and the sounds of a waning festival floating across a black and glimmering lawn. . . . And you also—have you heard also, beloved? . . . The faint pulse quickened, the emaciated fingers closed upon his, the touch was transmuted slowly, impalpably, into a caress.

The triumphal moment was too brief to sicken. Mara and Micha were coming across the room. On their way, they dried their hands on a napkin which they held between them. They paused at the table to lay the napkin aside, to pick up the jewels which they had taken from their hands, and to set their hair to rights with their pink, water-wrinkled fingertips. Their conversation had not been a lively one. They stood at the side of the couch, yawning and blinking. Mara held her rings in her hand, and jingled them back and forth in her palm as if to say, "I have already begun to undress, let me go to my bed."

Their farewells were cheerful. They all grew vivacious, seeing that the desired end of the occasion was close upon them. They even chose to linger in the bright and pleasant room, talking in hushed voices so that the servants might rest undisturbed, bestowing light touches and kisses upon each other, moving toward the door, and feeling on their faces the freshness of the summer night. On the path which led through the garden and into the street, Michal and David walked side by side. One of Jonathan's watchmen stood at the gate holding a torch, waiting to escort them to their house at the other end of the town. The torch turned before them, lighting up a whole veering stretch of leaves and branches; and David remembered another torch, lighting up other leaves, still glossy with a long-since-vanished rain.

"Ah, well. . . ." he said.

"Why did my husband sigh?"

"Did I sigh? Then I sighed out of a sense of blessedness, thinking how goodly a thing a bed is, and how pleasant it will be to put my head on the shoulder of my beloved."

He had a strange conviction that she was smiling to herself. "Yes," she said, and her voice had in it some of the weary, trailing cadences that once had fallen from Ahinoam's lips, "yes, it is a good thing to sleep."

⋙ VII ⋘

THE YOUNG SEASON matured into strong summer. The hour of reckoning was postponed, and the interval was sweet, filled with the first harvests, with feasts in the King's garden, with Saul's jests and Jonathan's remote, contemplative smiles. Sometimes it was as if the awesome moment before Shechem had never been; sometimes it was as if the time appointed by the angel of God would never be. The son of Jesse lay dreaming upon an island of peace, his spirit nourished by Jonathan's tenderness, his body lulled by love and the strengthening sun. When Michal called to him from the garden, breaking his sleep with the news that another morning was moving on toward noon and that fresh bread and cool curds lay ready in the shadow of the pomegranate tree, it seemed to him that there were no todays, no yesterdays, and no tomorrows.

He liked Michal's morning aspect, her body bent forward a little, her brown elbow resting on the table, her hand against her cheek, her face washed of all lines and tensions by sleep and made the more vague and childish by the changing light that fell upon her through the foliage.

Her anxieties always grew upon her as the day lengthened; by noon she was petulant, by dusk she had a feverish vivacity, by midnight her body looked thin and her face took on a haggard air. But at the morning meal she was a serene companion, chattering about her plans for the day and offering him the savory scent of the still untasted hours.

On that morning when the ram's-horn of danger first blasted in their ears, they were making light conversation of a heavy matter. It had come into her mind that there had been no quarrels between them of late. She counted the peaceful days and named the number to him. "Is it possible?" she said. "I have not called my lord an evil name since he returned out of Sharon."

Because the sun was strong and his bench was turned eastward, he had laid his hand across his brow to keep the light from his eyes. Now, in the ruddy darkness of his sheltering palm, he thought how that which is transitory becomes strangely dear. Even if policy had not taught him to hold his tongue, he would not have berated her during these weeks of waiting. "Perhaps we have no strength for quarrels, having spent so much in love-making," he said.

She laughed softly, but soon fell silent. He sensed that something had cut off her laughter before it had rippled freely out of her throat. He took his hand from his forehead, and saw that she had grown suddenly solemn.

"Somebody is at the gate," she said.

Her gravity alarmed him; he did not dare to turn. "Who would come up at such an hour as this?" he said.

She rose. "It is my brother Ishbaal. He must have come up from my father's house."

He turned then and saw Ishbaal walking up the pathway. The boy passed through the bands of light and shadow to the table under the tree, and stood at the end of the table without a word. His hair was disordered. He wore a rumpled tunic whose skirt was spotted with food. There were purplish circles around his eyes. It was plain that he had neither washed nor slept.

In the harsh light of the sun, Michal was sallow and unbeautiful. Her midnight look was upon her—the hard mouth, the angular cheek, the sharp line between her brows. "How is it that my brother Ishbaal runs through the streets of Gibeah in a tunic that would be a disgrace to the son of a smith?" she asked. "Is the fruit of Ahinoam of so little consequence to Rizpah? Are there no clean garments in the clothes chests?"

The boy simply stared.

"Is my brother bereft of his tongue?"

A frightening change came over his face. His jaws worked strangely, and his lips shook. Two large tears rolled down his quivering cheeks. Suddenly he flung himself forward and embraced his sister. He sobbed and turned his forehead from side to side against her breasts.

Even in this moment of exigency, there was room for only one thought in David's mind. He looked at the weeping boy and knew how like they were—Ishbaal and Jonathan. So Jonathan must have looked in his ninth summer, bewailing some forgotten tragedy; and he yearned to lay his hand upon the heaving shoulder, to have some part in the comforting. He even came forward and stood face to face with Michal, looking down at the tangled pale-brown hair. But he did not dare to touch the young mourner; he knew that Ishbaal had always loathed him with a nameless loathing, the more powerful because of its very namelessness. Beyond a grudged greeting and an eager farewell, he had never had anything from Saul's youngest son save a blank stare. He lowered his eyelids and waited.

At last the fit of crying subsided. The child turned and wiped his face upon the skirt of his tunic. He sat down upon one of the benches, resting his back against the edge of the table and turning his head away from the spot where David stood.

That softness, thought David, that dazed dreaming which came upon Jonathan only after Sharon—that has been upon Ishbaal since the time when Michal went forth out of Saul's house to lie with me and Ahinoam went forth out of Saul's house to lie with the dead. So it is with the King and the King's children; shame in Gilgal, wounds in Sharon, grief in Gibeah, draw the bones from them and leave them like the spineless creatures of the ocean which melt away in the sun and leave no sign. . . .

"Now," said Michal, taking another deep breath, "now let Ishbaal tell us what trouble has come upon him."

Before the child began to speak, he deliberately turned his back upon David. "The evil spirit is again with Saul my father," he said.

"So? Well, that is unfortunate. But, having seen it so often and knowing well that it will pass——"

The boy shivered. "No, now," he said, and the words were malformed by the shaking of his jaw, "it is not now as it was before. It is another spirit."

"How so?"

"My sister knows the first spirit, how it was a silent spirit and sat with a locked mouth in the dark. With this spirit, it is otherwise."

"How otherwise?"

Ishbaal's voice fell to an awed whisper. "It is a ranting spirit with a loud mouth. It goes raving up and down the stairs and through all the rooms. It laughs, and its chin is spattered with foam. Also, it prophesies."

"Prophesies?"

"It prophesies in a strange voice which is not my father's voice. The servants have said——"

"What said the servants? What said the fools?"

"They said that it was the voice of Samuel speaking out of my father's mouth, telling how all the seed of Saul shall be cut off." The shaken whisper paused in the still garden. "How Jonathan shall die, and with him Malchishua and Abinadab, how Michal shall have a barren womb, how the children of Rizpah will go early into their graves, and I, I also, shall soon go down to death."

For the space of a single heartbeat she laid her hand across her belly, as though to shield some life that might be stirring there. Then her old weapons came to her succor—the sour humor, the bitter smile. "It is indeed Samuel's voice," she said, "that blabs such stuff as this. He and he only would make such tales, and you and you only would believe them. Have you been witless enough to carry them to our brother Jonathan, to stir up his fever and tear his wound apart?"

"No." Now that he had breathed the horror out of his charged body, he was cleansed and relieved. "What is Jonathan's house to me? I come to my sister when I am afraid and wish to be comforted."

David saw with wonder that there was strong love between these two. She stood above the bench where he sat, encircled him with her arms, and rocked him back and forth as though he were a suckling babe, blowing her breath through his tangled hair, "It is an evil dream. Let Ishbaal call it an evil dream and say to himself, It is nothing, it will pass. Let him go up to my chamber and wash the dirt from his hands and face. Then, afterward, we will go up to our fields, we three together, to see how it is with the corn. And if there is time, we will also visit the cow that has a new calf, a very fair and goodly calf with a white star between his eyes and a long pink tongue——"

Suddenly the child turned and darted a hard, swift glance at David. "You and I will go, Michal," he said. "But not *he.*"

"Not he? Wherefore?" Her eyes begged her husband's forgiveness and asked him to excuse the child. "Certainly he will come. Otherwise all three of us will abide at home."

"He is to go up to Saul's house," Ishbaal said.

Her hands, which had been moving gently over the boy's back, suddenly fell like talons upon his shoulders. She grasped and shook him. "To Saul's house?" she said, and her voice was like the shriek of a mountain bird. "How is this? Wherefore?"

And now that the time had come, David stared down the green garden, and saw the sun and the leaves, the terrified woman and the startled child, the crumbs which Michal had strewn for the birds, the dishes from which they had eaten their morning meal—saw it all remotely, from a great distance, as a dove must see the city over which it hovers, as an angel, beating his wings against the arc of the firmament, must see the world. He was perfectly serene. "No, now, Michal," he said in a grave and vibrant voice, "let him be. If I am to go up, then I am to go up. It is the will of God."

She looked at him, and her hands released the child and fell open at her sides. "How is it, Ishbaal? Why is he to go up?" she said.

"As I went forth from the house, our father saw me and said that surely I would run like a girl to sit in the lap of my sister. That being so, Saul said, let me say to my sister's husband that he should come up. Let him come quickly, said my father, and on the way let him make a song concerning the great victory that came to pass before Shechem, when Israel was torn in two and Jahveh broke His spear in twain in heaven."

"But Saul is mad," said Michal. "Perhaps already he has forgotten what he asked in his madness. David, will you go?"

"I will go."

"He is to take his lute," Ishbaal said.

Michal came to David and laid her arms about his neck. Through the fine linen of her garment, he felt her tremulous body. The contact was poignant and sweet, but it pulled him earthward. He kissed her briefly with shut lips and put her aside. "Let us have no farewells," he said. "I will be with Michal again this night. Let my beloved go into our chamber and bring me my lute."

"Let me come up to Saul's house to be with my lord."

"No," he said, "Jahveh would not have it so. Should I be delayed until the third hour after noon, let Michal go down to Jonathan's house and tell him what has passed. Then, if there is need for intercession, the daughter and the son of Saul may come up together, if they choose, to intercede for me. Fetch the lute."

When she had gone into the house, the garden seemed even more silent and far away. The child, who sat with his back toward David, looked like an image carved from stone. The boughs stirred, and the shadow of the leaves moved back and forth upon the cloudy, pale-brown hair. "Jonathan," he thought. But this also he put aside, seeing that it drew him toward the earth.

She came again, carrying the lute close to her body. When she put the instrument into his hands, he felt warmth and moisture upon it. He knew that she had remained long in the shadowy chamber, close to their bed. She had held the lute against her breast and had washed it with her tears. Now her face was mild and untroubled. She walked with him to the gate.

"Let us eat the evening meal in the garden," he said.

Then he set foot upon the glaring road, white in the noonday heat. He heard the talk of the people of Gibeah and also the murmurous voices of the heavenly host. And that high house which stood upon the hill above him—it was not only the house of Saul; it was also the judgment seat. God sat in the common room, with the brazen surface of the earth beneath His feet and the brazen scales in His hand. And David trembled, not in terror but in awe, knowing that he was about to be weighed in the balance.

❧ VIII ❧

THE GREAT HALL of Saul's house was dark as a cave after the glare of the sun. David stood blinking on the threshold, vulnerable and blind. The room was one long quadrangle of shadow, slit here and there by stabs of light. Wherever a drawn curtain met the sill or the side of a window, wherever a door closed against floor and wall, there the white thrusts broke through. Who was within? What enemies, more accustomed to this dark than he, fastened their looks upon his naked face? Vague areas of light became discernible: the white of Rizpah's robe against the fireless hearth, the gleam of Abner's beard close by the door, and, at the very core of blackness at the far end of the room, the brazen tip of Saul's spear, the moist white rounds of Saul's eyes.

Such fear as he had never known assailed him then. Not the tense, honorable battle fear. Another fear, a lukewarm, sick, unwholesome dread. It was as if his heart had turned to pulp; it was as if not blood but stagnant water crept along the channels of his veins. I am the Lamb, he thought, I am the criminal and the sacrifice. The cord is knotted around my neck. I wait as Jonathan waited at Michmash. And somewhere, in some corner of this room, there is an executioner with a sword. . . .

At the far end of the hall, Saul stirred in his chair and sighed. After more hush he spoke, but his words fell faint and meaningless upon the quiet. "There was a certain brew of herbs. . . ." he said. He spoke to none of them, and none answered him. A vision of Ahinoam floated to the surface of the lutist's thoughts. She is risen from her burial cave, he told himself, she has come to lead me to mine. . . . Abner's whisper, no louder than the drone of the flies, told him to raise his voice and speak, for Jahveh's sake.

But he did not speak. He stood looking down at himself, seeing his hand curled around the frame of the lute. Golden and aerial, like Jacob's ladder springing from the somber earth—out of the blackness and the horror rose a succession of tones in his thoughts, such high music as neither he nor any singer in Israel had ever made before. Slowly the fear subsided; slowly the darkness lessened; slowly the room grew orderly, took shape, and settled round him.

"Who was it that whispered?" Saul said.

"It was I, Abner, my lord."

He barely heard them. He thought only of the song which was unfolding in his mind. The words were growing out of the soaring cadences: Behold the Lamb, the chosen of the Lord, he is lost. He has wandered into a den of lions. See where he stands, white in the blackness, white among the tawny watchers, white in the burning circle of their eyes. The daughters of Shechem weep. Their mouths are locked upon the antiphonal song. . . .

"Wherefore should Abner whisper?"

"I spoke to one that came this moment through the door, that he should go to my lord and make himself known."

Daughters of Shechem, go forth and gather lilies. Bind your brows with lilies and cease to weep. For surely the Lord has not fashioned His darling to be thrown to the beasts. Surely it cannot be torn and eaten, that which the Lord our God has made so fair. . . .

"Who is with us?"

The Lamb shall be delivered up whole out of the cavern. Come forth, daughters of Shechem, and dance with him in the green meadows. There is no mark upon him. And lo, the sacrificial garland that is upon his head, it shall be changed into a crown. . . .

Abner's voice, gentle and conciliatory, intruded itself upon the last phrase of the song. "The King's son-in-law, the lutist who was with my lord at Ephes-Dammim, the hero who was with my lord in the country of the Philistines, the shepherd whom my lord loves, it is he who has come," Abner said.

The captain's voice had trembled; the captain was afraid. Sooty terror obscured the burnished gold of the song. It was possible now to see two of the watchers. The old warrior stood against the wall. His hands hung at his sides, loose and weaponless. His head was bent. His beard trailed upon his chest. The concubine sat near the hearth, in the great chair that had once been Ahinoam's. Her face was bloodless, her eyes were closed, her body was very straight and still. Had it not been for the movement of her hands—she kept pulling the rings from her fingers and replacing them again—she might have been a corpse.

"So?" said Saul's voice, speaking out of the shadow. "And my daughter Michal, is she with her paramour?"

David found his voice at last. "She and my brother Ishbaal are together in that high house of stone and cedarwood which, in better days, was given to me by my lord."

Some movement took place in the heart of the shadow—gleam of rings on a lifted hand, jangle of bracelets. "And my son Jonathan? Has he come up with the darling of his soul?"

Abner and Rizpah both tore the stillness with a sharp intake of breath.

"No, my lord," said David. "My lord's servant has come to stand before my lord utterly alone."

It was a plea for pity, and he fancied that it begot pity. It seemed to him that the charged air was stirred by the unfolding petals of a great flower of tenderness. Someone sighed, and he could not tell whether it was Saul or the concubine.

"And you have brought your lute?" the King said.

"Yes, my lord."

"Come, then, and sing." The voice was gentle. "It was for your singing that I lifted you up out of the dung of Judah." The voice mocked him now. "Are you at the door again? How is it that this Bethlehemite is forever standing at doors? I remember a certain night in Sharon, and how the son of Jesse hung in the doorway of a certain tent. His face was white as curds." Laughter broke through the words, spilled cold and oily upon the quietness. "How is it with David now? Is his face white? Come, David, come, darling, come beloved of Saul and of the children of Saul, come,

Hope of Judah and Lamb of Israel. Come to me now, that I may satisfy my mind as to the color of your face."

Then I must go, David thought. But his knees were unstrung beneath him. He could not move.

"How is it, slayer of tens of thousands? Are you afraid?"

"Why should I fear my lord?"

The self-assurance, the ringing buoyancy, that he had achieved in his voice was magically transmitted to the rest of his person. He moved half-way across the room, but when he stood at the center of the great hall, close to the chair where Rizpah sat, he was able to discern the King—the unkempt hair and beard gleaming with sweat, the tunic clinging to the stark body in sodden folds, the mouth stiffened at the corners by dried foam, the rolling eyes. He knew then that what he went to meet was far wilder than he had thought.

"Come, my hero. Come, my brave and beautiful one, my eagle and my dove." The speech was a chant now, a terrible mingling of love and loathing. The mouth stirred in an avid smile.

David walked more slowly over the rustling reeds, past Rizpah, past the corner of the hearth, past the long table, to the tall chair which stood against the farthest wall. He stopped and knelt and lowered his eyelids. The dank and acrid smell of the sick man's sweat rose to him. How long he knelt there he did not know. Time went ponderously, upon the rise and fall of Saul's labored breath. Then the King's hands were upon him, light, swift hands, moving in disintegrating tenderness, putting his hair back from his face, touching his neck, unfastening the chain that lay about his throat, leaving his throat bare.

"Whence comes the voice?" Saul said.

"What voice, my lord?"

"What voice? Is there more than one voice in Israel? What voice but David's voice that sang the son of Jesse into the chamber of the King, into the bed of Michal, and into the tabernacle of the soul of Jonathan? And yet it is a voice like any other voice. Squeeze the throat, and the voice is gone."

"My lord!" The words came from him in a shriek just before the fingers closed around his neck. The room turned crimson with pain, turned purple with suffocation. The fingers released him, flung him backward, just as the whole earth was turning black with death. He fell across his lute, and the instrument gave out a wild, discordant clang. Then he heard a long sob, and wondered whether it was Rizpah who had sobbed. and knew of a sudden that it was himself.

"Come, sing," said Saul.

Rizpah had risen from the chair near the hearth. She bent and laid her cool, soft hands upon David and raised him to his knees. "Sing? How should he sing when you have strangled him?" she said.

"I have not strangled him, bitch. I have not strangled him, whore. If he has voice enough to wail, he has voice enough to sing."

The woman took the lute and held it up. "How should he sing?" she said again. Her fragrant, opulent body stood between the madman and his prey. "See how it is with his lute. One of the strings is broken."

Wherefore should she deal graciously with me? David asked himself. I have despised her for Ahinoam's sake and Jonathan's sake. Yet she has given herself to be a staff for me to lean upon. Because of me, she has been called bitch and whore. She has given me a little time in which to ease my throat and compose my face. Behold, God of Covenants, how I am committed to repay her. If I am delivered up and crowned, I will set her children in the high seats of holy cities, and call her my mother. . . .

"Give him the lute," said Saul in a quiet, shaken voice. "Let him see if he can mend the string."

David took the instrument from her and held it in his quaking hands. No string was broken—she had fashioned a lie to shield him—but the fine garland of leaves and lilies carved at the base of it was chipped.

"Can it be mended?"

"It can be mended, my lord." He was amazed to find that his voice had suffered no change. Save for an ache at the base of his throat, it was as if there had been no moment of violence. He watched his own hands making a show of restoring tautness to a string; he needed time to slow his hastening heart, to choose a song. "It will take a little while to mend it. If the King will permit his servant——"

"Mend it and hold your tongue. As for you, old bitch that only a madman could find fair, get back to your chair and rise from it no more."

Now that she was gone, now that there was no longer anything between himself and the rolling eyes, he felt feeble and forsaken. He had made a hundred songs, but there were not ten which he could remember; and there was some flaw, some trap, in every one he could recall. He raised his vulnerable face to the tormented face that glared down upon him; he looked and dared not look and let his eyelids cover his eyes.

"What can I sing for my lord?" he said in the candid voice of a child. "Let my lord forgive me. Since my lord laid his hand in just anger upon me, all my thoughts have flown out of me like birds. I have forgotten all my songs."

"Surely David has made a song since we returned out of Sharon. Sing a new song for us," Saul said.

Lord God, he thought, now I am surely undone. I have no new songs save the song of the Lion and the Lamb. . . . "There are many such songs," he said, lying to gain time. "Let my lord choose what manner of song will please him best. Will he have a song of love?"

"Love? No, now, we have had enough of that. Let us have no songs of love."

"Then will my lord have a song fashioned in his praise during the heat of the battle in Sharon?"

The dark body shot forward from the hips. "Come, David, come, my son," said the soft, insinuating voice. "Trouble me no more with lies. Be reasonable, my dear child, my ingratiating liar. I am troubled enough with this fury in my head. We know, we two, that there is no such song."

"My lord——"

"Has David never been afraid? In all these days since the virgins sang before Shechem of ten thousand slain, has he never made a song which says, 'Save me out of the mouth of the Lion, O my God'?"

Rizpah uttered a stifled cry behind him.

"Was David wrapped so softly in the prophecies of Samuel that he never wakened and shuddered and made such a song? Answer. Come, darling, answer. . . ."

Somewhere in the greenish sickness within him he found strength to say, "I have made such a song."

"Sing it, then, and quickly, without pause. I would have it as David made it, not as I have had so many other songs, fashioned to mean one thing in the heart, and changed a little here and there, so that they mean quite another thing when they fall at last from the lips. Come, lay your hand upon the lute."

He saw the spearhead glimmering through the shadow, and he knew that he must either sing or die. Well, then, he thought, I will sing it. I will hear it before I go down to Sheol, the new song. At the worst, he will transfix me with his spear, and I have seen him in battle, and his hand is sure. It is better to descend into utter blackness forever than to be stifled in the green slime of this hour. . . .

He laid his hand upon the instrument. Out of the marred body of the lute, golden and aerial, came the first high cadence of the song. It was indeed a Jacob's ladder. He ascended upon it, out of the terror, out of this sordid hour of lies and shame. Jahveh hovered in the open sky above him; great wings moved round him; he was borne upward on the softness of their roseate feathers; they brushed his lips and fanned his face. His voice flowed sure and vibrant out of his bruised throat. To sing the truth— to sing the truth at last! To sing yet once more as he had sung in the hills around Bethlehem—honorable and innocent—for his own pleasure and for the delight of the Lord.

> Behold the Lamb, the chosen of the Lord,
> He that is lost.
> He has wandered into the den of lions.
> See where he stands, white in the blackness,
> White among the tawny watchers,
> White in the burning circle of their eyes. . . .

It was as if he stood far off, at a vertiginous height, on the golden rungs of his song. This disembodied self looked down with remote pity upon that other self who sang in the black chamber, upon the aging woman who sat so heavily in her usurped chair, upon the old warrior who sagged against the wall, upon the King who had been beloved and loving once and who was a slayer now because he was forsaken and outworn. Wherefore should he throw the taunt of Shechem into a sick man's face? Judah would serve as well. The dying can afford to compromise, the dying can be kind. . . .

> The daughters of Judah weep.
> Their mouths are locked upon the antiphonal song. . . .

The spearhead shook against the blackness. The brown hand was on the shaft. But wait a little, wait yet a little, my lord. Hear me to the end. I would not die with all this blaze of poesy stifled in my insensate brain. I would not die on an unfinished song.

> Daughters of Judah, go forth and gather lilies.
> Bind your brows with lilies, and cease to weep.
> For surely the Lord has not fashioned David for the lions,
> Surely it cannot be eaten, that which God has made so fair. . . .

The Lion had shaken himself and risen. His eyes burned in the sooty darkness. An animal sound issued from his mouth—a foamy and leonine roar.

> The Lamb shall be delivered whole out of the cavern.
> Come forth, daughters of Judah,
> Dance with him in the green meadows.
> There is no mark upon him.
> And lo, the sacrificial garland upon his head,
> It shall be changed into——

There was a terrible whir over his shoulder, a clash of metal on the stones behind him. He knew that the spear had been thrown. He knew also that some ministering wing had interposed between his body and brazen death. Saul had fallen back into his chair and covered his face.

"For God's sake, be gone from this place," Abner said.

"Go, David, go," said the voice of Rizpah. Her hand came to him out of shadow, offering him the lute.

He took it and fled down the long expanse of blackness, through the glaring chink that Abner had opened for him, into the fierce assault of the afternoon sun. A cry rose behind him, a cry of bereavement, a desolate, self-castigating cry. It was the King of Israel, who saw the loathed one departing, and loved him, and wept.

◅§ IX §▻

Either way, thought the Princess Michal, whether he is slain here or escapes into the wilderness, either way, whether he wins or loses, I will lose. It has always been so with me. When I am dead they will say of me that I was the one who always lost. When I was a child, I was Saul's image and should have been Saul's darling. We used to hide in the caves and wait for him to find us. And when he found us, it was Jonathan whom he caught up and embraced; his kiss upon my forehead was an afterthought. At the black stone in Gilgal, I lost Agag, and Samuel was the victor. At Ephes-Dammim the palm went to Jonathan. Tonight I will lose again. If they drag him out into the street and drive a dagger through his heart, then I will wither soon, being eaten from within by an unquenchable fire. If he eludes them and finds his way into the land of the Dead Sea, then I am forgotten. He will not come again, not to me. A hundred years hereafter they will make a song concerning me: Saul had a daughter, and she was loving and reasonably fair, but she always lost. Pour vinegar instead of wine upon her burial stone, for her years were spent in bitterness. . . .

Her hands were not idle while she brooded over these matters. David lay spent and dazed upon the bed, and it was she who ran from chamber to chamber, jamming money into money bags, sewing jewels into the hems of tunics and cloaks, putting curds and bread and cakes of dried raisins into skins and baskets, flying often to the window to see whether death had yet come into the street. He had asked her once whether she thought that Saul would send an avenger in search of him, but he had asked in the tone of one who wishes to hear the question waived as an idle fancy; and she did not have the heart to let him find the confirmation of his terror in her eyes. "That is not likely," she had said, despising him a little and loving him the more for it. "Nevertheless, let us have all things in readiness, so that you may go quickly and without danger, even if such an impossible business should come about." Now it was night, and everything was finished. His cloak, his sword, his spear, his corselet, his lute, lay ready on the clothes chest. It had been arranged that Joab would, in the event of flight, follow him with a donkey laden with supplies. Now he had roused himself to look after one small task. He lay on the bed, leaning on one elbow and writing a message for Jonathan. His face was puffy and unbeautiful. His hand shook as he dragged the stylus across the clay. "Oh, God," he said after long silence, "what shall I say to him?"

She turned toward him and suppressed a bitter smile. "That is a thing which I cannot do for my lord. That is a thing which my lord must do for himself."

Before he returned to the letter, he gave her a humble, chastened look. He is a child, she told herself, and it is somehow less shameful to be wounded by such a child. . . . But how will this child fare in the wilderness? For always, since he was in swaddling clothes and the darling of Jesse's house, there have been fools to nourish him and sustain him. How will it be with him in the country of ashes and salt and lions? Who will serve him when he is no longer winsome and sweet, when he is sickened by meals of unwholesome roots and beaten lean by the winds and burned to leather by the sun? . . .

When he had finished his letter, he leaned from the bed and tried to lay the stylus and tablet upon the clothes chest, but there was no room.

He looked at the heaped paraphernalia of his departure which covered the carved lid, and the full knowledge of his state broke upon him.

"Your father will send a murderer to me," he said in wonder, as though the matter had not been mentioned before.

"It is possible. It would be better to go. You would be more secure in Gilgal or Bethlehem. I could easily send after you when his anger passes."

"His anger will never pass. I must go."

She pulled aside the curtain to look again at the street. Night—thick, humid, suffocating—leaped into her face.

"If only I might rest." His voice, lyric and solitary, rose in the room behind her, begetting pity. "No battle ever left me so weary as this. If only I might lie beside you and sleep through this one night."

She did not answer. She glanced over her shoulder and thought how sickly the room looked, washed in the light of a single lamp and strewn with the ruins of her hasty preparation. Perhaps, she thought, I should cheer the place for him by kindling a few more saucers of oil. But it seemed to her that the night beyond the window was inhabited by a thousand searching eyes. A few more flames would pull the legions of death closer to the house. She fancied that the voices of annihilation were already speaking in obscene and sibilant whispers in the street.

"Put on your clothes," she said and knew that her terror rang strident in her voice. "I would call in a servant to help you, but there is no knowing what man to trust."

"Let my beloved help me."

"No. . . ." The whispering was no longer a dream. Murder was actual and imminent. The terrible messengers talked in the darkness below her. She heard their voices, their muffled steps moving on the paving stones. In the light of a declining moon, she saw the gleam of their corselets and swords.

"If Michal will hand me my tunic and my girdle——"

"Make haste, in God's name. I cannot come. They are below."

"Wherefore make haste? If they are below, then let them come and take me. There is no other way."

She turned upon him in exasperation and fright and tenderness. He stood near the bed in his sandals and his tunic. She knotted his girdle, fastened his breastplate, hung the money bags at his waist, handed him his dagger. "The tower," she said softly. "We will take a rope and go up to the tower. It faces the field, away from the street. Perhaps they are not yet below it. You can let yourself down by the rope. If you move across the field in the shadow of the line of fig trees, they will never see, there is so little light."

She took him by the hand then and led him. The stair which they climbed was unfamiliar and difficult in the darkness. They had not come to the little tower room within the last three years. It smelled of mildew and dust. In the thin strips of moonlight cast through the two windows, they saw the wounding symbols of their failure: wedding gifts which they had meant to use and never used, a cradle which Ahinoam had sent to them from Saul's house in the first hopeful days, a doll which Michal had loved in her childhood. They stood together, still holding each other's hands. His face twitched in the moonlight. She thought, I will remember how, at the last, he wept. . . .

"What will become of you?" he said.

"Me?" She had not thought of that and had not been afraid. She saw now that he imagined Saul's spear would be cast at her also. Not so, she told herself, staring at the empty field below. The King never loved me, and the King slays only those whom he loves. . . . "My father will not touch me. I will wait here in Gibeah and do what I can for my beloved."

"Yes," he said, kissing her on the mouth, "wait for me." But the grieving stillness that hung between them afterward said: "Do not wait for me. I never loved you. I will never come again."

The field below them was still empty. The shadows of the fig trees stretched from the margin of the field almost to the sods below the window. She withdrew from him and fastened the rope to the bronze handle of a heavy chest. Ten knots, she thought, I will make ten knots and trust the rest to God. She pulled with all her strength. The harsh hemp cut into her hands so that her palms burned. "I never before let a man down through a window," she said, laughing. "A wife who was less chaste would have served you better in this."

"No wife could have served me better in this or in anything."

She knew that he had thrown his end of the rope from the window. Well, go, then, she thought. . . . He kissed her once more, but the taste of his kiss was the taste of their bitter and unfruitful years.

"God be with you," he said. But, she asked herself, what have I to do with God? . . .

He crouched and let himself down over the sill. She stood at the window and watched his white face and the streaming torch of his hair disappear into the dark. Then she leaned against the window ledge and pulled up the rope slowly, winding it into a coil over her hand. Suddenly she saw an image of the rope fastened around her own neck, and her body dangling against the dark wall at the end of it. "No," she said aloud, in a voice that sounded like her mother's voice. "No. . . ."

"Forgive me, my lady."

She started and tried to pull the tight roll of hemp from her fingers. It was one of the serving-women, standing in a patch of moonlight at the top of the stair.

"What is it?" she said.

"Forgive me, my lady, but they are knocking at the door. They are shouting and making a disturbance in the street."

"Well, let them shout. I will go down to them. Go to your bed," she said, casting the rope to the floor.

Now she was very weary. Her hair clung wet to her cheeks, and her body was drenched with sweat. She walked slowly down the stairway, and her damp palms gathered dust, pressing against the wall. She stopped in the cluttered bedroom and listened to their voices below—an insolent, aggressive roaring that brought the old regal air upon her. She went to the window and stood behind the curtain, smiling a chill and mocking smile. If I go down to the door, she thought, they will lay their hard hands upon my sore flesh and blow their stinking breaths into my face. But here I am Saul's daughter, here I am above them. . . . With one hand she snatched up the lamp, and with the other she tore the curtain aside.

The lamplight, falling upon them from the window, had robbed them of their awesomeness. What paltry murderers, she thought, and was hard put to it to stifle her laughter. All ten or twelve of them she had seen a hundred times before, standing sentinel duty at the door of her father's tent, helping with the sowing or the shearing, opening a heavy door for her and bowing as she passed. And it was plain that they remembered these old occasions at the sight of her. The first of them—the young captain who had wasted so many afternoons in making himself pleasing to David—stepped back a little and tried to hide his blade in a fold of his cloak.

Let him be the first to speak, she thought, staring coldly into his uneasy eyes.

"My lady," he said lamely, "where is your husband tonight?"

"Where should my husband be at such an hour? He is within and very weary. Even with all your howling, he continues to sleep."

"Then you must rouse him up, my lady."

"Rouse him up? Wherefore?"

"Saul has sent us after him, to bring him up to the King's house."

"Saul will wait. Go to my father and tell him that David will go up at dawn."

In the moment of stillness which followed, she felt that the first bloom of her power over them was gone. God help me! she thought, glancing over her shoulder at the great pomegranate-wood image of the god that stood at the foot of the bed, staring at her from beneath a peacock-feather crown. They were no longer under her spell, the little knot of shabby men in the street. They were consulting softly with each other.

"Well, what would you have me do?" she said.

"Ask your lord to come to the window, that we may conduct our parley with him." It was an old soldier who spoke. Once he had mended the leg of a broken chair for her, and she had made much over his skill.

"That is impossible," she said, tossing down to them whatever words came into her thoughts. "My husband is very sick. I will not have him wakened in his fever in the middle of the night."

They whispered again. It seemed to her that her lungs were raw with suppressed weeping: every breath of the humid air was a separate pain.

"Then, my dear lady——" An ingratiating voice, the oily voice of Doeg the Edomite, rose from the street. "Then, my dear lady, let us come up to behold my lord the armor-bearer in his bed, so that we may go back to

Saul's house and tell him that such-and-such is the case. In this manner we will discharge our unpleasant duties and also leave you to your rest."

She looked wildly at the staring image of the god. "Help me," she said again, and began to laugh, knowing that the god would help her whether he wished to help or not. "Come up," she called buoyantly into their faces. "Come up, but have the decency to wait until my servant comes down to unfasten the bolt."

She found the shuddering maidservant in the hall and told her to go down slowly and let them in. Then she seized hold of the god, dragged him across the floor, and threw him onto the bed. She spread a sheet and a coverlet over his long, hard body. There was a pillow of reddish goat's-hair on the clothes chest. Excellent, she thought, excellent, and put the pillow upon the sacred head. My lord is my god, she thought. It is only fitting that my god should become my lord. And truly the image on the bed was enough to provoke uncontrollable laughter. It looked so feverish with its tousled goat's-hair wig; it seemed to pant and sigh. . . . They entered just as she kicked the last remnant of the evening's confusion under the bed. She stood, disheveled and panting, between the sick god and the door.

"Behold," she said, biting her lips to stifle laughter, "behold how it is with my lord."

They looked at the exalted one in his shame and his misery, and were not such louts as to permit themselves to look for long.

"Look well, and carry the tale back to Saul, that you may delight his ears. Say to him how he bruised the throat that made his music, and dimmed the eyes that knew no other sun but his face. . . ."

Her voice broke on laughter in spite of all her efforts. But they took it for the wild laughter of the distraught, and shook their heads, and made their way with averted eyes from the room, through the hall, into the street.

When they were gone, with the last measure of her strength she rolled the image from the bed. For a long time she stood at the foot of the bed, staring at the white expanse of linen. It looked wide, empty, bare. Then, as the first gray light intruded upon her mourning, she flung herself into that emptiness and embraced it and bit at her hands and wept.

✌ X ☙

ABNER came with the wind of God into Saul's garden. The warmth of the gone sun lingered there, but the shadows were long and gracious to his eyes. He had settled himself under a fig tree at the margin of a fragrant plot of herbs to rest a while before the evening meal, to nurse a foredoomed hope, and to accustom himself to the prospect of its death. During the time of Saul's madness, this hour after the departure of the sun had been an hour of benediction. At the beginning of every evening, Rizpah the concubine had come out of the house. Since the remembrance of Ahinoam had made her hateful in Saul's eyes, she had come into the garden to sit with her old friend, the captain of the host. She had come without explanation or excuse, sometimes with Ishbaal or a maidservant, sometimes alone.

Yesterday Saul had risen serene and vigorous. He had lost all memory of the black month that lay behind him. He jested with the servants, bought a new girdle from a wandering Egyptian, bore with unwonted cheerfulness the news that the barley crop had been blighted. He had ordered that a particularly appetizing supper should be laid in the garden; it was the first day of the Feast of the New Moon, a three-day festival, and he would dine as usual with Abner, David, and Jonathan. He had come to the board with presents for each of them, and had looked at David's empty bench with evident regret. They knew then that he remembered neither that violent afternoon nor the even more violent night which followed it. The demon, not Saul, had sent murderers to his lutist. The demon, not Saul, had howled and foamed at them when they returned empty-handed, had told them to bring the sick man up for execution, to carry him up if need be on his bed. It was the demon who had beaten his head against the wall in impotent fury at the young man's escape. It was the demon who had laid a heavy hand upon his lying daughter and called her whore and filth and the fruit of a filthy womb. Yesterday morning, as though all this had never been, the King had sent up to Michal two combs of the finest honey and the first yield of his almond trees. Yesterday evening, as though all this had never been, he had observed gravely that he regretted to have his lutist absent from his table. "Well, let him be with us tomorrow then," he had said. "Surely he has a new song."

Yes, thought Abner, Saul is Saul again. He did not send for her yesterday, since he was busy with other matters. But no doubt he has sent for her this afternoon. And she will run back to him gladly, gladly. Only this morning she sat on the roof, drying her new-washed hair, making it sleek and fine. She will lie down in the light of her tarnished moon, and drink the old fever drink, and forget the tasteless water of my serenity. He started up and walked along the path, wondering how long he had wished in his heart of hearts that Saul were dead.

At the other end of the garden, the servants were moving round the table, chatting softly together while they set out the dishes for the second Feast of the New Moon. Gold fires burned in the arbor behind him. The silence was broken by the creak of the turning spits. The air which blew against his face was savory with the smell of roasting meat. A good king, he told himself urgently, a good king, frank and hospitable, ruthless in battle and compassionate afterward, a friend who has never haggled with me over the measure of my power, a brother-in-arms who put himself many times between the sword and my chest. . . . And yet he could not drive the vision from his eyes. He must see himself coming to Jonathan in the solemn afterhours of the King's death. "And what," Jonathan would say, "can I do to delight the heart of the captain of the host?" The forbidden words were so sweet that he must form them upon his lips. "Let me put down my sword and my shield, Jonathan. Let me go into the hills of Gibeah, where I dreamed high dreams and sought after a legendary bird in my youth. Let me take nothing with me, save only Rizpah, the dead King's concubine, who is old and outworn and beyond the bearing of children, yet dearer to me than all the women of Israel, seeing that I have yearned after her these twenty years."

At the end of the herb plot he started out of his fantasy. Lost in his guilty dreaming, he had come face to face with Jonathan.

"God be with Jonathan," Abner said. There was a tinge of annoyance in his tone. The young man always walked too softly, and now, since he had risen from his bed of sickness, seemed scarcely to tread upon the earth.

"God be with Abner." His voice was as courteous and musical as ever, but it, too, had undergone a subtle change. It had, day in and day out, precisely the same quality as when it had addressed the surgeon in the moments of peace between agony and agony.

"How is it with your wound?" said the captain.

"Oh, it goes well enough. It is almost healed."

Suddenly Abner knew that the young man had not come up from his own house in Gibeah. His lips were dry and cracked with the heat of a long journey. His tunic was drenched at the armpits, and his feet were powdered over with dust. He looked with longing toward the bench in the shadow of the fig tree.

"Shall we sit down together?" Abner said.

They sat, and Jonathan composed himself and turned to his companion with the old courteous solicitude. "And my captain's wound, how is it with that?"

"Well enough. It never troubles me in fine weather."

The uneasy silence which settled upon them was relieved by the cheerful noises of preparation for the feast. Dish clinked against dish, and the meat in the arbor made a sizzling, sputtering sound. The young man sighed and looked about him in bewilderment, first at the herb patch, then at the table, then at the long shadows lying across the lawn. "It is early," he said, with the bemused, self-deprecatory smile of one who has forgotten both the place and the hour. "I came with more haste than I had strength for, and that was foolish, since I am here long before the appointed hour." His hands, still white and limp from the long weeks of immobility, lay open in his lap. The House of Saul, Abner thought, has entered again into the vale of suffering. There is no rest for those who serve the seed of Kish. When Saul is sane, then Jonathan is tormented Must I sustain him? Must I forever be the comforter? Let him sustain me a little, seeing that tonight she will lie in his father's bed. . . .

"God of ages, but I am weary!" said Jonathan.

There was no help for it. "Whence comes Jonathan, and what has wearied him?" he said.

The look that the King's son turned upon him was enough to make him forget all other matters, even the vision of her new-washed hair spread upon Saul's pillow in the dark. It was not that the flat, brown, animal eyes searched him to see whether he could be trusted. It was that they beseeched him to be such a man as even the damned could trust in the hour of their ultimate guilt and misery. He had seen such a look on the face of a captured spy; he had seen it once in a woman stammering out an excuse that could not mask her adultery. But the King's son, the undefiled, the flower of the host—— Only the lutist who wrought fury in the humane Saul and shame in the proud Michal—only the lutist could bring Jonathan to this.

"I have been a long way," the young man said. "I have been in the hills, in a cave which is the hiding-place of David of Bethlehem."

He has looked into the magical gray eyes of the lutist, Abner thought, and he has forgotten his father and the crown of Israel. He has listened to the musical voice of the lutist, and knows neither his rank nor the hour nor what part of the earth he walks upon. . . .

"The captain of the host has been kindly in all his dealings with me, lenient when he might have been censorious, compassionate when he might have been just. It has come into my thoughts that I might consult Abner also in this matter."

Do not consult me, he thought. I am weary, I am old; this matter of David is beyond my comprehension, let me alone. . . .

But the rapt voice went on with the tale. In the hills above Gibeah, in that place of thorns and underbrush where long ago they had met and skirmished with the Philistines, there they had met again and eaten a sacred meal together and made a covenant before the Lord. Henceforth nothing could divide them. They were blood brothers; they had cut their wrists; and in the body of each flowed the other's blood. Seeing that each of them lived only in the other's eyes, surely Jahveh would not set them apart. . . . The voice pleaded for affirmation. Surely Saul's anger had passed with his madness? Surely he would take his lutist again, as in the old days, to his heart?

And the captain—held by the moving hands and the vibrant voice, held by the vision of those two against the world in the legendary hills above Gibeah—the captain nodded his head.

It would be well, there would be peace again, Jonathan had assured David. But David, strangely fearful, had refused to believe in the possibility of such blessedness. He had bidden his friend go down before him, to speak of him at Saul's table among the guests tonight, to watch Saul's face for any sign of lurking rage. But surely there would be no such sign. Tomorrow when they met again—for there was a meeting appointed between them at the end of a certain barren field near a stone called Ezel—they would come back to Saul's house together.

At the end of the long rhapsody, the young man sank back against the trunk of the tree, breathless and ashamed. He knew as well as the captain that he had not told this tale because he wished for counsel. He had used Abner as a vessel for his outpouring; he had barely cared whether the captain heard him; it had been enough that he had heard himself. And if, thought Abner, I used *him* as a vessel for *my* dreams, if I poured my longings into his ears, if I asked him to swear to me that she will come to me when Saul is dead . . .

"Perhaps," said Jonathan, flushing, "my captain does not understand what it is I would ask him. Does Abner, in the wisdom of his years and his experience, believe that my father will forget how——"

"I understand. I understand very well. But I must beg Jonathan not to lean on this wisdom of years and experience. Concerning a king who is possessed by an evil spirit and two youths who are inordinately bound to each other, who can be wise?"

The young face was transformed again; the transcendent, visionary joy had gone from it; it stared at Abner with a sinner's shamed and begging eyes. "Surely Abner knows my father——"

"And you—do you not know him also? It seems to me that you should know him, seeing that you are the jewel in the tabernacle of his heart."

Jonathan drew a sharp inward breath and turned his head slowly from side to side against the tree. No, now, thought Abner, laying a conciliatory hand upon his knee. I had not meant to wound him so, that was too deep a thrust. . . .

"Let the captain believe that I love my father. Let him know that I did not turn my face against Saul on many other occasions, not for the sake of Jahveh, nor for the sake of Ahinoam, nor even at Michmash, for the sake of my own life, when he would have taken it from me for a drop of honey and given it lightly to God. Only for David of Bethlehem, seeing that he is dearer to me than my own soul——"

And now the captain wished only to have the discourse end. "I know," he said wearily. "Believe me, I know."

The young man flushed again. "I have tired Abner, and I regret it. It was only that I wished to ask him what I might do to bring the thing favorably into Saul's sight."

"Then I will tell you. Go and wash the stains of the journey from your person. As you are now, you will make a sorry advocate for any cause. Surely it will not please Saul that you come into his presence in a soiled tunic. He will take the marks of dust around your eyes for the marks of illness. He will be uneasy for you, seeing you so worn. Go, then, and wash yourself."

The young man rose from the bench in evident distress. Surely there was cause for confusion; he had been chidden like a child and sent off by his elder to wash his face. Yet even this was not cause enough for his agitation. He rubbed his cheeks and looked at the dust on his fingertips. He laid the back of his hand against his forehead. He is afraid, the captain thought. He is terrified that he has broken his wound with all his running about. He knew his mortality in the tent in Sharon. Young as he is, they convinced him there of the certainty of his own death. . . . And the old warrior, who had lived so many years with a stubborn sore, who had learned to walk with death as with a companion, felt the soft touch of pity upon his heart. Perhaps it was really as the priests said in Judah. Perhaps the oldest son of Saul would die in the early summer of his years. . . .

"Once the dust of the journey is washed away, you will be a goodly advocate. My lord the King will be gladdened at the sight of you, for truly you are much changed for the better since he last set eyes upon your face. After a wound has begun to heal, the rest is easy."

Jonathan did not answer, merely cast him a grateful glance and sighed.

"Jonathan knows my room. Let him go up to it and take whatever he needs to make him fresh and fair."

"Abner is gracious."

"No," said the captain, feeling again the strange, disintegrating touch of pity. "No, Abner is not gracious. He is old and testy, weary with Saul's afflictions, and galled with certain small but incurable troubles of his own."

The young man turned back and regarded him with courteous and attentive eyes. "What can I do to serve my lord the captain of the host?"

Weariness and compassion unloosed his tongue. "Promise me," he said, "that when you come into your kingdom, I will be permitted to rest."

Jonathan bent forward and embraced him. "Before God," he said, "if I come into my kingdom, Abner shall live out all his years in peace."

When he had departed, the words continued to sound over the stillness of the garden. "If I come into my kingdom, Abner shall live out all his years in peace. . . ." The mournful voice that had said them had transformed both the reign and the serenity into foredoomed dreams, and Abner felt in his innermost spirit that neither the one nor the other would ever be.

❧ XI ❧

THREE sat under the swaying boughs of the olives—three and an empty bench provided for David of Bethlehem. If the captain had been uneasy because of the folded napkin and the untouched plate, that tension had been relieved almost at once. Saul had bestowed upon the untaken place nothing more than a raising of the eyebrows. He was determined to be merry; he was satisfied with the companionship of Abner and Jonathan. Easy and expansive in his new well-being, the King pushed his bench backward and leaned against the wall of the house, stretching and rubbing his sides. The spear and shield that had been set behind him interfered with the free play of his long arms, and he pushed them aside. The tip of the spear, on which converged certain recent and violent memories, no longer gleamed in the gathering dark.

Nor could the captain find cause for misgiving in the aspect or the manner of Jonathan. It was difficult to believe that this self-possessed youth was the same being who had stood an hour since in the garden, shamed and terrified. The sun that had fallen upon him during his journey had given him a pleasing glow. His hair was newly combed and free of dust. With his customary tact and grace, he chatted on of light, inoffensive things—a fair girdle that Mara was embroidering for Saul, an ancient book of incantations, a wonderful two-headed calf which everybody in the town believed to have been born last summer, but which nobody had ever seen with his own eyes. . . .

Yet Abner felt that there was something spurious about the occasion. It was as if the three of them and the table and the blown olive leaves had been set precariously at the edge of a chasm where chaos howled and causes were confused, where friend fell upon friend in obscure struggle, where unseen wounds bled and nameless spirits wept. It is nothing, he told himself. It is the gall of my jealousy, flowing out over everything, poisoning this pleasant hour. . . . And he forced himself to eat with the heartiness that his heaped plate demanded.

By the time they had finished with the meat and the bread, darkness had gathered upon the garden. The servants came out of the house with lighted torches. They planted the golden, wind-streaming lights on either side of Saul's bench and set themselves to the task of clearing away the crumbs and the bones to make way for the sweet. One of the young men who usually attended Saul at table was missing, and the King asked pleasantly concerning his whereabouts. It evolved that the young man had been married two days since and was therefore unclean, being filled with the spirit of generation, which was an offense to the virginity of the moon. "David of Bethlehem," Saul said, "no doubt he also is unclean for one reason or another. Well, let us hope that he will purify himself and sit with us tomorrow, since tomorrow is the last night of the feast."

The King had spoken casually, but something as pale and swift and transitory as heat lightning on a summer evening—something had flashed and faded in the eyes beneath the shaggy brows. Had the King truly forgotten that wild afternoon? Was it the first white cast of remembrance that had glimmered in his glance?

Necromancy and the follies thereof entertained them while the table was cleared of the leavings. Jonathan was in the midst of a long tale about a certain exorciser who had been tried in Bethel for calling up the spirits of the dead when one of the servants returned, carrying more wine and a great dish of delectable little cakes. The cakes, Abner knew, were the work of Rizpah—golden triangles of dough filled with chopped raisins and baked in honey. The servant set them before the King, and the King stared at them strangely, blankly. Again it was as if distant lightning flickered in his look. "Wait," he said to the retreating servant, "wait. Why have you brought us these? Where is the honey cake?"

Now, surely, Abner thought, they have all gone mad. For Jonathan went white, the servant began to tremble, and one of the maids who stood in the doorway fled into the house.

The servant opened his lips, but plainly could not find the breath for speech.

"Well, fool, what devil is in you that has taken your voice? Where is the honey cake?"

"Let my lord the King forgive his servant. There is no honey cake."

"What is this?" He turned a wild and frightened face toward Abner. "This morning," he said, "I sent down to my daughter Michal and asked of her that she make us a honey cake, which is a matter small enough, considering that only yesterday she had from me a bushel of almonds and such honey as would be a delight even to——" He stopped and covered his face with his hands. Then he shook himself and gripped the edge of the board and turned upon the servant. "What said my daughter Michal?" he shouted. "What was her excuse?"

"Nothing, my lord, she said nothing. I did not set eyes upon her. She was sick and could not rise out of her bed."

"Sick?" he said in a flat voice. "Sick? What manner of sickness?"

Abner could tell by the vacant stare which Saul turned upon him that the King had remembered how he had beaten his daughter, and feared that he had hurt her unto death. "No, now," he said, laying his hand upon Saul's open and clammy palm, "let the King cease to distress himself. It is some small thing. Women are forever looking for reasons to lie in bed. Yesterday I saw her sitting upon her roof, drying her hair." It was a lie; he had fashioned it out of the image of Rizpah in his thoughts.

If there had been any lack of conviction in the captain's speech, Saul had not detected it. "At what hour yesterday did the captain see her?" he said.

Abner pursed his lips and said that he could not remember for certain, but fancied that it had been some time close to noon. Jonathan blushed and took one of the small cakes and broke it into pieces. He will never make a creditable liar, Abner thought, since he blushes even to hear a lie. . . . But perhaps there would be no more cause for lying. The servant had departed. The King leaned back against the wall of the house and stretched again, as if by repeating an earlier gesture he could re-enter a past hour. The wind rustled through the boughs of the olives. The frogs made a deep-throated, somnolent sound in the stretch of marshland that lay behind the house. Abner drank a long draught of wine and sighed.

Both the King and the captain waited for Jonathan to put an end to the silence, but Jonathan was still. In the redness of the torches, his face looked less solid than in the last light of the evening; dark hollows were visible below his cheekbones and around his eyes. He leaned forward and made some hidden movement under the table. His right hand fumbled at the upper folds of his broad girdle; he was feeling for his wound; he was afraid that the violence had driven the healed flesh apart. Having reassured himself, he straightened. But Saul had seen the furtive gesture. He turned to the young man eagerly, almost thankfully, as if he saw in this new and comprehensible fear an escape from the more obscure and terrible one.

"How is it with Jonathan?" he said, in a voice shaken by anxiety and tenderness. "Is he in pain?"

"No, my father." He smiled a sour smile at himself. "It is a childish thing and I am ashamed when I speak of it, but I must forever be touching the wound to convince myself that it has not broken again."

"No, now, be assured, it will not break. Any man is ill at ease with his first wound. I remember that I was constantly touching the one I received at Jabesh-Gilead. So long as it is not inflamed and does not ache——"

Again he paused in the middle of his sentence and passed his hand slowly across his eyes. The captain knew that he was wrestling with the black fear that in the hours of his madness he might have laid hands also upon Jonathan. And God forbid it! Abner thought. There is enough agony as it is; let us have no unnecessary suffering. . . . "We spoil the festival with too much talk of sickness," he said, turning to Jonathan. "My lord the King and I have been separated from you these many days. Come, tell us how you have spent the time. Where have you been? What have you done?"

The words had no sooner fallen from his mouth than he saw how he had been dangerously stupid in an attempt to be kind and wise. He had meant to make way for soothing assurances. He had believed that the young man would provide Saul with a whole series of images as nourishing as the thought of Michal drying her hair in the sun. But Jonathan cast him a shocked and wounded look, and he knew that in his concern for Saul he had unwittingly betrayed Jonathan. Fool, fool, the eyes of the young man said, why have you so arranged events that I must either be silent or be a liar? Where have I been? In the hills above Gibeah, making a covenant with David of Bethlehem. . . .

Saul saw that glance. It was a brief, tormenting light cast across the lost days of his madness. His face took on the looseness, the wild and shifting look, that it had worn in those unremembered hours. His brown hand—the same hard, subtle hand that had put the hair aside from David's throat—fell lightly upon Jonathan's shoulder, felt the shoulder gently through the folds of cloth, turned it a little, so that the young man was pulled forward, his face close to his father's face.

"How is it, my dear child," said Saul softly, "that the son of Jesse came to meat neither yesterday nor today?"

Lie, thought Abner. Lie magnificently now, for God's sake. . . .

But the young man shrank beneath the tender and murderous fingers. He bent his head and lowered his eyes. The formal measure of that which has been rehearsed too often crept into his voice; and the lips of the madman sneered at the weakness of the lie.

"David earnestly requested leave of me to go to Bethlehem. His family has a sacrifice in that city, and his brother commanded that he be present at the sacrifice. . . ."

"No; now, truly?" The terrible hand left the young man's shoulder and clasped him by the chin. Slowly, inexorably, it pushed the fair head backward until the face was uplifted in the pitiless yellow light, the veined eyelids shaking over the eyes.

"He begged me to let him go. . . ." The words were strange and distorted, since the speaker could barely move his chin. "He said that if he had found any favor in my sight, I would let him go to his brothers. Therefore he has not come unto the King's table. . . ."

The hand slipped downward and closed upon the lying throat. It seemed to Abner then that a great wind was blowing, that the garden had shifted like a promontory broken away from the mainland by a tidal wave, that Jonathan gasped and Saul grappled in a confusion of waters, in utter dark.

"My lord," he cried out in a shaken voice, "take your hand from him. Take your hand from the Hope of Israel, my lord."

The King loosened his hold. The violence of the moment had driven them all to their feet. Saul stood against the wall, clutching his spear. Jonathan had retreated ten or twelve paces. He leaned breathless against the trunk of a tree, touching his wound and staring into Saul's face with accusing eyes.

"Son of a whining she-dog," Saul said, "take your false innocence out of my sight."

"Wherein have I offended my father?" The voice was courtly, remote, and cold.

"Wherein have you offended your father?" He flung the words back with horrible mimicry. A spattering of foam was breathed out upon his lips. "Do you think I do not know what lies between you and the son of Jesse? Do you think I am so mad that I cannot see how it is with you—how you have chosen him to your own shame and to the shame of your mother's nakedness? Why should you hide and coddle him and lie for him, when you know that so long as he walks upon the earth you shall not be established, neither shall your kingdom come into your hands? No, now, I know how it is with you. I know it as well as you know where the son of Jesse has hidden himself. Go then, and send for him, and fetch him to me, for he shall surely die."

The young man straightened against the tree. He smiled and leaned forward with a graceful, taunting movement of the head. "Wherefore should he be put to death?" he said in a cool and mocking tone. "What has he done?"

"What has he done?" It was as if the King had said aloud, "Do not ask me what he has done. His guilt is so monstrous that it cannot be named, not even by my foaming mouth, not even in this holocaust of shame and death."

"Yes, truly," said the guilty innocent, lifting his fair face and opening his candid eyes. "What has he done?"

The spear, thought Abner, God be merciful, not the spear . . .

It sped past him through the blown light and shadow. It missed the lithe, veering body. Its point bit deep into the tree. Jonathan, unruffled and unscathed, stood to one side of the trunk, looking calmly at the shuddering shaft of the weapon. Then he turned and cast a glance of loathing at his father and bowed gravely to Abner and was gone.

Abner stood wordless, pondering certain obscure matters in his heart. What was it that passed here? he asked himself. It was not only that the King of Israel, possessed by an evil spirit, strove to murder his son. At the last moment, before the spear hurtled toward the tree, it was impossible to tell who was the slayer and who was the victim. Tomorrow the servants who watched in terror from the windows will say how Jonathan was sinned against and Saul was the sinner. But who can journey into the dark world where they strove with each other? Who can enter into the black waters and see them there and truly know? . . .

He turned then to look to the needs of the King. But there was no king in Israel. That which had been a king was lying face downward on the ground, a wounded beast tearing at grass and biting sods. The captain knelt and laid his hand upon the heaving back, and looked at it in wonder. Behold how it has become with the Lion of Benjamin, he thought; see how it is with my lord. . . . But the sight was unreal and remote. The mouth of pity within him was dumb. Some other mouth spoke in his mind with terrible and persistent eloquence. "He is mad," it said in an exultant whisper. "He is mad and will cast her forth from him again. She will come into the garden alone tomorrow afternoon. She has washed her hair in vain. He is mad, and she will not go in to lie with him tonight."

⇜§ XII §⇝

Now tell me yet again," David had said, on that evening which Jonathan had described with such indiscretion and ardor to Abner. "Tell me yet once more what you will say to me when you come into the field for archery practice and I am hidden behind the stone called Ezel." And Jonathan, as anxious and uncertain as the lutist, had repeated a score of times: "I will shoot three arrows on the side of the stone, as though I shot at a mark. And I will send the little lad that I bring with me to gather up the arrows, saying, 'Go, find the arrows.' And if I say to the lad, 'Look, the arrows are on this side of you; take them and come,' then there is peace for David in Saul's house, and nothing to hurt him, I swear it as my soul lives. But if I say to the boy, 'Look, the arrows are beyond you, go your way,' then Jahveh has sent David out of Gibeah and into the wilderness." But even after the twentieth rehearsal of these simple phrases, the son of Jesse was still confused. When his lips touched Jonathan's cheek, the taste of that holy and fleeting kiss was blurred by the thought that he had not, perhaps, fixed the hour of the meeting in his mind. At the moment when their cut wrists, warm and aching, throbbed and bled against each other, he wondered whether the little lad would see him hiding behind the stone and would blab out the whole conspiracy. His uneasiness about the secret code floated like a mist between him and the solemn, tender eyes.

Jonathan had concluded that David would remain somewhere in the outskirts of Gibeah, hiding in one of the caves, waiting eagerly for what information Michal managed to send him, attentive to the pulse of his sick fortune and breathless for the slightest indication of change. The King's son was so convinced of this state of mind in his friend that he had come to the first meeting laden with little presents: a skin of wine from his own wine press, a fine cheese of Mara's making, an extra cloak, since the caves were damp and cold. But crouching in a cave was a wearisome business. If Gibeah was uninhabitable for the moment, there were other cities that could be visited. In this season of shame and trouble, David was not drawn to the brown streets of Bethlehem; there would be nothing there but wailing and shaking of heads. But there were other cities— Ramah, for example—where a man might spend a period of depression and barrenness. There he might meet, by chance and therefore innocently, a certain prophet. There he might step out of the wretched present into dreams of a more opulent time to come.

So to relieve his boredom he had journeyed to Ramah. So he had come to a certain house and entered through a certain door. In those still rooms, smelling of ancient tablets and dust, where a lamp from the ruined sanctuary of Shiloh burned in the blatant light of the afternoon, he had set eyes upon the face of that exalted farmer, that supernal herdsman, who had lifted Saul up in Israel, who was on such familiar terms with Jahveh that he could invoke an evil spirit from the Lord to drive the anointed mad. The hand that took the hand of the visitor was as dry and light as blown leaves. The eyes were sightless, filmed over with milky cataracts. The body was more ash than flesh, having been burned by the fires of God for ninety years.

"Does Samuel know who it is that has come up to him in the time of affliction from Gibeah?"

"Surely I know the voice of the son of Jesse. Come and kneel and be blessed."

The dry hand groped back to the little table that stood beneath the lamp, immersed itself in a cup of sacred oil, and lightly spattered the lifted face with the divine drops.

"It has been revealed to me how the Lion of Benjamin has sprung upon the Lamb of Judah. Now are the evil days, when the Lamb goes forth alone to dwell for ten years in the wilderness. But when his hour is accomplished, he will come forth, not into Gibeah but into Jerusalem, which is in the hands of the Jebusites, and which is the navel of Israel. In that city, all that I have said will be accomplished. It is not an uncertain matter, but a thing already finished in the mind of God."

David remembered how he had sworn to himself in the dripping garden to rebuild the House of God in Shiloh for Jonathan's sake.

"Lift your eyes to Jerusalem," said the tired voice. "When you come into your kingdom, I shall not see it. Soon I am to be released from the burden of this flesh and gathered unto the Lord. Nevertheless, in the hour of your fulfillment, remember me."

When he had returned to the cave near Gibeah, when he had settled down to the last and longest hours of waiting, with no company but the reproachful gifts of Jonathan and no sound but the monotonous drip of water down the rough walls, then he knew the full measure of his wretchedness. He mourned over the food as he had mourned over his mother's cheeses on that first night when he had lain, unknown and sick for home, in the camp of God. Dark and amorphous considerations disturbed him. It had come into his mind that perhaps there was another Jahveh, higher and more austere than He whom Samuel had set upon Saul, more terrible than the roaring bull who charged against His enemies and strewed the plains of Sharon spring after spring with the dead bodies of the Philistines. He could not fathom the nature of this God, nor see Him in any convincing shape, nor catch a glimpse of His face. Yet he could not rid himself of the conviction that He existed and saw certain sins that were not recorded among the lists of prohibitions preserved in the temples of Israel. He was the ward of such obscure matters as Jonathan's wine and the cheeses of Bethlehem. He concerned Himself with lies and half-lies whispered into the ears of Saul and Michal. He recorded in His thoughts the lines of songs as they sprang up in the mind and as they issued from the lips. Such a God was not hasty. He would wait for the proper hour and then mete out the proper punishment. Such a God might send a serpent into a cave to seek out His betrayer and strike him while he slept.

On the eve of his final meeting with Jonathan, he slept close to the mouth of the cave so that the first rays of the sun, falling across his face, would awaken him long before the appointed hour. Sleep had never lain so lightly upon him. Dreams passed like floating veils across his face, scarcely hiding the realities—the stubborn lumps of earth beneath the cloak, the cry of a mournful bird, the great, molten stars of summer burning into his opening eyes. Sun had fallen across his face. Here and there in the blackness of the cave, a little pool gleamed white. He rose and refreshed himself as well as he could with the unwholesome water that dripped over the rocks. Then he ate a morsel of bread and went to wait in the shadow of the stone called Ezel.

It was a great stone, twice the height of a man, very ancient and holy. The farmers in the section said that it had been set up centuries ago by one of the Rephaim—that race of giants who were the first offspring of God and who had come down to earth by chance and remained upon it, being enamored of the daughters of men. Perhaps it had been set up to commemorate such a union; it was phallic and generative; its tip had been worn to unbelievable smoothness by the rains of a thousand years. Sometimes, in the very early hours of the morning or late at night, a sterile husband or a barren farmer's wife would casually wander in its direction and furtively touch its side, hoping to draw from it some portion of its inexhaustible fruitfulness. But on the morning when David waited in its shadow, the field stretched out in utter emptiness under the thin sunlight. Had it not been for the little grove of pomegranates at the eastern end of it, the field would have seemed to stretch out to the very margin of the world. He sat down among sods and shale, resting his back against the black, smooth side. Perhaps, he thought, the power will flow into me also, so that when I return to Gibeah, Michal will conceive. But he knew in his heart that he would not return to Gibeah and that Michal, being of the accursed House of Saul, would go down childless to her grave.

Jonathan stepped forward, just as the watcher had expected, from the gray shadow of the foliage. His face wore the foreknown look; it was pale with watching and loose with hopelessness. He advanced slowly, to the heavy and solemn measure that had been set for him when the event was still a dream. His bow hung down from his hand, and the end of it dragged against the earth, cutting a little furrow in the sod. Everything had been predetermined, even the small morning gust that drove his tunic against his body and lifted the pale cloud of his hair. Wearily, heavily, he came to the center of the field and stopped on the predestined spot and signaled with disconsolate eyes to the eyes that watched him from behind the rock. Only the little lad, who had remained a blank in the lutist's thoughts during the days of waiting, possessed any reality.

It was foolish, thought David, to arrange for a code at all. Even before he saw me, I read the will of Jahveh in his face. . . . Nevertheless, the futile event must be carried to its completion. Jonathan raised his bow and aimed at some nameless target and sent the arrow flying over the lad's head. He, also, saw the uselessness of the performance. He stood for a long time, motionless and staring after the fallen arrow, and before he spoke he sighed.

"Is not the arrow beyond you?" he shouted after the lad, who had gone to bring it back. It was as if he, too, could not endure the nightmare unreality of the prearranged words, must twist them out of their stubborn shape, must give them some vestige of life and immediacy. The lad had taken up the arrow and stood shaking his head over it because the point was broken. "Make haste, speed, do not tarry," said the King's son, pouring all the bitterness and urgency of the occasion upon the little servant's head. The boy, amazed and affronted at the imperious voice, came back sulking, kicking up pebbles all along the way. "There," he said, throwing the arrow with too much force into the quiver at his master's side.

Jonathan put his bow and quiver into the hands of his little servant. "This is no hour for the practice of archery," he said. "I cannot see the mark. The sun dazzles my eyes. Take the weapons back to the city and give them to your lady Mara, and tell her that I will come in a little while."

The child looked at him in wonder. "Is my lord ill?" he said.

"No, not ill, only weary. Now take them and be gone."

The lad crossed the field slowly, uneasy with his burdens. Jonathan stood motionless long after he had disappeared from the grove. Then, certain at last that he would not come back, the King's son stretched out his hands toward the black stone. And David came forth from the shadow of the stone and knelt down at Jonathan's feet and wept.

"Come," said Jonathan, also weeping, "arise now and dry your eyes. We have only a little time together."

They went hand in hand back to the shadowy side of the stone called Ezel. The busy ants, the shale at which he had stared through the long waiting, the configuration of the distant hills, showing plainer now in the strengthening sun, were as disintegrating to David as the returning symptoms of an incurable sickness. He gazed at them steadily and could not bring himself to raise his eyes to his friend's face.

"Then it is finished. I must go forth," he said.

"Yes, and quickly. Avoid the towns. Hide yourself in the wilderness."

The tone of the speech was urgent and troubled. It raised in the lutist less fear for the future than curiosity concerning the past. What had the King said at the Feast of the New Moon? How had Jonathan borne himself? It was true that, in the final hour, he had come to stand beneath the banner of the Lamb. But how freely, how gladly, had he come? "What passed between Jonathan and my lord the King?" David said, still staring at the bits of shale at his feet.

"What does it matter what passed?" It was plain that, whatever his disloyalty, Jonathan loved the Lion of Benjamin and covered the marks of shame that were upon him even from the eyes of the dearly beloved. "It is sufficient to say that my father has shown me that his heart is set unchangeably against David. Let it be enough for David that I, who wished fervently to believe otherwise, have come to believe that there is no safety for David in my father's house."

"If Saul has set his heart against me," said David, "I have in some part deserved it. I am not without sin in this matter."

"Nor I."

And yet, as though to make it plain that he did not renounce the sweet sin nor wish any of its works undone, Jonathan took David's hand and held it, as he had held it on that magical night in the dripping garden, against his cheek.

"Let Jonathan forgive me," said David, weeping, "for all the sorrows that I have brought into his life, and for all the bitterness that came up with me out of Judah into the House of Benjamin."

"No, now, think no more of it. Even if David had never loved me, even if he had brought into Saul's house nothing but the sight of his face and the sound of his lute, even then there would have been enough. Let

David never believe that the remembrance of the delight will be clouded by the remembrance of the rest. I will think daily in his absence of the good hours, and see no mark upon them. I will remember nothing save that David was with me in the garden in Gibeah and at the door of the tent in Sharon and on that evening in my own house when he brought me the wine cup and set it to my lips. Let David also remember this and this only. So, should we meet afterward in Sheol, there would be no cloud to hide David's eyes from mine."

While the grave voice had spoken, a strange transformation had come upon the event. As it had been in the beginning, so it was now at its conclusion: Jonathan had taken it from the present and given it back to the past. It was not now, but long ago, that the two had embraced each other in the barren field. It was not now, but long ago, that they had risen to take everlasting leave of each other. And this present was in itself so remote, had receded so far in time, that those other incidents which existed behind it were legendary things, old tales turned gentle by the touch of centuries.

They embraced and kissed each other, and both of them wept; but of the two it was David who wept the more. He knew in his heart that Jonathan's sorrow was higher and therefore more serene than his own. Jonathan, believing at last the tale of the Lion and the Lamb, saw for himself only a few short years of bereavement, a brief walk toward his own burial cave, in which, without self-castigation, without glory, and without disloyalty, he could lie down and fold himself in peace. But for David there was the long life, the years of wandering in the wilderness, the crown that should have been Jonathan's crown heavy upon his brow, the other faces, as yet unrisen upon his world, that must at last obliterate this dear face. He wept quietly and without passion, but for so long a time that finally Jonathan must comfort him with tender lies.

"Come," he said, "shed no more tears. Set your heart upon that hour when we will be rejoined one with the other. Go in peace, since we have sworn, both of us, in the name of Jahveh, saying, Jahveh shall be between you and me, and between your seed and my seed forever."

Afterward, in the years when the son of Jesse was established in his kingdom, he strove on many sleepless nights to remember the last moments of this farewell. He came to the conclusion then that blindness had come upon him, that his eyes, about to be widowed of their dearest image, had rejected all the world. Surely he must have seen the son of Saul walking across the barren field, but he could not recall it. Nothing remained—not the blown tunic moving in the morning wind, not the pale cloud of hair. Black—black and bald and terrible as the sacred stone—the moment of Jonathan's going existed forever in his mind. Only when he had left the field and walked upon the shadowy road that led toward the cave did recollection return. There, on that road, a startled bird rose from a low branch, screaming past his face. It seemed to him then that his heart had flown

with just such a cry out of his breast, finding his forsaken body uninhabitable now that Jonathan was gone.

⚜ XIII ⚜

He should have gone without pause to hide himself in the wilderness.
Yet he could not bring himself to turn his face resolutely toward the
south. He moved eastward, he moved westward, he paused for a while on
the very margins of Philistia, and he slept for a night within earshot of the
bleating of his father's sheep in the hills above Bethlehem. He lingered
half a day by the walls of Gilgal because its chiming syllables brought
back to him the hours when he and Jonathan had awaited Saul's return
from the black altar. He had an almost irrepressible yearning to turn
northward to Beth-Shemesh so that he might see the city from which the
young weaver had come to die for Jonathan. And when he found himself
without food in the olive groves near the priestly town of Nob, he told
Joab that he meant to go up to the sanctuary there to ask the priests for
bread.

He might have found bread much more safely in one of the Canaanitish settlements that lay not four hours' journey to the west, but Nob
was dear to him. It was to Nob that Doeg the Edomite had borne Goliath's
head and Goliath's sword. Nob was Saul's chosen sanctuary. Of all the
priests of Jahveh, only those who dwelt in Nob still kept faith with the
Lion of Benjamin. The showbread on the altar there was made with Saul's
grain. The bullocks slain in the sacrifices had eaten the grass of the
meadows behind Gibeah. The wine in the sacred vessels had been pressed
from those grapes among which Michal had stood, long ago, like an
Astarte. If it was foolish to go, then let him be guilty of foolishness. If
Joab was so sickly-livered as to be afraid, then he would go alone. So at
dawn, three weeks after he had parted from Jonathan, while Joab walked
among the crowd of Ishmaelites, Calebites, Judahites, and Kenites outside the walls of Jerusalem, David went up to Nob to ask the high priest
for fresh loaves and a sword.

It was a small sanctuary set on a knoll completely surrounded by venerable olives. The roughhewn, ancient walls, wrapped in a swathing of
mist, were scarcely distinguishable from the gray morning sky. The sacrificial beasts lowed for their morning feeding in their stalls, but as yet
the priests had not risen from their sleep. The peace of disuse lay about
the place. Within the last ten years, it had been avoided by the ardent
Jahvists of the surrounding countryside. Its priests were sophisticates, and
they frowned upon fanatics, being themselves more scholarly than fervent.
They knew few incantations, but many things about the movements of
the stars. They were less skilled in exhortation than in medicine and surgery. The stone image of God that received their tastefully arranged baskets of grain, olives, pomegranates, and flowers had been blunted by time.

The features had assumed a certain vagueness and remoteness. It was as if He had seen the quiet look upon the faces of His ministrants, had found it good, and had taken it at last for His own.

David could see this image from the flight of earthen steps that led up the side of the knoll to the temple. It stood under a hanging lamp, paled now by the white light of morning. A little lad, bland and round-faced, devoted from infancy to the service of the temple, slept soundly on a mat of reeds on the floor. The altar, spread with spotless linen, bore six loaves of showbread piled in a neat pyramid, three bunches of grapes with their leaves and tendrils still upon them, a delicate cruet filled with oil, and a burnished copper plate strewn with grains of wheat. As David stood halfway up the flight of stairs, a bird flew over his shoulder, darted into the shadowy temple, and began to peck at the grains on the plate. The lutist made a sign against ill fortune, for the flight of a bird into any house was an omen signifying death.

He shrugged his shoulders and set his thoughts to other matters. He sat down upon the dew-moistened steps and reviewed again the story which he meant to tell the high priest. When he turned again to look at the interior of the temple, the lamp was quite paled out by the slanting rays of the sun, and the little lad was stirring in his sleep. He waited until the lad had risen and disappeared into the recesses of the temple. No doubt he had gone directly to waken the high priest, for the call for general rising soon issued from an unseen chamber; someone made a low clang with cymbals and someone else began to chant a morning greeting to the Lord. David rose then from the steps and came up to the very threshold of the sanctuary. Something stirred behind the open door which led to the back chambers, and his face took on the urgent, abstracted look which he thought would serve his errand best. The little lad, returning from the inner room, saw him and uttered a low cry. "Jahveh be with my lord," he said, recovering himself. "What does my lord seek in the House of God?"

"Is Ahimelech within?" He had never set eyes upon Ahimelech, but his voice implied long familiarity.

"His reverence the high priest of Nob is within and has just arisen."

"Then go and ask him if he will come forth for a word with Saul's armor-bearer, David of Bethlehem."

He knew by the lad's widened eyes that his name was legend. The childish face turned from him to look briefly toward the wall, where, among trophies of Amalek and Michmash, hung a great brazen sword. It is Goliath's sword, David thought. It is the sword that Doeg the Edomite brought up from Ephes-Dammim. And already the gentle liars of Judah have taken it from Elhanan and have given it to me. This child believes that it was I who slew the giant and gave this sword to God. . . .

"Let my lord the King's armor-bearer come and rest himself upon the bench that is by the wall while I go and say to Ahimelech that the hero is with us in the House of the Lord." The child remained a little longer, feeding his large eyes on the sight of glory. Then he bowed and was gone.

It is plain, thought David, settling himself upon the bench under the sword of Goliath, it is plain that Joab's fears were empty imaginings. None in this sanctuary has heard as yet of my disgrace. . . . And an exhilarating lightness lifted up his heart. The lie which they still believed was so sweet to him that he could not refrain from believing it himself. While he waited in the hospitable temple, it was as if he had truly come on some high errand for Saul. When he glanced up at the sword, he felt such gratification as he might have felt if he had taken it with his own hands from the slack fingers of the gigantic Philistine. And when the high priest, old and bald and slight, naked except for his sacred loincloth of white linen, advanced toward him with outstretched hands, he rose and bestowed upon his host a candid smile.

But Ahimelech was plainly uneasy. His face, dreamy and almost infantile with long study and seclusion, wrinkled like a whimpering baby's face under the shining dome of his brow. "How is it," he said, "that David has come to us alone, without so much as a servant to attend him?"

David assumed the air of hurry and preoccupation that he had been practicing since dawn. "The King has commanded me to look to a certain business," he said. "It is a matter of importance and requires the greatest possible care and haste. Unfortunately, I cannot speak fully of it to your reverence, since Saul explicitly said to me, 'Let no man know anything of the business about which I send you, and tell no man what I have commanded you to accomplish for me.' I have certain young men with me, and I have appointed a time and place for meeting them. Now tell me, what supplies have you here at hand? Let me have whatever bread you have in the sanctuary, for we are without food and have yet to travel a long way before this night."

If any doubts had arisen in Ahimelech's mind, they had been dispelled. He led his visitor gently toward the bench and called to the little lad to bring a cup of wine. Then he looked thoughtfully about him and shook his bald and shining head.

"Unfortunately," he said, "there is no common bread under my hand, but there is the holy bread, the showbread that we are about to take from the altar, since we will have new loaves within the hour to give to God. If only the young men that are with the King's armor-bearer have kept themselves from women last night, they can eat the bread of the Lord without sin. How is it? Are you and your companions holy?" He spoke apologetically, as though he considered this prohibition a wearisome and trying piece of superstition, but one which must be obeyed, inasmuch as the world is not in the hands of enlightened men.

To steal the bread which Saul had given to the priests of Nob was one thing; to steal the bread which Saul and Ahimelech had laid before God was another. David had a wild desire to say that he had lain with a woman and thereby save himself from the obscure sin of which the eyes of the timeworn image of God already accused him. But he was afraid that the hospitable old man who stood before him, offering him a cup of Gibean wine, would never permit him to leave the sanctuary empty-handed. It was possible that the priest would send to some other place for bread, making it necessary for him to remain and perhaps spreading the tale of his visit about. So he turned away from the blunt stone image and swallowed his wine and smiled his candid smile.

"Truly," he said, wiping his lips, "women have been kept from us these three days. When I came out upon this journey, the young men were undefiled, even though they thought it was merely a common journey that they had been sent upon. How much more, then, will they remain holy throughout this day, since they have learned from me something of the urgency of our business? We can eat holy bread without sin, let your reverence be assured of that."

Ahimelech turned then and told the little lad to take the showbread from the altar and wrap it in a napkin and give it to David. "And furthermore," he added, laying his hand upon the lad's curls, still damp and pressed down after sleep, "see that you guard your tongue concerning all this, for it is a heavy matter close to the heart of Saul our lord, whom we would not offend in anything. But I know that you will not speak of it to any man, since we have dwelt together in perfect confidence, you and I, ever since you came to live in the House of the Lord."

The world outside was washed in the white rays of the morning sun. The little community was awake and about its affairs, and priests and visitors strolled past the door. The light, oblique but intense, hurt David's eyes. He gazed at the moving figures. One of them looked troublingly familiar to him. It is strange, he thought, I could have sworn that the man who passed even now was Doeg the Edomite. . . .

The little lad brought the package of bread and laid it on David's knees. Once more he saw his dead glory resurrected in the child's rapt glance.

"And now," said Ahimelech, "is there any other way in which I can serve the armor-bearer of my dear lord? Has he wine and curds? Is there——"

"There is yet one more thing, your reverence. Have you a sword?"

"A sword?"

"I left Gibeah without weapons, since the King's business required such haste. But if there is no sword in the temple, then think no more concerning the matter. I thought only that, for the sake of safety, I——"

The old man lifted his smooth, infantile face toward the wall where the trophy hung, and smiled. "Will David take what Judah has given to David? The sword of Goliath, whom you slew, according to the song, in the vale of Elah, behold, it is here."

David rose and stared up at the gleaming length of brass upon the wall. Legend had made it his, and he could have sworn that he had wielded it in twenty battles.

"There is none like that," he said. "Give it to me."

They climbed onto the bench then and took it down together. The dust of many years, gathered upon it, sifted down on their lifted faces, and this seemed a portentous thing to David, who thought how, in the houses of the dead, the mourners mar their faces with dust. And he could not exorcise the gloom from his consciousness. It weighed upon him while he made his obeisance before the remote and blunt-faced Jahveh; it troubled him while he helped to wrap the gleaming weapon in a length of linen; it was not dissolved when he stood on the threshold in the fresh morning air.

"But wait a little," said the old priest when they had concluded their farewells, "wait a little, there is dust upon your face, my son."

The withered hand came to his assistance, wiping his cheek. He strove to disregard the remembrance that the gentle touch awoke in him—Jesse's hand, brushing a bit of grass from his flesh in those days when he deserved such tenderness, being still a blameless child.

"Forgive me, your reverence," he said in a muffled voice, "for any trouble that I have given you in this matter."

"It is nothing. It is you who have bestowed a gift upon me. I am rich when I am given an occasion to accomplish any small business for my lord or for those who are beloved of my lord."

And even when he had left the temple and the olive grove far behind him, even when he had exchanged the holy stillness for the noise of the bazaars, he could not rid himself of the vision of that guileless, infantile face, the round brow shining in the sun, the mild eyes clouded with an old man's easy tears.

⇜§ XIV §⇝

And now, thought Abner, there will be no more indolent summers. Even in the times when Amalek and Philistia both rose against us in the same year, we had war in winter and rest in summer. Now we will make war in all seasons. When the winter is upon us, we will march into Sharon; and when the new crops are green and the almond trees are white, we will march out of Sharon only to turn toward the wilderness, to make war against David of Bethlehem, which is another manner of saying that we will make war upon ourselves. Nor is there any longer a single hour in the day that a man may call his own. It has come to such a pass with the Lion of Benjamin that he can no longer endure to be left alone. We are called to council before the morning curds are dried upon our lips; we are sent for at noon when the sun is an affliction and sane men sleep; and when we take our sandals from our feet at moonset, thinking at last to get a little rest, then there is yet another council, and we must leave the bed which we have not even lain down upon, to talk of this, to talk of that, endlessly, uselessly, because for our troubles there is no help. . . .

So Abner thought on his way to still another council. He had been walking through the searing heat of noon to the appointed place—a promontory of limestone that jutted out over the city of Gibeah, a barren, ugly, holy expanse of gray shale and gray lichen, where the people of Gibeah came on days of sacrifice to pay their respects to an ancient altar and a sacred tamarisk tree. There was no telling why the King had chosen this particular place. He had taken to calling his warriors together at the gates of Gibeah, at the cistern, or in some unfrequented strip of forest in the hills above the town. He seldom held a council twice in the same surroundings. It was as if those surroundings, successively blasted by the hopelessness of the conversations, had been left as desolate as a land sown with salt.

During the two moons that had passed since Saul cast his spear at Jonathan, the captain of the host had been submerged in a strange torpor. He had seen and felt too much, and now he felt nothing at all. He saw plainly that this dullness was intolerable to the King, but he could not produce the passionate laments and accusations that Saul required. "Let me alone," he whispered to himself a hundred times, closing his eyes against the wild gesture, the demoniac look, "let me alone, let me rest." But he came to suspect that these everlasting councils were Saul's means of making it plain to him that never, so long as David lived, could he hope to be left in peace.

He walked slowly up the winding, weed-grown road that led to the top of the stone promontory, pausing often to wipe the sweat from his brow, since he had a spiteful wish to look fresh and undisturbed when he reached the meeting place. The prospect which broke upon him when he gained the top was even more dreary than he had imagined it. The gray of the shale and lichen seemed whiter, more leprous, in the searing sun. The tamarisk tree, burned by heat, twisted by wind, and ornamented here and there with bright scraps of cloth given it by the faithful, had the air of a weary hag tricked out in indecent finery. The old altar, greasy with recent anointings, looked squat and small against the blue immensity of the sky; and those gathered around it were few, shabby, and as ominous as a crowd of vultures waiting for the wind to bring them the scent of something dead.

In the days when David and Jonathan still sat at the King's councils, no man had observed that Saul's intimates were few; then the council had seemed select and brilliant. But now it was plain to the world that the Lion of Benjamin had taken too few companions to his heart and had loved those few too well. Those who remained, wandering restlessly back and forth between the altar and the tamarisk, were a sorry assembly: Saul himself, haggard with struggling against the evil spirit; the men of his bodyguard—he no longer walked even to the edge of his garden without them; a few young men who had distinguished themselves in the last campaign in Sharon; and three or four men of the household, including Doeg the Edomite. It angered Abner that the King should be standing not in the shade of the tamarisk but near the edge of the cliff, in the full glare of the sun. This was more of the self-abuse with which Saul tried to force upon others his own sense of desperation.

"God be with my lord," said the captain, unable to look up, through the heaviness of his torpor, into Saul's eyes.

"May God show more favor to Abner than he has seen fit to show to me."

He did not answer that. He thought, in his smoldering resentment, It is your way to make an issue of even a common greeting. . . . "Shall we walk into the shade and sit, my lord?"

"Why should we sit? If Abner must sit, let him sit. I am content to remain as I am."

"Very well, my lord." He found a patchy bit of shade, sat down upon the roots of the tamarisk, and closed his eyes.

The rest of the assembly, taking their cue from Abner, also proceeded to seat themselves within the tattered shade, each wandering as if by chance to the spot at which he had been looking with longing, each standing a little while before sitting down. Paltiel, one of the young heroes, a dark, stocky youth with a round, sad face, rested his head against the trunk of the tree and rubbed the sweat from his brow. Only Doeg the Edomite and the captain of the guard remained standing, their faces still set in a mask of alertness.

"Who gave you leave to sit?" Saul said, walking in long strides around the side of the altar. "None sits until the King is seated. Rise."

They rose, but without too much haste. They had grown so used to his ranting of late that they reacted to it with a show of fear rather than with fear itself. They moved aside to leave vacant the thickest patch of shadow. There, in that spot of relative coolness and dark, the tree had made a kind of natural throne by thrusting out two roots into an uneven seat beneath the canopy of the lowest bough. Saul sat upon these roots, and the others gathered into a semicircle about him.

"How is it," the King said, "that there is not one among you who shows any concern regarding the poison that is being brewed for us in the deserts of the south? Is there none among you who knows that we are in danger of our very lives? Is there no sane man in Israel save only I who am called possessed?"

But Abner barely listened. It is the old lament, he thought, staring over Saul's head at the boughs of the tamarisk.

"Hear now, you Benjamites." The voice that had sounded above all the other battle shouts before the burning city of Amalek, the voice that had urged the host on to the deliverance of Jabesh-Gilead, the voice that had praised the heroes and comforted the wounded and dropped strong, honorable words upon the faces of the dead—that voice had become the voice of a distracted suppliant. "Will the son of Jesse give every one of you fields and vineyards? Will he make you all captains over hundreds and captains over thousands, that all of you have conspired against me, and there is none of you that is sorry for me, or discloses unto me that my son has stirred up my servant against me, to lie in wait, as he lies this day?"

"My lord," said the moist, ingratiating voice of Doeg the Edomite, "there is a thing that my conscience tells me I must reveal to my lord, even though it should cause him pain."

Pig, thought Abner, oily, loathsome son of a pig, that it should come to such a pass that *you* could cause the King of Israel pain. . . .

And indeed it seemed to Abner that such a thought had formed itself in Saul's mind also. The King's mouth twitched, and his eyelids lay for a moment trembling over his eyes. Then the paroxysm passed, and he looked coldly at the speaker and bade him speak on.

"Not two moons ago my lord sent me on an errand to the sanctuary," Doeg said. "If I remember rightly, it was a matter of taking up certain measures of millet and wheat. It is possible that my lord the King remembers the very occasion, but that is of no consequence, and I will omit such digressions, since they consume the valuable time of my lord. But as I said, I went up to Nob on the King's errand, and I saw the son of Jesse coming to Nob, to Ahimelech the high priest. And Ahimelech consulted the oracle for the son of Jesse, to ask God what He would do for the Judahite. And Ahimelech also gave him victuals and gave him the sword of Goliath the Philistine."

"No!" It was a hoarse and terrible cry.

"But let the King believe me," said the wet voice, "for as my soul lives, terrible as the thing is, it is true. . . ."

At the moment of his outcry, Saul, springing up from his seat of roots, had struck his forehead against the lowest branch of the tamarisk. Now he stood against the trunk, swaying and holding his head between his clenched hands. Abner and the young hero named Paltiel both stepped forward, but it was Doeg who supported him; Doeg's hands lay like two soft bits of fungus upon the King's shoulders.

"Go," said Saul, shrinking against the trunk of the tamarisk.

"And where is it that my lord would send me?" said the Edomite.

"To Nob, to Ahimelech."

"Wherefore?"

"It is not the place of the master of the King's herds to ask the King wherefore. Go up to Nob, to Ahimelech, and say no word to him of what has passed in this place." He paused briefly, still stunned by the blow. "Say nothing of this, only tell him that he and all the priests of Nob are to come at once to us here, journeying by day and by night." He stopped again and drew his hand across his forehead and wiped his lips. "Tell him that I have need of him. Say that I must consult the whole brotherhood of priests concerning an important matter. Say that and no more. Now go, and come to me no more until you bring with you to this place every priest and every novice and every child that has been in service before Jahveh at Nob."

The Edomite bowed three times, kissed the hem of the King's tunic, walked quickly to the path, and was gone.

Saul covered his face with his hands, and those in the circle around him shifted and sighed and looked blankly at each other. Paltiel turned to Abner. "Does the captain of the host think it would be well to take a little water and wet a napkin and lay it on the King's head?" he said.

"No," said Saul hollowly, speaking into his cupped hands. "It is nothing. Let it alone. Furthermore, it will be best to save the water for drinking. There is little enough as it is."

Abner heard a murmur of consternation move through the group. It had become plain to them that Saul would not go down from the high place until Doeg had returned with the priests of Nob; they would be forced to wait on this dreary cliff, without food and with very little water, through the burning afternoon, through the evening and the night—the journey between Gibeah and Nob was long, and they could not hope for release before dawn. The captain of the host also permitted a look of complaint to form upon his face.

"You think of food," Saul said, not to him but to the whole assembly, "you think of food and the shade under your roofs and the linens upon your beds. And none of you considers what has come upon me, how those that I nourished to pray for me have whispered evil into Jahveh's ears against me, praying instead for the Judahite. It is nothing to you that Jahveh has been utterly estranged from me, that there is now no sanctuary in all Israel where I may burn bullocks before the Lord."

Perhaps because the blow had dazed him, Saul had spoken in a voice so cold, so empty, so flat that he might well have been discussing some ordinary matter such as the failure of a shipment of wood to arrive out of Lebanon. And this passionless voice stirred Abner deeply.

"Wait a little, my lord," he said. "It is not yet a proven thing. Why should the King of Israel put his trust in this Edomite?"

"Yes, truly," said Paltiel, "let us wait until we have heard the words of the high priest of Nob."

Now it was clear to all of them that there was no course for them save waiting. They stood in the circle a little longer, thinking that Saul might wish to speak again; but he was silent; he rested his head against the trunk of the tamarisk and closed his eyes. So they went, one at a time, to wet their lips against the thirst that was already upon them, and when they returned from their drinking they stretched themselves upon the shale and lichen in the meager shade and turned their faces from the sun. They lay in the heat through the whole afternoon, scarcely exchanging a word, moving only when the necessities of their bodies forced them to move; and long before the hour for sleeping, as soon as the wind of God stirred the gaudy strips of cloth upon the tamarisk, they slept.

On that morning when Jahveh departed utterly from Saul, Abner woke earlier than the rest. The heaviness of his torpor was no longer upon him; he saw the years that he had spent with Saul as an arc, rising slowly out of obscurity, attaining a bold height, and dropping back to nothingness; and he wished to be in the end what he had been in the beginning—the sharer of danger and meager bread. It seemed to him fitting that he and Saul should spend the first hours of this harsh day in each other's company, as, in other years, they had sat together in the white, charged dawn, reviewing their plans for battle while the host still slept. He rose and stepped over the sprawling bodies of the guardsmen. "My lord," he said softly, choosing precisely those words that he had said at Michmash, Amalek, and Jabesh-Gilead, "it is the hour, my lord."

The King started up. "How is it?" he said, running his fingers through his beard. "Have they already come?"

"No, my lord. I came to Saul out of old custom, because in the days of battle I used to come to him so, in order that he and I might speak a little together without the others."

A smile that gave more cause for grief than all the bitter lamentations crossed the ravaged face. "But this is not a day of battle. Of late the captain has shown himself to be very bitter because he was roused from his rest. There is no cause for rising early. Let him go and sleep."

"No, now, let there be no anger between us. Let me be with my lord in all things. . . ."

"Even in the slaying of the priests of Nob?"

The captain drew a long, sharp breath. "Surely," he said, "Saul will not lay violent hands upon God's anointed. No evil has yet been established against them. Surely Saul will not do such a thing upon the word of this servant, this Edomite."

The King turned then and looked his captain full in the face. There was no trace of madness upon his countenance. His cheeks sagged with fasting, and his eyes were bloodshot, but his gaze was steady. "Then Abner would not put his trust in the word of Doeg?" he said.

"No, my lord."

"Wherefore? He has been trustworthy with me in little matters, telling me always with great precision how many calves were born and how many lambs."

"But surely——"

"Abner would say to me that honesty in small matters is no assurance that in larger things a man will not be a liar?"

"Even so, my lord. There are those about the King of Israel who have served him well alike in small affairs and in great ones. In these let him put his trust."

A cold, mirthless laugh fell from the King's lips. "Truly?" he said, laying his hand on Abner's arm. "So there are truly those about me whom I can trust in great matters. Tell me now by what signs I shall know them. Instruct me, my dear friend. . . ."

The brown hand, sinking into the flesh of Abner's arm, looked like the talon of an evil bird. "Those who love my lord," the captain said, "them let my lord trust."

Saul leaned his head against the trunk of the tree and laughed so loudly that it seemed to Abner that all the sleepers must waken. "I am to trust those that love me? Truly, now? Even so? David of Bethlehem loved me—no, believe me, he truly loved me. I knew it when he anointed me, he was tender with the scars of my old wounds, truly I felt it in his fingers, his love. Jonathan, my son Jonathan, he also loved me, even after he made a covenant with the son of Jesse. And Michal loved me, to lay her head against my knees, to weep with me when Samuel gave the Amalekite to God; she was from her childhood open and honorable and told no lies. In all these three who loved me, in great matters and in small, I once put my trust."

"No, now," said Abner, laying his hand over the brown fingers that pressed his arm, "only one of these has been proved faithless. And even were all the children of Saul to set their faces against him, even if Jahveh Himself had hidden His face from my lord, yet is Abner with Saul, as in the old days. Let the King of Israel put his trust in his servant's love. . . ."

For a moment the talon that dug into his flesh loosened its hold, and a wan, indecisive smile softened the King's lips. Abner glanced across the edge of the cliff and saw a fluid, yellowish shimmer passing between the roofs of Gibeah. It is the torches, he thought. Doeg the Edomite is leading them with torches through the city. They are coming up from Nob.

"Abner has said that he loves me——"

"Saul knows. Surely Saul knows."

The laugh that burst out into his face was so loud that it roused the sleepers, who sat up on their haunches and stared at the King and the captain with blank eyes.

"Saul knows," said the King very softly, so that none of the watchers could hear, "Saul knows that Abner is a liar. Saul knows that Abner waits for the hour when the King is no more and the captain of the host inherits the King's concubine."

"My lord!" But he knew that however ardently he protested, the King would not believe him. The King had felt his guilt in his flesh and seen it in his eyes. And he remembered a thing that David had said to him once when they had met by chance in the garden: that it was impossible to tell whether Saul's madness was a matter of shutting his eyes against truth or of seeing truth more plainly than other men saw it in an equivocal world.

"Go," said Saul, turning his face aside. "Go and sleep that sleep which has grown so necessary to you now that the sun of the House of Kish is set."

At that moment the captain of the guard saw the procession advancing up the slope and cried out that Doeg had returned with the priests of Nob. Dull, ugly with half-dispelled sleep, haggard in the grayness of the dawn, the company on the promontory disposed themselves in some semblance of order: the King on his throne of twisted roots, the captain beside him, the young heroes sitting on the earth at his feet, the servants and the men of the guard standing in a semicircle behind the tamarisk tree. All this was accomplished in silence. Only the piping of a single bird broke the hush—shrill, insistent, as unseemly as the plucking of a lute at the door of a house of death.

Abner saw the length of the procession with wonder. He had known that the village below the temple held many priests, all of whom ate Saul's bread and served in his sanctuary; but he had never dreamed that there were some fourscore men in this brotherhood. They came up slowly, two by two, old men and young men, striplings and children, clad only in linen loincloths. They filed up with the docility of sheep, led by the eldest and the youngest, the high priest Ahimelech and his little temple servant; and when they all stood in one compact crowd upon the promontory, they said in a chorus, "Jahveh be with the King, our gracious and bountiful lord!" Abner searched their faces for some sign of terror, but he could find nothing. Surely, he thought, their untroubled countenances alone will prove them innocent. . . .

But Saul did not look at them. Saul rested his head against the trunk of the tamarisk, shielded his eyes from the glaring light of the newly risen sun with his hand, and breathed heavily, like one in pain. "Where is Ahimelech?" he said.

"Here am I, my lord." The high priest stood like the ram at the front of the flock, still holding the drowsy little servant by the hand.

"Why," said Saul wearily, "have you conspired against me?"

Under the round and shining dome of his brow, the old man's face wrinkled with something akin to laughter. It was as though he suspected a jest, and yet could not bring himself to believe that Saul would stoop to so cruel a jest. "I?" he said. "I, my lord?"

"You and the son of Jesse. You gave him bread and a sword and consulted the oracle for his sake." The King's voice was flat and empty. My lord is without passion, Abner thought, because for him this matter is already finished. In his mind, the priests of Nob are dead and buried and the temple where they burned his bullocks before God has become a house for dogs and birds of prey. . . .

"But among all your servants," said Ahimelech, "who is so faithful as David, who is the King's son-in-law, and is taken into your council, and is honorable in your house?" But even as he spoke, he saw the terrible possibility that this bond might have been broken. His weak eyes widened under his white brows, his voice wavered, and his hand trembled in the hand of the child. "Furthermore," he said in a shaking voice, "I did not inquire of the oracle for David's sake. Be it far from me to inquire of the oracle for any except the King my lord. Let not the King impute anything to his servant. His servant knew nothing of all this, neither more nor less. . . ."

A wave of consternation swept over the assembly of priests. The child tugged at Ahimelech's hand, so that the high priest, dragged sideward and downward, was robbed of the last shred of his dignity. His features twitched ridiculously, hysterically, between laughter and tears. Yet he remembered the child, and laid his free hand upon the child's head in a gesture of tenderness. Saul rose slowly, warding off the bough with a lifted arm, and stared long into the priest's face. Lord God Almighty, Abner thought, let the old man look up, let him show his guiltlessness in his eyes. But the eyes of the high priest, weak with long study, filmed over with tears, widened by mortal terror, could not meet the King's look.

"My lord," said Ahimelech, weeping, "my gracious lord——"

Fury—the fury of the wounded and betrayed, the blind rage of the cornered beast—rushed into the King's face. He shuddered, and a fleck of foam started from the corner of his lips. "Surely you will die, Ahimelech," he said. "Surely you and all your father's house will die."

The awesome word, the wild, contorted face, terrified the child. He uttered a shrill cry, and all the priests of Nob began to lament quietly among themselves, laying their hands upon each other's shoulders, lifting their faces now toward the King and now toward the morning sky, dividing their pleas for help between Saul and the Lord. They knew that all of them would be slain in this holocaust, since it was said that the priests of Nob were of one family, descendants of the house of Ahimelech's father. They saw that they were sharers in the same birthright of violent death.

Saul turned from them and walked to the other side of the tamarisk tree. "Come now," he said to the captain of the guard, "turn and slay the priests of Jahveh."

The young captain went white and trembled. "Wherefore?" he said. "Why should we fall upon them, my lord?"

"Wherefore?" The word was the roar of a lion. "Because they also are with David. Because they knew that he fled, and did not disclose it to me."

A murmur rose among the men of the guard. Abner, leaning against the tamarisk, heard it with terror. Now, he thought, the sedition that was in Judah and among the Calebites and the Kenites is come to us in Benjamin. When the King's guardsmen gainsay the word of the King, then who shall say whether there is any that reigns in Israel? . . .

The captain of the guard breathed heavily and stared at the ground. "We cannot do this thing," he said, "we cannot fall upon the priests of Jahveh, unarmed as they are and naked except for their loincloths. Truly, we cannot do this thing, my lord."

The King lifted both his clenched fists as though he meant to bring them down upon the young captain's head. For the space of several heart-beats the hands remained in the air, and the power of the royal house was poised with them, mighty and terrible, above the heads of all the Israelites. Then the hands faltered and came down, not clenched upon the offender, but open and flaccid at the King's sides. Saul shrugged and looked about him. His glance rested briefly upon the faces of two of the young heroes, lingered a little longer upon Paltiel, moved without pause over Abner, came to rest on the soft, sweating countenance of Doeg the Edomite.

"You," he said, "you that saw it and came to tell of it, you fall upon the priests of Nob."

It seemed to Abner that he had never seen a thing so loathsome as the face of the King's herdsman. He who had never drawn any blood save the blood of dumb beasts, he who had always crept quietly about, uttering sweet words and laying fearful fingers upon the arms of his superiors— he strove to assume a look of grave regret, but his lips trembled and his eyes shone with an irrepressible joy.

There was some question in Doeg's mind as to whether the squat altar or the twisted roots of the tamarisk would make the better execution block. He asked the opinion of the others, but received no answer. Saul stood like an image against the trunk of the tree, staring out over the edge of the precipice with glazed, unseeing eyes. Since it was plain that the King would not move, and since Doeg was afraid to spatter the royal robe with blood, he chose the altar for the place of death.

Now that there was no hope, the priests of Nob had ceased to whisper together and weep. They arranged themselves, as for some high festival, in even rows and began to chant the prayer for the dying. Without hesita-tion each of them advanced toward the altar, as if he came there merely to lay a new loaf or a dish of fruit before God. Only the children, little servants of the sanctuary, wept and whimpered, and these the high priest sent first to the altar, so that soon there were no more cries. The arm of Doeg was the arm of a butcher, and he managed the sword with great skill. The shale and lichen around the altar were stained now with a slow dripping, now with a sudden spurt of blood. Some, including the high priest Ahimelech, continued to sing after they had laid their heads upon the altar, so that their mouths were open in a chant even when their bodies had been pushed to one side upon the growing heap of dead.

The chanting grew thinner and thinner. As it lessened, Abner heard again the unseemly piping of the bird in the tamarisk tree, and this sound seemed to him an intolerable torment. He raised his hands to cover his ears, and heard another sound, the rush of torrential waters in his head. A black mist gathered before him, he swayed, and the captain of the guard sprang up to steady him. My spirit will go forth out of me, he thought, and the thought was blessed. But, before the last of the priests of Nob was slain, the darkness passed from his eyes, and he saw again the pile of bodies, the grisly heads, the naked legs thrust out at stiff angles, the hands, clenched or fallen open, the slow ooze and trickle of red. . . .

Doeg the Edomite laid his sword on the altar and came to the King, saying: "That which my lord has asked of me has been accomplished. In this as in all things I sought only to serve my lord."

Saul started then, stared long at the Edomite, and spat in his face. "Go," he said, "dog of Edom. Go to the sanctuary of Nob and take the wages of your hire. Take unto yourself and to your children and your children's children all the treasure that is laid up in the temple. And when you have taken it, go out of Israel and hide yourself in Edom, for the sight of you is as a death to me, and I would not set eyes upon your face again."

So Doeg fled out of Benjamin, and Saul went down with the guardsmen and the servants of his house to Gibeah. But Abner remained with the young heroes, laboring on the promontory until moonrise to bury the dead.

BOOK FIVE

BOOK FIVE

❧ I ❧

Aʜɪɴᴏᴀᴍ the Jezreelitess had been named in honor of the Queen of Israel. Her father had been involved in a litigation over a stretch of orchard land in the year of her birth; his cause was just, but the matter was obscure, and he was rightly convinced that he would never have gathered the fruit of his trees if Saul's wife had not interceded in his behalf. He wished to remind himself, whenever he mentioned or called the child, that he had reason for gratefulness. But the little girl was too slight, too diffident, to bear the weight of her royal name. Her mother and her eight brothers called her what she called herself; "Noi," she would say, "Noi is my name." Only the old man persisted in shouting all four of the regal syllables across the fields. And on his deathbed, when he blessed her and wished her many children, he cast a severe look at the assembled family and commended to their care "my only woman-child and your sole sister, whose name is Ahinoam after the name of the Queen of Israel, she who gave us our orchard and raised up our house from the dust."

Whenever an Israelite appeared in the sanctuary to lay an offering before God, he began the ceremony of gift-giving with an ancient formula: "My father was a wandering Aramean," he said. The purpose of this speech was to inform the Lord that the giver remembered the squalor and poverty of his beginnings, remembered how there had been a day when the whole nation was a band of migratory Bedouins, living in tents and sleeping in the stench of camels, despised in the Canaanite cities, squatting in the shadow of the forbidden walls. Certain of the children of Jahveh—and among them this Ahinoam of Jezreel—had preserved the remembrance of those desert days not in their minds only, but in their flesh. It was as if they had fallen back into the past, issuing from the womb as dark, as shy, as raw, as the children who must have clung to the skirts of Miriam when she walked behind Moses on her journey through the wilderness.

In her sixteenth year the namesake of the Queen of Israel was a wandering Aramean. Whenever she could, she ran into the wilderness, ostensibly to find certain healing roots and lucky stones, but really because of the lizards, the antelopes, and the hares. She had learned to walk so softly among the scrubby brush that the creatures of the desert seldom took fright at her presence. She taught the lizards to creep up and down her arm; she carried salt with her and fed it to the antelopes; the hares would sit quietly upon her knees, letting her run her comb through their fur. Her brothers were troubled because of her excursions. They knew her to be utterly innocent—her mother had died before she was old enough to learn the ways of men with women—and not one of them could bring himself to make the necessary explanations, although four of them had tried. Once an old woman whom she encountered in the desert had told her in coarse words that there were woman-hungry bandits about, and had given her to understand what use a bandit might have for her charms. But the talk had been so gross that she had been unable to comprehend most of it. That night at the evening meal, she had passed on to her brothers the only part of it that seemed significant: news that a horde of outcasts, banded together under a man named David, had grown weary of living near the Dead Sea and had come up to eat what meat and bread they could wrest from the farmers and herdsmen of the plains.

That was the first time she had heard the name of David. Perhaps because the person who uttered it was a hag, she had concluded at once that the outlaw was very old. Now, whenever she remembered the gnarled, scrawny, white-bearded giant whom she had conjured up in her thoughts, she smiled. For in the six months that had passed since that day, she had seen this David many times at her brothers' table. He was old—thirty is old to sixteen—but he was still supple and gallant. He was an outcast, but his manners were those of the court; he broke his bread into small pieces and made a flourish with his wrist before he poured out the wine.

She knew that the people of the plain were divided in their opinion of this exile. Some said he was a traitor to Saul and made his living like the worst of the desert rats, taking a heavy toll in crops from the farmers, who paid the required sum in fear, knowing that if they did not give it in peace it would be wrested from them in violence. Others told how he was the beloved friend of the hero Jonathan and had been driven from the court by the evil spirit that possessed the King. It was reassuring, they said, to have him and his three hundred between them and the marauders of the desert. One paid for one's safety willingly; it was a good investment; what, after all, were a couple of heifers, a basket of bread?

Her brothers were among those who paid the price cheerfully. Since four of them were soon to marry and two of them meant to go up after the Feast of the Ingathering to join the host of Jahveh in Gilgal, they were relieved that their fields, their flocks, and their precious orchard would not be left in the hands of a girl-child and two striplings. Because they were the children of a hospitable family, they considered it unseemly to pay their stipend to the comely and courtly warrior in some field or at the side of some spring, as one might pay a Canaanite. So they bade him sit once in the course of every moon at their table, and sent his hire after him with a servant when he left them, as though he had been one of their town cousins whom they could not permit to depart without some gift for the other relatives at home. Then, inasmuch as they enjoyed his company, they asked him to come up from his encampment on feast days or when they had slain a kid or were about to open the first skin of the new wine.

In the beginning, Noi seldom thought of the visitor himself. Her mind was occupied rather with the changes that he had wrought in their lives. Before his coming, they had been silent and abstracted; now the conversation around the table often rose to a roar. In the old days they had seldom eaten meat and had opened a wineskin only on a few fixed occasions. Now the spit behind the house often carried a crackling load, and the bowls were filled less often with water than with wine. For the first time in her life, she was allowed her little bowlful. The nape of her neck would grow warm and damp beneath the weight of her braid; moisture would rise on her cheeks and arms; and above the smell of the food she would sense the scent of her own flesh, disturbing and sweet. Under the red moon she would sit on the roof of the house with the rest of them, listening to the courtly talk—such talk as she had never heard before.

She listened most ardently on those occasions when the talk dealt with the adventures of the exiled Bethlehemite. She thought of him now as a beloved uncle, a mother's brother who is dearer than a father, since he is relieved of the duties of discipline and appears only in the glow of festivals with a garland on his head. On those mornings which followed the feasting, she would rise early, dazed with the need for more sleep and the fumes of last night's wine; she would go slowly about the business of setting the house in order; she would take up his plate, his cup, and fall into a dream. She had not yet outgrown the childish habit of turning yesterday's events into a tale which became the more real if she said it aloud. "He was born in Bethlehem," she would say, filling the basin with water and immersing the dishes. "He was the youngest as I am the youngest, and he lived in the hills and kept his father's sheep."

Now that she had begun to tell herself these stories, she stared at him whenever he was in the house so that she might have a clearer image to move through the pageantry of her dreams. She came to the conclusion that—for a man of his advanced years—he was unusually handsome. His body was long, supple, hard. His skin, turned to the color of cedarwood by the desert sun, had not lost its delicacy; when he leaned over the lamp, one saw the blue veins, the fine structure of the bones. His hair was a luxuriant, reddish mass of waves. It hung loose to his shoulders and took on coppery lights when he stood in the sun. His beard was short and pointed. His was an arresting face, manly and self-possessed. But the eyes gainsaid the easy smile and negated the long gold earring that hung jauntily from his left ear. The eyes were gray, somber as the bottom of a cistern in the cold light of early morning.

Now that she had glimpsed grief in his look, she searched him for other talismans of sorrow. There was a scar on his wrist, and once she asked him whether he had come by it in battle. No, he said, he had inflicted it upon himself; he had opened his wrist to take into his own body a little of the blood of a beloved friend; and she knew that this friend was Jonathan. Twice he had brought his lute up from the encampment and had sung strange songs to them under the feverish moon, and then it had seemed to her that there was a bitter core in the sweetness of his voice. As the months passed, she dwelt more and more upon his misfortunes, hoarding his words in her thoughts until her mind became a book of the sorrows of David.

"Lie still and let me comb your fur and listen to the story of my unfortunate uncle," she would say to the tame hare that lay across her knees. "He was married to the Queen's child, the most beautiful of all the daughters of Israel. He slew two hundred Philistines for her sake and loved her so that she grew like a healing herb in the flesh of his heart. But then the hand of the King of Israel fell heavy upon him, and he was cast forth into the wilderness. And while he dwelt by the shore of the salty sea, among the lizards and the lions, one came to him and said, 'The King has given her to Paltiel, who dwells with her now in the high house where you dwelt together long ago.' Then it was as though the healing herb had been torn from the heart of my uncle. Therefore, hare, should you come to his encampment while he sleeps, walk quietly, lest he waken and weep."

Or she would address a young lizard, asking him where were his father and mother and how it was that, being so weak and small, he crept about alone. "It is possible," she would say, "that all lizards are orphans, for I have never seen a small lizard crawling by the side of a large one. But if that is the case, do not grieve too greatly. I also am an orphan. As to my uncle the bandit, he has a mother and a father, but he has not set eyes upon them these twelve years. In the days of his bitterness, he sent his brother Eliab to take them from Bethlehem into Moab, lest the anger of Saul should fall upon them. Even then they were old, and they and their eldest have tarried long in a strange country. It is for this reason that his eyes are sorrowful when he looks toward the purple hills of Moab. He thinks how he is not by them to chop the meat for their toothless mouths and how his hand will not close their eyes when they are dead."

Once in her weekly round of cleaning she found and destroyed a spider web. When she saw the affrighted creature scurrying back and forth, she stepped back in horror at the thought that she had left a living creature without a home. For David also was homeless, had been driven out of Gibeah into the town of Keilah, a little Israelite settlement on the border of the wilderness. And even here, in the wretched mud-brick houses, he had not been permitted to find his peace. Saul had sent an army down against him, and, afraid that he might be taken within the gates, he had gone to wander roofless in the wilderness. In that bald country he had come upon a cave called Adullam, a many-chambered cavern in the rocks, where he and his company might stack their arms and store their provisions. But the host of Saul had scented him even there and driven him forth again. Now he avoided all places that could be encircled by an army, and he slept with his cheek against his shield and his sword in his hand. Once he had said to the two of her brothers who were going to join Jahveh's host, "I will see you when you come down against me next spring." The two young men had turned crimson, but he had taken the matter lightly, laughing and laying his arms about their shoulders. "Only," he had said, still laughing, "if we meet in battle, aim the spear at my chest. I have no fear of dying, but it sets my teeth on edge to think of a wound in the face."

There was one chapter in the history of his sorrows which she had not learned directly from his lips. It was the story of the burden of sin that was upon him. She had heard it by chance in the market place one day when she had gone up to barter fleece for oil. Two men were conversing behind her; she listened covertly because one of them had said the Bethlehemite's name.

"I paid him in honey for the most part," the first man said. "He knew that there was a blight upon my vineyard, and he was reasonable and did not demand either raisins or wine. I do not haggle with him; it is not worth the trouble. In the days before he stood between us and the marauders of the desert, we lost even more. Let him have his honey—it is little enough, I am content."

"But," said the second man, "whatever we put into his mouth is an affront to Jahveh. It is not the measure of wheat and the cruet of oil that I regret. It is that I feed the one whose hands are red with the blood of the priests of Nob."

She set her basket of fleece on the ground and pretended that there were stones in her sandals. She took them off and shook them and made a long business of getting them fastened again. Meanwhile she heard the story of the lie that was told for the sake of bread and a sword. "For his sake, fourscore fell at the altar above Gibeah," the farmer said. "The blood of the anointed is on his hands. The mark of Cain the murderer is on his brow."

On the following evening, when he came to them again, she waited until the conversation turned to the matter of a sickness which had stricken one of his comrades, and then she asked him whether there were any priests of Jahveh with him in the encampment, to make proper dispositions for the sick and the dead.

"Yes," he said, grown suddenly grave, "there is one with us who is of the house of Eli, a certain Abiathar, the son of Ahimelech—that Ahimelech who was once high priest at the sanctuary of Nob."

"And how is it that his father permitted him to leave the sanctuary and go into the wilderness?"

Before he answered, he closed his eyes. "He has no father. There is no sanctuary. Nob was ravaged long ago by Doeg the Edomite. All the house of Eli, save only Abiathar, are dead."

From that time forth, whenever she cleaned a kid for the table she would see his guilty, suffering face. And she, who had always loathed the sight of blood, would dip her hands deep into the basin and stare at her fingers and smear a little of the blood on her forehead, between her eyes. "The blood of the anointed is on my hands," she would say to herself. "The mark of Cain the murderer is upon my brow."

⊷§ II §⊶

IT WAS STRANGE, thought the son of Zeruiah, that the son of Jesse, who looked so mild, so tractable, should carry at the core of him a piece of stubbornness as hard as diorite. For months on end, there would be no disagreement as to the amount of the tributes or the manner of collecting them, no difficulty over the disciplinary methods to be taken with the vagabonds who made up the band. The hand that Joab loved would fall often upon his shoulder. The gray eyes would wink at him in council. Then, without warning and for the most stupid reasons, the dear uncle would draw himself up to the height of a Canaanite god and revile his nephew in the language of Saul's court, and would go off to some other part of the camp to consort with Abiathar the priest, or Abishai, or some other fool. These spells of lofty rage came upon him because he refused to realize that Joab knew what was to his advantage better than he knew himself. There was, for example, the time when Joab said to him that certain of the band were too old or too sick to be dragged up from the cave of Adullam into the plain. It would be better to leave them in the cavern; they could fend for themselves. The words had no sooner fallen from his mouth than he had reason to regret them. The son of Jesse had spat upon the ground, contemplatively, neatly, so that the spittle had fallen precisely between Joab's feet. Then, without answering, he had walked away. So it had been also when Joab had said that it might be possible to carry on trade with the city of Gath. "Philistia," David had said, turning his back, "is the hereditary enemy of every decent son of God."

Now he had incurred the wrath of his dear uncle again, this time because he had gone down by night and burned the field of a farmer who had refused to pay the price. He had set the field afire not out of any wanton impulse to destruction—indeed, it grieved him to see the flames eating so much sturdy grain—but to teach the villagers a lesson. When David heard of the matter, he went into an icy rage. "Dog and son of a dog," he said, "you have made me into a rat of the desert. Now get from this country and stay from it for seven days, for if none of the farmers fall upon you, I will be tempted to do so myself." So there had been nothing to do but to go forth out of the encampment, leaving his dear uncle in the company of Abishai, who was the favorite of the hour. And this ascent of Abishai was more painful to Joab than his own disgrace. He brooded upon it during his whole journey down to the sea.

He had brought it upon himself, he thought. He need never have invited his great hulking fool of a brother Abishai into David's encampment. But what was one to do with such a hairy jackass, a bad farmer and a wretched tradesman, good for nothing but chopping heads with a sword? Because the brain is softened by family feeling, there had been tender letters, and Abishai had come down from Bethlehem to hang like a millstone around his brother's neck. He had a talent for looking foolish; his body was large and muscular, and his head was too small—the shaggy, powerful length of him was topped with the round, rosy, ringleted head of a child. And embarrassment was transformed into bitterness when the son of Jesse took a fancy to the new recruit, waited patiently for him to wind out his stupid comments in council, and trusted him with important missions. It was true that in the most significant matters Joab was consulted; in the band, Joab held a position comparable to Abner's place in the host of God. Nevertheless, David was never at odds with Abishai and often at odds with Joab. And it was a heavy business to think that the two of them were together while he wandered off alone. "I will go down to Gath," he told himself; and he took the road to the coast.

Since the journey was long, he broke it by spending the night in the little town of Ziklag, an outpost citadel where the Seren of Gath kept a garrison to guard against possible incursions by the Amalekites. It was a clean town, walled and solid, with a decent house for sojourners. But Joab was uneasy in it. A sleepy, unwholesome, heavy-hearted atmosphere pervaded the place. The women were weary of the warriors, and the warriors were weary of the world. Ten years had passed since the Amalekites had ventured up against Philistia. There was no reason to expect another battle; men had grown old in the service there without staining their swords. Some of them took to games of chance, and others took to drinking. They grew irascible, were easily offended, often brawled with each other; and when they brawled, the whole population would surge into the streets and watch the spectacle with feverish eyes. They welcomed a traveler as the inhabitants of Sheol might welcome a breathing presence from the upper world. Joab had not been in Ziklag for more than an hour when he was invited to drink a cup of wine with a young captain who was standing guard that night on the western side of the fortress wall.

From the top of the bastion, broad and flat and draped for the young captain's comfort with a rug of plaited reeds, one could see a stretch of wilderness—stubble and sand and pebbles turned red in the light of the declining sun—a bar of pale beach, and a line of whiteness that proved by its constant undulations to be the sea. The wind came in from the coast, smelling of salt and seaweed. The silence was burdensome, and Joab fell to praising the wind and the wine. He was annoyed to find that he was paying excessive compliments; and yet he could not help himself, for there was something in the cool, alien face of the Philistine that made him uneasy. The man had the sinewy softness of a cat and never ceased to stare into his face with yellowish, feline eyes.

"No, now, let us talk no more of the wind and the wine. To me they are everyday matters," the young captain said. "Let my honored guest tell me where he dwells in Israel and describe for me the wonders of the city of his birth. Was he born in Shechem, where there is an oak that speaks with the voice of a man? Was he born in Gilgal, where the giants threw up a great circle of black stones?"

"In neither," said Joab curtly, believing that his host had heard the in-glorious accents of Judah in his speech and wished to put him in his place. "I was born in Bethlehem."

At the mention of Bethlehem, the eyes of the Philistine seemed actually to glow, as a lion's eyes glow in a thicket by night. "In the city of David? Then you are of the company that dwells in the wilderness with the hero?" he said.

"The hero is my uncle. I am the captain of his band."

"No, now, not truly?" said his host. "Not David's nephew and the captain of his band?" And he stretched his sleek arms above his head in satisfaction. Then suddenly, as though he wished to hide his gratification at the knowledge that he entertained so notable a guest, he began to speak of other things. But he seemed preoccupied with some pressing business, and paused often, staring steadily at the wavering, distant line of foam.

As the red light withdrew from the wilderness, as the wind fell and the stifling heat of the night settled upon them, this abstraction on the part of the captain began to breed uneasiness in the visitor. Darkness blotted out the surrounding countryside, and it seemed to Joab that he sat on the edge of nothingness with an alien at his side. The talk of the Philistine grew more and more disconnected and vague. It is possible, thought Joab, that he is drunk; but he remembered with increasing dis-quiet that, since the moment when he had made himself known, his host had barely touched the wine. "On fine days," said the young captain, "one can see the palace of Achish from this side of the wall. . . ." Suddenly Joab was possessed by an acute restlessness. He felt that he could not sit still for the space of another heartbeat. He rose and stretched and took two steps forward in the dark. All at once, like a lion pouncing out of the thicket, the Philistine was upon him. The sleek, sinuous arms closed around his middle; the long body pressed against his back; he could not catch his breath. God of Israel, he thought, this uncircumcised demon is going to throw me down from the wall! But before he could cry out, the violent embrace had turned almost tender. "No, now," said the Philis-tine, laughing in embarrassment, "it is not safe to wander in darkness on the edge of such a wall. One step more, and my illustrious guest might have fallen to his death on the pavement below."

But nothing could wash from Joab's mind the conviction of evil intent that he had had when the arms of the young captain closed around him.

When he lifted his bowl of wine, his hands shook. He thought now only of putting an end to the occasion. He yawned repeatedly, to indicate that he wished to go down to his bed. But his companion began to spin out a tale concerning a Canaanite woman, and embroidered every incident with so much detail that it became oppressively plain that he was using all his wits to keep his visitor beside him. "The sister of this same woman," he said, "is also notorious for her looseness. She—that is, the sister—was for a time the mistress of the nephew of Achish, the Seren of Gath. . . ."

"Of Gath?" said Joab, seeing a means of escape. "But, now that you speak of Gath, I am reminded that, with more regret than I have words to express, I must tear myself from your company. I am on my road to Gath, and if I am to reach the city by noon tomorrow, I must go down now and refresh myself with a little sleep."

"Gath?" said the captain. "You are going down to Gath?"

"Even so."

"Tomorrow?"

"Tomorrow."

There was a long silence then. Joab sensed that the feline and sinister presence was making calculations, weighing possibilities.

"But surely that is most fortunate. My servant also is setting out for Gath tomorrow to carry certain communications to my lord Achish. He will show you the way."

If I refuse the offer, Joab thought, it is possible that he will fall upon me again. I will tell him to send his servant to me at such and such an hour, and long before his servant comes I will have gone forth alone. . . .

"My host is generous," he said. "At what hour shall I await the servant of my host?"

"At whatever hour seems best to the son of Jahveh."

"After the morning meal, if it please the son of Dagon."

"Certainly. A very convenient hour."

"And now," he said, "if my host will lead me to the stairs, I will go down and sleep."

"Surely, surely." The soft and powerful hand closed upon his upper arm, raised him, drew him along the parapet, and continued to hold him at the head of the stairs. "I envy my guest the sights he will see when he comes into Gath, which is the city of my birth. Let the son of Jahveh bespeak me if he chances upon the street of the sellers of mussels, where I was born. . . ."

But on that journey Joab did not set eyes upon the street of the mussel-sellers. As he had planned, he rose in the night and made his way westward, alone and in darkness, led only by the starlit line of the sea. He could not find the highway. He wandered too far to the south; and he came to the city of Gath, hungry and bedraggled, when the day of his setting-out was almost spent. He was feverish with wandering in the sun, and, when he saw standing beside the sentry at the gates of Gath one who seemed alarmingly like the young captain, he told himself, **It is a** fever dream, it could not possibly be he. . . .

It was then that the captain and the sentry and a crowd of other soft and sinewy bodies fell upon him. They bound his hands, but gently, so that the flesh should not be cut by the ropes; in fact, they treated his person with a strange mingling of force and courtesy. They marched him between two files of plumed men through the streets of the town. He could see neither to the right nor to the left because of the towering shoulders on either side. "Let the son of Jahveh have no fear," the young captain said. "We are taking him to the palace of my lord Achish, where he will be given meat and bread." And they led him up a splendid staircase and through a long colonnade, and left him alone in a little room against whose windowless walls he could hear the breaking of the sea.

◆§ III §◆

A⊤ FIRST his terror made the little chamber in which they had left him the most loathsome place in the world. He hated its blank walls of polished gray stone. He hated the graceful couch, curved at the head like a swan's neck and covered with a piece of fine white stuff embroidered, in honor of the god Dagon, in ears of wheat. He hated the low table beside the couch and the delicate, boat-shaped lamp that burned upon it and the copper plate of unclean food—figs and a breast of roast fowl, two flat cakes of bread, six purplish olives and a heathenish little cake marked, like the stuff on the couch, with a bearded stalk of grain. But after a while his fright wore away into sheer weariness. He stretched his body on the couch, he spread the fine linen napkin across his chest, and beginning with the olives and ending with the unholy cake, he ate the food of the uncircumcised. He was finishing the meal when the door swung open. A manservant entered and made a low obeisance. "With the permission of the son of Jahveh," he said, "I will lead him now to my master, Achish, the Seren of Gath."

On his way through the long colonnades, Joab saw that night had come. There was no light save the light of the lamps, some hanging from brazen chains, some set in niches along the left-hand wall. On his right hand there was no wall, only a line of heavy columns; between them he could see a milky veil of stars, a crescent moon, a white beach, and the wavering line of foam. They stopped at a great brazen door ornamented with raised figures of women whose bodies converged at the waist into scaly tails. It stood open and threw a beam of light athwart the hall.

"Here, my lord, is the son of Jahveh," the servant said, motioning Joab into the room.

"So?" said a weary voice speaking from the other end of the chamber near a wide window. "Well, leave him with me and go and close the door."

The room was so vast that the furniture—the couches and tables and chairs—was like islands in an expanse of sea. The gray stone of the walls, the white stone of the floor, had been brought to such a polish that the seven lamps which burned in the room were multiplied. Yellow reflections of their flames leaped in the burnished grayness on either side of him and in the pink-veined whiteness under his feet. Bits of copper, too—polished plates and urns, spear tips and shields—made light and ghosts of light all around him. He stood staring like an ignorant Calebite.

"Is the son of Jahveh afraid?" the voice at the window said. "There is no reason for fear. Let the nephew of David come forward that we may drink together and talk a little. After we have spoken I will lay in the hands of the son of Jahveh a gift for his illustrious uncle, and send him forth in peace."

Well, thought Joab, if that is how all this will end, I will enjoy myself. . . . The vast chamber took on a distinctly festive air. The Seren of Gath, who had been sitting at the window opening on a stretch of rolling, starlit water, rose now from a carved chair, and smiled. Another chair had been set close to his, and between the two was a lamp on a table, flickering in the gusts blown in from the sea. "Come and sit," the Seren said; and he moved close to the lamp with courteous deliberateness. It was as though he had said aloud, "I will not confuse you with shadows. Behold my face." But the proffered countenance was alien and disturbing; the head looked at first glance like a sphere of blue-veined marble into which had been set a startling pair of blue glass eyes.

"God be with Achish," Joab said, sinking into the empty chair.

"With Joab also."

The voice had an almost feminine ring. The Israelite looked again and saw a pale aristocrat, bald and fifty, cool and clean-shaven. The eyes protruded a little and were rimmed in red. The nose was sharp and straight, and there was a touch of red also in the arched nostrils. The mouth was gentle, and the chin beneath it was round and full. The soft underpart of the chin was too white.

"I hear that you sojourned in Ziklag," said the Seren, as though there had been no violence there. "It is a very sturdy little city. Did the son of Jahveh notice the thickness of the walls?"

"Yes," said Joab, puzzled at the turn in the conversation. "They are very sound walls."

Achish bent toward the table, tipped a black-and-white cruet, and filled two exquisite bowls with a light and fragrant wine. His hands were white, veined, and speckled, laden with copper rings on which appeared the wheat of Dagon and the serpent of Astarte. His body showed through the fine linen of his tunic—a soft body, sagging with good eating and drinking.

"How is it with your illustrious uncle? Was he in good health when you left him?" he said.

Joab stifled the flow of phrases that rippled at his lips, sipped his wine, and said only, "In good health, my lord."

"And his wives and children and all the members of his house?"

"My uncle is childless. He has no wife save only Michal whom Saul has given to Paltiel, much to my uncle's sorrow. . . ." He stopped. A keen, thoughtful look had transformed the glassy eyes. He wished that he had held his tongue.

The Seren of Gath made a clucking sound of sympathy. "Indeed," he said, "that was a very sorry business. Surely there will not be peace again between David and him who has taken a beloved wife and given her to another."

Joab shifted uneasily in his chair. These veined and speckled hands, this weary and intelligent face, belonged to one who had led thousands into the plains of Sharon, sowing death in the ranks of God. And now the melancholy tenor voice had implied a troubling proposition: Since Philistia is the enemy of Saul, and Saul is the enemy of David, David and Philistia are not enemies.

"Surely the son of Jesse will take another wife," said Achish, "the seed of such as he——"

"I have taken a vow before Jahveh to speak no more concerning my uncle." His voice was too loud and coarse for the occasion. "I have learned that to speak of him is to bring misfortune upon him."

The Seren smiled. "Certainly," he said. "It is a wise vow, since your illustrious uncle is ringed about with enemies. I would not for the price of ten cities ask the nephew of the sweet singer to break his vow. Nor did I bring him here that he might speak of David. I know without asking how it is with David—that there are three hundred with him, and that he has gone up to the open plain and eats such food as is given to him by the herdsmen and farmers. All this I know. I brought Joab to my palace that he might bear such words as I have to say to David—words which, I assure the son of Jahveh, are the words of a friend, spoken from the heart." The Seren leaned forward and sought Joab's look with his alien, prominent eyes. Then he turned away abruptly and sent his glance over the length and breadth of the room. "The son of Jahveh sees how it is with us here in Gath," he said. "Let him remember this palace and give an account of it to his uncle when he returns to the plain."

"Wherefore?"

"That David may know that Gath is a wealthy city whose treasury is filled with rings of copper and rings of gold. Nor do our riches come to us from such uncertain enterprises as wars or raids upon the Canaanites. The soil has made us great, and the soil is with us forever. Year after year we gather the wheat in the plains of Sharon and load it upon our flat-bottomed boats and sell it at a profitable price to the people of Phoenicia and the people of the isles." He bent forward again and laid his white hand upon Joab's hand, and Joab was shamed to see the big knuckles thrusting crudely from his own spatulate fingers, the dark crescents under his own nails, the calluses and the scars. "Whosoever takes his hire from Gath has no need to go begging among the people of the plain for a little ragged wool, a bit of miserable meat."

Joab drew his hand back from the unclean touch. The old anger of the desert had blown hot within him, the bitter anger of the houseless wanderer in the presence of the soft, pale trader who jingles his coins in the safety of his walls. "We are not hungry," he said in a rough voice. "We are well fed."

"Not hungry, surely." The voice was conciliatory. "Certainly, well fed. But is not the Star of Bethlehem the first among the Israelites? Should he not walk in sandals of doeskin and sleep on pillows of fine linen and eat such food as is laid before the children of the House of Kish? What is there to prevent your illustrious uncle from living, not well, but magnificently?"

Nothing, thought Joab, but certain bonds. Bonds between David and Jonathan, bonds between David and God. He sat stiffly in the curved seat and stared at his knuckles and held his tongue.

"No, now," said Achish, "it seems I have given offense. But let the son of Jahveh believe that no offense was meant, that I spoke out of ignorance, being unacquainted with the manners of the country of my guest. When Joab carries my words back to his uncle, I trust that he will make them acceptable to his uncle's ears."

The veined hand took up the bowls and filled them to the brim. Joab sipped his wine and could not tell whether the audience was ended. The Seren of Gath sighed and ran his palm over the polished dome of his brow.

"The son of Jahveh, they tell me, saw what there was to be seen in Ziklag," he said.

"I saw the town and the walls. He who betrayed me into your hands—he drank with me on top of the wall."

"Must the nephew of David consider it betrayal? Has he not been used in the palace of Achish as an honored guest? I promised five rings of gold to any man who would give me the pleasure of the sight of his face. If there was some fear and some discomfort for the son of Jahveh, let him erase the matter from his thoughts. He will not go forth from my palace without gifts. Also, I have made a bed for him that he may rest beneath my roof this night, and I have brought up into the room in which he will sleep three young women, very fair, from the temple of Astarte. Let him remember only our talk and their embraces and forget the rest. Now, concerning Ziklag——"

Why, thought Joab, must he forever harp upon that town?

"Did the son of Jahveh observe the thickness of the walls?"

"Yes," he said wearily. "They are, as I mentioned earlier to the Seren, very good walls."

"Commend these walls to David tomorrow when you are with him in the open wilderness. For years they have shut out from my borders the marauders of the south. Whosoever is behind them is secure, even though Saul should send six thousand against him."

"Saul?" said Joab. "Wherefore should Saul come down against Ziklag? Were he to come at all, he would come against Gath."

"Where David is," said the Seren, "there will Saul come. And were Saul to come down and find David in the wilderness, then would the brave three hundred perish and the bright shoot of the House of Jesse be cut off in the summer of his years. But were Saul to come down, even with six thousand, and find the Star of Bethlehem established within the walls of Ziklag——"

Joab started up in amazement.

The Seren smiled. "Say to your illustrious uncle that I will give him the fortress of Ziklag. Say also that I will send him such supplies as I send the garrison now stationed there. Tell him that, in addition to this, I will pay him regularly, on the day of the new moon, thirty rings of copper and five rings of gold. Also, I will furnish his house and the house of his captain with such things as the son of Jahveh sees here about him, nor will I be tightfisted in any matter, nor will I require that the Star of Bethlehem should call me lord. Let him call me friend only, and come to dwell with his three hundred in my fortress, that I may draw from it my weary men and send them to fight upon some other field. . . ."

To fight, thought Joab, against the host of Jahveh, when Saul comes up to Sharon after the winter rains. . . .

"What," said Achish, "is there to bind David to the Benjamites?"

Nothing, thought Joab, save only Jahveh and Jonathan. . . .

"Tell him these things from me. Tell him also to take another wife, that his children and my children may visit in one another's palaces in the days to come, when there will be everlasting peace between Philistia and Israel." He rose and smiled. "My servant will bring the gift tomorrow when you depart, having refreshed yourself with sleep and with delight," he said. "Send to me, if you can, some word as to how the Star of Bethlehem receives the offer that I have sent him. A servant waits beyond the door to lead you to the chamber that is prepared for you. May the gods of your land and my land give you a joyous night!"

The servant stood in the dim hall, respectfully waiting. The old loathing, hot as the blasting wind of the desert, rose again in Joab. Cursed be the guts and the liver of the Philistines! he thought. He had half a mind to laugh in the servant's face and to leap between the columns onto the beach and lose himself and the whole unclean business in the blackness of the night. But there were the gifts, there were the temple women, there was the city of Ziklag—a very solid town with excellent walls. . . .

"Will the son of Jahveh go up to his chamber?" asked the servant.

"Go, I will follow," Joab said.

❧ IV ❧

On the second day of Joab's absence, David began to regret that he had sent him forth. It was Joab's ability to lie to himself that David missed. When Joab walked with him across the hill country of Judah, everything was well. Joab saw the fruitful areas, the vineyards and the orchards; Joab exaggerated the size of the flocks and turned every wandering heifer into a herd. And now that Joab had departed in anger, the bald truth thrust itself to the surface. The hill country of Judah was a land of dry water-courses and barren knolls, a land where the sour earth sent up, for the most part, only such dry and prickly weeds as would lie indigestible in the belly of a sheep. It could not support the families that had had the misfortune to be born upon it—to say nothing of three hundred freebooters come up from the south, men who raised nothing, but lived solely by the sword.

The second day of Joab's absence from the encampment had been a day of brooding and wandering about. Now, with the coming-on of night, his uneasiness had intensified to the point where he no longer cared to listen or speak. The evening meal was finished. He had forced himself to eat, and what he had eaten was like a stone pressing beneath his heart. Those who had broken bread with him had gone, to his relief, to take up the night watch upon the ridge of the hill. He stood over the dying embers for a long time, trying to decide whether he should go down to Hebron or rekindle the fire. Then he knew that he would do neither. He was sick of Hebron and sick of the camp. He would go up to the house of the Jezreelites, the eight brothers and their sister Noi, and forget his foreboding in high talk and wine. He tarried only long enough to find a pair of earrings that he meant to give to Noi. She was a child, and he took pleasure in bringing her such small surprises as delight a child.

Halfway between the encampment and the dwelling-place of his friends stood a certain house that roused his anger every time he passed it—a big, sprawling structure, half of sun-dried brick, half of stone, heavy and ostentatious, circled round with a low wall. It was the house of a certain herdsman called Nabal, whose name in the countryside was only a little lower than the names of the angels. This Nabal owned half the sheep between here and Hebron; his vineyards were the most fruitful in the district; his land was watered by abundant springs. All the village families were bound to him in one way or another. Servants who had been discharged from his house came home to tell that he was squat and ugly, given to violent fits of rage, often in a state of drunkenness, and likely at any moment to smash a lamp against the wall. Nevertheless, he was not lacking in friends. Tonight, as usual, there were lamps on the sills and torches in the garden. From one of the lower rooms a dozen male voices bawled out a stupid song. David walked more slowly to catch the words, knowing that their stupidity would aggravate his rage, but wanting to hear them nevertheless. Suddenly he forgot the song and stood still, looking over the uneven row of stones at the top of the low wall. A woman had appeared at the nearest window. She stood above the lamp, looking out into what she thought was an empty night.

She was a beautiful woman, broad-hipped and full-bosomed. Her face was of that waxen, faintly golden quality that makes the light upon it seem rather to be coming from within. She was a little heavy, and her eyelids were so full that they seemed to be drooping in the beginnings of sleep. But her ripeness was the tender ripeness of a late summer fig; it would yield sweetly to the touch. Her garments proclaimed the wealth of her husband a little too blatantly. The blue robe, the scarlet girdle, the bracelets that covered her forearms, the heavy earrings that swung against her round cheeks, and the rings that sank into her soft white fingers would have been considered garish at the court of the King of Israel. Yet they pleased the solitary watcher. He thought of lifting the weight of all that finery from her; he thought of the full, waxen body set free; and he leaned against the wall and drew a deep breath.

It seemed to him that a sorrowful look changed her face, and he saw that she was no longer young. Thirty, he thought, perhaps thirty-five, perhaps even forty, ripened by understanding, holding in that golden flesh the stored knowledge of all the subtleties of love. . . . A voice called from the bright chamber, saying "Abigail," and he knew by the slow turn of her head that she had heard her own name. She turned indolently then and walked back into the yellow glare. She bore her weight so lightly that her body seemed to float across the floor.

He stood for a long time, listening to the merrymaking and chewing a bitter leaf that he had plucked from a vine on the wall. The loneliness of the outcast was with him again—such loneliness as he had felt in the camp of God before Saul had lifted him up. Well, he thought, I will go to my companions. We will make as much noise together as any gaudy crowd of howling Judahites. . . . But he was weary, and his spirit was heavy within him, and he knew that he would make no noise at all until he had filled himself with wine.

At that point in his journey where he usually caught sight of the lighted windows, he saw only dark. There was not so much as a torch thrust into the soft earth of the terrace. He stood in the pasture, breathing rapidly and staring at the house, telling himself that surely some lamp would be kindled soon, surely one of the familiar voices would sound across the night. He put his hand into his girdle and felt the earrings that he had brought for Noi. He was filled with a disproportionate sense of slight that he had come bearing gifts, and they had gone forth on some business about which they had told him nothing. Well, he thought, I will leave the earrings on the table that they have set upon the terrace. She will find them tomorrow and know who brought them, and she will be sorry that they all went forth without me.

He crossed the pasture and started up the crumbling slope of the terrace. As he felt about for the table, his hand brushed against something yielding, something soft, and the stillness was broken by a cry. It was the little Jezreelitess. He was startled, and it was a moment before he could find breath to say, "No, now, Noi, be not afraid. It is only I."

"David?"

"Where are your brothers? How is it that you sit alone in the dark?"

"They are gone forth," she said in an uneasy voice. "They are gone forth to Nabal's house, because Nabal is celebrating the tenth year of his marriage this night. Since our dear friend was not also bidden to the feast, they did not mention the matter in his presence, lest it should cause him grief. . . ."

It is a sorry business, he thought, that I who sat at Saul's feet in Gibeah should be grieved that they have not called me to a vulgar country feast. It is a sorry business that I, who never blushed before any man save Jonathan, should feel my blood mount to my temples in mortification before this child. . . .

"So?" he said. "Then no doubt it was their voices that I heard from the road before Nabal's house, braying with the tongues of donkeys, singing some stupid song."

She made no reply.

Her stillness provoked him. "And you?" he said. "Why did they not take you with them to the great feast? Is it that all the women who are there are like to her whom I saw standing at the window, ripe for love-making, like figs that have fallen of their own will from the bough? Had they no use for a little green apricot who would fall asleep early and take up a bed that might otherwise be put to better use?"

He felt that the night had grown charged between them. He put up his hand and snatched at a cobweb that had fallen, soft and tantalizing, across his lips.

"Let my friend and the friend of my brothers cease to taunt me concerning my unripeness. I will grow ripe in good time," she said, sending up to him the stir of her breath. "Nor did I remain behind because I was not bidden to the feasting. I was bidden, but I refused."

"Wherefore?"

"Because that house which is too high for the Bethlehemite is too high for me also. I have taken a vow to enter no house save those whose thresholds have been blessed by David's feet. Furthermore, I have no need of the wine of Nabal. All through the evening I have sat upon the terrace, enjoying my own feast."

He was touched by her loyalty, and reached through the darkness and patted her cheek, and gently put aside a loose strand of her hair. "Since your brothers have gone forth," he said, "I also will get hence. I will come again another night." He waited for some courteous answer, but there was no word, no movement. Suddenly his fingers came upon the bits of copper and glass under his girdle. "But wait, I have brought a gift for my friend. Let me lay it in her hand before I depart."

"A gift? For me?"

He thought ruefully that in this, at least, he had not been disappointed. She had uttered the delighted cry of a child.

"But do not give me my gift in darkness," she said. "Come with me into the house, and we will take a twig from the hearth and kindle a lamp."

A nameless uneasiness pervaded him. The house behind him was no longer the familiar place to whose shelves he went to find his own dishes, from whose hearth he had often pulled the flat cakes of bread. Was it the darkness and emptiness that made the place alive with disturbing possibilities? "It is nothing, it is only a little gift," he said. "Let Noi keep it by her here on the terrace and look at it when her brothers have returned. It is not worth the trouble of making a light."

"No, now, it is no trouble to make a light. But if David would know the truth of the matter, I dare not go in alone. I am afraid. They have never before left me here by night."

He laughed. "Well, come then," he said, "we will go in together, and I will walk through all the rooms before I depart, to make certain that there are neither ghosts nor demons nor robbers nor lovers about."

She walked a little before him. "Bring the cruet with you," she said.

"No." He pushed her gently. His palm touched her bare, cool shoulder. "Noi has had enough wine for this night."

The fire within had sunk to a mound of pale ashes. He found a twig in the bundle of broken boughs on the hearth and kindled it. It sizzled and filled the room with a yellowish glow.

"Where is the lamp?" he said.

"Here."

She stood before him on the hearth, holding out the saucer of oil. He was utterly still while the twig kept burning closer to his fingers, for he saw that she was dressed only in the white shift in which she went to bed. Its simplicity bespoke the nakedness beneath it. There were no folds, no girdle, to hide the outline of the long, slight legs, the childish hips, the small, high breasts. Her skin looked warm and sweetly dark against the whiteness. Her big braids, hanging straight down over her shoulders, were startlingly black. At the end of these braids, below the strips of cloth that bound them, the hair escaped in short, glossy clusters of curls.

He started because the flame had licked upward to his fingertips. He held the twig to the wick until it burned steadily, then dropped the end and stamped out the remains of the fire. "Seeing that Noi is arrayed for sleep," he said in a voice which was harsher than he had intended, "let her go up to her bed."

"But David spoke of a gift——"

In the yellow light of the lamp he saw, as if for the first time, the unobtrusive loveliness of her face. He knew suddenly that her hair grew down into a peak in the middle of her brow, that her temples were delicate indentations, that her mouth—a little too wide for perfect beauty—was closed in a firm line upon the sweet, wine-scented breath within. And yet there was about that face, at once marring and increasing its charm, a certain hungry and baffled look. The large eyes which stared at him over the lamp were such eyes as he had seen in the faces of waifs who came up to the encampment to beg. He found that he was weary and thought that it would be well to rest a little in her company before setting out again. He drew the earrings from his girdle, closing his hand upon them. "Come, take them from me," he said, holding out his fist. He had seen her brothers tease her in this fashion, making her open their fingers for a bauble or a sweet.

She came to him and began to pull at his fingers, but he noticed that she was struggling with him only in a halfhearted fashion. She stood as far off from him as possible, plainly taking care that her shift should not brush his knees. At last she flushed and dropped her hands. "No," she said, breathing more heavily than the small skirmish warranted. "You must give me my present, or I will not get it at all."

Something—perhaps the unexpected collapse of the game—thrust him back into his old aching state. How is it, he asked himself, turning from her, that I have permitted myself to play the fool? How could I make merry with her when she has pitied me that I was not called up to Nabal's feast? And why is it that she holds herself aloof from me as though there were some uncleanness upon me? . . . "What is it that troubles Noi?" he said. "Is it an offense to her nostrils that I have not bathed and anointed myself with oil to stand in her presence tonight?"

She straightened her drooping shoulders and thrust out her chin, and this change in posture gave to her frail body a surprising measure of dignity. "Listen to me, my uncle," she said in a grave voice. "Know now and for all time that there is nothing in my uncle which could be an offense. If there is sweat upon my uncle, it is the sweat of his labors and his sorrows. My uncle is to me in all things sweet and lovely. Had my uncle ever deigned to lift his dear eyes to the face of Noi, he would long since have known that this is so."

Suddenly he saw himself as he must appear to the little Jezreelitess— a man of labors and sorrows, hard and tawny after the ravages of the desert, come at the end of a day of fear to enjoy a transitory peace. He saw the lordly body beneath his coarse tunic, and his spare hand, dark as cedarwood. Slowly he raised that hand, passed it over his face, permitted it to smooth the silky, pointed beard. Then he fixed his gaze upon the speaker, who had meanwhile lost every trace of dignity. She stood before him, slouched and sorry, her fingers pressed against her offending lips.

And now he wondered how he could have found that stooped and pathetic attitude unbeautiful, how he could have seen in the curved shoulders and the thrusting neck anything but loveliness. The white shoulder, left bare by the sleeveless shift—how cool it had been beneath his hand in the darkness outside. How fair the throat, how shadowy the hollow at the base of it, how touching the little round bones.

"Now, if my uncle's heart is not turned against me utterly by what I have said in my drunkenness, let him give me my gift and depart."

"Are you indeed drunken, Noi?"

"Yes, I am drunken. Surely my uncle knows that without the wine I would not have had courage to speak what lies in my heart. . . ."

"Come, Noi," he said, holding out his hand to her. "Tell me what it is that lies in your heart."

She came to him slowly, stopping as soon as the fold of her shift brushed against his knees. She raised her hand and laid it shyly upon his cheek.

"Would that my father had had nine sons, and I had been the last of them," she said, weeping. "Would that I had been a man-child, to own my portion of the fields and the orchard and to carry a sword. . . ."

He pressed her hand against his face. "Is it so sad a thing to be a girl-child, then? A woman was God's kind thought, Noi, given to Adam to comfort him in the first days of the world."

"No, it is not because I cannot bear to be a woman. Only, were I a man, then I might follow David. Without shame I might sell my portion and take up my sword and follow David into the wilderness, and be his armor-bearer to carry his shield and wash his feet. Without shame I might come to David in the hour of my loneliness. As it is, I——" She turned her face aside and sobbed loudly, like a child.

"No, now," he said, himself close to weeping, "do not weep."

"Let my uncle forgive me——"

"Since I am your uncle, come then and be a good niece to me. Sit in my lap and put an end to this crying. Here is your present, which we have nearly forgotten. Look now at the earrings of glass and copper, which were brought up for you out of Hebron."

She sniffed and bent over and dried her face on the hem of her shift. For a moment he saw her legs, slender and hairless. Then she dropped her skirt and sat down, as docile as one of her own tame hares, upon his knees. Her haunches were the haunches of a child; through the slight rounds of flesh, he could feel the bones. All at once she was merry. She snatched the earrings out of his hand and held them up so that the polished copper shone. She pressed them against her cheek, held them to her lips. And all the while, her body moved against his. She is innocent, he thought, let me remember that she is innocent, the sister of my friends, the only daughter of an honorable house, and furthermore so young that the measure of her years is barely half the measure of mine. . . . Nevertheless, the sweet mouth was open with delight and achingly close to his.

"Come, Noi," he said in a shaking voice, "reward me with a kiss."

She straightened and stared at him. Then, quiet and obedient, she sank back against his chest and gave him her lips.

The seduction of a virgin, he thought, like the burning of a field, is the deed of a marauder. I have forfeited all the credit that has been laid up for me with Jahveh in these harsh years if I do not put her from me. . . . Yet the very thought that she was forbidden made it less possible to renounce her. It was as if a great column of desire had risen up within him, solid, unassailable, ringed round with rippling lines of fire. He rose and set her upon her feet and clasped the length of her against him. She uttered a small cry at the violence of his embrace. He also made a sound—a wild and Canaanitish cry—but in her innocence she took it for a cry of pain.

"Is it that David desires me?" she said. "Is it as a wound within him, this desire?"

"No, no, no, as a pillar of flame. . . ."

"What shall I do to ease my beloved? I am ignorant in these things. Let my beloved forgive my ignorance. . . ."

Jahveh, he thought, the Jahveh who has laid up against me in heaven a long account—the lies that I gave to Saul in exchange for love, the gall that I left in the heart of Michal, the death that flew with me into the sanctuary at Nob—Jahveh will strike me for the use I have made of your ignorance this night. . . . And all the while he felt her yielding body against him, her narrow back beneath his palms, her face cool against his face.

"What shall I do?" she said again. It was plain that she was weary with standing so long.

"Do not be troubled, I will instruct you."

"But I would not be a burden to David——"

"It is a matter in which teaching is no burden, but a delight," he said. "Come, let us lie down together on Noi's bed."

❦ V ❧

Well, he thought, wandering aimlessly around the encampment in the slanting light of the afternoon, one good thing at least has come of last night's encounter. Fear has transformed itself into desire and found a passage for escape. Yet this day had been neither peaceful nor pleasant. Remembering Noi was like eating a melon: somewhere under the freshness and the sweetness was the bitter rind.

He was not in the least afraid that she would speak of their encounter. She herself, sitting on the edge of her bed to bid him good night, had offered a promise of secrecy. "I will say to my brothers that you came and gave me the earrings and departed," she had said. "No one will know that David has been with me. I will take new linen and put it upon the bed, and bind up my hair." And yet the large eyes had spoken to him in another fashion, staring earnestly into his face. "Do not leave me in this room," the eyes had said. "Take me up and carry me out of this house which can no longer be my home."

Once and once only, when he had gone to drink from a spring in the grove at the foot of the hill, it came into his thoughts that he might go up to the house of the brothers and ask that the little Jezreelitess be given to him as a bride.

The camp was crowded now. Most of the men had returned from the day's foraging and were laying out their booty—honey, figs, jars of olive oil, measures of flour, and skins of wine. He wandered toward the top of the hill, stopping to carry off a couple of cakes of bread.

Yet when he had made it obvious to all of them that he preferred to eat alone, he could not bear his solitude. He kept calling to one or another of the men who squatted on the slope of the hill below him, repeating his remarks because of the distance until their stupidity became painfully plain. He heard one of the men mention the roaring feast that had gone on at Nabal's house last night, and, in order to redeem the flatness of his earlier talk, he launched into a loud, cynical, bawdy description of the charms of the opulent Abigail. He was growing sick of the whole performance when he sighted Joab. His nephew, weighted down by a burden of cloth and metal plate, was climbing up the slope. "Am I to come up," he said, "or shall I go forth again for another four days and nights?"

David rose and stretched. "Certainly, come up. I have sent down to the farmer to pay him for the loss of his crop. He is paid, and you are forgiven." He paused. Now that his nephew was close to the top of the hill, that which he carried was plainly visible: a magnificent tunic embroidered in purple and red, a big plate of beaten copper, a handful of gold amulets, a broad girdle, and two pairs of sandals made of skin as white as milk. "God of battles," David said, "where did you come by such loot?"

"In Gath—yes, truly, I have been down to Gath and slept in the palace of Achish there. This is not booty but a gift from the Seren of the city to David of Bethlehem."

"A gift from Achish——"

"But do not shout it among these fools that are here with us on the hill. Let us go down to the grove, and I will tell you the whole tale."

But before going so far as to recount his journey down to the city, Joab spoke of another matter—how, when he entered the encampment tonight, it had been borne in upon him that the army of David grazed in the open country, a poor flock of defenseless sheep, waiting for the Lion of Benjamin to come down upon them.

"And what has that to do with the Seren of Gath?" said David. Fear was coming upon him again, and Joab, who had always laughed at fear, was now in league with it.

"Truly," said Joab, "there is a connection between the two. We are encamped here in the open, at the mercy of everyone—Saul, the villagers, the Philistines."

"What would you have me do? Fly into Egypt?"

"No, no, certainly not, only listen, my dear lord——"

But even then he did not proceed into a forthright account. He spoke at length of the regret that had assailed him when he went out from the encampment on that first night. Strange, he said, how distance will clarify a situation. While he stood in his uncle's presence, hearing his uncle expatiate on the burning of the field, he had scarcely listened; it had seemed to him then that the burning of a field was an insignificant thing. But, as soon as he came within sight of the walls of the fortress of Ziklag —and let him say in passing that they were very fine walls—he had been forced to admit to himself that the villagers were truly in a sullen mood and that anything might be enough to set fire to their stored resentment. David had been right—there was really nothing to keep the people of the plain from joining forces with Saul against the wretched little band. . . .

David sat in the darkness, tearing up handfuls of weeds by their roots. The circle of terror was closing round him. "Speak to me of such difficulties tomorrow before you set out to burn another field," he said. "Here on the ground between us lie certain things for which you have not accounted as yet—a little matter of a fortune in cloth and glass and copper and gold. I will be content if I am informed how Joab came by this."

"Certainly. I was about to tell my uncle," Joab said.

It was a preposterous tale, such stuff as Phoenician sailors tell the men of the caravans in order to drive a better bargain for their wares. "No, now," said David, leaning back against the grass, "let Joab save his sailor's tale for the women of Hebron. If my nephew stole the treasure that lies between us, let him say only where he stole it and how, that we may make an end of this foolishness and go back to the others."

But the voice that answered him out of the dark was not the voice of a liar. "As David lives and as my soul lives, I stole it not. It was given to me by the white hand of the Seren of Gath, whose eyes are the color of the sea. Would that David had heard the cordial voice in which the Seren inquired after his health and his happiness. Would he had heard how Achish grieved for David's loss of Michal, and for his childlessness, and for the division that has come between him and Jonathan. Would he had seen the man's face when he bade me tell my uncle to raise up seed unto himself, so that the seed of David and the seed of Achish might come together in the palaces of Philistia, in the day when David is King in Israel, and Israel and Philistia are bound together in everlasting peace. The desire for the alliance is so strong within him that he has offered David a gift—so great a gift that I fear to name it, lest I provoke my uncle's unbelief. 'The city of Ziklag,' said Achish, 'that city will I give to David, to belong to him and to Israel forever, that he may be delivered from the burden of terror which is surely upon him, that he may live like a lord within its excellent walls.' "

"Ziklag? He would give me Ziklag?" And suddenly he saw it plainly— the circle of terror was broken. One arc of it, a curve of plumed helmets and iron chariots, stood at his back to sustain him. Another arc, the bent line of sullen villagers, broke up and moved aside, pacified now that he had ceased to eat their bread. The third arc, the host of Jahveh, continued to move down, but it hurled itself vainly against Ziklag's sturdy walls. He saw also the blue and violet cities of the seacoast. He saw himself moving through their splendid streets in a chariot of iron, with a purple cloak flowing from his shoulders and a white plume nodding above his brow. He leaned forward in the darkness and put his hand upon the treasure that lay between him and the tempter.

"And he has promised to feed the army of my uncle even as he feeds. the garrison that now dwells in Ziklag. And he will be tightfisted with nothing. He will give my uncle not only a house but the furnishings thereof, carved chairs and couches such as he keeps in his own palace. . . ."

But David had ceased to hear the eager, ingratiating voice. His hand, groping in the pile of treasure, had come upon a pair of sandals made of soft leather. Something forgotten, something sorrowful, stirred in him as he touched the pliable, tooled hide. Jesse . . . Jesse making a purse of leather to hang on the girdle of his David, his darling. . . . Jesse who now lived in exile in the court of the King of Moab, who was perhaps turning in his sleep even at this moment to lay his arm across the withered body of his only beloved. . . . And I have seduced the virgin Noi. And I have stolen the bread of the children of Jahveh. And I have divided the host of God into two parts, so that those who are discontented in the north may move to the south. And even at this moment it has come into my thoughts to go down to Gath and make a covenant with the enemies of the Lord. . . .

"If my uncle could only look upon the walls of Ziklag——"

"Has my nephew forgotten," he said in a weary voice, "that he who lives within those walls will have sold himself into bondage to the uncircumcised?"

"Bondage? But who has spoken of bondage? The Seren Achish said to me explicitly, 'Say to David that I do not require that he should call me lord.'"

"What am I to call him, then?" he asked in bitterness.

"Friend," said Joab. "He bade me say to you, 'Let David call me friend.'"

Friend of the exalted ones, companion of the great. . . . Once in the Gibean years he had ceased to be a Judahite. He had sat like a son of Benjamin or Ephraim at Saul's knees. And now he was a bandit, and therefore less than a shepherd; now he was an outlaw, and therefore less than a Judahite.

"Let my uncle at least go down to Achish and talk a little concerning this matter. Let him at least look upon the wonders of the city. On the walls of Gath alone, six hundred bowmen stand, facing east and west and north and south."

And just such bowmen, thought David, came up that spring to the plains of Sharon when the almond trees were in blossom, and sent an arrow into the flesh of my beloved.

"Their bows stand as high as their shoulders——"

"God curse their bows and fill their bellies with arrows! No decent son of Jahveh breaks bread with the uncircumcised."

"Then," said Joab, "I am to take these treasures and hide them in some cave and let the Seren of Gath wait in vain in his palace for a word from the Star of Bethlehem?"

"Surely, take them into a cave," he said, and wondered why he had not said, "Carry them back to Achish" or "Throw them into the well."

"But a tunic will rot in a damp place. . . ."

"What is it to me if the tunic rots, fool?"

"It only came into my mind——" Again Joab's voice had grown hesitant and anxious.

Again the gray and stifling veil of fear floated around David. "What came into your mind, eater of unclean meat, wallower in the pigsty of Astarte?"

"Nothing, my uncle. Only that a day might come when David would wish to go down to Achish arrayed in this same tunic which he tells me to leave in a damp place. A day might come—God forbid that it *should!* —when, pressed on one side by the armies of Saul and on the other by the villagers, David may see this matter otherwise than he sees it tonight."

"Dog!" David said, leaping up from the ground. "We will not speak of that day until it comes."

"Surely, my uncle, surely. Shall we return to the encampment, then? My uncle is weary. My uncle has cause to be weary and distressed. As Achish said, the burdens that are upon David's shoulders are greater burdens than even a strong man can bear. . . ."

"Go, hide your filthy stuff in whatever place you will," he said. "As for me, I will go back to the hill to see whether your brother has yet returned. He went on a fool's errand for your sake. While you ate of the crawling creatures of the sea and kissed the mouths of the unclean, he journeyed down to seek you in Zeruiah's house in Bethlehem."

As soon as he reached the foot of the hill, David knew that Abishai had returned. A single supper fire glowed on the hillside at that spot where he usually broke bread. David walked toward it with the long, irregular strides of a man who can scarcely keep himself from breaking into flight. He nursed the illusion that terror lay behind him, that here, with this hairy, childish Judahite, he would be at peace. But as he sank beside Abishai on the shale and looked into his eyes, the fright within him was multiplied. Had Saul's armies come down so soon, and had Abishai heard of it in Bethlehem? Had he scented out an uprising of the villagers? Had Noi's brothers discovered what had passed and gone up to deliver the seducer into the hands of the King?

"What is it now?" he said in a whisper.

"I did not tarry long in Bethlehem, my uncle," said Abishai. "I went directly from Bethlehem to Ramah."

"Wherefore to Ramah?"

"Because we had news in Bethlehem——"

"What news?"

"Ill news," said Abishai, rolling his round head from side to side.

"News that will certainly be a bitterness in the ears of David. The prophet Samuel is dead."

❧ VI ☙

Aɴᴅ ɴᴏᴡ all the fears that had tormented him congealed into one great fear—the fear of God. Last night at sunset Samuel's spirit had departed from Samuel's body. Dour, unbending, and austere, that spirit had hastened down from Ramah to see how it was with his chosen one. Samuel's spirit had stood at the foot of the narrow bed and watched the anointed one seduce a virgin. Samuel had moved among the moist leaves near the spring while the Lamb of Judah handled the treasures of Gath and played with the thought of a covenant with the uncircumcised. Samuel and Jahveh had been whispering together. In the face of such unearthly terror, what were the little frights of the world?

He went alone and unarmed into the market place to buy a mourning garment—a tunic woven of the harsh hair of the black goat. He rejected the offers of all those who begged him to let them go down with him to Ramah. He meant to recite his sins in a loud voice on the way, and such a recital would be possible only in solitude. With his bracelets stripped from his arms and his earrings taken from his ears, in sandals whose soles were thin so that the stones might bruise his feet, he went up to Ramah to plead for mercy with the dead.

He deliberately set himself in the way of danger on the highroad; he made no attempt to hide himself from possible betrayers in the town; he announced his name in a ringing tone to the priest who officiated at the altar in Ramah, even though he could tell by the tribal mark on the man's wrist that he was a son of Benjamin and might well harbor some thought of vengeance against the liar who had brought Saul's hand upon the priests of Nob. Yet these excessive gestures did nothing to relieve the terror that made a shifting quicksand of his vitals. Some further penance remained undone even when he had groveled for an hour in the holy earth of the sanctuary and covered his hair with the ashes of the burnt sacrifice. He lingered at the high place until the going-down of the sun, trying to find some other means of appeasement. Then, seeing that if he tarried longer he would sin by failing to sit out a full night at the feet of the dead, he left the horned altar and the smoldering meat and went to the house of the prophet, which stood halfway between the sanctuary and the gate, at the center of the little mud-brick town.

A lamp had been set on the threshold of Samuel's house. The yellowish flame was scarcely discernible in the hot and luminous dusk. Outside, to the left of the door, was a mound of loose earth. So Samuel will not lie in a burial cave, he thought. They have dug a grave for him below the room in which he and I spoke together. The sisters and the sisters' sons and daughters who will inherit this house will feel, as they step back and forth across the rushes, the emanations of his holiness rising to them through the sod. . . . He steeped his hands in the earth and rubbed it into his neck and face. Even through the heat of the day it had retained its subterranean coolness. It had a dank smell, smell of Sheol, smell of the grave.

As David crossed the threshold, the eyes of the mourners deserted the body and fastened themselves upon the newcomer. "Who is it?" said a blind old woman crouching in a corner. "David, Jesse's son," a matron said in a whisper, "he whom Samuel anointed in Saul's place." They all turned then—farmers and herdsmen, wives and virgins, priests and novices—and greeted him with the upraised arms and rolling eyes that are reserved for welcoming the sons of the dead. Two young maids, the daughters of Samuel's sister's daughter, rose from their station of honor at the prophet's feet and motioned the Bethlehemite to come to take the empty place. In the house of Samuel, he thought, I am a king. . . . With the consummate grace and dignity that had come upon him in Gibeah, he moved across the room and dropped a lock from his beard and a lock from his brow into the grave. Then he knelt at the feet of the prophet and rent his garment, pulling it at both shoulders until there was a tear long enough to bare his whole chest. One of the novices reached across the body and laid the ritual knife in his hands. Conscious that the young maids were watching him avidly, he lacerated his arm from the elbow to the wrist, dabbled his fingers in the smarting wound until they were red, and smeared the blood on the calloused soles of the prophet's feet.

He forgot the others then—all the black mourners crowded one upon the other, all the lacerated arms and breasts and shoulders, all the curious and reverent eyes. He was alone with Samuel in the little room, growing darker as the luminous dusk faded. Now he forced himself to look steadily past the white beard to the face. Death had not softened the prophet. There was in that face a terrible austerity, an utter absence of clemency. The wrinkled eyelids had been forced down over a harsh stare; the mouth was open as if to give passage to some last, annihilating judgment of the Lord. To look at the dead face of Samuel was to know that the God of Israel was neither merciful nor loving—only just.

A disintegrating sickness took hold on David with that knowledge. It seemed to him that he could not continue to breathe the air of the room; under the smell of sweat and the smell of spices was the faint but inescapable odor of dissolution. I will arise, he thought, and go to the door. . . . But the stern face forbade it, bestowing on him a cold and bitter look, as though it said, "Will you go forth from me this night, which is my last?" No, father of my spirit, he said, forming the words only with his lips, I will remain. Furthermore, I will make a complete confession of all my sins, and perhaps, before your face is hidden under the earth, I will learn also the measure of my punishment. . . .

It was not necessary to confess aloud. These mourners who crouched shouting or wailing around him need not hear—would not even understand—the words that must pass between the prophet and his anointed one. Fixing his look upon the dead face, bending forward a little and uttering an outcry now and then to satisfy the requirements of the occasion, he began his silent confession.

Behold, he thought, I have sinned exceedingly, more than any other in Israel. . . .

How? When? Where? said the pitiless face.

I have gone into the house of my friends and taken there a virgin and an only sister. Like a pariah dog I have fallen upon whatever was at hand to feed my lust. . . .

Liar, said the pale, open lips. Tell me not that you had a dog's need or the need of one who has been abiding months within his tent, with no woman by. Your need was small. . . .

My need was small, as Samuel says. I fostered a little need that it might grow into a great desire. . . .

Wherefore? . . .

He remembered the moment when he had let the uncontrollable longing in. And it was strange and bewildering to him that he saw not Noi but himself—David, cleansed and transformed and exalted in Noi's eyes. A woman, hysterical with grief, uttered a strange laugh, and it seemed to him that the laughter had issued from the dead man's lips.

"Behold," David whispered, leaning forward and touching the cold feet, "I swear by the flesh of your body that I will make amends. I will go up to her brothers' house and beg that she be given to me as a bride. . . ."

Truly? said the disdainful face. It is not enough. The Judahite shepherd thinks in his heart how, when he reigns in Israel in a palace of stone and cedarwood, he will take another bride and be troubled with the sight of Noi no more. . . .

"As chief wife I will take her. I will raise her up and set her in Michal's place."

The woman laughed again. He lifted his head and looked about him. The sky beyond the bare windows had faded to a watery blue. The hanging lamp from the temple of Shiloh had grown brighter now, and the long body on the reed mat, marked by stronger light and sharper shadow, seemed even more austere. The niece of the prophet—a lean woman with a pair of scratched and sagging breasts—suddenly left off moaning and straightened. "Go," she said in an even and daily voice to the two damsels who had given their place to David. "It is time to refresh the mourners with a little wine."

Is she really grieved? he asked himself. And I—am I truly stricken? Is it not rather that I have lost all grief in the rituals of grief? And is this dour Judahite the man to receive a full confession? Was the sin I committed against Noi a greater sin than that which I committed against Michal? Is an alliance with the Philistines a more monstrous evil than the slaying of the priests of Nob? Yet in Samuel's eyes to depart from Michal was to withdraw from the accursed of God, and to bring down death upon those who dwelt in the sanctuary was to cleanse Israel of the fourscore vipers who soiled the holiness of the Lord. To come to God through the spirit of Samuel is to see Him shadowed forth only vaguely, as through a veiling of sackcloth, so that one knows the features but not the expression of the face. . . . One of the damsels laid her hand lightly on his shoulder and bent and offered him refreshment. He drank from the bowl only enough to wet his lips. The room, the crowd of mourners, the smell of spices and sweat and death, had closed again around him, and he turned back to the stark face.

Concerning this matter of an alliance with the uncircumcised . . . it said.

But the other mourners had not yet gone back to their mourning. One of them, a lean herdsman who had pastured his flocks close to Jesse's in the old days, bent across the prophet's legs and touched David. "The Star of the House of Jesse will forgive me," he said in a whisper, "for breaking in upon his grief. But it has come into my mind that he would profit by such tidings as I had yesterday from a traveler out of the north."

"Surely, surely," said David, plunged into fear again by the gravity of the man's tone.

"It is said that Saul's army is assembling even now in Gilgal. It is said that six thousand will come down against David into the wilderness."

"So?" He tried to master his terror by pretending that it did not exist. "Six thousand? Well, I had thought as much, but I am grateful——" His voice had risen slightly in spite of himself. The other mourners turned in his direction, smiling indulgently and shaking their heads. The room was quiet. The windows were blotted out in darkness, and the flame in the hanging lamp was intensely bright. He resumed his pious staring.

Beloved of God and dear friend of my father, he thought—and he heard his own voice speaking in his thoughts, tender, naïve, and ingratiating—if I have thought to make an alliance with the uncircumcised, surely Jahveh must understand such a weakness. Not Joseph in the deep well nor Ishmael in the desert was so beset as I.

No, now, the harsh mouth said, put by the ways of a little one. God is not Jesse, neither are you a child, that you should wheedle Him.

But since Jahveh is the Lord of hosts and therefore a man of war, he thought, laying his hand again upon the cold feet, surely He will understand how such a one as I must yearn after a stronghold. . . .

A stronghold? Truly, now, was that what you yearned after? I thought it was toward other things that your heart turned with longing. I thought it was palaces and chariots, and you seated at the side of the great, with fine linen against your flesh. . . .

I have suffered much and am exceeding weary. . . .

You have coveted much and are exceeding vainglorious. . . .

The friend of God and of my father has seen my heart. . . .

And turned aside, said the hidden eyes beneath the strained lids, and turned aside in monstrous disgust. . . .

He was startled out of his reverie by the knowledge that the mourn- ers' eyes were fixed upon him. He had sat motionless too long. In the in- tensity of his communion with the prophet, he had forgotten to tear his clothes and utter the required cries. He tore the clotted blood from his lacerated arm, dabbled his fingers in the fresh blood, and again anointed the prophet's feet.

It is not your blood that is wanted here, the stern mouth said.

What then am I to give Samuel and the Lord? . . .

Another vow. . . .

What vow? . . .

That you will turn your back steadfastly against the walls of Ziklag, and set your heart everlastingly against the unclean ones who eat the crawling creatures of the sea. . . .

He bent forward and looked searchingly at the dead face. If it was the face of a prophet, it was also the face of a herdsman—such a man as had bargained all his days over the price of a cow.

And if I go down into Gath and make an alliance with the uncircum- cised? . . .

The price of that is punishment. . . .

What punishment? Death? But surely if I do not go down, my wages are also death. . . .

How is it that the son of Jesse is so sickly afraid of death? To die is a small matter. Behold, I who am dead tell you as much. Moses is dead, and also Abraham. Deborah was a sweet singer, and she is dead. And Jephtha's daughter was a damsel, very young and tender, and yet she found it possible to die. . . .

Yet all these died fulfilled, and took the peace of their fulfillment with them into their graves, and I . . .

Remind me not of that which I have not forgotten. I know that I have sprinkled the holy oil upon the head of the son of Jesse. . . .

He felt the gaze of the mourners converging again upon him, and he uttered the necessary outcry, crouched, and covered his face. But through the chinks between his fingers his eyes sought the closed eyes of the prophet and narrowed as the eyes of a tradesman will narrow when he sees a buyer pondering a satisfactory price. Then we will bargain together, Samuel, he thought. You will throw all Israel from Dan to Beersheba into the scales against the walls of Ziklag. . . .

But the face which answered him was cold and scornful. As God is not Jesse, neither is God Samuel, it said.

And once again, as in the nights when he lay alone and sleepless in the cave outside Gibeah, David felt the presence of the Lord. That Other Jahveh Who concerned Himself with such matters as the cheeses of Bethlehem and the wine of Jonathan, that inscrutable One who had heard the sweet singer mar his own songs, that brooding, terrible, tender One was in the room. He hovered over the crouching mourners, over all Israel, over the whole flat surface of the world. Behold, He said, the walls of

Ziklag are very strong walls, but howsoever thick your walls, you cannot hide from Me. This night moves on toward morning, the false dawn is already white on the rims of the hills, and with the morning this holy herdsman will be taken from your sight, and he and all his reproaches will be covered up with earth to trouble you no more. For prophets pass, but I remain. Ahimelech also, he who put bread and a sword into your hands at Nob, he who lifted up his hand to brush a speck of dust from your cheek, death has also hidden away his weak and watery look. The priest is gone, but I shall not pass. Saul, too, shall pass, and all the seed of Kish, but I shall stand indestructible upon their graves. And where I am, there also is My punishment. And My punishment is even as Myself, all-pervading and lasting even unto the ends of the world. . . .

Now, body and soul, the son of Jesse was given over to terror; his tongue clung dry to the roof of his mouth, and his knees began to shake. One of the damsels, seeing that he shuddered, came and knelt down beside him and held a bowl of wine to his lips.

He drank a little and raised his eyes and looked uneasily toward the window. But outside there was nothing to fear; there was only a lighter sky behind paler stars; the roofs of Ramah were whitening in the dawn. He took the bowl and drank again. His heart, which had been beating weakly and unevenly, gradually took up its old, steady rhythm. God had departed from the world, had returned to His throne in the firmament, had resumed His former shape and crowned Himself with His usual crown of peacock feathers. The Other Jahveh was no more.

Then, he thought, putting the bowl back into the girl's hand and fixing his eyes once again upon the face of the prophet, then I will make my covenant with Samuel and leave these matters between God and me until a day when I can examine them in peace. . . .

Now, concerning this matter of a covenant with Achish . . . said the open, uncompromising lips.

Certainly, David said, it will be as Samuel wishes. Such was my intention from the beginning. How could it be otherwise? As I live and as my soul lives . . . He stopped and tore at his wound again, and for the last time anointed the prophet's feet. As I live and as my soul lives, I will make no alliance with the unclean ones who eat the crawling creatures of the sea. I will set my back utterly against the uncircumcised. . . .

He had not made his vow too soon. Dawn was already at the window, a burst of whiteness quenching the stars. The mourners rose and cried out and rent their garments, for it was time now to lay the seer of Ramah in his grave.

BOOK SIX

BOOK SIX

✆ I ❧

A HINOAM the Jezreelitess sat up in her bed and stared at the window. She could see nothing but the stars. The village, the plain, the stretches of brush, the whole world, were blotted out in the dark of the moon. She had lain down early, hoping that a long night's rest might clear her mind of the nightmare mist that was upon it; but now she knew that she had been listening only to the obscure voices of her own body; she had been wondering and questioning again; she had not even striven for sleep. In the big room below the loft in which she slept, one after the other of her eight brothers had lain down for the night. She had counted the number of times that the door had closed behind them, and the small thuds of their sandals upon the floor. Now there was no sound in the house save the sound of their slow, multitudinous breathing.

In the past she had always walked barefoot through the house, un-afraid of the little creatures of the wilderness—the spiders, the lizards, and the mice—that came into the rambling house. But now one fear had begotten a score of others. She put on her sandals and walked across the room in mortal dread lest she should feel the light feet of the creeping things upon her. Once at the window, she dusted the sill with the hem of her shift before she could bring herself to lean against the wood.

No, she thought, I cannot deceive myself any longer. It *was* the dark of the moon when he came to me—I remember the soft black sky and the yellow stars. Since that time, another moon has risen and has fulfilled herself, and has descended into the caverns of Sheol. And I must say to myself, A moon is surely past since I lay down beside David of Bethlehem, and neither he nor the day of my pouring forth has come. . . .

It was useless to strive against the questioning and the remembering. When, she asked herself for the twentieth time since she had lain down that night, when was it that the manner of women was last upon me? It was when we took the olives down and laid them in the press. From this knowledge there was no escape, and yet it seemed to her that there must be some escape, some way to restore peace. It is because I am hungry, she thought, that I am so wretched. All this day I have swallowed nothing but a little honey and bread. I will go down and take a bit of cold meat and lull myself to sleep with a bowl of wine. . . . Although the night was heavy with the stored heat of late summer, she shivered. She found her cloak and laid it around her shoulders, and opened the door that led to the outside stairs. But on the landing she was assailed by the open blackness of the night and the raw, weedy smell of the wilderness. . . . She stepped into the dark lower room of the house, closed the door firmly behind her, kindled a lamp, and sat down in a chair by the window. The smell of the night came to her across the sill. How was it? What did she say to me, the old woman who gathers mustard seeds? She told me again how I must not wander about alone, lest one of the bandits fall upon me and leave me with a full belly. It was then that I said to her, "How does a wife come to know it when she carries a child?" . . .

But it was to comfort myself with food that I came down, she thought. She rose then and went to the shelf and took down a joint of kid, a bowl, a wine cruet, and a flat cake of bread. As she carried them to the table, it seemed to her that her terror was subsiding. But the slippery meat in her mouth made her sick, and she fell to shuddering again.

She pushed the meat aside and turned to the wine. The bowl which she had taken from the shelf was the one from which *he* had always taken his draught in the good days when he had sat, first as a remote hero and then as a dear uncle, at their table. Brushing her mouth against the rim of it, she fancied that she established some faint, sad contact with his lips. She drank slowly, savoring each sip, calling up a vision of his face. Strange, she thought, strange and sorrowful that, having come to know all his body, she could remember so little of it with pleasure. Strange that, as a child clings to an old toy, dear beyond any new one, she dwelt most upon his face, his hands, his hair. She relived in solitude only the first hour and the last moment: his breath upon her neck, his hand upon her shoulder in the dark of the terrace; his wandering touch passing over her face when she sat, like a good niece, upon his knees; his quiet kiss, light on her obedient, closed eyes. "Go to sleep," he had said.

Go to sleep, go to sleep, go to sleep. . . . Her head nodded, and it seemed to her that in a moment she would obey him, she would sleep. Then the veil of peace was rent by one sharp stab of longing; she sat upright and wide-eyed at the table, longing for his voice, his face against her face.

To think that the beloved might return, to plead with him for another sight of his face, was a sweet indulgence. Her tense body drooped in the warmth of it; her hands tingled with the languor of the wine. A few more moments of sitting on the hearth in the heat of the fire, and she would be able to sleep. She took her bowl with her and sat down in the glow, on the warm stones.

But she had no sooner settled there than the spiral began to whirl again, carrying her thoughts inexorably back to the day when, tending the bread

242

at this same hearth, she had raised her eyes to see the detestable Joab standing at the door. What had he meant to say? What obscure message had glimmered behind his eyes? What had he said?

She drank the last of the wine from the bowl and gave herself up to the remembrance. Night of the Festival of the New Moon, night when the kid was roasted and the bread was kneaded for *his* sake. Surely, she had thought, even if he is weary of me now that we have lain down together, surely he will come up, if not out of kindness, then at least to collect the tribute, the oil and figs and wine. . . . Fair, horned crescent floating like a white feather in the arc of blue, footfall on the path, hand at the latch —it is the beloved, it is he. . . . But when the door was opened, she saw that it was not he; he had sent his nephew in his place. As for Joab, he sauntered into the house as though he had dwelt there all his days. He took a handful of raisins from the table. He went to the chair near the window and lolled in it, stretching and chewing and staring at them all with his big, luminous, insolent eyes.

"And where is the Star of Bethlehem?" one of the brothers had said at last.

The loathsome intruder finished his chewing and wiped his mouth before he replied. "First he was in Ramah, waiting for the prophet to be buried. Then, the prophet being duly buried, he returned to the camp for the night. But it seems that while he tarried in Ramah, he heard certain news concerning the armies of the King of Israel. The news was such that he found it necessary to go down without delay into the country of the Kenites and the Calebites, to seek for recruits and to see to the smelting of some swords. So he is with the men of the south at the moment, and cannot come to gather the tribute. I am come in his stead."

She trusted her remembrance of this first stage of the incident. But the rest was so strange that she did not know whether to call it fantasy or reality. Had he truly risen then and walked toward the table, ostensibly to take another handful of raisins, but really because he wished to stare into her face? And the words that she remembered—were they words he had actually said? "My lord and uncle has charged me to tell you that he regrets his absence from your table this night. . . ." Surely he had said it; surely, even in her exigency, she could not have invented the slow, deliberate voice and the subtle, sidelong glance. "His heart yearns after the pleasures which he has known beneath this roof, and he bade me say expressly that he will not rest until he has tasted those pleasures again." No, it had not been a dream. She saw him too plainly, lifting the raisins one by one from his brown palm and smiling a slow and evil smile.

"And when will the Hope of Judah come up out of the desert?" the eldest brother had said.

"Before the moon is full he will come again."

But the moon has fulfilled herself, she thought, leaving the hearth and going unsteadily to the window, and whether I dreamed or heard makes no difference now, because he has not come. . . . Out of the vast emptiness beyond the window came the early wind, smelling of mustard seed and dry brush. The dawn was a glimmer at the edge of the plain. She turned back to the table and stopped long enough to snuff out the lamp and tilt the wine cruet against her lips. Then, slowly and fearfully, clinging to the wall and shuddering at the thought of the creeping creatures of the night, she climbed the outer stair. "Go to sleep, go to sleep, go to sleep," she said, closing the door behind her. But the dawn had broken and the new day had been born under a caul of fearful whiteness before she slept.

❧ II ❧

DAVID tarried long in the land of the Kenites and the Calebites simply because there was so much profit for him there. The Lord had stirred up a driving storm of anger among the men of the sands. They were bitter against the House of Saul as the desert is bitter against the city, as the camel-driver is bitter against the great buyer, the soft-handed lord. And of late their bitterness had been whipped into a fury by an incident in Gilgal—a Calebite chieftain had been slain in a private quarrel by Saul's second son, Abinadab. The Kenite smiths not only smelted David's old blades, but also provided him with a hundred new swords. As for Caleb, the whole tribe would have followed him in a fit of fervor to his encampment on the plain if he had possessed the wherewithal to keep them fed. As it was, a hundred lean brown youths came northward with him in a frenzy of religious zeal and tribal rage.

It was the first night of the new moon when he came into camp with his zealots and his swords. He had meant to go up to the house of the eight brothers as soon as he had bathed. But his old comrades fell so eagerly upon him, Joab had so many matters to discuss with him, Abishai and the priest Abiathar had prepared him such a fine dish of savory lamb, that departure would have been sheer churlishness. I will go to her tomorrow, he thought, and stretched himself comfortably before the campfire. He felt no great eagerness to set eyes upon the girl; the excitement of his journey had almost driven the thought of her from his head.

It was unfortunate that he found it impossible to go to her on the second night also. The Calebite recruits resented the fact that he had spent his time exclusively with the Judahites, and it was necessary to soothe their hurt pride by sitting among them and raising his voice in a few of their songs. He felt a certain uneasiness because of this delay. He went so far as to call Joab to him and inquire whether Noi had received his message and had sent any reply.

"What reply should she send?" Joab said. "Did my uncle expect that she would coo like a dove, with all eight of her brothers standing by?"

"Then she was not alone?"

"No, she was by no means alone."

He was disturbed by a certain vacant, absent look that came, on uncomfortable occasions, into Joab's large eyes. "And is my nephew certain that she heard the message and understood it?" he said.

"Heard? Certainly she heard. As for understanding, my uncle knows the limits of her mind better than I. I spoke the matter plainly, in such language as one would use to a drooling infant. If she did not understand, then surely her wits are weak, and it is the better for David that she did not understand."

He thought that he might go up on the following morning, but that intention, too, was blocked—he was needed in the camp to settle a dozen arguments over the distribution of the swords. And at moonrise he encountered another delay: Abishai brought him a traveler who had come down by the Way of the Mountains out of Ephraim—a breathless traveler who reported Saul's armies encamped in the forest of Ephraim and ready to move south within seven days. By the time he had finished his talk with the traveler, it was very late; no doubt Noi and her brothers were all in their beds. Nevertheless, he set out, knowing that if he remained in the encampment, terror would assail him again.

The late summer night was windless and mellow. The crescent moon, setting into the distant hills of Moab, touched the edges of those hills with a faint cast of gold. All around him, from brush and garden and roadside tree, came the smell of drying foliage and ripe seeds. A tremulous, aching tenderness possessed him. And that, he thought, is as it should be, since I am going on a journey of love. . . . Yet, try as he would, he could not teach his tenderness to congeal around the thought of Noi. He conjured up in his mind the moment when she had dropped her shift from her shoulders and stood before him in her nakedness. But all his remembering could not draw his desire to those slender, sloping shoulders, those childish arms, those pointed, insufficient breasts. Longing remained diffuse and beyond satisfaction, spread out upon the glimmering edges of the Moabite hills. I knew, he told himself, that I did not desire her. Then who is it that I desire? . . .

He was roused out of his brooding by a chorus of laughter and a burst of light. Nabal's house—he had come upon Nabal's house again. The windows flamed yellow, and great golden swaths of light revealed a sun-dried vine on the crumbling stones of the wall. That other time when I paused here, he thought, Nabal's wife was at the window, she whose name is Abigail, and she had a luminous face and opulent breasts. . . .

He stopped at the wall, unmindful of the light that lay full upon him, uncertain whether the shape in the window before him actually existed or had been placed there by remembrance. No, it was no illusion; the wife of Nabal stood, as she had stood on that first evening, staring out across the fields; and a woman who is forever looking forth from the windows of her house surely cannot have much joy within. Suddenly he knew that her eyes were upon him. She drew her veil across her face, but under the filmy, shimmering stuff he could see the corners of her mouth indented by an indolent smile. The seed-scented night was quickened by the glance that passed between them. He had found favor in her eyes—he knew it by the leisurely manner in which she turned from him, as if to make plain that she was sorry to depart. He watched her until she had become a dim shape against the flaring lamps, until she merged with the others who rose to greet her.

Suddenly he knew that his longing had settled and congealed at last—not upon Noi, but upon this wife of Nabal, this soft white shape made incandescent with love wisdom, this knowing one with ample breasts. For the first time in many months he felt the stirring of music within him. An aching, brooding phrase took shape in his mind, uncurled and stretched there, as a woman uncurls and stretches after love.

> What have I to do with children?
> I am weary of the sapling.
> Cover me with the shade of an opulent tree.
> Nourish me with ripe fruit.

For a long time, walking through the dry thickets and across the stretches of starlit shale, he carried the song within him, tending and perfecting it. He did not reproach himself. Another time I might have hidden such a matter from God and from myself, he thought. Now I will not deny it if on the way to one beloved I have felt my flesh stir toward another. . . . He walked slowly, because he wished to untangle a few knots in his skein of song. Before he had set his foot upon the slope of the terrace, that which he had created lay smooth and golden within him. And now, he thought, standing beside the little table where he had found Noi on that first unfortunate night, what shall I do, since the house is utterly dark and all of them are asleep? . . .

He went round to the side of the house and stared at the window of the loft—a narrow chink crossed by trails of vine. He remembered how it had looked from the inside of the room; a half-moon had hung beyond it—how many days had he been gone? He bent and picked up a bit of shale. Throw it through the window, he said to himself, rouse her from her sleep. . . . But his hand hung slack at his side. He could not, try as he would, imagine himself lifting his hand. He walked forward a few steps, still staring at the loft, and stumbled into a patch of brush. The dry branches cracked. He cursed softly, knowing that she must have heard.

The door creaked, and she appeared on the landing, only vaguely discernible in the light of the young moon—a length of white shift, a heart-shaped face, a mass of black hair. She did not speak. She stood at the top of the steps, swaying a little and clinging to the balustrade.

Well, then, he thought, since it must be done, let it be done graciously. . . . "Noi? Come down to me, beloved," he said.

But she did not come down. She sat upon the stair and let her head fall forward until it touched her knees. Her body rocked back and forth, her shoulders heaved, and he knew that she wept. He came then and sat beside her on the topmost step, but she neither moved toward him nor raised her head. She continued to crouch and to give herself over to her disconsolate, soundless weeping.

"But I have come back to my beloved," he said in a whisper. "Therefore it is foolish that she should weep."

"To cast me out," she said, dragging her fingers through her hair. "David has come to cast me out in my shame. . . ."

He did not know what to make of such wild talk, and laughed it away. "No, now," he said, "if we tarry here upon the steps, your brothers will waken and hear. Let my beloved come with me a little way into the wilderness, so that I may lay before her such matters as will comfort her heart."

It was plain that she was too shaken to walk beside him. He rose and lifted her, and she seemed as light in his arms as one of Jesse's lambs. Now that he held her, he could not speak. All words, all thoughts, went out of him; he knew nothing but the feel of the childish body, the head that rocked against his chest, the tears that moistened his neck, the small, thinly fleshed bones under his fingertips. He had never been so close to a grieving body before. Pity, new and disintegrating, surged up within him.

There was no grove or thicket or cluster of rocks about, so he contented himself with a bleak patch of pasture some fifty paces away from the house. He put her down upon the dry weeds, crouched close to her, and offered his knees as a pillow for her head. For a long time he sat above her, stroking her hair and waiting for the sobbing to cease. Then, seeing that she would weep forever unless he broke his silence, he said the words that were required by the Lord.

"Noi," he said, "is this a proper manner in which to welcome a bridegroom? It is true that I have been overlong in coming. But I have come to ask you to be to me as my mother was to my father, the true wife, the only bride. Tomorrow I will come up at moonrise to ask your brothers to give you to me. If they are willing, well and good, and if they are not willing, I will regret it, but I will carry you away nevertheless, since it is a thing which has been foreordained by God. It seemed to me when I came to you for the first time that you loved me. Why is it, then, that you continue to weep?"

She sobbed and shook her head.

"Then has Noi ceased to love me?"

"No, oh, no." Her arms closed round his waist. She turned her face against his stroking hand and kissed it.

"Then why should you weep?"

"Because I am no longer such a one as David or any man in Israel will take unto himself for a bride. Because it was an evil thing that I did when I lay down beside you. Because of my shame. . . ."

"What is this foolishness?" he said. "What is this shame?"

"The seed—believe me, it is the seed of David—the seed has taken root in me. A moon is past, more than a moon is past, and it is sealed up within me, the fountain of blood. . . ."

247

He started up. "Noi," he said, clutching her shoulders. "Noi, is it possible, are you with child?" If she made any answer, he did not hear it. He heard only his own voice saying loudly and joyously the name of the Lord. For now he was freed at last of an apprehension which he had never dared to name. He had carried within him the secret belief that his seed was sterile—it had fallen upon many, and never before had it borne fruit. Suddenly he remembered her, knew that she still lay weeping against his knees. He took her face between his hands and kissed it and broke into laughter. "No, now," he said, "surely this is a matter for joy."

"But the old woman who gathers the mustard seed in the wilderness said to me even this same day that no man will take unto himself one who carries quickened seed within. She said that no man will believe such seed is his, since she who is evil enough to lie down with one will surely lie down with another. . . ."

He laughed again and shook his head. "No, now," he said, "how should I believe such a thing of Noi? She is so difficult to teach that I know of no other man in Israel who would take upon himself the labors of her instruction. But is it so? Are you indeed with child?"

"It is so. I am with child."

"Get me a son," he said, "nourish me a son in your womb. I will feed him before the campfire and teach him to hold the bow and the spear. I will carry him on my shoulders from Beersheba unto Dan, and he will be a warrior king, such a one as will lead the hosts of Jahveh even unto Egypt, even unto the islands of the western sea. . . ." He paused because she was silent. A cricket made an insistent, sorrowful sound in the weeds behind him. A long-forgotten incident flashed across his thoughts; he saw his father sitting on the hearth with a lean little she-dog lying across his knees. "Poor bitch," said Jesse, fondling her ears, "she is too young for whelping. The milk of her mother is scarcely dry upon her tongue."

"Noi," he said, "are you afraid?"

"I was afraid, seeing that my lord was gone from me for so long. It came into my mind—may my uncle forgive me—that he would not come again, that I must go forth into the wilderness to eat wild locusts and roots until I had accomplished the thing alone."

She was no longer weeping. She lay as limp as a dead bird across his lap. Her face was wet and swollen; her body was thin and angular beneath her shift; her bare feet, white and narrow, trailed on the grass. Merciful God, he thought, she has grown so thin with grieving that she is very like to die of this, both she and the one that she carries within. "But I expressly bade Joab say to you that I would surely come again," he said.

She sighed. "The fault is with me and not with Joab. He came as my lord bade him and said what my lord desired should be said. But matters had come to such a pass with me that I knew not whether I heard or dreamed."

"Forgive me," he said.

"What is there to forgive? It was not my uncle's intention to leave me in doubt. And now he is with me, and trusts that this seed is his seed, and puts my heart at rest. What is there to forgive?"

More than you know, he thought, and more than you will ever know. Forgive me that, had Samuel not reproached me at the edge of his grave, I would never have set eyes upon you again. Forgive me also that, even on this night, I yearned toward one who stood at a window, and that I will yearn toward her again, should she still be at the window when I turn home. Forgive me that I will make of you what Saul made of his Ahinoam. . . .

The cricket continued to chirp sorrowfully in the weeds. The earth was growing cold beneath him. The air was damp, and a mist had blurred the edge of the setting moon.

"Come, my beloved," he said, "let us go back. It is not good that one who bears quickened seed should lie in the cold."

She rose and stood before him. There was an air of waiting in the stillness of her body. She stared at him with big, unwavering eyes.

She is waiting for some pledge or promise, he thought. He took a bracelet from his arm and laid it in her open hand, and told her again that he would come to speak with her brothers at the time of the evening meat. But when all this was finished, she still stood motionless before him, lifting her face. He moved a little closer to her and saw a scarcely perceptible stirring of her lips. I have forgotten to kiss her, he thought. He laid his mouth against her mouth. Their kiss was as flat as yesterday's bread.

No words passed between them while he carried her over the stretches of dry earth and shale. May the Lord be satisfied, he thought. But it is no joyous thing, this that I do to satisfy the Lord. . . .

❧ III ❧

ALL THAT PASSED in the house of the eight brothers on the night of the wedding feast was unreal and remote. The bride was ill and looked more unbeautiful than ever, sallow in her multicolored robe, slight under the weight of her amulets. Her brothers, who were trying to make the best of a sorry business, drank too much and talked in loud voices that jarred the bridegroom's dull and aching head. When I have taken her home, he assured himself, then I will find some measure of peace. In the cave where we will lie beside each other on the coverlets and pillows that were stolen from the caravans of the south, in the quiet cave I will teach myself at last that I have married her. . . . So he thought, staring at the ravaged table, the gnawed bones, the skins of pomegranates, the pools of spilt wine. He looked at her who sat sagging under the heaviness of her necklace, and she bestowed upon him, for the twentieth time that evening, the necessary smile.

"Come," said David, touching her sharp little elbow, "much as I have enjoyed this food and this merriment, there are other pleasures that deserve a little of our time this night." They laughed—all the eight brothers and the three companions that he had brought with him from the encampment. But their laughter was without conviction. He knew by their faces that they were inventing excuses for the tepidness of this wedding feast; neither mother nor father sat at the board to warm the occasion with their happy tears; the shadow of Saul's army lay over the festivities; there was no place for ribaldry, inasmuch as the bride was very young. . . .

The eight brothers made only one faint effort to detain those who were so eager to depart. Bridegroom, bride, and wedding guests would have been out of the house in less time than it takes to fill a vessel at the well if it had not been for Noi. Noi paused on the threshold and said that she must go up to her room in the loft to fetch a thing which she had forgotten. It was unthinkable that the bride should serve herself; three of her brothers and two of David's men offered to run the stairs and asked her what it was that she required. "A little piece of fleece," she said, flushing under her veil. "The tail of a lamb. . . ." And then, because they stood staring at her as if she had gone mad, her youngest brother took it upon himself to explain. "It is the tail of a certain lamb of hers," he said. "Its mother died, and Noi nursed it. She made a kind of tea for it out of a skin used for curds. She——" Abishai, far gone in wine, stumbled through the door into the dark. When the lamb's tail had been fetched and the others had left the house, they found him covertly wiping his nose on his sleeve. "A lamb's tail has unmanned him," Joab whispered at David's ear. "Look at the fool. Before God, he is in tears."

David would have preferred to walk at her side in the dark, saying little or nothing, holding her hand and nourishing whatever small roots of tenderness might begin to grow within him. But Joab, Abiathar, and Abishai walked close behind them, wounding the silence with jests and laughter, agitating the blackness with red flares of torchlight. Now and then he looked over his shoulder to answer some piece of banter, but he was always glad to turn his eyes again to the empty road before him.

"Will my lord have music sung before the bridal cave?" said Abiathar.

"No. We are very weary. Let us have the music when we have strength to enjoy it."

One of the wedding guests behind him moved a torch to avoid an overhanging branch, and a clump of dark foliage on the side of the road sprang into being in the light. Where have I seen such veering swaths of leaves and boughs before? David thought. Where, in what garden fresh with the smell of thyme, cool with raindrops rolling from the leaves? Was there truly such a garden once? Turn to me in my wretchedness. Rise up out of Mara's arms and go to the roof of your house and turn to me tonight, Jonathan. . . .

"My lord," said she whom he must teach himself to call his bride.

"Yes, beloved?"

"It has come into my mind that this has been a sorry wedding feast for David, not such a one as was spread for him in Saul's house when he took the King's daughter to wife."

He shrugged and closed his fingers more firmly around her hand. "As I remember it," he said, "I was not very merry then, either. A man is grave when he marries, and it would be better if there were no torches, no feasting, no wine to goad him into merriment."

"With a woman also, that is so."

"I would rather have walked back to the cave with only Noi at my side this night."

It was a shabby bit of love talk, a bone to throw to a dog, and yet she was satisfied. "David is gracious," she said.

But she had set him to remembering that other night when he had led a king's daughter from her father's house, in the light of fifty torches, through a town whose every citizen stood waiting in the streets to bid the Star of Judah and the Rose of Benjamin be fruitful and multiply. And in the high house of stone and cedarwood built for the King's son-in-law, the King's daughter unbound her veils one by one, and stood naked upon the white rug. Who comes to stand against you on the white rug now? he asked himself. Who quenches the light and plunges with you into the windy cavern of desire? Michal, Michal, turn to me in my wretchedness. Rise from the arms of Paltiel and go to the roof of the high house and turn your face toward the wilderness tonight. . . .

"There," said Joab in a whisper, "lies a house that should yield us many fat sheep. Beyond this same gray wall is the house of Nabal."

"Ask him for nothing. We give him no protection against the marauders of the desert. He has men enough in his hire to protect himself. Furthermore, he is a man of consequence and has an evil temper. Let him alone."

"As my uncle says."

David raised his eyes to the house of Nabal and saw no lighted windows. It is strange, he thought, that when she stood leaning on the sill, I dreamed I desired her, and sought to draw her eyes upon my face, and made a song. How is it possible that I, who lay with my head upon the breasts of Saul's daughter, could have yearned even for a hour after this soft, aging, bedizened Judahite? This little one who walks beside me in the dark is less offensive than she. This one has at least the cleanness of an antelope, the quiet ways of a hare. . . . He laid his arm around her shoulders and bent and kissed her lips.

"My lord," said Abishai in the sudden, explosive accents of one who dreads the silence, "I hope there is yet a little room within you for food, since the men of Caleb are like to be waiting at the camp with fruit and cake for the bridegroom and the bride."

"Then we must eat again?"

"I will eat," said Noi. "Let my lord only taste, and I will eat in his place."

The ground over which they walked had begun to slope gently upward. He raised his eyes and saw the crest of the hill on which his army was encamped—a low, flat crest, like the back of some crouching beast, shaggy with brush, sinewy with ridges of stone. Here and there, scarcely larger and brighter than the yellow stars, burned a few fires. He sighed and shook himself. Suddenly he knew that Noi was worn with walking. Her breath hastened; she clung to his arm; she stumbled on a piece of shale. He lifted her up then and felt again that he carried the very body of sorrow against his chest.

Abishai had been mistaken concerning the men of Caleb. If they had waited to spread a feast, they had grown weary of waiting and had lain down on their cloaks to sleep. The whole slope of the hill was strewn with the inert shapes of sleepers. Only a few of the outlaws sat yawning around the dying fires, and it was plain that they had kept watch for their own reasons, not through any desire to welcome the bridegroom and the bride. Here and there one of them would stop in the middle of some tale or argument to bid David and Noi be fruitful and multiply. Some of them rose and bowed, some of them made raw jests, some of them smiled. But there was no general welcome. He knew what he had known from the beginning—that they looked with cold eyes upon this marriage. Why should their lord choose precisely the time when Saul's army moved down from the forest of Ephraim to make himself unclean in the sight of the God of battles, to squander his powers with a skinny, sallow child?

Well, he thought, at least there will be no need for more eating. He bore Noi past the last of the campfires, over the crest of the hill, and down the other side. Here at the foot was the opening of the cavern in which they would sleep. Joab, Abishai, and Abiathar followed him, holding their torches low, casting a red light upon the embroidered pillows and coverlets of goat's-hair that lay within.

"Is there anything that my lord and lady require?" Abiathar said. "There is nothing for nourishment within the cave except a cruet of wine."

"We need nothing more."

"Be fruitful and multiply," said Joab, and his jackal face was insolent in the torchlight with the knowledge that this wish was a matter of form and had been fulfilled long before it was spoken.

"Be fruitful and multiply," said Abishai, turning aside like a shamed boy and lowering his head.

"Yes," said Abiathar, thrusting the base of his torch into the earth before the cave, "be fruitful and multiply."

All three of them bowed, first to David and then to Noi, then climbed up the side of the hill and were gone.

He looked long at his bride in the light of the torch that Abiathar had left behind. Her disordered finery hung grotesquely upon her. It will be better, he thought, when she has laid her clothing aside. . . . But nothing, not even the thought of her robe falling from her shoulders, could beget so much as a faint stirring of desire within him. Her grave eyes, staring steadily into his face, seemed to be asking for something, and he felt confined and futile, thinking that surely she must be asking him to feel desire.

"My lord," she said at last, "there is a thing that I would ask of my lord. . . ."

"What is it, beloved?"

"That he take pity on my weariness and let me lie against his side without love for this one night."

For the first time in all his days, it seemed to him good that a woman did not desire him. He nodded and kissed her, first on the forehead, then lightly on the lips. "Come," he said, "I will put out the torch and we will go into the cave together. There we will lie quietly beside each other and rest. Some other night I will take my delight with Noi. Some other night I will also bear her into a strong house and set her down upon a goodly bed."

"It is enough for me that I should be with David in the hour of his bitterness," she said.

He uprooted the torch and smothered the flame against the earth. With the last sputter, all light died. The side of the hill rose up before him, a black wedge between him and the stars. Small noises filled the sudden silence—chirp of insects, rustle of animal feet, stir of creeping things, sounds of an alien and inimical world.

"Come, then," he said in a voice not quite his own. "It will be better when we lie down together."

But what had given him the illusion that the cave would be a place of safety, a place for rest? A cave is a door to Sheol, a cave is a tomb. The coverlets and the pillows they knelt upon while they unfastened their garments were damp and cold. He did not dare to speak. He had begun to shiver and was afraid that the words would fall in jerks from his lips.

Lord God of righteousness, when will I be punished enough to satisfy Your wrath? I have made a joyless marriage for Your sake. Was it needful also that I should have a cave for my marriage bed? Perhaps this same night the serpent or the lion or the murderer will fall upon me here, and I will die. And if I do not die tonight or tomorrow or within three-score years, what profit is there in such a thought? How can that which is human ever be comforted, since in the end it will be sealed up with all the generations of the dead? . . .

"Shall I lie down now beside David?" she said.

"Yes." His teeth chattered. "Come."

She crept toward him in her nakedness through the confusion of chilled cloth. Her body lay warm and dry against his side; the ominous quiet was broken by her stirring; the certainty of death was suspended by the coming and going of her breath.

"Are you warm, Noi? It is not good that one who carries a child should be cold."

"I am warm, I am blessed."

And now that he had remembered that she carried his son in her womb, he was no longer afraid. There is another life with us here, he thought. The pulse that beats secretly within her belly will still beat when both of us are dead. When I am closed within the burial cave, that which I have begotten will move about in the heat of the sun. When I am nothing—neither a shepherd in Judah nor a bandit in the wilderness nor king in Israel—my son will breathe and beget, and his son's son will carry the glimmering thread of life out of my slack, cold hands, across the abyss of death, golden, triumphant, even unto the ends of the world. . . .

He passed his arm beneath her body and drew her closer, so that her head rested against his shoulder and her unbound hair lay across his chest. "It is a good thing," he said, "to have Noi beside me. I had thought that I would nourish and comfort her, but now it is plain that I am the one who is to be nourished and comforted."

"Truly, my lord?"

He knew by her voice that all this time she had been quietly weeping. He raised himself and kissed her wet cheek. "Yes, truly," he said.

"But I am a poor bride for the Star of Bethlehem. I am as nothing beside the King's daughter. . . ."

"No, now, that is not so. Although Noi has not been the first to give me delight, she is yet the first to lay healing herbs on my heart." And indeed it seemed to him that the scent of her was the scent of herbs. Turning his face against her head, breathing against her hair, he thought that he drew into his nostrils the scent of peace. He felt the first tingling warmth of sleep. "Tomorrow I will bring a present to Noi. I will give her a collar of turquoise and gold that once hung round the throat of the Queen of Israel."

"And tomorrow I will make David a dish of savory lamb. Also a paste of honey and pistachio nuts."

He raised himself upon his elbow, thinking to kiss her yet once more. But even as his mouth brushed hers, their quiet was broken by footsteps, their eyes were assailed by red and wavering light.

"May my uncle forgive me," said the voice of Joab at the mouth of the cavern, "for coming upon him on his wedding night. Surely my uncle knows that I would not rouse him up tonight if it were not for a grave matter——"

"What matter?" He sat bolt upright, blinking into the torches. "What evil has been sent against me now?"

"No evil save the awaited one, my lord. Saul's army will be upon us by dawn. The sentry has wakened me even now to say that he has seen the torches from the ridge—the scouts have passed the mountains and begun to cross the plains. Surely my uncle will wish to lead his men swiftly to the appointed place."

"But Noi—what of Noi?" he said.

The voice of Abishai spoke at the entrance. "Trust her to me, and I will bring her up to you in safety. No evil shall befall her, I swear it as I live and as my soul lives."

And David was glad in his heart that this stupid, hairy, tender one should be the one to look to his bride.

❦ IV ❧

It was a somber country—that stretch of the southern wilderness in which the army of David sat waiting face to face with the host of the King of Israel. The leprous dryness of the desert lay upon it. The brush was scrubby and powdered with a fine gray dust. The earth ran swiftly through the fingers, as loose and dry as sand.

There were certain old tales which said that giants had dwelt here in the infancy of the world, and it was easy to believe that some voracious and terrible generation had left its marks upon the place. Great chisels might well have hacked at the cloven tops of the hills. Angry fists might have hurled the boulders down the slopes and twisted the few black trees awry. The birds screamed continually, as though obsessed with some primeval, unforgettable fright. The watercourses were deep and bone-dry. Once there had been yellow torrents rushing between these banks. But in a time of draught and famine in the years when the earth was beginning to grow old, the last of the giants—so the old tales said—had flung themselves upon the sun-dried shores and lapped the failing waters dry.

There was just such an empty watercourse at the bottom of the deep chasm that divided the army of David from the host of Saul. Each army looked down a steep slope, ragged with shale and accessible only to the goat and the antelope, at the pale and dusty riverbed that lay some two hundred feet below. Each army stared across less than half a mile of emptiness at its adversary—an adversary so close that it was possible to see banners and crests, even to distinguish familiar faces.

Joab had chosen the site of the encampment. It was he who had pointed out to David that whosoever held the southern ridge held those encamped to the north in the hollow of his hand. No man, not even Saul in his madness, would be foolhardy enough to charge down the northern slope in full sight of the enemy, to cross the dry watercourse within range of the slingers and the bowmen, to clamber up the southern side into a shower of spears. The great cleft between the two margins of rock was blank, impassable. True, in a day or so, the scouts had found a way to move around it. Six miles to the east, the cleft rock joined again—an army could climb over gentler slopes of lichen-covered rock, could move southward under cover of a screen of trees, and could emerge in the rear of the rebels on the other side. But such a maneuver would be successful only if it were planned in secrecy and executed as a surprise. And secrecy was impossible in the camp of Saul. The rebels on the southern ridge saw everything—called across the chasm to inquire whether the King had stayed in his tent all day because he was mad, sent condolences to Ahitophel on the death of three mules, made ribald comments whenever Rizpah showed her face, and asked Abner whether he meant to roast or stew the two fine mountain goats that had been brought to him last night.

The days of waiting were sickly days. The sun burned equally upon the two ridges; both the rebels and the King's men were growing lean on brackish water and unfamiliar meat; all eyes shared the same monotony—the chalky slopes, the pale riverbed, and, to the west, the gray and naked mountains that rose out of the miasmal country around the Dead Sea. The scream of the mountain birds, the yapping of the jackals, rent the veils of sleep alike for the men of Judah and the men of Benjamin.

And yet only half a moon had passed since David's wedding night, and four days of that time had been spent in maneuvering—brief and deceptive encampments, mock stands and mock flights, shows of readiness for battle which never developed into battle, serpentine wanderings over stretches of brush, gray plateaus, and shale-strewn hills. Joab had been the planner and the leader in all these sallies. Nervous and wily as a jackal, too tense for either food or sleep, he had grown thin with the exercise of outwitting the captain of Saul's host.

In those days the rebel army thanked God for Joab, since it was plain that the son of Jesse had indeed become a bleating lamb in the wilderness. He was listless, he was remote. He often stood staring at the ranks of the enemy with a mist as of tears blurring his eyes. Perhaps he yearned after his bride, whom Abishai had taken back to the relative safety of her brothers' house; perhaps he thought of the gone days when he had sat at Saul's feet. However it was with him, his companions in arms knew that, for the present, he was not good for anything. Yet there was no murmuring against him, no thought of complaint. Whatever his sorrows were, he bore them with surpassing grace. It was as if the very presence of the Israelite court had revived in the Judahite armor-bearer all his old courtly ways. No one but a dolt could fail to see that the crown of Israel belonged on his head. He had been ailing; the brackish water had infected him with dysentery; and the disease had made his skin translucent, had brightened his solemn gray eyes. It was true that the rebel army depended upon Joab; had Joab deserted them, they would have been trapped by Abner, they would have died. But had the son of Jesse gone forth from them, they would have ceased to be soldiers or men. If he had not been among them, kingly in his wretchedness, comely in his secret grief, they would have dispersed in the night; and with the army of the Lamb, the hope of Judah and the promise of God would have melted away.

During the sojourn at the edge of the Valley of the Rocks, he was assailed less by sickness than by wonder. On the journey down to the southern wilderness, he had learned with amazement that for a long time he had been walking like a ghost among the living. This discovery had broken upon him during a wayside council, when Joab had pointed out to him how, once the armies were assembled on either side of the chasm, they would be so close to each other that it would be possible to distinguish faces.

"Faces?" he had said, starting from the rock he sat upon. "The men in Saul's host—we will be able to see them face to face?"

"Even so, my lord."

"That is close indeed," he had said in a casual voice. But for a long time he sat on the stone and stared at the ground and gave himself up to the miracle that was being accomplished within him. His years in the wilderness had gone by as if he had wrapped himself in a winding sheet; now he moved painfully, stiff with long dark and cold, in aching resurrection.

But the hope that he would see Jonathan had not been with him long. Three days after they had set up their encampment on the edge of the ridge, a renegade Danite from Saul's ranks had found the detour and come over to David's side, to tell, among other things, that Jonathan was not with the host. And for David it was as if all color had suddenly been drained from the world. Be still, he told himself, be still. It was better with me in the years when I was dead. . . .

But that resurrection, once accomplished, could not be undone. However tightly he bound the winding strips during his waking hours, they were torn apart while he slept. The white face, the cloudy hair, rose to the surface of all his dreams. Often he wakened in a state of lassitude, unable to rise from the ground, worn out with the interminable journeys he and Jonathan had taken together. They went hand in hand to the peak of some white, infertile mountain. They toiled up endless flights of stairs. Or they hastened, wordless and solemn, over stretches of frosty forest land in bitter cold, toward some stone of covenants where they could keep their old and broken vows of death.

Then one morning he ceased to struggle. What is, is, he told himself, and lay all day in the shadow of a stone, giving himself up to remembrance, healing the terrible divide between the day and the night. And it was strange and wonderful to him that this old longing, which in the past had divided him from Saul and Michal and all the world, should work another magic now, should beget in him a pervading tenderness, a tremulous love for all men. He remembered the dusty wedding gifts in the tower room in Gibeah, and paid at last his long-due debt of tears. He turned eastward toward the hills of Moab and said to his mother and his father, Keep your blood warm a little longer, wait for me, do not die. . . . He thought of Noi, showing the all-too-early signs in the house of her eight brothers, and he yearned to defend and comfort her, to carry her like a sick lamb against his chest. His gravity and kindliness stirred up concern among his companions. "How is it with the Star of Bethlehem?" they said. "He has the look of one who has turned his back to the world and has prepared for his death."

But on the evening of that same day all their fears were dispelled. He rose from the shadow of the stone and washed himself and was merry. A faint tinge, the color of an apricot, showed on his cheeks. He took his evening bread on the edge of the cliff with Abishai and Joab, eating quickly and ravenously and tossing his crusts and bones over his shoulder into the chasm. For the first time he saw that the army on the other side of the riverbed was not the army that had gone down, in the days of his glory, to meet the Philistines in the plains of Sharon. Those who stood guard at the edge of the northern ridge had the look of molting eagles; the pattern of the camp, so studied and precise in the old days, sprawled and wavered now. The baggage wagons had been set at the center of the host. Around them, in bulging circles, Saul's thousands were disposed. The supper fires were small and few, and Joab pointed out that the supplies of the Israelite army were doubtless waning fast.

Before the meal was over, Joab excused himself and set out for a council with his captains; but David and Abishai lingered long over the raisins and the curds. Silence came upon the two of them, and David was grateful for the silence. It was late; on both sides of the ravine the supper fires were going out; the moon had risen. Mellow, golden, very close, it hung above the chasm, evoking long shadows in the dry riverbed, touching the edges of bush and vine, giving the dead leaves a metallic glow. The son of Jesse folded his hands and stared as solemnly as any heathen worshiper into the warm, ripe disk of the moon.

Just such a moon had hung on many a night above the garden in Gibeah, when he had lain stretched on the grass beside the King's son, when Abner had dozed and dreamed of ancient battles, when Saul had rested his head against the knees of his concubine. Long since, he had sealed up those nights in the opaque stuff of forgetfulness, as the honey is sealed up in the cells of the honeycomb. But now the walls were down at last; now he took, and tasted, and knew the old sting of sweetness. All the lost music, all the forgotten talk, came back to him. The wind passed singing through the boughs of Saul's terebinth; and the air was fresh with marjoram and thyme. The King of Israel rose from the bench beneath the tree and bent above him, smiling and saying, "Tomorrow let the son of Jesse bring us yet another song."

And suddenly that tenderness which had risen first from the thought of Jonathan and had flowed out over Michal and Noi, Jesse and the mother, and all the poor creatures who dwelt for a few precarious years upon this gleaming moonlit world—suddenly that tenderness converged upon the King of Israel, who walked this night among the dying fires on the other side of the chasm. Saul, he thought, how is it with Saul tonight? My lord who delivered Israel out of the hands of the uncircumcised, my lord whose body is seamed with the scars of Michmash and Amalek, my lord who came to the succor of the men of Jabesh-Gilead—how is it with my lord? . . .

At that moment he saw through the thickening shadows that he and his hairy kinsman were no longer alone. A Hittite bowman stood beside them at the edge of the cliff, carrying a dead mountain goat upon his shoulders.

"Look, my uncle, he has caught a fine mountain goat in the ravine."

"Yes, I see." But he scarcely heard his own voice. The word "ravine" hung static in his thoughts. He looked down into the moonlit, jagged gully, and thought how on the other side of it the King of Israel paced back and forth among the host. How have the years dealt with him? he asked himself. Is he greatly changed? They say that his beard is grizzled now, frosted over with patches of white. Is it still upon him—that cloak that I used to lay across his shoulders? How is it that I have forgotten his murderous fingers round my throat? How is it that I can remember nothing but his tenderness and would give my right hand for a sight of his face? . . .

The Hittite was boasting of his own valor in the thick accents of his kind; how, in full sight of the Israelites on the other side, he had gone halfway down the side of the cliff to claim his quarry. "And not one among them turned his eyes upon me," he said. "They huddled in the shadow of the rocks and stared at their own feet. . . ."

"Where does the King of Israel sleep?"

Abishai gaped at him. "I have not fully heard the words of my lord," he said at last.

"I inquired of my nephew in what place the King of Israel lies down to sleep."

"Why, at the center of the host, among the baggage wagons. So at least my brother Joab has said." And with the calmness of a mother who thinks to undo the naughtiness of her child by disregarding it, he turned back to the Hittite and mended the broken conversation, asking courteously whether the rocks had proved slippery and whether it was true that there was the imprint of a monstrous hand on the dry bank below.

But the son of Jesse saw neither Abishai nor the bowman. He saw the circle of baggage wagons on the other side of the chasm; he saw them not as they were now, but as they would look an hour or so hence, when even the last of the supper fires would have burned out and there would be no light save the triumphant light of the high moon. He saw himself standing within the circle of the wagons, leaning against a big wheel and looking down at the sleeping face of the King of Israel. And so it will be, he thought, so it will be tonight. . . .

"Well," said the bowman, "I will take myself back to the campfire. May Jahveh walk with my lord and with my captain."

"Wait," said David, rising. "Who will go down with me to Saul, to the camp of the Israelites?"

The Hittite stood staring at him, his mouth loosened by amazement, his eyes shifting with fear.

"Wherefore, my uncle?" Abishai said.

"Because a longing has come upon me—I am possessed by a great and unreasonable longing—to look upon the face of him who was once my lord."

The Hittite bowed himself out of sight. David and Abishai stood face to face, but neither looked at the other. Abishai's stubby fingers plucked at the hairs on his chest.

Well, thought David, if he will not come with me, then I must go down alone. . . . But the thought had scarcely formed itself in his mind when the pudgy hand touched his elbow.

"I will go down with you," Abishai said.

◄§ V §►

LONG AFTERWARD, whenever he told his children of that brief and precarious journey, David paused in wonderment, remembering that no fear had been in him then. The light of the moon fell pitilessly on the bottom of the chasm, so that those above could easily discern what passed below. A single arrow, aimed well in moonlight, might have sent the son of Jesse into Sheol to make the prophet Samuel a laughingstock among the ghosts. And yet he who had shuddered at the thought of a snake lurking in a cave felt no fear at all.

He knew the source of this high courage, but he never spoke of it to his children, since it was a tenuous and subtle matter—such a matter as children cannot be expected to understand. How can one teach a child that only those who have wrapped themselves in winding sheets, only the living dead, are afraid of death?

When he and Abishai dragged themselves above the ledge and stood in the presence of Saul's host, not even the fear of fear fell like the shadow of a pointed finger across his heart. He felt only triumphal music—blast of joyous trumpets, high shrilling of pipes—in his blood.

He should have thought, Gracious is Jahveh who has laid a miraculous deep sleep upon them. Instead, he thought only, How sorrowful they look in the light of the moon! . . .

Abishai whispered behind him, "God has sealed up their eyes for the sake of my lord."

He nodded without turning his head and began to walk slowly toward the outermost circle, where the lowest of the low—old slinger of Issachar, sickly water-carrier of Dan—lay asleep.

"Let us not linger," said Abishai. "Let us go directly into the midst of the encampment, even into the presence of the King. To tarry is to tempt the Lord."

He looked across the sleepers, lying in dark concentric rows. Here and there moonlight made a white glimmer upon a sword, a breastplate, or a shield. At the core of the circle he could see the great wheels of the baggage wagons and the banners, limp upon their staves in the windless air. Something glittered in their midst—it was the point of Saul's spear, as permanent in his remembrance as the blue vein that branched across Jonathan's brow.

"No," he said, "we will not tarry." But he tarried, looking into the faces of the sleeping menials, finding even among them the savor of the gone days; for one of them had brought him a draught of water during the battle on the plains of Sharon, and another had carried a basket of figs from Saul's garden to that high house in Gibeah which the son of Jesse had once called his home.

He walked on, stepping always into smaller circles, moving always closer to the banners and the wagons and the glittering leaf-shaped head of Saul's spear. How solemnly, how profoundly, all of them slept—the Ephraimite captain with his arm laid across his shield, the Benjamite slinger with his hand on his companion's wrist, the Danite physician with his little bags of herbs at his side and his face, spare and sorrowful, lifted to the full light of the moon. That face—where was it that my eyes beheld that face? David asked himself. In the plains of Sharon, in the pale light of a spring evening, when the wind of God moved through the branches of the almonds, tearing the white and bitter blossoms from the bough. This is the mouth that said the words I could not say, lulling my beloved as though he were a little child. This is the hand that drew the red lump of death out of his side. . . . The son of Jesse bent and laid his fingers lightly upon the surgeon's hand.

"My lord!" Abishai said.

"Be not afraid. He will not waken. This is he who healed my brother Jonathan."

The physician turned on his side and breathed deeply, but did not waken. None of the others stirred, even though the two intruders walked now among those who should never have closed their eyes by night—King's armor-bearer, keeper of the King's accounts, captain of the host. David stood motionless in the shadow of the wagons, staring at the big wheels and the black heaps of dried figs and grain. Then he raised his head and looked above the wagons, above the limp banners, above the tip of the spear, at the stars.

"Jahveh," he said in a whisper, "wait for me. Let them sleep."

He felt it then, stretched over the whole encampment, hovering between the sky and the plateau—the great, still presence of the Lord. Sleep issued from it as dew issues from a cloud; captain and bowman and water boy were drenched for David's sake in beneficent, impenetrable sleep. Since God was with him, he could take his time. He knelt on the ground beside the captain of the host.

"My lord!" said Abishai. "The King is not here. He is within the circle of the wagons. Come!"

"I know."

How is it, David asked himself, that I loved Abner and knew it not? Old, scarred hand that drew me into the King's tent at Ephes-Dammim—blunt, solemn face that watched me make a covenant of death—grave, decent mind that saw my darkest dream and was too honorable to call it by its evil name—God keep you, live for a hundred years, and spend them all in well-earned rest. . . .

"My lord," said Abishai, rubbing his sweating palms upon his tunic, "will you kneel here beside the captain all night?"

The rough Judahite accents fell like a stone into the still pool of remembrance. "No," he said coldly, "it is only that I have been wondering——"

"What is it that the son of Jesse wonders?"

Why I am condemned to live in the company of fools, he thought, why a son of Zeruiah should stand with me at this exalted hour, why I did not come up alone. "I have been wondering whether such a mound of flesh as my nephew can crawl between the wheels. Perhaps it is impossible. Perhaps it would be well for Abishai to remain outside."

"Let me go with my lord."

The voice was shaken and humble. Without turning his head, David knew that the childish face had puckered. Now, he thought, I have put a grievous wound upon the heart of my companion. It is as though I had said aloud that I find his fat body disgusting and that I would not have the King of Israel see me in such tawdry company. . . . He turned and laid his hand upon the plump and hairy arm. "No, now," he whispered, "it was a jest. Let us crawl between the wheels together, on all fours, like the Judahite dogs that we are."

The ground beneath the wagons gave off a sweet and homely smell. It was covered with all that had dripped or sifted through the cracks in the wood—flour and oil, herbs and dried curds, raisins and powdered spice. He had breathed such a scent often in the camp of God; and for weeks after a long campaign, he had found it again on the cloak and the tunic of the King of Israel when he laid them in the clothes chest at night. Once, he thought in the darkness beneath the wagons, once I was the warder of his sleep and the guardian of his unarmed nakedness. . . . He crawled slowly forward on his belly until he issued into sudden emptiness. Then he stood up. After the crowded rows through which he had passed, this last circle of the encampment seemed open, vast. At the very center lay Saul, with his spear thrust into the earth at his head and the cruse of water at his feet.

David stepped backward and closed his eyes. It was as though he had received a blow beneath the heart. That which he beheld was not the hero of Jabesh-Gilead, nor God's anointed, nor Samuel's honorable adversary. That which he beheld was a sick man in an uneasy sleep. Saul lay on his back, with his head fallen a little to one side, so that his face was naked to the merciless brightness of the moon. The long beard, spread over his shoulder and trailing on the ground, was streaked with strands of white. There was whiteness too in the moist and tangled locks that fell back from his brow. His skin hung loosely upon the big bones of his face. His breathing was painful, uneven, as though breathing were a labor, as though there were no end to labor, even in sleep. And David was ashamed that he had come up to invade the privacy of the King of Israel, to see him in his most vulnerable hour. As the ailing lion hides his sickness in the brush, so Saul slept alone among the wagons to hide his face.

The breath of Abishai was on David's neck. "God has delivered up your enemy into your hand this night," Abishai said.

Like a flash of forked lightning the thought tore through his mind: This is the enemy, and God has laid him here before me. God has walled him about with wagons, and stopped the ears of the host with a deep sleep. No cry would waken them, even if there were to be a cry. This is the enemy who strangled me and hurled me down to grovel and weep. This is the enemy—and not my enemy alone—enemy of Samuel and of Judah, canker in the bowels of Israel, madman upon the throne. . . . And suddenly he felt the presence of the God of hosts, the great body of the Warrior, covered with dragon scales and blowing the hot breath of the bull. The God of Battles was with him, panting for blood.

"Come now, let me smite him," said Abishai. "I pray you, let me smite him to the earth with one stroke, and there will be no need to strike him a second time."

With one stroke—God, God, David thought, what things might be accomplished with one thrust of the spear! One stroke, and I am avenged and Israel is cleansed and Jonathan is on the throne. A nameless murderer lays Saul low by night and flees; and David is recalled to live in a high house of stone and cedarwood, to walk with the great, to sing again in a green garden, to turn Israel into Caphtor, to wear a double crown. . . .

Saul stirred in his sleep. The loose lips closed and were indented briefly at the corners by a faint and transitory smile. Such a smile had transformed his face on many a sun-reddened evening in the garden at Gibeah, when he lay with his head in the lap of his concubine. Such a smile, solemn and tender, he had bestowed a hundred times upon his lutist at the end of a song. With such a smile he had risen from the council table or walked across the field of battle to greet a hero, to welcome Abner, to embrace Jonathan. So he had smiled long ago in the tent at Ephes-Dammim, when he fell silent after telling how the men of Jabesh-Gilead had brought him their sour wine and washed his feet with their tears.

"My lord," said Abishai.

David made his shoulders hard and high against the son of Zeruiah and lifted his eyes to the stars. Jahveh still hovered between him and the firmament. But He was no longer the God of Battles—He was the Other Jahveh now, formless and all-pervading. Weep, son of Jesse, said the Lord. Weep for the hero of Jabesh-Gilead and Michmash and Amalek. Weep for him who lifted up the tribes of Israel and joined them together. Weep for this broken tabernacle in which I dwelt, for it was fair and clean and high, and I dwelt comfortably there. Cease for one moment to be David of Bethlehem. Cast off the fair flesh that stands between you and Me, and between you and all men. Put by your too-well-beloved self, and creep bodiless and selfless into that which lies before you. And if this is impossible, if you are still imprisoned in yourself even at such an hour, then weep for yourself. For you also are anointed. You also in your day will become the ravaged temple through which the sounding wind of glory and the devouring fire of shame have passed. . . .

The voice of the world, speaking in Abishai's mouth, said yet once more, "Let me lay him low, my lord."

But David turned and smiled at Abishai and shook his head. "Destroy him not," he said. "Who can put forth his hand against Jahveh's anointed and be guiltless? As Jahveh lives, Jahveh will smite him, or his day shall come to die, or he shall go down into battle and perish. God forbid that I should put forth my hand against Jahveh's anointed. Come, now, let us go out before we rouse him from his sleep."

Abishai sighed and set out toward the wagons, but David remained a little longer, staring down at the dreamer's face. As in the old days when he had watched beside his lord on a night before battle, he bent and folded the edge of the cloak back upon the King's body, so that it might shield him from the cold. Then he took up the cruse of water that lay at Saul's feet and the spear that stood at his head. While he crawled beneath the wagons and walked past Abner and Ahitophel, he drew the remembrance of the lost years from the pottery and the wood. Clasping them to him as he moved through the ranks of the sleepers, he held all Gibeah, all the forgotten songs, all the long summer evenings, to his breast.

"How was it, my lord," said Abishai as they let themselves down toward the riverbed, "how was it that you would not let me smite him in his sleep?"

"Because our God sometimes changes His shape and becomes other than the God of Battles. . . ."

The small eyes, stupid and good, said plainly, "I do not understand."

"Because," he said, remembering how Abishai had wept for Noi on her wedding night, "my heart went out to him; he looked so pitiful as he slept."

Abishai nodded and sighed. "I am glad then that I did not put forth my hand against him," he said.

❧ VI ❧

THE SON OF JESSE did not close his eyes that night. Abishai slept at his feet, his round face puckered now and then with a remembrance of the tender and incomprehensible rebuke that had been put upon him by his lord. The rebels slept under the setting moon, so deeply that it seemed that the sleep of Jahveh had fallen upon them also. Toward morning, God sent His silence upon the jackals and the birds; and in the misty hush David sat alone at the edge of the ravine and fondled the water cruse and ran his palm up and down the shaft of the spear. Sometimes his face wore the subtle smile that he had seen upon Saul's lips, and sometimes he rested his forehead against his knees and wept.

When the sun sent the first diagonal rays across the riverbed, and the prelude to awakening—the lifting of arms, the turning of heads, the deep inhalations of the changed air—stirred the armies on either side of the chasm, he could no longer bear to sit still. He walked to the very edge of the ravine, and it was as though his spirit went forth from him to hover like a hummingbird, with beating wings, over the beloved ones who were wakening now in the camp of God.

How would it be, he asked himself, if I lifted up my voice and spoke aloud to those on the other side? Surely they would hear me, for we have hurled our taunts across the cleft, and Saul used to say that my voice was strong enough to carry even to the footstool of the Lord. . . . For a long time he played with the notion, growing heedless and heady. What would come to pass, he asked himself, with laughter rippling under the question, if I should call out to the King of Israel and hold up my booty and bid him look upon what I have in my hands? . . . He swayed back and forth on his heels at the very edge of the cliff; the mist billowed below him, and it seemed to him that he was poised upon the rolling surface of an effulgent sea. Yet he doubted in his heart that it would be well to shout the King's name. To hold the cruse and the spear before the King's eyes— that would be a piece of insolence. Abner, he thought, I could call upon Abner and rebuke him that he slept. . . . And even before the thought was fully formed, he had shouted the name of the captain of the host.

A murmur went up on the other side. Saul's host was awake; the men of Israel were stumbling to their knees; six thousand pairs of hands were groping after bows and swords and spears. Even now, the son of Jesse thought, the King's hand reaches out to touch this shaft which I embrace, and he finds it not. . . .

"Abner," he said again, "how is it that you do not answer?"

"Who is it," said Abner, "that cries out to the captain of the King's host?"

And David said to Abner: "Are you not a valiant man? Who is there like you in Israel? Then wherefore have you not kept watch over the King your lord? For last night one came up from among my people, to destroy the King. As Jahveh lives, you deserve to die because you have not kept watch over your lord, the anointed of God."

At first there was no answer. They will not parley with me, David thought. The lordly ones of the north will keep their regal silence before the renegade Judahite. . . . Then he saw through the mist that the host of Jahveh was dividing to make way. Abner came forward and stood at the edge of the chasm, and David and the captain of the host were face to face.

Under the long stare of Abner, the son of Jesse became again that which he had been in the camp at Ephes-Dammim—a confused and embarrassed child. He lifted up his trophies and said lamely, "See where the King's spear is, and the cruse of water that was at his feet."

Now both the armies were fully awakened. Before him and behind him there arose a babbling and a questioning: What has come to pass? Saul's spear? The water cruse that lay beside the King? Who then has crossed the impassable barrier by night? Who but David? Who other than our valiant lord? But David scarcely heard them, for another voice, loud with grief, shaken by tenderness, had risen at the center of the host of God.

"Is that your voice, my son David?" the King of Israel said.

Then David wept and answered, saying: "It is my voice, O my King. Wherefore should my lord pursue his servant? What evil have I intended? What have I done to deserve to be exiled from the land of God? Would my lord truly send me forth to dwell among the heathen, to worship other gods, and to shed my blood upon unholy earth?" He waited, staring earnestly across the sea of mist, but there was no movement among the warriors on the other side, and no reply. He saw himself, worn and shabby. He saw his army, an assembly of the condemned and the rejected, driven to the last extremity, standing at the very edge of the southern sand. "Why," he said, "should the King of Israel bring an army down against such a one as I? To come down to me with an army is to call out the host of Jahveh to pursue a miserable flea or to hunt a partridge in the mountains."

In the ensuing hush, he heard his companions stirring and murmuring behind him. He knew in his heart then that he had been borne out too far on the exaltation of the moment. He had broken faith with his warriors; he had humbled them and himself in the presence of the enemy. When I turn again, he thought, I may be utterly alone. Even these wretches may have taken up their weapons and made ready to depart. . . . Yet the thought roused no fear within him. He stared at the long diagonal rays of sun, stronger and more golden now, lying like the swords of the heavenly host across the mist. It is in God's hand, he thought. . . .

"Go in peace, my son David."

He started and had to tell himself that it was the King of Israel who spoke. The voice—grave, sorrowing, and remote—might well have issued from the mouth of the Lord.

"I have played the fool," Saul said. "I have erred exceedingly. Go in peace, for I will do no harm against you, because my life was precious in your eyes last night."

A shout of exultation, a clash of spear against shield, went up from both sides of the chasm. It had dawned upon the warriors that what they witnessed was a treaty of peace. Those on Saul's side shouted, "God be with the Star of Bethlehem!" and those on David's side shouted, "A long life to the Lion of Benjamin!" The son of Jesse raised his voice above this babble, and talked, as incoherently as the rest, of many things: Let Saul send a young man from the ranks to fetch the stolen spear; let the King remember in the tabernacle of his heart that his armor-bearer had not put forth his hand against God's anointed; let Jahveh remember it also, and look favorably upon His servant, and deliver His servant out of all these tribulations . . . He scarcely knew what it was that he said. Then each man took up his weapons and turned his back upon the Valley of the

Rocks—David's men to return to the plains of Judah and Saul's men to return to their fields and houses in Dan and Ephraim, Issachar and Manasseh and Benjamin.

As they departed, Saul's voice spoke once more above the clatter.

"Go with my blessing, my son David. You shall do mighty deeds, and when your day comes, you shall surely prevail."

◆§ VII §◆

THREE DAYS had passed since the Star of Bethlehem had led his warriors back to their encampment in the plain of Judah. Three days, and he had not walked forth to re-establish his authority over the herdsmen, had not gone down to the house of the brothers to fetch his bride, had not spoken with Joab concerning the state of the army—had done nothing but wander aimlessly about the camp or sit brooding by himself.

On the journey from the Valley of the Rocks to the plain, the radiance within him had not perceptibly faded. For he had said in his heart, I that was cast down am lifted up. When Saul yearned over me in the presence of the hosts and called me his son, I was summoned again into the fellow-ship of the great. . . . And yet at the sight of the camp his exaltation had dwindled. The others were glad enough to settle down upon the familiar slope, still scarred by the black ugliness of their burnt-out camp-fires. They had gone cheerfully about their business, collecting the regular fees from the farmers, informing the herdsmen that there would be addi-tional payment due, since double protection against the marauders of the desert would be necessary during the coming Festival of the Sheep Shearing. But the son of Jesse had remained in the encampment, sitting on a stone from morning until evening, finding the sight of the wilderness loathsome, and deploring the day of his birth.

He had come at last to see that his high adventure in the Valley of the Rocks had brought him nothing but a passing illusion of magnificence. As he had gone forth from the encampment—poor and discredited and alone—so he had returned to it. It was true that he had been delivered from certain fears; but the deliverance was indecisive, since Saul's madness might at any moment cancel Saul's clemency. The King of Israel had indeed called him "my son," and the words themselves were memorable and dear. But his pleasure in this also was transitory. The words could too easily be transformed into mockery. Behold, he thought, putting on his threadbare clothes, behold the garments of the son of the King of Israel. . . . And, stretching himself out under the inimical sky, he said in his heart, Look, now, my lord, where your son lies down to sleep. . . .

On the third day of his sojourn on the slope, the camp was almost empty. It was the Festival of the Sheep Shearing, a mild and sunny day through which the sounds of singing and laughter passed on an erratic wind. David lay alone on the side of the hill and heard the songs that used to rise in the green stretches of land around Bethlehem, saw the damsels dancing before the brown gates, saw Samuel's white hands blessing the flock, saw Jesse, merry and reverent, moving among his washed and shimmering sheep.

There were none left on the hillside with whom he cared to speak. Abiathar the priest had gone down to one of the villages to bless a flock, and Joab had set forth in protest against his uncle's surliness. Those among the warriors who had families had returned to dwell beneath a roof for a night, to eat bread cooked on a clean hearthstone, to set eyes on their fathers and their mothers. All the rest were busy among the farms and villages of the plain. There was double booty to be brought home tonight. The plainsmen, eager to appear openhanded in the eyes of their visitors, generous with religious ardor and wine, would pay without complaint. Tonight the caves of the encampment would be packed with raisins, cheeses, plump wineskins, cruets of oil, bushels of flour. All of the freebooters would return heavily laden—all except Abishai and the six young men whom he had taken with him to Nabal's house. That was a fool's journey, and David had warned them against it. If they returned empty-handed, they had nobody to blame but themselves.

He had meant to go up today to the house of Noi's brothers. But he could not bring himself to bathe and put on his tunic and girdle; he lay on the slope, naked except for his loincloth, his body seeping up the rich indolence of the sun. And toward the hour of the noonday meal a hunger such as he had never known stirred in his vitals—no mere hunger after food, but all the hunger of his last seven lean years—a yearning to embrace, to own, to enjoy the teeming riches of the world.

Then suddenly all desires converged into a single desire. He yearned after a woman, and knew that since morning he had harbored this longing, had watched it ripen like a pomegranate in the heat of the sun. Shall I go down then and bring up my bride? he asked himself, turning on his side and hearing the tribal chant borne on the wind across the plain. And at this notion he laughed a brief laugh, dry and bitter. Child, child, he thought, as meager as a twig, as hard to the lips as a green apricot—a good companion to one who shudders in his sepulcher, but nothing save a reproach to one who has arisen. . . .

What woman, then? He closed his eyes against the sun and called up a vision. He imagined that he was a child again, and had gone down to the temple of the Baal of the Vine, in spite of the warnings of Jesse, to stare at the bossed brazen door on which man and fish and beast embraced and flowed into each other in a lawless festival of universal oneness, universal delight. He was a child and laid a child's hand upon the latch. And then he was no longer a child; he had opened the door; he had gone in. They had made an arbor of their temple in honor of the god. Walls, ceiling, and altar were lost under leaves; the place was heavy with the smell of incense and wine. On the lofty beams, among the clouds of fragrant smoke, the sacred pigeons fluttered and coupled. On the altar, two snakes intertwined. And on the leafy floor they lay together—the brave and the beautiful—and a constant murmur of exaltation, a laughter untainted by the remembrance of death, flowed from their lips. "This is the forbidden blessedness," said a woman's voice. "Come, eat of the fruit."

She who had spoken came toward him through the smoke, stepping lightly over the lovers. Her body showed full and golden under its veils and bangles, but she moved so gracefully that she seemed to float upon the air. Her breasts rose like two pale melons, pressing against each other, closing upon the chain which hung between. Her face was covered with a fine veil, but he could see the mouth beneath the folds. It parted and breathed a delicate moisture against the cloth. Then some voice behind the altar summoned her, and she was gone.

Who was she? he asked himself, starting up from his fantasy. And his heart answered him, saying: Fool, fool, it was the wife of Nabal who was with you, she whose name is Abigail, she who stood at the casement in the generative night and looked out upon you with favor in her eyes. And even this morning you have let Abishai and the young men go down to demand tribute fom her husband, because you are bemused and care not who goes where and have no more governance over your affairs than a child. Now they have gone down, and there is no stopping them, and they will bring scorn upon your name. For Nabal will curse them and cast them out and make laughingstocks of them before his guests. And henceforth the name of David will be a mockery in Nabal's house, and the wife will laugh with the husband. . . .

The thought was as sudden and intolerable as the sting of a hornet. It stung him out of his dreams; it drove him to his feet. He found his tunic lying on a stone near by, pulled it over his head, and girded it so tightly that the leather belt bit into his sides. And now where shall I go? he thought. How shall I waste the rest of this accursed afternoon? . . . He considered again the possibility of going to the house of the eight brothers; but that thought had no sooner entered his head than he told himself that he could not go. He must walk down to the caves instead; he must clear the debris from the caves, must make them ready for the fine store of food the freebooters would bring home from the villages tonight.

He paused first at the smallest of the caves, the one which had been reserved for booty other than food. Under the curving arc of rock lay seven small heaps neatly spaced in a semicircle—vases, amulets, baskets, girdles, sandals, tunics, cloth. And this, he thought, is the sum of my imperishable riches. All save this has been eaten up, or will be eaten before another moon. . . . The next cave would be a disorderly mass of slippery skins of wine and curds. He grew weary at the thought of it, and sank down upon the moist earth and leaned his elbows upon a heap of cloth. Soon I will go forth, he thought, but now I will rest. . . .

The cloth yielded gently under his weight. He moved forward a little and pillowed his head upon it. It was cool and delicate. It gave off a strange fragrance, such a fragrance as he had scented in his childhood upon a porous weed which, said the traveler who brought it into Bethlehem, had once grown at the bottom of the western sea. He raised his hand and drew a loose length of the cloth over his shoulder and held it up in the half-light of the cave. A strange cloth, he thought, yawning. Here it is grayish, but it would show green or blue in the sun. A valuable cloth, heavily embroidered. Is it a sea dream that turns the vague shapes upon it into darting fish—or are they sea creatures indeed? . . . A fluted fin glinted at him through the dark. It was sea cloth, Philistine cloth, heathen cloth. It was the cloth that Achish had sent from the city of Gath. "And he bade me tell my master," said Joab's voice, "to come down and dwell among the great, to be the friend of his heart, to ride in a chariot through the streets of the cities beside the sea. . . ."

"David," said a voice.

It is the voice of Samuel speaking out of Sheol, he thought, and he will say to me, "Behold how you have kept those covenants which you made with the God of Hosts at the edge of my grave. For you swore to take the child Noi and to cherish her as the true and only wife, and even this day she goes heavily among her eight brothers, with her shame upon her, while you lie idle on the slope and dream of coupling with the wife of Nabal at the wine feast of the Canaanites. Remember also how you have said, laying your hands upon the soles of my dead feet, 'I will turn utterly from Philistia. I will have no dealings with those who eat the crawling creatures of the sea.' And even now, when God has delivered you out of the hands of Saul, you are not content. Glory also you must have, and plumes, and a chariot, and a soft bed." . . .

"David," said the voice again.

But it was only the voice of Abishai, speaking near the entrance. Nevertheless, David threw the cloth from him and came forth from the cave in a confusion of anger and shame, as a man might come from illicit and interrupted love.

Abishai stood staring disconsolately at the ground. His bearing was that of a kicked dog. Is it possible, thought David, that kin of mine could look so foolish and woebegone? . . . Farther up the slope stood the young men who had accompanied Abishai, and they also had a hangdog air.

"Well, then," said David, with more harshness than he had intended in his tone, "how was it, Abishai? What came to pass at Nabal's house?"

"It was a fool's errand. We got nothing out of Nabal's hand, my lord."

He wondered why he had put the question; it was painfully obvious that their journey had come to naught. To shrug now, to hold his tongue—that would be wisdom. And yet his blood, suddenly hot within him, would not let him be still. He had a bitter need to punish them and to goad himself. "Tell me the manner of it," he said.

"Why should my lord concern himself with the manner of it? Let it suffice to say to my lord that we spoke very humbly and graciously to the churl and that he cast us forth without so much as one raisin."

The thought of this great oaf standing as his despised advocate before Abigail's eyes—the thought was enough to drive him mad. "Dolt, donkey!" he cried at the top of his voice. "When I say the manner of it, I mean the manner of it. Tell me from the beginning to the end what came to pass."

Abishai sighed, shifted from foot to foot, and looked about him. The encampment had come to life in the warm light of the afternoon. Many of the men had returned with their booty while David dreamed in the cave, and were making it ready for the Star of Bethlehem's delight; and still others could be seen coming round the side of the hill, bearing baskets on their heads.

Abishai said lamely, "At least some were more fortunate than I. . . ."

"Fool! How many times must I repeat a command?"

A small, sly smile, almost as infuriating as the thought of Nabal's highhandedness, twitched the corners of Abishai's soft lips. "Well, then," he said, "here is the manner of it, and may it please my lord. We came into Nabal's fields, and we found him with his guests, shearing his sheep. We made a very gentle speech to him, saying how we had watched over him and his guests and his shearers, that no harm from the south should come near them on the day of the festival. We asked him only to give us whatsoever seemed proper in his sight. 'Give,' we said, 'whatever is in your hand unto your servants and unto your son David.' That we said, and no more."

David saw the whole scene—the circle of bedizened guests; the stocky master of the house, dressed in his vulgar finery for the feast; the fair wife standing beside him, keeping her face blank for the moment, waiting to learn whether she should sneer or smile. . . .

"Well, how was it?" he shouted. "What of Nabal? What said he?"

"Why should my lord wish to offend his own ears with the mouthings of a fool?"

"My most offensive fool stands even now before me. Tell me what Nabal said."

"As my lord wills. Nabal answered David's servants, and said, 'Who is David? Who is this son of Jesse? Nowadays there are many servants who run away from their masters and come to hide in the wilderness. Shall I feed them all? Shall I take my bread and my water and my meat that I have killed for my shearers and give it to men who come from I know not where?' This is what Nabal said, and may it satisfy my lord."

Runaway slave, and, most galling of all, no different from all the other threadbare wretches who scratched for a living in the barren land. Not the King's son-in-law who slept once in a regal bed. Not the anointed one, beating down the bitter years that stood between him and the throne. For the first time he saw himself undistinguished, colorless, a dog in a pariah pack. The realization drove him into a churning fury. He began to rage in a voice that drew all his wondering host from their dallying on the hill, to stand about him, to stare into his face.

"Go every man of you and gird on his sword. Take a little bread, a little meat, but until I am avenged let no man who is my man and a soldier wet his tongue with wine. For the foul pig Nabal has sent my own servants to tell me that I am a dog, and while he lives I cannot live. Surely I have been a fool to stand between his belongings and the men of the south. Let God do so to me and more also, if I leave anything that is his to see the morning light, even so much as one man-child."

For a moment they continued to stare at him. A few raised their voices in the required outcry, but most of them looked covertly over their shoulders at their newly kindled fires and their heaps of unsorted booty; and he could read the signals of disappointment flashing from eye to eye. Now he felt doubly shamed. Surely they are a pack of dogs, he thought, and it is only by sufferance and not by devotion that I am the leader of the pack. . . . He turned on his heel and went from them. The violence of his rage had left him shaken.

Perhaps this weakness is the weakness of hunger, he thought, walking back to the cave and sitting on the earth before it. He rested his back against the slope and was disproportionately grateful for a hollow in the rock that made a kind of niche for his head. He longed for food, and wished to be angry that none of them had thought to bring him food; but the capacity for anger had gone from his body, and he could feel only a childish hurt at their neglect.

The heroic rage that he had felt against Nabal had also dwindled. The clean and searing pain had been transformed into a dull and sickly ache. I would make a great matter of it, he thought; I would hide it under curses and brandished swords; but nevertheless it is only a tawdry thing, it is only that I have been shamed by a rich Judahite. . . . He gazed disconsolately at the last slanting rays of sun. The wind had come up from the sea and was bearing the final chants and cries of the festival across the plain. "God of hosts," he said aloud, "what a day this has been for me! Wherefore did I ever go forth out of my father's house into the King's camp at Ephes-Dammim? Would that I were this night in the city of my ancestors, making merry over so small a thing as the fertility of my father's sheep!"

Over the sound of his own voice, over the distant and diminishing cries that were rising from the villages, he heard another sound—a tinkling of little bells. He held his breath and listened. Heathen bells, ringing in the temple of the god of wine? Philistine bells, dangling from the fluted skirts of damsels who danced at the edge of the sea? He shook his head against the tinkling, but it only grew clearer and more persistent. Then it mingled with another sound—the soft clop of hoofs in the dust. Travelers, he told himself, have turned off the highway and are coming toward the slope, perhaps to ask for the security of our company for the night. . . . He stood up and went in the direction of the highway to see.

A small company was approaching across the barren plain, coming up between the boulders and the patches of brush, moving slowly toward him through the long red rays of the sun. No caravan—a train of six donkeys, heavily laden and richly caparisoned. At the head of the train walked a slim young Israelite, curled and bejeweled, plainly the pampered servant of the great. The first five of the donkeys bore baskets of dressed meat, cakes of dates and raisins, flasks of wine, bushels of parched grain. The last of the donkeys was bridled and saddled, and bore upon its back a shape made vague and mysterious by floating veils, a woman who sat as erect and still in her saddle as though she had been an Astarte carved from stone.

David went forward to greet the newcomers, shielding his eyes from the crimson blaze of the sun. The little bells on the necks of the beasts continued to jingle until he and the young servant were not ten paces apart. Then the servant raised his hand and stopped the donkeys in their tracks. It seemed to David that all sounds had ceased, that a wing of silence had swept down upon the world.

"Where," said the young man, "can my lady find David, the son of Jesse, even he that is the pride of Judah and the Star of Bethlehem?"

David dropped his shielding hand from his face. He saw himself as the great shining eyes behind the veil must see him—a comely man made the more comely by roseate light, a lean and manly man standing astride the harsh earth of the wilderness. "Behold, even here," he said with dignity. "I am he."

The servant bowed three times, touching the earth with his fingertips. "Then all these gifts that are laden upon the donkeys are for my lord, the son of Jesse and the Star of Bethlehem. They are the gifts of my lady, she who sits upon the last donkey of the train."

"And who is your lady?"

"Abigail, the wife of Nabal, she is my lady. Let the son of Jesse not turn his back in rage against her because of the doings of her lord, for she is innocent."

She prodded the side of the donkey with her foot and came forward until the little beast that bore her stood very close to him. Then, without a word, she slipped from the saddle and knelt before him, all the bright folds of her draperies trailing in the dust. The wind drew the veil from her face, and for one moment he saw it plainly, pale, with a slight shine upon it, like the inner part of a halved almond, the lips ripe, the eyes wide, the brows two wing-shaped curves above the eyes. Then almost at once her beauty was hidden from him, because she had laid herself down at his feet, covering her face.

"Upon me, my lord, upon me be the iniquity," she said. Her words were urgent, but they fell from her lips unhurried, like honey falling from the honeycomb. "Hear the words of your handmaid's mouth. Let not the Star of Bethlehem trouble his heart over my worthless husband. For Nabal means folly, and as his name is, so is he. It was Nabal who saw the young men whom my lord sent up to the house. I, my lord's handmaid, saw them not."

On the hill behind him, all those in his army who had witnessed his shame were gathered now to look upon his glory—to see the woman lying at his feet. He looked briefly over his shoulder at them, and then turned back to the woman. Her soft, rounded back showed through the blue and saffron stuff of her veil.

"Arise, now," he said in the tender and insistent voice of a masterful lover. "Come, Abigail, arise."

She chose to raise herself only to her knees. Her ringed hand came up slowly and touched the hem of his garment in a gesture of supplication. There was in this gesture a rare charm; it was at once innocent and mature; in touching him she became both a damsel laying her chaste fingers upon the garment of her beloved and a mother straightening the disordered tunic of her child.

"As Jahveh lives and as my soul lives," she said, "I bore no part in this matter. Only after your young men had gone forth from my husband's sight, only then did I hear of the monstrous thing which had come to pass. My servant, even this young man before you, came to me in secret and told me how it was, and said that surely the Star of Bethlehem would come up against us for vengeance, with fire and sword."

He held out his hand to her, meaning to lift her up. She shook her head, but took the proffered hand and held it between her own. Her fingers were soft, pliant, eloquent.

"But God is gracious," she said. "He has sent me in good time to save the Star of Bethlehem from bloodguiltiness and from avenging himself with his own hand. Surely my lord will not go up against Nabal. . . ."

"No," he said, pressing the supple fingers, "I will not go up against Nabal now."

The veil across her face was borne slightly outward by a sigh of relief; then it was drawn inward against her lips, and curved with her lips in her slow, indolent smile. "May all my lord's enemies be of the stature of Nabal," she said, and the scorn in her voice had a sweetness for him, so that he also smiled. "And now let my lord take this present which I have brought down for him, and divide it among the young men who follow my lord."

"But wherefore," he said in the old courtly accents of Saul's house, "wherefore should my lady trouble to bring gifts to me?"

"If your handmaid has been forward, forgive her forwardness. Consider them as gifts for one who fights the battles of Jahveh. Consider them as earnests of the pleasures that are to attend my lord through all his days. For it is plain that no evil will ever touch my lord. Though one should rise up to pursue him, yet will he be safe, seeing that his soul is in the safekeeping of Jahveh, and that his life is bound up with the life of God."

He stared across her head at the crimson and purple bars of cloud that lay at the edge of the plain. The weight of the wretched years in the wilderness had fallen from him. He saw with wonder and delight that he had done needless penance and burdened himself with needless vows. That Other Jahveh who had stood behind him in the cave—that God of tears and pity—gave place to the God of his fathers. God loves whom He chooses to love, he thought, and God has chosen to love me. Jahveh has laid her hand in mine and has sent her to tell me to put off my remorse, since I am indeed the anointed, the Lord's darling, one set above the sacrifices and the grovelings that are for other, lesser men. . . .

The slow, sweet voice went on yet a little longer, speaking for the indulgent Father-God. "The souls of all your enemies, them will you sling out as a stone is slung from the hollow of a sling. And it will come to pass that Jahveh will lift you up, even as He has promised, and will appoint you King in Israel. Seeing that all this is certainly to come to pass, it is fortunate that my lord has saved himself from bloodguiltiness, so that no bitter remembrance will mar the perfection of that day when he shall come into his own."

She rose at last then, balancing the tremulous weight of her body for a moment upon his arm. Her face was close to his. Through the veil he saw again—bright as on the night when he had stood wretchedly beside her window, bright as in the visionary festival of the Baal of the Vine—the still shining of her eyes.

"When Jahveh has dealt well with my lord, then let him remember his handmaid," she said.

The last sentence had been spoken so quietly that neither the warriors on the hill nor the young Israelite who was unloading the donkey could hear. The words had an intimacy which had not sounded in the phrases that had gone before. It was as if she had said, "When you come into your kingdom, reach out your hand and lift me up also, out of the misery of a fool's house, out of the shame of a fool's bed."

"Blessed be the God of Israel who sent you this day to meet me," David said. And then, because the speech had been too ardent, he tempered it for the servant and for those who looked down from the slope. "Blessed be your discretion which has kept me this day from bloodguiltiness and from avenging myself with my own hand. For, as Jahveh the God of Israel lives, if you had not hastened here to meet me, surely there would not have been left to Nabal by the morning light so much as one man-child."

Now all the store that she had brought with her lay heaped among the stones and the brush. She turned toward the donkey which had borne her, but she did not mount at once. She stood with her hand on the bridle, plainly waiting for another word.

He helped her into her saddle. His arm knew the yielding softness of her waist. "Go up in peace to your house," he said. "See, I have hearkened to your voice, and I have accepted your person."

"I have accepted your person." It was a strange and equivocal phrase, he did not know why he had uttered it. It might have meant either "I have been moved by your supplication" or "I have taken your voice and your face and your body into the very tabernacle of my heart." However she interpreted it, she was satisfied. She permitted her large eyes to shine full upon him for a long moment; then she nodded to her servant, set her heel against the donkey's side, and departed as quietly as she had come. He stood motionless, gazing after her; and those on the hillside did not come down to look at the booty until the last tinkling of the golden bells was lost, until the last puff of dust left by her donkey's feet had settled upon the darkening plain.

⊸§ VIII §⊷

THROUGH the long evenings in her brothers' house, the child Noi sat always at the end of the table, her elbows propped against the wood, her hands cupped around her face to shield her eyes. "She is ashamed," her brothers said among themselves. "It is a pity that she is so flat and thin. Had she been a little fuller, she might have hidden her state. As it is, anybody can see that she is four moons gone with child." But they were mistaken when they believed that it was shame which drove her cold fingers to her face. Ever since the night when she had been visited by the dream of the eagles, she had been putting up her hands to save her eyes from the terrible, metallic beaks, the iron claws, the hard, sharp wings.

She had dreamed of the eagles in the first week after David's departure. One afternoon, exhausted by a fit of vomiting, she had lain down under a tree to sleep; and while she slept a wind had come up and sent the dry leaves down upon her face. Sleep had transformed these leaves into the eagles. The furious birds had darted toward her by tens and twenties, with red, gaping throats and filmy eyes, to claw her, to rend her flesh. Nor, in the two moons that had passed since that afternoon of fright, had she been able to rid herself of the dream. Whenever she heard a rumor concerning her lord, the eagles were again upon her; and her fear of them was such that she thought she would surely lose the child.

On the tenth day after the Feast of the Sheep Shearing, the wool was ready for the market. Her brothers had heaped it onto the backs of seven borrowed donkeys, and had set out in the direction of Hebron to sell it in the great bazaar. It had troubled them to leave her alone in the house, but she was glad to see them go. She thought, I will be alone with the child in silence. We will enjoy our peace. . . . All that day she sat in the closed house, holding such conversations with her unborn child as she had once held with antelopes and hares. But toward the hour of sunset the house became intolerably hot, and she was forced to open the door. So on that evening, as on all other evenings since her wedding night, she sat at the end of the table, waiting for the eagles to return.

How long she had been sitting there before she saw the shape on the threshold she did not know. Suddenly the man was there, and the eagles were there, rushing upon her, so that she rose and cried out in a wild voice and put her arms across her belly to protect the child.

"But, my lady, it is only I, it is only Abishai." He stood, big and awkward and remorseful, in the doorway. "I have come to Noi from the camp of David, to bring her a message from her lord."

She was sorry at once that she had given him so poor a welcome. It was plain that he had set great store by his visit. She noticed that he had washed and combed and put on clean linen so that he might be acceptable in her eyes. His round and shining face, his gleaming ringlets, his fat body under the clean tunic, touched her strangely. "Peace be with my dear nephew," she said.

"See," he said, holding up his hands, "I have brought presents for my lady from her husband. A bracelet for her arm, sandals for her feet, and a bolt of fine cloth from which she is to sew the garments for her child."

Then he is still my husband, she thought, and remembers even after these many weeks that I carry his child. . . .

"Why should my lady stand before me?" Abishai said.

She sat down, trembling, and put the loose strands of hair from her eyes. "Come, Abishai, and sit also. There is bread and fruit on the board before you."

"Let my lady look upon her presents," he said in the voice of a child who repeats a meaningless lesson. "David bade me lay them in the hands of Noi as tokens of his love."

He no longer loves me, she thought. And this poor soul has been sent up to lie to me, and cannot lie in his simplicity. . . . It was difficult to see the gifts; long, bluish shadows darkened the room; only a few wan patches of light remained. She took up the bracelet and examined it closely. It was ornate and strange—a heathen bracelet with dolphins and shells graven upon it. "Whence came the bracelet?" she said. "Is it not the handiwork of the uncircumcised who dwell at the edge of the sea?"

"It is the work of the heathen, as my lady says. It was given to my lord by Achish, who is the Seren of the city of Gath. There was a day when David said to my brother, who brought the bracelet up from the city, 'Take these stinking gifts of the unclean and hide them in a cave, out of my sight.' But that day is past. Now it is otherwise with David . . ." He stopped suddenly and set his teeth into his soft, childish lip. "Of that we need not speak," he said. "Let Noi not burden her heart with it. It was not Noi, but David, who took the bracelet at the hand of Achish. Noi takes it without sin from the hand of her husband and her lord."

"Am I to go to my lord, Abishai?" she said.

"Go to your lord? Assuredly you will go to your lord. When in Israel has a wife not gone down to live with her husband? In good time, Noi will certainly go down to David. . . ."

Even through the menacing approach of the eagles she saw and pitied him—poor liar, flushing and stammering and ready to weep. She leaned across the board and touched his arm. He took her hand and closed it in his own and turned toward the door, so that she might not see his face.

"No, now, tell me truly, Abishai. It is a better thing to know than to be forever afraid. . . ."

"Be not afraid," he said, plainly weeping. "He will send after Noi in a little while—a moon, perhaps two moons. Before God, I swear that he will send after Noi. Believe me, I would not deceive my lady who is dear to me. . . ."

He was blinking against the light, striving to get possession of himself. Then suddenly he withdrew his hand from hers. He was David's man again, reciting by rote those lessons which his lord had taught him.

"It is necessary to wait," he said, "until David has prepared a house that will be suitable to receive my lady. It is not well that she should sit in the sun and lie in the damp of the caves while she carries my lord's child. He has asked me to say to my lady that Achish has promised him the city of Ziklag. In that city is a great and comfortable house. Another moon or so, and he will lead her down and lay a fine coverlet over her feet and place a soft cushion beneath her head."

"Tell him from me," she said, "that I need no house and no cushions. Without my lord, my heart is eaten by wild birds, even though I am sheltered by walls and rafters. Without my lord, though I sleep upon linen, I sleep upon stones."

"Yet let the bride of David be reasonable and discipline her heart for the sake of her child. . . ."

She laughed, and the laugh caught like a sob in her throat. The words were David's words, laid upon this poor unlettered tongue. She rose and stood erect above the table. "No, now, tell me no more lies, my friend," she said. "If my lord will not have one wife come down to him, it is because another wife has taken her place in his bed."

He stood up and caught her by the shoulders. It was as if he had thrown his big, kindly body between her and the eagles. "So it is," he said thickly, "even so." He stroked her head and pressed her cheek against his chest. "So it is. Nabal is dead, and David has taken unto himself the wife of Nabal. Believe me, he did not seek her out. It was she that came down to him, with presents and blandishments. Let that much be said in his defense before God. And when her lord heard of it he was stricken with rage, so that his body became as a stone, and he died. It is as my lady says, even so—Nabal is dead, and David has taken Abigail to wife. We cannot change it now. Only let my lady take comfort, only let my lady cease this shuddering, lest she should lose her child. . . ."

And indeed it seemed to her that the child was struggling within her, that, wild with her own loathing for life, it sought to cast itself from her womb.

"Let my lady turn to her servant who loves her and would rather lose his right hand than inflict pain upon her. . . ."

It was as if a milky whiteness was gathering upon the world.

"Let my lady permit her servant to lift her up, to carry her out of this heat into the air. . . ."

The eagles were coming down upon her again, but this time they were harmless—not flying now, merely falling, falling with limp wings and broken necks through the abyss, falling and falling, like leaves through a windy night, like leaves upon her face. . . .

She opened her eyes and knew that it was night, that she lay upon the terrace under moving boughs, that her head rested upon Abishai's knee. A vision of the wife of Nabal, whom she had once seen at a festival, stood balefully bright before her, gleaming against the dark. Round arms, round breasts, round white shoulders, veiled face as round and luminous as the full moon. And she possesses all things—wealth and grace and an opulent body—and I possess nothing but the child, and perhaps even the child has slipped from me. . . .

"How is it with my lady?"

Slowly, fearfully, she lifted her hand and passed it over her body. The strange and familiar mound was still there.

"Is it well with Noi?"

"Yes," she said, turning her cheek against his knee. "I have not cast the child forth. It is still with me, the poor child."

"Surely, surely," he said, drawing her hair from her damp cheeks with such tenderness as she had not known since the day when her father's hands lay upon her in blessing at the hour of his death. "The child is a prince in Israel, and our God will certainly preserve the child."

She raised herself and moved back against him, so that her head rested against his chest. His heart beat under her head with great beats like the strokes of a hammer. Surely, she thought, the heart in his body is a strong and mighty heart.

"Believe me that I did not lie to my lady when I said that my lord would take her into his house. He will come down to her as soon as he has settled this business of Ziklag, and he will deal honorably with her, in loving-kindness, since one love need not drive out another love."

I will think of that tomorrow, she told herself. Tomorrow I will think how it will be to dwell in a house in Ziklag as the second wife. I am far too weary to think of it now. . . .

"Shall I lift up my lady and bear her to her bed?"

"Yes, in a moment. Only there is a thing that I would say to Abishai."

"Let my lady speak."

"If the child that is within me should come to birth, he will have two fathers—even the son of Jesse who begot him and the son of Zeruiah who bade me not to cast him forth."

Abishai's heart stood still for a moment; then it began to·beat again, loudly, irregularly. "Blessed be my lady," he said, "that she has bestowed such words upon her unworthy servant. Now let her know that her servant is hers and hers alone, to serve her so long as Jahveh breathes the breath of life into his body, even unto his last hour."

"How shall I tell my gratefulness to the son of Zeruiah?" She lifted his warm, plump hand and held it against her lips.

For a long time they remained so, in utter silence, under the tree. Then the wind strengthened and she began to tremble, and he lifted her up and bore her into the house and laid her upon her bed. He went down the stairs without a word, and she thought that he had left her. But he returned again, bearing a kindled lamp in his hand.

"It is not a good thing," he said, "for one who has a heavy heart to close her eyes upon darkness." And he sat at the foot of the bed until she slept.

⤚§ IX §⤙

CERTAIN doubts troubled the mind of Joab while he journeyed down to Gath with his uncle. The son of Jesse was a God-ridden man and might well take sudden flight once he actually beheld the heathenishness of the place—the knots of male and female prostitutes preening themselves before the temples, the soft, unclean sea creatures being sold as food in the market place, the constantly recurring patterns of wheat and serpents, sacred to Dagon and Astarte. And even if all went well during the walk through the city and the first meeting between the Star of Bethlehem and the Seren, there was another reason for doubt. He, Joab, had never dared to question his uncle as to how thoroughly he had detached himself from the family of the King of Israel. If Achish should ask him outright whether he would be willing to march one day in the ranks of Philistia against the host of God, he might leap up and shatter the delicate structure of the alliance with one loud "No!"

But if my uncle, Joab thought, is scrupulous in matters of piety, he is also luxurious. The sight of painted men and the smell of frying mussels and crabs may revolt him, but these may well be lost in the splendor of plumes and flowing robes, chariots with brazen wheels, windows bright with a dozen lamps, great colonnades facing upon the sea. It is true that the person and the bearing of Achish may disappoint him when he remembers the majesty of Saul. Nevertheless, he cannot be insensible to the consummate elegance of Achish, the perfection of his gestures, the pure and precise manner in which he employs the language, the subtlety of his smile. For Achish is a subtle man, somewhat womanish, somewhat tender; and perhaps because of his delicacy the chief difficulty may not even arise. As on the night of my first coming into Gath he did not make mention to me of the fact that he wished David to stand with him against the House of Kish, so he may hold his peace with David also. He may wait for weeks, moons, even years before mentioning the matter to my lord. . . .

These conjectures had seemed accurate enough when he made them. Yet afterward, when he had leisure to remember and reconsider, he saw plainly that he had based them on a faulty conception of the nature of the Star of Bethlehem. It was true that David scarcely noticed the fawning prostitutes and the unclean meat; but he failed, too, to take the expected cognizance of the splendid guardsmen and spacious palaces. Instead, he was obsessed with a wild excitement at the thought that he was about to behold the sea. Gath, the city of sin and splendor, became in the mind of David that which it really was—a frail, ornate bit of grill-work between Israel and the wonder of the waters. The temples were nothing to him; he was drawn past them to the beaches, to the white and wavering line of foam. The cries of the mussel-sellers were lost upon him. His ears, like the sounding shells of Philistia, held nothing but the everlasting, murmurous voice of the western sea. He amazed and confused his nephew with such strange talk as "Which way does the isle of Caphtor lie?" and, "Wherefore did Achish build his palace beyond the beach, when he might have built it even here, where the steps could descend into the waves?"

And when they stood at last in the gleaming lamplit room and looked upon the person of the Seren, who had risen to stand before them with his back toward the sea, then the son of Zeruiah cast a sidewise glance at the face of the son of Jesse and knew that he had been misled in this matter also. Achish was, indeed, even smaller and more effeminate than he had remembered; the great window dwarfed him; there was a troubling softness about the fold of flesh that hung between his neck and chin. But the Star of Bethlehem in nowise found him disappointing. It was instead as if David, advancing across the white carpets, drawing closer to the red-rimmed eyes and the pale hand, had cried out in his heart, "This is my soul's true brother!"

"The dimness of many years drops from my eyes when they behold my friend," said Achish.

"When I behold Achish, my eyes are blessed," David said.

They embraced then, not in the brief and perfunctory manner that the occasion required, but with so full and sincere an acceptance of each other's persons that jealousy smote Joab. Never, thought the son of Zeruiah, did he fold me in such an embrace, not when I returned from the south laden with spoils, not when I presented him with a magnificent plan of battle, not after I had come to his assistance in the struggle, putting my sword between the enemy and his breast. . . .

They sat down, all three of them, in the graceful curved chairs around the little table, which was furnished with the same black-and-white cruet and the same shallow bowls, with napkins and little round cakes, each one stamped with a sheaf of Dagon's wheat. The space between the chairs was scrupulously equal, and yet it seemed to Joab that he sat at a great distance from the others. My lord, he thought, sits with the lord of Gath, and I sit by forgotten. Since I am no more than a servant here, why does this bald and pallid one not throw me a cushion and bid me sit at their feet? . . .

The blue, prominent eyes sent a conciliatory glance in his direction. Plainly this Philistine could read a man's thoughts before they rose to his lips. "Blessed be the captain of David's host," Achish said, "who has brought us together. Had he not wandered down to the city of Ziklag one evening, who knows when we three might have sat at table?"

David also turned toward the son of Zeruiah and laid his long, sun-darkened hand upon his nephew's knee. The old adoration for the son of Jesse rose in Joab like a spring in the wilderness. How comely he is, he thought, how fit to dwell in palaces, how fair in the embroidered tunic that Achish sent him, how graceful and how lordly, reclining at ease among the cushions in the curved chair. . . .

Achish had begun to build the conversation tentatively, delicately, with the skill and care of a priest who builds, bit by bit, a pyramid of fruit and flower offerings to the Lord. And how, he asked, was the health of the son of Jesse? No, his own health was only indifferently good, but he was sustained by the knowledge that his friend remained sound, even after all his sufferings. And the mother and father of the Star of Bethlehem—it had come to his ears that they were dwelling in a far country. In Moab, indeed? Perhaps, when David dwelt in Ziklag, when he had a solid house and a bright hearth of his own, the pride of Judah would send to Moab after his father and his mother. . . . (Here the pyramid of fruit and flowers began to topple, for here the Seren soon saw that no Israelite could bring his pious parents into a house given to him by the uncircumcised.) Ah, well, all things take time. Meanwhile, they would be well cared for. He would send ingots of gold and ingots of copper regularly to the King of Moab for their keep. And the bride of David? See, he was well informed. It had come to his ears that the Star of Bethlehem had taken a bride, and that her womb was blessed with a child. . . .

Not so very well informed at that, thought Joab. The dainty pyramid is sliding askew again. My lord Achish has mentioned the wrong bride. . . . David bent and stared into his wine bowl. He blushed, and the blush became him—clear rosiness of an apricot spreading under the sun-begotten gold. Achish turned aside and smiled, half amazed and half pleased, as though he said to himself, It is at once strange and touching to see that a youth's delicacy dwells within him, that he should flush to hear mention of the fact that his seed has taken root. . . . Joab felt a short laugh rising in his throat, and transformed it into a cough. Achish lifted the cruet and poured another round of wine.

In a moment he was back to his subtle building. But this time he narrowed his pyramid, constructed it a little more closely around the core. He had learned that something between three and four hundred valiant men of war followed the Star of Bethlehem in the wilderness. Did David believe that all of them would come with him into the city of Ziklag, or were there those who would turn their backs on the alliance and go home?

David flushed again and fixed his eyes upon the face of Achish. The eyes were wide, childish, and startlingly beautiful in the light of the many lamps. Just such eyes, thought Joab, he used to turn upon Jesse and Saul. . . . "Let the Seren of Gath not deceive himself," said David, "as to how it stands with me. Some four hundred men I have, but they are not truly men of war. They are marauders, and nowise like those plumed and disciplined guardsmen whom I beheld in the streets of Gath. Pariahs they are, dogs of the wilderness, nor am I one whit more than the leader of the pack. They will come into Ziklag with me as dogs come, being faithful. None will return home, inasmuch as, being dogs, they have no homes."

How wise is my uncle, Joab thought. How subtle is his policy. He has laid his bleeding heart upon the table among the white napkins and the little cakes, knowing that Achish is a soft man, womanish and tender, one to be utterly unnerved at the sight of a bleeding heart. . . . And so indeed it came to pass. The Philistine protested in a tremulous voice, laying his white hand upon David's knee. Not in his house would any man, no, not even the son of Jesse, lay the name of dog upon those fearless ones who, without thanks from Israel, had these many years secured the southern border against the inroads of the men of the sands. How much the son of Jesse must have suffered that, even in jest, he should put the name of dog upon the very flower of Israel.

From that moment the council was no longer with Achish; it had passed from the soft white hands to the hard golden ones. Now it was David who built and balanced, but so casually that his mind seemed scarcely to be with him in the tall chamber—seemed instead to be hovering over the distant waters toward which he often turned his eyes. It was true, he said, that he had grown bitter in the wilderness. Such a life was not truly a life, and he had sometimes wondered whether it was to be preferred above the peace and dignity of the sepulcher. Nevertheless, Achish must not err in placing the responsibility for these misfortunes upon Israel. Saul, not Israel, had sent him into exile. Saul, not Israel, had pursued him to the very margins of the sand.

Joab took two of the little cakes from the table and crammed them into his mouth from sheer nervousness. Now, he thought, while he dreams upon the sea, he has blundered into the perilous moment. Now he will say, "I will not go forth against Israel with the host of the uncircumcised." . . .

But once more he saw that he had misjudged the son of Jesse. David did not turn urgently to Achish; he merely stared gravely at the sea and sighed. To ask of a man that he should forget his lord, he said, that—even that— is a hard demand, but one which he was nevertheless prepared to accept. There had been moments in the high house in Gibeah—his voice was elegiac, vibrant, tender—there had been moments so golden that a man found them returning in his dreams. Sometimes he fancied in his sleep that his finger still wore the ring that Saul had put upon it. No matter how splendid the new lord is, yet it is a sorrowful matter to forget the old. That which is known in the very blood, even though it has declined, even though madness has overshadowed it—that which is known is dear. . . .

Behold, thought Joab, he plays before Achish. He beguiles Achish with sweet songs. And here again it is not that he ensnares his listener only; he also deceives the son of Jesse. This is his power, this is his magic—that he falls down in wonder before the graven image which he makes of himself.

The hard, slender hands stirred on the arms of the chair. To turn one's back against one's lord—that was bitter, but possible. But what could the helpless exile say if he were asked also to turn against his people, to become a base traitor in the eyes of Judah, to grow hateful to the very walls of the brown house wherein he was born? Old mother, whose wrinkled face still bent over him in his dreams, old father, whose withered hand still sought in the hours of sleep to smooth the lines of grief from the forehead of an unworthy son—how would it be when this son had so conducted himself that reunion was impossible, that there could be no reconciliation, that the mildest spirits among the dead must curse him, even out of their two sealed graves?

Achish pressed his fingers together with so much vigor that the knuckles started hard and shining against the white flesh. It is as I thought, then, Joab told himself. It was the purpose of the Seren of Gath to ask the son of Jesse to march forth with him against the host of God. The price of a walled city is a great price, nor is there any reason to believe that he will toss such a city away for a sweet and sorrowful voice. And yet, for the sake of this voice, Saul gave away his only daughter. . . .

"It is true," said David, "that when a man goes from one master to another, he must expect to lay offerings upon the altars of strange gods. Yet surely Achish knows that no man can truly depart from the one god which is his own." How is it possible, he asked, to forget the ravaged temple at Shiloh, where the cobwebs hang upon the rafters and the wind walks like a ghost through the stirred dust? Can the eyes be so base as to forget the austere face of the prophet Samuel? Can the fingers be so foul as not to remember the soles of his dead and holy feet? And the altars of Judah, the little hillside shrines, the rocks anointed with our poor wine and rubbed with the fat of generation after generation of our sheep. . . . To be cursed henceforth at these very shrines, to be forbidden the right to shed tears upon the prophet's grave, to be denied forever the righteous joy of kindling the fire beneath the slain lamb. . . . Nevertheless, he said, he was in the hands of Achish. "If Achish should say to his vassal, 'March forth with me tomorrow against the host of God'——"

The Seren of Gath rose from his chair and walked to the window and stared out at the sea. "Vassal?" he said. "Wherefore does the Star of Bethlehem say such a word as vassal? No vassal is he to me, but a true confederate, a companion in arms, equal to me in all matters. There are no kings in Philistia, but only united brethren, each holding authority in his own city. When David dwells in Ziklag, he will speak for Ziklag in the high councils. And in Philistia, as in Caphtor of old, each voice in the high council is a free voice, speaking untrammeled from the heart."

The Star of Bethlehem turned upon the Seren a wan, persecuted smile.

"Wherefore," said Achish, coming back from the window and laying his hand upon David's shoulder, "wherefore does David turn this sad questioning of his smile upon me? Is it that he trusts me not? What I have said, I have said."

"But what is it that my lord has said? He has spoken to me of my own voice, poor and unwelcome, raised solitary in the councils of Philistia. If all Philistia should march forth against the host of God, what is my voice that it should detain them? As a hare speaking against the roar of lions. . . ."

The Seren of Gath walked round the little table and stood before David. The solemnity of the ritual dignified his small, plump body. He poured wine into a bowl and lifted the bowl and spilled the wine upon the gleaming floor. "As I have poured forth this wine," he said, "so may Dagon and Astarte pour forth the blood of my body. May they make me as an empty vessel, broken in battle"—he hurled the delicate bowl to the ground, smashing it to bits—"may the gods do so to me and more also, if I or my brothers of the council force the son of Jesse to go out to meet the host of Jahveh against his will."

It was enough. The Lamb of Judah rose and embraced the Seren of Gath.

Joab rose also, knowing that the evening's business was finished. Nothing remained but the courtesies. A room had been prepared for the son of Jesse, close to the room of Achish. The captain of David's host would sleep where he had slept before, and with the same companions, should he desire to spend the remaining hours of darkness in delight. Which would the Star of Bethlehem prefer—to talk with the captain of the guard concerning the manner of taking possession of the city of Ziklag, or to go down and choose such women as might please him from among the priestesses of Astarte? The son of Jesse courteously refused the women and requested the company of the captain; he had no taste for women; his heart brooded upon his bride—he did not find it necessary to say which bride.

There were lengthy farewells and involved blessings, with frequent mentions of Astarte, Dagon, and the God of Israel. And Joab found it difficult to suppress the rippling chuckle that rose in his throat. Jahveh is a wily God, he thought, very shrewd and clever. Jahveh can wind them both around His little finger—the tender, foolish Dagon and the sensuous Astarte. . . .

BOOK SEVEN

BOOK SEVEN

❧ I ❧

WHEN David opened his eyes, he saw that the room in which he lay was crossed by rays of morning sun softened by a whitish mist. Winter, he thought, and the mists of winter. Heavier mists than we knew in Judah, for Ziklag lies close to the coast, and these are the mists of the sea. . . . He propped himself on his elbow, moving carefully so as not to rouse Abigail, who lay beside him. The images of an unhappy dream pressed against the margins of his consciousness, trying to break in. He rubbed the last vestiges of sleep from his eyes and stared down the length of the room—a strange room and heathenish, a room gleaming with white draperies and pale rugs and burnished pottery, a room in which he had never taken root, even though he had slept in it these last three years.

All things considered, he should have felt very secure in this place, yet he seldom wakened now without a sense of impending evil. The room was too white, too aerial, and opened to the outer world by too many windows. He sighed and turned to shield his eyes from the glare of the fog. Abigail shifted against her pillow and sighed also in her sleep.

Even in her dreams, he thought, she grieves with patience and dignity over her childlessness. . . . She had grown a little heavier, and her serenity had passed almost imperceptibly into blandness. When he was in a cheerless humor, it seemed to him that she had only two aspects—one that bestowed upon him a resigned sigh and one that gave him an equally resigned smile. And he wished that one day she might be moved beyond patience and dignity, might break a dish or curse an unwelcome guest or pinch the lean brown arm of Noi's child.

Nevertheless, he thought, turning a little and looking down upon her, she has not lost all the magic that belonged to Nabal's wife when she rode across the plain bearing wheat and figs and grapes and God's goodwill and the promise of a festival of love. . . . He thought of kissing her, but knew that she slept lightly and would surely waken. Then she would be certain to ask him her eternal question—"How dear am I to the heart of my lord?" Dearer than the King's daughter, he told himself, and dearer than the little Jezreelitess from whom I drew a son. Yet not so dear as to make me cease to desire to be alone. . . .

He lay on his back, staring across the room at a piece of whitish drapery that covered half the broad window, hanging between the grayness of the wall and the whiteness of the mist. As the light intensified, it seemed to him that the folds suggested a figure—a tall, solemn mourner rigid with the shock of loss.

He turned his mind to other matters—how the Seren of Gath had been a guest in his house last night, how they had talked together of a treaty with Phoenicia, how the grandchild of Achish had played with the son of David in the common room before the fire. But the austere presence in the drapery still stood before him. He turned his head against the pillow, trying to obliterate it by seeing it from some other angle. Yet it would not be gone. How will I pass the day? he asked himself. Perhaps I will take the child Amnon down to Gath, to look upon the horses that are in the stables of the charioteers, to see the fires that are in the bellies of the foundries, to eat among the fishermen on one of the moored boats, perhaps even to sail out a little toward the unknown isles. . . . The wind stirred the drapery, and the figure swayed in grief.

Through the closed door of the bedchamber he could hear the comings and goings of his servants. He thought of rising and pushing the door open a little way, so that the comfortable life of the house might flow into his uneasy solitude. Soon the hallway before his threshold would be sweet with the rising fragrance of the morning bread. Soon the awesome quiet would be broken by the crackle of the hearth fire and the clink of dishes and the yelp of pariah dogs gathered before the door for their share of last night's crusts and bones. He sat up and thrust one leg from beneath the coverlet and set his foot upon the rug at the side of his bed. But Abigail moved, breathed less evenly, let her round, soft arm fall across his waist. He sank back cautiously against the pillows. He was not yet prepared to give her the joyous greeting with which she expected to be welcomed out of sleep. A vague somnolence, a heaviness in which he often took refuge now, came upon him. . . .

The veil of drowsiness was rent apart by a clang. He knew at once that something had fallen, something had been dropped by one of the servants in the adjoining room. No doubt it was the great brass bowl from which, on the preceding evening, he and Achish had taken their fruit. And yet he saw something other than an awkward boy letting a bowl slide from his hands. He saw the city of Gibeah as he had first seen it—pale, ancient heap of stones under a leaden sky, streets in which generation after generation had walked, dry earth beneath which sons and sons' sons to the twentieth generation had fallen into white bones and dust. The sound of brass which still rang against the morning hush was the resonant clashing of a great cymbal; it was the suspended beat of his own heart, saying, "Behold, the hour approaches, the hour of death."

Then, as the last brazen vibration quivered into stillness, he heard another sound. He heard again, after years in which it had been silent, the long, shrill flute note that had sung in his ears in Gibeah on that evening when he had looked across the table at Jonathan's worn, dust-marked, mortal face. He saw again the dry lips and the frail flesh stretched across the bones and the vein that beat away time in the sunken temple—saw the flat brown eyes focus upon him, saw the lips and cheeks changing in a smile. The remembrance was swift and terrible, so that he must close his hand hard upon the coverlet.

The woman on the bed had become a stranger; she murmured in her alien sleep; her soft arm pressed upon him. God of Hosts, what do I want with her? he thought. . . . But the God of Hosts stood white, inexorable, and austere beyond the window, in the mist. The God of Hosts was the God of Samuel, as inaccessible as Samuel's sealed eyes. Two vows, the God of Samuel said, two broken vows. . . .

The woman drew closer and embraced him. He put her from him, still cautiously, still fearing that she might wake. He could remain beside her no longer; he went from the warmth of her body into the chilly moisture of the air.

"Beloved," said Abigail, yawning, "surely it is very early. Why should you rise?"

He did not reply at once, hoping that silence would let her slip back into the deep waters of her dreams. But she was fully awake; she raised her round golden arms and stretched them into a bar of sunlight. Her large eyes shone upon him. Her lips were already pursed to receive the expected kiss.

"No, now," he said in a voice that was not his own, "let my beloved forgive me. I feasted too well last night with the Seren of Gath, and the wine is sour on my breath. Let me go forth and refresh my mouth with a little water, and then I will come again."

She nodded and smiled, but he could not smile. He glanced over his shoulder at the figure in the cloth. The wind had effaced the greater part of it. Nothing remained now but the head—a face muffled in a veil, a lined and stricken brow. The white, aureate fog beyond the window, the mist in which the pitiless God had stood, was beginning to dissolve. Familiar shapes were discernible within it—the clumps of hedge and herb in his own garden, the bronze gate, the twisted branches of an olive tree. It was a child's bad dream, he told himself, crossing the chill bedchamber and opening the door which led into the common room. I will smell the good scent of the morning bread, I will spread my hands before the fire on the hearth and put this matter from my heart. . . .

But the common room was not as comforting as he had expected. The fire had only begun to kindle; the maidservant had only begun to knead the dough on the table; and in the wan light the faces of the servants looked as dull and pasty as the dough. A chubby and awkward fellow stood near the window, holding the brass bowl in his hands and ruefully examining the havoc he had wrought upon it. Something in the droop of the youth's plump shoulders struck David as particularly foolish and loathsome.

"Dolt," he said, "are your fingers anointed with butter? Look how it is with the bowl. You have put a scratch upon it that no polishing will ever erase."

The fat shoulders went up in an exasperated shrug. "It is a grievous thing, but it is done. I assure my lord that I repent it. What more can I say to my lord?"

The maid who was kneading the bread stopped and wiped her fingers on a napkin. She was an aging woman, afraid of quarrels, constantly bolstering a precarious peace. "If my lord wishes to warm himself," she said, "there is a brazier of burning wood in the chamber of my lady Noi."

The young man continued to turn the bowl round and round against the light, and David felt a disproportionate anxiety lest he drop it a second time.

"Set it upon the table!" he shouted.

"Yes, my lord."

Then, before the boy had crossed the room, because he wished to escape even the mild vibrations of brass set against wood, he hastened into the chamber where Noi and her little one slept. Mother and child lay close to each other, their heads upon the same pillow, their arms intertwined. He could never stare into Noi's face without uneasiness. His glance passed swiftly over her prominent cheekbones, her heavy eyelids, the shining masses of her hair, and focused upon the head of the child. Yet to look upon the son was to look upon the mother. It was not only that the body was the same—the narrow shoulders, the arc of the ribs showing plainly through the skin, the half-opened mouth, the weighty mass of curls. The child had partaken also of Noi's spirit; and this thought was a burden. It was true that he had deceived the mother, had made her the second wife, had taken the keys of his house from her hand, had failed to go in unto her even when it grew plain that Abigail would give him no issue and that the hope of his house lay sealed within Noi's womb. But he had loved the child and enriched him with lands and titles. He had spent as many hours with the child as he had spent with Abigail. If he had erred in any way in his dealings with Amnon, it had been that he had shown himself too solicitous, too tender. And yet, even in his sleep, the boy wore his mother's rejected look. He was forever turning his face away from the good things of the world. He was obedient; he smiled when a person bade him smile; he played when his father required him to play. But it was plain that he preferred to sit quite silent on the hearth beside his mother's chair, making endless series of patterns in the reeds that covered the floor, resigned to seeing his labors destroyed a dozen times an evening by passing feet.

David moved quietly toward the brazier at the foot of the bed, fearing that Noi or the child might waken. How is it with me then, he thought, that I have filled my life with a multitude of beings whom I constantly wish asleep? Let Abigail sleep, let Noi sleep, let Abishai and Joab and Abiathar take themselves to their dreams, let the Seren of Gath make himself most pleasant in my eyes by announcing to me that he is weary and will straightway go to his bed. When will it be again as it was on those mornings in the tower room in Gibeah when I held my breath, waiting for the beloved to stir the hushed pulse of the world with his waking? What passes now in the gray city of death and dust? In what exigency do you turn toward me, and wherefore am I hounded by the vision of your mortal face, Jonathan? . . .

The child started up, uttering a feeble and quickly stifled cry. He sat among the rumpled bedclothes, thin and overtall for his three years, forcing his small, bony face to assume a smile.

"Do not be afraid," said the son of Jesse, feeling the old embarrassment in the presence of the child. "It is nothing. It is only I."

"My lord?" said Noi, flinging back her hair. For the space of a single heartbeat, her face was naked. A wild dream of the wanderer come home at last flared up and went out in her eyes.

"God be with Noi."

"And with David. Is there any way in which I can serve my lord?"

He could not bring himself to tell her that he had come into her room to warm his hands before her fire. Then surely, he thought, I will make the journey that I considered when I wakened. I will take the child to Gath, and this will be reason enough, and a kindly reason, for standing at the foot of her bed. . . .

"It has come into my mind," he said, "to go down to Gath this day. Since there is no pleasure in going down alone——"

Again the dream of reconciliation widened her eyes and parted her lips. It was plain that she saw herself beside him on the white beach.

"I have come to ask Noi that she give me leave to take the child."

She lay very straight and still beneath the bedclothes, drawing the coverlet up to her chin. "The child is my lord's," she said. "Give me an hour, and I will make him clean and fair."

He stared at her rigid body, seeking some word that might serve as a balm upon her many bruises, finding none, and wishing at last that she might hurl some bitter imprecation at him, or weep. How is a man to deal with women? he asked himself. Wherefore does each of them set a mask upon her face, so that it is impossible to deal frankly and honorably? The King's daughter quarreled and ranted, and this one lies stiff as a corpse, and Abigail sighs and smiles. . . .

He remembered then that he had promised to return to his bedchamber. She lay waiting for him among the embroidered coverlets—the first wife, the opulent one—stretching her golden arms in the sun.

"I will come within an hour, then," he said.

"Yes, my lord."

Yet before he left her chamber, in order to refresh his mouth he tilted her water cruet and filled a little bowl that stood upon the sill, since he did not wish to go seeking after water in the common room.

◆§ II §◆

ALL AFTERNOON he wandered, with the little Amnon sitting upon his shoulder, through the streets of Gath—chill streets with the mist still upon them, windy streets where the clothes of the passers-by were caught by sudden gusts, streets in which one constantly heard the scraping sound of the tide. Great white-bellied clouds, pregnant with the winter rains, moved in a dull procession over the bazaar and behind the colonnades; the wind came landward, bearing the smell of the creeping creatures of the sea; the weather was the weather of Sheol—neither winter nor summer, neither day nor night; and the lamps at the windows cast a dismal light through the mist.

In spite of the little scarlet coat and the shoes of doeskin and the hood of goat's-hair cloth, the child was cold. He sat on his father's shoulder as rigidly as though he had been carved out of wood. He needed the warmth of a hearth, and there was a hearth at which he would have been more than welcome in the house of the Seren of Gath. Yet the son of Jesse could not bring himself to walk up the palace stairs. He wanted none of Achish. A strange, disturbing aftertaste clung to the hours that he had spent with Achish last night.

Moving among the blown stalls of the bazaar, he stopped to stare at a length of Phoenician cloth and saw instead a vision of Achish's face, the mouth tight and sorrowful, the cheeks sagging, no color upon them except the little crimson spots driven out by the wine. And he knew suddenly that Achish had brought some unknown grief into the house, some trouble which he could not bring himself to reveal. He remembered the veined hand raised often for attention and then falling again, the lips parted to say some word and closing on nothing save a sigh.

What, then, had ailed Achish last night? Perhaps he was ill. He suffered from an affliction of the bowels, and perhaps he had been borne down with the burden of his own death. And should Achish go down into the Sheol of Philistia, how then would the son of Jesse fare among the uncircumcised? Between David and the Seren of Gath there had been more than an alliance. Achish had indulged his confederate as a father would indulge his most beloved child.

A sharp wind sent the reeds and wisps of straw down the street. Amnon shivered. David raised the corner of his own cloak and tucked it around the child's legs. "Shall we go down to the stables," he said, "to see the fine horses?"

"Yes." He spoke in a diction so pure and precise that it was disturbing to hear. His speech was not a child's speech; it fell from too-careful lips.

When they had come to the great stable which sprawled near the sea at the side of Achish's palace, when they stood in the steaming warmth under the crude brown rafters and between the stalls of stone, with the smell of fresh dung in their nostrils and the whinnying and stamping in their ears, then Amnon asked to be taken down from his father's shoulder. He drew very close to one of the stalls and stared at the gray mane, the twitching ears, the rolling eyes. He stepped forward and leaned against the stone of the stall, to show his father that he was not afraid.

"No, now," said David, drawing the child back against him. "Do not go near him. He is a heathen beast and very fierce. He has hoofs to trample and teeth to bite."

He wondered now why he had come down to see the horses. The men of Philistia loved the beasts, would lean their heads against the silken, nervous sides, would let the tremulous lips lick sweets from the palms of their hands. He had striven to emulate them; he knew a good horse when he saw one; he had even persuaded himself to mount the wild and foaming mares that were the pride of Achish and to ride them along the beach. Yet his flesh crept whenever he touched them. Horses were the battle beasts of the unclean; there was evil magic in them; they carried in their glossy flanks the dark power of Ethiopia and Scythia, the sorcery of the unknown islands of the western sea. Still, if the child was to ride forth eventually with the sons and grandsons of the Seren of Gath, it was well to stifle early the Israelitish creepings of his blood. . . .

One of the Seren's charioteers waved a greeting from the far end of the stable. Four or five young men were working there in the thick shadows under the rafters, diligently cleaning a double row of empty stalls. It was strange to see them at that end of the stable. There were some twenty more stalls than there were horses—the empty stalls had remained untended since long before the day when David first came up to Gath.

He cupped his hands at his lips and shouted, "What is it that the servants of Achish do among the useless stalls?"

The voice of the charioteer answered him, begetting echoes among the rafters. "We are making ready for the morrow."

"The morrow? What comes to pass on the morrow?"

"On the morrow they will come in on the ships—the twenty horses brought out of Egypt by my lord."

David started. That Achish should have been awaiting the arrival of twenty steeds out of Egypt, and yet should not have made mention of it in the house in Ziklag last night—— He was shamed before the charioteer. He was shamed even before his son, who looked at him with wondering and pitying eyes. Suddenly his dislike for the horses turned into positive loathing. He closed his nostrils against the reek of their urine, he turned his sight from them, he stared at the heavy, ominous procession of clouds that passed the open door. Wild and terrible, among the piled clouds, he saw a vision of horses—spread manes, rolling eyes rimmed round with blood, hoofs trampling something helpless and unutterably dear.

"Let us go now, my father," Amnon said.

He lifted his son and held him high against his body, wondering whether the little one could feel his heart knocking in his chest.

The charioteer shouted from the far end of the stable, "Do you go forth from us so soon, my lord?"

"Yes," he said, and could say nothing more.

"Come again on the morrow to see the new steeds. Bring the little one with you, and we will show him a horse newborn. I have a mare that will surely foal this night."

He nodded and set Amnon on his shoulder and went again into the misty street.

"Where will my father take me?" Amnon said.

"To the foundry. To the great ovens in which they smelt the shields and the swords. There my son can warm himself before the fires. It is a goodly place, with red embers and much warmth. . . ."

He set out in the direction of the glow that the foundry cast upon the mist. The roar of the flames in the furnaces mingled with the desolate sound of the coming and going of the sea. Then he heard it again—the brazen clang that had broken upon him this morning—the blow of doom, the blow of a hammer against bronze, thud and clang, so that the air above the city pulsed with noise. He said the name of God aloud and stood perfectly still in the middle of the street. The alien faces, white and untroubled, kept flowing past him. The sound of the waters ebbed and flowed. And he knew that the hammer blow of death had fallen on no heart but his and that he alone heard the high flute note begotten by the wind blowing in from the shore.

Never in his life had he seemed so remote from the rest of the human race. He hastened toward the Street of the Foundry, jostling whoever came into his path, cursing under his breath. In the warmth of the foundry, he told himself, I will lose this nightmare, I will hear with a sane man's ears and see with a sane man's eyes. . . .

During his stay in Philistia he had come to this place a score of times to replenish the armory of Ziklag. He knew it well—the barren rise of ground on which the foundry stood, the cluster of sheds where anvils sent off yellow sparks, the two great ovens, open at one end to shed a lucid orange glow upon the entire street. He had always enjoyed the smell of molten metal, the music of clanking anvils, the loud, jesting voices raised above the roar and hiss of fire. Now for the first time he knew the desolation of the empty slope strewn with shale and ashes and bits of twisted bronze. The furnaces had suddenly turned inimical; the sickly warmth that issued from them was like the exhalation of a volcanic cone.

"My father," said Amnon, "let me see the fire."

He started, because the blows had assailed his ears again, sharper and closer now. They were coming from one of the sheds to the side of the ovens. Whatever thing the hammer struck was no piece of small arms. A weapon for giants, such a weapon as the Rephaim must have wielded in the days of their ascendancy in the Valley of the Rocks. . . .

"My father, let me——"

"Wait a little," he said in a harsh voice. The blasting heat thrown off by the ovens had brought a weakening sweat upon him. He shivered, and knew that the child knew that he shivered. "First we will go up to the sheds, so that I may see what work is at hand—whence comes that noise."

Halfway up the slope he saw that the ground before the largest of the sheds was cluttered with great wooden wheels. No doubt they were wheels for chariots, but they were larger and heavier than any chariot wheels he had seen before. He could not bring himself to consider why they were there or how they were related to the shattering sounds. Instead he set himself to counting them, and had counted a score and seven before he reached the threshold of the shed.

For a long moment there was nothing but silence and the brownish darkness inside. Then the crash broke again, full in his face, and a shower of saffron-colored sparks went up, revealing the smith at the anvil. A huge glowing sheet of hammered bronze, still hot and malleable, was bent over the anvil and covered half the floor. Then the sparks cascaded into nothingness in midair, and the noise was still, and the voice of the smith said: "Do my eyes behold the Seren of Ziklag and the hope of his house? Come in, come in out of the wind, my lord."

The man was well known to David; he had made him a helmet and a corselet, had fashioned the braziers for his house in Ziklag, and had thrice sharpened his sword. For years he had worked at the mouth of the furnace, so that his lean face was without eyebrows and eyelashes, and had turned the color of red clay. His arms were developed out of all proportion to the rest of his body. They were long and hairy; and when he stood in the semidarkness, dressed only in his leather apron, he looked like one of the creatures who had roamed among the rocks before the sons of God had come upon the world. Nevertheless, he was kindly. When he was at the anvil, the children of the neighborhood came without fear to watch the sparks. Now he stood at ease behind the strange metal sheeting, and bestowed upon the little Amnon a dry, cracked, tender smile.

David set the child down and led him into the shed. The part of the ground that was not covered by the sheet of metal was crossed and recrossed by a long serpentine strip of bronze, hammered flat, and about the width of a man's thigh. This also was strange and new. He stepped carefully over the coils. The bronze of the stripping was quite cold, but he avoided it as if it would have seared him to the bone. He could not bring himself to ask concerning these things at once. He stood close to the anvil, close to the glimmering sheet of metal that lay upon it, staring and wetting his lips with the tip of his tongue.

It was the child who uttered the question. "What is it that he makes, my father?" he said.

"Ask him, for I know not." He regretted the words at once. There was a note of grievance in his voice. It was as if he had said, "Ask the smith, who is more exalted than I in the confidence of the Seren of Gath."

But the man behind the anvil took no offense. He spoke with the eagerness of one who loves his craft and can think of no happier duty than that of expounding it to a wondering child. "Sheeting—it is sheeting that I make," he said. "My lord the Seren of Gath has learned it from the Seren of Askelon, who, in his turn, learned it from the princes of the far north—how chariots are twenty times more terrible if there is a sheeting of bronze upon their sides. Henceforth the chariots of Philistia will go forth to the wars clad all in bronze, shining and indestructible. Behold the stripping which lies at your feet. That also is for the chariots. It will arm the wheels thereof. Look down and behold how there are holes in the stripping, to bind it to the wheels with nails of bronze. Spikes also we will make, to set into the wheel at the point where the rim meets with the spokes. And I assure the little rose of the high house of Ziklag that they are wondrous spikes, very long, and sharp enough to tear a man's flesh." In his eagerness to rouse admiration in his lord's child, he had for the moment forgotten his lord. Now he turned courteously to David. "Surely," he said, "the Seren of Ziklag has heard all these matters from the lips of the Seren of Gath. Nevertheless, it is a delight to me that I should be the first to show him the stripping and the sheeting. A few of the spikes also I have by me. Wait a little, and I will bring one and lay it in the hand of my lord."

David stood utterly still, waiting, while the smith clanked about in the shadowy corner. He saw the green hills of Judah and Benjamin and Ephraim rutted by the brazen wheels; he saw Bethlehem and Gibeah and Gilgal and Shechem consumed by tongues of fire; he saw the tower room of Saul's house in Gibeah toppling toward a distant vision of the sea. And when the smith came and laid the heavy spike upon his rigid palm, he said in his heart, This is for the tearing of the flesh of my lord and my beloved. . . .

Suddenly he realized that the smith was speaking, had been speaking for some moments, freely and energetically. And David knew in his heart that this smith, like all the other sons and daughters of Philistia, had completely forgotten in the course of three years that the red-haired, honey-skinned darling of Achish was of the race of Moses and Barak and Abraham.

"And we will be kept laboring here day and night," he was saying, "through all the season of the winter rains, so that at the moment when the rivers subside we may march eastward, armed as no nation in Canaan has ever been armed before. Nor will we pause this time in the plains of Sharon. For it is our purpose now to cross the land, even unto Shechem and Gilgal, even unto Gibeah where the mad King dwells. We will enslave them as they were enslaved in the days after Shiloh, when they dared not come up to the highways, but crept like beasts through the forest and lived in caves upon berries and roots. This time we will burn their cities and utterly put them down, these dogs of Israelites. . . ."

298

The hand of the son of Jesse faltered. The spike fell from it and rang against the coil of metal on the floor.

The face of the smith went putty-colored. His lashless eyelids blinked. His lips fell apart. For a moment he stared in shocked silence. Then he said, "Dagon forgive me! I had forgotten. I am a fool, my lord."

"Do not think upon it," he said in a flat voice. "It is forgiven."

"But it is not as if my lord is truly of Israel. My lord is the dear brother of the Seren of Gath. . . ."

"How can that be?" he said, wondering at himself that he should discuss such a matter with a smith. "A man is the seed of his father in the womb of his mother. A man is the food he eats and the air he breathes and the earth he walks upon. I am Israel, and these spikes that you have made, my friend, these spikes——"

The smith picked up the spike and tossed it into the corner. "Let my lord forgive me. Let my lord say to himself, 'It was an old fool that spoke.' Let my lord believe that in these three years I have asked myself only how I could better please and serve my lord."

"I know. I know."

They looked down then and saw that the child was standing close to them, looking from one to the other with large, moist eyes.

"Will we go to see the fire now?" Amnon said.

David lifted him up and held him hard against his chest. Flesh of my flesh, he thought, green shoot of my homeland, grown sickly in an alien place. . . .

"No," he said. "Forgive your father. He has no heart now to go and look upon the fire."

Then he turned and went out of the shed, holding the child against him. The scent of the child's body was the scent of Noi's body. He breathed it in the foreign, windy street, and wept.

⋞ III ⋟

A MOON passed before the Seren of Ziklag and the Seren of Gath beheld each other face to face. Had it not been for Joab, David's knowledge of the affairs of Gath would have been confined to what little he had learned from a smith and a charioteer. But the son of Zeruiah went often to the cities of the uncircumcised. *His* heart had not been bruised by Achish's silence; *he* saw no reason to brood in solitude behind the walls of Ziklag; *he* could speak with the Philistine captains as freely as before. Three times in the course of every week he came to eat the evening meal at David's table. There, warmed by excellent wine and cheered by the cordiality that had arisen between him and Abigail, he delivered his news to the Star of Bethlehem. His skill in finding facts was surpassed only by his skill in passing them on, polished and adorned, to his lord. It was only after he had departed that David saw the enormity of the dilemma. Then,

299

in the hushed house, among the foreign rugs and pottery, the son of Jesse walked back and forth, oppressed and grieving and unable to sleep.

There was at least this small comfort at the core of the calamity; it had not been Achish who had planned this major assault against the Israelites. The Seren of Gath had at first stood firm against the undertaking, but the Serens of Ashdod and Askelon, younger men and fiery in council, had proved incontrovertibly that now, if ever, was the time to put the yoke upon the Israelites. Were not the tribes divided—Judah and Caleb and the Kenites utterly estranged from Saul? Were there not quarrels and uncertainties and delays even in Benjamin and Ephraim, where the King's hold was strongest? What policy could issue from the dark mind of a mad king? And the King of Israel was plainly mad. Victory was certain, would have been certain even without the chariots of bronze. And if each of the five cities could supply twenty such chariots, victory would be cheap.

Yet the Seren of Gath had delayed, absenting himself from councils on the plea of sickness. His peers were courtly and considerate men, and referred only obliquely to his fondness for his ally. Surely the gallant warrior who held the gates of Philistia against the south would lose nothing by the defeat of one who had sent murderers against him and hounded him into the wilderness. But the people of the city were less restrained than the Serens of Ashdod and Askelon. They scratched inscriptions on the palace stairs and the palace walls; they drove their malice into the stone with bits of broken shell. "The lord of Gath," they wrote, "having lain with all the temple women in Philistia, has taken a son of Jahveh to his bed." And "The city waits only to be informed of the hour when Achish will be circumcised."

So it was that, worn out with entreaties and insults and illness, Achish sent his galleys for steeds out of Egypt and instructed the master of his foundry to begin work on the sheeting and the spikes. Thrice, he told one of his captains—who told it again to Joab—thrice he had made attempts to lay the matter before David. But his heart had failed him on each of these occasions—he simply could not imagine himself saying the necessary words.

There was one more tale concerning Achish that the son of Zeruiah knew but did not repeat to his uncle. He heard it from the wife of the Egyptian physician who had been attending the Seren of Gath. It seemed that Achish had made certain groundless commitments, had said in council that he had never held back for the sake of his confederate of Ziklag, that the son of Jesse was more Philistine than Israelite, that when the hour came for going forth, David and David's host would march against Israel with the rest. Afterward he had sorely regretted his speech and had said as much to the physician; he knew not why he had made it; perhaps he had used the irresponsible words to embody a wish. Was it strange that, after three years of friendship, he should wish that the Star of Bethlehem were more devoted to him than to Saul or Jonathan?

Joab did not carry this tale to David's table. It was a stubborn tale that would not be twisted. No matter how he tried, he could not bring it in smoothly. "Of course," he said, when David commended him for his skill in ferreting out news, "of course I cannot discover *everything*. No doubt there are certain matters which are so private that they never reach the ears of a wife or a servant or a captain or anyone at all. . . ."

So they wore away the time in gossip and conjecture, until that evening when David went from his hearth to answer a knock and saw the Seren of Gath standing like any common visitor at his door.

◄§ IV §►

ON THAT EVENING David was left alone in the common room earlier than usual. Joab had gone off to keep an assignation with one of the Canaanite women who had come—at first singly and in pairs and finally in large numbers—to dwell in the town. Noi always rose from the meal promptly. She went to her room scarcely an hour after sunset to sit on the bed with the child until he fell asleep. Although evening after evening she was courteously bidden to return to the family again, she never reappeared. She remained on the bed, doing some bit of handiwork and singing tonelessly, either to the child or to herself. It was Abigail's custom to sit up late, embroidering or weaving, pausing in her work now and then to comment on politics or household matters; but tonight she also had gone to her bed. He had only himself to blame, he thought, standing on the hearth and staring disconsolately into the fire. She had spoken cheerfully, and he had not smiled. She had spoken gravely, and he had answered only in a monosyllable. She had hummed over her work, and he had contracted his eyebrows. Then, with that dignified resignation which irked him most, she had risen. "Since both I and my lord are weary," she had said, "I will go into the chamber and sleep."

He blamed them all for departing, even though it was he who had driven them forth, having dismissed them from the sanctuary of his heart either this night or long ago. An oppressive quiet inhabited the room; the last servant had performed the last duty and departed; the shelves were starkly bright and orderly; the table was austerely bare.

It was then that he heard the shy, soft knocking at the door. The summons was so tentative that he fancied one of his servants must be standing on the other side of the portal, delayed on some mischievous errand of his own and afraid to show himself. He waited until the knock had sounded a second time, and then crossed the room and opened the door. The brightness of many lamps fell full upon Achish.

"Behold," said the Seren of Gath, "I have come alone, as friend comes to friend, to ask a little quiet talk. For my heart has yearned strongly toward my brother David. . . ."

"Not more strongly," said the son of Jesse, drawing him in out of the gust, "surely not more strongly than mine toward my lord."

He laid Achish's purple cloak on a clothes chest near the entrance, took the cold elbow of his lord in his palm, and drew him toward the fire. It had been many days since his hand had lain upon the flesh of the unclean, and now, in spite of himself, he stiffened a little.

For what seemed a long time they sat silent on either side of the hearth, staring at the yellow flames that rippled over the driftwood and seaweed from which the peoples of the coastland made their fires. Scent of alien waters, David thought; even to our hearths it pursues us, the strange and insatiable sea. . . . And he thought again of Gibeah, of the smell of wet earth coming through the wide windows on the first nights of the rain, of the snap and hiss of green twigs.

"It would seem," said Achish, "that my friend is sorrowful at the sight of my face."

"No, now," said David, still staring at the fire, "how is that possible? Even at the moment when your hand was at my door, I was saying in my heart, 'When shall I again behold my lord?'"

For a long time there was charged stillness between them. Achish looked at a fan of seaweed burning scarlet among the flames, at the wall, at his own white hands. "If I have remained absent from Ziklag these many days," he said at last, "it has been partly because my old affliction has been upon me and partly because I know that all Philistia—even I—must be hateful now in the sight of David, who journeyed to the coastland in his flesh only, leaving his spirit behind him in Gibeah and in Bethlehem."

"No, now, my brother——"

"I have said to myself, 'How can I tell him this thing? Let him hear it from another mouth than mine.'"

"I have heard it," he said quietly. "More than a moon since, I heard it from the lips of a smith and a charioteer. I have heard of the chariots sheathed in bronze, and the steeds brought up out of Egypt. I have heard how the armies are to move eastward, even into Israel." He had meant to fall silent then, but suddenly he found that he could not hold his peace. "I have been told how they will burn Gibeah and Bethlehem and Shechem and Gilgal, how they will ravish those that are my sisters and enslave those that are my brothers. It is plain to me now—I assure my lord that it is very plain to me—that the land which is my land is to be soaked in the blood which is my blood. . . ."

"David, it was not I——"

"No, now, shall I smile because the sword which tears my flesh comes not out of Gath, but only out of Ashdod and Askelon?"

"My brother——"

"They are my brothers who will go down under the wheels sheathed in bronze. They only are my brothers who will be trampled to death by the beasts that my lord of Gath coddles with sweetmeats. . . ." He wished that he could stifle this wild and futile raging, but there was no stopping now. He knew that his voice was loud enough to rouse the whole sleeping household, that his hand was pounding against the arm of his chair, and yet he could not cease. "Willing or unwilling, Gath will march out—Gath will march out to set the torch to the cities of Dan and Ephraim and Benjamin. Saul was my lord, and Saul will be slain. What is left to me except the ashes of Israel? Would to God that I also might be consumed in that holocaust!"

Through the blur of his pain and fury, he saw the face of Achish—a stricken face striving to compose itself. "Surely, even as the son of Jesse tells me, there will be little left to him," Achish said. "Nothing save Judah and Caleb and the land of the Kenites. . . ."

The words of the Seren had ceased to sound before the son of Jesse took their import to his heart. "Nothing save Judah and Caleb and the land of the Kenites. . . ." And this, in grosser language, meant "When the hour of victory is come, then, for a certain price as yet unnamed, I will lift David up and make him king over half of Israel."

Achish was speaking again; his voice was meditative and very low. "If the son of Jesse thinks that my resistance was light, that I bridled a little and shook my head twice or thrice and meant from the beginning to give my consent, then he is mistaken. For two moons I strove against them. And if in the end it was they that triumphed, it was because they were many and young, and I was solitary and old. Also Dagon, whom I have sorely offended, sent the old evil upon my bowels, and I was weak, and hateful to myself. . . ."

It is as he says, thought David. Surely he has suffered for my sake. The marks of his suffering are plain upon him. . . .

"A hundred times they said to me in veiled words that I had forgotten Philistia in remembering David. Nor could I protest too strongly, since I have always been one who lies with bad grace. I knew in my heart that had I never set eyes upon the Star of Bethlehem, I would have gone forth. Not gladly, for I am weary. But I would have gone forth, seeing that it was Dagon's will, that the hour for the lifting up of Dagon had indeed come."

Surely he has loved me, David told himself. And I have given poor measure in return for his love. I have eaten his bread and hidden behind his walls and dwelt secure in the tabernacle of his heart. But my heart has been closed against him, yearning after Israel and Jonathan. . . .

"Nor was it only the Serens who stood against me. The people also were stirred up, to scrawl my name in shameful inscriptions upon the walls of my house. They wrote that I had turned to Jahveh and set my face against Dagon and Astarte. They said that the love I bore for David was a guilty love. . . ." He flushed and stared even more steadily into the fire. "Nor could I say to myself that they were utterly unjust. How can a man distinguish surely between one sort of love and another sort of love? This I know: that I loved David freely and without question, that I rejoiced in the sound of his voice and the sight of his face. I set him above my sons.

and my peers and the women of my house. Nor, when I came to examine my heart, did I know surely that the son of Jesse was less to me than Dagon and Astarte. . . ."

"Let Achish forgive me," said David. "I have made a poor return for his love. I have brought nothing but grief upon his head."

The Seren rose then and walked close to the fire and spread his unsteady hands against the glow. "It would yet be possible," he said, "for the son of Jesse to silence the slanders which they speak against me."

Now, thought David, leaning forward in his chair, now he will name the price. . . .

"I said a thing in council—I know not why I said it——"

"What said my brother and my lord?"

"A piece of folly, such as I would give my tongue to have unsaid. For many hours they had wrangled with me, and their patience had grown short, so that they forgot their wonted courtesy. And one of them laid a plan of battle before me and said, 'We will go by such-and-such a route and meet the enemy in such-and-such a place, provided that it is suitable to the Seren of Gath and to that Israelite who rules his heart.' Then a foolish yearning possessed me, and I thought, If David only loved me as he loves Saul. . . . And the longing was so strong upon me that I strove to transform it into reality. Before I could bite my lips into silence, I had said to them all, 'Concerning the son of Jesse, my friends the Serens are sorely mistaken. I am dearer to him than Saul or any other Israelite. When we march forth against the circumcised, he and all those who are garrisoned in Ziklag will march forth with us. The Star of Bethlehem is with Philistia, and in no wise have I refused for his sake.' And those that were with me in the council smiled knowingly and answered me, saying, 'Is it indeed so between Achish and David? We knew it not. In the hour of setting forth we shall see.'"

This, then, is the price, thought David, that I should march with Philistia against Israel. . . . Suddenly he was assailed by an inward cold, so strong that he shivered and knelt upon the hearth at Achish's side and spread his hands before the fire. Achish remained silent, still staring at the little tongues of yellow and blue that rippled over the embers.

"Surely they did not believe my lord?" David said.

Achish shrugged and thrust out his lower lip. "It was such a lie as they would wish to believe. For should David march up with us toward Gibeah, no man among the Judahites or the Calebites or the Kenites would take his sword and come forth to meet us. The south would give us free passage for David's sake."

David started, seeing plainly that this was so.

"My brothers the Serens made plain to me how, if David went up with us and the cities of the south stood not against us, no towns would be burned in the land which is David's land. Nor would any temple or shrine of Jahveh be razed in the name of Dagon and Astarte. . . ."

"Truly, my lord?" He had not meant to say it. For what profit was there in the salvation of the south alone? Was not Israel one living body, stretching from Dan to Beersheba?

"Surely the son of Jesse knows that I have dealt honorably with him and have never beguiled him. My brothers the Serens have sealed it with vows. When David returns to his own, he will see the plains and hills of Judah as they were before he departed, white with flocks and green with the olive and the vine. . . ."

They will not touch the brown house in Bethlehem, he thought, nor the tabernacle of the Lord in Hebron, nor the prophet's house in Ramah. . . .

"Let David forgive me if I bring before him so gross a matter—the words are the words of the other Serens, who know not, as I know it, the mind of the Star of Bethlehem. They have said to me, 'If he goes up with us, all the south will fall into his hands. He will be king thereof, and keep forever the peace that has been these three years between the south and Philistia. And when we give him a land, it will be no place of rutted fields and charred villages, but a flourishing and peaceful land.'"

The son of Jesse looked up at the Seren of Gath and saw that he had turned his head aside and closed his eyes. He could not tell precisely when the reddened eyelids had descended over the blue, protruding eyes. He did not know whether the Seren of Gath had actually seen it in his look—the fierce joy at the thought of Judah and Caleb and the land of the Kenites saved and laid untouched in the hollow of his hand. He knew only that Achish, had he seen, would have refused to see.

"I have striven to see the matter as David would see it," Achish said slowly. "Inasmuch as the north will certainly be put to the sword, whatever David does, what profit would come of it if, for the sake of a king who has turned his back on the Pride of Judah, Judah is ravaged with the rest?"

What profit indeed?

"It is said in the south that the seer Samuel foretold once how the son of Jesse would reign in Israel. If it is the will of Jahveh that David is to reign, then wherefore should David fly in the face of his God?"

Wherefore? thought David. And yet Israel has been one body since the day when Saul went up to Jabesh-Gilead, and called the tribes together to march with him, and delivered the men of Jabesh-Gilead out of the hands of Nahash, so that they were grateful to him and gave him their sour wine and anointed his feet with their tears. For a little while the songs of Judah and Caleb rose in the encampment side by side with the songs of Ephraim and Dan and Benjamin. Now it will be as it was before Jabesh-Gilead, even as it was when the uncircumcised set the torch to the high place of Shiloh. The south will look to its reaping while the north dies. Judah and Caleb and the Kenites will say among themselves, "What is Israel to us? We are David's. Our swords and our spears stand idle against the wall for David's sake." . . .

"Therefore, if David will go up with me——"

He wished now only to be finished with it, to see the uncircumcised depart from his house, to go to some place of utter darkness and weep. "As my lord says, there is no help for it. I will go up," he said.

Achish bent then and raised him and kissed him three times, once on each cheek and once on the brow. He mastered himself long enough to return the embrace, to summon servants to accompany the departing one with torches on his way to Gath, to stand long on the threshold, waving after the little procession that moved against the black and gusty night.

But when the door was closed, when he was alone in the foreign room near the fire that gave off the scent of the sea, he yearned greatly after Israel. He sought then to flee into the gone years, to make himself one with his ancestors—the wild and holy ones, the keepers of camels and asses, who had dwelt at peace with Jahveh in the sand. He flung himself upon the Philistine hearth as if it had been a strip of the desert. Lying at full length upon it, he raked up dust and ashes in his hands; he scattered the dry stuff of grief upon his head and drew the immemorial symbols of mourning upon his cheeks and brow. What it was that he mourned, he could not rightly tell—dying Canaan, the great and honorable King, the beloved, himself. In the name of each of these he cried out to Jahveh, but the face of God had turned from him utterly. And without the Lord and the laws of the Lord, what was life? Life was a mockery, a deception, the web of a spider spread gleaming across blackness everlasting. Nothing was real but death.

❧ V ❧

THE WINTER went by, solemn and monotonous, resonant with the clang of beaten bronze, crossed by the cold arrows of the coastal rains. The son of Jesse seldom showed his face beyond his own walls. He had fallen again into that numb and dreaming state which had come upon him once before in the wilderness of Judah. Once again he had called his nephew Joab to him and had said: "I lay it in your hands. Whatsoever is to be done, do. Only come not up to ask me concerning this and that. He pleases me best who leaves me most in peace."

He was given peace—he was given too much peace. Joab, busy with a thousand duties, came less and less often to his uncle's table; he was forever in haste, forever preoccupied. Achish also kept more and more to his own house in Gath. Whether it was because the Seren was ailing, or was pressed with the business of war, or was fearful that his confederate might try to withdraw from the alliance, David did not know. The gifts and the messages that went between Gath and Ziklag were as they had been in the past, generous and tender. But David's heart was uneasy concerning Achish. He saw my eyes, he kept telling himself. On that wretched night when he said that I would be king in the south, before he turned his head away, he surely saw the unseemly eagerness in my eyes. . . .

Only two other visitors came with any regularity to the high house in Ziklag—Abiathar the priest and the hairy Abishai—and David was weary of them both. The more the son of Jesse wished to retreat from conversation, the more the priest strove to drag him in, boring him with minute accounts of the beliefs and customs of the Philistines. Nor was the company of Abishai more gratifying. If the priest talked too much, the fat, retiring warrior talked too little. He would sit for half an hour at a time staring earnestly and uneasily into the faces of those about him, waiting for them to speak, and offering nothing at all. During the whole dreary meal, David could think of nothing but the moment when the servants would clear the table. Then there would be a respite; Abishai would sit on the hearth with Noi and the little Amnon, and devote himself to playing with the child or gaping into the mother's eyes. This interval was always far too brief for David. Noi refused to stay in the common room longer than usual; she rose from the hearth at the accustomed time and disappeared into her chamber with the child. And David could not forgive her for sending Abishai back to plague him. "I cannot understand the woman," he would say in a testy tone. "Is she a bird that she must be asleep at the going-down of the sun?"

But on those evenings when neither of the two unwelcome visitors arrived, he was even more acutely miserable. Then there was only Abigail, busying herself with her eternal needlework, nursing her eternal grievance, turning upon him her resigned and unvarying smile. The winter rains had fallen like a heavy curtain around her life, closing her in. Now she had nothing to relate concerning the houses she had visited in Gath, or the doings of the Seren's grandchildren. She could speak only of the inanities of the household, the symptoms of her fancied illnesses, the incoherent stuff of her nightly dreams. And when his mind wandered from this bodiless talk to some other matter, she fell silent and brooded over her childlessness. The burden of the blame, which she had taken upon herself in the beginning, had slipped almost imperceptibly onto his shoulders. Since the night when he had agreed to go up with Achish against Israel, she and all women had ceased to stir him. Now her large shining eyes turned upon him at least once every evening with the unspoken reproach: "If my lord will not come to me, how can I bear him a child?"

Evening after evening, no matter who spoke or moved around him, he sat in solitude, thinking of the time when he would go out to betray Saul and Israel. He had only to stare into the fire to see how it would be: the sun rising before the gates of Ziklag, the host coming forth from the city, their banners hanging limp in the moist air of the morning—banners on which the star of David stood side by side with Dagon's ear of wheat. He saw himself riding forth on one of the steeds out of Egypt; he saw himself as he would look in the eyes of God—small and mean as a red ant that crawls upon the earth. He watched his own troops filing over the highways of Philistia and Judah, heedful of the rich crops of Philistia and Judah, saving their violence for the streets of Gibeah and the fields of Benjamin. He saw himself and his host pausing in the appointed orchard to join forces with the five Serens of Philistia. He heard the neighing of the beasts and the thunder of the brazen wheels, and saw the congregated host, greater than any host that had ever trampled the soil of Israel. . . .

These images, and only these, were real to him while he sat out the winter in his house in Ziklag. And, since he had brooded over them so long, when they came to pass at last—when the rains ceased and the wheat turned green and the warriors went forth—these things also ceased to be realities. In a dream he set forth from the walled city. Insubstantial faces moved around him and wept behind him, and insubstantial banners floated above his head.

❦ VI ❧

It was not strange that the Serens of Philistia should have called their armies to a three-day halt in that section of the plain of Sharon where Saul had bidden his host to pause ten years ago. Since the days of Saul's anointing, now Israel, now Philistia, had raised their banners here. The grove of almond trees at the foot of the slope had been in full bloom that year; now they flowered again, casting white petals on the wind of God. In the meadow beyond the grove, the warriors of Philistia lifted up their songs against the thought of death. They sang, as the men of Israel had sung before them, of the hearth fire in the homeland, of the waiting wife and the waiting child, of heroes fallen in other battles, of the eternity of glory and the mutability of love. Over field and grove and meadow hung the big, close stars, watery and tremulous, as though they had been touched by the tears of the world.

Had it not been for the white tent among the almond trees, the son of Jesse might have imagined that all the years of his exile had been undone, that the hand of God had lifted him out of an uneasy dream and borne him back to a lost, unforgettable spring. He stood on the slope among the wheat now as he had stood long ago. He stared down at the grove and strove to forget that Joab stood beside him. Over that same stretch of weeds and grass, beneath the almond boughs, the King of Israel had carried his wounded son. Light had fallen upon them at the entrance of the tent— a sudden brightness on the trailing, cloudy hair. But Saul's tent had been black and coarse, woven from the rough wool of the goats of Kedar, and the great tent in which the Serens were to sleep was white and fine and hung with streamers of scarlet and blue, the colors of Dagon and Astarte. Many lamps had been kindled within; the shapes of the five Serens were shadowed forth on the linen, sitting together over the evening meat. They had sent their servants away an hour since, plainly because there was some matter which they wished to consider alone. And at any moment,

Joab would ask the questions that had been tormenting him since the going-down of the sun: Why should the Serens eat in secrecy? Why had the Star of Bethlehem not been asked to come and break bread? How would it be with the men of Ziklag if they learned that there had been a high council from which their lord had been excluded?

That he should not have been bidden to the table of the mighty ones, that he should have been left to wander back and forth across the slope of wheat with no company save the burdensome company of his captain—this was indeed cause for hurt and misgiving. But David could not bring himself to consider the slight with any constancy. He even felt a perverse pleasure in the pain of being the rejected one, the one who waits outside. For had he not tarried without on that other evening? All had gone into the tent—Saul and Ahitophel and Abner and the surgeon—all had been close to the stripped and suffering body of the beloved save himself. . . .

"Look now, the Seren of Ashdod has come out of the tent for a breath of air," Joab said.

He had indeed come out—a solemn and sinewy man plainly driven forth by impatience with what passed within—but David saw him for no longer than a breathing space. What was the Seren of Ashdod and his impatience beside the remembrance of the King of Israel, swaying above the clothes chest, refusing to close his eyes against the torment, refusing to set the quaking lamp in another's hand?

"The Seren of Ashdod has gone in again."

"Let him go. What is it to me?"

They had begun to speak loudly and earnestly in the white tent below him; their voices, now separately, now together, were borne up to the wheat field. It might have been possible to piece the fragments of their talk together, but he could not bring himself to listen. He paced the slope and heard the swishing of the stalks beneath his feet—that, and the long, harsh gasps that had issued from the beloved's laboring throat, and the tired voice of the surgeon out of Dan saying, "A little longer, only a little longer, my dear boy, my brave heart."

"Believe me, my uncle, I would give ten years of my life to be able to hear what they are saying below."

He did not reply. He heard them again—as he had heard them countless times in his dreams—the wild, sharp animal cries that had torn through the hush of that other night.

"Three times," said Joab, "I have heard them say distinctly, 'On the day of battle'——"

David uprooted a handful of wheat stalks and crushed them in his palm. The day of battle . . . Now for the first time he knew in his heart that there would be a day of battle, that this would not end where his thoughts concerning it had ended, that there was something beyond the mustering of the armies in the plain below the Gilboan slopes. And how will it be with me on the day of battle? he asked himself. If even the remembrance of that long-healed wound is as an arrow through my heart, how will I fare when the ranks of Israel go down before the chariots of bronze? How will it be when the cries of the dying are numberless, and every cry is your cry, my brother Jonathan? . . . And suddenly he saw the face of the beloved smiling upon him, grown reasonable and serene after an assault of pain. My friend, said Jonathan, you give yourself too much trouble. It is written in the mind of Jahveh that I am to die young. . . .

The quarrel in the white tent had subsided. The son of Zeruiah, weary with fruitless efforts to see and know, settled his lank body on a knoll and chewed on a stalk of wheat. "Perhaps we should go to the encampment and break bread with the host," he said. "My uncle has denied himself to his warriors since the hour of noon."

David looked across the tent and the pale, flowering boughs at the meadowland. They had been singing there all the while, but now for the first time he listened to their song. What was it that they mourned in the strange and sorrowful modes of Philistia? No matter what the words imported, it seemed to him that they sang always of the island home from which they had made an ancient and heartbroken journey—lost motherland where the iris grew between the flagstones of the streets, where the steps of the palaces went down into the sea. . . .

"Surely my uncle should take a little food, seeing that nothing has passed his lips since the morning bread."

At the thought of the meat turning upon the spits he felt a sickly stir of hunger. Yet to go to the encampment was to see the grove from the other side, to lose the white almond boughs and the triangle of glow that fell from the opening of the tent upon the grass, to turn away from the thought of Jonathan. "If you are hungry, go," he said. "I have no stomach for meat."

Joab cast his wheat stalk from him and heaved an impatient sigh. "If my lord remains, I will certainly remain with him. It is not suitable that David should pace up and down alone, like a pariah dog, within sight of the tent of the uncircumcised."

"Nor is it suitable that Joab should constantly speak to me concerning my shame. I am mindful of my shame. Only it seems to me tonight a small thing that I should be shamed in the eyes of Philistia, seeing that I am already shamed in——"

"No, now," said Joab, rising from the knoll, "my uncle is mistaken if he thinks that I consider him shamed in the eyes of the uncircumcised. Surely the Serens of Philistia have in no wise intended to lay a slight upon him. It is only that my lord does violence to his own dignity when he walks back and forth before the tent as though he waited like a servant upon the pleasure of those who sit within."

David stood still again, this time in sheer amazement. It was borne in upon him that for the first time in all his days he felt no concern for his own dignity. Since there was a choice between losing his pride and keeping the sight of this grove haunted with remembrances, then he would cast his pride away. "If Joab blushes for me," he said, "let him go down and hide his face among the host." He wheeled round and stared at the tent. The sound of contending voices had risen within it; the Seren of Askelon was plainly at odds with the Seren of Gath; their shadows, distorted and magnified, gestured at each other on the glimmering cloth.

"What would my uncle do," said the son of Zeruiah, "if the Serens of Philistia refrained from bidding him to come into the tent this night to sleep? It would be a sorry business if my lord's warriors were to witness so great a slight."

"It is a sorry business," he shouted, as though the words had been driven from him by an unexpected onslaught of pain, "it is a very sorry business that your lord's warriors should be here at all."

"No, now, why should David torment himself? When Judah lies in the hand of the son of Jesse, he will see that his bargain was just. It is the manner of David to require too much of himself. No man would have chosen otherwise than he, no man in Israel——"

"No man save Saul and Jonathan."

"Let the son of Jesse cease to measure himself according to the measurements of the House of Kish. In overmuch honor, in prodigal softness and tenderness, they threw themselves away."

"In God's name, hold your peace! They threw themselves away for my sake."

They walked back and forth then in silence. There were no sounds other than the faint and sorrowful cadences from the meadow. Whatever quarrel had taken place within the tent of the mighty was over now; the voices were still. When the shapes of the Serens moved again upon the lamplit cloth, their motions were the seemly motions of a courteous departure. Four of them, magnificent in their plumed helmets and purple cloaks, came forth and went off toward the distant fires of the encampment, no doubt to show their faces to their hosts. Only Achish, smaller and older than the others, cloakless and without a helmet, remained within the grove. He stood at the entrance of the tent, with the lamplight glancing from his bald brow. For a while he stared at a patch of whiteness at his feet—petals fallen from the almond boughs. Then he lifted his worn face to the slope where David and Joab walked, and raised his hand, and beckoned.

"He summons us," Joab said.

"He summons *me*." There was bitter pleasure in slighting the witness of his humiliation. "Let Joab go to the camp. It is plain that Achish would speak to me alone."

On his way down the slope and across the grove, he saw that what he had said in malice was actually so; the Seren bent his head a little in approval. Without a word, he motioned that David should enter before him. Whatever had come to pass within the tent had been for him a painful and exhausting business. He breathed as a man breathes after battle, in the long, shaken breaths that are akin to sighs.

There were six couches within the tent—Joab need not have troubled himself; it was plain that the Star of Bethlehem would be asked to lie down with the great ones of Philistia this night. He stood near one of these couches, looking across the table at the silent Achish and thinking how the sons of Jahveh carried no couches in the baggage wagons that followed them into battle. In the season of war the sons of Jahveh slept, as their ancestors had slept before them, upon the ground.

"It is clear to me," said the Seren of Gath, lowering his head and drawing long lines upon the table with his fingertip, "it is clear to me at last that the heart of David is not in the camp of Philistia. It has gone northward, even to Gilboa, to brood above the host of Jahveh. Nor do I hope to recall it and chain it to me, for I am old and have come to know that a man's heart will go where it will, no matter what chains are put upon it. Nevertheless, let David turn again to me for a single hour. Let him listen as he listened in the first days, when we broke bread together at his table in Ziklag and at my table in Gath, before the shadow fell between us. For I have a thing to tell him. It has been given to me to take a little from the cup of his bitterness and to pour it into mine." He left the table then and came to one of the couches and sat upon it. He laid his old, veined hand upon a pillow and felt the embroidered cloth and sighed. "Come," he said, "come and sit beside me. A pillow is a goodly comfort, even in the hour of wretchedness."

Cold, hard and cold, thought David, are the sods on the floor of the burial cave beneath the shoulders of the dead. . . .

While he stood motionless, the Seren moved far to one side of the couch, so that it would be possible for David to sit without brushing against him. He thinks he is unclean in my sight, David told himself, now that my spirit is gone out to Israel. He thinks also of the shameful words that they wrote upon the walls of Gath concerning him and me. . . . And suddenly his heart was swollen with pity. He crossed the room and sat close to Achish. He accepted the shaven cheek, the bald brow, and the alien scent of myrrh and cedarwood, and he lifted the worn hand from the pillow and held it briefly against his lips.

"Behold," he said, "there is no shadow between us. I listen with my heart to the words of my lord."

"Only this——" The hand withdrew from his and returned to the pillow. "If David so wishes, he may deliver his eyes from the sight of the destruction of Israel. It is no longer needful that he go up to Gilboa with the host. He may go back—even he and all that came up with him out of Ziklag—to dwell in his own city until the battle is done."

David started up. For the space of one heartbeat he wondered, At what price? At the loss of the kingship in the south? Then he sank back against the cushions, knowing that this deliverance was cheap at any cost— that he would buy it now even if the price were his own death.

"How is it," he said after long silence, "that my lord should send me back to Ziklag?"

"I?" A self-deprecatory smile passed over the face of Achish. "No, now, it was not I. The other Serens—they who were not blinded with affection for the son of Jesse—it was they who saw what had come to pass within his heart. They saw how his spirit had flown forth to the camp of Israel, how he walked as a man in a dream, bemused with grief. And it came into their minds to ask themselves and me: 'How will it be with him in the hour of battle? Will he not turn then from the ranks of Achish and flee to the ranks of Saul? How shall we put our trust in him when it is plain that he is broken with the burden of his sorrows, and does not know himself?' "

He could not answer. Like all other men, he thought, the Serens of Philistia have taken me for something better than I am. I never said in my heart, "I will flee to Saul in the final hour, I will turn at the last and die with Israel." And yet it is possible. I might have turned. Seeing the cloudy hair go down beneath the chariot wheels, I might have turned or fallen upon my sword. . . .

"And I," said Achish, "contended with them and with myself, saying that David was mine, that he had turned utterly from the House of Kish and had bound himself everlastingly to Gath. Now I will contend no more. David is not mine. He is Saul's and Jonathan's. Nor do I bear him any rancor because of this, for, as I have said, a man's heart will go where it will. I grieve only that I have added more to the vessel of his pain. Let him know this at least: If the son of Saul should fall into my hands on the day of battle, I would not smite him. Him I would claim as my prize of war, that I might bring him to David. . . ."

For an instant the son of Jesse saw the bright curve of the sea, saw the palaces of the lost island rising wet and golden out of the waves, saw a ship moving toward the coral and the iris, with the beloved standing upon the prow. If it were possible, he thought, if we might dwell in Caphtor together, if God would restore him to me yet once more, fresh, incorruptible, sweet to embrace, from the grave—— Then the vision departed from him, and he knew that the Seren was speaking.

"Out of my tenderness for the son of Jesse," Achish was saying, "I have deceived my brothers the Serens, and myself, and Dagon and Astarte. Yet since the Serens have forgiven me this night, I will no longer brood upon it. I will forgive myself also, nor am I uneasy as to how it stands with me in the minds of the gods. As a man grows older, his gods also age and grow more kind. If it should come to pass that I fall at Gilboa, I think that those divine ones who will sit in judgment upon me will have wrinkled hands and hoary heads—for are they not the father and the mother of all men? I think they will say to each other, 'Behold, here is Achish, our aged and foolish child. Why should we chastise him? Has he not been well chastised upon the earth? All that he loved when he dwelt among men has faded or is changed and broken. Therefore we will let him go and sleep.' "

"No, now," said David, lifting the veined hand from the pillow and pressing it between his own, "what is my life to me if any evil should befall my brother and my lord?"

But Achish rose and went from him, ashamed, and eager to hide his face. He walked quickly to the table and filled two bowls with wine. When he returned with the bowls in his hands, he had the air of one who has sat long at a congenial feast. His mouth was closed and merry, as though he stifled laughter over a remembered jest. "Let us drink together," he said, "Let us drink to the hour of my return out of Israel, and to the day when David is made king in Hebron."

The son of Jesse knew with amazement that he had utterly forgotten the matter of the kingship. "Surely," he said, "they will not give me Judah, seeing that I——"

"How should it be otherwise? I have claimed Judah and Caleb and the land of the Kenites for David this night. It is signed and sealed, nor would I let any man of them go forth from the tent before his word was given. Whether I live or die, the land is David's. This was promised to David in return for peace in the south. There is peace in the south, and David will have his crown."

"May all the gods conspire to keep the spirit in the body of my brother and my lord," David said. He drained the bowl to the bottom, and coughed a little because his throat was tight with tears.

"I had thought," said Achish, staring at the couches, "to invite the son of Jesse to sleep this night in the tent of Philistia——"

"Gladly, if it will please my lord."

But the Seren turned abruptly and walked toward the entrance of the tent. "No, now," he said, speaking into darkness, "let David go forth and lie down after the manner of Israel, on his cloak, under the stars." Nor would he permit himself to tarry over the leave-taking. He set a brief kiss upon David's forehead, wished him a peaceful night, and departed into the tent without another word.

But David could not bring himself to go at once to the encampment. He wandered about in the grove, turning often to look back over his shoulder at the white tent, luminous against the night. Once he saw a shadow moving upon it. It is the Seren of Gath, he told himself. He is bending over the couch where we sat together and rearranging the pillows that are upon it. May they be soft indeed, and a consolation to him in the hour of his bitterness. . . .

❧ VII ❧

ON THE MORNING of his going forth out of Sharon, Joab received a gift from his uncle—a splendid red steed out of Egypt that the son of Jesse had ridden in the host of Philistia. Although it was plain to him that the Star of Bethlehem had parted with the horse only because he detested it, the captain accepted it with delight. His pleasure in the beast was so great that it flowed out over everything; he rode in the forefront of the host, jingling the heathenish amulets that hung from its trappings and enjoying the rippling flex of its muscles under his thighs. It seemed to him that the world was a very felicitous place, and he considered himself the most fortunate man in the world.

Twice or thrice he had tried to share his exuberance with his uncle. But there was no satisfaction to be had from the son of Jesse; he trailed along toward the rear of the column on his stupid dappled donkey: it was plain from the beginning that he would tolerate no nudges, no side-long glances; he kept turning in his saddle to look toward the ridges of Gilboa, still faintly visible against the dazzling sky. Some change had come upon him on that night when he had paced the slope of wheat before the tent of the uncircumcised; his face, strangely sharp and white in the dusk, had been the face of a wounded warrior who prefers death to the violence of his pain. That look had passed, but the sharpness and the whiteness had remained. It was as if the hand of God had passed over the face of David, taking all youth and softness from it, leaving it austere and chill and spare. And yet, thought Joab, he grows even more comely with the years. When he is old, when the red glory of his beard is turned to frost, there will still be that radiance upon him which melts the hearts of men and leads fools to lay the world in his hands. . . . Still, there was no pleasure to be found in his company. The very presence of the steed out of Egypt at his side made David's lean hands tighten on the reins and brought a heavy furrow into his brow. And Joab left his uncle, half out of boredom and half out of pity, and rode again at the forefront of the host.

Evening and the end of the journey drew on together. In the first coolness of the wind, the captain's spirits revived, and he rode far ahead of the rest. Now the unknown regions flowed almost imperceptibly into land well known—the desert strip to the north of Ziklag, a place in which the configurations of dune and rock and brush were as familiar to him as the palm of his hand. From the crest of a certain sandy slope, it would be possible to see the city. In the days before the going forth to Gilboa, he had spent half his time upon that slope, watching the archers at their practice and training the new recruits to use the weapons of Philistia after the manner of the Philistines. When I have come to the top of the slope, he thought, I will rejoice in the sight of the city. It is a goodly thing to be delivered from battle, to come into a high house and to sit at a fair table. And when my hunger is appeased I will go into my chamber and wash the dust from my body. I will lie naked in the cool of the night upon the clean linens, and name my good fortunes to myself until I sleep. . . .

But when he reached the crest, he stopped and cried out and pressed his hands against his temples, thinking that surely he had gone mad. The city was not as it had been. It showed strangely black against the pale-green arc of heaven. There were gaps in the walls. There were no roofs where there had certainly been roofs before. Here and there, among the broken blocks that had once been houses, a few fires still smoldered. The city had been put to the torch, and had been burning long—so long that there was little left to burn, and only a small cloud of smoke still hung above the plain.

The steed out of Egypt, sensing his terror, reared beneath him.

"No, now, my friend," he said, "we will not permit ourselves to lose our heads. Come, we will break this matter to our lord."

He raced back then, past the straight files and the dull, dreaming faces. The son of Jesse had fallen back in the later stages of the journey almost to the rear of the column. It was difficult to find him, but Joab discovered him at last, riding beside Abishai among the ranks of the slingers, his head hanging down and his eyes closed, so that one could not tell at once whether he was awake or asleep.

"My lord," Joab shouted across the heads of the slingers, "bid the host to halt and come forth out of the ranks, that we may have a word together."

With maddening slowness, David lifted his head and stared across the marchers into his nephew's eyes. Then he raised his brows and shrugged and sent the word to halt along the line.

Joab slipped down from his horse and stood in the sand beside a flowering bush of thorn. "My lord," he said, "in God's name, come, for it is no small matter that I have seen from the crest of the slope."

The Star of Bethlehem dismounted and gave his donkey into the hands of one of the slingers. He came slowly out of the ranks and turned his white face toward the thorny bush and smiled a madman's smile upon the scarlet flowers.

"Let my uncle prepare his heart, for the wrath of the Lord is certainly upon us. . . ."

"Well," he said, turning from the bush and fixing his large, unseeing eyes upon his nephew's face, "what is it now?"

"Ziklag is no more. I have seen it from the slope. That which was Ziklag is a heap of charred wood and fallen stones."

David said nothing.

Surely, Joab thought, surely I am mad. It is not possible that he should hear such tidings and smile. . . . "Let David listen; they have put the torch to Ziklag. While we were thence, the Bedouins of the south have forced the gates and left the whole city afire."

"So?" said the son of Jesse. But he did not speak to Joab. He lifted his face and flung his question upward to God. "Will Jahveh take Ziklag then? Is it with Ziklag that I am to pay for my iniquities?" . . . He turned his transported and frightening eyes again upon his nephew. "Burned?" he said. "Gone up in smoke, to be a burnt offering before the Lord?"

"My lord," said Joab, "only God knows where they are or what thing has come upon them—all those whom we left within." He knew that he was speaking too loudly. The men who stood nearest the blossoming bush had heard. Like flame itself, the news of the burning of the city was

316

spreading. Abishai had dismounted. "How is it?" he said, forcing his way between the moving heads and shoulders. "Ziklag afire?"

"Consumed," said Joab. "Burned even to cinders and ashes. And here stands my lord——"

From the mouth of the fat and hairy Abishai came the cry that should have issued from the mouth of David. "God of Hosts! How will it be with the women and the little ones? Where shall we turn to look for Noi and the child?"

"Abigail also," the son of Jesse said. Yet he said it strangely, as a man might recount in his last years a tragedy that had come to pass in the days of his youth. "She also, and Noi, and the little one—all these have been taken from me and given into the hands of the marauders out of the south in payment for the iniquities which are laid up against me with the Lord."

"In God's name," shouted Joab, "let my uncle rouse himself! If Jahveh has indeed put the women and the children into the hands of the Bedouins, then let us search after them in the lands where the Bedouins dwell. God has not snatched them up utterly, so that they cannot be found upon the face of the earth. Let us not stand bemused like witless children. Let us go in all haste and find the thieves and smite them until no man among them is left to boast——"

Abishai laid his hand upon David's shoulder. "Indeed, my lord," he said, "you must put aside this stupor of grief that has come upon you. Even as my brother says, we may yet find them. . . ." He fell silent because the host was shouting, calling for pursuit, calling for vengeance, calling upon the Star of Bethlehem to lead them down into the desert. "For surely," they said among themselves, "it is better to go forth against the Bedouins for the sake of Israel than to go up against Israel for Philistia's sake."

David sighed then and straightened. "Say to the host that we will go down," he said to Joab. For the first time during the encounter, his eyes actually beheld his nephew's face. "Perhaps we will find them, even as Joab says. And yet we may not find them, and if we find them not, which of us could say that the ways of God are not just? For if the north were to be delivered at Gilboa out of the hands of the uncircumcised, if the spirit were to be kept in the bodies of Saul and Jonathan, if, in exchange for the salvation of the House of Kish, Jahveh were to burn my city and take from me everlastingly the women and the child——" He started and stepped backward, so that he struck against the bush. "No, now," he said, flushing, "as Joab says, I am bemused. Certainly we will come upon the thieves. Certainly we will fall upon them and smite them and take our own out of their hands."

BEFORE the time of the burning of Ziklag, the son of Zeruiah had lived through many hazardous hours. But no time in his life seemed so perilous to him as the moment when the army came down on the other side of the slope and halted beneath the broken walls of the city. There, for the first time, the bond between the host and the Star of Bethlehem was strained almost to breaking. There, for the first time, the men who had borne with his aimlessness in the wilderness and his dallying with the uncircumcised said: "It is enough. God is against him. We will stand with him no more."

In the thick heat and the acrid smell of the fire, the exiles had mourned in loud voices over their sons and daughters, their women, the common treasure that had been laid up in the storehouses of Ziklag, the private treasure that had adorned the houses whose falling rafters kept sending up showers of sparks against the night. They had turned upon the son of Jesse and reviled him; it was he, they said, who had brought this calamity upon their heads—God's hand was heavy upon them because they had gone up against Israel for his sake. And he—he had sat motionless upon the donkey, his chill, remote face lighted fitfully by the fire. There had been that in his bearing which had cried out to them, Revile me, hurl curses and stones upon me; and one of them actually cast a stone and bruised the still, defenseless hand.

Well, thought Joab, riding among the files of the archers over the moon-blanched, rock-strewn desert, that peril at least was past. The rage in the ranks had been averted from the son of Jesse—not because he had so much as raised a finger to save himself, only because the priest Abiathar had laid the whole matter in the lap of God. While David stared and the host milled and murmured, the priest Abiathar had gone down on his knees to consult the sacred dice. All would be well, he had told them in his piercing voice. Whatever had been taken from them would be restored to them threefold—so said the holy cubes of stone that had informed the armies of Israel of the intentions of the Lord since the days of Abraham.

And now let Jahveh show His mettle, Joab thought. Let Him lead the host of David to the camp of the marauders. Let Him keep the women and the children untouched and render back the loot threefold. For the men in the ranks are in no mood for trifling. Twice they have been on the point of violence—once at the borders of Philistia and once beneath the walls of Ziklag—and their swords are thirsty for blood. If not the marauders, then certainly the son of Jesse, he and all his kin, will satisfy their swords. And if that should come to pass, would I save myself? Would I flee? Who could overtake me? There is not another steed out of Egypt in the host. . . . But he knew that whatever came to pass that night, he would remain. I am nothing without him, he thought, looking over his shoulder at the moon-whitened figure of the son of Jesse, riding among the grim faces and the glinting spears. And should they slay him, even though I sat at the knees of the King of Moab, yet would my heart be slain, and all that came thereafter would be as a shadow and a dream, nothing more. . . .

If the silence of the host had been oppressive by day, it was almost unendurable by night. The footfalls that had sounded on the roadways of Philistia and Judah were muffled now in sand. The clanking of the weapons had ceased, since every man bore his weapons carefully, hoping to come stealthily upon the thieves while they slept. Joab rode far ahead of the rest, looking in vain for any prints of the feet of men or camels or asses that the evening wind might have left unobliterated upon the sand. In the distance, beyond a dune and a grayish cloud of brush, he saw a glossy line of darkness cutting across the whiteness, and he knew it to be a certain brook called Besor. He had never seen the brook, but the name of it was often upon the tongues of the men of the south. Here they watered their camels before they set out toward the cities of Philistia and Judah; here they came on certain days which they considered holy to appease the spirit that dwelt within the water with pellets of bread and strips of bright cloth. His heart sank when he beheld the utter emptiness of the stretch of land beyond the brook. He had thought to find them here, casting some part of their spoil to this same spirit; and now that they were not here, where else to look for them he did not know.

As he drew closer to the dark coil of water, he saw that something lay upon the farther bank of it—a dim and huddled shape half-hidden by another patch of brush. What can it be? he asked himself. Have the men of the desert indeed been here and left a great slain ram for the spirit of the waters to feed upon? He bent down to soothe the horse as he prepared to cross the brook. But, unlike the foolish donkeys of Israel, the steed out of Egypt felt no fear in the presence of the goddess of the water. He forded her sinuous black body lightly, easily, and stopped beside the brush to arch his neck and sniff at the huddled thing that lay before him.

"God of Hosts," said Joab aloud, "it is a man! No, not a man—something between a man and a child." And he dismounted and knelt beside the huddled one, and saw that the breath of life still dwelt in the body. The face, turned upward toward the moon and crossed by shadows of twigs, was a face out of Egypt, brownish against the whiteness of the sand, languorous and sloe-eyed, with a broad nose and a pair of ripe and feverish lips. "It is a slave boy out of Egypt," Joab said. And now he could discern, preserved all about him in the moist sand around the brook, the prints of many feet—the feet of camels and the feet of men. They have indeed been here, he thought, and it seemed to him that the stench of camels still hung upon the air. They have departed not long since and left this one behind because he is sick unto death. . . .

He laid his hand upon the hot brown shoulder, and the lad stirred fretfully against the sand.

"My son," said Joab, "can you speak in the tongue of the men of the desert?"

He nodded, but it was plain that he was too weak to speak at all.

"They that looted Ziklag—was it they that left you here?"

He nodded again. Two large tears coursed down his cheeks.

In the utter stillness of the vast sand, the spirit of the water made a rushing, plashing noise. Joab dipped his hand into the brook and passed it over the feverish face.

The slave boy turned his head a little and looked at the red steed. "A horse out of Egypt," he said.

And the son of Zeruiah, hearing the ache of exile in the lad's voice, was stirred. "Come," he said, "I will lift you up and set you upon this horse out of Egypt and carry you to my lord."

But when he had returned with the Egyptian to the host, he saw that it was no small matter to seek out the son of Jesse. The warriors were not as they had been before. They also had sighted the brook and named it. By the brook, they knew how far they had come into the desert, how futile was their errand, and how great was their weariness. The files had broken into knots of gesturing and complaining men; the weapons that had bruised their shoulders and stiffened their arms through a journey of twenty hours were thrown onto the sand in careless piles. From all sides Joab heard the cry that it was impossible to go farther, that there must be a long halt for food and rest. As he rode through the disordered company, the lad out of Egypt shuddered against him. He is afraid, thought Joab, and I—I also am afraid. While they fill their bellies and sleep, it will be well for the House of Jesse; but when they waken and know that their women and children are utterly lost—what they will do then only God knows. . . .

He came upon David at last among the baggage wagons. The Star of Bethlehem had dismounted and was leaning against one of the big wheels, overseeing the dispensing of water and bread. His voice, raised now and then to direct the men who were unloading the food, was flat and without power. He held his left hand stiffly and awkwardly; the black bruise upon it showed plainly, even in the light of the moon.

"My lord," said Joab, "I have here a slave out of Egypt whom I found upon the margin of the brook called Besor. He was a servant among the Bedouins, even they who burned Ziklag, and it may well be that he can tell us into what land they have carried our own. Therefore, let my lord come and take him from the saddle, for he should be taken down gently, seeing that he is sick almost unto death."

David came and took the lad and bore him to the baggage wagons. One of the wagons was filled with sacks of flour, and the son of Jesse laid his burden upon these, very gently, and put a soft, loosely filled sack beneath his head. He sat upon the wagon, staring into the slave's feverish face. "Go now," he said to Joab, "and bring me a flask of water, and bread, and clusters of raisins, for it is clear that this poor wretch has been long without food and has no strength to speak."

While the men of Ziklag filed sullenly up to the keepers of the baggage to take their rations, the son of Jesse fed the slave out of Egypt. He fed him tenderly, holding small rusks of bread and single raisins against his lips. He fed him as a father might feed an ailing child. So, in the sight of his nephew, he had sometimes fed the little Amnon, when the boy had been ill or uneasy and had refused to eat. And now it was plain to Joab that the remembrance of such an hour had come also upon David, that suddenly it was borne in upon him that his only son, who had taken bread at his hand, was this night at the mercy of strangers under the open sky. For suddenly the flask shook in his hand, the water dripped upon the face of the slave, and the Star of Bethlehem bowed his head upon his knees and wept.

For a long time he sat at the edge of the wagon, shaken by fierce and soundless weeping, unmindful of those who came into the circle of the wagons to receive their water and bread. Each of them glanced up at him in amazement, and one of them asked in a hushed, shamed voice, "What is it that has come upon my lord?" Then the son of Zeruiah turned upon them all and berated them for David's sake. Why, he asked in bitterness, why indeed should David weep? What had he suffered save a little reviling, a little stoning? Nor had the men of the south taken much out of his hands—merely two wives and an only child. And the men of Ziklag bowed their heads and went forth from the wagons, saying to one another, "I am glad at least that it was not I who cast the stone."

It was the lad out of Egypt who brought an end to David's weeping. Suddenly he raised himself from the sacks of flour and leaned forward and laid his hand on David's hand. "Behold, I have found my voice," he said in the language of the men of the south. "How can I serve the lord of the Israelites, who gave me water and bread?"

The son of Jesse straightened then and wiped his face upon the hem of his cloak. "My son," he said in steady voice, "who is your master? Out of what land have you come?"

"I am a bondservant sold out of Egypt," he said, "and I am the servant of one of the men of the south. I fell sick in the heat of the desert, and my master left me when we paused to salute the spirit that dwells in the brook Besor. We made a raid upon the lands of the Cherethites, and upon that which belongs to Judah, and upon the south of Caleb, and we burned Ziklag with fire."

"Will you bring me down to the camp of the Bedouins?"

"If my lord will swear to me by his God that he will neither kill me nor deliver me into the hands of my master, I will bring my lord before morning to the encampment," he said.

The son of Jesse slid down from the wagon and raised his eyes to the very center of the sky. "I swear by the God of the Israelites," he said, "even by Him who has been merciful to me far beyond my deserving, that I will neither lay violent hands upon you nor render you up to the vengeance of your master. Be henceforth the servant of him that found you, he that is my nephew and the captain of the host. Go with him now and ride before him on his horse and show us the way."

The son of Zeruiah came to the wagon and lifted the Egyptian in his arms. "My lord," he said, looking across the lad's head into David's face, "the warriors may refuse to go down. There has been much murmuring in the host."

The Star of Bethlehem leaned against the wheel of the wagon. He shrugged, then turned and gazed upon the whole disordered army, scattered dark against the whiteness of the sand. "I will go down," he said. "Those who wish may follow me and those who will follow me no more may remain at the side of the brook Besor. And, if there are none here who are not weary of following after me, then nevertheless I will go down alone, to seek after the child and Abigail and Noi and——" He fell silent. In the tabernacle of his heart, Joab heard the last unspoken words: "my own death."

But there was no question of his riding out alone. Even while he spoke of the breach between him and the host, they sat in the sand bemoaning the hour of senseless rage against him. Those who had gone up to the circle of the baggage wagons had come down with the tale of David's weeping, and whispered to the others how it was no small matter to lose an only son, begotten late and much beloved and destined to wear the crown of Israel. They restored that legend which they had shattered under the walls of Ziklag; they took him again to their hearts, purified and humanized—the suffering Lamb of Judah, their weeping lord. And when it was asked of them whether they would go forth or stay, four hundred of them rose and shouted in a great voice that they would follow wherever the Star of Bethlehem should choose to lead them, even unto death. As for the other two hundred—they made it plain that they tarried not out of disloyalty, but out of overpowering weariness. They remained, only because they had not strength to move, to guard the baggage beside the brook. And when the column of warriors had disappeared over the swelling sand, those who had stayed behind prayed aloud, and they prayed for the son of David as often as for their own.

❧ IX ☙

During the two days of captivity in the hands of the men of the south, Abigail wept and sickened. Since her infancy, she had been bred in plenty and in kindliness. She had never tasted strange meat or slept upon the ground under the open sky; and now that there was no familiar food to eat, no pillow beneath her head, no roof between her and the sun, it seemed to her that surely such a calamity could end in nothing but her death.

322

With Noi the Jezreelitess it was otherwise. She had known the wilderness since the days of her childhood, and for her the desert was nothing but a harsher and more beautiful brother to the wilderness. There had been months of poverty and famine in her father's house when she had learned to relish the boiled root and the flesh of the hare. Nor was she a stranger to calamity. When the marauders ran howling through the gates of the city, when they set torches to the houses and dragged the women and children forth into the streets, when she and the little Amnon set out with fire behind them toward the blank unknown, she said to herself that this, and worse than this, had come to pass before.

Nor could she permit herself to indulge her feelings. It was necessary for her to maintain a stedfast and easy air for the sake of the child. When he looked back over his shoulder at the burning city, she spoke to him of the wonder and loveliness of fire. She could not blame Abigail for raising an outcry over the collapsing roofs of Ziklag; Abigail had lost much—the fine robes, the great chair upon the hearth, the carved bed, the rooms in which she had spent her opulent days and her magical nights. But she, Noi, had really lost nothing. She knew that her lord hated the city in the secret places of his heart; she herself had hated it since the first night she had slept there. She had no possessions save a few baubles and the lamb's tail that she had carried with her out of her brothers' house. She had snatched the lamb's tail up and thrust it into her girdle, along with the earrings which her lord had given her on that memorable and bitter evening when she had rendered up her virginity. So it was not too difficult for her to say to the child, "Look, now, my darling, never again will you see such great bright flames as these." And it was easy for her to march southward with a serene and cheerful face.

She was fortunate, too, in that the mere thought of the Bedouins did not put her into a fright. She failed to detect the jackal smell that was supposed to cling to their lean, hard bodies; their taunts were simple and childish; they were kind to their camels; one of them, seeing that she was very tired, offered to carry her son, and Amnon slept comfortably in his brown arms. "Surely," said Abigail, "when night comes they will fall upon us and possess us." Noi smiled. You they may rape, she thought, but me they will leave in peace. . . .

There was, however, a single hour toward the end of the first day of the journey when her stedfastness departed from her. It was at the time of sunset, when the marauders halted to make a sacrifice to the spirit who dwelt within the waters of the brook called Besor. Since the rites were secret and very holy, it was not fitting for the uninitiated to look upon them; so the captives—a weary and grimy crowd of Israelites and Philistines and Canaanites—were sent to sit against a line of dunes, with their backs to the stream. Something—perhaps the humiliation of this little exile, perhaps the vast emptiness of the sun-reddened sand that stretched before her eyes—something shattered the shield which she had set before her heart, and let the cold thrust of terror in. Until that hour she had told herself, They will certainly hold us for ransom. When David is returned out of the north, he will borrow gold from the treasuries of Achish, and we will come again to our lord. . . . But now the other captives were saying on all sides, "They are carrying us down to sell us into bondage in Egypt," and it seemed to her in her solitude and her weariness that this was so. Amnon was not with her. He had gone with a girl-child, a daughter of Canaan, to play in the sand. She rested her head against the dune and thought how it would be to dwell as a bondservant in an alien land. But she could call up no images. One thought, and one only, existed in her mind: If we are sold into Egypt, I will never again look upon my lord. . . . She knew then, by the utter desolation that descended upon her, that she lived neither for the child nor for the kindly Abishai nor for anything beneath the sun except the delight of beholding David's face. For with me, she thought, it is otherwise than with beloved women, whose longings abide in their bodies and go forth out of their lips and their breasts and their fingertips. Since he has turned from me, all the yearning that is in me has come to dwell in my eyes; and if my sight may go out to him no more, then surely I will go down into the darkness of Sheol to dwell among the dead. . . .

They marched far to the south that night—so far that it seemed to Noi they had certainly come into the land of Goshen. The face of the desert grew more stark with every mile; even the rocks and the brush fell away; there was nothing now but the everlasting fall and swell and ripple of sand. Then, bright and unbelievable in the moonlight, a green and watery spot was transformed from a desire into a reality, a place of palms, a cluster of rocks turned glistening by a rushing spring, and here they slept.

The second day was much like the first, only it seemed infinitely longer. Those who had been bred in the comfort of the cities began to suffer: their mouths were dry, their eyes burned, sores broke out upon their tongues, and white blisters rose upon the soles of their feet. The captives became sullen and quarrelsome. The talk, when there was talk at all, was nothing but a recital of pains.

All through the morning Noi comforted herself with the belief that surely at noonday they would lie down and sleep. But when the sun stood at the center of the arc of burning blue, there was still no word of rest. Indeed, the men of the south seemed merrier and more vital than they had been in the morning. And suddenly it was borne in upon Noi that their hearts had been lightened by the knowledge that they were close to their homes.

Within the hour, she saw that this was indeed so. Green—wet and green and golden—another oasis sprang up before her eyes, larger and more luxuriant than that in which they had spent the night. Here there were more than a score of palms, dark and soft against the hard brightness. Here great clumps of black rock covered with creeping vines thrust themselves out of the desert. Springs gushed from the rocks and poured over the vines and ran into reddish ditches and deep wells. In the shadow of a grove of palms stood a little temple built of shining black stones. The place was sacred to the moon god Sin; his crescent was embroidered on the banner that stood before it. On everything—temple and trees and ditches and vines—was the glimmer of water; and water seemed to her so fair a thing to behold that her eyes filled with tears.

The eyes of the Bedouins were not for the oasis, but for the tents beyond it. Spread in a vast semicircle behind the palms and the temple, amid the scrubby brush nourished by the waning flow of the springs, were the hairy black homes of the south. A shout of delight tore out of the throats of the riders. The answer was flung back from the tents— a shrill, multitudinous cry. Then the men of the desert forgot all things— their camels, their captives, their booty, their stolen herds—and ran to their tents to embrace their wives, to drink sweet water from stone cups, to rest in the shadow of the black cloth from the searing light of the sun.

Throughout the rest of the day, the captives were left more or less to themselves. They were given to understand that the enclosure around the little black temple was sacred to the god Sin and that any stranger who set foot therein would not live to see the rising of another moon. They were told that they had better unload the baggage and water the camels, and it was made plain to them that they must not lay their unclean hands upon any Bedouin child. But for the most part they were given a burdensome liberty—to come and go in the oasis much as they chose, to take a moderate portion of the food in the baggage wagons, to drink and bathe at the springs. While they rested and appeased their hunger, they were reasonably cheerful, but by sunset their despondency had settled upon them again.

Noi the Jezreelitess waited to go to the spring with Amnon and the little daughter of Canaan until all the others had washed and drunk their fill. Her greatest longing now was for solitude and silence; the sound of women's voices, the press of women's bodies against her, had become unendurable; besides, she wished to spend a long time beside the waters —she had made up her mind to wash both the children from head to foot so that they might be cool and comfortable throughout the night. She was glad that Abigail had not offered to go with her to the spring. The first wife had fallen in with two women out of Caleb and sat with them beneath a palm tree, bemoaning herself and recounting all the wonders that had been lost in the burning of her house. It was plain that the three of them had much to mourn and would continue to tell one another their afflictions until the hour for sleep. As she walked toward the wet and gleaming rocks, holding each of the children by the hand, she saw that twilight had come down upon this strange world, that all the flamelike light had gone from the sky and given place to a transparent, watery blue. Beyond the oasis, the marauders were making merry. They had taken the meat from the spit and carved and divided it. Now each man had his portion and had gone off to eat it with his family. They were spread abroad in small groups over the face of the desert. There was dancing among them, and the sound of the pipe and the lute; but the manner of the music was lost in the babbling, for their voices were raucous with wine.

When she reached the rock of the spring, she stepped backward. She was not alone. A lean, dark woman of the south sat at the foot of the rock and stared into the unpeopled whiteness of the desert, her back to the revelers, her face to the rising moon. She was unbeautiful and solemn; she wore a crimson robe and a yellow veil, and even through the veil it was possible to see that there was a scar upon her cheek. She also, thought Noi, is a rejected one, even such a one as I, and it is a sorry matter that I should break in upon her grief. . . .

"Come," she said to the children, "we will drink and go, and leave the quiet of the spring to this daughter of Sin."

The woman started and smiled upon her. "No, now," she said, "if the daughter of Jahveh would bathe, let her bathe, and if she would wash her children, let her wash them also. I would not keep another from the waters. The waters are not mine, but were called up from the rock for all men by the bounty of the god."

"The lady is gracious," Noi said, and set about the business of stripping Amnon and the little Canaanite. She felt that the eyes behind the veil followed her every movement, and she was ashamed to have the stranger think that any child of hers should be clothed as the girl was clothed and should be eaten up by such a multitude of lice. She was tempted to make some remark that would indicate the actual situation, but she stifled the desire, feeling that there was unkindness in it—unkindness toward the child's lost mother who must be lying now among the charred timbers of some Canaanite town. In order to conceal her embarrassment, she grew very energetic; she pushed the children about under the spring and dug her fingers into their scalps; and while she worked she hummed.

"How cheerfully," said the Bedouin woman, "the daughter of Jahveh bears herself in the hour of her affliction."

She flushed and smiled. "What else is to be done?" she said. "One bears oneself in such-and-such a manner for the children's sake."

"And what is the name of the daughter of Jahveh?"

"Noi—Ahinoam the Jezreelitess, out of Ziklag, the handmaid and the second wife of him that is called the Star of Bethlehem."

"Then," said the solemn one, "let Ahinoam the Jezreelitess put all misgiving from her. No harm will befall her. For I have heard from the mouths of my brothers that she will be kept with us in the encampment until the day when her husband returns out of the north. On that day she will be sold back into the hands of her lord for the price of thirty camels, and the price of thirty camels will be asked also for the unfruitful wife, whose name is Abigail, and also for the little one. This is an established thing, and will certainly come to pass."

Is she a prophetess, thought Noi, and has the fury of prophecy possessed her? . . . For the daughter of Sin had leaped to her feet and was shrieking at the top of her voice. Her eyes stared through the veil at the desert, stared so wildly and steadily that Noi and the children wheeled round to see what it was that she looked upon. And even as they turned, the emptiness of the desert was no more—the desert was blackened by a flying steed and banners and spears and file upon file of charging men. As the shriek died away, another sound rushed in. It was the host of Ziklag, shouting the name of God. The woman of Sin fled toward the tents of her people. But Noi remained by the spring, clasping the wet and naked little ones against her and weeping for joy because her eyes were satisfied —among the onrushing host she had seen her lord.

❧ X ☙

I_T WAS TOLD_ afterward in the first songs and legends that sprang up among the men of Ziklag how the battle was bitter and long. All through the night and through the next day until the evening, the host of David smote the sons of Sin, smote them with the violence that had been withheld in the plains of Sharon and under the walls of their ruined town. It was reckoned that a thousand of them dwelt by the oasis, and only four hundred escaped—young men who, when the tide of battle turned irrevocably against them, took to their camels and fled to the south. The temple of Sin was looted and destroyed; scarcely a stone was left standing upon a stone. The women and children were dragged from the hairy tents, and the tents themselves were consumed with fire.

At dusk on the second day, when the desert around the encampment had already begun to grow noisome with the slain, the last of the sons of Sin went down beneath the sword of Israel. The shamed and sickly after-silence of battle came upon the living. They walked grimly to the springs and washed and drank; they bound up their wounds; they went among the captives to seek out their wives and children, and, having found them, they wept a little and slept.

It was not until the morning of the third day, when they were ready to depart out of the accursed place, that they knew the magnitude and the splendor of their victory. Jahveh had done unto them even as He had promised by the sacred dice. It was considered a miracle that no Israelite warrior was among the fallen and that no Israelite captive had been lost. Each man received his own at the hand of God—his children unharmed, his wife undefiled. Furthermore, the loot was such as might have delighted the heart of a King of Egypt—not only the treasure of the black tents, but also all that the marauders had brought down with them from Judah and Philistia and Canaan: herds and flocks, slaves and young women, camels and horses, shields and swords, linen and glass and gold.

All the host went rejoicing on their northern trek save only the little

327

Jezreelitess and the Star of Bethlehem. The men of Ziklag could understand the quiet melancholy of the second wife; she had never had much reason for gaiety; and she had set her heart upon two small requests, neither of which had been fulfilled. She had asked to possess as her bondservants a Canaanite child who had been separated from her in the heat of the battle and a certain Bedouin woman with a scar on her cheek. But the woman had been seen lying among the tents with an Israelite arrow through her belly, and nobody could find the child. Seated together with the Hope of Judah on Abishai's donkey, Noi looked pitiful and small, and the men were tender of her and brought her such things as might please her from among their spoils—the one pair of sandals small enough to fit her feet, a comb fashioned from the shell of a turtle, and a box upon which some son of the south, lying behind them among the dead, had carved the palm trees of his home.

But if they understood the sorrows of Noi, they were utterly baffled by the grief of the Star of Bethlehem. He had been strange and incomprehensible on the journey out of the plains of Sharon. He had been restored to them when he wept among the baggage wagons on the edge of the desert. He had been entirely theirs in the heat of the battle, striking left and right and laying death upon some fifty of the sons of Sin. But now that the battle was finished, he had grown strange and incomprehensible, again. True, he had shown joy when the child and the two women were given back into his arms, safe and untouched. Yet something had been lacking in that joy, and the men had said among themselves, "He does not yet believe his good fortune; he must teach himself that all this is so." Nor had he shown the proper enthusiasm over the miracle that God had accomplished for him. He kept questioning the tallies; he kept asking Joab and Abishai and the priest Abiathar: "Not one of the captives lost? Not one Israelite among the dead?" As to the booty, when they led him down to look upon it, he walked amid his wealth with his head bent, as a man might walk through a driving rain. "Behold," said Abiathar, "here is the very clothes chest that stood in the house of my lord in Ziklag." And David said: "Indeed? And I thought the Lord had taken all my possessions out of my hands in punishment."

They saw in him also a meticulous concern over Jahveh's laws such as he had never shown before. He insisted that the prohibitions of the holy season of war should be kept to the letter until the army had come again to Ziklag; he forbade any man to lie with his wife or to wet his lips with wine. When he was asked what part of the spoil he would take unto himself, he turned the talk to some other matter; and when they pressed him, he grew angry and bade them hold their nagging tongues. What trinkets they had taken in war, he said, they might keep. But the great spoil —the flocks and the herds and the rich booty that had been gathered after the battle from the store tents and the temple of Sin—would not be divided until the host was united with those who had tarried beside the brook Besor.

At sunrise on the following morning, they departed out of the oasis and set their faces toward the brook Besor. Certain considerations that had been banished by the glow of their good fortune returned to obtrude upon their cheer. There were some among them who had smarting wounds and others who were burdened by the knowledge that at the end of the long trek they would have the dull and arduous task of rebuilding Ziklag. At the noonday meal, eaten in blasting heat, they complained about the lack of wine and the division of the fruit and water and bread. Joab berated Abishai, Abiathar reproved David for his solemnity in the face of Jahveh's overwhelming graciousness, Abigail found fault with Noi, and Noi grew short-tempered with the child. Two of the captains over hundreds came up to David and stood before him with ill-concealed impatience. "The men have sent me to ask my lord when we will slay an ox and eat meat," one of them said. The son of Jesse turned cold eyes upon them. "It is a strange thing that the men should wish to eat meat without their brothers who are beyond the brook," he said. "Say to the host that we will slay an ox when the army is one army. We will not set up a spit until we have come to the brook Besor."

During the remainder of the journey, all the rancor that rose up within them was vented upon those Israelites who had remained behind to guard the baggage wagons. A persistent murmuring against them sounded in the ranks. *They* had not marched by night across the terrible face of the desert; *they* had not risked their lives in battle; *they* had not dragged the heavy spoil an interminable way across the accursed sand. *Their* wives and children would be restored at no cost to them—for who could consider it a heavy task to sit for three days beside a stream of fresh water, chatting and drowsing from dawn to the going-down of the sun? Warriors who faint at the beginning of an enterprise should have no share in the fruit thereof. Their women and children would be rendered up to them, yes, but they could not in justice ask for more. Surely the spoil of the battle was not for loiterers. Surely it should fall into the hands of those who had bought it with sweat and blood.

But at evening when they sighted the appointed meeting-place, they saw that the son of Jesse thought otherwise. He rode to the forefront of the host and called aloud to those who had tarried. He was the first to cross the water. On the other side, he embraced one after the other of them and clasped their hands. Those who had not yet forded the brook could hear him assuring the loiterers that all was well, that no wife or child had been touched. "As to the loot," he said, "it is such a mass of booty as has never before been brought up into Israel."

"As to the loot," said one of the young captains over hundreds, crossing the brook and standing at the side of his lord, "those who went down into the southland and bled in the battle are agreed that it is theirs, and theirs alone."

His audacity had sprung from the anger he felt when he saw the loiterers sitting comfortably by the cool water. Now that he had spoken, he was thoroughly frightened—afraid of the silence in which his words seemed to speak themselves over and over, afraid of the chill gray eyes turned haughtily upon his face.

"Is it so indeed?" the son of Jesse said.

The young captain would have faltered had he stood alone. But now the others had come up behind him, were still coming up by scores, and many voices in the host were raised in support of his own. "Because they went not down with us," said many among them, "we will not give them anything of the spoil that we have recovered, save only to every man his wife and children, that he may lead them away and depart."

The sons of Zeruiah, thinking to take the matter out of the hands of the dazed and incapable son of Jesse, pushed through the press and crossed the brook. But before the hoofs of their beasts had passed over the dark coil of water, it was plain that their distress was needless, that the Star of Bethlehem was in complete possession of himself. He climbed upon one of the baggage wagons and stood above them all. He had wrapped a strip of linen around his bruised hand, and the linen showed white in the shadow. They could not turn their thoughts from it; it was as a rebuke spoken against them all. They stood in utter silence now, staring up at him; for he was remote and solemn as an angel in the dusk, and his hair and beard were stirred by the wind, and his face was white and fair.

"You shall not do this thing, my brothers," he said in a voice which was at once austere and tender, like the voice of an angry father addressing a beloved child. "You shall not do this thing with the spoil which Jahveh has given us, with the gift of the Lord who delivered our enemies into our hands. Who is there in Israel who will side with you in this matter? For as his share is that goes down to battle, so shall his be who tarries by the baggage. It is God's wish and the wish of all upright men that those who go forth and those who wait shall share alike."

There was no protest among those who heard it. The young captain stepped back and concealed himself among the others, and those who had raised the strongest outcry bowed their heads.

Joab, still bearing the sick Egyptian lad before him on his saddle, brought his red steed to the side of the baggage wagon and addressed his lord. "Then, since we are all agreed in this matter," he said, "let us divide the spoil. Thus each man, knowing his share, can go up to Ziklag with an easy heart."

The son of Jesse made no reply.

"Let us begin by giving David's share to David," said the son of Zeruiah. "What does the Star of Bethlehem claim as his share of the loot?"

"All the herds," said David. "All the flocks, both goats and sheep. All the camels. Also all the gold."

It was a monstrous claim, and they gasped to hear it. True, he had slain fifty, and it was his city that had been burned, and he was their lord. Nevertheless, it was such a portion as had never been rendered to one man in Israel. One voice and one only was raised on the other side of the brook, where the speaker was safely hidden among the host. "Surely the son of Jesse will walk like the Pharaoh of Egypt, with a canopy above his head and sandals of gold upon his feet."

A nervous spurt of laughter leaped from the mouths of the multitude and was hushed at once because David had begun to speak again, more gravely than before. "Surely," he said, "the men of Ziklag, having dwelt with me both in the city and in the wilderness, cannot believe that I would take such a spoil unto myself. Behold, I sought it not. I went down into the desert to take my women and my child, and them only, out of the hands of the sons of Sin. And this other was given me though I wanted it not—this other was forced upon me when I asked only that God should smite me for all the sins that are upon my head. You also have sinned, my brothers, even though your sin is less grievous than mine. You also have eaten stolen bread in the wilderness. You also have gone up with the uncircumcised against the anointed of God."

He paused, and they thought that a fit of sacred madness had come upon him, for his gaze was fixed and vacant. But he sighed and passed his hand across his face and looked upon them again with serene eyes. "And it came into my thoughts," he said, "to gather together all the flocks that God has given us and slay them and set torches to them and make a holy hecatomb of their flesh. But I thought I heard the angel of the Lord say, 'Burn it not. Render it instead unto those from whom, in the days of your trials in the wilderness, you wrested meat and bread.' Therefore I will divide this spoil which I have taken for my own, and send it to all those villages which we were wont to haunt in the days when we were bandits who stole from the hands of the children of God. This I will do, unless the host gainsay it. And if the host gainsay it, I will go forth out of the land of Jahveh into the land of Moab and dwell forever among the heathen, that the sight of my face afflict my God no more."

For a long time they were silent, each man considering his lot. If the gold and the flocks and the herds were to be sent in remission of sin to the towns of Judah and the Kenites and the Calebites, and if that which was left was to be divided equally among those who had gone down and those who had tarried, no man would receive more than the wherewithal to restore his ruined house. And slowly it was borne in upon them that he had asked nothing for himself, that he had claimed not even the treasure that had been taken from his own house, that he had indeed journeyed back from the desert with nothing more than Abigail and Noi and the child. So, when they came at last to raise their voices, they raised them only to acclaim him. They pressed around the baggage wagon and lifted up their arms to him, and that one among them was accounted blessed who was given the bruised hand to kiss.

So they set up a spit beside the brook Besor and washed and drank and sat together to eat meat, and night came down upon them. Meanwhile, in the mountains of Gilboa, still moist and cool with the winter rains, the host of Saul lay down to sleep, and the armies of Philistia, flanked on either side by brazen chariots and steeds out of Egypt, moved steadily across the starlit plain of Esdraelon.

ᦒ XI ᦒ

DURING his reign over a united Israel, the Lion of Benjamin had been the author of many wise and temperate statutes. He had striven always to extirpate dark and retrogressive ways and beliefs; he had set his hand energetically to tearing out the roots of a bloody and superstitious past. Not three moons after his anointing, he had decreed that any man or woman who dabbled in the questionable magic of the underworld should be straightway exiled from the land. Wizards and necromancers and those who had familiar spirits no longer dared to work their spells and brew their potions in the light of day; if they practiced at all, they practiced in secret; and it was said of Saul that he had cleansed the nation of an unwholesome preoccupation with the dead. And yet matters had come to such a pass with the King of Israel that, on the night preceding the battle of Gilboa, he journeyed stealthily around the outskirts of the Philistine encampment and came disguised into the village of Endor in order to break his own just law. From his own camp at the foot of Mount Gilboa, Saul and all the ranks of Israel had watched the host of Dagon assembling around the village of Shunem—the plumed and burnished ranks, the sleek steeds of battle, the gleam of brass on the chariots of the uncircumcised—and the King and all the host of Israel were overcome by fear, so that every man felt a trembling in his heart. Then Saul yearned greatly after the men of God who had counseled him in his better days; he remembered the prophet Samuel who had raised him up after Jabesh-Gilead, and the gentle Ahimelech and all those other priests of Nob who had drawn oracles from the mouth of the Lord for his sake. Even though a shadow has fallen between me and the God of battles, he said to himself, yet will I lift up my voice to Him once more, inasmuch as I will inquire of Him not for my own sake, but for the sake of the host and all Israel. . . . And he called what priests and prophets were left to him and bade them ask the intentions of the Lord before the assembled host.

First he sought after a revelation through the sacred dice—two worn pieces of stone, marked with ancient symbols, such as had counseled captains and shepherds of the people since the days of Barak and Deborah. At sunset he stood before the congregated ranks, watching while the priests shook the dice from their linen loincloths, lifting up his heart earnestly to Jahveh and praying for auspicious signs. But the priests were nonplused and the host was plainly frightened—it was impossible to read the signs. That which the Lord uttered through the sacred dice was mockery—such meaningless and malevolent gibberish as children utter in order to confuse and torment their elders. And the King of Israel was shamed before the host.

"It is possible," he said, "that the Lord has turned aside from me because I did not first seek to come to Him face to face, without intermediaries." And he lay down alone in his tent and closed his eyes in sleep, trusting that the Lord would speak to him in a dream. But when he revealed his dreams to the men of God in the morning, their faces assumed a baffled look. "It is with the dreams of our lord the King," they said, "as it was with the sacred stones. No meaning can be drawn from the images which have come to the King in his sleep. What he has dreamed is utterly dark and incomprehensible."

Anger rose within him—anger against this malicious One who humbled a man before his host and mocked him with gibberish and meaningless dreams. "No, now," he said to the priests, "what am I to do, seeing that the Lord of Hosts laughs in my face?" And they bade him fast through the day and seek out diligently every man in the encampment who had ever seen visions or fallen into an ecstasy or prophesied. So from morning until evening he sat before his tent, sick with terror and weak with ·hunger, consulting minor prophets and innocents who believed that they had heard the voice of God. But whosoever prophesied for the King of Israel prophesied very strangely, with babblings and enigmas and unholy spurts of laughter. And when dusk descended upon the camp of Israel and upon the plague of Philistines gathered around Shunem, Saul knew that there was nothing to be gained from further converse with the Lord.

He said in his heart then, I have no portion in the God of Israel who sits enthroned in the clean arc of heaven. I have no portion in light, or in reason, or in any of the beneficent influences that pour from the firmament upon other men. . . . And, even as this thought came to him, he felt a stirring within his bowels, sickening, yet sweet. For if that which is good is utterly estranged from me, he thought, then I need no longer withhold myself from that which is evil. . . . He walked back and forth before his tent in the blood-red dusk, and his heart went out to all shameful and forbidden things—cruel rites and obscene incantations and the abandon and abasement of Canaanitish orgies. Wherefore have I persecuted wizards and necromancers? he asked himself. Are they not my brothers and my sisters, those lost, rejected ones who, being sick within, brew potions for incurable ills, and, being cut off from the living, commune with the dead? . . . Then he called his servants to him and said unto them, "Seek me out a woman who has a familiar spirit, that I may go and inquire of her, seeing that God answers me not." And his servants said unto him: "Behold, there is such a woman at hand, beyond the encampment of the men of Dagon. She dwells in the village of Endor, and our lord the King could come to her by passing round the ranks of Philistia in the black of the night." So he disguised himself, darkening his beard with dye and changing the shape of his lips with the juice of the bitter berry. And he arrayed himself in the habit of a merchant of

Gilead, and journeyed with two servants toward Endor, traveling all through the night.

It was sunrise when they came to the caves which lay on the outskirts of the village of Endor. The King was weary and weak—he had walked a great distance in the dark and had taken no food for more than twenty hours—and the gray hillside, hollowed out like a honeycomb and shrouded by the morning mist, blurred before his eyes. It was not hard to distinguish the cave of the woman of Endor from all the other caves in the side of the hill. Being a creature of the night, she had not extinguished her evening lamp. It shone like a solitary eye in the pale light, like the eye of a madman staring through disordered tresses of wild vine. And when they came up the side of the hill, she stepped forth into the light, knowing well that these strangers had come to seek her. She was a small, neatly made woman in her fortieth year; there was no line upon her face, nor any hint of gray in the great coils of soot-black hair piled round and round her head. She would have been considered handsome and distinguished if it had not been for her mouth. It was as long and thin-lipped as the mouth of a frog, and she had painted it scarlet, so that there seemed to be a bloody gash across her face.

Her eyes, black and lively, kept darting back and forth from the faces of her visitors to some task that she had in hand. As they drew closer, they saw that she held a dead snake and was swiftly, skillfully peeling away the skin with a sharp little knife of stone.

"Well, now," she said, smiling at the mutilated serpent, "what can the travelers be seeking at this hour of the day? Shelter? I have no shelter. There is but one room within."

Then the King of Israel looked at her with unveiled eyes, as a man comes to a harlot, without shame. "Divine unto me, I pray you, by your familiar spirit, and bring up to me whomsoever I shall name unto you."

The witch of Endor fixed her eyes on the snake and continued to peel away the skin. "But the stranger knows," she said, smiling her frog's smile, "that Saul has cut off those that have familiar spirits, and wizards, and diviners, and sent them forth out of the land. Wherefore should you lay a snare for my life and cause me to die?"

And Saul swore to her by Jahveh, saying, "As Jahveh lives, no punishment shall come upon you because of this."

She nodded briskly, as a highborn lady nods when the point of a subtle jest is made plain to her. She laid the snake and the knife upon a stone and wiped her small, deft hands on her skirt and drew very close to the King of Israel. "Whom shall I call up from the dead for you?" she said.

"Samuel."

Her hands, still cold with the blood of the snake, fell upon the King's arm. Her mouth flew open in terror and then closed into a writhing, scarlet line. "Why have you deceived me?" she said, staring at him steadily. "You are Saul. You are the King of Israel."

334

And he closed his hands upon hers and held them in brotherly tenderness, and said: "Be not afraid. Only tell me what you see—what spirit is raised up out of the dwelling-place of the dead."

Then, clinging together—so absorbed were they in each other that they had forgotten the King's servants—they went into the cave, through the locks of wild vines, into the very gaze of the wild, yellow eye of light. Standing apart from him, so that there were some ten paces of umbral emptiness between them, she lifted up her face and rolled her eyes upward, so that nothing could be seen but the gleaming whites. Her mouth opened and became a raw cavern, and a loud cry issued out of her throat, for the familiar spirit that was with her had brought up the dead.

"Whom do you see?" said the King of Israel.

"I see a spirit coming up out of the earth."

"Tell me the form thereof."

"An old man comes up, and he is covered with a robe."

And Saul perceived that it was Samuel, called up out of Sheol, and he bowed his face to the ground, and did obeisance at the prophet's feet.

And Samuel said to Saul, "Why have you disquieted me and brought me up?"

And Saul answered: "I am sore distressed, for the Philistines make war against me, and God is departed from me and answers me no more, neither by prophets nor by dreams. Therefore I have called you up, that you may counsel me yet once more."

And Samuel said: "Wherefore do you ask me, seeing that Jahveh is departed from you, and has become your adversary? Jahveh has done unto you all that He spoke through me—He has rent your kingdom out of your hand and given it to your neighbor, even David. Because you did not obey the voice of Jahveh and did not execute His fierce wrath upon Amalek, therefore Jahveh has done this thing unto you this day. Moreover, Jahveh will deliver Israel also with you into the hand of the Philistines. And tomorrow you and your sons will be with me in Sheol, and Jahveh will deliver the host of Israel into the hands of the Philistines."

Then the spirit departed, and Saul fell straightway his full length upon the earth and was sore afraid. He was unable to rise for weakness, for he had eaten no bread all the day, nor all the night. And he lay on the floor of the cave until the morning was far spent, nor did any man speak to him or touch him until he lifted up his head.

He saw then to his amazement that the witch of Endor had not departed from him. As a sister watches over a dying brother, so she had knelt before him, guarding him lest any other being should intrude upon his pain. And the first sight that he beheld was her scarlet mouth, smiling upon him in tenderness.

"Behold," she said, "your handmaid has hearkened unto your voice and put her life into your hand. Now, therefore, I pray you, hearken also unto the voice of your handmaid. Let me set a morsel of bread before you, and eat, so that you may have strength to carry you on your way."

335

Inasmuch as I am damned, he said in his heart, it is only fitting that I should break bread with the damned. . . . And the woman had a fatted calf in the house, and she hastened and killed it. She took flour also and kneaded it and baked unleavened bread thereof. And she set a meal before Saul and his servants, and they ate the noonday bread in the cave, at the hand of the witch of Endor. And such was the bond between the rejected ones that Saul was in no haste to depart, but tarried with his sister until night descended upon the earth.

ej XII je

WHENEVER he gave himself a moment's rest from the task of rebuilding Ziklag, the son of Jesse beheld a vision of Jonathan. He no longer saw him on the slopes of Gilboa, going down beneath the chariots of the uncircumcised. Now he saw him always in the King's house in Gibeah, wandering through the dim corridors, stopping before a pile of ancient armor and searching among the tarnished weapons until he came upon a corselet or a sword.

What was it, he would ask himself, falling silent in the midst of a conversation with a mason or a carpenter, what was it that the beloved was wont to do with all those things which he took at one time or another from the venerable rubbish in his father's hall? . . . Then suddenly it dawned upon him that Jonathan had sought to salvage all that he had carried away from the heap, had mended it and polished it and restored it to the hands of men. He remembered also how, in the harsh days of waiting for Saul's return out of Gilgal, Saul's son had labored in a barren field, seeking to clear it of its age-old curse of stones. So it was with him always, he thought. In the time of his affliction, he said in his heart: It is a sorry world. All things decay, all delights depart, the gain is forever devoured by the loss. Therefore let us salvage what we can, even though it is only a piece of rock-ridden earth or a tarnished sword. . . .

These visions were so persistent that he began to consider them omens sent from the Lord. He could not bring himself to carry them to the priest Abiathar; he strove with them alone. Surely, he thought, it augurs well for him that I no longer see him torn by the chariots—perhaps the chariots never came near him—perhaps he is delivered out of the hands of the uncircumcised. Nor is it an evil sign that I should see him as he was in our good hours together, young and fair and with the bloom upon him, going vigorously about the business of restoring that which had fallen into disuse. No, now, it is a good omen. I am a fool to question the nature of it at all. . . . And yet he could not detach from the vision the sense of sorrow that always brooded above it; and his heart was troubled because the beloved never spoke, but came and took his piece of armor and bore it down the long hall without a word.

If he were to speak, thought David, no doubt he would interpret the vision thus: "Let it be with the son of Jesse as it was with me in the old days. When I grieved or waited, I set myself some worthy task and thereby relieved the ache that was in my heart. Let David also labor in the hour of his tribulation. Let him put his shoulder to the rebuilding of Ziklag, so that, when Achish leads me down, the place in which we meet will be whole and fair." . . . So the Star of Bethlehem labored at the rebuilding of the burned city, labored with the men of the ranks, laid his hands to the clearing of the streets and the restoration of the walls. From dawn until the last light of the sun was quenched he labored. Little food passed his lips, and his sleep was brief, and it was in those days that Abigail found the first streak of white in his hair.

Some ten days after the return to Ziklag, the dwellers in the towns round about, having received their gifts of herds and flocks and gold, began to make manifest their devotion to the Star of Bethlehem. Linens and chairs and clothes chests came to him out of the villages. The city of Hebron sent him a load of timber that they had bought from the kingdom of Lebanon. The great families of Gath made him a magnificent present of vessels of pottery and metal, and the wife of the Seren sent two splendid carved beds. The women of the villages came down, bearing fatted kids and cheeses and baskets of fruit. Farmers and herdsmen journeyed unsolicited from the plain to labor at the houses and the walls. At first the son of Jesse was gratified by this show of concern and generosity. Then misgivings assailed him again, and he asked himself: Do they turn so eagerly to the House of Jesse because they know that the House of Kish is no more? . . .

As soon as this thought possessed him, the presence of the people became a burden to him, and he sought every pretext for being alone. One night he did not go down with his family to sleep in the black tents that had been pitched around the burned city in the shadow of the walls. He insisted upon remaining in the spot upon which his new house was to stand, among the six roofless pillars and the shavings of wood, in the blank oblong marked off by the foundation stones. On the morning of that same day, some of the men had brought up to him certain pieces of furniture that had stood in his common room before the conflagration—a clothes chest, three chairs, a bench, and a long table. He dragged these objects into the oblong and examined them by the light of a torch which he had thrust into the earth near one of the pillars. He went to the chest and opened it and found, among folded cloaks and tunics, some hard and strangely familiar thing—his lute. Its strings were unbroken, for Noi had wound them with reeds and wrapped them in linen; the only mark upon it was that which it had received long ago when he had fallen upon it at Saul's feet. He carried it to one of the chairs and sat down and plucked at the strings. They were out of tune, and the tones, sounded at random, bore a strange and unaccustomed relationship to one another. He plucked the same strings again and knew that he had come by chance upon a dark, elegiac thread of melody. Long after he had extinguished the torch and lain down upon his cloak to sleep, the tones continued to sound in his ears, as persistent as the smell of charred wood that would not depart from the town.

He dreamed a dream that night. Perhaps because he slept as he had often slept in the Gibean days, with his lute under his hand, he dreamed that he lay wakeful in Saul's house, in the moonlit chamber that looked westward toward the sea, plucking mournful music from the strings of the lute. Then his hand was quiet because there was a knocking at the door, and his heart leaped up within him, saying, It is the beloved.

The great door opened slowly, creaking upon its ancient hinges; and it was indeed Jonathan who came into the room and stood beside the bed. But he was changed almost beyond recognition; there was no radiance upon him, neither in his eyes nor in his cloudy hair, even though he stood in the full brightness of the moon. The lights of God have gone out for him, thought the son of Jesse. The moon knows him not, nor will he draw back his luster from the heat of the sun. . . . And he wept.

Then the son of Saul drew closer and knelt beside the pillow and spoke: "My brother, weep no more. What profit is there in weeping? God has created the world in such-and-such a manner. It is created, it is finished, I cannot change the world. Let us turn our thoughts therefore to the business of mending. There is a thing to be mended. Behold, it is in my hands."

And David turned on the bed and saw in the hands of Jonathan the figure of a fair woman, molded out of clay and broken in two between the breasts and the hips. He saw also how grievous was the change that had come upon the beloved, how the hands which held the image were stiff and awkward, how there were bluish patches below the eyes. And his heart stood still within him, for he saw that the pulse in the beloved's temple had ceased to beat.

"My brother," said Jonathan, "it is no great matter that it is broken. It was broken before, and into more fragments than this. It can be mended again, if only the son of Jesse will have done with tears."

But he cried aloud, "Beloved, I cannot mend it! Let Jonathan set his hand to it, since it is he who heals and I who destroy."

"No, now," said Jonathan in the sweet and reasonable voice which he was wont to use in council, "surely my brother sees that I cannot mend it, inasmuch as my hands are numb." And he bent and breathed his breath upon the pillow, and his breath was dank with the odor of charred wood and death.

And David woke in the red sunrise, sobbing and saying to himself: It is only the smell of fire. The city is in flames. It is not the smell of death. . . .

That day he could not bring himself to remain near the unfinished house where he had dreamed the dream. All morning he wandered through the city, among curled shavings and brown clay bricks and foundation stones. Wherever there was heavy work, he stopped and put his hand to it. He helped to raise a dozen pillars; he heaved a ponderous door into place; he went down into darkness, with a rope tied round his waist, to speed the business of purifying a well. While the work lasted, the world about him looked much as it had looked before; but between task and task everything—the truncated houses, the pillars lying athwart the street, the very earth and sky—seemed to be suffering from some disintegrating malady. It is the dream, he thought. I will speak of it tonight to Abiathar. I will ask him to interpret it for me. Perhaps the omens in it are not so baleful as I think. . . .

By noon he had wandered as far as the northern gate of the city. Three soldiers and a mason were working there, mending a gap in the wall. Beyond the gap was a stretch of wilderness, arid and unreal in the intense light.

"Let me set my shoulder to these," he said, nodding toward the cyclopean blocks of limestone that were to be set into the wall.

"Gladly, gladly," said the mason. "They are very heavy. It takes four men to haul up a single stone. This morning the business has gone but slowly, since now and again one among us must stop for rest. But we will surely finish by sundown with the help of my lord."

He set himself to the work eagerly enough, but a strange ineptitude came upon him. Although the weather was hot and clear, with a foretaste of high summer in the strength of the sun, he was cold. The great blocks kept slipping from his hands until those who heaved with him could no longer trust him to lift, but set him to putting the mortar between the stones. Before sundown he had gone to the gate a dozen times to plunge his hands into a great jar of water that stood at the edge of the cistern. He could not endure the sight of the dried mortar upon them. They are as dull as a leper's hands, he thought; they reject the light of the sun. . . .

At dusk they left their unfinished task and sat down before the gate of the city to break the evening bread. They spread the food upon a plank of cedarwood and asked the son of Jesse diffidently if he would sit and eat. Much as he wished to go from them and seek out Abiathar, he could not refuse. He strove with the conversation as a sick man strives with the coverlet which he takes in his delirium to be the source of his pain. If only they would be still, he thought, if only they would leave me in peace. . . . He avoided their eyes and stared across the stretch of stony wilderness dotted with smoky clumps of brush turning purple and crimson under the setting sun. Over just such a stretch of rock and brush and sand, he thought, Abigail came down to me from Nabal's house, bearing spurious tidings concerning the fond indulgence of the Lord. . . .

Someone touched him, and he started. "My lord," the mason said, "does my sight deceive me, or do I behold a runner coming toward us out of the wilderness?"

David narrowed his eyes against the red and purple glare and saw a figure advancing between the scattered rocks and bushes. This, then, he told himself, is the runner come out of the north with tidings of the battle.

"He is clothed in the garb of a mourner," one of the soldiers said.

Surely, thought David, he is clothed in the garb of a mourner. How else should he be clothed? I never dreamed that what came to pass upon Gilboa could end in anything save the ruin of Israel. Then why should my heart stop to hear that he comes in mourning? What old, half-remembered terror rises up, now that he draws near, now that I behold the hairy garment and the mourning hood? . . . He rose and stepped forward and cast away the bread that was in his hands.

"Will my lord go forth to meet him?"

He did not know who it was that had spoken behind him. He turned and looked at them, and saw that they had ceased to eat and were wiping the food from their lips. He turned again and saw that the runner was upon him—the foreknown robe, the foreknown hood, and a face, no longer muffled, streaked with ashes and earth. He moved toward the stranger, and the stranger fell before him as one falls before a king, at full length upon the sand.

"Have they sent you down out of Gilboa?" said David.

And the stranger answered, speaking into the earth, "I am escaped out of the camp of Israel."

"What of the battle?"

The stranger did not reply. He reached out and took up a handful of earth and strewed it upon his head.

"No, now, tell me," said the son of Jesse, and his voice seemed strange to him, like a lute which has gone out of tune and makes unearthly music.

"The people have fled out of the cities," said the stranger. "The cities of Israel, all that are on this side of the Jordan, have fallen into the hands of the uncircumcised. The host of God is fled from the battle, and many are fallen and dead. . . ."

The world also had changed. An unnatural shadow was passing over it, such a shadow as in the sinister hour of an eclipse sickens the face of the moon.

"How is it with the King of Israel?" David said.

"The King of Israel is counted with the slain, even he and his son Jonathan."

Insensate, dull, unanswering—it is not so with the breathing being of the beloved! Achish has promised to restore him whole out of the battle. Achish will lead him down and lay his living hand within my hand. Achish has given his word for it, and what is the word of this craven who did not stay to die at Gilboa—what is his word against the word of the Seren of Gath? . . . And David turned upon the runner and railed at him. "How should such a one as you know what came to pass?"

The stranger lifted up his head and spoke again. "Behold," he said, "as I happened by chance upon Mount Gilboa, I came upon Saul leaning on his spear, and there was a wound in his side, for he had fallen upon his sword to make an end of himself. And, lo, the chariots and the horsemen followed hard after him, and when he looked behind him, he saw me and called upon me. And I answered, 'Here am I.' And he said unto me,

'Stand, I pray you, beside me and slay me, for anguish has taken hold on me because my life is yet whole within me.' So I stood beside him and slew him, because I was certain that he could not live. And I took the crown that was upon his head and the bracelet that was upon his arm, and I have brought them hither to my lord."

His hand, gray with ashes, fumbled in the folds of the hairy garment and brought out two golden circlets and laid them upon David's feet. And the crown and the armband were horrible, like serpents crawling upon him. He spurned them with his foot and called aloud upon the name of Jonathan.

"The son of Saul also," said the mourner, "is certainly among the slain. I saw him not, but there were many that beheld him. He lay at the foot of the mountain, and there was no life left in him, inasmuch as he had been torn by spears and crushed also beneath the chariots of the uncircumcised."

It was as if the earth had shifted and were falling apart. He raised his clenched hands to contain the tumultuous surging in his head.

"Malchishua and Abinadab, his brothers, they too were found among the fallen. None is left of all that house, save only Ishbaal, who is unfit to reign." The hideous hand groped out and found the circlets and laid them again upon David's feet. "Therefore, in the hour of her tribulation, Israel turns her eyes toward the House of Jesse. The House of Kish is no more."

◆§ XIII §◆

That night the firmament was open, starry, windless. The city had been stricken into silence. Men and women gathered in small groups and spoke in whispers. Yet when he remembered in later days what had come to pass after the bringing of the tidings, David imagined that all voices had been drowned in a continual rush of noise.

In this churning world there were certain matters that demanded his attention. He looked to each of them, calling upon others to assist him, seldom using his own hands—he needed his hands to press hard against his head. It was required that he put on a mourning garment. But the pain in his head was so persistent and the noise in his ears so deafening that he grew confused and rent what he had upon him and cast it away before another garment had been brought to take its place. He sat, clothed only in his loincloth, in the unfinished house until it was borne in upon him that this was no house, that those who passed by in the street could see him in his nakedness. Noi stood between him and the street to conceal him while Abigail went to look for a tunic of hairy cloth. It was the second wife whom he asked to serve him in putting it on; her utter silence, her solemnity, her large dry eyes, were less burdensome to him than Abigail's plentiful tears.

341

It was necessary also to learn where the uncircumcised had carried the bodies, and he bade Joab question the runner. The bodies, said the stranger, had been carried to the great temple of Astarte in Beth-shan, to be hung as trophies of victory upon the wall. It came into his thoughts, too, that the runner must be slain. For was it not a law in Israel that whosoever lifted up his hand against the Lord's anointed should be put to death? Partly to give satisfaction to God, partly to cleanse himself of the loathing that had come upon him when the runner had laid the two golden circlets upon his feet, he called one of the young men to him and bade him go and smite the dog who had laid his foul hands upon the body of the King. Within an hour, one came to him and told him that the thing was done. But he was not content to hear it, he must go to behold it with his own eyes. Nor did he feel that the cleansing was complete even when he saw the corpse lying at the city gate, with blood drying on its lips. Perhaps they have laid hands upon the wrong man, he thought. Perhaps they should have slain another. What other? The Seren of Gath? Myself? . . .

The last of his obligations was fulfilled by midnight. He sat in a chair and looked about him at the roofless pillars, the foundation stones without walls, the threshold without a door. Abigail had taken some bedding and had spread it in one of the corners. "It seemed to me," she said, "that my lord would rather sleep here alone than among the others in the tents beyond the gate." He looked at her in amazement. How had she come by the preposterous notion that he would sleep at all? Abishai had wandered into the unfinished house and was helping Noi build a fire. David went to him and took him by the arm and led him apart.

"Tell me," he said, "what is the shortest road to the city of Beth-shan? Is it easier to go up by the Way of the Hills or by the Way of the Coast?"

"But why," said Abishai, "should the thoughts of my lord turn to Beth-shan?"

"Because it is there that they have taken my brother and my lord and hung them upon the temple wall."

"No, now, let my uncle cease to brood upon it. When the spirit is flown forth out of the body, the body is nothing; it suffers no more."

But he would not be pacified. He continued to press the matter until Abishai sat down and explained the relative advantages of the Way of the Hills and the Way of the Coast.

After a little, Noi came to them, bearing a bowl filled with a tea of herbs which she had brewed upon the fire. She set it in David's hand without a word.

"No, my child," he said, "I cannot drink it. If Noi would serve me, let her——" He wished to give her another task, and could think of none. He set the bowl upon the ground and tried to remember what she took pride in doing. . . . "Yes," he said, starting up, "if Noi would serve me, let her go and find my lute. Let her find it and wrap it as she did not long since, in reeds and linen, so that it will come to no harm."

342

"I have found it," she said, "and it is laid away in a safe place."

"Nevertheless, wrap it again."

"Surely. And when it is wrapped, shall I lay it aside or bring it to my lord?"

"Lay it aside. . . . No, bring it again, that I may see it," he said.

His mourning garment was bound around his waist with a wide belt of leather. A leather pouch hung from it, and he fell to pressing it flat between his hands. Suddenly he knew that it was empty and must be filled; no man ought to set out on a journey, even though it should be his last, without the wherewithal to pay for a room at an inn. He knew that there were certain pieces of gold—amulets in the shape of suns and crescents—hidden in the clothes chest, and he left Abishai and went to search for them. But when he came to the clothes chest, he saw that the lid of it was open and laid back, and that Amnon was sleeping upon the cloaks and tunics inside. He was sleeping very quietly, with one arm laid across his face to shield it from the wavering light of the torch that burned above him. David knelt and began to feel about among the garments. Every movement was painful to him; his head ached the more because it was necessary for him to bend over the chest. His hands were awkward and kept striking against the child's feet, and this troubled him. The little one drew his feet out of David's way and stretched and sighed.

Abigail came up behind him. "What is it that my lord would have?" she said. "Let me serve my lord."

"A few amulets—a few of the crescents and suns that we laid within the chest."

"Surely," she said. "But what should David do with amulets?"

"My pouch is empty——"

"But why should the pouch be filled? Surely there is nothing that David wishes to buy this night——"

"No, now," he said in anger, "if the child had not been laid like a doll in the chest, there would have been no need for me to make endless explanations."

"It was not I," she said coldly, "who laid the little one there."

The thought that she could concern herself with laying blame upon Noi while Saul and Jonathan hung on the wall of the temple of Astarte seemed so monstrous to him that his mouth began to tremble, and he wept.

Noi came and pushed the child roughly to one side and brought out a handful of amulets. "It was I," she said, "who laid my little dog in the chest. I will take him up and carry him hence to the tents as soon as I have finished with the lute."

"No, now," he said, rising and wiping the tears from his face, hard, with the flat of his hand, "let my wife not lay the name of dog upon the Hope of Judah and my beloved son. Let her put the amulets into my leather pouch, for there is such a pain in my head that I can scarcely move. Let her give me my lute and send Abishai to fetch my donkey, that I may go forth to Beth-shan."

"But why," said Abishai, "should David needlessly afflict his eyes and smite his heart with what he will behold?"

"Do you think I go to gape at them?" he said. "I go to take them down from the walls, to cover them from the eyes of the uncircumcised. I go to wrap them in linen and spices, to carry them up to Gibeah, to bury them in the garden of Saul's house where Ahinoam lies, she and the weaver and Kish."

"No, no, my lord," said Abigail, falling upon him and weeping. "For if my lord goes up, surely he will die at the hands of the men of Beth-shan. The people of Beth-shan will never permit him to take down the bodies and live."

But Noi brought his lute and laid it in his hands. "How can we keep him here?" she said. "Let him go, for he can do no other."

◦ XIV ◦

He came to no harm on the journey up to Beth-shan. Those whom he encountered on the way—Philistine soldiers plundering in the farmlands, Israelite deserters hiding in the tall wheat, old men and women and children fleeing with what they had salvaged out of their burning houses, Phoenician tradesmen forced to remain in a strange land because the roads were blocked by war—all these took him for a man possessed by a spirit sent from God. He was mad, and therefore he was sacred. They nourished him with goat's milk and honey and bread. They pointed the way to him and held up their children that they might touch him and be blessed. For God was surely in him—nobody but an innocent of God would travel through the pillaged land unarmed, clothed in a mourning garment and carrying nothing but a lute.

If any city had reason to rejoice over the ruin of Israel, it was the city of Beth-shan. Both of Israel's enemies dwelt within its walls—the Philistines, whom Jahveh had beaten back to the coast, and the Canaanites, whom He had ground into filth and poverty. It was a very ancient city, older than Shechem and Gilgal. Men had dwelt for so many centuries in Beth-shan that they had made a hill for themselves out of their own rubbish; it was told how there were walls lying buried beneath the present walls; and children digging in play upon the slopes outside the gate sometimes came upon strange rings and brooches or were terrified at the sight of human bones.

Once it had been a city of thriving tradesmen who sent their tooled leather and pottery and embroidered cloth over a web of highways that stretched into all parts of the land. In the years of their prosperity, the people had shown their gratefulness by dedicating a broad square in the highest part of the city to the uses of many gods. They had crowded this square with a forest of steles and pillars and standing stones, each one sacred to some divine being; and they had raised up temples to the most powerful and beloved of the gods—Shan, the Serpent, for whom the city was named; Mekel, the wise and aged lord of scholars and craftsmen; and Astarte, the young and voluptuous Lady of Desire. But in the days of their subjection, when the roads were blocked by Saul's armies, and leather and flax and potters' clay must be bought at outrageous prices from the Israel-ites, most of the steles had been forgotten and most of the temples had fallen into disuse. Only Astarte, comfort of the despised and the defeated, continued to receive her usual offerings. Her terraced temple alone remained wealthy and crowded; and whenever some small piece of good fortune came to relieve their misery, they laid such votive offerings as they could muster at her feet.

The last terrace of her ziggurat could be seen, rising over the brown roofs, from any part of the city. David saw it from the gates in the violet light of early evening, and knew that he had come at last to Beth-shan. The goddess herself stood at the highest window of her temple, looking out upon her people—young, slender, high-breasted, holding a dove in each of her uplifted hands. The Serpent Shan had come up from his neglected temple to lodge with her; he coiled around her golden feet and laid his head against her thigh. The wall beneath her could not be seen from the gate because a cluster of brown roofs came between. But the son of Jesse knew what it was that she would behold if she leaned forward and lowered her eyes. The corpses of Saul and Jonathan and the fallen banners of Israel were surely fastened to this wall.

It was with him in Beth-shan as it had been on the journey. He was received with awed kindliness because of the spirit that dwelt within him. In a city drunken with the wine of victory, he was led courteously to an inn. In a city overflowing with soldiers and visiting revelers, he was given a room. A small room, the innkeeper said, but high and airy, with a window that opened upon the temple of the Lady, with a table and a chair and a bed. The holy stranger might put his golden suns and crescents back into his pouch; the room was given to the god who possessed him. What god it was that had entered the filthy and emaciated traveler, the innkeeper dared not ask. But he was puzzled. The robe was plainly a robe out of Israel, yet he who wore it wore also tooled-leather sandals out of Philistia; and no son of Jahveh had ever had so red a beard, such silky hair.

"Will the stranger eat?" said the innkeeper.

David sat on the edge of the bed, with his face turned away from the window. To die, to turn stiff and cold, with a belly full of food—that was horrible. He had never understood how men could walk up to the sacrificial stone with their bodies heavy with food.

"No, no food," he said.

"But the wayfarer is very weary, and surely the god will not speak clearly within him if he fasts day and night. A little goat's milk, fresh, and cooled in a vessel of water? A fig or two? A little bread?"

His tongue had been cleaving to the roof of his mouth for the last four hours. "Milk," he said. "A little milk, but nothing else, no bread or fruit."

When the innkeeper had departed, he rose and turned toward the window. With his eyes closed, he groped in the direction of the glow, and did not stop until his thigh struck against the sill. Even then he did not raise his eyelids at once; he stood with his face turned toward the temple of Astarte, wondering whether at this height all barriers had fallen away, so that he must see at last. Now, he told himself, grasping the sill and opening his eyes. But he saw only the terraced wall, half lost in shadows. The sun had gone down; the fire that had burned upon the face of the goddess had been quenched; what hung at her feet was a cluster of shadows against shadow, a dark mass toward which a single raven floated down, black against the purplish sky.

He knew then that all through the journey he had prepared himself only for this moment. He had put from his mind the matter of taking down the bodies and the thought of his own death at the hands of the uncircumcised. And now that he had been delivered from the horror, he began to tremble. A great, warm, dissolving weakness was upon him. He stepped backward and sat upon the edge of the bed, with his knees apart and his hands hanging down between them. Tears coursed over his grimy cheeks, and he could not lift his hand to wipe them away. He sobbed aloud, without concern for those who might hear him. He wept fiercely, entirely, with his whole being, as he had not wept since he was a child. The innkeeper returned and held the bowl of goat's milk to his mouth. He took the liquid and wept the more to find it marvelously cool upon his swollen tongue. "Come, now," said the Canaanite, plainly awed at so wild a show of holy sorrow, "the man of God will burst the strings of his heart with the violence of his grief. Let him lie down. Let him lie down awhile and sleep."

He wished to protest, to thrust away the well-meaning Canaanite who lifted him up and laid him across the bed. But all strength had departed out of him. He felt his body sinking into the softness beneath him, sinking endlessly down, past a window in which a goddess stood, past a mass of formless shadows, past a lute gone out of tune and sounding three strange notes, past the wide, dry eyes of Noi, past everything, surely into the bowels of the earth.

"Sleep a little," said the voice of the innkeeper.

But surely he knows, thought David, still going down through darkness, surely he knows that there is no sleep after such weariness except the sleep of death. . . .

WHEN he opened his eyes again, it seemed to him that a profound change had been wrought upon the world. It was not only that night had come—night robbed of its oppressiveness by the lamp left burning upon the table. It was not only that the heat of the day had given place to a moist and pervasive coolness. It was that the world, after suffering from a fatal malady through many nights and days, had miraculously grown serene—the fever had passed from the world. The revelers were still up and about; the yellow glow of their torches still moved through the ancient streets. But the tumult and the glare had departed from the face of the earth. And in the ensuing darkness and stillness, he knew that he had ceased to distract himself with feverish raving, that his spirit had risen up within him, sane and whole, to accept the death of the beloved.

He is dead, he told himself, staring at the unwavering flame of the lamp. He is dead, and I will hear his voice no more. It is not that they have torn him with spears and broken him with brazen wheels and hung him at the feet of Astarte. It is that he is gone out, like a wick crushed between the finger and the thumb. It is that the radiance and the sweet reasonableness and the tenderness that dwelt within him have been quenched and will shine no longer upon the dark faces of other men. This is a thing accomplished. It was completed when the first spear struck him. This is finished and cannot be undone. . . . And while he pondered these matters, the stillness within him grew even more profound, and he felt that God had taken pity on him and established within him the peace of ultimate loss.

He rose then and went to the window. The innkeeper had refilled the bowl with goat's milk and set it upon the sill, so that it might take unto itself the coolness of the night. He lifted it and drank slowly, and the fresh draught took the last taste of sickness from his mouth. In the street below him, the heathen were lifting up their voices in a taunting song concerning the slain. But it does not matter, he thought, they cannot hear it. They are remote, sealed up, set utterly apart from the malice of men. All that can be done unto them has been done. . . . Yet this inner certainty in no wise delivered him from his obligation to take them down. His duty seemed even clearer and simpler now. One went down into the street and walked to the ziggurat; one climbed the winding ramp that coiled like the Serpent Shan around the temple; one knelt on the sill of the window where the goddess stood, and reached down and gathered up certain lifeless masses of flesh and bone. . . . And all the while he thought of it, he listened to a sound that had begun to make itself heard in the deep hush within him—three notes plucked on a lute gone out of tune, and then another note, wild and high and sweet. There is strange music within me, he said in his heart, so strange that I myself cannot understand it. There are three notes that say, "Life is nothing, there is only death," and there is a fourth note which says, "Believe it not. Death is nothing. There is only love." . . .

He drank again and leaned upon the sill and watched the yellow light of the torches flickering up and down the labyrinthine streets. When the torches are out, he thought, when the revelers have reeled to their beds, then I will go up to the temple of Astarte. For if I go now, there will be many there to behold me and lay me low before I reach the top of the ramp. But if I abide here until the hour before sunrise, it may be that I can take them down or at least lay hands upon them before I am slain. Meanwhile, seeing that I am the only mourner who sits this night with my brother and my lord, I will do what is yet left to be done according to the law of Israel to do reverence to their bones. . . .

But he was very weak, so weak that he could not stand as a mourner should when he sends up his lamentations in behalf of the slain. Thinking that Jahveh saw how it was with him and would grant him forgiveness, he seated himself upon the sill and rested his head upon his hands. He grieved that he had forgotten to bring a sacrificial knife up out of Ziklag, such a knife as one uses to let out blood as an offering to the dead. But his fingernails had grown long during the journey, and with these he lacerated his shoulder and his cheek until the tips of his fingers were moist with blood. He also closed his hand upon a heavy lock of his hair and plucked it out and cast it forth from the window, saying, "Take it, my lord and my father. Take it, my brother and my beloved." He fell silent then, wondering whether those who sang and shouted in the street below had heard him. But he knew that they could not hear, that the silence was an inward silence only, that the world which seemed dark and still to him was actually alive with torchlight and noise. It is well, he thought. Then I can mourn aloud. The song of praise that is written in the Book of Rituals for the Dead—I can sing it even as I sang other songs in the garden in Gibeah, lifting up all the voice that was in me for Saul and Jonathan. . . .

And yet—perhaps because he had been so long from Israel that all its songs had receded from his memory, perhaps because the strange notes sounded persistently in his ears, obliterating all others—he could not recall the required song. No, now, he thought, I am a sorry mourner, and there is none here but I. Forgive me, my God. Forgive me also, poor shapeless shadows, dishonored flesh. Wait a little, and surely I will recall it. Bear with me a little until I fetch my lute, for surely I will remember it when my hand is on my lute. . . .

Yet when he brought the lute to the window and took its funeral swathings from it, when he was seated on the sill with the taut strings under his palm, he was no closer to the elusive melody than he had been before. The tumult in the street had grown louder. Someone—no doubt a foaming prophet of one of the gods of Canaan—was shrieking his exultation above the babble of the rest. "Your glory, O Israel," he shouted, "is slain upon your high places!" And the three disintegrating notes sounded in

348

David's mind beneath the words of the prophet, sounded inexorably, sounded until the words and the notes were one, and, being joined together, were the first line of a song of lamentation for the dead.

Your glory, O Israel, is slain upon your high places. . . .

He said it aloud. He plucked it forth from the body of the lute.

Your glory, O Israel, is slain upon your high places.
How are the mighty fallen!

Even as it issued out of him—a living entity, born complete and unchangeable, above skill, beyond himself and more than himself—even as it came swiftly forth from him, he knew that it was a stranger upon the earth and brother to no other song. All that he had created before it had been fashioned, wrought in the mind as a vessel is wrought in the hands. But he did not fashion this lament—he only uncovered it and lifted it up before the world. Before one of the moving torches had gone out, before the prophet had ceased to rant, it was a finished thing. He rose, borne up on the strength of the song, and lifted up his voice, and sang above the noise of the revelers, keeping his eyes fixed upon the distant and invisible temple of Astarte.

Your glory, O Israel, is slain upon your high places.
How are the mighty fallen!
Tell it not in Gath,
Publish it not in the streets of Askelon,
Lest the daughters of the Philistines rejoice,
Lest the daughters of the uncircumcised triumph.

You mountains of Gilboa,
Let there be no dew, neither let there be rain upon you, nor
     fields of offerings;
For there the shield of the mighty is vilely cast away,
The shield of Saul, as though he had not been anointed with oil.
From the blood of the slain, from the fat of the mighty,
The bow of Jonathan turned not back,
And the sword of Saul returned not empty.

Saul and Jonathan were lovely and pleasant in their lives,
And in their deaths they were not divided.
They were swifter than eagles,
They were stronger than lions.
Daughters of Israel, weep over Saul,
Who clothed you in scarlet, with other delights,
Who put ornaments of gold upon your apparel.

349

How are the mighty fallen in the midst of the battle!
O Jonathan, slain in the high places!
I am distressed for you, my brother Jonathan.
Very pleasant have you been to me.
Your love to me was wonderful,
Passing the love of women.
How are the mighty fallen,
And the weapons of war perished!

If there is satisfaction for the dead, he thought, then Saul and Jonathan are satisfied. My voice is not as it was when I sang in the tent at Ephes-Dammim or in the Gibean garden, yet it was a peerless song and well sung, considering that the singer is very weary and about to go up to his death. . . . He laid his lute upon the bed and went again to the window to learn whether he had been heard by any of those who still celebrated the fall of Israel in the street below. No faces were turned toward the window. A crowd of soldiers were brawling over certain temple women; four lean and filthy boys were begging in shrill voices; an old woman had thrust her head from a window and was calling her granddaughter home. . . . This is the last tawdry hour of the carnival, he thought. Very soon they will sink into drunken sleep. Soon the fires of heaven will be quenched, and the temple of Astarte and that which hangs upon it will grow visible in the pitiless whiteness of dawn.

It would be sweet, he thought, it would be very sweet to spend these last hours that are left to me with the softness of the bed beneath me and the coolness of the pillow against my torn cheek. But if I lie down, sleep will surely overcome me, and who knows at what hour I will awake? . . . He seated himself again upon the sill. As a child is curled in the enfolding darkness of the womb, with its fists against its breasts and its head upon its knees, so he curled himself in the square of the window, shutting out the torchlight and the noise, making for himself a final place of peace. Certain quiet and disconnected images floated through his mind: his mother brushing the crumbs of the evening bread from the table; a newborn lamb staggering after a ewe; a crowd of pilgrims—comely and decent in their holiday garments—walking toward the high place in Ramah; the cistern at Ephes-Dammim; Saul's cloak lying across a bed; the veined hand of Ahinoam; Michal comforting the little Ishbaal; Noi mending a tunic; Amnon asleep. . . . While he beheld these things, he wept, effortlessly and serenely, in the tabernacle of darkness which he had made for himself. For it was a fair world, radiant with green shoots, glimmering forever under the life-restoring sun, musical with numberless voices lifted up in grief and tenderness and delight—and how could a man do otherwise than weep, seeing that he was about to depart?

Suddenly he started up. Surely, he thought, my reason has gone forth from me. Am I mad that I should hear the songs of Israel in the streets of Beth-shan? . . . He set his feet upon the floor and leaned far over the sill and listened. The night, already rimmed about with the white light of dawn, was filled with an unbelievable sound. Somewhere near the northern gate of the city a hundred voices—no, three hundred voices—were shouting a song from the Book of Rituals, the song that he had not been able to remember, the song in praise of the valiant dead. How long he had been sitting in darkness before the sound aroused him, he did not know. There were only a few scattered torches still burning in the city, and these jerked and wavered as though their bearers also had heard men of Jahveh singing in the night. And now he could no longer take it for a dream. The street which led from the northern gate into the city was abloom with the light of many torches. Dark heads crowded against each other, file upon file. He saw the gleam of shields and the glitter of spears and swords. He saw a single banner floating above the singing faces— a banner embroidered with the likeness of a tamarisk tree. It is the banner of Jabesh-Gilead, he told himself. These thirty years the men of Jabesh-Gilead have remembered how Saul delivered them out of the hands of their enemy. Out of all Israel they alone have come to reclaim the bones of their lord. . . .

Without slackening the pace of their march, without lessening the ardor of their singing, the men of Jabesh-Gilead advanced upon the temple of Astarte. There was a murmuring from the windows of the houses; a few drunkards reeled in impotent anger against the moving columns; certain Philistine captains shouted orders; but it was plain that the abandon of the carnival had delivered the city into the hands of three hundred farmers and herdsmen out of the hills. They formed in solid ranks around the House of the Lady. The light of their torches fanned upward to the second terrace and made a roseate glow upon the ancient stones. Then some ten of them withdrew from the others and went, bearing their lights with them, up the ramp that coiled round the building like the Serpent Shan.

They knelt, even as David would have knelt, on the sill at the feet of the Lady of Desire. For the space of a few heartbeats, the red of their torches revealed to the eyes of the son of Jesse that which had been hidden from him by the going down of the sun—a white shoulder bone half-covered by a grizzled beard—an eyeless face and a cloud of pale-brown hair. Then the horror was taken from him. They had covered it with the folds of the banners, and tenderly, in the folds of the banners, they gathered it up and laid it upon the broad sill. There they bound it into something removed from mortality—white linen marked with the insignia of the defeated tribes of Israel—and raised it upon their shoulders and carried it down the winding ramp.

So it was not given to the son of Jesse to reclaim the bodies of his brother and his lord. It was the men of Jabesh-Gilead who reclaimed them and bore them out of Beth-Shan and carried them without pause across the hill country, even unto that town where Saul had come as a savior in the vigor of his youth. At the gate of their city they made a great pyre of such wood as they had by them, and they burned the glory of the House of Kish upon it, casting thyme and myrrh and aloes into the flame and making loud lamentation throughout a day and a night. Then they gathered the bones out of the ashes and folded them in linen and buried them in the high place of Jabesh-Gilead, beneath the sacred tamarisk. For here, they said, he stood among us in the days of our deliverance and his triumph. And they anointed his grave with their sour wine and their tears.

BOOK EIGHT

BOOK EIGHT

❧ I ❧

IF THE captain of the host had been slain along with his lord in the
mountains of Gilboa, the seed of Kish would have passed completely from
the annals of Israel. Only Abner would have sought for another king
among the fragments of that shattered house. None save the captain would
have closed his eyes to the clear intention of the Lord. For never had a
single family suffered so many afflictions. Four had been laid low in battle
in one day, and those who remained among the living were scarcely more
fortunate than the dead.

Even the most ardent partisans of the House of Saul had come to accept
the fact that Michal was barren; two husbands had failed to raise up seed
by her; invocations and sacrifices had been vainly made for her in twelve
temples and thirty high places. Mara, the wife of Jonathan, had been
delivered of one fair but sickly son. From the hour of his birth, she had
never risen from her bed; and on the day when Israel went forth to the
final stand against Philistia, she had turned her face against the wall and
died. Her little one, Meribaal, might have been crowned, in spite of
his frailty, for his father's sake. But during the black hours when the
remnants of Saul's family fled out of Gibeah before the armies of the
uncircumcised, Jahveh had stricken the child from his nurse's arms and
cast him upon the paving stones, so that he was lamed in both his feet.

As for Ishbaal, the last of the sons of Saul and Ahinoam, he had barely
reached his twentieth year when the cataclysm descended upon Israel. In
the first chaotic months after Gilboa, the men of Ephraim and Benjamin
had almost forgotten him. They lamented that the sons of Saul and
Rizpah—vigorous and black-bearded men—were illegitimate and could not
wear the crown. For no one had ever dreamed that the youngest child
would reign. All his days he had been slow-witted and shy, such a one
as leans upon others, never willing to set up a household for himself. But
Abner had not forgotten him. Abner had gone up to the house of Michal
and Paltiel and had led the young man thence, crowned and anointed, to
the city of Mahanaim, a stronghold on the eastern side of the Jordan,

where those who had survived Gilboa had found a resting-place. "Behold the King of Israel," Abner said, taking him by the hand and presenting him to the scarred and disillusioned host. And they had smiled a wry smile to behold him. Pale and soft and solemn, given to staring and to pausing long before he uttered the most insignificant word, forever tormented by foolish fears—the youngest of Saul's sons had seemed a sorry one to wear his father's crown.

And yet once the deed was done, a kind of ghostly peace settled upon them. They made a shadowy home for themselves in the strange land. It was true that there was no sense of permanence in the life they led in Mahanaim. They knew that they held the town by the sufferance of David, who ruled in the south, and the Serens, who had occupied Manasseh, Ephraim, and Benjamin. Some day an army would march out of the south or the west and raze the wall; some day the torches of the invaders would consume the arbors and the houses. But meanwhile it was mildly pleasant to sit in a daze all day upon these unfamiliar slopes, to plan a garden, to tell again the tales of Michmash and Jabesh-Gilead, to let old wounds bake in the heat of the sun. The world that they inhabited now was a world of dreams and silences; it could not be otherwise; it was a world shaped by the hands of an ancient captain and a dull-witted youth. Like old men and children, they lived peacefully within it, rising late, inventing games to pass the heavy hours, caring less for what came to pass in Israel than for the roast kid that was to be eaten with the evening bread.

Only the endless and meaningless councils were burdensome to them. There was nothing to discuss; yet the King and the captain would keep them at the council table until the setting of the moon. One council was much like another. At some point in the discussion, Abner would say, "Let us keep peace in Israel at any cost," and Ishbaal would be sure to break in at least twice to indicate that he wished to see a wrestling match on the following night. During the first year of their exile, it amused the men of Mahanaim to refer to their King as "Wrestling-Match" and to their captain as "Peace-At-Any-Cost." But before twelve moons had passed, the jest had lost its savor. The men of Mahanaim, like their captain and their King, had come to think that nothing on earth was so dear as peace, or so significant as the wrestling match which would be held tomorrow night.

For three years the host of Jahveh dwelt in Mahanaim on the eastern side of the Jordan. They had ceased to call themselves the host of God. To the south and west of them, in the plains around Hebron, another army, young and undefeated, had inherited that name. As Samuel had prophesied, Jahveh had gone out of Benjamin and Ephraim to hover over the black tents of the Judahites. But there were certain compensations. Those who had survived Gilboa became good carpenters, good gardeners, excellent tellers of tales. They kept the peace scrupulously, for the sake of themselves and their captain, and they wrestled for the delight of Ishbaal every third night.

Come in now, old woman," Abner called from the threshold of his house. "Tomorrow you will be complaining again that a devil out of the evening has crept into your bones."

Rizpah did not answer him at once; but even though she was screened from him by boughs veiled in new green, he could sense her slow smile. His garden, like all the gardens in Mahanaim, seemed insubstantial, impermanent. Tonight he could not quite believe in his garden, or in the serene and opulent figure that sat on a bench at the end of it. Evening after evening during these last three years he had come forth to call her in. Yet he had never lost the wonder of it. He had never ceased to say in his heart, Jahveh has indeed given her to me, after all the waiting. She who will come now to sit down by the hearth with me is the same woman whom once I dared not touch. . . .

For out of the fire that had consumed the glory of Israel one man at least had taken his happiness. Not that he had not mourned. He had mourned bitterly through twelve moons, both for Israel and for the beloved dead. While their bones remained in Jabesh-Gilead beneath the tamarisk, he had gone down three times to stand at their graves; and when the son of Jesse decreed that the bones should be carried to the burial cave in the Gibean garden, he had wept aloud and clothed himself again in hairy cloth; for Gibeah was a long journey from Mahanaim, too long a journey for an old man who had an idle army on his hands and was forever fearful lest they break the peace. . . . But slowly it was borne in upon him that the world remained, though the pride of Israel had departed from it. Slowly he learned, and rejoiced to learn it, that, though the hosts went forth no more, there was still the sowing and the reaping, the summer and the winter, the rising and the setting of the sun. And into this new-found world, into a house new-built and still fragrant with the smell of the living wood, he led his dead lord's concubine.

At first they were constrained and solemn all day long, and by night they slept lightly, each keeping to an opposite side of the bed. At table, the meat grew cold while they held long, uneasy, empty conversations. It is not as I dreamed it would be, he said in his heart. The magic that was upon her when she was Saul's has gone forth from her now. . . . And yet there were certain moments when the magic returned and his heart yearned over her—moments when he wakened at night and saw her soft, still face in moonlight, moments when he sat beside her on the edge of the bed and watched her unbind her graying hair.

It was the coming of the seven tall sons of Saul that restored them to each other. Some three months after the marriage, the young men journeyed up to Mahanaim to show the captain that they bore no grudge against him, that they rejoiced to see their mother a first wife at last. From the moment they crossed the threshold and shattered the stillness with their loud talk and louder laughter, there was no longer any place in Abner's house for shyness and solemnity. Their way with Rizpah was jocular and boisterous. They pinched her cheeks and flung their arms around her shoulders, and surely her husband could do no less. Their talk was familiar and not entirely free from rudeness. "How is it with you, old woman," one of them said, "that you cannot make a decent loaf of bread? My wife bakes better bread than this, even though she is no more than a child." And that same night, when the fire on the hearth had fallen to embers; Abner rose among them and turned to her and said: "Come now, old woman, I find myself very tired. Come with me, that I may have the warmth and comfort of you beside me in our bed."

Abner grew very unwilling to have them depart. Perhaps, he thought, we will be constrained again when they are gone. . . . But when the last of them had stepped over the threshold, he saw that these were groundless fears. She turned to him then and laid her cool arms around his neck and kissed him full on the lips. "It was pleasant to see them come," she said, "and it is equally pleasant to see them depart. Now we will enjoy our house in peace." And such peace as he had never known before descended upon him.

They had learned to dwell comfortably with each other. They had learned also that it is sometimes good to be alone. Her thoughts turned often toward the grave of Saul; twice or thrice he had caught her weeping; and he was glad that he could not find it in his heart to begrudge the dead King his rightful measure of tears. So in the cool of the evening he released her to the garden and to her remembrances. Meanwhile he would sit at the table, recalling old battles or considering what was to be said tomorrow in council.

But when the last ray of sun had gone out upon the sill, he went to the door of his house. . . . Israel lay prostrate under the yoke of the Philistines. Saul and Jonathan, Malchishua and Abinadab, lay in the cave where Ahinoam slept, and the honor of the House of Kish lay buried with their bones. A shadowy King ruled over a shadowy army in an outpost town whose name had been a laughingstock in the days when the Lion of Benjamin ruled the land. And yet, and yet . . . There she sat at the end of his bare little garden, and his heart was light within him, and he could not chide himself into grief.

"Come in now, old woman," he called from the threshold.

She arose and came and lifted up her face for his kiss.

As they walked in together hand in hand, he knew that the legendary bird that he had sought in his childhood in the hills around Gibeah had floated down to him, had folded its wings and settled at last against his breast.

❧ III ❧

WHEN David of Bethlehem entered Hebron to be crowned King over Judah and Caleb and the land of the Kenites, he was a wealthy man in spite of himself. Three times the value of the loot that he had taken from the men of the south was rendered back to him. Achish paid him the price of a king's ransom for his services in Ziklag; the Bedouin King of Geshur, eager to keep the peace, gave him a fair daughter named Maacah and a dowry of four hundred camels; the people of Judah presented him with a high house in Hebron, twelve fat fields, and seven orchards; and the Calebites and Kenites sent him herds and flocks as numerous as those that had belonged to Abraham.

While the army of Abner and Ishbaal languished for three years in Mahanaim, the host of David prospered in the plains around Hebron. The black tents of the captains over hundreds and the captains over thousands stood in an always broadening circle around the city. The young men of the north soon grew weary of the yoke of Philistia and came down to take their swords and shields from Joab's hand; and even the Jebusites, entrenched since the beginning of time in their near-by fortress of Jerusalem at the very navel of Israel, began to cast uneasy glances at the splendid warriors who practiced archery and the throwing of the spear within sight of their walls.

Within the portals of the high house in Hebron also, Jahveh accomplished much for David's sake. The womb of Abigail was opened at last. She brought forth a son, and this was considered a good omen, even though the little one died before his eyes had beheld one setting of the sun. Maacah, the Princess of Geshur, had been with her lord no more than ten moons when she bore twins, a girl named Tamar and a boy named Absalom. Then a fourth wife, a young woman of Hebron named Haggith, the high-born daughter of a great family of the city, sickened in her father's house and made it known at last that she was heavy with David's child. The Star of Bethlehem was gallant. He did not deny it. There had been a certain evening when he had come to consult her father on a matter of business, and none had been in the house save the young woman, and they had walked together in the garden. The fruit within her womb was certainly royal. He rejoiced to acknowledge it. He led her up to his house to dwell among the others, and none save Noi—who had also brought forth in her day not too long after her marriage feast—could resist the delight of heaping subtle insults upon her poor, proud head. But her lord would look at her across the long table without flushing. He would say to her, "You are quite as fair as you seemed to me in your father's house, my girl." And when she bore him a son, he called the boy Adonijah, to show all Judah that he considered the whole matter a blessing sent from God.

Of the four wives who dwelt with David in Hebron, only Noi had no swaddling clothes to make. Yet she was happier in that city than she had been since the days when she dwelt with her brothers in the wilderness. While the others were occupied with bearing and suckling, the business of the house and the fields and the orchards fell almost completely into her hands. David looked to the herds and the flocks, and Abigail tended the garden. But all the rest—the gathering of the fruit, the making of the oil and the wine, the sowing and the reaping of the grain—was Noi's province, and, with the help of Abishai, she administered it well. In time it came about also that she tended all four of the children. Not that she raised a finger to draw any of the little ones to her; she was satisfied in Amnon and would have been more likely to rob a man of his gold on the highway than to come between a mother and her child. But Haggith was young and unsure of herself, and was forever laying the infant Adonijah in Noi's lap; and the Princess of Geshur spent as much time in her father's household as in her own. Every spring a fit of restlessness came upon the Bedouin woman; she wept so often that David bade her go up to the hairy tents of her people and tarry there for several moons. She always left Tamar and Absalom behind her, begging Noi to tend them well. So the little Jezreelitess was constantly surrounded by children; and the ambassadors who came to dwell in the court at Hebron believed at first that she was the fertile wife and treated her with a marked respect that they could not gracefully abandon after they had discovered their mistake.

Early in the third summer of the sojourn in Hebron, it came into Noi's mind to journey down to the orchards to watch the gathering of the first fruits. Every year the overseer of the orchards asked that some member of David's family be present when the first pomegranates were plucked. For the gathering was a sacred occasion. The best fruit was packed into great wicker baskets and carried to the temple in Hebron to be presented to the Lord. Noi would have liked to go down alone this time. David had journeyed to Gath with Abigail to spend seven days with Achish, and Maacah was off to her people's hairy tents again. But Haggith, who was nursing Adonijah, made it plain that she was afraid to dwell alone in the house with so young a child. So Noi and Haggith journeyed down together, with all the children. They rode in a wagon drawn by a dappled donkey and half-filled with the wicker baskets that were to be taken up to the tabernacle. Amnon, a tall lad of six, sat with the driver. Adonijah slept on a pillow in one of the baskets. The twins, Tamar and Absalom, sat on the floor of the wagon and played with two dolls, exactly alike, which had been sent to them by the King of Moab.

It was said that Jahveh had never before created such beautiful children as Tamar and Absalom. Even though they had scarcely passed their second birthday, the round shapelessness of infancy had already gone from them. They were dark, and they seemed the darker because they were always dressed in tunics of austere white linen. Their faces were precise and expressive under the thick masses of black ringlets that curled over their foreheads; the line of their lips was as clean as the line of a leaf; whoever touched them—and there were few who could resist the longing to touch them—felt, beneath the apricot softness of their flesh, the delicate structure of their bones. Yet there was always something wounding in their presence; they made it plain to all who fondled them and waited upon them that they loved each other and merely tolerated the rest of the world.

Only Noi did not plague them with futile courtship. If they were dirty and made it known that they thought themselves dirty, she washed them. If they were caught in a hedge of thorn and asked for help, she pulled them free. It was not that she was proof against their dark sorcery; it was only that she had encountered inaccessible beauty once before and had learned that the salvation of the rejected lies in passiveness. And she was glad that her son Amnon sat with the driver during the journey, for if he had remained inside the wagon he would surely have thrust his attentions upon them.

The four hours of the journey were pleasant and uneventful. Of all David's wives, Haggith burdened Noi with the greatest number of cares and gave her the least pain. For the young woman who had dwelt in the luxury of one of the wealthiest houses in Hebron had been bred so tenderly that there was no malice in her. She clung to Noi, and Noi counseled her and tended her and defended her against the others.

So it was not burdensome to Noi to have her for company on the way to the orchards. It was even possible to take pleasure in her beauty: her smooth brown hair parted at the middle of her brow, her pale, urban skin, her long, fine neck, forever thrust forward in an attitude of humility and attentiveness. She kept a smiling silence because she knew that Noi wanted quiet; when she suckled the infant Adonijah, she veiled the white fullness of her breast lest it should be an offense to Noi's eyes; she leaned forward only twice or thrice to pass her hand across the irresistible curls of Tamar and Absalom. And when they came to the end of the journey, she greeted the wife of the overseer of the orchards as though she were being presented to some great lady of Hebron. She praised the house and gave earnest thanks for the compliments which the fat and flustered woman poured out upon her little one.

Noi remained in the overseer's house only so long as courtesy required. She ate and commended the food that had been prepared for the visitors; but her heart yearned after the long, cool avenues of trees. I will lie down, she thought, and pretend that I am asleep. Then they will leave me in peace, and I can remember whatever I choose. She yawned into the face of the overseer's wife, and rubbed her eyes.

"My lady is worn with the journey," the good woman said. "Let her come and lie a while upon one of the beds."

"No," she answered in haste, "I will lie down, but under the trees. Let the lady Haggith lie upon the bed, for it is not good that a nursing mother should have too much sun. As for the little ones, Tamar and Absalom, they will do well enough if they are left to themselves, and Adonijah can lie beside his mother, and my lad can go with the driver to see the donkey watered and fed. I will go on to the orchard."

"Then," said the wife of the overseer, "let me go down with my lady Noi——"

But the gentle Haggith forestalled her by begging her help with the bathing of the infant, for she had seen that Noi wished to be alone.

The laborers spread a carpet and a pillow for her beneath a lordly tree. They made a little pyramid of figs at her elbow and brought her a water cruet and a cup. "And if there is any other wish that comes into the thoughts of my lady," the tallest of them said, "let her but lift up her voice."

She nodded very gravely, setting her mouth into a prim line. Another wish had come into her thoughts, such a wish as might sting any modest woman into austerity. She had wished that the lean brown youth would draw her to him and set his lips against her lips. "Surely I am well served and need nothing," she said. They bowed and went their way, and she stared after them, telling herself, It is nothing, it is the turn of the year. In a week, when the first bloom is gone from the fruit, it will pass. . . . And she turned her thoughts to the time when David had come down to her out of Beth-shan.

She saw around her again the roofless pillars of the house in Ziklag. She felt again the tension of long waiting and the oppressive heat of that summer night. Then, in the light of the single torch that burned against a pillar, she saw the Star of Bethlehem, and barely knew that it was he. Filthy and so wasted with fever that his bones seemed to strain outward against his flesh, he crossed the threshold of the unfinished house and knelt before her and wept against her knees.

It was I that he wanted then, she thought. It was to me alone that he whispered in his delirium about the torn flesh and the birds of prey and the face without eyes. I know what none of the others know—not Abigail, not Maacah, not Haggith. I know that it is a shadowy and useless business to struggle for the possession of his heart. His heart is for none of us. It lies in the burial cave with Jonathan. . . .

Night after night she had lain wakeful beside him on the bed, and sometimes he had reached out and laid his hand upon her, lightly, guilelessly, even as in her sleep she laid her hand upon the child. And I wanted nothing more, she told herself. I was satisfied. If he rose up one morning and sent after Abigail, surely it was no unexpected blow upon my heart. And if he is King in Judah and has taken two fair wives to raise up seed to the throne, that cannot shatter my peace. He was mine, I possessed him in the hour of his grief, nor has there been any that possessed him more fully than I, save only Jonathan. . . .

Far off, in some other part of the big orchard, the young men had begun to sing one of the festival songs in praise of Jahveh, the Giver of all fruit. Now there was nothing troubling in the thought of these youths. She took from her arm a bracelet that David had brought up to her from Gath, and laid it under her cheek, and almost slept. . . .

"My lady Noi," Haggith said.

She had come in the manner of the daughters of the high houses of Hebron, on careful and noiseless feet. Her voice was so quiet and humble that it turned away any wrath that might have risen over her intrusion. Noi raised herself on her elbow and looked at the mild comer, who carried her infant with one arm and shepherded the twins before her with the other.

"My lady Noi, the little one is all covered with red spots. The wife of the overseer says that it is nothing, that it is so with all infants who lie in the sun. But I am inexperienced in these matters, and until I had the judgment of my friend I could not rest."

Noi took the infant and patiently examined the little points of red upon its belly. "The wife of the overseer knows whereof she speaks. It is only a little prickly heat, brought out by the sun."

And now, she thought, go up to the house and let me be. . . . But the young woman did not move, only took the proffered child and stood staring at the ground. Her lips said nothing, but her gentle eyes said, Permit me to stay, let me tarry with you until all my fears are gone. . . .

Noi sighed. "Come then and sit with me and hear the young men sing," she said.

Tamar and Absalom had already seated themselves upon the grass. They no longer had their dolls, but they had begun at once to pick up the leaves that had fallen from the shaken boughs. Each laid a pile of leaves in the lap of the other, and now and then their dark and glowing faces almost met, and they smiled.

Haggith sat down on the edge of the carpet on which Noi lay. "It is a fine day for the gathering," she said.

But if you must speak, thought Noi, then speak at least of some matter that is worth the mentioning. . . .

"What a pity," said Haggith, "that our lord did not come down with us."

The young woman turned to her baby and made much of him, pressing her lips against the soft folds of flesh under his chin. But the baby was vexed by the prickly heat and whimpered and turned aside. She bent forward then and gathered leaves and offered them to the boy Absalom. He took them out of her hand without touching her fingers and scattered them upon the ground. The gentle eyes grew bright with restrained tears.

Child, child, thought Noi, it was an unfortunate time for you when he led you into your father's garden. When will you learn that the war for the son of Jesse is to no purpose and has no prize? . . .

"Listen," said Haggith in a tremulous voice, "the young men have begun another song."

I must find her a comforter, Noi thought. Jahveh gave me a comforter in Abishai. Many times I would have been pointed out as the rejected one who has only children by her if Abishai had not stood at my side. And if I, who bear the harsh strength of the soil of Judah in my blood—if I need a comforter, how much greater is her need than mine, seeing that she is an only daughter upon whom all the household waited, of whom all the city said, "How gracious she is, and how fair!" . . .

"Does my lady Noi know what it is they are singing?"

She started. She had not been listening. In her search for a comforter, her thoughts had settled upon the third son of Zeruiah, a youth who had come only three weeks since to David's court, a lithe and comely boy named Asahel. But there would be danger in that, she thought. There would be a ripple of fire beneath their words and looks. He also is a child, and indulgent toward whatever yearnings he feels within him. Besides, he is too like his eldest brother—another wily son of Ishmael. . . .

"Let Haggith forgive me," she said. "I barely heard the song. I am dull today and half-asleep."

The mild voice had grown even more tremulous. "I will go up to the house then and take the children with me, that my lady Noi may rest."

"Indeed you shall not." She bent forward and embraced the young woman and kissed her cool cheek. "Why should I sleep? We will all of us sleep long enough in our graves. There are many matters of which I would speak with Haggith, and——"

She fell silent, for she had seen the little Amnon walking toward them. He came up slowly, kicking the fallen leaves before him. He was too slight to bear gracefully the marks of favor that David had put upon him; the broad bracelets hung loose on his arms, the necklace lay heavy upon his collarbones, and the sandals were too richly embroidered to suit his thin, dark feet.

"Are you tired of the donkey?" Noi asked him. "Come, sit by me, and I will give you a fig, and perhaps Haggith will let you hold the little one."

He stood before her, holding out his hand. "Give me two figs," he said.

"Surely, but wherefore?"

"One for Tamar, and the other for Absalom."

She looked at him with stern displeasure in her eyes. She hated his reverent manner of naming the two children of Maacah.

"Let them alone," she said coldly. "They make it plain enough that they have no need of you. When will you learn to let them be?"

Haggith lifted up her round white arm and laid it about his waist. "Come," she said, "sit by Adonijah."

And her voice also was painful to Noi. It was as if she had said, "Let the fruit of the womb of Noi stand with the fruit of the womb of Haggith against these children of the desert, who are fair enough to outshine any child who stands alone." . . .

"Give me the figs," he said stolidly, moving out of the arc of the young woman's arm.

"Let him learn, then," said Noi. "Let him see how they want none of his figs. Let him learn it for himself." And she snatched up a handful of the fruit and crushed it into his palm.

She turned her face aside then because she did not wish to be a witness to his foredoomed disgrace. Even as she turned, she saw a vision of herself standing at the table in her brothers' house, peeling the brown inner skins from the almonds to make them white and fine for David, who sat feasting under their roof that night. "No, now," one of her brothers had said, "why should you peel the almonds? He wants no almonds. Let him alone." Nevertheless . . . Plainly, so plainly that she could see the gray, preoccupied, courteous eyes turn briefly upon her and turn aside, she remembered how she had brought him the almonds, nevertheless. . . . Fool, fool, beggar and fool, she thought, and knew not whether she heaped these taunts upon herself or upon her son. For Amnon knelt stricken before Tamar, who had swept the figs onto the grass with her delicate, cruel hand.

She should have gone to comfort him, but the wherewithal for comfort was not in her. There was nothing in her but a fierce protest against the child, herself, and the whole intolerable world. "Have you learned, then?" she shouted to the kneeling boy. "Will you come away from them and let them alone?"

He did not stir. He knelt, shaken and staring, before the little Tamar, and his eyes were big with self-inflicted suffering. She rose and flew at him and struck him across the mouth. He sat back upon his heels and covered his face and wept.

"My lady Noi!" Haggith said.

"My lady Haggith!" She said it in bitter mockery, so that the delicate accents of the high houses of Hebron were made ridiculous upon her tongue.

But the young woman either did not hear or refused to believe what she had heard. "How is it with my friend," she said, "that, for the sake of a desert brat, she should strike him who is to be King in Israel?"

King in Israel—she had forgotten that. . . . She strove now to see him with Haggith's eyes, but she could not bring herself to believe in his royalty. The anklets and bracelets of copper and gold, the girdle of many colors that only the eldest of the King's house might wear, the circlet of bright ribbon—forerunner of a crown—that hung to one side in his disordered curls—these were the dreams, and the frail, ineffectual child beneath them was the reality.

"Indeed," said Haggith, "I think the milk has dried in my breasts from sheer amazement. I have never seen Noi so moved to anger before."

"It was not anger," she said, flushing. "It was shame. When the child turns beggar, how can I do otherwise than blush for his sake?"

"But how should such a little one know what is cause for shame? Look, now, how he weeps."

Noi went to him then and lifted him up. She dried his cheeks and set the circlet straight upon his head, and made him sit beside her under the tree. He soon grew quiet and fell to watching the young men at work. They were finished with the gathering now; they knelt in a circle upon the grass, filling the wicker baskets with the finest of the fruit. The afternoon was almost spent; the eastern rim of the sky had begun to pale. My fair green day is gone, she thought. And yet there is still an hour before the evening bread. Perhaps we will sit quietly here. Perhaps I can still salvage an hour of peace. . . .

But Haggith had grown sorrowful again. She rested her head against the trunk of the tree and sighed. "Would I were in Gath," she said.

"Gath is a wearisome place."

"But I have never beheld it. Why is it always Abigail who is chosen to go up to the house of the Seren with our lord?"

ᴗᴗ IV ᴖᴖ

Tʜᴇ ᴅᴀʏ which Noi and Haggith had spent idly in the orchards had been a day crowded with business for Joab. Before the breaking of the noonday bread, he had been called up from the encampment by the steward of David's house. An ambassador had come from Phoenicia on his way down to Egypt; he must be received with honor, even though he had come unannounced; since the King was in Gath, his nephew must take his place. Through the remainder of the morning and most of the afternoon, Joab had sat in conversation with the ambassador in the common room of David's house, listening with only half an ear to the usual formalities, and wondering all the while when the curled and perfumed nuisance would rise up and depart. Then it had dawned upon him that this Phoenician was making a tour from Syria to Egypt to bear the greetings of the lords of Tyre and Sidon to the rulers of the south. Perhaps he had also paused to pay respects in Mahanaim. Perhaps it would be possible to learn from him certain details that might be passed on to David concerning the weakness of Abner's host.

The son of Zeruiah lolled in his chair, and asked in a casual voice whether the respected son of the goddess Atargatis had come down from Syria on the eastern side of the Jordan. Had he passed through any cities on that side? Succoth—Jabesh-Gilead—Mahanaim?

The Phoenician flushed a little and toyed with the end of his beard. Much as he blushed for it before a man of the House of Jesse, he must admit that he had stopped at Mahanaim at the express request of the lords of Sidon and Tyre. Not that they felt any great warmth toward the old warrior and the ineffectual young man who called themselves captain and King there, but merely because courtesy and ancient custom demanded it. In the old days, before Saul had united the tribes, it had been the policy of Phoenicia to call upon all the Israelite lords. . . .

Certainly, certainly, Joab said. And had the ambassador tarried in Mahanaim long?

Not long, no. Only long enough to deliver the greetings, to see a wrestling match, and to witness the preparation for a journey that Abner meant to make with half his troops. . . .

A journey?

Yes, a kind of journey, a pilgrimage, to be more precise—a little pilgrimage down to the pools of Gibeon, in which they meant to cleanse themselves for some festival or other. . . .

366

The Feast of the First Fruits?

Indeed, indeed, the captain of the host had taken the name of that world-renowned festival from the very tip of his tongue.

Joab stared at the top of a polished table and saw instead the pools of Gibeon gleaming through the leaves, saw half the host of Abner, naked and helpless, immersed to their waists, saw his own host—no, a mere handful of his own host—moving with drawn bows through the thick foliage. One command—a few rounds of arrows—that would be all that was necessary to make the son of Jesse King over all Israel.

For a long time after the Phoenician had gone forth, Joab remained standing in the middle of the room, staring at the chair on the hearth. It was as if the King of Judah were sitting there and fixing a gray and solemn look upon him.

David's presence was comely still, but austere and self-contained. The face, the body, the long, lean hands and feet, were spare and hard; little was left to hide the tendons and the bones. God had put ten years upon the head of the son of Jesse within a single moon. There was a streak of white in the lock that hung over his brow; his eyelids had grown red and raw; the peerless symmetry of his face had been marred by the scar that ran slantwise across his cheek; his mouth had dried like a plucked flower left lying in the sun. To think that such a man could be maneuvered against his will into a struggle with Abner was an illusion.

No, thought the son of Zeruiah, I cannot say to him, "Give me six or seven hundred to go up to Gibeon and smite the house of Kish." There are certain matters that may not be mentioned in this house: Saul and Jonathan, the city of Nob, chariots and steeds out of Egypt—even though the host of Jahveh would be seven times as strong for a hundred horses and twenty chariots. Mahanaim and those who dwell therein are also not to be mentioned. Asahel spoke of them once, and the King turned such a look upon him as left him frightened for days. If we are to meet the army of Ishbaal and Abner beside the holy pools, we must meet them there by chance. . . .

By chance. . . . It would be possible to convince the son of Jesse that such a journey had been made by chance. None save the son of Zeruiah had heard the ambassador say that the army of the north was coming down to visit the pools of Gibeon. It was by chance that Ishbaal's men were traveling down; they had suffered some accidental pollution and must cleanse themselves in holy waters before the Feast of the First Fruits. Some of the men of David, a hundred or two hundred, must also be made unclean, must eat forbidden meat or lie with a leprous woman.

A leprous woman. . . . There was a certain Canaanite harlot who dwelt near the southern gate of the city; she was whey-faced and languorous with plying her trade every night; many in the host had visited her; he had visited her upon occasion himself. If it were possible to say that she was leprous and to be believed . . . But who should say it? Who but his brother Asahel? He called the steward of David's house to him. He was

367

weary, he said, and had no wish to journey down to the encampment. It would please him to break the evening bread in David's house. And since he found it burdensome to dine alone, he would put the steward to the trouble of sending a servant down to the camp to bring up the young Asahel.

He was troubled also that he must depend upon the discretion of Asahel. The youth would be certain to sense that there was more to the business than uncleanness and purification. He was never willing to take the word at its face value. Surely, thought Joab, he will try to worm out of me what he ought not to know; I must guard my tongue. . . .

Two servants entered the room and began to lay the table for the evening bread. He closed his eyes against them, and strove to see how a battle could come to pass, by chance, between two armies met at a holy pool to cleanse themselves. We must take no arms, he told himself, save the short daggers which even a pilgrim may carry to guard himself against violence. But it is one matter to smite the host of Abner from a distance with spears and arrows, and quite another to attack them with daggers, face to face. Who knows whether an occasion will arise? Perhaps Abner will withdraw when he beholds us, leaving us only an unnecessary purification for all our pains. . . .

"My lord," said one of the servants, "the steward of the house bade me say that he regrets there is only the meat of yesterday's kid, which he will make as palatable as he can with a savory sauce."

Joab did not answer. He snapped his fingers and started halfway out of his chair. A wrestling match, he thought, did not the Phoenician speak of a wrestling match? Well, then, we will give them a wrestling match that will put an end to all the wrestling. . . .

"However," said the servant, "there is an excellent melon also, and there will be new bread."

"Set the meat forth as soon as my brother is come," Joab called after him. "Set it forth and depart. We are warriors and can serve ourselves."

He lolled in the chair. He need no longer grope after a plan. God had given it to him. God would make the son of Jesse King in Israel in spite of his fool's devotion to the House of Kish. In the cool of the evening, by the pools of Gibeon, the two armies would sit down face to face. And he, Joab, would arise and say to the old man, "Come, now that our sins are washed from us, let us be merry. Let us have a wrestling match and pit the young men of Mahanaim against the young men of Hebron."

Asahel was at least discreet enough to ask no questions before servants. He wandered around the room, doing all that propriety had not permitted on other occasions; he fingered the stuff of draperies; he lifted the bowls and boxes on the tables and examined their undersurfaces and their insides. All the while he kept up an easy chatter that relieved his elder brother of the obligation to speak. But when the servants were gone, he fell silent.

"It is no light matter that I would lay before my brother," said the captain, serving out the savory kid and disciplining his face into somberness. "Let him prepare his heart. He and I and more than a hundred of the host may well be unclean and in danger of leprosy."

The lad sat very erect and opened his large eyes. "How should we be in danger of leprosy?"

"The harlot out of Canaan, she that dwells beside the southern gate of the city—she is stricken. Her face was always pale, as my brother may remember. But now her hands and the soles of her feet have turned as white as snow."

"Not truly?" said the youth. All the glow fled out of his cheeks, and he raised his hands from his lap and stared at them.

Something—perhaps tenderness for the young brother so like himself, perhaps the sight of the death fear upon a beardless face—something disarmed the captain of the host. He made an involuntary sound that might have been taken for either a cough or a laugh. He served the meat energetically and bent his head to hide his own eyes. "It is nothing," he said. "All that is necessary is that we go up to the pools of Gibeon to wash ourselves. Once we are washed, we will be strong against the leprosy."

Asahel's red, ripe lips stirred against each other, striving to suppress a smile. In a moment of childish pity, Joab thought, I have betrayed myself. . . .

"What is it," said Asahel, "that my brother goes to seek at the pools of Gibeon—he and I and a hundred of the host?"

"Purification, even as I said."

"No, now, she is not truly leprous, the harlot by the gate."

"She is indeed."

"I am not deceived. Let my brother tell me what he means to bring to pass."

Annoyance was useless. Joab bent across the table and rubbed his hand over the boy's thick mop of curls. "Seeing that you have found me out, I cannot do otherwise than be plain with you. She is not leprous, but I would have the warriors think her so," he said.

Asahel sat quiet for a moment. Then he smiled. "Let my brother permit me to guess who it is that we will meet by the pools of Gibeon."

If he lights upon the truth, Joab thought, then the truth is easy to find, and another man may find it also, even my lord. . . .

"Abner!" said Asahel. "It is Abner who will be in Gibeon—he and a goodly part of Ishbaal's host. We will smite them at the pools."

"Even so." And yet, he thought, it is not so brave a business as it was an hour hence. I must march up with whatever the harlot gives me, leaving my bows and spears behind. As for you, stripling—you must go up with the rest. . . .

"It is a very good tale—the tale about the harlot," Asahel said. "Fear will come upon them, and they will not even question the matter. I will take five or six stupid ones with me and go up to her house and drive her into the wilderness. Then, when the son of Jesse returns out of Gath, she will be beyond all questioning. But where is our brother Abishai this night?"

Joab smiled. The lad saw all eventualities. He knew that if Abishai should hear of the business, there would be justice even for the harlot at the gate. "Abishai is gone forth to the fields in the north to oversee the gathering of the first crop of wheat."

"Then we are secure indeed."

"No, now, let my brother not deceive himself. We are not secure. Since we will go up as pilgrims, we will have no arms save daggers upon us. No man has ever bought a kingdom at no price at all."

The boy shrugged, and munched at the melon he was eating. His cheek was warm and soft against the pale rind.

"Before we arise and go forth from this house," said Joab, "I would make a covenant with Asahel."

"What covenant?" The big, luminous eyes were scornful of all covenants.

"Let Asahel swear to me that he will remain always in the rear of the host. He has not gone into battle before. . . ."

The flat and shining look of false sincerity—that look which he himself had so often turned upon the son of Jesse—rose now in his young brother's eyes. "Behold," said Asahel, "I am Joab's. I know my brother's wisdom and my own foolishness. I will be in the rear of the host, even as my brother desires."

"Swear it."

Asahel shrugged. "I swear it," he said. "Before God, I swear it." And he spat out a melon seed and sent it across his plate with his fingertip.

◄§ V §►

From the moment when the matter was broached to him, Abner protested against the pilgrimage to Gibeon. If his host had suffered from real uncleanness—if there had been any leprosy or contact with dead bodies or spilling of innocent blood—he would have led them to the waters willingly enough. But the particular uncleanness from which they professed themselves to be suffering was so questionable that he could only believe that they had spun it out of their own fancies. They were not unclean; they were merely restless with the monotony of their days.

Every summer of their sojourn in Mahanaim, this same restlessness had stirred their blood. The first year they had soothed it by making gardens; the second year they had taken to Canaanite women. This year they had lighted upon uncleanness. Some fool among them had spoken to the Canaanite who herded the flocks, and had come back to the city with a tale that the herdsman was a sorcerer and that all the goats were possessed.

The Canaanite, so the tale ran, had a flute with which he conjured the Baals and Astartes out of brooks and trees. He played strange, lively tunes to the goats and the gods and the goddesses; they leaped about the meadow in the moonlight, all together, in a kind of demoniac ecstasy. And he did not send the divinities back into their proper places. He forced them to jump down the throats of the beasts, where they continued to dwell. Whosoever in the host had eaten the meat of one of his flock was in grave danger of having eaten a heathen god.

Abner reported this childish stuff to Ishbaal, much as in the old days he would have reported it to Saul, with an amused smile. But where Saul would have laughed aloud, Ishbaal merely stared. The young man had always been superstitious, had picked up lucky pebbles and worn Horus eyes. It did not seem to him at all unlikely that the gods should leap down the throats of the beasts.

"Let the captain of the host go down with them to Gibeon," he had said. "Whether they are clean or unclean, it can do them no harm to lave themselves."

Abner had reasons of his own for wishing to remain in Mahanaim. Within three or four days, he thought, Michal will come up to Mahanaim with Paltiel, to dwell in the house of the King until the Feast of the First Fruits. And I would be here to behold her, I would see the shadow of Saul's smile upon her lips. Nor is it a small thing to ask such a one as I to go down and cast his clothes aside and stand naked among young men whose bodies are still whole and fair. Rizpah has forgiven my body for the sake of the love that dwells within it. But to those who have seen me only in the panoply of battle, I will be a sorry sight. . . .

He had yet one other reason for wishing to remain in Mahanaim. A strange and womanish fear had come into Rizpah's head; she kept saying that the host of David might also come to the pool; she insisted that he break the holy prohibitions by carrying at least his spear. He could not consider this fright of hers with any gravity. It was extremely unlikely that two hosts should conceive themselves unclean within the same moon; and even if such a coincidence should occur, there was no reason to believe that they would choose the same holy waters. But even though the cause for her terror seemed ridiculous, the terror itself begot such uneasiness in him that he began to believe he could not make the journey without his spear. And when certain of the captains protested against his going armed upon a pilgrimage, he replied that the pilgrimage was not of *his* making, that *his* bowels were undisturbed by the presence of an undigested god, that he would go down with his spear or would not go down at all.

Once the men of Ishbaal were beyond the walls of Mahanaim, they were in no haste to come to the place of absolution. They dallied along the road and tarried in every town; they paused at every line of stalls and fingered everything within reach. It was fortunate, thought Abner, that the pools of Gibeon did not lie far to the south. As it was, they slept for one night by the highway, rose late, and did not come to the green groves of Gibeon until the second afternoon.

The water shimmered through the trees, smooth, bright blue, motionless. The grove was cool with green shadows, and the earth was covered with glossy vines. As soon as they found themselves under the boughs, the warriors began to strip off their clothes; but the captain went forward, spear in hand, to the very edge of the grove, wishing to delay as long as possible the moment when he would reveal his frailties to the rest. Suddenly the green arching boughs ceased to interlace before him. He saw the bank, and the water beyond the bank; he saw the whole pool, an oval of blue crystal lying against the dim, dark green. And then he saw—and could not believe that he saw it—a host assembled on the other side. Surely such a thing could not come to pass upon the face of the earth. These were the men of David, naked except for loincloths, and shining with their recent immersion in the holy water. The host had come up out of the south, even as Rizpah had said.

His first impulse was to command his warriors to put on their garments and depart. But before he could so much as turn, six or seven of his young men had waded into the water up to their hips.

"Behold," said one of them in a voice intended to be heard on the other side, "Judah has done Israel an honor. The dung of Judah has journeyed up to Gibeon."

"Truly?" said another. "And what have the men of David to do with the holy pool where Barak cleansed himself?"

"Why," said a third, "inasmuch as they have eaten meat at the hands of the uncircumcised these six years, it has suddenly come into their minds that they should be cleansed before the Feast of the First Fruits."

The naked warriors on the opposite bank sat perfectly still; their faces, so far as his weak eyes could tell, were friendly and serene. The old captain hastily cast off his clothes and waded out to those who had called across the water. He stood before them, shaking with anger and chill, with the icy water around his thighs. "Pigs and sons of pigs," he said, "may your tongues fall out of your mouths if you say a single word to break the peace."

"Abner!" It was the voice of Joab. He had risen and stood at the very edge of the water.

"What would the son of Zeruiah have with me?" Abner said.

"Peace, peace, nothing but peace." The lean, dark Ishmaelite held out his arms and offered a symbolic embrace to the whole of Ishbaal's host. "My men have come up to bathe, since they were in danger of leprosy. They have bathed, and very soon they will depart. Only, we have traveled a long way, and we would rest a while. Therefore, let there be a truce between us. Let us sit by the pool peaceably together, even as we sat in better days in the camp of God."

The old captain had to believe him. For indeed if the son of Zeruiah spoke falsely, then the host of Ishbaal was in a sorry case. Heedless, drunken with the delights of their journey, they had plunged into the water under the very noses of the enemy. Their daggers lay on the bank behind them. They were naked, and could find no sure footing on the slippery bottom of the pool. Even though it was known from Dan to Beersheba that the word of Joab was a reed and must not be leaned upon, he accepted the truce in as cordial a voice as he could bring up out of his shaking body. Then he turned at once and bade his men not to tarry. "Ishbaal will be very wroth with us," he said, "if we are not within the walls of Mahanaim by tomorrow night."

One after another, the men of Ishbaal returned to the bank to dry themselves in the sun. And last of all, the captain of the host—half-blind with the glint of the light on the water—also found the bank and lay down upon it, so weary that he could not close his fist upon the spear that lay at his side.

"My lord," said one of the young men who sat by him, "it is my belief that the captain of the host of David spoke in good faith. They have been entertaining themselves innocently enough with riddles and tales. Also, the second son of Zeruiah, he that is called Abishai, has ridden up with five or six men to join them. He is a man of honor and will surely keep the truce."

The light on the pool had faded. It was possible now for Abner to look across the water and to see plainly what passed on the other side. They had moved back from the bank and sat in a broad semicircle under the trees. One among them—a lithe brown stripling whose brow was covered by clusters of curls—had risen to dance a wild dance out of Ishmael, audacious and sensual. At the end of the dance, he flung himself down with his head against the knee of the captain of David's host.

"It is Asahel," one of the warriors said to Abner.

"Who, then, is Asahel?"

"A son of Zeruiah, the youngest of the lot."

"One of them has danced for us, my lord the captain," said another of the warriors. "Would it not be well for us to call up a dancer for their delight?"

He shook his head. "It is better," he said, "that we sit on one side of the pool and they on the other, and that no words pass between us. Let us arise soon and go to Mahanaim, lest we tempt the anger of Jahveh by tarrying too long." He stood up then and put on his garments. They were comforting against his flesh, for they had soaked up the warmth of the sun.

"Abner!" The eldest son of Zeruiah had come again to the edge of the pool.

"What would Joab have with me?"

"Behold, we have asked our youngest brother to dance for your delight. Therefore it is not courteous that Israel should depart from Judah without an equal show of good-fellowship."

Abner could see the smile upon the Ishmaelite's face—a false, tender, utterly evil smile. "What can we do," said Abner, "to give pleasure to the men of David's host?"

"We have heard that there are mighty wrestlers in Mahanaim."

For the first time in his life, the old captain made an appeal to the pity of the enemy. "We wrestle a little in Mahanaim," he said, "to fill up the emptiness of our days."

"Will you wrestle now?"

"Surely. If it pleases Joab, we will choose two champions among us and let them wrestle for the delight of the men of the Star of Bethlehem."

The champions of Mahanaim had already risen behind their captain, and were about to step forward when Joab spoke again.

"No, now," he said, "must we sit forever, each upon his own bank, with the pool between? Why should not the young men of David wrestle with the young men of Ishbaal, proving their strength in friendly rivalry before we depart?"

Even as he spoke, another—the hairy Abishai—had risen up behind him. "No, my brother," he said. "Were the son of Jesse here, he would surely forbid it."

But the voice of Abishai was lost in a babble of voices from both sides of the pool, calling aloud for a trial of strength and skill. The old captain turned to Ishbaal's men and lifted up his hands to plead with them, but they did not heed him. "Send over twelve to us to wrestle for the glory of Judah," they shouted, "and we will send twelve to you to wrestle for the glory of Benjamin."

All that came to pass thereafter had upon it the brightness of an evil dream. The light, about to lose itself in the black caves of Sheol, flared up once more. The grass and the trees were sharply green, the waters intensely blue under this final radiance of the sun. As in a dream, the captain of the host of Ishbaal saw the young men wade out into the water, their bodies white in the glow. As in a dream, he saw the twelve for David pass the twelve for Ishbaal in the middle of the pool, each twelve going toward the opposite shore. He picked up his spear then and leaned trembling upon it. He saw the twelve for David climb upon the bank and go toward the wrestlers who had risen to meet them. He saw without surprise that their daggers bulged under their loincloths. Without surprise he saw the hard lines of their mouths, the glitter of their eyes. And when they seized their opponents by the hair, and bent back their heads, and drove their daggers deep into the taut throats, there was no amazement in him. He merely stepped back because his own face had been spattered by spurting blood.

One wild cry went up on the other side of Gibeon. Only one of the twelve who had crossed the pool to wrestle with Judah for the glory of Benjamin—only one of the betrayed had been given time to shriek before he was slain. Abner started out of his dream and saw a Judahite bearing down upon him. He thrust his spear into the evil face. Nine or ten of the twelve that had clambered onto the bank a moment hence were still unharmed, still thrusting their daggers into naked chests and sides. Their fellows across the pool, having slain the Benjamite wrestlers, were wading out, carrying their daggers before them. Joab walked in the forefront of the host.

"Flee!" Abner shouted. "Behold, the others are almost upon us!"

374

And, stepping over the bodies of his own slain warriors, he took his spear and fled.

⋞ VI ⋟

THE COUNTRY through which Abner fled—he and what was left of the host of Ishbaal after the slaughter by the pool—was fertile, rolling land. Great boulders thrust themselves out of the soil, but even these were muffled in moss and vine. There was greenness everywhere—in the ripened fields, in the clumps of trees, in the sky itself, pale and lucid now after the setting of the sun. It was good country for flight; there were winding roads and masses of shadow to confuse those who gave chase and to shelter those who ran before. Pursued and pursuer alike flew over the green slopes in utter silence. There was no sound but the beating of feet upon the hard soil of the roads and the swish of legs moving through the millet and the wheat.

At first the captain of the host found it difficult to keep pace with the others. He felt as if all the blood in his body had been driven into his chest and was surging and pounding there. But after he had put a mile behind him, a marvelous lightness came upon him; Jahveh had breathed a second strength into his body; the painful fullness under his ribs was gone. He felt so certain of the grace of God that he even paused at the top of one of the knolls to look about him, and he saw to his wonder that he had outstripped the rest.

A hundred or more of the men of Ishbaal were running in groups of six and seven across the darkening plain. The host of David had also scattered. He was thinking that he might turn back and give the flight some semblance of an orderly retreat when he saw that he had been sighted and was being followed. Some slight, half-naked stripling of the host of David was upon his traces. Less than a hundred steps behind him was a youth whose pace was the pace of a wild doe. As he plunged again into flight, the captain said in his heart, It is Zeruiah's youngest. It is Asahel. . . .

The captain thought to lose himself by going circuitously among the boulders; the shadows were growing thicker; the light-footed one behind him might well lose sight of him. But the stripling turned neither to the right nor to the left and kept drawing closer and closer, until it was possible to hear the rustle of his footsteps in the weeds. He is a green fool in battle, Abner thought. Does he not see that I have my spear in my hand? . . . Yet both prudence and pity held his hand. The lad was of the House of Jesse, and the captain did not wish to incur bloodguiltiness against that house; furthermore, there was no beard upon his face—he was as slight as the crescent which hung pale above the field of flight—and it is a bitter business to slay the young. The captain took shelter behind a great stone and lifted up his voice.

"Is it Asahel who follows me?" he said.

The lad stopped in his tracks. The sound of his footfalls no longer broke the hush. "It is I," he said.

"Then turn aside from following me. Follow one of the younger men of Ishbaal's host and take your glory out of his hand."

There was no reply. The swish of moving feet sounded again, and again Abner fled.

But now the second strength which the Lord had breathed into his body was ebbing away. The fullness in his chest had begun again to afflict him. He could not tell whether the darkness before him was the darkness of night or the purplish mist of exhaustion. Surely, he thought, if I continue to run before him I will fall out of weariness, and he will take me even as I lie and make an end of me with the dagger that is in his hand. . . . He ran panting to the next boulder, and lifted up his voice a second time.

"Turn back!" he shouted. "Cease from following me. Wherefore should I take my spear and smite you to the ground? How should I hold up my head in the sight of your brother Joab if your blood is on my hands?"

Once more the footfalls ceased to sound. The old man held his spear high, so that the point of it glittered above the top of the boulder. Behold death, he thought, and turn aside. . . . Then the moment of reprieve was over. The captain fled again and saw his pursuer, not twenty paces behind him, a white spar of vulnerable flesh darting through the dusk. He knew that the risk was too great, even if the end of this must be bloodguiltiness. And yet pity was still strong upon him. He stopped and reversed his spear in his hand. I will not smite him with the point, he thought. I will hurl the spear in such a manner that he will be stricken with the blunt end of it. If I strike him so, he may yet live. . . .

He paused and took aim. With the last strength that was in him, he hurled the spear. The boy fell upon his back, with his arms and legs spread wide, and Abner knew that he was dead.

He should have gone on then. He saw a high knoll, not a hundred paces beyond him, around which it would be possible for him to rally his troops. He knew that they must be rallied before they were utterly lost to each other in the blackness of the night. Yet he turned back and walked slowly to the place where the dead boy lay. The blunt end of the spear had been as effective as the point. The shaft had gone straight through the lad's body and pinned him to the earth. Blood ran from his mouth, his ears, the corners of his eyes. His hands lay open on the ground, with the fingers spread wide and the weeds standing between.

I have slain multitudes, thought Abner, I have slain multitudes in my day. Were I to heap them up, warrior upon warrior, there would be such a hill of them as would obscure the face of the moon. And this is a grievous thing to lay upon the top thereof, this lad whose cheeks are still downy, this naked child. . . . And he could not pull the spear out of the body. He could only gaze upon the bleeding mouth which gaped in amazement at the actuality of death.

He was still standing above the corpse when a young captain over a thousand came up to him.

"My lord Abner," said the young man, "let us go up to the knoll and rally the host before we are overtaken by night."

"Behold," said Abner, "behold what I have done. I have slain Asahel."

"Surely he is slain in a strange manner," said the youth, raising his eyes in wonder to the point of the spear. "How was it with my lord the captain that he should use the hinder end of the shaft? Why——" He started then and took the old man by the arm. "No, now," he said, "I will ask another time concerning that. Let us go without pause to the knoll, to save what is yet left us after this day of woe."

From the top of the knoll, the dim green earth stretched down before them for miles. Abner could see the whole course of the flight—the scattered groups of the pursued running far before the scattered groups of the pursuers. Neither had yet reached the little spot of whiteness which was the body of Asahel. All that Abner beheld seemed to him strange and remote. How small are the sons of men, he thought, how small is man fleeing from man in terror across the earth. . . . The young captain beside him made a trumpet of his hands and shouted to the host. The men began to move in slowly converging lines toward the hill on which they saw the white hair and beard of their captain.

They passed the corpse of Asahel without stopping. But those who followed them paused—white bodies crowding against one another—and congregated around the slain. While the men of Ishbaal climbed upon the knoll or lay down panting at the base of it, the men of David stood among the boulders in the plain and raised outcry above their dead. Then two detached themselves from the mourners and ran on, beating their breasts and tearing their garments as they ran. These are the sons of Zeruiah, Abner thought, even Joab and Abishai. Soon the host of David will come up behind them, to fall upon us in vengeance for the dead. . . .

He looked at the host which had gathered around him; it was unbelievably small; he knew that most of those who had journeyed with high hearts out of Mahanaim would behold the walls of their outpost fortress no more. I am sick of strife, he thought. Since the day of my first battle, I have been sick to death of strife. Let us in God's name make any covenant, even to going down in chains to David in Hebron, so long as we shed no more blood. . . .

"Joab!" he called aloud.

Joab and Abishai paused and raised their faces to the hill. "What would Abner have of me?" said Joab. But Abishai said nothing, and Abner knew that he could not raise his voice because he wept.

"Shall the sword devour us forever?" said Abner. "Can war between Judah and Israel end in anything but bitterness? How long will it be, then, before you bid the men of David turn back from pursuing those who are their brothers in the sight of God?"

Night was coming down swiftly, like a hawk upon spread wings. Out of the thickening darkness, the voice of Joab said: "Even if you had not spoken, we would have turned aside. We also are weary of following after those who are our kinsmen. Depart in peace, and we will depart in peace."

So the sons of Zeruiah went back and lifted up their dead brother and bore him toward Bethlehem, to be buried in the family burial cave; and the host of David went with them, wailing for Asahel and for the others, for there were among them nineteen who had been slain. But the host of Ishbaal remained a little longer upon the hill, to be numbered; and among the men of Mahanaim there were three hundred and threescore dead.

❧ VII ❧

AFTER HIS RETURN from his brother's burial in Bethlehem, Joab waited for a night and a day in Hebron before he received a summons to present himself before his lord. He had expected that a messenger would come to him early in the morning, asking that he eat the noonday meal with the Star of Bethlehem. When no messenger arrived, he said to himself, It is a good omen. If he were very wrathful, he would be eager to fall upon me. Since he has waited, I may reasonably conclude that we will break bread together in peace this night. . . . But no courier from the house of David appeared at Joab's door during the long afternoon; and, as the molten light began to pale in the room and upon the adjoining garden, he entered upon an entirely new set of conjectures. My lord, he thought, is not yet finished with wrath. It may be that he will withhold his chidings until the weight of my loss is less heavy upon my heart. . . .

Once he had convinced himself that the absence of a message was a piece of good fortune, he spoke to the servant concerning the evening meal, and was pleased to find that there was beef in the house—sacrificial meat left over from the Feast of the First Fruits. He sat down in an almost cheerful frame of mind. The food was much better than that which he had eaten in Bethlehem; the last of the sun lay in mild squares upon the table; the room was beginning to grow pleasantly cool. But he had scarcely swallowed his first bite when the messenger appeared—an old man, solemn and uncommunicative, with nothing to say save that the King of Judah wished the eldest son of Zeruiah to come up to the high house within the hour.

It boded ill for him—it was a distinct slight—that the son of Jesse had not called him up to partake of the evening bread. Nevertheless he refused to give way to fear. The Star of Bethlehem might have had other guests to sit at his table tonight—some priest, some merchant of the city, some visitor out of a foreign land. The son of Zeruiah twined a bright girdle around his waist to indicate that he was not in a heavy mood. He bade the young Egyptian whom he had found at the brook Besor follow him, for the sight of this lad might well awaken in David certain kindly remembrances. He went slowly through the dusky streets, stopping to look at the trinkets in the bazaars, and he did not falter in the least when he crossed the garden of David's house.

It was not yet dark when he entered the common room. He had dreaded most that he would find the son of Jesse sitting there alone, portentous and inflexible in his carved chair. But the scene that he beheld was pleasant, even merry; the witching Maacah had returned from the tents of her people, and sat on the hearth at the feet of her lord. Her children were with her, and she was decking them out in some lengths of purple stuff, no doubt a present from their dark grandfather. For a moment after he entered, Maacah continued to chatter, David continued to listen, the little ones continued to finger the gay cloth. Then the young woman's bright, almond-shaped eyes settled upon the visitor, and she fell ominously silent. Without a word, she rose and gathered up the cloth and the children, and hastened from the room as one might hasten from a breaking storm.

The son of Zeruiah stopped upon the threshold so suddenly that the Egyptian bondservant trod upon his heels. The room was shadowy, and all that was white within it seemed to float upon the surface of the darkness—the white napkins still lying folded upon the table, the white bowl which Asahel had taken up only a few days since in his living hands, the white tunic falling in straight folds around the body of the King of Judah, the white, impassive face. There was no greeting. To stand wordless on the threshold was to admit guilt and fear. He entered and forced himself to walk at an unhurried pace toward the motionless one who sat near the hearth.

"Send him hence," the son of Jesse said. "Send your servant hence. Did I not say to you that you were to come up to me alone?"

He turned to tell the Egyptian to depart. But there was no need. The words—as hard as flying splinters from a chipped stone—had driven the slave forth. The captain stopped where he stood, ten paces from the carved chair.

"Come and speak," the King of Judah said. "Speak, for I will not let loose my wrath upon you until I have heard you plead your cause."

It had seemed to him that he had considered every eventuality, but he was not ready for this. It had not once occurred to him that the son of Jesse would simply sit motionless before him, waiting for him to defend himself. What should I say to him? he thought. How should I begin? Can I say to him, as one tells a tale, "There was a leprous harlot at the gate"? Shall I tell him, "We met the host of Ishbaal at the pools by chance"? He may have heard that it was not by chance. What, then, can I say? . . .

He said at last, "Whatever I did at Gibeon, I did for my lord."

The King sat perfectly still, his hands upon the arms of the chair, his feet crossed at the ankles upon the woolen rug. And Joab knew that his first sentence had been an unfortunate one, that he had indirectly admitted his guilt, and that his appeal had been in vain. Very slowly, the long, crossed feet upon the rug withdrew, without uncrossing themselves.

"Surely," said the captain, "my lord knows the tale as well as I. . . ."

"Your lord," said the cold, flat voice, "knows the tale far better than you think. Can Joab have believed that those who went up with him to Gibeon would keep silent?"

"Then why should I recount to David that which he already knows?"

The King leaned forward in his chair. His eyes narrowed, and he smiled. "Because," he said, "for once in my days, I would see the son of Zeruiah caught in the toils of his own cleverness. I would see him trip and stumble upon his own lies."

The knowing smile that had begun to form upon Joab's lips in answer to David's smile went out like a smothered lamp.

"Come, tell your tale," the King of Judah said.

Joab stared at the hands, lying lithe and ready against the white folds of the tunic. They will close upon my neck, he thought, they will strangle me to death. . . .

"Begin. I do not mean to sit out the night."

He cleared his throat and said, "There was a certain leprous harlot who dwelt by the southern gate——"

"Leprous? Was she indeed leprous? She seemed whole enough to me when they brought her up out of the wilderness."

He said in a whisper, "They found her, then?"

"No, they did not find her." The gray eyes looked pale and exultant in the dusk. "There was no need that they should find her. Why should I send ten men to wear the day away with combing the wilderness when I knew well enough that Joab would betray himself?"

It would have been far better, thought the captain of the host, to have come up to his house in a mourning garment, to have fallen at his feet, to have said that I was guilty of a grievous sin against him. This alone would have been sure diplomacy. How is it with me that I did not see it? . . . And, grasping wildly at the knowledge that grief and grief alone would move the King of Judah, he coaxed tears into his own eyes, and said: "It was not I who called the harlot leprous. It was my youngest brother, he that I found with the spear through his body, even Asahel. . . ."

"Asahel," said David in a grave and meditative voice. "Who was it that slew Asahel?"

The son of Zeruiah started. Surely, he thought, he cannot have learned much if he has not yet heard how Asahel was slain. . . . And the exigency of the moment was such that he was willing to use anything, even the horrible image which had been hounding him night after night, to stir up pity in the breast of his inquisitor.

"Abner smote him, my lord," he said. "It was the captain of Ishbaal's host that smote him, and strangely, with the hinder end of the spear. And when I found him, he was pinned to the earth."

The son of Jesse rose and sighed. "Do not deceive yourself," he said. "It was not Abner that slew Asahel. He who took him forth on an errand of murder—it was he who struck him down. The blood of Asahel is upon Joab's head."

The wind was at its strongest. The curtains that hung at the window billowed inward upon the gust. And the son of Zeruiah saw Asahel alive, saw him wandering from window to window, ardent and restless, pausing by the sill and leaning toward the garden, as though the whole magical world called to him out of the summer night. Tonight, thought Joab, there is no motion and no desire in him. And that same blood which ran from his ears and eyes—it is indeed upon my head. . . .

He saw the hard, white face of David moving toward him through the thickening dark. "If it is as my uncle says," he whispered, "if it was through me that my brother came to death, then surely my lord should hold his hand in pity from me. For the lad was dear to me, dearer than any save only the Star of Bethlehem."

The King of Judah stood motionless five paces from his captain. "Why, then, did you go up to Gibeon?" he said.

"To be cleansed of the foulness that was upon us."

"What foulness, inasmuch as she was not leprous?"

"The host thought that she was leprous. . . ."

"Joab taught his brother to spread that tale."

"No, now, my lord cannot believe what he says. Wherefore should I fashion such a tale to tell the host?"

"Wherefore indeed, unless it was to come upon the men of Ishbaal naked and without weapons in the pool, and to slaughter them in cold blood?"

"Let David ask himself how it should come to my knowledge that there was uncleanness in the army of the north. . . ."

"I have asked my servant. I have no need to ask myself. Does Joab think that I keep blind bondsmen? How should the son of Zeruiah sit all afternoon with an ambassador out of Phoenicia, in this very room, without the matter being plain? It is known to all the world that Sidon and Tyre send greetings to Mahanaim as well as to Hebron. Does the son of Zeruiah take me for a fool?"

The long, spare hands of the son of Jesse were clenched to strike. The knuckles shone.

"Strike me, then," said Joab. "I have sinned grievously. I knew that they were naked in the pool. I lied concerning the harlot. I went forth to slay them, as my lord says, in cold blood. This I did as I would do anything—even to the rendering up of my youngest brother—out of devotion to my lord."

He had thought that by inviting the blow he might forestall it. But the white fist flew at him through the darkness and struck him with such force that he staggered backward and uttered a cry. Then David's hands fell slack at his sides. He stepped back and sank into his chair.

"I will not have it," said the son of Jesse in a weary voice, "I will not have it that this blood should be put upon me. What the son of Zeruiah did he did in my absence and against my will. Had he waited for a hundred years, Joab would never have had any sign from me that I wished him to go up against Israel."

The captain stood before the carved chair, dragging at his jaw with both hands. "Now that my lord has chastised me, shall I depart?" he said.

"No." The voice was toneless. "There is much to say which has not yet been said. Sit, if you wish."

Joab sat on the hearth, at an appropriate distance from the King of Judah's feet.

"Now lie to me no more," said David, "for I am sick unto death of lies. Did you believe it, in the tabernacle of your heart—did you believe that I would be gratified by such slaughter as you have wrought in the ranks of Israel?"

The captain drew up his knees and rested his aching face against them. Perhaps now it would be wise to lie, to say that he had foreseen the wrath of David, to take the whole burden of the deed upon himself. And yet the son of Jesse had asked for an end to lying, and he himself was also weary of lies. "I thought that my lord would rage at me," he said. "I thought that he would have preferred the matter settled in some other way—perhaps in an open battle between our host and the host of the north. But I thought also that in the end he would thank God that so many of his enemies had been slain."

There was a long silence between them. The King of Judah rose and walked to the window and sighed. He stood now behind the captain, and Joab did not dare to turn. He could not tell what was passing over the chill and kingly face—rage, resignation, unbelief—but the voice that came from the unseen mouth was a voice urgent with pain.

"Before God, I am not such a one!" he said. "It is true that through me the priests of Nob were slain. It is true that I went down to Gath, and that I marched a little of the way against Saul with the uncircumcised. I have done much that was evil, and I have permitted more. I have taken bread out of the hands of the sons of God. Israel might now be one land, united and whole, if I had never been born. All this is so. But I am not such a one as Joab thinks."

"I never thought ill of my uncle and my lord. I thought only that he would do even as all kings must do in order to increase their kingdoms. Whatsoever the son of Jesse has done in the past has seemed to me only that which any man would have done in his place."

Surely, he thought, this will move him. For this is the truth, given to him without stint out of the very core of my heart. . . .

"I had thought," said the King of Judah, "to take the son of Zeruiah and stand him against a great rock before those among us whose sons and brothers were slain at Gibeon. I had thought to say to the mourners, 'Smite him with arrows until there is no breath left within him, for he has brought dishonorable death upon your sons and your brothers, and bloodguiltiness upon the host.' This I had thought to say to them, inasmuch as it was not war but murder which you brought to pass beside the holy waters. And I would have dealt with you even as with a murderer. I would have left your body unburied in the wilderness, that the beasts might lick your bones."

Joab rested his forehead against his knees and closed his eyes. The voice of the son of Jesse had thrust the sentence into the past—it had been a possibility ten days since, but it was a possibility no more. What punishment, then, was to be meted out instead of death? Perhaps all that had passed within this room tonight had prepared the way for clemency. Perhaps there would be no punishment. . . .

"Inasmuch as the son of Zeruiah murdered at Gibeon for my sake, the bloodguiltiness is in part my own. Therefore I cannot slay him in justice, for he who is guilty must not also sit in the seat of judgment. Only let him remember henceforth that I am not a jackal of the desert who feeds upon carrion and laps up blood. . . ."

Surely, thought Joab, he is about to forgive me utterly. And he hid his mouth against his knees and smiled. . . .

"Nevertheless . . ."

The voice was very close to him. He started and looked up and saw the King of Judah standing over him, and the smile died upon his lips.

Like pieces of crystal, the pale eyes blazed upon him. "Stand up, murderer! Stand up, dog!" the son of Jesse said.

He stood and staggered backward, raising his hand before his face.

"No, now, I will not strike you. Why should I befoul my hand upon you? I am already foul with you—you have plunged me deep in blood. Go into the house which I gave you and close its doors upon you, and do not show your face in the streets of Hebron until the fierceness of my wrath is past. And when you come forth again, do not go down into the encampment. It is enough that your poison should have festered among my host these thirteen years. Break your sword and cast it forth from the window. Throw your shield into the street. For henceforth I have no captain. I am captain of my own host."

✑§ VIII §✎

GRIEF had been violent and all-pervading in Mahanaim; there was scarcely a family that did not count some kinsman or dear friend among the dead. When they took off their mourning garments and looked about them at their city, they saw that it was changed and desolate. There was uneasiness in the houses and indecision in the tents, for there was a quarrel —there was a bitter, galling, unspoken quarrel—between Ishbaal and the captain of his host.

It was taken for granted among the men of Mahanaim that their King was a slow-witted and frightened child. They knew what all Israel knew —that it was the captain of the host who kept the spurious crown upon

Ishbaal's head. They had said a hundred times among themselves, "How would it be with us if a day should come when the captain grew weary of Mahanaim and turned his back upon his lord?" Now the dreaded breach had indeed come between them; but it was the fool, it was the poor, bemused fool, who had turned aside from his support. Since the moment when the runner had come before the defeated host, wailing over the calamity that had come to pass at Gibeon, Ishbaal had locked himself within his house and refused to set eyes upon Abner's face.

If the Princess Michal had not tarried in Mahanaim longer than she had intended, if she and her husband had not remained in her brother's house throughout the period of mourning, the charged silence might have lasted for three or four moons. It was she who took measures with her brother. She went up to him one afternoon and matched a new terror against his present terror—she threatened him with his father's ghost. "For Saul will not rest in his grave," she said, "while his captain is shamefully barred from the house and given no chance to raise his voice in defense of himself."

On the following evening the young King came to his sister and told her that he would send for Abner, that he would prepare a little feast for Abner and Rizpah on the following night. "Let my sister and her husband also sit with us and rejoice," he said, "for the captain of the host is forgiven. Only let us have no words whatsoever concerning what came to pass at Gibeon. Why should we waste the hours in mourning over what cannot be undone?"

He took pains to make the feast as gracious an event as possible, planning it after the fashion of the feasts which his father had held in Gibeah long ago. He had the board spread in the garden, under the summer trees. He ordered all the Gibean delicacies—new curds and honey and roast lamb; he even requested that his sister delight the company with one of her peerless honey cakes. He spent longer than usual in the business of instructing the servant who was to carry the message down to Abner's house. He had worded it very carefully, and he wished to make certain that it would not be marred. "Come up to feast with us as in the old days," he said. "Michal and Paltiel will break bread with us under the trees at the hour of the going-down of the sun. All that has brought trouble between us Ishbaal has forgotten. Let Abner forget it also. Let there be no talk of war or of mourning tonight, but only such talk as will add savor to the meat and the wine."

But the captain was so furious when he heard the words that he could scarcely hold his tongue before the messenger. To have been silenced and forbidden the presence of the King was bitter enough; to be called up lightly to a feast, to be instructed that the whole business was something to be forgotten—that was enough to drive a man half-mad. He strode into the house, leaving the servant upon the threshold, and laid the matter before Rizpah. Had she ever heard of such downright, unspeakable, insupportable arrogance? Did the simpleton take his captain for a dog? The woman laid her cool hand upon his arm. If we deal with fools, we must expect foolishness, she said. As her husband had truly said, Ishbaal had but half his wits. He could not be expected to proceed with tact in such a situation. Certainly it would be wiser to go up to the feast. To refuse would be to sustain the uneasiness in Ishbaal, in himself, and in the host. . . . He listened and shrugged and sighed. He had felt, even at the time of his anguish after the battle, a persistent longing to behold Saul's daughter. Surely Michal would give him some opportunity to justify himself. . . . He returned to the door and gave the servant a brief message of acceptance, courteous but more restrained than any he had ever sent to the young King in the past.

Abner and Rizpah appeared together in Ishbaal's garden at the appointed hour. They had fallen into the habit of walking hand in hand in their own garden, and when they saw Paltiel coming from the house to greet them, they drew apart with some regret.

"They have sent me forth to welcome you," he said, smiling upon them. "The King is with the servants, giving them the final instructions concerning the feast. As for my wife, she is decking herself out as though Abner had been her lover. She has asked me a hundred times this day, 'Am I still fair? Will he find me old?'"

"No, now," said Rizpah, laughing, "were she ancient, she would yet seem a damsel in my company."

"The lady Rizpah," Paltiel said, "is ageless. As for the captain, it is plain that God has given him a second youth." He turned then and gazed at the door of the house. The daughter of Saul had just crossed the threshold and was coming quickly toward them, with her hands held out in a gesture of eagerness.

She greeted Rizpah pleasantly, but did not kiss her. The sorrows of Ahinoam still hung between them. But Abner she greeted as in the past after long campaigns. She drew his face down toward her own and kissed him full upon the lips.

Surely, he thought, she is my partisan and will give me an occasion to justify myself. . . .

Rizpah praised the cluster of gold stars and crescents that hung about Michal's neck on a delicate chain. Paltiel blushed with pleasure to hear it commended. "It looks well around a slender throat," he said, touching it lightly with the tip of his finger. "Only a slight woman could wear it. So he told me—the trader who brought it down out of Lebanon."

Michal smiled at him, and the old captain saw that she blushed for him a little too, that there was both gratification and embarrassment in her look. Then all four of them turned, for the King had come into the garden. In the dying light, with his hair spread out on the evening wind, he looked more than a little like his brother Jonathan. Not that such an illusion could be sustained for long. He was larger and heavier than his brother, and utterly lacking in Jonathan's grace. His face was soft and undistinguished; his brow was low, and there was a troubling emptiness in his brown eyes.

He placed the captain in a seat of honor, between Michal and himself. He seemed so eager to see Abner comfortable and well served that all the day's anger subsided within the old man's heart. When the servants have set the dishes before us and departed, he thought, then the King will speak. He waits to ask indulgence for his moodiness only until he may speak before his peers alone. And that is well. I have no desire to see him humble himself. . . .

Nevertheless, he found himself looking forward to the hour when he and Rizpah would sit together on the edge of their bed, reviewing all that had come to pass. He would ask her whether she thought that Ishbaal regretted his behavior, and she would ask him whether he believed that the daughter of Saul had utterly forgotten the Star of Bethlehem. He was so certain that he would be required to give a penetrating answer to this question that he gave grave consideration to it. He came to the conclusion that Michal's heart still turned now and again to the son of Jesse, but why he thought so, he did not know. . . .

The feast progressed, and the light turned dim and purplish upon the garden; course after course was lifted from the table; and yet there was no sign that the young King meant to speak of the incident. No doubt, Abner thought, he is waiting until the last of the food is gone; he has a passion for eating. . . . But the thought that the matter might be postponed until a much later hour was galling to the captain.

He took a deep breath and turned toward Ishbaal. "My lord," he said very distinctly, breaking in upon one of Paltiel's sentences, "when will we speak of the shadow that has been between us? The matter lies heavily upon me, and, until it is removed, I cannot enjoy the feast."

Rizpah glanced at him across the table. Her look was half tender, half displeased. Michal flushed and stared at her own hands. Her husband gazed across the plates with the falsely frank and attentive eyes of one who wishes to show respect to the nonsense of the venerably old. As for the young King, he started and put down the piece of honey cake that he had been lifting toward his lips. He said, looking vacantly before him, "I am aware of no shadow that is between me and the captain of the host." Then he turned toward Paltiel and asked quietly and deliberately, "What was it that my brother was saying concerning the trade in wine among the uncircumcised?"

"Wine?" said Paltiel, plainly disquieted, for they had not been speaking of wine.

Abner turned toward Michal. "What ails the King?" he said. "Surely he has not forgotten that he has forbidden me his house and has given me no occasion to lift up my voice in defense of myself?"

"No," said Michal very softly, "he wishes to forget. Perhaps it would be more prudent to let the matter rest."

"To let it rest?" He knew now that Ishbaal had been foolish enough to believe that he might deal with his captain as with a dog, kicking him at one moment and then whistling him back again. The fool is a fool indeed, he thought, if he thinks to appease me with a feast. . . . All caution left him, and he said aloud, "I cannot let it rest."

Ishbaal continued to speak of crops and markets, but there was no doubt that he had heard. He stammered, and that which he said had even less meaning than the inanities he had been uttering for the last hour.

"My lord," said Abner, "how can it be said that there is nothing to divide us when I have been denied the sight of Ishbaal's face?"

All of them fell silent. The young man had assumed an air of quiet dignity which Jonathan would have borne well, but which in him was sheer arrogance. "No, now," he said coldly, "is it not enough that I have forgotten the business? Must we mar the evening with talk of that which is far better put out of our thoughts forever?"

Michal reached beneath the table and laid a light, warning hand upon the captain's knee. But the fury that boiled up in him now was beyond control. That this dull-witted youth should address him in such a voice as Saul had never dared to use—it was intolerable, it made the blood churn in his head, it turned the landscape red before his eyes. "I will not be silenced," he said. "I will have it named—the sin for which I have been punished before all Israel. Nor will I wait to hear my lord whisper it to me in some dark corner. Let him name it now, before my peers, or I will call a council and demand that it be named before the host."

The King continued to maintain the mask of haughtiness, but it was plain that he maintained it at no small cost; and the captain thought with exultation, He is afraid! . . .

"Let us rise and go into the house," said Michal.

"Let me hear my offense before we rise," Abner said.

Ishbaal straightened then and pushed his plate aside. "It is an offense in a captain," he said in an unsteady voice, "that he should make war without the express approval of his king. When did I ask that there should be war between Judah and Israel?"

"Surely the King is not such a fool as to believe that it was I who made war at Gibeon. The host of David came up as murderers. We made no war —we merely turned and fled."

Before the sound of the words had died, Abner regretted them. The King was haunted by self-mistrust, and no man might say "fool" to his face. The King was a coward, and whosoever said "murderer" in his presence incurred his hate.

Ishbaal hid his shaking hands beneath the table. "The captain of the host," he said in a shrill voice, "takes far too much upon himself."

"The King speaks truly. I have indeed taken too much upon myself. All the sorrows of the House of Kish I have carried upon my back these forty years. Saul saw my burden and was grateful. But on the day when his son was anointed in Mahanaim, I received a bitter portion for a man in his declining years—a heavier load and a far lighter measure of gratitude. . . ."

"And yet," said the young King almost in a whisper, smiling the sickly smile of the terrified, "and yet, before the bones of my father were buried in Gibeah, the captain inherited one thing which the House of Kish owed him not."

Michal rose in fright, tilting the table so that there was a clatter of dishes. "No, now, before God you shall not name it," she said, speaking to her brother but turning her look upon Rizpah, whose fair, mild face had suddenly gone white and old.

"Wherefore should I not name it? I am the King, and I name whatsoever I choose. The captain of the host took too much upon himself when he led into his house that which belonged to me according to the laws of Israel. It is written that when a king dies he who inherits his throne also inherits his concubines."

Rizpah had risen and was walking away from the table. Abner also stood and watched her go. Wait a little, beloved, he thought, wait a little and I will follow. Only first I must deal with this pig upon whose head I have set the crown of Israel. . . .

"No, now," said Michal, "it is enough. Let us in God's name depart out of this place."

But the captain of the host laid a firm hand upon her shoulder and thrust her down, so that he and the King of Israel might stand face to face. "Do you take me for a dog out of Judah?" he shouted. "I have ministered to the House of Kish and preserved it and delivered it out of the hand of David. In return for all this, you reproach me with a fault concerning a woman. God do so to me and more also if I do not take Israel from you and lay it before the son of Jesse, so that he may reign from Dan to Beersheba, even as Samuel prophesied."

He remained at the table long enough to see the face of Ishbaal go blank and imbecilic with terror. Now, thought the captain, I am avenged and she is avenged. He will not dare to walk forth without a bodyguard by day, nor will he close his eyes in sleep by night. . . . Michal had laid her head upon her arms and was weeping. Paltiel's blunt hand reached across the table and strove to touch her hair.

The captain turned then and followed his wife. She had come to the end of the garden and was fumbling with the latch on the gate when he joined her. "No, now," he said in a tender and unsteady voice, "wait a little." And he took the corner of her veil in his hand and wiped the tears from her face before he led her into the street.

⇜ IX ⇝

On the evening of the quarrel between Abner and Ishbaal, Michal's grief had broken through her reserve with the force of a living spring. She had wept long at the table and in the common room of Ishbaal's house. She had gone up to the roof to compose herself, and there too she had wept. Her weeping had broken out afresh when she lay beside Paltiel in the great bed. And long after her husband had fallen into an uneasy sleep, she had begun to weep again.

Paltiel had said what he could to console her: Perhaps, now that the King was plainly terrified, he would bear himself with more humility and prudence. Perhaps it was even possible that the violence had cleared the air of hidden resentments and doubts. But she remained inconsolable. She had come at last to know that her grief had not arisen out of the quarrel.

During the thirteen years of her life with Paltiel she had called herself happy—as happy as any mortal could hope to be in a pain-ridden world. She had said to herself, I am safe, I am warm, no chill out of the past can penetrate to me now. . . . But her pleasure in the serenity of her days was a kind of discipline; she had learned it through constant practice, as her brothers had learned the art of the spear and the bow. She had taught herself another art also. As a gardener lops away unwanted shoots with the pruning shears, so she cut away her yearnings and her dreams, without mercy and without compromise, so that there was a certain impervious look of quiet cruelty upon her face. People had grown wary with her, fearing that she might be cold and merciless. They were amazed to find her cordial and gentle. She had no desire to impose her disciplines on others; she turned her rigor only upon herself.

She had come to rely entirely on her self-control. She had believed that her serenity could not be shattered even by the sight of the son of Jesse himself. So she might have believed for the remainder of her days if Abner had not come into Ishbaal's garden, bringing back all Gibeah in an hour.

All Gibeah—the golden meadow where she and the son of Jesse had tended her father's goats; the moonlit arbor where, for the first time, the whiteness of her breast had been laid bare for a young man; the broad common room with the rustling reeds and the glowing hearth where, on a day of rain, he had consented to take her as his bride. And when the captain of the host had shouted the name of David into the young King's face, she had scarcely perceived that here was treason and the downfall of her father's house. She had heard nothing but the name, and it was as if a door had swung open to show her at last what god it was who had stood, naked and shining and silent all these years, in the tabernacle of her heart.

She was glad that she had been given an ostensible excuse for her excessive weeping. She was glad, too, that Paltiel, eager to return to his fields and orchards, saw in her wish to tarry behind him in Mahanaim nothing more than a desire to remain with her brother until overtures for a peaceable settlement had been made to the captain of the host. But in reality she was little concerned with what would come to pass between Abner and the King. She needed solitude, and knew that it was to be had in this drab and somnolent city. Sometime it would be possible for her to go down to her husband; sometime she would take comfort again in his tenderness by day and in the warmth of his body by night. But that would be neither today nor tomorrow—that would be only when the revolt within her had been utterly put down. . . .

Meanwhile, she waited. It seemed to her that she waited for a return of the old quietness. Yet she kept listening to the outer world as well. She kept expecting a face at the window, a step among the dried leaves in the garden. And all the while she stood apart and heaped mockery and contempt upon herself. Behold, she said to herself, how it is with the daughter of Saul, how she yearns after the son of Jesse who has four wives for his bed in Hebron. Behold how she looks toward the window to see whether he has come up to carry her home—he who took her only to gain a kingdom, he who never loved her, he who forgot her thirteen years ago. . . .

One hot summer morning when almost a week of this waiting had passed, she went to walk alone in the garden. The air was heavy, and the sun was too bright for her eyes. She found herself weak and languid. Her cheeks were hot, and there was a dryness upon her tongue. There is a fever of yearning within me, she thought. I sicken now as I sickened in Gilgal long ago, when my mother took me up to the black city, hoping that I might forget. . . . She sat down then upon a bench close to the gate. They are all dead, she thought, Ahinoam and Saul and Jonathan. None of us are left to walk among the ashes of the House of Kish, save only the poor fool and I. . . . And it came upon her again, the uncontrollable weeping. She wept now as she had not wept when they had brought the tidings down from Gilboa, or when she had watched them lay the little linen bundles of bones in the burial cave.

How long she had been weeping when she heard the strange sound, she did not know. There was a metallic, repeated clicking. She looked up and saw that the latch on the garden gate was being moved from without. A tall warrior stood beyond the brazen grillwork of the gate.

"Let my lady forgive me," he said. "These three days I have waited for her to show herself in the garden. The captain of the host has sent me to ask my lady if she will follow me to a certain place where she will find my lord the captain. For there is a thing which must be said in utter secrecy."

She rose and hid her swollen face in the folds of her veil. "Now? Must I come now?" she said, and her voice was thick with weeping.

"If my lady would come without delay, the captain of the host would be more than grateful. The matter is urgent, and has waited long."

Perhaps, she thought, I will walk behind you to my death. There was talk of treason that night in the garden. What should prevent the captain of the host from murdering me and my brother? . . . But the thought was without conviction and stirred her so little that she merely sighed.

"No evil will befall my lady."

What evil can befall me? she thought. Surely I have suffered all the evil that is in the world. . . .

390

"I must ask my lady to walk a long way. My captain awaits her in the outskirts of the city, in a cave beyond the northern gate."

"Go on before," she said, "and I will follow."

X

AFTER the long walk through the streets in the heat of the sun, the cave was a place of coolness and quiet. There were crevices in the dome-shaped roof, and the darkness was crossed by three shafts of dazzling light. Bits of radiance were caught up, too, in scattered pools where the moisture of last winter's rains had gathered; and there was a pale and bluish gleam upon a few wet areas of the wall.

The warrior left her at the entrance, waiting only long enough to draw back the curtain of vines that hung before the opening. Plainly the matter to be discussed between the daughter of Saul and the captain of the host was of so secret a nature that even a trusted messenger might not hear. She stepped into the cool darkness and stood wordless for a moment. Then Abner walked into one of the shafts of light. His beard and hair were white in the radiance; his hands were held out in a gesture of welcome; his eyes were guileless, and he smiled.

"Would that I had a more seemly place," he said, "in which to receive the daughter of my lord. I have brought a rug and a few cushions, so that she may sit, at least."

She went to him and laid her hand in his, and he led her through patches of brightness and patches of shade to the square of aqueous, shimmering light in which the rug had been spread. He stood at ease before her, looking down upon her, his thumbs thrust into his girdle, his legs set wide apart. "If I am the enemy of Ishbaal, am I also the enemy of Michal?" he said.

She considered the matter gravely for a moment. Then she smiled at him and shook her head.

"But if I have committed treason——"

The treasonous words that he had uttered that evening in the garden had been provoked, and therefore might be excused. Furthermore, they were unreal, remote. The revolt in Mahanaim had paled beside the more immediate revolt within her heart. "Let Abner forget what passed in the garden," she said. "Let him go up and grant forgiveness to Ishbaal, who cannot sleep or eat because of the terror that is in him. He will make any concessions. He waits only to be forgiven."

"But if the matter has passed beyond forgiveness——"

The old eyes regarded her steadily. She started, seeing a fearful and unbelievable possibility.

"If I have done even that which I vowed I would do—if I have indeed sent down and offered myself to the son of Jesse—what then?" he said.

"Surely Abner has not sent down to the son of Jesse." But she knew that her amazement was spurious, that somewhere in the silent, waiting core of her spirit, she had known as much.

"I have sent down," Abner said. "Now, therefore, if Michal is bound utterly to Ishbaal, let her rise up and run forth from the cave and call me traitor before the host. Yet, before she departs from me, I have a message to give to her."

"What message?" she said in a whisper.

"I have a message for her from the Star of Bethlehem."

She did not answer. For the moment it was enough that she and David should have known even such remote contact as infinitely distant stars must know when their rays converge upon the same blade of grass. Behold, she thought, at the instant when I cried out to him in my heart, he remembered me. We are not utterly divided, for he has said my name. . . .

"The son of Jesse has said that he will make me welcome in Hebron upon one condition: that I bring down with me his wife, even Michal the daughter of Saul, whom he purchased from her father in return for two hundred foreskins of the Philistines."

She was hard put to it to stifle a sudden surge of laughter. The message was so characteristic of the son of Jesse as she had known him in Gibeah that it eradicated the years and rendered him back to her unchanged—irrepressibly and laughably the same. The old gallantry was there; he had called her "the daughter of Saul"; she was still royal in his eyes, even though she stood amid the rubble of the House of Kish, without so much to her name as a field in Benjamin. He possessed the old blithe scorn for realities; plainly, she was Paltiel's wife, but he had swept that matter aside and had agreed to consider her his own. Nor had his memorable tendency to equivocate grown less—if he had bought her at the price of two hundred Philistine foreskins, he was indeed in debt. She remembered his having paid two, as it were, on account; but she could not recall that any mention had ever been made of the rest.

"No, now," she said, "let the captain forgive me if I have given way to unseemly levity. It is only that I find him quite unchanged."

The old man fixed a solemn and beseeching look upon her. "Has my lady heard? Has she seen what choice is laid before her?" he said.

She saw it then, and all laughter died within her. She saw Paltiel returning out of his fields to reassure himself of her presence within his house. She saw him holding out such small gifts as he always brought back for her—a perfect pomegranate still warm with the sun, a fair pebble turned up by his plow. And if I were not there to make much over his gifts . . .

"Surely," she said, "the son of Jesse cannot believe that I will arise and come to him, after all these years."

Abner shifted his look to the ground. "I do not know what the son of Jesse believes. I know only what he desires. And I am certain that he desires the return of my lady, for he said expressly, 'Unless you bring her down to me, you shall not see my face.' That he has need of me, I know.

There is enmity between him and the eldest of the sons of Zeruiah—he has taken no other captain for his host."

She could not bring her mind to dwell upon hosts and captains. The word "desire" was a potent word; Abner had done well to utter it. In the Gibean days, the son of Jesse had sometimes gone so far as to say that he "wished" her to come to him. But he had never used so urgent a word as "desire."

"Wherefore should he desire that I return?" There was sweetness in saying the word.

"He has great need of my lady. . . ."

"How can that be so, seeing that he has taken four wives to his bed?"

The captain of the host moved deliberately into an area of darkness. "What woman in Israel," he said, "could take the place of the King's daughter with the Star of Bethlehem? It was to her that he came in the springtime of his days. If he had taken four hundred others, he would remember nevertheless. She would be first in his house and dearer than all the rest."

It is not so, she told herself. He never loved me. . . . And yet she could not deny herself the boundless luxury of believing that, during all these barren years while she had taken the pruning shears to her yearnings, his had grown green and luxuriant. To be the first wife, dearer than all the others. . . . To sit beside him through the long evenings in the quiet of his common room. . . . To yearn again, to possess again. . . . What had there been for her in Paltiel's house? Pity and courtesy, kindliness for the slow mind and the blunt body, patience by day, forbearance by night. . . . Peace, peace, what has a woman to do with peace? What are thirteen years of peace beside one Gibean night? . . . She rose and felt the shaft of light break dazzling upon her face.

"Will my lady go with me then to the town of Bahurim to be reunited with her lord?"

The matter had gone far—there was actually a place in Israel where they were to meet and embrace. . . . She closed her eyes and saw Paltiel crossing the threshold of his house. But how can a man thrive on deceit? she asked herself. Surely he knows that I only suffered him to possess me. . . .

Nevertheless she said to the captain: "What of my brother? What of Paltiel?"

"Your brother is afraid, and I will deliver him out of his fear. The Star of Bethlehem has a mighty army. Against such an army, the walls of Mahanaim are as the shell of an egg. I will say to Ishbaal that the King of Judah takes Michal as a hostage. So long as Michal dwells in David's house, there will be peace between Judah and Israel."

"Is it so? Will there be peace?" She sought for justification now.

She could not see him, but she sensed that he shrugged. "So the son of Jesse has told my messenger," he said.

"And Paltiel?"

There was long silence, in which for the first time she heard the dripping of water. Slow, single drops were running down the walls of the cave and falling into the pools below.

"Paltiel. . . ." he said at last. "Certainly it will be a grave loss to Paltiel. And yet a man might lose a beloved wife with less pain if it were given out to him that he lost her for Israel's sake. This I know—that David waits only for the death of Achish to hurl his host against the Philistines and drive them forth from the land."

She wished that the captain would come again into the shaft of light. Her heart had gone out to him in gratefulness. He has been straight and plain with me, she thought, even as he was straight and plain with my father in other days. Why, then, should he hide his face from me in the dark? . . .

"Abner has dealt very honorably with me," she said.

Again there was stillness and the drip of water. Then she heard him draw a sharp, quick breath. And she knew that he had not dealt honorably with her; she knew that in his exigency he had used her, that Rizpah was more to him than the House of Kish, that he had sold the House of Kish for a price at last. But how, how? She groped back through the conversation to the moment when he had retreated into the dark. What had he said? "He has great need of my lady. . . ." What need? Her unruly heart had not stopped to ask; she had seen only one possible need. But there were others. There was, for instance, the need of an upstart Judahite to have Saul's daughter beside him when he reached out his hand to take Israel. . . .

"Nevertheless, if my lady finds that her heart is bound to Paltiel——"

She laughed. "No, now," she said, "Abner knows my heart. He has taken it in his hands and has molded it to his purpose. He knows well how it was with me—in Gibeah and now and forever; how I turned always and utterly toward the Judahite. And it is plain to me that it is not out of longing but out of policy that the son of Jesse calls me to him."

"You are the first true wife," said Abner, miserably clinging to the fragment of his deception that had contained a shred of truth. "There was none whom he loved more than Michal, save only Jonathan, and Jonathan is dead."

She strove to repress the look of exultation on her face. Dead, she thought, dead, and surely in some measure forgotten. He cannot work his terrible magic against me now. What are they to me, the four whom I will strive against in Hebron? There is no adversary upon the earth who is to be compared with Jonathan. . . .

"Come, now," she said, "why should we tarry over the matter? It is settled. I will go to David. To Paltiel and to Ishbaal we will say that I go to bring peace in Israel. But between Abner and me let there be no lies. The son of Jesse has called me down so that he may strengthen himself by me. And I—I go down for the old reason. I go down because I yearn after my lord."

ᴥᶴ XI ᶚᴥ

Wʜᴇɴ the son of Jesse rode into Bahurim, he regretted that he had chosen it as a meeting-place. The houses were brown and squat; the streets were short and narrow; and the inhabitants looked mean and oppressed by the heat of the summer sun. He wished that he had arranged to bring Michal and Abner down to Hebron. He would have felt more secure with the magnificence of his house around him—the brazen gate, the green garden, the cool, shadowy rooms and the pillared halls.

The wealthiest of the elders of Bahurim had been swift to offer his house for the uses of the King of Judah. The elder himself had tarried only long enough to inform the son of Jesse that the servants would serve a respectable repast whenever the King required it and would on all other occasions keep themselves strictly out of the way of the reunited lovers. The word "lovers" and the faint smile that accompanied it were distasteful to the Star of Bethlehem, and he was glad to see the old man gone.

Of late the business of Joab had occupied his mind more than even so momentous a matter as the offer which Abner had sent to him out of Israel. There had been hints in Abner's message; Benjamin and Ephraim were disaffected; the army in Mahanaim was decimated; what man could suppose that Ishbaal would reign in the north for long? But Abner's offer was still indefinite; to dream about it would have been to indulge in a luxury. The problem of Joab was, on the other hand, a stubborn fact, a piece of unyielding insolence against which the King of Judah bruised himself at least once in the course of every day. The eldest son of Zeruiah must somehow be humbled. But by what means?

Any man save Joab would have been utterly shattered by the shame and the reproof that had been heaped upon him. In the urgency of his sorrow, David had punished Joab for more than Gibeon—he had let loose upon him the accumulated bitterness of all the shameful maneuvers in which he himself had borne a part. In stripping the command of the host from Joab, the son of Jesse had striven not only to punish his nephew but also to cleanse himself. And it was this knowledge that had led him to lighten the discipline a little, to do nothing more than raise his eyebrows when the Ishmaelite came again to the encampment. The matter had ended in equivocation. Joab was at the same time the captain and not the captain. Within the course of two moons, his position was as it had been before, with only this difference: that, since he was forbidden to address himself to David, he could do much as he pleased without troubling himself to consult his lord.

And now that Abner was about to come down to the camp of Judah, the matter had become pressing. The wounds upon the body of Israel would be healed far more swiftly if Abner would take the army of the south into his practiced and honorable hands. The world knew that the old man

395

would never march northward against his tribesmen. He would let Ishbaal live out a harmless and inglorious life behind the walls of Mahanaim. Like David, he would wish to hoard the strength of Israel until the day when Achish died. And yet the King of Judah had not called his nephew to him to say, "Behold, it is as I said; you are no longer the captain; I have found another captain in your place." He had not so much as mentioned that messages had passed between himself and Abner; he had simply sent the troublesome Ishmaelite on a long campaign against the dwellers in the southern desert; he had gained no more than a breathing-space. . . .

The sight of the wooden gate intruded itself upon his meditations. The time when the gate would swing open to admit the King's daughter could not be too distant now. He strove to visualize the meeting, to see the Princess Michal standing on the path under the shadow of the fig trees. But he could see nothing but a pair of dark, resentful eyes. Certain of his own men had ridden down out of the north with a strange story concerning the beginnings of her journey. It was said that Paltiel had insisted upon accompanying her, that he was behaving in a most unmanly fashion, clinging to her hand and weeping like a child. The poor wretch, David thought. To love is continual anguish. It is well to be finished with love. . . .

The afternoon was waning. The light was broken now into a series of oblique rays, shining over a bank of purplish clouds in the west. The time of the meeting had been left vague. "We will come," Abner had said, "between noon and the setting of the sun." Now that the sun had begun to set, it was necessary to make the final preparations, to wander to the copper basin which stood on the clothes chest, to dabble his fingers in the tepid water, to wipe the shine of sweat from his face. He leaned over the basin and saw himself. The image which floated darkly upon the surface startled him with its starkness and solemnity. Surely, he thought, this is no face with which to go forth to meet a woman. . . . And even as he stared at it and sought to change it, he heard the creaking hinge of the garden gate. Abner's voice, Michal's voice—voices out of Gibeah— came to him through the window. He closed his eyes and saw Saul's garden on a summer night. Then I am not completely turned to stone, he thought, feeling the hoped-for resurrection, the stirring in his blood. . . .

❧ XII ❧

THE GLOW of remembrance survived the moment when they met upon the dusty little path. It was not lessened when they stopped ten paces apart to gaze at each other, to measure the changes that had been wrought by the years. He found her far less changed than he had dreamed; she carried herself with the indestructible pride of the highborn; she had changed only in that she had grown more distinctly and immutably herself. He came forward and embraced her with spontaneous ardor. The fact that she did not invite him to kiss her made it possible for him to do so with actual pleasure. He was gratified too by the cool reserve of her lips.

As for the old captain who stood behind her on the path—his presence served to increase the glow. He had changed far more than Saul's daughter; his hair and beard were sparser and whiter, and his skin was bleached and shriveled; to look at him was to feel the full weight of the thirteen years. And yet he seemed closer to Jonathan than Jonathan's sister. He greeted the King of Judah with the same smile that he had been wont to bestow upon the lutist; and for an instant, in the light of the dying sun, all remembrances, unspoken and unspeakable, flared up in his reddened eyes.

The son of Jesse found himself moving through the intricacies of the situation with more than creditable grace. The strangeness of the house, which had seemed a liability before the coming of the guests, was a blessing to him now. He made witty conversation out of his ignorance of the where-abouts of napkins and servants, basins and food. Within half an hour, they sat down cheerfully to the respectable repast that had been promised by their host, all three of them expressing surprise and delight at the excellence of the service and the savor of the meat.

David was fortunate, too, in being delivered for the moment from direct and earnest conversation with the woman who sat beside him. The con-versation was all between him and Abner. The captain had announced soon after his arrival that he meant to set out for the north before the fall of night—four of the warriors who had journeyed down with him were awaiting him at the gate—and there was much to be settled before he could depart. He gave his information briefly, as if it were of little significance beside the matters that would come to pass in his absence be-tween the lovers. Still, it might please the King of Judah to know that the elders of Benjamin and Ephraim were by no means averse to a union be-tween the north and the south. Such a union could be brought about in a matter of months. Nor was there any reason to believe that there would be bloodshed. The army of Mahanaim would not come into the field so long as their city was not attacked, so long as there was clemency for their harmless young King. . . .

. The news was so gratifying, the occasion was so innocent of the expected stress, that David found himself wishing to shower endless honors and favors upon Abner. "And the captain?" he said, smiling across the lamps which the servants had carried into the darkening room. "How can I ever show my gratefulness to the captain? What will he take at my hands? Will he stand in the place of the son of Zeruiah? Will he take my host?"

The old man smiled and closed his eyes. "I am exceedingly old and burdened with years," he said. "Let the son of Jesse believe me: I want nothing at his hands but a house and a garden and the assurance that I may spend my latter days in peace."

"But there are wounds upon the body of Israel——"

"I know, I know. And if it is the will of the Star of Bethlehem, I will labor yet a little to heal those wounds—a few moons, a year, as long as my lord requires. Meanwhile, the troubles that have arisen in the House of Jesse will be forgotten. The day of my reward will be the day when the son of Zeruiah takes back his host."

In this also the son of Jesse found reason for good cheer. One could say to the Ishmaelite: "Behold, I have relented. It is only a small punishment which I have meted out to you because of the slaughter at Gibeon. For the sake of Israel, I have given the army to Abner for a year. When the year has run its course, I will render back to you all that I have taken— yes, that and more, for it will be a far mightier host, increased by thousands out of Benjamin and Ephraim."

He saw with some regret that the meal could not be protracted. Night had come down upon the garden beyond the window; the lamps burned with a steadier glow; the captain had pushed his plate aside and was wiping his lips.

"Must Abner depart so soon?" said David.

Abner's smile turned the question into a piece of kindly and meaningless courtesy. "If I depart in haste, it is that I am eager to be about my lord's business," he said. "When shall I come again?"

David pondered for a moment. He counted fourteen days as the shortest possible time that might pass before Joab's return from the desert.

"Within ten days," he said, "in Hebron."

Abner raised his wine cup with the haste of one who merely wets his tongue before he departs. While the captain drank, David glanced sidewise at Saul's daughter. She sat motionless, with her chin resting upon her clasped hands. There was a fixed look, a solemn shining, in her eyes. He grew uneasy then at the thought that the time had come when he must deal with her alone. What is she waiting for? he asked himself. Does she believe that I can work miracles? This is not Gibeah, nor am I in my twentieth year. . . . And when he rose to walk to the door with the captain, it seemed to him that the highheartedness of the occasion was departing with the old man into the night.

He walked to the opposite side of the table and stood looking down at her across the lamps and the empty plates. "Have I changed so greatly that my lady Michal must accustom her eyes to my face?" he asked in the courtly accents of Benjamin.

"Changed?" she said gravely. "We have all changed. How could it be otherwise, in thirteen years?"

"I have come a long way," he said, "since that night when I parted from Michal in Gibeah. . . ."

Her eyes, solemn and pitiful, were lifted to his face. He resented the look. He wanted no pity from a woman. It had been difficult enough to endure the shy ministrations of the little Jezreelitess, who, knowing her own unworthiness, had sorrowed at a proper distance over the griefs of the Star of Bethlehem. It was unthinkable that he should accept the pity of a woman who had no great awe before lesser kings, inasmuch as her father had reigned over all Israel.

"The Lord has seen fit that I should prosper in spite of the enmity of the House of Kish," he said. "I have my host and my kingdom. I have three sons and a daughter——" He stopped. He had blundered into cruelty. He had not meant to fling this blatant reminder of her barrenness in her face. "I am eager to show the daughter of Saul the chambers which I have prepared for her in Hebron. . . ."

She was not listening. She bent her head a little and set her teeth into her lower lip.

"There are two broad, fair chambers, and one of them opens upon the garden——"

"No, now," she said, "let my lord forgive me." And she covered her face and wept.

He should have gone to her then. He should have embraced her and comforted her. It might have been possible to move swiftly from pity into love, to dry her cheeks and lead her to the bed. But he stood motionless, appalled by a sudden realization: it was small wonder that she wept. He saw the world as it must appear to her eyes. He saw himself, grown hard and arrogant and cold, and Paltiel making a solitary journey toward an empty house, and night coming down upon an alien room, and honor and tenderness spent to no purpose upon a dream. . . . God of Hosts, why did I bring her down? he asked himself. Even though, without her, I might never have claimed the allegiance of Ephraim and Benjamin, I should have left her in peace. . . . And he could not endure the sight of her uncontrollable weeping. Anger assailed him, and he strode into the garden, knowing not which he hated most—Saul's daughter or himself.

He walked to the gate and leaned upon it. Then I will return to the room and say to Michal, "That which I said concerning my children was not said in malice, but in awkwardness. It is true that I have brought only evil upon the House of Kish, and that I have heaped nothing but sorrows upon your head. Nevertheless, I did not wish to be cruel. Come, then, let us be kind with each other now, for the world is a bitter place, and there are not too many nights before the eternal night." . . .

But when he came again into the shabby room, he found that she was no longer there. The servant who was clearing the table told him that the lady had taken a lamp into the bedchamber and lain down to rest. And when he found his way at last into the room where she lay, he saw that she had delivered him from the necessity for speech.

She lay upon the bed with the coverlet drawn to her chin. Her eyelashes quivered upon her cheeks; she was feigning sleep. He stood above her for a little before he quenched the lamp, but she did not stir. She had made it possible for him to take her and to lose her in the blackness of the night.

✥ XIII ✥

O**N THE TENTH DAY** after the meeting in Bahurim, Abner came down to
Hebron as he had promised, bringing twenty men with him, all elders
and captains out of Benjamin and Ephraim. The King of Judah gave
them an impressive welcome. He spread a feast for them at high noon
within the green shadow of the common room. Even though it was a day
of stifling heat, the occasion was as festive as he could have wished. Saul's
daughter sat at his side at the head of the board. She knew many of the
visitors and soon put them all at their ease.

The terms of the covenant were made clear to the assembled company
in a formal, almost ritualistic conversation between Abner and David, a
conversation which took place before the serving of the meat. The King
and the old captain rose from their seats and faced each other across the
long board. David asked a series of questions, and Abner furnished the
foreknown replies. It was agreed that there should be henceforth but one
king in Israel, that the son of Jesse should reign from Dan to Beersheba,
and that his children and his children's children should reign after him,
even unto the end of the world. It was also agreed that no violence
should come upon those who chose to seclude themselves behind the walls
of Mahanaim. For the time being, the combined hosts of the north and
the south would encamp at Hebron. But Hebron was to be looked upon
only as a temporary capital. Jerusalem, the navel of the world, was still in
the hands of the Jebusites, but sooner or later the men of Jahveh would
march up against it to make it their own. Jerusalem was the only proper
capital for the united nation. It had belonged neither to the north nor to
the south; it had been in the hands of the heathen since the beginning of
time; and he who set his throne upon its soil rooted his house deep in
victory. As for the captaincy—that, too, was a settled matter. None but
Abner, the hero of Michmash and Amalek and Jabesh-Gilead, would
stand at the head of the host of God.

At the third hour after noon the men of Ephraim and Benjamin rose
to depart. They paused only long enough to go up to the roof of David's
house, from which there was an excellent view of the encampment. They
looked down upon the thousands of warriors practicing archery and the
throwing of the spear. They saw the innumerable black tents, the herds
of grazing donkeys, the magnificent piles of armor blazing under the sun.
They saw, too, a sudden surge of excitement pass over the army. The
ranks broke and moved toward the tallest and most splendid of the tents,
and a babble of welcome rose from the host. The visitors did not ask the
son of Jesse what it was that had come to pass, nor did he tell them. But
he could barely refrain from sending them on their way with discourteous
haste; for he knew that the son of Zeruiah had come back too soon from
his foray into the south.

Now that they were gone, he walked the floor and spent his sense of

400

urgency upon irrelevant matters—the common room must be set to rights; the women and the servants must move about more quickly; the little Amnon must be sent to bed. Once or twice he asked himself if it might not be best to go down to the encampment, seek out the son of Zeruiah, and lay the situation plainly before him. But then the talk would begin with a discussion of Joab's foray, and it would be difficult, after a series of congratulatory speeches, to inform the returned warrior that Abner had been given command over the host. Furthermore, it was possible that the son of Zeruiah would hear nothing for some time of the visitors who were even now leaving the gates of Hebron. Perhaps he would remain in his tent for hours, telling the tales of his raid to an avid crowd of listeners. Perhaps the wisest procedure was to wait, to do nothing at all. . . .

But not much time was given to him for waiting. Noi had barely led Amnon off to his chamber, Maacah and Haggith had only begun to heap the soiled plates, and Abigail had not yet finished gathering up the crumpled napkins when Michal returned from the garden—she had been lingering there, staring after her departing tribesmen—to say that the son of Zeruiah was at the gate.

"Joab, indeed?" he said. "Let him come to my bedchamber, and I will receive him there." For his temper will be vile enough from the beginning, he thought, and it will not be sweetened by the sight of the leavings of a festival in which he has taken no part. . . .

The curtains of the bedchamber had been drawn, and only a greenish, watery light seeped through them. All colors were muted—the coppery gleam of the big water basin, the whiteness of the rugs, the crimson of the coverlet. David stretched himself upon the bed, with a pillow beneath his head. He wished to appear both splendid and serene before the son of Zeruiah. He did not wear the circlet which signified that he was the King of Judah, but he left it lying within full view, among the folds of the coverlet. Now let him come, he thought, let us have done with this matter once and for all. . . .

Joab entered the shadowy room, closed the door behind him, walked noiselessly to the foot of the bed, and stood at the King's feet. It was plain that he had neither rested nor bathed, that he had come up from the encampment as he had ridden in from the desert—dusty and sweating and burned red by the heat of the sun. Three moons of disapprobation had not erased the insolent look from his eyes. Instead of waiting for the King of Judah to indicate to him that the interdiction of silence had been lifted, he raised his voice at once. "What have you done?" he said.

Not since the day when Saul had cast the spear had David been required by any man to justify himself. He kept the chill silence of one who does not feel himself called upon to answer.

"I know what has come to pass in this house in my absence," Joab said. "Abner has sat with you in council. How is it that you spread a feast for my enemy while I kill swine for you in the desert? Wherefore have you sent him away secretly at the hour of my return?"

The King of Judah put down his rising anger and continued to lie motionless upon the bed.

"Surely," said Joab, "you know what Abner is and what he seeks in the camp of God. He has come down to spy upon you, to watch your goings-out and your comings-in."

He is far gone indeed, thought David, if he believes I can be hoodwinked by such lies. . . .

"Whatsoever Abner has learned in Hebron," Joab said, "he will carry back to Mahanaim to whisper it in the ears of Ishbaal his lord."

"Abner will return neither to his lord nor to Mahanaim," said the son of Jesse, "and Joab knows as much. A covenant has been made this day between Judah and the captains and elders of Ephraim and Benjamin. When he has carried the news of the covenant into the north, then Abner will return to Hebron, he and all the sons of Jahveh who bear arms, to dwell with us in the camp of God."

"So?" said the son of Zeruiah. Now he clung to the footboard with both hands. His eyes were no longer insolent; they were wide with consternation.

"Many things have been established this day," said the son of Jesse in a quiet voice. "Judah and Israel are one henceforth. Hebron is the capital of the united kingdom until the hour when we shall wrest Jerusalem out of the hands of the Jebusites. The host—how could it be otherwise?—is in the hands of Abner. It will remain in his hands until such time as there is no more mistrust between the north and the south."

For a moment such thick and oppressive silence as comes before the roll of thunder brooded upon the room. David could not bring himself to look into his nephew's face. He stared gravely, remotely, at the brown hands. They clutched the footboard; the swollen veins stood out upon them; the nails drove down upon the polished wood. Let him glare at me, thought the King of Judah, feeling Joab's eyes upon him. Let him glare his fill. He will come to know at last that I will not relent and am not afraid. . . . Then suddenly, unaccountably, the air was clear. The dark hands relaxed and flung themselves upward in a gesture of resignation.

"If it is established, then it is established. What can I do but bow my head before the judgment of my lord?" Joab said.

David started up from his pillow in amazement. It had never come into his mind that his pronouncement would be met with acquiescence, unstudied and complete. For the space of a few heartbeats, he wondered whether the very wholeheartedness of the acceptance did not mark it as spurious. He fixed a long and searching look upon his nephew, but he could find no shadow of guile in the large and luminous eyes.

"Why should my uncle gaze upon me in wonderment?" Joab said. "Did he think I would gnash my teeth and rend my garments? What profit is there in mourning over that which cannot be mended?"

The King of Judah sat upright now on the edge of the bed. A certain uneasiness made it impossible for him to sit still. He began to smooth the creases from the crimson coverlet. "The host is Abner's," he said, "for the present only. When the breach between Judah and Israel is completely healed—within a few moons, within a year at most—I will render it back into Joab's hands." He had said quite enough to appease one who had shown so plainly that he required no appeasement, and yet a nameless fear drove him to speak on. "I will give back to Joab much more than I took from him after Gibeon. The host will be increased by thousands out of the north——" He paused because he had sensed that the son of Zeruiah was not listening. He glanced up and saw the dark pupils turn swiftly in his direction; Joab had been looking toward the door; now he came round to the side of the bed, seated himself upon the coverlet, and slouched forward with his elbows upon his knees, in an attitude of intolerable weariness. "Were my uncle to promise me a host of fifty thousand for tomorrow, it would not stir my heart," he said. "Save for the brief interval of this hour, I have been upon my horse since the rising of the sun. The heat of the desert was such that I am burned almost to ashes. Let my uncle believe me, I can think of nothing but sleep."

For the first time in many moons, the son of Jesse laid his hand upon his nephew. "Indeed," he said, "I meant to inquire at once how it went with you in the south, but the thought was driven from my head."

"It went well enough," said the son of Zeruiah, lifting the hem of his tunic to wipe the sweat from his face. "The spoils were enough to fill four wagons, and some three hundred Bedouins are no more. There is a bar of silver as thick as my arm which has been laid aside for the King of Judah. I will bring it up to him whenever he wishes—tomorrow morning, tomorrow night."

"Let us break bread together tomorrow," said David. "Come up to us at the hour of the going-down of the sun."

In the unaccountable moment of silence between his invitation and Joab's acceptance, the King of Judah reassured himself with the thought that tomorrow night they would sit peaceably at the table, with this unhappy matter half forgotten. His nephew rose, and David did not urge him to tarry longer. He himself had grown suddenly weary; the day had been noisy and crowded; he had not been vouchsafed a single hour for his own use. He embraced the son of Zeruiah and went with him as far as the door of the bedchamber. Then he bade him farewell, and turned and lay down again upon the crimson coverlet, closing his tired eyes against the fading light. But he was troubled by small things—the clatter of dishes and the laughter of Tamar and Absalom in the garden—and it was long before he slept.

◄§ XIV §►

THE EMBASSY out of Ephraim and Benjamin tarried near the cistern of Sirah longer than they had intended. They had meant to stop there only long enough to wash themselves and to break the evening bread under the meager fig trees that stood around the circle of yellowish and ancient stones. But there were many old men among the travelers from the north. The longer they sat beneath the fig trees, the more they felt their weariness; and they were still at Sirah, talking and rubbing their aching legs, at the hour of the rising of the moon.

Abner sat on the edge of the cistern with one of the Ephraimite elders. Their talk had been desultory; neither of them really listened to the other; each had used his neighbor merely as a pretext for giving voice to his own thoughts. The elder out of Ephraim had spoken of his garden and his grandchildren, and Abner had spoken of the day when he would lay down his sword and return to the hills of Benjamin. In the dreaming silences that came upon them, Abner wondered what crops he would raise on the land of his fathers. Well, he told himself, I will consider the matter with my old woman. . . . And now that he had thought of her, he began to worry over the house in which the two of them were to spend the remainder of their days. No one had lived in it since the coming of the Philistines; the rafters were sagging, the garden wall was down, and the garden itself was a wilderness. "We will restore it," he said aloud.

"What is it that the captain will restore?" said the elder in a patient voice.

"My house in Benjamin. We will set it to rights, my wife and I."

"Indeed," the Ephraimite said, "there are many fine houses that have fallen into ruin in Benjamin."

The phrase, said idly enough to indicate attentiveness, took on a strange weight in the somber place. The captain gazed at the dark water and thought how much that had been dear to him had been devoured by the years. He was still lost in his brooding when he was roused by the sound of his name. A stranger stood before him, a young slave out of Egypt, with a flat, impassive face and a pair of slanting, heavy-lidded eyes.

"I have come from Hebron with a message for Abner," the slave said.

He had appeared so soundlessly at the edge of the cistern that Abner was startled. "What would the King of Judah have of me?" he said.

"I do not come from the King of Judah, my lord."

It was the manner of Egypt, the captain thought, to make a mystery out of the simplest of things. Only a son of Amon and Set would stand as still as a stele in the fading light, waiting for his message to be drawn out of him word by word.

"Then who sent you?"

"Joab, the son of Zeruiah. He charged me to give a message to the captain of the host."

Well, give it, then, thought Abner, peering at the expressionless face through the gathering dark. He had a conviction that whatever the slave was about to say would be sullen and ungracious, and he was startled again when the words came smooth and fair out of the solemn lips.

"When my lord Joab returned this day out of the south," said the slave, "and heard that the captain had departed, his heart was smitten with grief because he had not spoken with Abner, nor looked upon his face. 'God forbid,' said the son of Zeruiah, 'that he should hold the matter of Gibeon against me. If I see him not, how shall I know that I am forgiven?' So strong was Joab's yearning after a word with Abner that he would have ridden forth to seek him. But he could not ride, inasmuch as this day he has come in from a raid in the south, and cannot sit upon his horse for weariness. Therefore Joab bade me say to the captain of the host, 'Return this night to the gate of the city, that I also may make a covenant with you before you depart.' This is the message of my lord Joab, who has sent his steed with me to carry back the captain of the host."

"Can I return again this night to Sirah?" Abner said.

"Surely, my lord. The steed of my master is very swift. My lord can go down to Hebron and return to Sirah again in a matter of two hours."

The slave made a gesture in the direction of a distant and solitary olive tree. A red horse was tethered to it, a powerful and forbidding beast that neither grazed nor wandered, but stood motionless among the thorn and the stones.

The thought of riding back through the growing darkness with the heathenish beast beneath him and the Egyptian sitting behind was strangely repellent to the captain of the host. But to offer an excuse would be to strike the son of Zeruiah in the face.

"There is no help for it," he said, turning to the elder. "The son of Zeruiah has found it in his heart to be courteous and kindly with me, and I would not give him offense. Say to the others that they should tarry for me here. I will return within two hours."

When they came to the tree to which the red horse was tethered, the captain knew that he could not manage the beast. It expressed its hostility in certain subtle movements—its eyes rolled in their red sockets, and the muscles in its flanks began to twitch.

"No, now," said Abner, "this steed will have none of me. Let the son of Amon mount and take the reins, and I will ride behind."

They rode so swiftly past the few villages that lay between Sirah and Hebron that the yellow windows were mere blurs of light. He wondered at the vastness of the land and at the slightness of the dominion that man had established over it. The trees, meager and scattered as they were, seemed far more numerous and more permanent than man. Once he lifted his face to the sky, but such giddiness overcame him that he had to cling hard to the Egyptian. The moon and the stars careened before them down the great arc of sky, and he was obsessed by the irrational notion that the inexorable laws of the firmament had been loosened—that the moon and the stars were rushing headlong upon the world.

He thought of raising his voice against the pace. But he had a persistent conviction that nothing he could say would move the Egyptian. He believed—and he knew not why he believed it—that the slave had sensed his fright and was taking pleasure in it; that the flat, imperturbable disk of a face which flew through the twilight before him wore a fixed and cruel smile. No, now, he asked himself, how is it with me that my mind is open to these strange imaginings? If the heart within me is such that it is confounded by a horse and an Egyptian, then I am an old man indeed and fit for nothing but tea made of herbs, and quiet talk, and sleep. . . . And he conjured up a vision of Rizpah, who would at this hour be coming in from the garden. He told himself that surely she had invited one of the neighbor women to sit with her that night, for it seemed to him unbearably pitiful that she should be moving through the withered foliage alone.

He had closed his eyes in order to see the image of Rizpah more clearly. When he opened them, the lights of Hebron were before him, floating in a dissolving mist. The last glimmer of the twilight had been withdrawn from the firmament, and he knew that the bazaars were shut. Somewhere in the bright city toward which they sped there was a long black vista, an empty merchants' street. . . . The pace of the horse slackened. The Egyptian turned his head slowly over his shoulder. His face was barely visible in the dark, but the captain was certain that the ripe lips were curled in a taunting smile.

"Behold, we have come to the city," the slave said, and began to guide the horse slowly down a slope covered with fig and olive trees toward the twin pylons that stood at the gates of Hebron.

The captain saw the gleam of dark water between the end of the slope and the gate. The King of Judah, in order to double the small yield of water that rose from the springs of his city, had ordered that two deep pools be dug outside the walls. The work was not yet complete, and the land before the city looked raw and torn. The light of the moon, falling obliquely upon it, revealed a stretch of clay broken by two black oblongs and cluttered with piles of squared building stones. At the foot of the slope, the Egyptian dismounted. "My lord must walk to the gate," he said. "The way is between the pools. Let my lord go before me, and I will tether my horse and follow."

After the long ride, Abner was dazed and shaken. He walked unsteadily between the pools. He could hear the moist clay sucking beneath his weight; some of it seeped over the edge of his sandals and clung to his feet. The pool to his right was filled with still water. The one to his left had been dug in midsummer and had not yet received the winter rains. The stone lining had not been set in place, and the crude oblong bore the aspect of a gigantic grave. He turned aside from it and fixed his eyes upon the entrance to the city. Against one of the towering gray pylons a solitary figure stood—thin, tall, motionless. It is the son of Zeruiah, he thought, and forced himself to walk more swiftly toward the gate.

Far above Joab's head, in the tower chamber of the gray pylon, a lamp burned and a figure moved back and forth, sometimes obscuring, sometimes revealing the yellow light that shone in the square, curtainless window. It is the watchman at the gate, thought Abner. And for a moment he was soothed by the feeling of reassurance that rose in the breast of every son of Jahveh who looked upon such a light—the ever-present, unshutting eye of the city on guard against the evils of the wilderness and the night. Then he knew that the Egyptian was coming up behind him. The moist, sucking footfalls drew closer, and he hastened to the end of the pathway between the pools, wishing to keep the greatest possible distance between the son of Amon and himself.

Now that he was not twenty paces from the gate, he fixed his eyes upon Joab. It is as they say with the son of Zeruiah, he thought; he is less Israelite than Ishmaelite. . . . The face toward which he advanced was as alien as the disk-shaped face that came up behind him. It was as narrow and keen as the faces of the jackals that walked through the southern sands. It wore a wide smile, and the teeth shone white in the light of the moon.

"Do my eyes behold my lord Abner?" said Joab, spreading his arms wide in a gesture meant to symbolize an embrace. "Has he indeed come all this weary road to make a covenant with me this night?"

The captain raised his eyes once more to the warm glow in the window of the watchtower. Then he went forward and laid his hand in the lean, hard, waiting hand. The pressure of Joab's fingers was such that he winced. God of Hosts, he thought, how long will he hold me? Will he never let me free? . . .

"The son of Zeruiah," he said, "has dealt with me very graciously. I have been brought against my will to do him certain injuries. That he has forgotten them shows plainly the greatness of his heart."

Without releasing his hand, Joab had linked arms with him and had drawn him into the shadow of the pylon. They turned and stood together with their backs against the rough stone. The Egyptian loitered in the moonlight, not ten paces from them. It was strange that his master had not dismissed him. It was stranger, and more terrifying, that the ripe lips plainly wore a cruel smile.

"What injury has the captain of the host put upon me?" said Joab. "The matter of the captaincy? The matter of Asahel? No, now, these are trivial matters that can be settled between us in a moment." The son of Zeruiah sprang forward and confronted the captain, and there was a dagger in his hand. "Settled in a moment, with one blow," he said.

Swiftly, unbelievably, even as Abner cried out, Joab was upon him. There was a cold, inward thrust, a white blaze of shock across the sky.

"Murder!" shrieked a voice from the watchtower. "Murder at the gate!"

Abner lifted up his voice to protest that the breath of life, the knowledge of the moist clay that he lay upon, were within him still. But no words issued from him. Nothing came forth but a strange gurgling and a pool of black blood. Then it is so indeed, he told himself. . . . And he turned his face toward the hills of Benjamin and gave himself up to the dark.

At no time had the hand of Jahveh worked so plainly for the son of Jesse as in the days after the slaying of the captain of the host. The violence at the gate of Hebron might well have cut off all hope of a united kingdom. Surely Joab had shown that Hebron was a haunt of bandits, a hornet's nest on the edge of the wilderness. Surely, when a day of covenanting ended in murder there was no reason to believe that the men of Judah would fulfill any promise or abide by any law. Yet the north sent no messengers down to pour out its indignation before the son of Jesse. The north waited, weary and passive, to see how the King of Judah would conduct himself.

He conducted himself—and they had no reason to believe him otherwise than sincere—like a man bereaved of a beloved father. He lay on the floor in sackcloth and ashes. He ate no meat. He bade the men of Hebron tear down a summerhouse that he had begun to build two years ago, and set up in its place an impressive tomb for the captain of the host. On the day of the burial, he ordered that the entire city should put on mourning. He walked, disheveled and white in the face, before the bier; and the dirge that he composed for the occasion cried out fiercely to all the world that he was innocent. Abner, it said, had been slain in violence by a child of iniquity. And his sorrow over Abner was such that he made all Hebron see the enormity of the loss, and the multitude stood around the tomb all day and wept.

Yet another danger was manifest in the situation. The men of Mahanaim had been devoted to their captain, and all Israel believed that the tidings of the murder would rouse them out of their long dream. They might have marched southward and demanded the execution of Joab at the gates of Hebron; they might have crossed the Jordan and offered their services to the affronted elders of Benjamin; they might even have led Ishbaal back to Gibeah and reaffirmed the dominion of Saul's seed over Israel. But they continued to sit idle within the charmed circle of their city; not one of them rose up and shook off the spell. They had learned to bear calamity with a numb serenity—Gilboa had passed, Gibeon had passed, and this also would pass. . . .

There were those in Benjamin who believed that Ishbaal at least would be moved to some gesture of desperation. But God had sent a torpor upon Ishbaal also. He wandered about in his withered garden, sucking ripe figs and pomegranates and wearing a tunic forever spotted with the juice of the fruit. Now that Abner was no more, it was plain how desperately the captain must have striven to keep a mask of kingliness upon this empty, staring face.

By the end of the summer, there were few who would have denied that there was but one king in Israel. Even in Mahanaim the pageantry of royalty fell imperceptibly away. The servants in the King's house neglected their duties, so that dust gathered upon the polished wood, and the same reeds, soiled and trampled, remained from week to week upon the floor. The King's bodyguard ceased to walk behind him, and his armor-bearer no longer sat at his feet while he slept.

So it was a simple matter to make an end of the last of the sons of Saul and Ahinoam. There were two Benjamites of the House of Rimmon who were willing enough to slay a useless and burdensome fool for a good price. They took it as a matter of course that a good price could be had from the hand of the son of Jesse. A bandit who had stolen from the children of Jahveh in the wilderness, a traitor who had marched up with the uncircumcised almost as far as Gilboa, a double-dealer who had wailed loudly at the edge of Abner's tomb but had not slain the son of Zeruiah for his bloodguiltiness—certainly a lordly price could be extracted from such a one. So they said between themselves, and patiently awaited their hour. Their hour was high noon, when the bodyguard lounged in the shadow of the arbors, when the servants drowsed, and the armor-bearer lay in the garden fast asleep. They knew that Ishbaal also had taken himself to his bed. There was no one to question their coming in—only an old crone who sat spinning in the common room, and to her they said that they had come up from the house of one of the young captains to borrow a basketful of wheat. When the deed was done—and it was done easily, for he did not so much as utter a sound when they held the pillow over his face—they cut off his head and laid it upon a bed of wheat in the wicker basket. Then they covered it with more of the grain and bore it out of the house and carried it southward, across the barren reaches of the Arabah, journeying without pause through the whole night.

And how did the son of Jesse bear himself when the sons of Rimmon laid their trophy before him? The tale of that encounter spread steadily northward, carried by wandering shepherds, by itinerant prophets, by leaders of caravans. How had he borne himself? Like a king—like the king of all Israel. The words in which he had denounced the murderers were passed unchanged from mouth to mouth:

"As Jahveh lives, He who has redeemed my soul out of all my adversity, when one came and told me, 'Behold, Saul is dead,' thinking to have brought me good tidings, I took hold on him and had him slain in Ziklag, which was the reward I gave him for his tidings. How much more, then, when wicked men have slain a righteous person in his bed, shall I not now require vengeance for his blood at your hands, and take you away from the earth?"

The sons of Rimmon were slain before the going down of the sun. The law required that their bodies should be dealt with as the bodies of criminals. The hands and feet were cut off, and the corpses were hung upon the two gray pylons that towered above the pools, so that every traveler who passed the gates might look upon them and know that the King of Judah was just. But the head of Ishbaal was washed and anointed with spices and bound in strips of linen. Michal carried it down in a round clay vessel and laid it in Abner's tomb, and those who followed her remarked that it was strange that she should shed no tears, that she should stand unmoved even at the moment of the closing of the grave.

Before the winter rains set in that year, there was much traveling over the highways. The drowsy villages which lay along the sides of the roads were given the pleasure of supplying brief repasts to a series of distinguished visitors: ambassadors from Tyre and Sidon, representatives from Gilgal and Shechem, elders and captains out of Ephraim and Benjamin. The hand of God had stretched out over the land and was drawing the brave, the rich, and the wise southward to the court at Hebron. Night after night, the King of Judah sat feasting in his garden with amicable strangers. Night after night, he received assurances of allegiance. They had ceased to address him as "my lord the King of Judah." They spoke again, as they had not spoken since the days of Saul's greatness, of "my lord the King." There was but one king in Israel.

And early in the spring, on the propitious occasion of the Feast of the First Fruits, they all returned to Hebron in one great convocation, singing hymns of rejoicing, their swords wreathed in olive leaves and their heads crowned with flowers. They called the son of Jesse forth from his house and led him in a procession to the high place of the city. "In times past, when Saul was king over us," they said, "it was David who led us out to battle and brought us back victorious. Plainly God has said to the son of Jesse that he shall be a shepherd of his people and a King in Israel." And they poured the holy oil of Shiloh upon his head and crowned him with a golden crown.

BOOK NINE

BOOK NINE

BOOK NINE

❧ I ❧

IN THE EARLY YEARS of his reign over a united Israel, it was said of David with affectionate wit that he carried the scales of justice into the council chamber and onto the field of battle, and that he did not put them by when he entered the portals of his high house in Jerusalem. He dealt with his wives as even-handedly as he dealt with his captains. The honors that he bestowed upon them were measured out so impartially that no man could tell which wife was the most dearly beloved.

When he was crowned king in Hebron, it was Michal who stood at his side and cast the dimmed luster of the House of Kish over the sacrifices and the feasts. When Achish died in Gath, it was Abigail who walked with her lord in the long pomp of the funeral procession. When Jerusalem fell to Joab's valor and strategy, it was Noi who helped to choose the hill on which his palace was to stand; she was with David when the earth was broken and blessed; and it was she who first beheld the magnificent logs of cedarwood that came down as a gift from Hiram, King of Tyre. After the great battle in the valley of Rephaim, where the Philistines were utterly confounded and driven back to the sea, Haggith sat at the head of his table, rewarding his captains with her quiet smile.

If the witching Maacah did not receive her share of the honors, she had none to blame but herself. She had gone off one summer afternoon to the tents of her people, meaning to return to Jerusalem within three moons. But the Queen of Geshur died during her sojourn; the old King, her father, had no other daughters; it was necessary for her to remain with him at least until he was resigned to his loss. She tarried for a year, and at the end of the year made it plain that she had gone home once and for all. She left her children behind her, knowing that they would receive motherly care at the hands of Noi.

If the King of Israel portioned out with irreproachable equality the favors which he bestowed upon his wives, he was, during the first years of his reign, even more scrupulous in his dealings with his children. No man could doubt that Absalom was the favorite son. The boy was so

413

comely that people turned to look after him in the street. Yet Amnon was the first born, whom Jahveh had sent to inherit the throne, and the son of Jesse used every possible occasion to remind Israel of this fact. It was Noi's child—gangling, stoop-shouldered, painfully shy—upon whom he bestowed the albino foal that was born in his stables. When he appeared on the portico of his house to greet an ambassador, it was Amnon whom he held by the hand. When the spoils of the Philistine campaign were brought up to Jerusalem, there was a certain little coat of scarlet, embroidered with white crabs and shells, which had belonged to the son of the Seren of Askelon. This coat the King of Israel held long across his knees, glancing up from it to the red lips and agile torso of Absalom. But in the end he laid it upon Amnon's narrow shoulders. "It is such a coat," he said, "as can be worn by none other than the Hope of Israel." And when the ark of Jahveh became the preoccupation of the land, the King announced at once that it would be Amnon who would accompany him on his holy journey to Baale-judah. First the King of Israel, and then the heir apparent, would behold the long-veiled mystery of the dwelling-place of the Lord.

The ark of God had been held prisoner in the land of the Philistines since the fall of Shiloh. Saul had set eyes upon it in the years of his youth, but Jonathan had never beheld it. Now that the uncircumcised had been defeated in the Valley of Rephaim, they were willing to use the ark to gain concessions from the Israelites.

The son of Jesse might have gone down with an army and demanded the ark without making any concessions; but it seemed to him both mean and impious to haggle over the sole physical manifestation of his God. If he gave more for the ark than the elders of the tribes would have permitted themselves to give, it was because he yearned more than any other Israelite to possess it. His capital was magnificent, populous, sweet with the smell of new cedarwood, rich in brazen gates, girt round with sturdy walls. His capital was musical with living waters and green with luxuriant palms and olive trees. His capital was the navel of the world and the center of Israel—but it had no holy place. Pilgrims used it merely as a way station on their road to the tomb of Rachel, the speaking oak of Shechem, the springs of Kadesh, the stone on which Jacob had laid his head. But if the ark of Jahveh were set upon a high hill in Jerusalem, then Jerusalem would become the holy of holies. The box of acacia wood whose contents were too sacred to be looked upon had been borne out of Egypt and carried before the tribes during their wanderings in the wilderness. It was Jahveh's gift to Israel when Jahveh and Israel had both been young, in the very bridal time of their life together. And whatsoever city possessed it became the lodestone of all pious hearts.

The court was swift to see his reasoning. But no man guessed that his eagerness to reclaim the ark was sustained by another and more private longing. When they have brought it up, he thought, and set it in a high place in the city, I will journey down alone to Gibeah and stand above

Jonathan's burial cave. I will say to him, "Behold, brother and beloved, I have come to tell you that I remember the night when we talked of the broken temple of Shiloh under the dripping trees in your father's garden. Shiloh I could not rebuild, inasmuch as the prophet Samuel bade me establish the House of God in Jerusalem. But the ark I have taken out of the hands of the uncircumcised. What we dreamed of accomplishing together I have accomplished for your sake. The ark is in Israel." . . .

When the time drew near for the men of Jahveh to bring up the dwelling-place of their God, the King made it plain that the occasion was to be considered a national festival in which each of the tribes was to bear an equal part. He called for three thousand of the strongest and most comely of his warriors to meet him on an appointed day on the olive-shadowed slope above the city, so that they might journey with him and his son to Baale-judah to receive the ark of God. He admonished them to purify themselves, to fast and pray and put on linen that had never been worn before. The land was at peace, and no man was to bring any weapon with him. Every man was to come in white, with a white girdle and a crown of olive leaves. He selected and carefully trained an orchestra of priests to lead them with music. The instruments were to be made anew, of the purest metal and the finest cedarwood, and several of them he fashioned with his own hands. There were harps and psalteries, timbrels and castanets and cymbals. He himself would walk at the head of the procession, clothed like the other pilgrims and playing on his lute. But since the journey was long, he decided that Amnon should go mounted on the albino donkey. And when the lad asked for permission to wear his scarlet coat, David could not refuse. It would be well to have the Hope of Judah singled out from all the rest.

When they came to the border town of Baale-judah late that afternoon, they learned that the sons of Dagon and Astarte had arrived with the ark some hours before them and had placed it in the house of a certain Abinadab, an old man noted for his piety. The house of Abinadab was brown and low, just such a house as had been the dwelling-place of the son of Jesse in Bethlehem. When they came to the street in which it stood, David bade all his followers save Amnon retrace their steps and wait for him before the gates of the town. "Leave the oxen and the cart at the door," he said. "I will bring forth the ark and set it thereupon and lead it up to the gates. But we will remain here for an hour or so, my son and I, inasmuch as it is fitting that the King of Israel and the green shoot of his house should pray a while alone."

The multitude departed then, and David lifted the child from the donkey and removed his scarlet coat, so that Amnon also would come before the Lord in white. The child looked more slight and disheartened than usual after the long journey. But there is no good in veiling him before the eyes of Jahveh, David thought. The Lord knows well how it is with my house. . . .

Those who dwelt within—the old man, his wrinkled wife, and their two stalwart sons—were already in such a state of transport because of the presence of the ark that they had little emotion left to spend upon the arrival of the King of Israel. They rose from their seats, wordless and with shining eyes, and led the King and the King's son to the end of their common room. There, on a clothes chest, in a nest of green vine leaves, the holy of holies stood. They pointed at it with unsteady fingers, bowed, and departed into the garden.

David knelt down before the ark, holding Amnon by the hand. His first response was disappointment. It was only a battered box fashioned out of acacia wood. Certain mystic symbols had once been carved into the sides of it, but time had almost obliterated them; there was nothing left but a few vague lines. The priests of Israel were at odds over the nature of the contents; some talked of a piece of metal hurled from the smoking cone of Sinai, others of a meteor stone cast out of the sky by the hand of God. He had disciplined his heart and could renounce all questioning. He bowed his head, and when he lifted it again, he saw that the afternoon sunlight had strengthened upon the box, so that the old, dulled wood was transfigured in the glow. Then he knew that the ark was beautiful because it was old, that the years had washed all harshness from it, that the corners were softened by the touch of countless pious fingers. Moses touched it once, he told himself. Barak bore it before him in the early battles of Israel. Deborah drew strength and sweetness out of this same wood on the day when she lifted up her voice in an unforgettable song. . . . He also touched it, and felt himself one with Israel. The devotion of innumerable souls flowed over him, so that he was no longer a creature isolated in time, but a partaker in the everlasting life that passes from generation to generation from the beginning of the world.

He saw that the child was sitting back upon his heels, and that his face was white. "No, now," said David, drawing the boy close to him, "I had not meant to keep you kneeling here so long. Let us arise and sit a while." And inasmuch as there was but one chair in the room, he sat and held the boy upon his knees.

In such a room as this, he thought, Jesse lifted me up and offered me the warmth and comfort of his body in my weariness. . . . And he fell to yearning after Jesse as he had not yearned since he had left Bethlehem. I will send again to him in Moab, he thought. I will say to him, "Come and dwell in the King's house in Jerusalem, that I may set my children upon your knees." . . . And it seemed to him that Jesse would surely consent to come at last, now that there was but one land and one king, now that the capital was established and blessed with the presence of the ark of God. This certainty filled him with such joyous eagerness that he could no longer sit still. He lifted Amnon up and carried him into the little garden, where Abinadab and his household sat meekly waiting.

The King of Israel turned to the two sturdy sons and invited them to go up with the ark to Jerusalem. Uzzah, the eldest, hung back because of shyness, and spoke of their father's need of them during the spring reaping.

But both his brother and his father made naught of all his objections, and the matter was settled in a flurry of bows and compliments and smiles. The King returned into the house with the sons of Abinadab to bring out the ark. All three of them covered their hands with linen napkins, for it was impious, said the father, to touch so sacred an object with bare hands. David smiled, thinking how many hands must have touched it during its journey through the wilderness and how his own palm had drawn holy nourishment from it not an hour ago.

But who shall understand the ways of the Lord? It was His will that the ark should not be brought up at once to His new capital in Jerusalem. The day that had begun in rejoicing ended in confusion. Not an hour after he had departed out of his father's house, Uzzah the son of Abinadab was reckoned among the dead. Without mischance, the King and the King's son and the two youths led the oxcart to the gates of Baale-judah. Without mischance they continued with the procession over the hilly road that led toward Jerusalem. But at the top of one of the hills, near the threshing floor of a certain Nacon, one of the oxen stumbled, and the ark began to topple from its place. Then Uzzah stretched forth his hand to steady it, and the anger of God was kindled against him because he had dared to touch the holy of holies with his bare hand. And Jahveh smote Uzzah for his error, so that he died in the road beside the ark of God.

It was impossible, in the face of so plain an indication of the Lord's displeasure, to go farther. The ark was taken back to Baale-judah and placed in the house of a certain Philistine named Obed-Edom, a governor who spent half of the year in the border town and the other half in his native city of Gath. There it remained for three months, and there it might have remained for a century had it not been that Obed-Edom the Gittite and all his house were blessed with unbelievable prosperity because of its presence. Then Israel saw that God's anger had abated, and went again to bring up the ark when the three moons had passed.

&ε§ II §ε&

WHILE the ark of God remained in the house of Obed-Edom, most of the sons of Jahveh put it from their thoughts. But the son of Jesse could not forget it. When he found an hour's release from the multiplicity of tasks that had settled upon him with his crown, he walked alone in the gardens of his palace, brooding upon the ark, thinking of that moment when he had been drawn forth from himself and immersed in the life of undying generations. Those who happened to encounter him in his solitary wanderings smiled to themselves, believing that some young daughter of Jerusalem had caught his fancy, for he had the aspect of a lover. He had begun again to anoint and adorn himself. He went in robes of scarlet and purple; he never appeared beyond the portals of his house without his crown; and he wore the gifts sent to him out of Moab and Sidon and Tyre—long chains of crystal and gold, sandals sewn with vari-colored thread, turquoise rings, and bronze bracelets.

Those who beheld David in his garden were not mistaken when they took him for a lover. He yearned to behold the time-rounded corners, the vague symbols, the wavering, dented sides, as a lover yearns to behold the face of the beloved. It came into his mind that he would build a high house for the ark to dwell in. For weeks he occupied himself with the thought of this dwelling-place as eagerly as a betrothed youth plans in his father's house the halls and chambers that he will build for his bride. He was disappointed when a certain prophet called Nathan reproached him for harboring such a dream. The ark, said the prophet, had dwelt in tents since the day when it was brought up out of Egypt, and God willed that it should continue to dwell in tents until a great day of peace and plenty which the son of Jesse would not live to see. When David slept in peace with his fathers, then and then only would the seed of his bowels raise up a temple in Jerusalem to the God of Hosts.

David accepted the interdiction, and turned his mind to the hour when the ark would pass through the gates of Jerusalem. The welcome that he had planned for it before he had looked upon it seemed meager now. He composed new music, at once more solemn and more tender. In addition to the three thousand warriors who were to walk in the procession, he summoned three hundred priests from all parts of the land, to stand at the top of the hill where the ark would come at last to rest. Since he could offer his God no more than a tent for a dwelling-place, he decreed that the tent should be wrought of the heaviest black goat's-hair, lined in crimson and fringed in gold. The chorus of seven hundred youths and virgins who had been trained for the occasion was not large enough to carry the burden of his new song. He added a chorus of young matrons of the city—wives of his captains and ambassadors, all in the very bloom of their beauty—to stand in a double row upon the slope of the hill and to hide the harsh earth beneath strewn leaves and flowers.

He made a vow that he would not permit himself to behold the ark until it passed through the gates of Jerusalem. He believed that so great an abnegation would find favor in Jahveh's eyes, would be a surety against any new mischance. He bade the members of his household remain in-doors during the entire day of the festival; they might stand at the win-dows, but they must not draw the glances of the multitude to themselves. They must wear white garments and lay their jewels and their amulets by, so that the God of Hosts might be pleased by their humility.

The Lord gave him another mild and radiant day. At the beginning of the journey, he had thought that he could keep his vow only by the most painful discipline. But when the procession left the house of Obed-Edom, he knew that he could wait—to feel that the ark was behind him was enough. He heard the lowing of the oxen and the creaking of the wheels, and sometimes he fancied that he caught the sweet, grassy smell of the beasts' breath. A holy influence issued from the ark and transmuted the brown road, the delicate green of the fig and olive trees, the sun-washed roofs of the villages, the whole world. Once, completely confident that he was master over his eyes, he turned and looked across the cart at the long procession of uplifted faces. When he saw the young counte-nances, his heart was uplifted within him. The breath of God, he thought, was indeed breathed into us on the day of Creation. And he felt the divine breath stirring within his own body, so that he was light as a cloud; and he longed to dance as he had danced as a child before the gates of Ramah on the days of the high festivals.

At noon, before the watchtowers of his capital, he turned at last and permitted himself to see. In the glare of noonday the wood of the ark seemed to stir and breathe in the shimmering waves of heat. Before him and behind him were the multitudes—white, silent, comely, with parted lips and shining eyes. There was a trumpet blast and a general hosanna, so loud that it seemed to shake the earth beneath his feet. Then the wellspring of love that had been sealed up within him these many years sprang forth —joyous, uncontrollable, so abundant that he needs must let it flow out-ward over the city and the world. And he cast away his tunic and stood before the Lord and all Jerusalem in his linen loincloth, and danced before Jahveh with all his might. So David brought the ark of God with shouting and dancing and with the sound of the trumpet through the palm-strewn streets of Jerusalem.

First he danced heroically for the God of Hosts who went out to battle before the armies of His people. Then he danced slowly, with large, un-folding, magnificent movements, for the Creator of the world. He danced the Creation in the streets of Jerusalem—the dividing of the great waters, the establishment of the plains and the mountains, the awakening of man out of his dull and earthy sleep. The seeds of these dances were known to the children of Israel; every man who stood in the streets of the city had seen some primitive form of them before the tribal altars and around the tribal fires. But as the procession approached the foot of the hill, David danced a dance that had never before been seen in Israel—he danced before the Other Jahveh now. He addressed himself, with the simplicity of complete understanding, to the brooding and sorrowing Presence who had stood behind him in the cave on the outskirts of Gibeah, who hov-ered over the dead on the field of battle, who was beyond vengeance and beyond appeasement, who merely looked upon the world and wept. For the first time in all the days of Israel, there were tears upon the face of the Lord. And the son of Jesse paused at the foot of the hill, knowing that there were tears upon his own cheeks.

He stepped aside and took his tunic from the hand of his servant. The high priest Abiathar was coming up behind him, bearing the ark high above his head upon folds of streaming white linen. The clash of cymbals ceased, and the surge of singing voices subsided into stillness. The King of Israel had commanded that the highest moment of the festival should be a moment of silence, in which there would be no sound but the beating of multitudinous hearts. He looked about him and saw that he stood among the young matrons who had strewn the hillside with flowers. The woman who stood beside him brushed his arm in shifting her basket and glanced at him briefly with grave, comprehending eyes.

He looked upon her only long enough to say in his heart, How beautiful are the daughters of Jerusalem! . . . Perhaps it was the shimmer of the sunlight upon her that endowed her with a tremulous and quiet loveliness. Afterward, when he stood beside Abiathar at the opening of the tent, he could not recall her face, could recall only a slow and subtle smile. And this remembrance also was lost in the ecstasy of the moment of fulfillment, when the tent in Jerusalem received the ark of God. He flung himself down before the tent, and heard a vast rustling as every man and woman and child within the gates fell prostrate before the Lord.

From noon until the hour of the setting of the sun, he remained upon the high place. He made burnt offerings and peace offerings upon an altar set up before the tent. He lifted up his hands to the great clouds of saffron smoke that rose from the sacrifices, and he called upon the God of Israel to bless the people of the land, all those who dwelt that day within the gates, and all those who waited, from Dan to Beersheba, to hear news of the wonders that had come to pass in Jerusalem. He also opened his storehouses to the people, that every man and woman might take at the hands of his overseers a cake of bread, a cake of raisins, and a portion of the sacrificial meat. Those who dwelt in Jerusalem returned to their houses to break the evening bread, and those who only sojourned there for the festival spread their repasts under the green fronds of the palms. And when the people had withdrawn, peaceable and murmurous as a flock of doves, to the reaches of the city below him, he yearned to behold his children. So he blessed the multitude yet once more, and returned to his home.

❧ III ❧

HE FOUND his gardens cool and empty in the twilight. All the foliage had taken on the dim greenness of moss, and the water in the pool had grown pale with the sky. He walked slowly toward the portals of his house, eager to behold the children and the women, and yet troubled by a quiet regret. For my spirit went forth to God this day, he thought, and now it must come back again to the world. . . . Even as he strove to resign himself, the doors of his house were opened and Michal came out to meet him. He hastened toward her, smiling, but there was that in her bearing which killed his smile.

As she came out upon the portico, she was tying a bright girdle around her waist. Her hands dealt with the crimson cloth deliberately. It was as if she said aloud, "I have gone in white all day for the sake of your festival. But now your festival is over, and I, for one, am glad to see it depart."

When she had finished with the girdle, she came forward and stood before him. Instead of lifting her face for his kiss, she took an amulet from the bosom of her robe and slipped it over her head. He looked at her in amazement, asking himself what had come to pass during his absence to turn her cold with spite.

"How glorious was the King of Israel this day," she said in the precise accents of the royal House of Benjamin. "How glorious was the King of Israel, who went naked before the eyes of the servants of his servants, who uncovered himself for the multitudes as some base prophet out of Judah uncovers himself."

She sneered at him, and he knew that she had sneered at him from the vantage point of some high window of his palace when, in his ecstasy, he had been most vulnerable. White fury possessed him, and he could scarcely refrain from striking her across the face.

"When Saul my father was King of Israel, it was otherwise," she said.

All the authority of the House of Kish rose up once more from its ashes to humble and wound him, to transform him again into a base Judahite. Saul had been skeptical, manly, self-possessed; Saul had been mistrustful of priests and ecstasy. And now Saul mocked through his daughter's lips at the leaping, naked Judahite who had come by evil chance to wear the crown.

But I am alive, the son of Jesse thought in furious exultation. I am alive and King, and all the men of the House of Kish are counted among the dead. . . . "It was before Jahveh," he said, "that I uncovered myself. It was before Jahveh that I danced—even Jahveh, who chose me above your father and above all his house to be King over His people and over Israel."

Her face went very white, and he knew what images had risen before her: the high house in Gibeah looted and burned by the uncircumcised, Jonathan crushed by the wheels of the brazen chariots, Saul falling upon his sword, the head of her youngest brother staring up at her from a basket of wheat. He knew, but he had been stung beyond pity, and he could not hold his tongue.

"I will dance before the Lord," he said, "whenever I choose to dance before Him. If I have been vile this day, I will be yet more vile than this; I will leap naked before God even until I am vile in my own sight. But the servants of my servants of whom you spoke—they will see no vileness in me. For the King of Israel is base in no man's sight, and I am the King of Israel."

Without taking her eyes from his face, she thrust her hand again into the folds of cloth around her bosom, drew forth a long gold earring, and began to raise it toward her ear.

He snatched the earring from her hand and flung it to the ground. He knew what would shatter her hateful self-possession. He knew well what would make her weep. "If the daughter of Saul makes herself fair for my eyes," he said, "she labors in vain."

She stood motionless before him, her hand still lifted, as though the earring still dangled between her finger and her thumb.

"Come no more into my presence!" he shouted. "It was an evil hour when I called Abner to bring you down to me in Hebron. Whatever bond there was between you and me was broken long since and should not have been mended. If I lay my hand upon you from this day forth, may God strike me dead!"

She did not weep, but her lips quivered; and he knew that he had quenched the last light within her. He turned from her then and entered his house, thinking to lose the thought of her among the little ones. But when he beheld them all laughing with Noi and Haggith upon the hearth, he had no heart for their merriment. He merely called to them that he was very weary, and went up to his bed.

❧ IV ❧

THE ARK OF GOD had been carried up to Jerusalem in the third year of David's reign over a united Israel. The five years thereafter were years of war—war with the tribes of the desert, war with the Syrians, war with the kingdoms of Moab and Edom. And the angelic host went out with swords and spears before the strong ranks of Israel and smote the enemies of Jahveh and crowned the city of Jerusalem with the trophies of many victories.

It was a time of power and splendor. The booty of a score of battles fell to the Israelite captains, and their houses of stone and cedarwood rose high around the palace of their King. Caravans carried rich burdens up and down the highways: linen as thin as a spider's web from the land of Egypt, oils and perfumes from the cities of Syria, purple cloth from Phoenicia. The sons of Jerusalem no longer returned to their fields and flocks when the season of war was over; winter and summer they dwelt in the capital and practiced the arts of war in the valleys beyond the walls. And the daughters of Jerusalem, clad in purple and scarlet, anointed their heads with oil of roses and weighted themselves down with trinkets of brass and gold.

In those years the Lord dealt very graciously with the son of Jesse. The hand of God was lifted against him only once: Not three moons after the ark had come to rest in Jerusalem, the messengers whom he sent into Moab to bring his father home returned in mourning to say that the old man was dead. Jesse had been ailing when they arrived at the court of the King of Moab; but his sickness, he said, was not grave and would soon pass—let them tarry a little and he and his wife would go up with them. So long as there was breath within him, he inquired after the King and the King's family, particularly after the little ones. Afterward, the messengers repeated his questions a dozen times before the King, who seemed to draw comfort from every word that had issued from the old man's lips.

And yet the words were so simple that the messengers blushed a little to repeat them. The lords of Tyre and Sidon, the chiefs of the desert and the kings of Syria had said so often "May all the gods on the earth and under the earth and above the earth lay the wealth of the nations and everlasting happiness and a hundred years of life before the throne of the glorious King of Israel," that it seemed somewhat childish to repeat "May Jahveh walk with my son David to the end of his days."

As for the old mother—she asked an indulgence at the hands of the King. The earth of Moab was indeed alien earth, but it was blessed inasmuch as it held the body of him whom she had loved and served through seventy years. If her son would bestow a kindness upon her, he would permit her to remain near the grave of Jesse. If he would offer her yet another kindness, let him stretch out as bounteous a hand to his brothers as he had offered to his sister's sons. So the King of Israel sought out all the sons of Jesse and made them governors in the border towns and captains over the garrisons in Syria. But he asked none of them to dwell with him in Jerusalem, partly because they had not been bred to be courtiers and partly because the sight of them filled him with an aching sense of loss.

At the end of the five years of war, the children of Israel knew such peace and plenty as they had never known before. It seemed to David that the prophet Nathan could not truly hear the voice of Jahveh, inasmuch as he had implied that the golden years of the nation would not come until the son of Jesse had been laid in the burial cave. And surely this was a golden year—Moab, Edom, and Syria were conquered lands and paid heavy tribute into the storehouses of Jerusalem; Canaanites and Philistines dwelt peaceably among the Israelites like younger brothers; courteous embassies passed between Israel and Egypt, Israel and the coastal cities of Philistia, Israel and the land of the Ammonites. Between Tyre and Jerusalem there was a bond of fast friendship. Hiram, King of Tyre, who had furnished the cedarwood for the King's palace, fell into the habit of writing long epistles to David, and even came once to dwell in the capital for two full moons. Once, on the occasion of a national festival, David took it upon himself to jest with the prophet. "Am I to die tomorrow then," he asked, "seeing that Israel prospers and there is universal peace?" The prophet weighed the jest with unexpected gravity. "No, my lord," he said. "My lord the King will live for threescore years and ten, and his life will be complete, so that he will bow his head in resignation to accept his death. But another will die in an alien land, and his going-forth will shatter the peace that is upon Israel." And two moons thereafter, messengers came out of the kingdom of Ammon to say that Nahash, lord of the Ammonites, was dead.

David did what he could to indicate his sympathy. He dispatched an embassy of reverend elders to the son of Nahash, and sent down with them spices and myrrh for the funeral. He had never set eyes upon the son, but he had known the father well, and his words of condolence were affectionate and intimate. But within half a moon, runners came out of the city of Jericho near the borders of Ammon with an unbelievable tale. The young King of Ammon had used the occasion to fling a challenge of war into David's face: He had reviled the ambassadors and had clipped off half their beards; he had ordered that their garments be cut away up to the waist, and had sent them forth half-naked into the streets of his capital at Rabbah, to be mocked and spat upon. The King of Israel sent the runners back to Jericho in all possible haste, bidding the ambassadors tarry in that city until their beards were grown. And he summoned his host to march out, under the command of Joab, against the Ammonites.

During the recent campaigns, the son of Zeruiah had been given complete jurisdiction over the host. David was in his forty-fifth year, still lithe and hard and slender, still masterful with the spear and the sword. But in the recent wars against Edom and Moab, he had shown the strain of long marches and protracted sieges. On three or four such occasions he had said outright that he would go out to battle no more; he served Israel better by looking after the complicated and delicate matters that demanded his attention in Jerusalem. And yet when the tidings of Ammon's insolence were brought to him, he did not say plainly that he would remain in the city. He used the ambiguous "we" when he discussed the plans for the battle, and he ordered a new shield to be fashioned for him in Askelon.

Ten days before the time appointed for the departure of the host, he was still undecided. He had hoped that Joab would say that his presence in the field would be a bulwark to Israel. But Joab had not raised his voice, and David was not certain that his nephew's silence was based solely upon solicitude; it was plain that the King's cautiousness was exasperating to the audacious Ishmaelite. On several occasions it had entered David's mind to say flatly that he meant to take part in the Ammonite campaign. But always when he was on the point of announcing his decision, he found that he did not really wish to ride down into Ammon. The war would be bloody and tedious. It would end, no doubt, in an interminable siege of Rabbah—Rabbah was notable for its mighty walls. And yet he felt depressed at the thought of tarrying through the long summer in Jerusalem. After the talk of marches and sieges, the conversation of the court would be savorless.

Nevertheless, he thought, as he stood at Joab's door on that fine summer evening, if my presence is not truly necessary on the field of battle, I will remain at home for Israel's sake. . . . But he had not yet convinced himself that the host could do as well without him, and his heart was high with the hope that Joab might plead with him before the captains this very night.

The room that he entered was spacious and sweet with the smell of cedarwood and wine. Even though the light of day had not completely faded, lamps burned on the window sills and on the long table. Food and drink had been set out in a haphazard, openhanded fashion for those who could tear themselves away from their talk long enough to eat. There were great platters of cold roast mutton, several excellent melons, and steaming cakes of bread. But none of the thirty-odd men assembled in Joab's common room had yet turned to the board. They stood in small groups, near the hearth, in the corners, at the windows, talking with such vigor that they did not see that the King was with them. He paused on the threshold to consider the varied and vivacious company. It was very different from the crowd that had assembled around Saul's table in Gibeah. Then the host of God had been led by none but Israelites; now the sons of Jahveh were almost outnumbered by their allies. Philistines, Hittites, Ishmaelites, and Phoenicians chattered in their exotic versions of the tongue of Israel, and the pale lamps illuminated many an outlandish garment, many an alien face.

The son of Zeruiah hastened across the room. "Our lord the King is with us," he said in a loud voice. All conversation stopped, and all the speakers offered the necessary glances, the required smiles. "Let my uncle forgive them, for they are beside themselves with excitement. We have been informed not an hour since that Ammon has sown the seeds of revolt in Syria. More than thirty thousand have come down out of Syria to stand with the Ammonites—men of Beth-rehob and Zobah and Tob.

Surely, if Israel was to march out against such an array as this, the King would not be permitted to remain behind, thought David. Surely the son of Zeruiah would say, "Let my lord come down to cheer us through the long siege of Rabbah."

But the awaited words were not forthcoming, and the captain did not tarry long with his lord. There was a matter concerning the baggage wagons that Joab must discuss with Ahitophel—for Ahitophel, bald and rheumatic now, had long since come from the north to serve David as he had once served the Lion of Benjamin. The King of Israel found himself, in the midst of a dozen close and engrossed groups, in embarrassing solitude. It came into his mind then that a crown was no security against such humiliations, that even a king might wander about unwanted and alone. He turned and walked toward the table, assuming an air of preoccupation. Surely, while he busied himself with a slice of melon, one or another of the captains would wander to the board. And two of them did detach themselves from their companions in order to break bread with him—Abishai and a lean and swarthy Hittite whose name he did not recall.

"My lord the King remembers Uriah, whom he made captain over a thousand after the siege of Jerusalem," Abishai said, seeing at once that his uncle had forgotten the name.

"And how is it with Uriah?" asked David, striving to connect the face of the Hittite with some illuminating incident out of the past. There were four or five Hittite captains at every council, and he had not yet learned to distinguish one from another. To him, all Hittites seemed to have been cast out of the same mold—the same black, wiry hair, the same thick eyebrows meeting above the same beaked nose, the same ripe and somewhat womanish lips.

425

"How could it be otherwise than well with me," said Uriah, "seeing that I have received so many gifts and honors from my lord?"

David could not remember what gifts and honors he had bestowed, and he glanced in Abishai's direction for enlightenment. But before the lumbering warrior could fashion an acceptable phrase, his brother Joab summoned him, and David and the Hittite were left at the table alone.

David's uneasiness in this man's presence was not due alone to his inability to recall Uriah's high deeds. He belonged to a certain class of warriors for whom David had small affection—outlanders and former heathen who had grown overzealous in their desire to observe the ritual of their chosen land. The season of war would not officially begin until the night of the full moon, and yet the Hittite had already adopted all the prohibitions. He wore the rough white tunic in which the ranks marched out to battle. His hair and beard had not been anointed for many days. Furthermore, David found it disquieting to look at the captain's face, with its perpetual mask of courteous attentiveness.

"How is it with the family of Uriah?" he said, sensing that the silence had been kept too long.

"My wife is in excellent health," said the Hittite, indicating with disturbing candor what another man might have wished to suppress—the fact that he had no child.

Perhaps, thought David, I will know the wife and be reminded through her of the deeds of the husband. . . . And he said that though he knew the name of Uriah's lady well, he was unable to bring it out of the shadowy places of his memory.

The Hittite smiled. He had seen that the King knew neither him nor any member of his household, and he accepted the fact with annoying humility. "My wife is called Bath-sheba," he said. "I am fortunate in that Jahveh has given me a true daughter of Israel. Her family is of the tribe of Benjamin, and Ahitophel is her uncle. Although my lord knows her not, there was an occasion which she has never forgotten—an occasion when she came face to face with my lord."

The King turned his eyes from the swarthy face to the long, crowded room. He felt a growing resentment against all those who stood chattering around him that they should leave him with no companion save this self-effacing Hittite. "And on what occasion did I behold the wife of Uriah?" he asked, unable to keep the note of impatience from his voice.

"On the day of the coming of the ark of God. Bath-sheba my wife was among those matrons who stood upon the slope of the hill, and when my lord the King rested after his dance, he stood at her side. My lord will not remember it, but she shifted her basket and brushed against the arm of my lord the King. She said that there was no anger in the King's eyes, that he smiled very graciously upon her, in spite of her awkwardness."

David was bewildered to discover the recollection whole within him after five years. "I remember the occasion," he said. Surely I remember, he thought. There was a shimmer of sunlight upon her, and she looked at

426

me with comprehending eyes, and my heart cried out for the first time after many barren moons, "How beautiful are the daughters of Jerusalem!" . . .

And now that the Hittite had taken on new significance in his eyes, they were no longer left alone. Joab went from group to group, complaining that his food was being wasted, and the board was soon surrounded by a milling crowd.

For the remainder of the evening David avoided the others. A tender and aching mood was upon him; he was possessed by a persistent desire to sigh. When he was drawn into conversation regarding the campaign, he no longer used the equivocal "we," and he thought of bestowing his new shield upon Ahitophel. He found himself looking often toward the bald and sickly master of the baggage wagons. It stirred him strangely to think that the little, shortsighted eyes which had looked upon Jonathan's anguish in the plain of Sharon should also have beheld Bath-sheba in the days of her innocence, before she had yet become the Hittite's bride. He wandered slowly through the assembly, feeling his long crimson robe and his golden ornaments as heavy burdens upon him, and yet this sense of weakness and weariness was dissolving and sweet. He went often to the window to take deep breaths of the evening air. The dusk beyond the window had become meltingly beautiful in his sight. The boughs of the figs and pomegranates in Joab's garden were in full bloom, and their fragrance was borne in on the wind. How is it with me, he asked himself, that I have not breathed this scent for many years? How is it that I have not gazed at a cloud of blossoms against a darkening sky since that time when I looked down upon Achish's tent in the plain of Sharon and remembered Jonathan? . . .

The King was not among the first to take their leave; a sense of incompleteness was upon him; he could think of no other house to visit at so late an hour, and he could not bring himself to go in this restless state to his bed. He tarried until the room was almost empty. He stood long at the door with his hand on Joab's arm, talking absently. On the threshold he glanced once more over his shoulder. Ahitophel had gone forth, but Uriah remained. He and one of his countrymen were discussing some matter of strategy with a condescending Israelite.

Outside, in the fragrant darkness, he walked slowly across the garden and paused at the gate. Footsteps sounded behind him. The Hittite had followed him, was coming up to join him, was saying, "Inasmuch as we go in the same direction, may I have the great honor of walking a little of the way with my lord?"

And now he knew at last what high deeds this captain had accomplished for Israel. Israel had good cause to be grateful. The Hittite and his company of mercenaries had been the first to follow at Joab's heels through the underground watercourse that led into the very bowels of the Jebusite citadel of Jerusalem. He it was who had sown death and confusion through the whole city while David and the rest of his host breached the walls.

For this signal service, he had been made the King's neighbor; David had given him a high house of stone and cedarwood not fifty paces apart from his own. "I will delight in the company of the hero of Jerusalem," he had said.

"On many an evening," said the captain, walking a little behind him through the hushed and empty street, "we have seen our lord walking in his garden."

There was a wall of flowering bush between Uriah's garden and his own. Had she indeed looked upon him through the frail, open greenness of that wall?

"The iris which my lord planted around his spring are flourishing very well this year."

They had come to Uriah's gate, and the King rested his hand on the ornate grillwork. "Permit me to send a sheaf of them to your house in the morning," he said.

"Indeed," said Uriah, coming up behind him, "I am overwhelmed by the generosity of my lord the King. Bath-sheba's heart will be gladdened when she hears that my lord will send us a sheaf of his own iris." He fell silent, but it seemed to David that there was something else that the Hittite wished to say.

"Perhaps," said Uriah, "before the King returns to his own house, he will pause for a moment in mine. He ate but little at Joab's table. Perhaps he would do me the great honor of taking a little of my meat. . . ."

David opened the gate and held it wide for the captain. "Very gladly," he said.

❧ V ❧

URIAH's house had been built for splendor. Pillars of cedarwood soared to a lofty ceiling; great blocks of limestone had been set into the floor; and the hearth and window sills were of polished stone. But it was plain that those who dwelt there had turned their backs upon magnificence. The furnishings were few and small; chairs and benches looked slight and isolated; there were no vases, no ornamental boxes, no cushions, no rugs upon the floor. Three small lamps cast an insufficient circle of glow around the long, bare table. Had he not known that the captains of Israel were well provided for, David would have thought himself in a household pinched by poverty. An ancient serving-woman rose up from the shadows and turned the querulous, persecuted face of the unhappy old upon her master. "My lady is not here," she said quickly, as though to shield herself from blame. "My lady is in the garden. Shall I go and tell my lady to come to my lord?"

"Go and fetch more lamps," said the Hittite. "If she is in the garden, I can easily summon her myself." And he went to the window and called his wife's name, sharply, as he might call the name of a serving-maid.

And now the King regretted that he had come into the Hittite's house. With Uriah's possessive, unceremonious summons, the last trace of the magic was gone. I have come on a fool's errand, he told himself, to set eyes upon some little Benjamite who was valued so lightly in her father's house that she was given in marriage to a Hittite. . . . And indeed, when she came and stood upon the threshold, he thought that there was nothing in her to stir any man overmuch. She was a slight young woman, neither short nor tall. Her face was comely enough—perhaps a little more delicately molded than the usual face, but certainly not dazzlingly fair. Nor could he convince himself that these were the eyes that had looked upon him when he had rested from his dance before the Lord. "Our house is honored above its deserving by the presence of the King," she said. Her voice was clear and musical, and her accents were the pure accents of Benjamin. She stood wordless for a moment, plainly confused by the presence of so illustrious a visitor. Then she recovered herself and begged leave to go and fetch meat and bread.

She bore herself with marked dignity, as though she were conscious of his glance upon her. The white linen of her robe was heavy, but certain clean lines were visible through the folds. Her hair hung in one gleaming round over her neck and shoulders. When she had passed out of his sight, he could recall nothing but the light of the lamps upon it; he could not remember whether it was black or brown, straight or curled.

"Will my lord the King come to the table and sit?" Uriah said.

They moved toward the bare board and seated themselves on either side of it, Uriah with his back to the shadowy room, the King with his back to the wall. The old woman returned with two more lamps, and set them between her master and his guest. It was plain that she had been told the identity of the visitor; her lips were compressed, and her hands shook with fright. When the sound of her retreating footsteps had died, there was long and oppressive silence.

"Are they all countrymen of Uriah, those who serve in his battalion?" David asked at last. In the bare room, his words had a hollow sound.

"No, my lord. Half are Hittites. The others are sons of Moab and Philistia."

Their feeble effort at conversation had collapsed. Both opened their mouths to fulfill the pressing need for speech, but neither could find a word. Bath-sheba returned, moving almost soundlessly through the gray shadow and emerging in the circle of glow. She was carrying a large platter on which there were slices of cold meat, a cruet of wine, and three cakes of bread. As she bent to set her burden upon the table, the light of the burning wicks shone upward full upon her throat and face. And the King saw how it was that her face had seemed to shimmer before him. Her cheeks were as delicate and unblemished as the cheeks of a child, and the color of her flesh was the cool, transparent whiteness of the foam on new milk.

Like any well-bred daughter of Benjamin, she went about her household duties. She brought out bowls and plates, wiped a long knife clean on a napkin, and laid it close to her husband's swarthy hand. Like any well-bred daughter of Benjamin, she stepped back to survey her handiwork. Then, with the same conscious dignity that David had observed in her walk, she put the brown and shining fall of her hair back from her face, took her place at the board beside Uriah, looked at her plate, and smiled.

Now that she sat at the table, the sense of constraint was intensified. David knew that he should not stare at her, but he could not refrain from examining her smile, from seeking to identify it with his remembrance of the slow and subtle stirring of her lips. That also was an illusion, he thought. She smiled then as she smiles now, out of embarrassment. It is the custom among the daughters of Ephraim and Benjamin to cover awkwardness or insufficiency with a smile. . . .

"The King has been so gracious as to say that he will send us a sheaf of iris from his own garden," Uriah said, turning his head slightly toward his wife.

"The King is very kind."

David started, for he had completely forgotten the matter of the iris. Remembering the surge of ardor that had driven him to make the promise at Uriah's gate, he smiled sourly at himself. And now, he thought, I must be on guard lest I forget a second time. I must speak of it to a servant before I go up to my bed tonight. . . . The food was tasteless and flat. The King ate quickly, making a show of appetite. The Hittite chewed with the pleasureless persistence of one who eats solely for the sake of nourishment. The young woman ate almost nothing. She broke the bread into small pieces, as though she were preparing to feed a child or a bird, and slipped the morsels between scarcely parted lips.

And now David thought only of the moment when he could arise and depart. The vast emptiness of the room, the gray shadows pressing in upon the bald circle of light—all these were as the elements of an uneasy dream. The Hittite had begun to speak. He spoke with the earnestness of a converted heathen of Jahveh's anger against the kingdom of Ammon. He spoke with the ardor of an outlander of the might of Israel. And the King knew that Bath-sheba also was pained by the strangeness of his accent and the inflections of his overcourteous voice. Her white cheeks flushed slightly, and she resorted once more to her self-conscious smile.

For the remainder of the unquiet hour, David roused himself enough to say such gracious words as they might care to repeat to each other for reassurance after he had gone. He complimented the lady on the richness of her bread; he wished the captain glory at the battle before Rabbah; he made vague references to the satisfactions of the simple life. When he left the table, he was not sure that he had tarried long enough. He had lost all sense of time; it seemed to him that he had been detained in the room for hours.

430

They rose promptly, perhaps too promptly. It occurred to him that the occasion had been painful to them also, that they were eager to reconstruct it and refurbish it, that they could take no pleasure in his visit until he had left them to themselves. As he walked with them across the interminable length of resounding limestone blocks, he thought of the moment when he could wash away the taste of the food with a bowl of his own good wine. On the threshold, they exchanged the usual courtesies. It was as if they had entered into an unspoken agreement to avoid exchanging glances. The Hittite stared at the garden, the little Benjamite stared at her husband, and the King stared at the not-too-distant windows of his own house, still yellow with light.

As he passed the clump of iris which grew near the spring in his own garden, he knew again that his promise had gone completely out of his mind. If I carry one of the blooms into the house with me, he thought, I will be certain to remember. . . . He bent and broke a moist, crisp stem and raised the flower to his face. The petals were crumpled, cool, clinging. A subtle and disquieting fragrance rose from them. He stood for a long time breathing this fragrance. And suddenly his heart was heavy within him, as though he had suffered a great and irretrievable loss.

๕฿ VI ฿๛

THE NIGHT of the full moon came and departed; the host of God went out against Ammon; the streets of Jerusalem ceased to sound with marching feet. An unseasonable spell of heat descended upon the city. From noon until evening those who dwelt within its gates kept to their houses. It was enough merely to live through the burning hours. Having this burden of heat to bear, the people of Jerusalem rejected all other burdens. The public work on roadways ceased, the merchants closed their bazaars, and friends no longer ventured forth to meet each other. Men and women sat breathless and panting in the shadow of their houses and waited for the night.

While the oppressive weather lasted, the King of Israel made it his custom to retire to his own chamber after the breaking of the noonday bread. There were cooler places in the palace. The common room faced eastward and was shadowed by thick clumps of trees. Yet David seldom came here to rest. In the evenings it was the haunt of courtiers, and during the daytime the women and children of the household considered it their own. His family did not intend to trouble him; yet there was not one among them who could keep the silence necessary for his repose. Amnon and Absalom carried on hushed and subtle hostilities in his presence; Tamar came in from the garden, singing at the top of her voice; Adonijah fell over the heaped pillows; and each of the wives felt that she had been more than considerate if, in the course of a long afternoon, she had addressed no more than three comments to her lord. So he no longer tried to sleep on the couch in the common room; he said that he needed the more resilient softness of his bed.

He could not always escape to his own chamber immediately after he had risen from the noonday meal. One afternoon, more than a moon after the host had marched out, he was detained longer than usual by the arrival of a messenger who had come through the scorching heat from Rabbah. Good news and ill news were intermingled on the clay tablet that he laid before the King. The Syrian armies had been decimated and routed in a bitter battle before Rabbah; but the Ammonites, scarcely scratched by the arrows of Israel, had retreated in full force into their citadel. The unseasonable weather had settled also upon the land of Ammon. The siege would be long, and the men of Jahveh had no relief from the sun in the treeless plain.

The message that David dictated to be sent down to Joab at Rabbah seemed to him singularly empty and feeble—not worth the fatigue of the man who would carry it across the burning roads, not worth the tablet it was written on. He recast the wording of it several times, and let the final version go with the sense that it was less effective than the first. As he crossed the common room, he saw that Amnon and Absalom were quarreling in a remote corner. They were forever quarreling, and today he had not the strength to mediate between them. He turned his back upon them and went up the stairs.

He bolted his door behind him and stood in the middle of the high and shadowy chamber, disburdening himself of his ornaments and his robes of state. The windows were so closely curtained that he could barely see his own hands striving with the knots and clasps. Yet the glare of the day thrust itself in sharp stabs of light through the chinks between sill and curtain. Naked except for his loincloth, he lay at full length upon the bed. The pillows had soaked up the warmth, and there was a disturbing scent as of dust upon them. He shook them and turned them, but the warmth and the dry scent remained.

Since the heat had first descended upon the city, he had drowsed fitfully through the greater part of the day and been unable to sleep at night. Always, when the wind of God moved like a benediction through the rooms of the palace, his torpor was lifted from him. Today he had determined not to surrender himself to drowsiness while the light lasted, so that he might sink into deep and wholesome rest with the coming-on of the dark. He lay on his back, looking up at the dim beams of the ceiling, trying to call up such soothing considerations as might give him rest without bringing hot and heavy sleep upon him. But an hour later he was still striving with the pillows, still turning restlessly. A score of images had passed through his consciousness, and not one of them had brought him either pleasure or repose.

He turned his head to shield his eyes from a blade of light, and saw his own bare arm stretched across the sea-green stuff of the coverlet. A fearful thought burst like a bubble in his head: Saul's arm was just such an arm as this when I anointed him with oil, in those days when his strength and his glory had already begun to pass. . . . He examined the long, pale arm severely, as though it were not his own. It had grown thin —he had taken little nourishment during the time of the heat. The muscles had become flaccid—for months he had not lifted a spear or a sword. A hard, bluish vein ran almost the length of the forearm, and the skin on the back of his hand was roughened. Suddenly he knew that nothing could restore the clean strength that his arm had once possessed. Henceforth, whenever he looked upon himself he would see the tokens of his decline. Disintegration had already begun its work within him, and there was no staying its hastening advance toward death.

He set himself then to the sorrowful arithmetic to which every man must come at last. He subtracted the staggering sum of the gone years from the round but questionable threescore and ten. Twenty-five years are left to me, he thought. Twenty-five, at best. . . . Five times five, he thought. But, divided into five equal parts, twenty-five years were nothing. Take five years, he thought, any five years, the five years of splendor which have only just passed. . . . But he could not grasp them—they had no reality. Remote, phantasmagoric, like converging images in a dream, he saw the incidents of his struggle for Israel. Armies clashed in the purple Moabite hills; the Philistine dead lay by the thousands in the Valley of Rephaim; the red griffins before the gates of the cities of Syria were licked by tongues of fire; the ranks of the men of the south fled down twenty moonlit nights over endless expanses of sand. Perhaps all warriors recalled their battles only as dreams; perhaps every war in the wretched history of the world had been bled of its actuality the moment it ceased. But all the other occasions that he summoned up—the national festivals, the pilgrimages with his children, the nights when he had relieved his jangling nerves or fulfilled his obligations in brief encounters of love—all these floated bodiless through his remembrance. The five years remained as unreal as before. Lord God of Hosts, he cried out in his heart, how will it be with me if those years that remain to me are as insubstantial as these which I have conjured up? How will it be with me if I live only to multiply an unquiet dream by five, if I go down, bewildered and unfulfilled, into my grave? . . .

Yet surely, he thought, I deceive myself when I call my days a meaningless dream. Surely I am blessed above any man in Israel. I was a shepherd, and I am king over a strong nation. My seed was barren, and I have begotten sons to wear my crown. Israel was shattered, and Israel is whole again. I have laid all the enemies of Jahveh low. I have builded the city of Jerusalem at the navel of the world and adorned it with palaces and gardens and set the ark of God upon a high hill. My songs are in the mouths of the multitude, and my name is spoken with reverence from Lebanon to Egypt. What is there left for me to yearn after? What have I missed? . . .

And he was haunted again by an old sense of insufficiency, a conviction that some radiant and elusive essence had passed from him. Time had grown flaccid and empty, now that it was gone. He turned his face on the pillow so that he might look northward toward Jonathan's burial cave. He strove, as he had often striven when the sense of loss was upon him, to conjure up a vision of the beloved. But it was many months since he had turned toward Gibeah, and he knew that the dust of Jonathan was dust indeed, and that time had left him empty of even the desire to weep. For behold, he told himself, Jonathan has been dead these twelve years, and nigh unto half a lifetime has passed over me since last I looked upon his face. . . .

He strove to remember by what stratagems of the spirit he had brought himself in better days to accept the inevitability of death. He remembered how as a child he had always wished to die in battle, to be hurled on the crest of some prodigious deed out of life and into history. He could recall the images with which he had made himself weep: the comrades in arms lifting up his body, the long procession of virgins and heroes bringing offerings to the burial cave. But in those days, he thought, it seemed to me that I could be a partaker in my own posthumous glory. Since that time, I have sat at the feet of many corpses—the valiant, the righteous, and the wise. And I have seen that the living dog that is kicked away from the door by which the mourners sit is more than the insensate body upon which they fix their sanctimonious eyes. When I am dead, I will be a piece of corruption, veiled for the sake of the living in a web of tenderness and renown, but beyond all songs, all tears, all legends—fit only for the shut darkness of the grave. . . .

He pushed the pillows aside that he might breathe more freely. The heat lay like a solid weight upon his chest. The panic that he had tried to alleviate had only multiplied within him. It seemed to him now that death was an ineluctable presence, that he would behold it henceforth whenever he lifted his eyes. How shall I deal with this presence? he asked himself. How did I deal with it when I dwelt in Gibeah? For there was a time when I lay in the tower room, lost in serene contemplation of my own mortality, wishing that I might receive a mortal wound and lie dying for days. . . . He remembered the blur of warm and easy tears that had always glimmered between him and his vision of death. To lie dying for days upon the bed in the tower room, to be freed at last by the certainty of dissolution from all prohibitions, all laws. To utter the unutterable, to turn on the pillow and touch the exquisite hand, the cloud of pale brown hair. . . . For while love is in us still, he thought, we see in death only an ultimate and perfect means of going out to the beloved. . . .

But I have no beloved, he told himself. My beloved has lain in the burial cave so many years that I cannot even grieve greatly over his death. The emanations that once flowed out to me from his ashes have grown fainter, have grown utterly still. Nor is there any being left among the living to whom I could render myself up in my final hour. Love is no longer with me—nothing is with me now but tenderness and forbearance. Lord, Lord, I have been tender and forbearing long, but I age, I grow weary, I may be neither tender nor forbearing at the last. Take pity upon me and deliver me in the hour of my death from the required farewells, from the empty words and the unreal embraces. Let me die alone. Let me die like a coward in my sleep. . . .

It seemed to him then that the room had undergone some change. The bright blades of light had lost their edges; the rugs shone with a muted whiteness; the curtains had begun to stir in the wind of God. Then it is evening, he thought. They will come to me soon to call me to the table, and then there will be another nightmare—a long board laden with food that I cannot eat, a long row of faces remote from me and ignorant of my terror, faces that I am required to love, faces of strangers that I must smile upon and kiss. . . . Perhaps if he went up to the roof or walked about in the garden he might grow calm enough to sleep. He rose from the bed then and stood staring at his raiment—the gold ornaments heaped upon the little table, the crimson robe left lying upon the floor. If I go into the garden, he thought, I must dress and adorn myself. If I go up to the roof, none will behold me; I can go in a short linen tunic, I can leave half my body bare to the cool of the dusk. . . . So he arrayed himself in a linen tunic and a loose white girdle, and washed his face and arms in the water that had grown tepid with standing in the brazen basin. He was weak as after a long battle, and his knees trembled as he crossed the room.

When he opened the door, he found his armor-bearer drowsing across the threshold. "Go now," he said gently, "and sleep in a cooler place. Say to them below that I will not sit at meat this night, inasmuch as the heat has left me without stomach for food. Say that I will come down after an hour or so has passed. For the present I wish to be left in peace."

When he came out upon the roof, he saw that eventide had indeed settled upon the city. The sky curving over Jerusalem and the neighboring hills was the pale, yellowish green of half-ripened fruit. He knew also that the delectable coolness which touched his damp body was more than the transitory coolness of evening; the wind of God had brought new weather with it from the mysterious reaches of the western sea; the time of the heat was past. Fresh currents of air swept across the roof of the palace, waving the fronds of the palm trees, flapping the rugs that hung over the parapet, rippling the white canopy that had been raised on one corner of the roof to shadow a long couch heaped with cushions of green and gold.

He thought of stretching himself upon the couch. Yet he could not bring himself to lie at full length upon the cushions. At full length he had suffered the assault of fear, and it seemed to him now that to lie down was to be afraid. He moved to the part of the parapet that overlooked his own garden. The wind, moving full upon him, drove his tunic against his body and cooled the film of sweat upon his face.

The city which he had wrested from the heathen and made strong and lovely for Israel lay below him—pale, opalescent, its palms and walls and streaming banners all softened in the lessening light. Some sun still lingered upon the roofs of the adjoining palaces; their parapets and the green clusters of fronds which swayed against them were touched with a powdery gold. Somewhat lower than his own and divided from him by green clumps of palm leaves lay the roof of Uriah the Hittite. He started, because someone was moving across it. A tall, solemn Ethiopian slave woman was stepping with the litheness of a cat over the strewn rugs and cushions, bearing a great empty basin at her side and balancing upon her head a copper vessel that glowed with the last richness of the sun. She set the basin at the edge of Uriah's roof, directly under the King's eyes. Then she tilted the vessel and poured a stream of water into the basin. She is about to bathe, he thought. . . . But she straightened, retraced her steps across the roof, and was gone.

He leaned against the sun-warmed stones, waiting. A strange, brooding expectancy was upon him. He lifted his eyes to the green sky and met the grave stare of the first star. And now another figure, slight and lost in the flutter of a long white garment, walked with conscious dignity across the roof. It is she, he thought. The little Benjamite has come out of the dark rooms of her house to bathe on the roof in the cool of the eventide. . . . And at the thought that he was about to behold a woman secretly in her nakedness, he was awed, and overwhelmed by a feverish excitement.

He stepped backward soundlessly, so that he might be screened from her sight by the cluster of fronds and the parapet. When he looked at her again, there was a mist before his eyes. Her long, loose robe and her pale face shimmered before him. The wind, blowing behind her, drove her shining hair forward against her cheeks, and her cheeks were as fresh and delicate as the foam on new milk. She stood long over the basin, letting the benediction of the wind pass over her; and her countenance was transformed by the slow and subtle smile. She had but one garment upon her. She unfastened a brooch at her shoulder, a knot at her side. The white linen billowed down behind her, and she stood naked against the cool green sky.

When the beating of his heart had subsided a little, he wondered at himself that he should be so deeply moved by a slender and somewhat childish young woman. Then he knew that if her hair had been longer and richer, if her breasts had been more opulent or her thighs had been fuller, her seemliness would have been utterly effaced. She had been fashioned sparely, so that every part of her was barely sufficient and therefore inestimably precious. Her charm was the charm of a finished and changeless entity. She had the cool perfection of the crescent moon set in the vast arc of the firmament.

She bent over the basin, took water in her cupped hands, and let it trickle over her throat, her young shoulders, her compact breasts. All her movements were self-conscious and restrained. She straightened again and went about the business of spreading the gleaming film of water over her belly and into the crevices between her torso and her thighs. She stepped into the basin and bent to one side, reaching after the brazen vessel; and, as she turned, the line of her body became the clean, curved line of a drawn bow. With both hands, she raised the vessel and poured a heavy stream of water over her shoulders. Now her whole body was wet and luminous. Drops of water ran down her sides and shone upon the three misty areas of pale brown hair.

To take her, he thought, to take her in the cool of the evening, with the freshness of the water still upon her. To quench the heat of the day against the cool length of her. To know her, to know her utterly, and then to sleep. . . .

She stepped out of the basin, turned her back to him, took up a square of white linen, and began to dry herself. Seen from the back, her body seemed even more delicate and slender. Her shoulder blades showed plainly through the flesh, and her haunches were the small, unripe haunches of a child. She looked at them over her shoulder. The water still gleamed upon them, and she made a kind of sling of the square of linen, held it below the slight globes of her buttocks, and drew it from side to side until the last of the moisture was gone.

And all in a moment, desire gave way to pity in him. He pitied her because he had looked secretly upon her nakedness, because he had seen the meagerness of her haunches and watched her while she dried them, because there had been in her manner of drying them something strangely pathetic, something that shattered her fragile dignity and transformed her into a vulnerable child. And as in Saul's garden his spirit had gone forth at the sight of the mortal vein beating in the temple of the beloved, so now it went out in pity and tenderness toward this little Benjamite. I have used her ill, he thought, in staring at her and in longing to possess her. . . . She had bent down to gather up the long white garment; and he stepped backward, meaning to depart.

But in his retreat his foot struck against a small table. She rose, with the white folds of the garment only partially drawn around her, and looked across the palms, across the parapet, until her glance found his face. He expected her to cry out, but her lips remained immobile. He expected her to bow her head, but she did not so much as close her eyes. Nor did she lift her hand to draw her robe around her. She stood simply, submissively, with her arms at her sides, her head tilted backward a little, one breast and shoulder bare. And the beating of his heart was suspended within him, because his eyes had encountered her eyes.

In that look, she freely rendered up more to him than he had taken in secret when he beheld her in her nakedness. It was as if she had said aloud to him, "Here am I without a veil to hide me. Behold, my spirit rises naked in my eyes to stand before my lord." And he knew that he also had gone forth unveiled to her in this look. She beheld him now as no other living being had ever beheld him. Nothing in him was withheld from her—not his bond with the burial cave in Gibeah, not his

437

abject terror in the presence of death. Their look was more intimate than the most passionate words, the most abandoned touch.

She stood for a long time motionless and gazing up at him; and before she gathered the folds of her robe around her and turned to depart, the corners of her lips were indented by the slow and subtle smile. He knew that she would not look back at him. That which had passed between them was complete and would only have been lessened by another glance.

When she was gone, he walked slowly across the roof and down the stair that led to the rooms below. A hushed exaltation was upon him. He passed the open door of his own bedchamber, and he remembered with amazement that here he had told himself that whensoever he lifted up his eyes he would behold the certainty of his own death. But death was no longer with him. Liquid, lambent, golden, love had filled the cup of his life to overflowing; love had washed out the bitter dregs of death. He walked a little way through the shadows, and then stopped and rested his forehead against a pillar. A sweet shuddering came upon him. He breathed the scent of the cedarwood as he might have breathed the scent of her body. "I love you," he said, and wondered at himself, for he had never said these words to any other woman. "I love you, you have closed me away with you, let me come to you in reverence, let me embrace your knees, let me kiss your feet."

⤙ VII ⤚

WHEN he opened his eyes on the following morning, he knew at once that the whole color of his existence had undergone a profound change. The room in which he found himself seemed as radiant as a piece of crystal in the sunlight. It was as if swifter, fresher blood had been poured into his veins; it was as if some angelic messenger had taken the heavy heart from beneath his ribs and left a light and ardent one in its place. He realized with wonder that he was sitting upright, that he had wakened, vigorous and undrugged by sleep, at the first light touch of his armor-bearer's hand. It was only after he was fully aware of the transformation that he remembered her naked, self-surrendering glance. He rose then and stretched his arms toward the sunny ceiling, and the gesture was at once triumphal and humble.

Those who had occasion to speak with him that day—his wives and children, his armor-bearer and his servants, the ambassadors from Phoenicia and the collectors of tribute who had come out of the cities of Moab to render their accounts—found him lively and penetrating, ready with a score of witty sallies, capable of settling in a few moments such matters as he had been wont to ponder for days. It seemed to them that he had put aside some heavy dream and turned at last to give his full attention to realities. But in truth he had never been so little concerned with the business that went on around him and so totally given over to the affairs that lay within him. While he suggested to Noi that she and Haggith and the children should take themselves off to the orchards against a possible return of the heat, he remembered what had passed on Uriah's roof in the cool of the eventide. When he paused in his morning walk to settle a quarrel between Amnon and Absalom, he found himself salvaging out of oblivion and washing in the bright liquid of his happiness the time that he had spent in Uriah's house. When he spoke with the ambassadors, his tone was grave and dubious, because he was striving with the incontrovertible fact that Bath-sheba was the wife of Uriah the Hittite and was therefore not to be touched. When the collectors of the tribute laid their accounts before him, he was full of questions, for he was saying in his heart, Wherefore am I King of Israel if I am to be denied the sole possession which I desire? Why should I deny myself? When last I denied myself, what came of it? Nothing but barren weeping over a burial cave. . . .

As the day ran its course, the joy within him grew less exuberant, but more profound. All questioning, all efforts to justify himself had ceased. He no longer asked himself whether he would send a messenger to summon her. He knew that he could no more refrain from summoning her than he could refrain from filling his lungs with draughts of the sweet air.

And that thought—solemn, tremulous, tender—cast a kind of aura over the present hour. He would have thought that to love her would be to misprize all other living beings. And yet the more he brooded upon her, the more his heart went out to all the others. He remained long at the table, letting his eyes dwell upon each of them. He pitied Abigail because she had grown old and obese, and, because the business of eating was her sole remaining delight. He grieved over the hard, set face of Michal, and said in his heart, May God forgive me, inasmuch as it was I that turned her into a pillar of stone. . . . He strove to make way for Haggith's quiet voice in the hurrying stream of conversation—she was so well-bred that she seldom managed to make herself heard. He took up the finest slice of meat and laid it upon the plate before Noi. For she tended me in my sickness, he thought. All my children, both her own and the children of those who have driven her still further from me, she has washed and soothed and fed. She has looked to my orchards and flocks by day, and has sat beside my ailing bondsmen by night. . . . And he could not return her glance, because his eyes were bright with tears.

He yearned greatly over the children also. He stared at their delicate hands, their small faces lifted in the glow of the newly kindled lamps. How beautiful, he thought, are the children of Maacah. . . . Absalom, still smarting under the rebuke which his father had laid upon him that same morning in the garden, sat in proud isolation, looking upon no one. And it is no great wonder that he bears resentment against me, David thought. He was fashioned to be a king, and it seems to him that it is I who deny him his kingship. . . . His lovely sister, grown grave in the shadow of her brother's trouble, sat wordless beside him and took no meat.

The folds of her white tunic had already begun to be thrust forward a little by the first budding of her breasts. Behold, thought the King in wonder, my seed was sown and became a woman. . . . And this seemed to him an obscure and holy mystery. He turned then to the mild Adonijah, sitting contentedly in the curve of his mother's arm. How blessed am I in my children! he thought. . . . And it seemed to him that even the shy and tormented Amnon had rare virtues. He bore his triumph over Absalom without arrogance; he seemed even to regret his ascendancy; he kept asking Tamar whether she would not have more of the fruit, inasmuch as she had eaten no meat.

David tarried at the table so long that the evening wind was already stirring the draperies at the window when he rose to depart. He said that he was weary and would spend the evening upon the roof. He paused to lay his hand upon each of them, and his touch took the sting from his desire for solitude. Then he motioned to his armor-bearer and walked across the darkening common room, between the towering trunks of the pillars, toward the stair. At the foot of the steps, he said to the young man in a quiet but easy voice: "Go now to the palace which stands to the right of mine, and say to the lady who dwells therein that I would have her come to me. Her name is Bath-sheba, and she is the wife of Uriah the Hittite."

The armor-bearer did not reply. The King fancied that through the gathering shadows he could see a blush upon the young man's face, and he strove to keep a quiet, ordinary smile upon his own. "Her husband is at Rabbah with the ranks of God," he said. "He has sent me a message to deliver to his wife—such a message as cannot be entrusted to the usual runner. But you need not tell her so. If she knows that I have word from Uriah, she is likely to be troubled. Simply say that the King would speak with her upon the roof of his palace."

"Tonight?" said the armor-bearer.

"Surely. Within the hour. Go now, and bring her back with you."

"But if she cannot come?"

"She will come."

He had never doubted for an instant that she would come to him. Now, as he climbed the dusky stair, his joyous expectancy was suspended. She may not come, he told himself, walking across the roof. And it was impossible for him to sit or rest in the presence of the doubt. He leaned against the sun-warmed stones and stared at Uriah's roof. A mournful, apprehensive mood descended upon him because the vessel and the basin were gone. But, like a token of their unuttered pledges—white and undeniably real in the green dusk, held to the roof by the weight of a cushion and rippling in the wind—was the square of linen with which she had dried herself. She forgot it, he thought, because of the look that was between us. . . . And again the sweet shuddering came upon him. He yearned after the linen. He wished to bury his face in it, to seek for the scent of her flesh in its folds.

He continued to gaze upon the waving square of linen until he heard footfalls on the roof behind him. He turned and steadied himself against the parapet. The armor-bearer came to a halt behind her, bowed to the King, and was gone. She came forward then, slowly and with conscious dignity, the folds of her stark white garment blowing around her body, her veil floating before her shimmering face. As the new moon comes into the sky—foreordained and yet miraculous—so she came, shedding a hush and a radiance before her. He could not speak. He could only form the syllables of her name with his lips.

She did not look upon him. Her head was bowed when she stood face to face with him, and her eyelids, pale and heavy, covered her eyes. "My lord the King has summoned me," she said. "I have come to the King my lord." And in these words, spoken simply and in the pure accents of Benjamin, she gave him the same submissiveness, the same self-dedication, that she had bestowed upon him in the look. She also had been assailed by the sweet shuddering. She also had waited through the long day, knowing that the night must find them brow to brow and knee to knee.

He spoke then, uttering such words as he had never before spoken to a woman. He called himself blessed above all men. He poured out his humility and his gratefulness. He lifted her small hands and held them against his face. He kissed her cheeks and breathed their milky fragrance; he kissed her eyelids, her forehead, her hair. And their love was like strong wine within them, so that they reeled with it and could not stand, and walked unsteadily to the couch beneath the canopy, holding fast to each other's hands.

And when they had utterly known each other, when the wind of God had ceased to blow and the night hung above their dazed and exalted faces, she turned to him and spoke at last. "I have loved my lord the King since the hour when I first beheld him. . . ."

It seemed to him then that the cup of his life had indeed been filled to overflowing. And he arose and knelt before the couch and kissed her feet.

✌ VIII ✈

For the first time in all his days, David called himself a happy man. During the long conversations with ambassadors, he kept saying to himself, When this day is past, I will go up to the roof and behold my beloved. . . . In council, in the midst of some serious deliberation, he would suddenly see a vision of her small foot emerging from the folds of her skirt. How beautiful it is, he would say in his heart. There is a blue vein, scarcely perceptible, running across her ankle. I will hold her foot in the hollow of my hand tonight. . . . Sometimes an irresistible desire to sing would come upon him. He found himself lifting up his voice above the others in the choruses that were sung before the ark, and twice or thrice he wakened half the household early by bursting into resonant song.

If there were certain difficulties—if limits of time and place were put upon his passion—he had lived too many years to be unaware that these very confines were the source of some of his happiness. Had he been free to seat her among his wives, their intimacy would have been less. They would no longer have been conspirators together against the world, nor would he have felt that the eventide was set apart from all the common hours of the day, a tabernacle in time to encompass her alone. The first phases of their love-making were so stark, so direct and bare, that every addition was a new delight. When they wished to distinguish one occasion from another, they used such phrases as "the time we saw the falling star" or "the time we began to laugh and could not stop." All the small pleasures which those who dwell in a house together come soon to take for granted remained for them rare gifts. The brazier carried up from the King's bedchamber burned with a singularly golden fire. Bread brought up stealthily from the hearth and eaten by moonlight became a feast. And when they ventured down, in the first pearly light of the dawn, to walk together in the King's garden, they felt such hushed ecstasy as the first man and woman must have felt when they wandered hand in hand into the unpeopled, virgin reaches of Paradise.

In the early days of their union, there was little talk between them. But it was not long before they spoke constantly, pouring themselves out in searching and profound conversation, so intimate that they felt no need to touch each other, so swift and ardent that they dared not pause to kiss. It seemed to David now that his life had been a very silent one. In the shadow of the dripping trees in Saul's garden, he had once known what it was to go out in words to the beloved; and twice or thrice he had advanced toward close communication with Achish, sitting late in the palace at Gath and staring not at the listener but at the wavering line of the sea. But there had always been matters that must be skirted; there had always been a hidden core that must be left untouched. Now, for the first time, his tongue was utterly loosened, and whenever he spoke with her he sought her eyes. And he knew in his heart that everything—all that he laid bare to her and all that she guessed—she accepted with the same comprehending smile.

There was only one matter that they avoided in their talk—neither of them could utter Uriah's name. When it was necessary to mention him, they referred to him with a sorrowful *"he." He* was at Rabbah, besieging the stubborn citadel of the Ammonites. The war might last forever—Joab was furious with the persistence of the heathen and had sworn that nothing would make him raise the siege. When the bitter business of Rabbah was settled, there was still the need to scourge the Syrian tribes for their revolt against Israel. *He* might not return until spring. . . .

Toward the end of the third moon of his happiness, it occurred to David that she had never set eyes upon his bedchamber. He was overcome by an irresistible wish to see her slight body lying on the great bed. All through the morning he pondered the matter, and by noon it seemed to him that it could be effected with complete safety. Noi, Haggith, Abigail, and the children had gone off to the orchards. Michal was making a pilgrimage to Gibeah to anoint her father's grave. The captain of the bodyguard, in order to restore discipline, had moved for the time being into the quarters that housed his officers—they had grown lax and quarrelsome of late, and he felt that his presence was needed there. No ambassadors, no governors of outpost cities, no captains of garrisons in Philistia or Moab or Syria were sojourning that week in the King's house. The halls would be empty at an early hour; before moonrise the servants would be free to close themselves up in their own rooms. There was little business to occupy David through the long hours of the afternoon. He spent them in carrying the makings of a feast to his bedchamber—a cruet of wine, a fine ripe melon, a haunch of roast kid, and a loaf of honey cake. An eager, buoyant mood, such as he had not known since childhood, was upon him.

But when she came to him on the roof that night, when he drew her down to his knees and told her of the feast that he had prepared for her below, a sense of disappointment settled upon him. It was not that she did not make much of the occasion; she told him that she had always wished to look upon the room in which he slept, had always longed to lie down with him upon his own bed. Yet he felt an indefinable uneasiness—his festival was not as he had hoped it would be. For the first time he felt abashed in her presence. Am I childish and overeager? he asked himself. Could she consider me a fool? . . .

On the way down the dark stairway she gave him her hand. Her palm was moist and cold, and it came into his mind that she might be ailing. He was stricken with the realization of her mortality. "Is it well with Bath-sheba?" he whispered, careless now of whatever servants might be listening behind closed doors. She closed her small hand reassuringly around his fingers and whispered that she was very well. But he drew her quickly through the shadow and into the lamplit room.

He sat upon the edge of the bed and watched her while she wandered about, touching the curtains, testing the softness of the rugs with her small, arched foot, holding the bowls and the vases up to the light. But her expressions of delight over his rich possessions only filled him with an aching sense of remorse. He thought of her walking about in the bald rooms of her own house, dressed in the stark white linen provided for her by the austere Hittite, unable even to wear the crystal and turquoise and gold bestowed upon her by her lover. No, now, he thought, if I have had cause to rejoice in the secrecy of our oneness, she has had no cause to rejoice. . . . And when he gazed upon her again, slight against the towering windows and the long draperies, the sight of her was a bruise upon his heart.

He went to the table and began to carve the melon. He found a disproportionate consolation in preparing her slice, in removing all the slippery seeds and pulling away the stringy pulp that had held them in place. Suddenly he heard a strange sound, a low, animal whimper. He looked up and saw that she was leaning against the window sill, clutching the folds of the draperies, and weeping.

"What is it? What has come upon my beloved?"

She did not answer. She pulled the curtain across her quivering face and shook her head.

He was assailed again by the knowledge that she was mortal, that her sweet presence was created out of perishable flesh and sustained by ephemeral breath. "Is there some sickness upon my darling?"

"No, no, no," she said, and wept the more.

Another fright, less terrible, but sickeningly ugly, came upon him. "Has *he* sent you a message? Is *he* about to return?" he said.

She shook her head.

"Then what is it? Why do you weep?"

She dropped the curtain and came toward him. She held up her hands before her breasts, the palms open as though to protect herself from a blow. "They will take me away from my lord," she said. "They will take me for an adulteress and stone me in the streets. They will know now what has been between me and my lord."

He looked at her in amazement. "Why should my beloved torment herself with such terrors? Who has seen us? Who should know?"

"Even though none has seen us, all the world will know. They will take me away from David and stone me to death. . . ."

"No, now, it is hidden and will remain hidden. . . ."

"How should it remain hidden? I am with child," she said.

IX

For the three nights that followed his blighted night of festival they talked on the roof from the hour of dusk to the setting of the moon. Now more than ever they were conspirators against the world. A spell of mist and chill had been borne in upon the city from the sea. They kept the brazier burning, and it became a kind of hearth for them in the vast night that was their household. They sat cross-legged, on cushions, with the brazier between them. They gazed earnestly into each other's firelit faces and assured each other that there was a way, that this matter could not come to such a preposterous end as infamy and death.

There were ways, there were a dozen ways. All of them looked simple at first, and in the end all of them proved to be quite impracticable. She might, for example, send to her husband saying that the heat of the city oppressed her, and that she had gone to dwell for a while with a cousin of hers in Benjamin. But what if, moving northward in pursuit of the Syrians, *he* or Ahitophel should stop at this same cousin's house? It would not do, it would not do at all. Nor would it do for the King of Israel to conduct himself like the lords of Egypt, to reach forth his hand and take what he desired. Israel and the prophet Nathan would be affronted for Jahveh's sake; there would be a great cry against it among the people—it would not do, they turned from it quickly because it conjured up the hideous vision of a stoning in the streets. Once and once only she spoke of going to a necromancer to secure such a potion as would bring a child forth incomplete out of its mother's womb. He rejected it utterly with a low cry; his face sagged in the flickering light and looked pinched and old.

There was a way—there was a loathsome and intolerable way—but workable nevertheless. Each of them brooded upon it and dared not put it into speech. Each of them watched covertly for some sign of it in the looks and words of the other. If *he* could be called home, if *he* could be brought to spend a single hour in his wife's bed. . . . And whenever a new plan ended in the certainty of shame and destruction, they fell silent and stared at each other across their little heap of fire, thinking of this. . . .

On the third night, when they had exhausted themselves with their wild searching and had found no answer, he rose, saying that they were plainly too weary to consider the matter further and that it would be well to lie down upon the couch and sleep.

"Wait a little," she said, holding out her hand to him. "There is a thing which has come into my thoughts——"

He turned away, knowing well what it was. "We will speak of it tomorrow," he said. "Come, let us sleep."

"My lord will sleep the better if he will listen. There is a way. . . ."

"What way?"

"If David will call *him* back to Jerusalem, soon, before my body has begun to change. . . . If David will send him up to me. . . . No, now, do not turn such a look upon me. I have thought of it long, and I also will suffer. But it will be finished soon, it will be finished in a single night. . . ."

He cried out again, in pain and disgust, as he had cried out when she had offered to cast out the child. But the next morning he dispatched a messenger to Joab before the gates of Rabbah. "Give my greetings to my nephew," he said to the messenger, "and tell him to send me Uriah the Hittite."

⋖ X ⋗

AT FIRST, it had seemed to David that his period of waiting for the coming of Uriah the Hittite would be a waking nightmare. But once he had begun to occupy himself with the details, he put from his mind the end that the plan was to accomplish, and even managed to achieve a kind of calm assurance as to his ability to carry it out with success.

After the breaking of the noonday bread he went to his bedchamber and set himself to the study of a long report from the overseer of his estates. He read the interminable list of items with complete attention;

he felt untroubled, clearheaded, confident. It was with amazement, then, that he found himself starting out of his chair when his steward knocked at the door. He was shocked, he was unmanned by the sudden, violent speed of his heart when he heard the foreknown words "Uriah the Hittite is in the common room, my lord."

It seemed to him now that the situation was filled with dangerous possibilities, and that his preparations were hopelessly inadequate. He bade his steward inform the visitor that he would descend within a few moments. Then, seeing how futile it was to try to reconsider so much in so short a time, he changed his mind and caught up with the steward on the stair. "Go and look to the evening bread," he said to the man, who gazed at him in surprise. "I will go down to greet the captain myself."

The figure that rose from the couch to bow before him looked insignificant in the long reaches of the room. A Hittite like any other Hittite, he told himself. . . . But the swarthy face was immediate and unforgettable. And he loathed it, because it was the face of the Hittite who had possessed his beloved.

Before he asked Jahveh to walk forever at the side of his gallant captain, he sighed and drew his hand across his eyes.

"Is my lord the King weary? Have I roused him out of his sleep?" said Uriah. "If it please the King, I will wait until such an hour as he chooses. . . ."

"No, no, no. I was drowsing, it is true, but I am well awake and more than anxious to hear how it goes in the camp of God."

They sat down together on the long couch, which was heaped with cushions and covered by a piece of bright-blue cloth embroidered in violet. At once, the coverlet became distasteful to the King. How ugly it is, he thought while he asked in a cordial voice after the health of his nephew. Tomorrow I will tell the steward to take it out of the common room, out of my sight. . . . The Hittite was giving a detailed account of the deeds of the eldest son of Zeruiah. Although it was plain that he had come with exasperating zeal directly to the King's house without so much as drying his face or washing his feet, he did not permit himself to relax against the cushions. He sat upright, his elbows close to his sides and his hands lying palms downward upon his thighs. The hands were hard and leathery; there were dark crescents under the nails and knobby bones at the wrists.

"Have there been breaches made in the walls of Rabbah?" said David in an urgent voice, for he could not be silent, seeing these hands clasping the beloved's slight body.

No, Uriah regretted to report that there were as yet no actual breaches. On several occasions the ranks of God had thrown themselves with all their strength against the walls—the King could see by Uriah's modest downward glance that he had led at least one of these sallies—but nothing had come of it. The heathen were stubborn and showed no inclination to offer a truce, even though there were tales that they were in sore straits and had begun to eat rats and dogs.

446

"And did the hero of Jerusalem ride forth in any of these sallies?" David asked, reminding himself that a man was more likely to make merry in his own house if he had received the King's praise.

"Thrice I rode out, but it was nothing, inasmuch as it was to no purpose, my lord."

"No, now," said David, "who shall say that the futile battles are not the most glorious? If the wall could have been breached, I know that Uriah would have breached it long ago. . . ." He fell silent and stripped off one of his rings, a serpentine coil of copper and gold. For a moment he sat staring at it. Then he lifted Uriah's sweaty hand and began to force the ring onto the middle finger. He had to strive long to make the ring pass over the grimy knuckle, and while he strove he remembered after what fashion he wished this Hittite to make merry, and his own hands turned damp with disgust.

And now he wished only to be alone so that he might wipe his flesh clean of the loathsome touch. How long has he been with me? he asked himself. When can I send him forth? I must not send him forth too soon. . . . And suddenly he saw the extent of his distraction; he knew that only a few minutes had actually passed. Nor had he followed the plan that he had conceived for this interview. He had proceeded without order, touching wildly and briefly upon the middle, the end, the beginning—and the crowning ceremony, the giving of the ring, which he had meant to use as a signal for departure, had already been performed even though the conversation had barely begun.

He saw, too, with fright that he had not as yet given the Hittite a reason for his sudden recall from the scene of the battle. He had intended to ask his opinion concerning the effectiveness of certain vests of quilted cotton that were being used for the first time at the siege of Rabbah. Now he launched into a series of questions regarding these vests, speaking with an unnatural degree of ardor, and working himself into so intense a state that he fancied his visitor must surely suspect him or think him mad. But he soon saw that Uriah found nothing unnatural in his behavior. To Uriah, these vests were highly significant, like all the accouterments of the host of God. His ardor outstripped the King's in his defense of the vests.

And when the matter of the vests was settled, the Hittite sank back for the first time against the cushions. He was spent with his energetic talk and tried to dissemble the fact by looking straight into the King's face. David stared back at him with steady and cheerful eyes, for all at once he had seen a graceful way to make the Hittite depart.

"May God forgive me," the King said in a solicitous voice that reminded him unpleasantly of his visitor's, "may God forgive me that I have kept you here so long. I was eager, certainly, to hear the news of the camp, and I wished particularly to receive an expert opinion concerning the vests. But I did ill to forget that the captain is weary, that he has not so much as set eyes upon—upon those that dwell within his gates." The Hittite raised his hand as if to wave away both his household and his weariness, but the King

447

talked on. He rose in his excitement. He actually brought himself to lay his hand upon the swarthy shoulder. "Go down to your own house," he said, "and take unto yourself a little well-deserved cheer, a little meat and wine." And now it seemed to him that his inventiveness had quite outstripped the careful but unimaginative plan which he had found himself unable to follow. "Go and wash and prepare to eat," he said, "and I will send up to you and—and to your household a dish from my own table. My steward has promised me a savory stew of kid. It will gladden my heart to think that Uriah eats my food, even though he is absent from my board this night."

The thought of sending down a dish from his own table seemed to him particularly felicitous; it indicated an almost tender regard for the captain, and it would be certain to break down the air of austerity that hung over the Hittite's house. Sitting over the King's dish, telling Bath-sheba of the King's favor, flashing his serpentine ring across the board, how could *he* be otherwise than genial, expansive, in the proper frame of mind for . . .

David did not permit himself to dwell longer upon that. He passed his arm through the arm of the visitor and led him to the door. But when the door was shut, he found that he had no control over himself. Before he could go to the steward to direct that a dish of savory stew be sent to the house of his neighbor, he stood long over the basin near the threshold, washing his hands, washing his arms, washing his face, filling his mouth with water and spewing it out again.

The day was drawing on toward the hour of the evening bread. He left the house and walked restlessly up and down the garden. Will she come down to the portico to meet him? he asked himself. What will they say to each other? Has it been her custom to wash his feet and help him to anoint himself, or does he leave that matter to the servants? Will he kiss her? . . . And the King wrung his fingers until the knuckles cracked. He knew suddenly that the very sight of Uriah's house was increasing his wretchedness, and he turned and walked back into the common room. The steward was sitting on a bench close to the threshold.

"Have you carried the savory stew to the house of the captain?" David said.

"I have taken the stew, but not to the house of the captain, my lord." He started. "Not to the house of the captain? Wherefore?"

"The stew was intended for the captain, was it not?"

"Surely, even as I said——"

"The captain did not go up to his house. He went to the quarters of the officers of the King's guard, to spend the evening in their company. There he eats, and there he will lie down to sleep."

And now things had come to such a pass with David that he laughed aloud in the steward's face. "To the quarters of the guard?" he said. "To spend the night?"

The steward coughed and pretended to be staring at a length of drapery.

448

"Even so, my lord. Therefore, I have carried the King's dish to the mess hall of the guardsmen. . . ."

He continued to speak, but David did not hear him. Still laughing and striving wildly to control his countenance, he went out of the house, down the garden, through the great brazen gate hung between stone pylons, into the street. The long, low building which housed the officers of his bodyguard lay a hundred paces to the left. Quickly, quickly, he thought, I must go quickly, before my resolve has ebbed completely from me, before I have said in my heart, "Let him sleep where he will, so long as he does not lie down upon her bed." . . .

He stopped breathless in the doorway of the building. The interior of the long room was dark after the brilliant outer light; the table and those who sat about it were barely visible to his dazzled eyes. He blinked and sought the curly hair, the curved nose, the weakly sensual mouth of the Hittite. He could not see him anywhere at first, and then was violently startled to find him close at hand—sitting on a bench at the threshold while a servant dried and anointed his feet.

"My lord the King," said the captain, rising.

David stared into Uriah's face as though he could not believe his own eyes. "Is the captain here?" he said. "How is it that he has not gone up to his own house, to eat and drink and greet his wife after these many weeks of war and weariness?"

The Hittite smiled the smile of one who is somewhat ashamed of himself. "The ark and the men of Israel and Judah abide tonight in tents, and my lord Joab and his warriors are encamped in the open field," he said. "How, then, while they suffer the rigors of the siege of Rabbah, shall I go into my house and eat and drink and lie with my wife? As the King lives and as his soul lives, I cannot do such a thing. . . ."

If the words had been spoken loudly and freely, they might have been called vainglorious. But they were said so apologetically that they were utterly unassailable. Such stedfastness, such dedication to Jahveh and to His host were virtues seldom found of late among the ranks of Israel. And a man must bow a little before them, even if they dwelt in the swarthy and repulsive body of an alien fool. . . .

"Well," said David at last, turning his bracelet round and round on his wrist and staring at the ground before him. "Sleep here tonight then if you wish, but tarry in Jerusalem tomorrow. Come up to me yet once more tomorrow evening, and we will break bread together, we two. . . ."

He saw the blush of pleasure rising in the dark cheeks, and was ashamed to behold it. He was remembering how in the plains of Sharon he had walked forth from the tent of Achish, wishing to sleep like Saul and Jonathan on the stubborn ground. "I will not keep you long," he said, turning back toward the street. "The day after tomorrow, at dawning, I will let you depart."

Long afterward, when he looked back upon his third encounter with Uriah the Hittite, he found it hard to believe that it was actually he who had sat at the lamplit table that night. He had called Uriah "dear friend" and "beloved brother." He had begged him to set aside the prohibitions put upon the warrior; he had said, "It is a wound upon the heart of the King that his guest should refuse to partake of his wine." Time after time, he had filled the captain's bowl with the thick and aromatic wine of Syria, watching the signs of drunkenness that appeared upon the dark and narrow face. He had come round to the corner of the table in order to sit cheek by jowl with Uriah. He had spoken close to his ear in a soft, companionable voice. Casually, subtly, he had turned the talk to obscene matters—the voluptuous dances performed by the daughters of Sin, the skill of the women who dwelt in the temples of Astarte.

He was never certain how many hours this nightmare lasted. He knew only that when he led the drunken Hittite across the garden, the waning moon had already risen. They stood together at the gate, and the white light cast the shadows of the brazen scrolls and bars across their feet.

"Go up to your house and sleep," said David.

Uriah nodded and began to stumble in the direction of the long, low building—lightless now—where the officers of the bodyguard ate and slept.

Such consternation came upon the King then that he could find voice only to whisper, "Where are you going? Go up to your own house. Why should you rouse the guardsmen? Their doors are bolted. They have long since gone to their beds."

"Then I will sleep upon the threshold, before their bolted door," said Uriah. "I will cover myself with my cloak, even as Joab covers himself."

"No, now. . . ." And while he stood protesting, Uriah had walked some ten paces toward the moonlit threshold on which he intended to sleep. "Stop, wait a little," David said. To let him go was to break down the last barrier against infamy and death. . . .

Uriah turned, catching at the hedges for support. "Yes, my lord?"

"Come again tomorrow. Come to me tomorrow at dawn, before you depart." For surely, he thought, the night will yield up some answer. Surely I will find a way before he has shaken the dust of this city from his feet. . . .

"Even so, my lord," the Hittite said. He lurched down the stark, bright street and was gone.

When David stood alone in his garden—he knew it then and he never denied it thereafter—he was himself, sane and entire. The moon shone low and with a tarnished brilliance through the black screen of the hedges. Except for the constant, throaty sound of the spring, the garden was utterly still. He walked up and down the path, feeling the sleeve of his robe catch again and again on the same blossoming branch, seeing the same white glimmer upon the moving water. A thought, or rather the foreshadowing of a thought, was stirring within him. He actually felt a physical sensation of stirring—a nauseating sensation, as though some finned and slippery creature were turning over in the region below his heart. What am I thinking? he asked himself. . . . And the thought darted up, fully formed: To make an end of the Hittite. . . .

He wondered why it had never come into his mind before. If the mouth of Uriah were to be stopped in death, there would be no man left on earth to say that the child was not Uriah's child. He began to pace the path again, swiftly now. Other realizations, melting and tremulous, had risen within him, but he put them resolutely aside. A man did not either commit or command murder in order to take a woman into his house, in order to break bread with her and walk with her in the garden and lie with her night after night. . . . No, whosoever took another man's life to ensure his own pleasure was such a one as Joab; he passed forever out of the pale of God's consideration. . . . But to quench the life in the body of the Hittite in order to sustain it in the body of the beloved . . . He stopped on the path and covered his face with his hands; he saw the rise and fall of her breasts; he felt her sweet, moist breath passing between his half-opened lips. And now for the first time, now that there was some hope of succor, he permitted himself to see her set upon in the street and bruised by stones. What was the life of the Hittite beside *her* life? Whose life would he not forfeit now—and gladly, gladly—to make her secure against death? . . .

He walked to the edge of the spring and stared at the white gleam of the moon upon the wet rocks. He must not deceive himself; he must admit that there were other ways to keep the breath stirring in her beloved body —other ways than the Hittite's death. She could go to dwell for the rest of her days in the court of Hiram, King of Tyre; she could find such refuge as Jesse had found long ago in the kingdom of the Moabites. It would be possible to give out that she had fled with some young lover in her husband's absence—such things had come to pass in Jerusalem before. But the thought of endless separation was not to be borne.

He sat down upon a bench before the spring and gazed steadily at the clumps of withering iris leaves. He remembered the night when he had taken a moist bloom and held it against his face, and that night seemed as distant as the nights in the hills around Bethlehem. That was three moons ago, he thought, and then I did not love her. . . . But all the days in which he had not loved her seemed without content, without meaning; these last few nights had been intolerable without her; and the sweet shuddering came once more upon him when he thought that tomorrow she would come up to him again. What is my life unless I possess her utterly? he asked himself. Why should such a one as I be sacrificed to such a one as Uriah the Hittite? . . .

He conjured up an image of the captain—not as he had seen him tonight, befuddled by wine, for that would have been unjust, but as he had appeared on that first evening at Joab's table. He saw the woolly hair, the curving nose, the narrow, oily forehead. Even then, he told himself, before I had so much as set eyes upon her, I knew what manner of man he was. It is a pale and circumscribed existence that I would take from him. It is a cold and dull reflection of the world that lies behind that sweaty brow. . . .

And now it seemed to him that the times were burdened and clogged by too many such men, that such men stood everywhere in the path of the vital and the lordly ones, casting their shadows over the gleam of things, slowing the pulse of the world. Why should I let him live? he asked himself. Why should I spare him more than I would spare a fly that has buzzed into my face? Why should I concern myself with preserving his life when it is plain that he does not even live? He has made a sepulcher of the high house that I built for him; he has used the exquisite body that I love as a bondsman might use the body of a serving-maid; he has transformed Jahveh Himself into a crotchety priest concerned with nothing but the keeping of the dietary laws. Why, in order to keep the breath within him, should I confine my ardent heart? No, now, if we cannot lift our hands against such men as this, we become even as they, and the world is peopled henceforth with a race of lizards crawling and blinking out their days. . . .

He drew the folds of his robe closer around him and walked toward his lamplit door. The common room had a ravaged and disorderly look. Most of the lamps had gone out for want of oil, and those that continued to burn cast a sickly light over smeared plates and cups, crumpled napkins, and bits of gristle. The thick and aromatic scent of the Syrian wine still clung to the place. Sprawled on his face upon a rug, like a man struck down from behind, a single servant slept.

He did not wish the bondsman to waken. The thought that any eyes should look upon him now filled him with a creeping terror. He went stealthily, on the balls of his feet, to that corner of the room in which a tall cabinet stood. The doors creaked faintly as he opened them. Out of the dust-scented darkness he drew a stylus and a clay tablet, such a one as is double and may be sealed up to contain its secret. He carried these things back to the table and laid them on the board between a joint of meat and a dark puddle of wine.

And suddenly the knowledge of what he was about to do broke full upon him, so that the hand which groped after the stylus turned motionless. I am about to command murder, he told himself. I am about to do that which Joab did unto Abner at the gates of Hebron. . . . He heard the voice of the Hittite saying, "The ark and the men of Israel and Judah abide this night in tents. . . ." He is an honorable man, he thought, and he has always served me well. His blood courses through his veins, his breath comes and goes, he sleeps on the threshold under the stars. I will write and his blood will be still—he will have no breath—he will lie henceforth under the earth. . . .

"Ah, God . . ."

It was the servant who had spoken. He sighed and turned over in his sleep.

And quickly, before the bondsman could waken, before any human eye could see, the King of Israel took up the stylus and wrote upon the tablet. In large, uneven letters, driven deep into the clay, he wrote a message to Joab: "Set Uriah in the forefront of the hottest battle, and retire from him, that he may be smitten and die." Then he folded the tablet and sealed it up and carried it back to the cabinet. Nor did he look upon it again until he laid it in Uriah's hands.

⋙ XII ⋘

FOR THE FIRST TIME in her life, the lady Noi had taken to lying late abed. It had been her custom since her childhood to rise with the coming of the dawn. When she had dwelt in the wilderness, there had always been her brothers to feed, and since the birth of Amnon there had been children, her own and the others. But now the children were old enough to dress themselves without her, and during the whole morning they sat in the garden with Hushai the counselor, whom David had chosen to instruct them in the history of Israel, the laws of the land, and the nature of God. So, even though she woke out of long habit as soon as the light fell across the foot of her bed, there was no need for her to rise. She lay propped up against the pillows, listening to the morning sounds of the household: the voice of Haggith mildly remonstrating with the servants, the incisive voice of Hushai putting sharp questions to the children under her window, the confident voices of Tamar and Absalom, and Amnon's nervous, tentative replies.

Sometimes Haggith would come in for a brief visit, bearing a cake of steaming bread, a piece of choice fruit, and a bowl of hot herb tea. The question of Haggith was no longer a worry to her; there was no longer any uncertainty as to what would become of the poor young woman once she ceased to stand in high favor with her lord. Since the unseasonable spell of heat that had descended six moons ago upon the city, Haggith had not been called once to David's bedchamber. Another young woman—the widow of Uriah the Hittite—had plainly taken her place. But Haggith had borne it all with the dignity of the high houses of Hebron. If she had wept, she had wept in the privacy of her own chamber; and she had permitted herself only one uncharitable remark: that a slight pregnant woman always looked more ridiculous than a tall one.

After Haggith had gone back to her household duties, Noi would sit with the pillows behind her back, sipping the tea. The sun would fall across her hands, and she would say to herself, Really, I am growing far too thin, I must eat. . . . She would set out then to eat everything that Haggith had carried up, and she would feel a childish pride when she set the plate, clean and bare, upon the little table beside her bed. But within half an hour she would begin to wonder if she would not have done better not to have eaten. A certain gnawing sensation would begin to work within her. It was less like pain than like hunger—a strange, unnatural hunger which the taking of nourishment only increased.

It is nothing, she would tell herself. Thousands of people have just such pains and never so much as mention them. . . . And, having addressed this formula to herself, she would feel comforted and restored. In these last six moons she had grown very adept at minimizing all painful things; whether the ache was in the flesh or in the spirit, she contemplated it until it shrank away. Why should I grieve over that? she asked herself a dozen times a day. It is nothing, nothing at all. . . .

She did not suffer over the ascendancy of Bath-sheba as she had suffered over the triumphs of the others. She had seen all of them come and go— it was an old tale with her, she would not waste her tears. The new bride did not seem to her such a one as could stir a remote and self-possessed man to a transcendent passion; she was slight, quiet, and almost ugly in her pregnancy; her lips and eyelids were often swollen, she was very short of breath and breathed through an open mouth, and she carried the child in a painfully obvious manner, as Haggith had said. If he doted on his sixth bride more publicly than he had doted on the others, kissing her fingertips at table and insisting that she sit beside him on ceremonial occasions even in her present state, that was only to be expected. A man grew more fond and less concerned with the opinion of the world as he grew older. This wife, like all the others, would be put aside when the first bloom was gone. This wife, like all the others, would never be permitted to draw the veil away from the tabernacle of his heart. She alone had truly known him among the roofless pillars in burned Ziklag. And he would turn to her yet once more when he closed his doors against the merrymakers. We will lie together on the same bed, she told herself, through the quiet nights of our latter years. When he is beyond desire, he will reach out again and take my hand. . . .

When such thoughts as these came into her mind, she would turn up the cool side of the pillow and lie back against it. The warmth of the tea, the cessation of the pain, the quiet sounds in the garden below, would lull her into a light and pleasant drowsiness. If she kept her eyes half-open, she could be certain of another hour of rest. But if she permitted herself actually to sink into sleep, she would start up with some distressing matter in her thoughts, and the process of reducing the imponderable to the trivial would have to begin all over again. . . .

There was, for instance, this business of the siege of Rabbah. It had gone very ill; a thousand of the sons of Jahveh, including the brave Hittite captain, had fallen before the walls. Nobody could say when the war would end. Already the great clouds, pregnant with the winter rains, brooded upon the horizon around Jerusalem in the gray mornings; already the penetrating wind had begun to blow in from the western sea; yet the heathen had not offered truce. And the longer the siege of Rabbah lasted, the more credence was being given in the streets of the city to certain obscure and disturbing rantings of the prophet Nathan. God was angry, the prophet said. He had turned His face against Israel and Jerusalem; He had seen a sight in Jerusalem that had offended His eyes. But prophets have always ranted when the wars went ill, she told herself. Those who go about in sackcloth have always found fault with those who go about in crimson and purple. It is the way of the world, it is nothing at all. . . .

And yet, and yet . . . One of the guardsmen who had been disciplined for drunkenness last spring was spreading an ugly tale. If Uriah the Hittite had indeed sown the seed that was ripening so obviously, so hastily, in the lady Bath-sheba's womb, then it had been his spirit and not his flesh that had done the deed. His body—God rest it where it lay in the sun-baked plains around Rabbah!—had certainly not journeyed up to his house while he tarried in Jerusalem. He had loudly and repeatedly deplored all congress with women during the season of war. And, so far as this guardsman could determine, the Hittite had been as good as his word—he had slept the sleep of the chaste among his fellow warriors on both those nights. . . .

Talk, nothing but idle and malicious talk, Noi would tell herself, starting up out of her dream. She would rise then, knowing that the lesson in the garden had almost come to a close, that the children would be running in to plague Abigail and Michal, that Haggith would be wanting her advice as to what should be served with the noonday bread. Once on her feet, she always found herself stronger and more energetic than she had dared to hope. But when she sat on the edge of the bed and bent over to fasten her sandals, the gnawing ache would begin again, sharper than before. It is nothing, she would tell herself. I am a weakling to make so much of it. When I think of the warriors at Rabbah, and what wounds they carry about . . . Thousands of people live out half their lives with just such little pains. . . .

✧ XIII ✧

DURING these weeks, the King of Israel found himself thinking constantly of his predecessor. The memory of Jonathan lay at peace within him at last, but now Saul would not sleep. At first it seemed to him that he was being reprimanded by the uneasy spirit of the dead, and he appointed two priests to devote themselves to the tending of the Gibean burial caves. But the sorrowful and majestic shape still would not rest. And he came at last to know that this was no visitation out of Sheol. It was simply that he and Saul had entered into a new kinship. The life that he lived now was a repetition of the life that he had watched Saul live in the Gibean days.

When he sat among his children on an idle afternoon, he would find himself staring too long and too earnestly at the beautiful Absalom. No, now, he would think, I look at him far too fondly, with a kind of baffled tenderness that might well be taken for doting. . . . And he would see the face of the first King of Israel turned searchingly and beseechingly upon Jonathan. . . . But Saul was more fortunate than I, he would tell himself. Saul had the wit to sow his best seed first. How would it have been with Saul if Jonathan had been a second son—if he had been forced to push the radiant one aside in order to make room for Malchishua or Abinadab? . . .

And one evening toward the end of summer, as he stretched himself at length on a bench beneath a palm tree, with his cheek just touching Bath-sheba's knee, he remembered how Saul had lain in the mellow light of the Gibean garden with his head in the lap of his concubine. And truly, he told himself, I am now as he was then—I have but two women, the true wife who has looked to my house and nurtured my children, and the beloved. . . . Michal, Abigail, Haggith—all of them had departed from the innermost places of his spirit. He looked upon them now as he might have looked upon a group of aging sisters. He was kindly with them; he never failed to make mention of the fact that one or the other of them had dressed her hair in a new fashion or was wearing a particularly elaborate robe. But he said in his heart: I will carve out seven burial caves in the hills above Jerusalem. I will carve them out on either side of a brook or a spring; and there will be four on one side and three on the other. Even as Saul sleeps, so I will sleep—for there is a cave which waits for Rizpah in the Gibean garden—between the true wife and the beloved. . . .

If there was one matter in which he had always considered himself unlike the son of Kish, it was the matter of piety. The zealous and God-fearing man of Judah—or so he had told himself—would never set his face against the priesthood after the manner of the skeptical and worldly Benjamite. And yet, as the winter rains began to fall slantwise across the windows of the common room, he pondered much upon the bitter struggle between Saul and Samuel, and found it far less reprehensible than he had found it in the past. A man's love of God might lie fallow within him, needing renewal. So, at least, it was with him for the present. To think of Jahveh at all was painful to him; that thought always brought another in its wake—at every ceremony, every sacrifice, he saw in his mind's eye the grave of Uriah the Hittite, a mound of red clay, a scarcely perceptible undulation in the barren reaches of the Ammonite plain. And he was glad that the high priests Abiathar and Gad had tarried with the host before Rabbah. He would have found it more than burdensome to sit with them through these gray, sodden evenings, discoursing upon the nature of God.

And if priests could be considered a burden, prophets could be called a downright affliction. Within the past four moons, David had learned as much. The prophet Nathan continued to walk through the muddy, somber streets of the city, ranting and prophesying: God was angry, He had seen sin sitting in high places, His warriors would continue to fall before the walls of Rabbah until those who had offended Him had confessed and purified themselves. . . . He could not bring himself to believe that the man was so insolent as to refer to what had come to pass within the royal palace. Yet Samuel had raved in just such vague and awesome terms against the House of Kish some thirty years ago. And whenever the King heard the fanatical voice above the clatter of rain on the dried palm fronds, he was disquieted for Bath-sheba's sake. Her lips turned blue at the first sound of it, and she would fall to weeping and saying that she would never bring forth a living child. . . .

There were times when he almost made up his mind to summon the prophet to the palace and settle the matter with a stern prohibition against preaching in the streets. For by the time the second moon of winter had appeared—a misted, tarnished crescent seen briefly between the tattered clouds—the city was in a deplorable state. More than a thousand of the men of Jahveh had fallen and been buried before the stubborn walls, and the voice of the prophet had become a call to general lamentation. Fathers and mothers, wives and sisters, ran into the rainy streets and followed after him, grieving afresh each evening, tearing their hair and beating their breasts.

Whenever the King looked down upon them from the upper windows of his palace, he felt his lips curving in the same cold smile that he had seen upon the lips of the Lion of Benjamin. Behold the people! he would say to himself. If good news should come out of Rabbah this very night, they would all forget their dead and parade in the streets with torches in their hands and wreaths upon their heads. . . .

And so, indeed, it came to pass. The messenger, riding in from Rabbah in the windy, rain-spattered dusk, encountered just such a crowd of mourners in the street. They saw the palm branch that he bore across his breast; they saw the wreath of victory upon his brow; and the looks of grief and penitence upon their faces gave way to vacant, stupid smiles. In very little time, the streets of Jerusalem were rosy with torches. The voice of the prophet Nathan was drowned in the universal thanksgiving. He stood in a gutter, his dour mouth twitching above his drenched beard, his eyes blinking against the streaming, flickering light. By midnight, every house was lighted. The lady Noi opened the doors of the King's palace and dispensed to every comer a measure of wine, a cake of figs, and a loaf of bread. But the King of Israel did not show his face that night to his people. Like Saul, he went into his bedchamber and closed the door. Like the wounded Lion of Benjamin, he stretched himself upon his bed and covered his quivering face and wept.

❧ XIV ❧

IN THE TEN-DAY INTERVAL between the fall of Rabbah and his nephew's return, David laid plans for such a feast as had never before been spread in Jerusalem. He sent messengers to every outpost town, inviting the governors to present themselves at the palace. He entreated all his visitors to stay on for the occasion; his house was crowded with distinguished strangers—friendly potentates out of Syria, ambassadors from Egypt, kinsmen of the lords of Tyre and Sidon and the Serens of Askelon and Gath, elders from Judah, Caleb, Ephraim, and Benjamin. He was satisfied only when he knew that no room in his palace would be empty, that no moment of the appointed day would be without its piece of ceremony or pageantry. For he had a cold dread of encountering Joab alone.

Since the morning when a certain sealed tablet had gone out from his hands to the camp of God before Rabbah, every communication that he had received from his nephew had given him cause for apprehension. Not that the captain of the host had ever been so gross as to make mention of the matter after the first simple statement—"Your servant Uriah the Hittite is also among the dead." But all his other messages were less constrained and more importunate than in the past; the tone of them was a tone that could exist only between conspirators.

During the last days of the siege of Rabbah, his loathing for Joab fastened upon him like a physical malady. Twice he dreamed that a messenger had come up to him out of the battle saying, "The son of Zeruiah is also among the dead." He went cold when he thought that it would be necessary to kiss the returning warrior. He will hold me in the circle of his arms, he thought; we will embrace as two murderers embrace. . . .

On the day appointed for the feast, the weather could scarcely have been more wretched. A heavy procession of gray clouds kept moving across the whitish sky; the whole city took on a drab and brownish cast; everything —the streets, the surrounding hills, the houses themselves—seemed on the point of dissolving into mud. Even the glowing braziers could not prevail against the chill. Small groups of guests stood in the circumscribed areas of warmth, spreading their fingers over the fires.

At the second hour after noon, it was made known that the son of Zeruiah was already within the gates. The steward of the King's house had gone down to meet him and bid him pause under his own roof to array himself for the occasion. The conqueror of insolent Ammon would be with them within the hour. Yet, even now that Joab's arrival was at hand, the King of Israel did not come down to mingle with his guests in the common room. He tarried in one of the upper chambers at Bath-sheba's side. She was not well, and he could not bring himself to leave her, even though the good Haggith had also seated herself beside the bed and kept saying: "Truly, believe me, her time is not yet come. A bowl of brewed herbs, a little rest, and she will be restored."

He was annoyed that Haggith should think him stupid enough to mistake this sickness for the beginning of labor. He knew the source of it well —she was sick with fright. The child had stopped moving within her, and she was convinced that it was dead. She lay with her hands folded upon the great, pitiful mound of her belly. Her lips and eyelids were swollen and her mouth was open, so that her face reminded him of the puffed face of a frog. She had never been so ugly, and he had never yearned over her with such tenderness. He rose from the bed and kissed her damp forehead. "No, now, little frog," he whispered, "it will move again, and very soon. Rest a little, go to sleep."

She stared at him with dark, afflicted eyes. "Go down," she said.

"I go because I must."

He could tell by the cheering in the streets that the hero of Rabbah was not far away. He hurried through the hall, down the stairs, across the common room, nodding this way and that to his guests. Then suddenly he stopped and stared, unable to believe his own eyes. No one had bidden the prophet Nathan to the feast. Yet there, alone beside a pillar, the prophet Nathan stood, dressed in a garment of black goat's-hair cloth.

"My lord," said an elder of Benjamin who was standing at his elbow, "behold, the captain of the host."

He moved forward to the glaring square of light revealed by the creaking portals. He saw the long, loose shape, the jackal's face, the large and lustrous eyes. "My dear nephew," he said, and gave himself up to the murderer's embrace.

Almost immediately, before Joab's kiss had dried on his cheek, the cere-monial procedure began. The guests moved in an eager but orderly line to embrace, question, and congratulate the captain of the host. The King of Israel walked discreetly away from his nephew, assuming the modest and retiring mien of one who wishes to yield the place of honor to a man more worthy than himself. He smiled at the ambassador from Sidon and laid his hand upon the shoulder of the young nephew of the Seren of Askelon. He bowed to a visiting merchant out of Egypt and said a kindly word to a palsied elder from Dan. Then he stopped in the shadow of a pillar and took a deep breath. But even as he rested his back against the column, he knew that the prophet Nathan stood on the other side of it. He felt himself pursued—pursued by Joab and by the prophet. He passed his arm through the arm of a Syrian potentate and led him into a corner, talking all the while, with less sense than vigor, of the intoxicating powers of Syrian wine.

All through the afternoon, he was possessed by fear. A young lutist out of Ephraim sang a song in praise of the valiant who had died before Rabbah, and behind the singer's rosy face and loose curls he saw Uriah's grave. A bearded captain read a list of spoils that had been taken in the heathen city; but he was conscious of nothing but the prophet's steady and impenetrable glance. He took the amulets from his neck and the rings from his fingers and bestowed them upon a long procession of heroes; and all the while he thought of the moment when he must lay the finest of the gifts—a lump of raw gold—in the loathsome hand of the captain of the host. And under all these immediate fears moved another. How is it with Bath-sheba? he kept asking himself. Has the child yet moved within her? Could God be so cruel as to take the life of the child? . . .

459

So he worried away the hours before the breaking of the evening bread. As a man submits to some involved and agonizing piece of surgery, so he submitted to the stages of the ceremony, saying to himself at the end of each event, At least that, too, is done. . . . And at last, as the servants began to move into the common room, bearing the steaming dishes before them, as the elder from Caleb finished his speech in praise of the heroes of his tribe and the elder from Benjamin arose to take his place, the King began to see the approaching end to his anguish. This last speech and an hour or two at table, and then the wretched business would be over.

During the speech of the venerable Benjamite he grew so weary that, without realizing what he did, he sank into a chair. The little group of listeners who stood in front of him moved courteously aside, so that he might look down a length of empty room directly into the speaker's face. He was not grateful to them for their courtesy. For in full view now, just behind the Benjamite, attentive and erect, the prophet Nathan stood.

He fell to wondering then why the Lord had chosen such a man as this to be His trumpet upon the earth. Samuel had been dour enough, and yet he had possessed a certain austere majesty. But this one grew all knobbed and gnarled, like the prickly thorn. One shoulder was higher than the other, so that he seemed always to be twitching his body in an exasperated shrug. His beard was streaked and ugly, half black, half yellowish white, and his forelock was forever plastered down by the sweat of his brow. Samuel, thought David, was a scourge to the Lion of Benjamin. But this one is a fly buzzing at my ear, persistent and pestiferous, mean and crotchety and old. . . .

"Therefore, a reverent silence is the best praise that we can offer up to our dead," said the venerable Benjamite, having praised them aloud for the better part of an hour. His speech was finished; the assembly sighed. The steward, standing at a distant door, rang the little bell that was to summon the guests to the board. But no one moved. For suddenly, unbelievably, the ceremony had gone awry. The prophet Nathan had stepped up to the place left vacant by the retreating elder, and was saying in his strident voice that he had a boon to ask of the King his lord.

David's jaw began to quiver; it was necessary for him to prop his elbow against the arm of the chair and steady his chin on his hand. While he labored to find his voice, the company drew back on either side. Between him and the prophet there were twenty paces of empty floor, and yet it seemed to him that Nathan was breathing into his face. "A boon?" he said. "What boon? Let the man of God ask whatsoever he will."

The prophet cleared his throat and fixed his impenetrable glance upon the King's brow. "I will tell the King of an instance of grave injustice." He spoke with the slow precision of one who has memorized his speech. "There were two men who dwelt in one city, and one was rich and the other poor. The rich man had exceeding many flocks and herds. But the poor man had nothing save one little ewe lamb which he had bought and nourished up. And it grew up together with him and with his children, and ate of his morsel and drank from his cup, and lay in his bosom, and was to him as a daughter."

The King of Israel let out his suspended breath in a long sigh. No, now, he thought, if it is a matter of poor men and rich men and ewes. . . . And he sank back and folded his hands upon his knees.

"And there came a traveler," said the prophet, still staring at David's forehead, "there came a traveler to dwell in the house of the rich man, and the rich man thought to make him a savory dish, that he might eat. But the rich man went not out to take of his own flock or his own herd to prepare the dish. He spared his own flock and his own herd, and took the poor man's lamb instead, and dressed it and gave it to the traveler who sojourned in his house. . . ."

The prophet paused. Those among the assembly who were Israelites lifted up their voices against such a state of affairs. The outlanders were plainly embarrassed. The matter was a local one and no concern of theirs, and yet to keep silence was to seem coldhearted. Some of them sighed, and others went so far as to shake their heads. And now the King of Israel, in full possession of himself, rose from his chair. He was incapable of feeling anything but a sudden, buoyant surge of relief. Nevertheless, he managed a good counterfeit of righteous wrath. "As Jahveh lives, the man who has done this thing is worthy to die," he said. "There is no pity in him. Name him, then, so that he may be required at least to restore the lamb fourfold."

The prophet thrust his bony arm straight out before him and pointed his forefinger at the King's face. "You are the man," he said.

A murmur rose in the assembly. Israelites and aliens alike turned wide-eyed and open-mouthed upon each other. What demon had possessed the prophet? To raise his voice against the crowned head of Israel—and in the midst of a solemn feast! Plainly the man was mad!

But Nathan's voice blared the murmur down. "God has been very gracious to the son of Jesse. God has anointed him King over Israel and Judah and has delivered him out of the hand of Saul and has given him a high house and many wives for his delight. Wherefore, then, has he despised the word of Jahveh and done that which is evil in the sight of the Lord?" The muscles of his throat worked horribly. For a moment it seemed that his voice would be strangled by his own rage. Then he began to rant again, thrusting his forefinger at the King. "You have smitten Uriah the Hittite with the sword," he shouted. "So that you might take his wife, you have smitten him with the sword of the children of Ammon, and from this day the sword shall not depart from your house, there will be evil in your house forever." He stepped backward toward the portal as he spoke. The assembly divided and shrank from him, for he reeled, and the foam of phophecy was upon his lips. "Thus says Jahveh to the son of Jesse: 'I will raise up evil against you out of your own seed. I will set your sons and your daughters against you. That child which you begot upon Bath-sheba—that child shall die. Your sin was committed in secret, but I will wreak My vengeance against you before all Israel and in the light of the sun.' Thus says the Lord."

Someone—a young Egyptian standing close to the threshold—had the presence of mind to pull open the great door, to make way for the raving prophet as one might make way for a raging beast. The blinding square of light broke upon them. The voice of the prophet trailed away. There was no sound but the sound of the driving rain. A draught blew through the long room, stirring the garments and draperies, and a bondsman hurried forward and helped the young Egyptian close the creaking door.

It was the son of Zeruiah who rose to the occasion. He appeared out of the ranks of awe-stricken starers and made his way up the cleared aisle to the King's chair. He walked loosely, debonairly, rattling the bracelets on his wrists. He shook out his hair and smiled a scornful smile. No, now, said his eyes, we will put a brazen face upon it. . . . And he bent and took the King's hands and raised him up from the chair.

"These days," he said, "every madman in Jerusalem is accounted a prophet."

The steward rang the little bell that was to call the guests to the feast. The awesome hush was broken by a universal chattering; everybody announced himself very hungry; everybody sniffed the delicious smell of the roast meat. The King of Israel also looked in the direction of the table. He opened his mouth, but no words would issue from it. He strove to walk, but he could barely keep himself erect because of the trembling in his knees. Joab supported him, Joab led him forward. He walked to the board, leaning upon the murderer, with the murderer's knowing glance upon him.

⊰ XV ⊱

IF THE CHILD had been stillborn, he could have endured it. But the child had come, male and perfect and beautiful, out of the womb. It had learned to close its delicate hand around Bath-sheba's finger and to focus its blue eyes upon David's face. They had been gay with it; they had called it quaint and tender names; they had seen that the soft down on its well-shaped head showed reddish in the light of the sun. Their love had gone out in tremulous, fearful tentacles to fasten upon it until it became a part of themselves. The child had lived for three full moons before the morning when Bath-sheba came running into David's bedchamber, disheveled and white, to say that a fever had come upon the little one. The little rabbit, the little fish—come, look at him, come—he was hot to touch, and he lay staring straight out before him.

For the first three days of the sickness, he could not bring himself to face the possibility that it could end in the child's death. Other children had sickened and recovered. Tamar had lain in a stupor for three days during her fifth year. She had been more feverish than this, he told himself, laying his hand upon the small, burning feet. He sat at the child's side day and night, and comforted himself with every change. Yesterday the child had tossed about violently, thrusting the coverlet aside, and today he merely turned his head against the pillow; surely this indicated that the pain was less. He called in one physician after another and waited for each new arrival, believing that he would be the one to uncover the mysterious thing that burned in the little one's body. He stared into the small face after every remedy was administered and told himself that the rheumy eyes had grown a little clearer, that the cracked lips were stirring in a smile. But on the fourth day he could no longer deceive himself. A terrible sound, a high, thin scream, issued and continued to issue, with very brief intervals, from the child's twisted mouth, and his eyes, dilated with rage and hate, were fearful to look upon. David knew then that no medicines could restore this screaming thing to humanity. Only a miracle, the physicians said. . . . And he rose up and went to lay his anguish at the feet of God.

A certain little room, remote and windowless, had been built onto the back of the palace as an extra storeroom some years ago. It jutted into the garden; a palm tree and a bed of herbs had been uprooted to make way for it; and since no paving stones had ever been laid, the floor was a square of earth, still redolent of the scent of roots. Whoever entered the place saw nothing at first but darkness and one long shaft of light that entered through a chink between the roof tiles and the brown clay wall. But when the eyes had accustomed themselves to the shadows, other shapes emerged— great earthenware jars filled with oil, the pale curves of swollen wineskins, and flour baskets that powdered the brown earth around them with a whiteness like the whiteness of frost.

It was to this storeroom that David came on the fourth day of the sickness of his son. He chose it partly because it was narrow and oppressive; to lie on the floor was, after a manner, to lie at the bottom of a grave. But he chose it also because no sound could come into it from the other rooms. The chink between the walls and the roof let in some sounds from the garden; but the door was proof against even the screaming of the child. In darkness, far below the level of the light, he lay prostrate on the floor and covered his head with the flour-streaked earth and humbled himself before God.

Time moved slowly in the windowless cubicle. Whenever he had occasion to leave it—and he left it only to see to the necessities of his body— he was amazed to find that the sun was still high, or that the afternoon had not begun to wane. And yet he felt that he must make haste. That which he wished to accomplish was being brought about in the most tedious and painful manner—if, indeed, he could say that it was being brought about at all. When he had closed the solid door behind him, it had been his purpose to abase himself utterly, to lift up a chastened and contrite heart to his God. Hour after hour he had made the outward gestures of mourning; he dug pits in the earth, he scratched his face and gnawed his fists; but his heart was neither chastened nor contrite within him, nor could he summon up the slightest conviction that what he did was of any concern to the Lord.

He spent the first day and the first night in repeating the rituals of confession over and over. He clung to the words as though they possessed in themselves the magic that could work his salvation. He said, "O God, I bitterly repent," and waited for remorse to well up within him, like a spring called forth out of the desert by a sacred rod. But nothing came of it. He could not weep for his sinfulness, even though he wept out of terror when he was forced to open the door and hear the screaming of the child. "I have sinned most grievously in Your sight," he said, tearing at his arms. "I have offended You, even I that am nothing, a blade of grass, a grain of sand. . . ." But it would come upon him suddenly that he was not thinking of the words he uttered. "O God, I bitterly repent," he said, beginning at the beginning, lest the magic power of the formula would be shattered by his wandering thought. "I have sinned most grievously in Your sight. . . ." But, before he could finish, exhaustion, born of long watching and little nourishment, was upon him, dragging him down into sleep.

On the second day he did not waken until noon. Someone was knocking at the door. They have come, he thought, to tell me that the little one is dead. . . . But it was only the steward of his house, bearing a bowl of milk and a cake of bread. "The hour of the noonday meal is already past," the steward said, "and my lord will surely fall faint unless he eats."

"How is it with the child?"

There was no need for an answer. The scream cut across the air— shriller, more unearthly, than it had been last night.

"Nevertheless," said the steward, "let the King take a little bread."

He accepted the food, and the steward departed in haste, seeing how eager he was to close the door.

David sat on the ground, resting the back of his head against one of the tall baskets of flour and sipping the milk. God has turned His face aside from me, he thought, because I have said His words with unseemly haste, nor troubled myself to seek after the divine essence that lies hidden within them. . . . And when he had drunk the last of the milk and eaten the last of the bread, he lay down on his back, with his hands clasped beneath his nape, and gave himself up to contemplation of the confessional.

"O God, I bitterly repent," he said, and paused, knowing that he had already broken his resolution against haste. "O God," he said again, staring at the pale motes that gleamed in the shaft of light. "God? What is God?" For the first time in all his days he realized that he did not truly know the Lord. I have served Him, but I have not known Him, he said in his heart. . . . And all that he had accomplished for Jahveh's sake shrank to nothing—the battles that he had fought against the uncircumcised, the ark that he had brought up with cymbals and psalteries, the great citadel that he had built to be His dwelling-place at the navel of the world. For in all this, he thought, I have been to Him as the steward of my house is to me when he comes to the door with a fresh face, untouched by any knowledge of my nature and my grief, thinking to discharge his debt to me with a little milk and a little bread. Even as I wish my steward gone from my sight, so has the Lord wished me gone from His sight. All that I bring to Him is nothing and less than nothing, unless I lift up my eyes and know and accept His face. . . .

Through the remainder of the long afternoon and evening, the King of Israel sought earnestly after the countenance of the Lord. He remembered those times when he had drawn nigh unto Him—the night when he had sensed the brooding presence hovering above the Gibean cave in which he waited for his last meeting with Jonathan; the evening when he had sat beside the open grave in Samuel's house, touching the dry soles of the prophet's feet; the afternoon when he had knelt in the brown house of Abinadab, pondering upon the half-obliterated symbols carved upon the ark of God. And he was amazed to see how few and far apart were the occasions when he had looked upon his Creator. They rose, distant and widely separate, like the few mountain peaks that lifted themselves out of the plains of Israel; and seas of mist, seas of impenetrable blankness floated between. They are beyond me now, he thought; my eyes behold them as through the fog. Strive as I will, I cannot be lifted up, nor can I truly see them from below. . . . The long ray of light paled while he strove to remember. The voices in the garden ceased; the outlines of the earthen jars and the wineskins grew vague and were lost. Surely, he thought, if I call upon Him with all my spirit, He will come again. . . . But the longer he persisted in his search, the more dim and remote that which he sought became. He turned on his face and beat his fists against the earth in rage and bafflement. "O God, God, God," he said aloud. But the word refused to yield its blessed essence.

Yet on the third morning, when he came forth to take a little nourishment, it seemed to him that his search had not been utterly in vain. At least the child was silent now; the fever had not abated, but the pain was less. The little one, said Hushai the counselor, who came to sit with him at the table, had grown quiet, had even slept. As he cooled his mouth with the fresh milk, David glanced sidewise at Hushai, an aging scholar, as slight and inoffensive as a dried leaf, with white hair and a pair of startling blue eyes. This morning his eyelids were reddened and his cheeks were chapped and spotted; it was plain that he had wept. And David thought how, even though this man could not truly drink of the cup of his own sorrow, he was acceptable, inasmuch as he had contemplated it and had offered up a decent tribute of tears. Perhaps I also, he thought, have become more acceptable in Jahveh's sight, seeing that I have at least striven to know. . . . And he returned quickly to the storeroom, eager to continue with his examination of the confessional.

"O God, whom I earnestly seek to know, I bitterly repent," he said. Now, when he lowered himself to the ground, he felt the ravages of his long mourning. He did not stretch himself at full length because of the drawing ache in his shoulders and his thighs. He sat instead with his back against the wineskins. He had grown so used to the darkness of the room that he could see the crevices between the brown bricks. He covered his face with his hands to shut out all distractions. "Bitterly repent, I bitterly repent," he said.

To feel profound remorse . . . It was not so with him, it had never been so for an instant, he knew it now. On that miasmal night when he had taken the tablet from the dusty cabinet, he had felt only terror. When the prophet Nathan had railed at him before the assembly, he had known shame, rage, fright, but not remorse. Bitterly repent . . . In the darkness behind his cupped hands, he called up a vision of the treeless plain of Ammon, the stretches of red clay, the low and solitary grave. He forced his mind's eye to penetrate the mound, to look upon what lay within. "O God, I bitterly repent that I have done this thing to Uriah the Hittite, that Your creature who walked and breathed has become at my hands a piece of putrefying flesh to be compounded soon with the earth of an alien land. . . . O God, I bitterly repent. . . ." And the husk of the word was broken at last, so that its essence was poured forth upon him, and he bowed his head upon his knees and wept.

He wept long. Whenever he felt the tide of remorse ebbing within him, he urged it back. He wished to weep himself into such a state of shaken peace as he had known in his childhood when he had wept against Jesse's knees. Then suddenly he remembered that as a child he had always come at last to wish his evil deed undone. He had always turned back with longing toward those hours, quiet and blessed, before he had broken the bowl or scratched his brother's face or set the pariah dogs against each other. And how is it with me now? he asked himself. Would I raise him up out of his grave if the price of his resurrection were this: that I should be what I was before I took the beloved? . . .

Evening settled upon the storeroom while he pondered this question. The windowless cubicle became a grave again, save that through the chink between wall and roof there was a strip of pale-green sky, the color of unripened fruit. As on that evening, he thought, when she unveiled herself before me, when she stared at me across the palms and freely gave me with her eyes more than I had taken in secret. . . . He turned his back then to the luminous strip of sky. He lay at full length on his face and strove against such remembrances and dug at the earth. "O God," he said, "I bitterly repent." But the vision of her body would not pass from him. And he could pray no more that night, for he was assailed by yearning. He longed only to be finished with mourning, to go up with her to the roof, to be healed by her touch. He lay as he lay upon the great bed in his chamber, with his arm extended as though to support the weight of her head; and, thinking of her body pressing against his side, he fell again into sleep.

He slept profoundly, in dreamless darkness; but with the first gray sign of morning, he started up wide-awake. Ah, God, he thought in terror, I have not yet finished with the confessional, and the fourth day is already dawning, and perhaps the child is dead. . . . He rose and walked back and forth across the narrow floor. He dared not either sit or lie, for fear that sleep might come upon him, and the child might perish while he slept. "O God, I bitterly repent, I have sinned most grievously in Your sight," he said. Then suddenly fierce rebellion broke within him. "O God," he said, staring straight before him, "O God whom I do not know, I bitterly repent that I have murdered Uriah the Hittite. But I rejoice in the depths of my bowels that I have taken his wife to be my beloved. I have sinned grievously in Your sight. And yet I am a better man in the days of my sin than I was in the days of my guiltlessness. For when I knew her not, my spirit was sealed up as in a charnel house. I went not forth out of myself, nor did any other come in. And if I have sinned in taking my beloved, behold, I have bought my resurrection with my sin. I am alive again, she has drawn me forth out of myself, she has borne me into the liquid, golden tide of life that laps around the crags and deserts of the world. Therefore, smite me for my sin, for I cannot renounce it. I bitterly repent that *he* lies in the red plain before Rabbah, but I rejoice that *I* have risen from the dead."

Now that he had made an honest confession, he saw no further reason to remain in the storeroom. Without looking back over his shoulder, he went out and closed the door. The brightness of morning was strengthening perceptibly. White veils of light seemed to be unfolding over the stairway, the halls, the common room; ribbons of light streamed down between the dark pillars; beyond the windows, the garden was shrouded in mist. At one of the windows, he saw his steward talking earnestly with Hushai the counselor. Two bondsmen and a serving-maid stood by. The woman was weeping, and the men were sighing and shaking their heads. At the sight of David, they fell to whispering together. He walked toward them, and they ceased to whisper and stared at him with solemn eyes. He stood before them then and asked them in a steady voice, "Is the child dead?"

It was Hushai the counselor who answered him, saying, "The child is dead."

David turned to one of the bondsmen. "Go and find my armor-bearer," he said, "and tell him to prepare for me in my chamber, for I will bathe and anoint myself and put on clean apparel. Also," he said, addressing the steward of his house, "prepare hot food to set before me, that I may eat."

The steward looked at him in amazement.

"Food—set food before me," said David. "Is it strange that a man who has fasted four days should ask for meat?"

The steward was embarrassed and confused. "My lord," he said, "how is it that while the child yet lived, you fasted and wept, but now that the child is dead, you arise and eat bread?"

And David said to his servant: "While the child was yet alive, I fasted and wept, for I said 'Who knows whether Jahveh may not be gracious to me so that the child may live?' But now that he is dead, wherefore should

I fast? Can I bring him back again? I shall go to him, but he will not return to me."

So he washed and anointed himself and put on clean apparel, and went up to the high place and bowed himself before the ark, and returned and ate savory meat and hot bread. And that night, after the little one had been laid in the burial cave, he went to Bath-sheba and comforted her and slept with her head upon his arm and her body against his side.

⤜§ XVI §⤛

ONE EVENING some seven moons after the death of the little one—summer had come again, and the old green had fallen away to make room for the new—one evening the King of Israel found himself alone. Noi and Haggith and the children had journeyed down to the orchards. What had been at first a casual holiday with them had been transformed into an obligation; it was unthinkable to the overseer of the estates that they should not be present for the gathering of the first fruits. There was no business of state to fill the palace with ambassadors and governors. For the first time since the birth of the child, Bath-sheba had gone forth to spend the evening abroad. There was a family gathering in the house of her uncle Ahitophel, and she would not return until the second or third hour of the night. There were, to be sure, other possible companions in the palace: Hushai the counselor was drowsing in the garden, and in an upper chamber Abigail and Michal were sitting out the evening together. But the King of Israel was content with his solitude. He lay on a couch in the empty common room, listening to the evening music of the birds. When his steward came in bearing lamps, he sent him forth again, saying that he wanted no light. The full moon would soon be rising beyond the open portal, and he wished to behold these long vistas and lofty columns in her white light.

In the days before the child had died, it had been his custom to devote such solitary hours to meditation upon God. But now whenever he found that his thoughts were moving toward sacred matters, he turned them sharply aside. From the moment when Hushai the counselor had said to him, "The child is dead," he had closed his heart against Jahveh. It had not been only out of a desire for comfort after long pain that he had refused to mourn the little one's going-forth, that he had anointed himself and eaten hot food and returned without delay to the beloved's bed. All that he had done he had done in testimony of the fact that he held resentment against the Lord. For in the matter of the child God had shown Himself as rigorous and merciless as His prophets. A dead spirit, closed in the charnel house of a sick, insensate body, was better in God's sight than a living one which, though it had sinned grievously, was yet capable of coming to Him freely and without deception. With such a God, it was impossible to hold intimate communion. One gave Him His due—the solemn service, the slain heifer, the new tabernacles and the wayside shrines. But to lay one's living heart at His feet was as unthinkable as to lay it at the feet of Nathan. Henceforth the King of Israel would serve, but never seek to know, his Lord.

Perhaps he was drowsing, perhaps he was lost in thought, when the moon actually appeared. He knew only that he had missed the moment of her coming. The whole room was washed in a watery radiance. The shadows of the pillars, the tracery of leaves, lay all around him on the gray stone floor. He started up with a hushed sense of waiting upon him. The moon was well above the hedges now, and her light was like growing music. He waited for something, he knew not what—the turning-back of the years, the resurrection of the dead, the sound of an angelic horn blown across the arc of heaven. Then he knew that Hushai had crossed the threshold and was looking about the dark room in wonder. He said in a low and questioning voice, "My lord?"

"I am here, Hushai, staring at the moon."

The old counselor moved forward, led by David's voice. "There is a youth in the garden," he said. "He has journeyed a long way out of Benjamin to look upon the King's face. Ask me no more concerning him, for I have asked and asked, and he will tell me no more."

A thought flickered across David's consciousness—a thought so preposterous that he smiled at himself. Because of the moonlight and the nameless awe that was upon him, he had imagined for a moment that the youth who had come by night to the King's garden was a heavenly visitor such as had come down in ancient days to mortals with tidings from the throne of God. He rose and shrugged. "Bring him to me, then," he said.

"It would be very gracious of the King to go forth to meet the young man," Hushai said. "For he is hard put to it to walk—his servant lifted him from his donkey and set him on a bench near the spring. He cannot come to the King unless his servant supports him, inasmuch as he is lame in both his feet."

"Then surely I will go and greet him," said David, and he went into the moonlit garden alone.

He could not see the bench at first; it was hidden from him by a clump of flowering thorn. Then he passed the thornbush and saw the dark rocks and the water gleaming upon them—saw the known shape, the pale face, the cloud of pale-brown hair—Jonathan!

He stood utterly still upon the path, and there was no breath in him. He stood so long that the young man strove pitifully to rise up from the bench, and said in the pure accents of Benjamin, "My lord the King, I cannot rise." He knew then who it was that God had sent to him. This was Meribaal, the child of Mara and Jonathan. This was Meribaal, who had fallen from his nurse's arms in the retreat from Gibeah after the battle of Gilboa. This was the little one who had been lamed in both his feet, and that had been long ago, so long ago that here was a youth, only a few years younger than Jonathan had been on that gray morning

469

when, near the cistern at Ephes-Dammim, he had taken his girdle and torn it for David's sake.

"Meribaal? Are you Meribaal?" said David.

"Even Meribaal, my lord."

And David stood before the bench and embraced him and wept over him.

Afterward they sat long in the moon-whitened garden, talking earnestly to each other. There was much to be said, and the youth had something of his father's easy, gracious manner of speech. Before the lights had been quenched in the window of the upper chamber where Abigail and Michal sat, he had told the whole tale of his life—how he had sojourned in house after house with this cousin and with that aunt, how the fortunes of the children of Kish had waned, how he had gone from one family to another, leaving always when he began to feel that he was a burden upon them. There was no self-pity in his talk. He neither made much of his affliction nor sought to hide it. "And so," he said at last, "inasmuch as the orchard of my grandaunt suffered another blight this year, having no other place to turn, I have come down to the King my lord."

"Would you had come long since," said David. "Come under my roof this night, and go from me no more. Dwell in my house and be as the dearest of my children and eat at my table with me until the end of my days."

The lad turned aside to hide his tearful eyes. "They assured me in Benjamin," he said, "that my lord the King would deal kindly with me for my father's sake. But I had never thought that he would show me such kindness as this. . . ."

While they had been speaking together, the illusion of Jonathan's presence had faded. Though he was very like his father, Jonathan's son was not Jonathan. His face had been somewhat marred by poverty and pain; the nose was sharp, the lips were thin and inclined to tremble, and a certain softness blurred the delicate modeling of the cheeks and chin. And yet the comeliness of the beloved still flowered in him. His hand was the slight, eloquent hand that had long since fallen into ashes. And the King lifted it up and held it between his own, saying, "Not for Jonathan's sake alone, but also for Meribaal's sake."

They sat a little longer beside the spring, listening in silence to the purling of the water over the rocks and breathing the elusive fragrance of the iris blooms.

"What are you thinking?" David said, glancing sidewise at the lad's face.

"Nothing. . . . Only that God has indeed shown favor to me this night."

"And to me also." To me also, David thought, He has shown favor this night. Though He has borne away her child and laid it in the burial cave, yet He has come to me in pity, to bring to me in the little one's place the child of the dead beloved. . . . He knew then that his heart was no longer hardened within him. It had fallen open like a flower at the merciful touch of the Lord.

BOOK TEN

BOOK TEN

❧ I ❧

The heirs to the glory of the House of Jesse showed no great eagerness to marry. Amnon was in his twenty-fifth year and still turning this way and that. Sometimes he gave out that he was on the point of paying court to a cousin of the King of Egypt, sometimes to the grandchild of his father's good friend Hiram, King of Tyre. But nothing came of either suit; the girls involved were very young; and the King of Israel, who had found his true beloved in his middle years, would not lightly urge a young man to marry. If the heir to the throne had shown any inclination to make easy use of the daughters of Jerusalem, it might have been advisable to hurry him into the safety of a respectable bed. But he was chaste; love had for him a dark and sickly cast, so that when others jested about it he sat by with flushed cheeks and a lowered head. He is waiting, the King of Israel thought, for a woman who possesses the magic to transmute shame into glory. I will allow him to wait in peace. . . .

The Princess Tamar gave cause for deeper uneasiness. At twenty-two, she still went about in the varicolored garments that it was the custom of the virgins of the high houses of Jerusalem to wear. Every lutist in Israel had composed at least one song in praise of her beauty. To behold her was to carry a flowering thornbush forever within; her hair was the flowing blackness of a flock of sacred goats; her breast was the breast of the dove. Below her straight brows, childish and candid, her eyes were almond-shaped, mysterious and wise. Her voice, too, would have been more becoming in a wife than in a damsel; it was soft, throaty, slow; a mere request for another piece of bread became in her mouth a kind of caress. And yet, ripe as she was for marriage, she would not marry. She loved her life as it was and shrank from any suggestion of change. And whenever a dull evening descended upon the royal palace, she went off with her brother Absalom. They appeared often in the streets of the city, walking arm in arm under the palm trees, or sitting in a splendid chariot side by side; and the lutists of Israel made many a song concerning the great love that was between these two.

Absalom had never been able to dwell peaceably under the same roof with Amnon, and their enmity had increased with the years. Their father, growing old and yearning after serenity, had seen fit at last to set them apart. He had been more than generous in the provisions he had made for Maacah's son; it had seemed to him that he was driving the young man forth from his home; and in order to mitigate the blow, he had given him a high house of stone and cedarwood within the city and a great, rambling place, with flocks and herds, to the north of Jerusalem. During the summer Absalom played at being a herdsman at Baal-hazor; but during the remainder of the year he dazzled Jerusalem with his splendor—his chariots, his Egyptian steeds, his robes of scarlet and crimson, his windows ablaze with light. It was toward these windows that the sons and daughters of merchants and smiths and captains over hundreds turned their yearning eyes. The life of the King's palace was the life of royalty, solemn, legitimate, and dull. But the life in Absalom's house bloomed among them like some exotic plant—rootless, detached, and all the more exquisite inasmuch as no man knew how long it could flourish. As for the master of the house, he was more beautiful even than his sister. He was slender and lithe, and his armor-bearer had given it out that there was no blemish upon him. His hair was the wonder of Jerusalem—it streamed over his shoulders in a black, unbelievable ripple of waves and curls. His face was the smooth, spare face of the sons of the desert—the nose was delicately aquiline; the cheeks and brows were so dark that they lent a startling brightness to the whites of his eyes. He smiled on one side of his mouth, and all the sorrows of the elect one who has been thrust into second place, all the subtle sufferings of the aristocrat who must abase himself before a fool, were embodied in that one-sided smile.

The most that could be said for Adonijah, the son of Haggith, was that he caused no one any grief. He was a good lad, affable and a little plump, for he loved his food and could never refuse a second helping of the sweet. He and Abigail would jest over their common failing at the table. He called her "Grandmother," and she delighted in the name. "Come, Grandmother," he would say, "join me in a second piece of this fine pastry." There was reason to hope that he, at least, would marry in good time. He had just turned eighteen and already showed a fancy for one of Hushai's nieces, an undistinguished girl in whom it was possible to find certain mild charms if one searched for them with the proper patience. She and Adonijah and Meribaal spent a great deal of their time together. There was a sturdy bond between Haggith's son and the last frail shoot of the House of Kish. At table they entered into long discussions concerning the nature of God and the structure of the universe—discussions which were embarrassingly amateurish. Still, they were charming youths, even-tempered and courteous, and it pleased the King of Israel to see them together. For, he thought in his heart, when I am no more, the son of Jonathan will not be forced to wander roofless under the stars. He will dwell with Adonijah, so long as Adonijah lives. . . .

The bedchamber that had once belonged to Absalom was given to Bathsheba's child, the little Solomon. It was a broad and sunny room, directly across the corridor from the King's own chamber. It was filled with gifts— a table of cedarwood, a cabinet with two polished doors, a chair covered with a lion's skin, a bright bird in a cage of brass—such gifts as a man would choose to bestow upon a youngest son who was also the only living issue of the true beloved. On certain nights the King would not come down to sit at the head of the long table in the common room. He would break the evening bread in Solomon's chamber with no company save the beloved and her child. It was a merry custom; the bright bird chattered and screamed on its perch, and David would lift the boy up to appease it with bits of cake. Sometimes, when the meal was over, he would remain through the entire evening, sitting on the edge of the bed beside Bathsheba and playing games with the child. Sounds would float up to them from the street—the laughter of young men and women on their way to a feast at Absalom's house, the talk of captains coming up from the encampment to drink with Joab, the chatter of women who were crossing over from the neighboring houses to visit with Noi or Michal or Haggith or Abigail. . . . But the King of Israel was folded in a profound peace, such a peace as he had not known since he left his father's brown house in Bethlehem. As Jesse was to me, he thought, an old father with a whitening beard, so am I to the little one. As my father was to my mother, so am I to my beloved. . . .

Thus it was with David, and with his house, in the fifty-fourth year of his life and the seventeenth year of his reign over a united Israel.

❧ II ❧

AMNON, the heir to the throne of Israel, stood alone in his bedchamber. He was naked except for his loincloth. His outer garments—a long blue robe and a yellow girdle—lay ready for him upon the bed. He knew that he should put them on at once; he could tell by the voices below that the family was assembling for the evening bread. But such a weariness was upon him that he longed to lie down beside the robe and the girdle. All day he had held a conspicuous place in the ceremonies of the Feast of the First Fruits. His arm ached with the weight of the basket of pomegranates he had carried, and it seemed to him that he could not sit erect through the three or four hours allotted to the domestic feast.

All through the day, in the blatant noise of the streets and the shadowless heat of the high place, he had been asking himself the same questions: Am I sick? Has God put a poison into my body to punish me for my sinfulness? Will I die? . . . Before his conversation with Jonadab, his friend and armor-bearer, he had never thought himself ailing; he had only thought himself infinitely wretched. But since that evening not three weeks past—an evening which he would not permit himself to remember, especially not on a holy day when he had stood before the ark of God—he had constantly touched his forehead to see if it were feverish and felt for unevenness in the beat of his heart.

Now he went and stood above the table on which the big brazen basin stood. It was still filled with the water in which he had washed himself. The surface had turned into a dull, greenish mirror in the evening light, and if he bent close to it, he could study the reflection. Pale, he thought, I am very pale—or is it only the shadow? . . . He crouched over the dark water; the face that floated there was unlovely—a high, narrow forehead, a jutting nose, a loose mouth above a sparse beard. But I have always had a sickly countenance, he told himself. I was never such a one as *he*, straight as an arrow and without a blemish upon him. I am sick, I am weary, and tonight *he* will be at the table, fresh, glowing, not in the least depleted by the burden that he carried in the procession. . . .

And she also—oh, God! he must not remember it, not on the day of a high festival. He must not remember how, when she shifted her basket of flowers from one arm to the other, her breasts had been pushed together so that one saw above the neckline of her robe the two dusky swells of flesh and the shadowy crease between. . . .

He went swiftly to the bed and began to dress himself. He fastened the robe at waist and shoulder and bent to take up the girdle. The melting tide of weariness broke again upon him. It would be possible simply to say, through the mouth of a servant, "My father, forgive me, but I cannot sit at table, inasmuch as I am utterly weary this night."

To lie down, to rest, perhaps even to sleep. . . . Surely, he thought, there is some sickness upon me. No sound man could be so drawn to his bed. . . . He laid his palm against his cheek and sighed with relief to find that there was no fever. And yet, to lie down . . . He heard the voice of Jonadab, his friend and armor-bearer, saying the accursed and unforgettable words—a black serpent crawling across the clean holiness of the day—"Lie down upon your bed and feign sickness, and when your father comes to you, say to him, 'Let my sister Tamar come and give me bread to eat.'"

He made a sacred sign against the words. He opened a small jewel chest with leaves and pomegranates carved upon it, and took out an amulet, a little golden crescent that had been blessed in half the tabernacles of Israel. He hung it around his neck and thought, I am well, I am safe, I will not die, I will think these evil thoughts no more. . . . Then he hastened through the door and down the stairs.

At first it seemed to him that the common room was empty. The feast had been spread in the garden; through the open door, he could see the table. The diners were still wandering up and down the paths in groups of twos and threes. Neither of the children of Maacah was to be seen in the little assembly. They will come late, he thought. No matter how late I come, *he* will always come a little later. While they hang upon *his* coming, they will while away the time as best they may with me. . . . Then he saw that the King of Israel was sitting on a couch in the shadow of a pillar, regal in his long robe of deep purple. He came forward to greet his eldest son, and as he moved into the brightness between the columns, his hair and beard caught the light and shone like a sun-pierced mist.

"And how is it with Amnon?" David said, laying his arm across his son's shoulders. "I was troubled in my heart for him when we stood together in the high place. I turned and looked, and he was green in the face."

"No, now, I am well enough," he said. But he told himself, I am sick indeed if I grow green in the face with standing in the sun. . . .

"Perhaps it would be well for Amnon to go early to his bed."

He did not answer. He heard the voice of Jonadab saying, "Feign sickness, and when your father comes to you, say to him 'Let my sister Tamar come and give me bread to eat and dress the food in my sight that I may take it from her hand. . . .'" Her hand, he thought. The little cushions of flesh at the top of the palm—the pliant, curling fingers. . . .

The King drew him in the direction of the portal. Amnon cast a covert glance at his father's face. Above the flowing beard, the mouth was at once firm and tender. The whole face would have been benign if it had not been for the keen slate-gray eyes. Once, and once only within his remembrance, he had seen those eyes blurred and misted. He had come suddenly into the King's chamber to announce the arrival of a visitor, and had found his father sitting on the edge of his bed—vague-eyed with dreams—plucking strange music out of a lute. Had the look remained, had the music continued to sound, it would have been possible to say all things, to lay before this gentle dreamer even a meager and sinful heart.

"Shall we sit in the garden?" David said. "My son will be the better for a cool breath upon his face."

The words were so kindly that Amnon could scarcely refrain from taking his father's hand. Then the old bitter knowledge crept upon him, and he sneered at himself. It is not for my sake, he thought, that he leads me into the garden. He has heard the sound of chariot wheels beyond the gate and knows that Absalom is coming. . . .

"Surely, let us go out, inasmuch as Absalom has come," he said.

Light, hastening footfalls came up behind them, and he knew that it was *she*. She had tarried in her chamber, waiting for the sound of the chariot wheels. And yet she was gracious; she would throw a bone to a dog if she had nothing better to do. She moved close behind them, so close that her breath stirred on the nape of Amnon's neck as she said: "God be with my father and my brother. That is a fair girdle which Amnon wears tonight." They moved apart then so that she might walk between them. Amnon turned aside from the crisp curls that brushed his cheek. "Absalom is with us," he said.

The narrowness of the path gave her a pretext for separating herself from them and hurrying on ahead. She set one foot upon the brazen grillwork and gazed into the street, where the wheels of the chariot had raised up a sunlit cloud of dust. Clearly articulated beneath the webby stuff of her varicolored garment, he saw her haunches and her thighs. He pressed the sharp end of the crescent into his breast and turned his eyes aside.

Under the palm trees, beside the spring, near the beds of herbs and the clumps of bushes, he saw the others—blessedly uninvolved in his sin and his pain. The lame Meribaal and the gray-eyed Adonijah were showing a tame antelope to Michal and Abigail. Haggith was moving serenely down the length of the table, counting the bowls and the plates. Bath-sheba had already seated herself near the head of the table and was brushing a loose lock from the little Solomon's brow. For her, thought Amnon, the King my father dipped his hands in blood; but it is forgiven; she sits and toys with the child's hair; he stands on the path and smiles, while I, I . . . Some ten paces from him, his mother rested her shoulder against the red trunk of a palm tree and conversed with the steward of the house. Mother, wretched little mother, Amnon thought, how is the pain in your side to-night? What are we doing, you and I, in the King's garden? Would we two could go back into the wilderness to dwell in the house in which he found you! Would we might close the door behind us and cling to each other the rest of our days. . . . He sought earnestly after her look, but like all the rest, she had lifted up her eyes to watch the coming of Absalom.

He came up the pathway, letting the gate clang shut behind him. He had put off the princely and flowing garments that he had worn in the procession; and all those who had said this morning "He is at his best in crimson," thought now "He is most comely in simple white." He wore a short tunic of Egyptian linen, bound to his slender waist with a broad belt of leather. The neckline was cut low to reveal his throat and part of his brown and hairless chest. The wind blew the delicate stuff of his garment against his flawless body. His face, his arms, his naked chest, glowed against the whiteness of the linen as the brown rocks of the desert glow against the whiteness of the sand. He kissed his father and embraced Noi. Then he came up to the wretch who stood between him and the throne and saluted him with blank, respectful eyes and a one-sided smile.

"And how is it with Amnon?" he said, moving toward the table. He did not wait to be answered. He turned at once to greet Bath-sheba and to lay his hand upon the head of the little Solomon. "Shall we eat? I have eaten nothing but holiness all day long," he said.

Eat and be damned, thought Amnon, moving to his rightful place at the head of the table and sitting down at the King's side. His father had begun to slice the joint of lamb, and he remembered with fright that it was holy meat. He rested his elbow on the table and shadowed his brow with his hand. She had chosen to sit directly opposite him, between Meribaal and Haggith. An hour, two hours perhaps, at table—and all the time he would be forced to look upon the shadowy line between her breasts. . . .

His father turned a solicitous glance upon him and laid the best cut of meat on his plate. "If my son is sick," he said, "let him eat a little and go up to his bed."

"I am well, my father. It is only that I am weary."

Tamar bent across the board and regarded him with an obvious counterfeit of concern while he filled his mouth with the meat. "But truly Amnon has looked somewhat wan of late," she said. "What is it that makes him grow leaner from day to day?"

"Nothing, nothing." She had asked the same question as his friend and armor-bearer, Jonadab, and now he could neither thrust aside the unholy remembrance nor spew forth the holy meat.

"Why," the voice of Jonadab had said, "does the King's son grow leaner from day to day?"

"I love Tamar, the sister of my brother Absalom."

"Then lie down upon your bed, and feign sickness, and when your father comes to you, say to him, 'Let my sister Tamar come and give me bread to eat and dress the food in my sight that I may take it from her hand.' And when she is come, draw her down upon the bed. . . ."

No, no! he said in his heart. Surely God will never permit me to arise living from this table, seeing that I have thought such a thought. . . . He reached out with a shaking hand and lifted his bowl of wine to his lips. When he set the bowl down, he saw that the guests at the other end of the table were very merry. Michal was smiling and Abigail was choking with laughter and Adonijah was shouting across the length of the board, begging his father to listen to the witty thing that Absalom had just said.

❧ III ❧

At about the fourth hour after sunset the children of Maacah rose and left the King's garden. It was not considered strange that they should take their leave; they were always the last to arrive and the first to depart. Nor was the company in the least surprised when Tamar rode off in her brother's chariot. It was her custom to go up to Absalom's house whenever she pleased, and sometimes a night and a day would pass before she showed her face again in her father's palace. Her brother had set apart for her use a chamber in the upper part of his house—a small but exquisite room carpeted in white and draped with crimson curtains out of Tyre. He had gone to great lengths to furnish it completely; brushes and combs and pots of unguent were laid upon the lid of the clothes chest, and the white vase on the table was always filled with flowers.

The Princess Tamar loved her brother's house. To enter it was, to experience a sweet release. The little common room with its four chaste pillars and its pale pottery and burnished brass was to her the fairest chamber upon earth. Beside it, the long hall of state in her father's palace was as dreary as a cave. There one sat erect and listened to interminable harangues on the condition of Israel; here one heard all the poetry and wit of the nation while lolling on a padded couch or sitting among the cushions on the floor. The spirit of the young master—buoyant and dashing—had left its stamp upon everything. His rugs were thicker and more brilliantly embroidered than any other rugs in Jerusalem. His wine was light and dry, free of the thick and vulgar sweetness which pleased the palates of the uninitiate. And as for his food—there was no food like his in any other house in Israel: the almost transparent slices of cold lamb dusted with a powdering of green herbs, the small squares of fish dipped in oil and wine, the dates stuffed with pistachio nuts, the little cornucopias of flaky pastry brimming over with honey, the brown cakes of bread flavored with cheese and crusted with delectable sesame seeds.

On the evening of the Feast of the First Fruits she had eaten very little at her father's table, partly because uneasiness had dulled her appetite, partly because she had hoped that she might be bidden to Absalom's house. And now that her brother had indeed led her home, now that they stood together in the lamplit room, she rejoiced to see that the table had been spread for two only. They would be alone in the still, bright house, to talk until dawn if they pleased. He had invited no other guests tonight.

Absalom took her cloak from her shoulders. His hands did not brush against her; long ago—so long ago that she could not remember how or when—they had made a silent compact to forgo touch. Slowly and without a word they moved across the room to the table. Still wordless, but smiling secretively, they settled down at the board, one on each side, face to face. A lamp and a dish of pale grapes stood between them; he reached out his brown and beautiful hand and set these barriers aside. He bent above the platter of meat, found a fine, thin bit of lamb, and held it up to the light. "For you," he said, and laid it on her plate. Then he leaned back and uttered a short and painful laugh and tossed his hair back from his brow.

"What thoughts have stirred up laughter in the throat of my brother?"

"What thoughts? No thoughts, my dove. Only the remembrance of our glorious brother, the Hope of Israel, faint with carrying a basket of pomegranates. It is enough to make a man laugh himself into his grave."

She wished to laugh with him; there was a covenant of bitter laughter between them. Yet tonight she would have preferred that there be no mention of Amnon. The uneasiness that had crept upon her in the King's garden came back again, and she knew for the first time that it had risen from Amnon's tormented face. She tossed back her hair and smiled with one side of her lips.

They sat silent, gazing across the table at each other. They had assumed identical attitudes—their right elbows resting on the board, their right cheeks lying against the palms of their hands. Since the days when they had lain side by side in the same cradle, focusing their infantile stares upon each other's faces, they had known that to be silent was to be one. Pulsing emanations, blind antennae, went out from them toward each other—went out and met, so that he started and she sighed. He lowered his glance to the platter of bread. He chose a piece on which not one sesame seed had been burned or broken, and laid it on her plate.

"Did our father make the Feast of the First Fruits another occasion for urging my sister to marry?"

By the casual ease of his utterance, she measured the pain that lay beneath it. She shook her head.

"Did he trouble my sister with a request that she urge me to marry?"

"No. . . ." She took the bread and ate. "He said nothing whatsoever concerning that utterly dull and outworn subject tonight."

He nodded and piled her plate high with bits of meat and fish. It was as if he had said aloud, "What else is there on earth to trouble my sister's heart? Come, let us eat and be glad."

For the first time in her life she sought to deceive him. The fright that had come upon her at her father's table—she knew now that it had been actual fright, a tingling at the roots of her hair and in her fingertips—was nameless still, and she would not force him to share it until she had learned its name. Whenever they had grieved together, these two princely ones, they had grieved only over the day when they must turn their backs upon each other, when they must render up their bodies, virgin and without blemish, to the crasser children of the world. That day had been for them the day of ultimate evil, and, brooding upon it, neither of them had guessed that there could be any evil other than this. But now it seemed to her that even this transitory security was being assailed from without. . . . She strove to shut out a vision of Amnon's red-rimmed eyes.

"How is it with Tamar that she does not eat?"

She ate then and strove to regale him with the talk that was his chief delight, but the dark and radiant face across the table was expressionless. The antennae had gone out again, and nothing could deceive them. He had not heard a word she had said.

"There is some trouble lying heavy upon the heart of my sister."

"Yes, I have been troubled."

"Wherefore should Tamar veil her heart before me?"

"It is nothing," she said. "It is only that our brother Amnon——"

White fury flashed in his eyes. His hands closed into fists. His lips parted, and his teeth shone.

"No, now, Absalom makes too much of it. It was only that Amnon stared at me tonight, and I was foolishly troubled by his eyes."

They had always deplored violence. It was unsubtle, it was vulgar. There was a note of tender chiding in her voice, and he responded to it at once.

"Let my sister put her fears at rest," he said pleasantly, as though the matter in question were a bit of chipped pottery or an ill-tuned lute. "Our brother Amnon knows that he is a dog. Tamar dreamed that he looked upon her. He would not dare to raise his eyes." He lifted a cluster of grapes from the fruit bowl and held them up against the lamp. He plucked off a bruised grape and smiled. "And if he should lay a finger upon my sister, if he should so much as say one questionable word——" He laid the fruit, green and perfect, upon her plate. "Then I would kill him," he said.

IV

ON THE THIRD DAY after the Feast of the First Fruits, the King arose and broke the morning bread alone in the common room. It was a fair morning, cool for the season. A wind stirred the palm trees beyond the opened door. The air was radiant, crystalline, and for a while he gave himself up to sheer enjoyment of the weather. He had gone to the window and was looking at the white miracle of an almond tree in flower when he heard a light step upon the stair. It was Noi, and he fell to wondering why she had come down at such an hour, for she was always the last of them to rise.

She stood before him and bowed. "God walk all through the day with my lord!"

"And with Noi," he said, drawing her down upon a bench close to the window. "How is it that you have come down so soon?"

She did not answer him at once, and he saw that she was embarrassed. "Amnon is ailing," she said at last, smiling to ward off any alarm that might be rising within him. "A fever—distaste for food—a little weakness—nothing more. But he was awake before sunrise, wanting herb tea, and I went in to take him the brew, and——" She looked at the floor and flushed. "And it seemed to me that he would be gladdened by the sight of my lord."

How have I dealt with her, he asked himself, that she should blush to ask me to put myself to the trouble of walking up a flight of stairs? Surely she must consider herself a slave in my house, and our son the son of a slave woman, if she cannot run to me and say outright, "Come and stand at the bed of him who is to be King of Israel." . . .

"At any hour of the day when my lord can find a moment——"

"Surely I will go up, and at once," he said.

"My lord is very gracious."

"Gracious? I am concerned in my heart for my eldest son, who is heir to Judah and Israel." And because he could not endure the grateful look that she fixed upon him, he turned and hastened toward the stairs.

Is it possible, he thought, that not only she but all the world has seen this thing that I sought to keep hidden? Is it plain, in spite of all the honors and gifts which I have bestowed upon Amnon, that my tenderness is a spurious tenderness, that he is less to me than Absalom or Solomon? . . .

The door of Amnon's room was closed, and this also was a reproof to him. She had not dared to trust that he would come; otherwise she would not have closed the door. He rapped softly, and wondered why he rapped at all.

"Come in," said the flat voice on the other side of the door.

But the fault is not mine alone, he thought, stepping into the room. He, also, is to blame. He has been withdrawn and secretive from the days when he was a child. . . .

"My father is very gracious."

He could not see the speaker. The curtains had been drawn against the brilliant light. The bedchamber was shadowy, musky, warm. Slowly his eyes adjusted themselves to the darkness. He saw the pillows—crimson and blue and yellow—piled up at the farther end of the couch. He saw Amnon's head propped against them—the narrow brow, the sunken cheeks, the small, sparse beard, the shining whites of the eyes. He leaned far forward, stretching out his hand until his fingertips touched the young man's forehead. But Amnon turned his head aside. "There is no fever in me, my lord and my father," he said. "The fever passed from me during the night."

David straightened and sighed. The poor wretch had the air of one who confesses a fault. Does he think, the King asked himself, that I would visit him only if he had a burning brow? . . . He said in a hearty voice: "That is an excellent omen. If the fever passes, the rest will soon pass. Is my son in any pain, or is it only weariness?"

"Only weariness."

For a moment David sat silent, knowing for the first time the breadth and depth of Amnon's weariness. The voice was the voice of a warrior who has come up out of a violent and futile battle. Surely he had been waging a long war with shadows—his face had been yellow and sickly these many moons. And none had lifted a hand to succor him, none had so much as asked him what desperate conflict had been waged in his heart. . . . David bent forward again and groped after Amnon's hand. But even as he moved, his son turned aside and thrust both his hands under the coverlet.

"I have a request to make of my father," he said.

"Whatsoever Amnon should choose to ask, now and unto the end of my days, is his own."

"Oh, it is a small matter. It is only that I have taken no nourishment save a little herb tea, and all food is loathsome to me, so that there is only one dish of which I could eat——"

"Let my son only name it."

"The little cakes which my sister Tamar makes—those that she kneads from honey and nuts—them I could eat."

"I will go at once and tell her to make them."

"Let her make them here, my father, over the brazier, in my sight, and give them to me with her own hand."

Poor wretch, the King thought, moving toward the door. It is not that he longs for the cakes. It is only that he would have her make much over him in his sickness, that he would claim from her a little of such tenderness as she pours out upon Absalom. . . .

He turned on the threshold and smiled upon Amnon. "Indeed, I know how it is to long for a certain dish. I too have had such desires in time of sickness. I will send her up to you," he said.

483

V

When his father took leave of him, the heir to the throne of Israel thought in his heart, I will eat her cakes and send her out untouched, with the help of God. . . . When the King paused on the threshold in a slanting ray of sunlight, his dappled beard and hair alight and his splendid body turned back toward the room in baffled solicitude, the fetid dream had almost gone down before him.

It was significant that David had not completely closed the door behind him. He had left a line of light and a streaming current of cool air, a bright chink through which a contrite spirit might re-enter the world. Indeed, the world itself—the wholesome world of clinking kettles and easy voices—floated in through this opening to the sufferer. He heard Meribaal and Adonijah praising the fair weather. He heard Hushai explaining the history of the Creation to the little Solomon. And then he heard the King's voice and *her* voice raised in the not-too-distant chamber where she slept.

That King had a request to make of his daughter.

His daughter was entirely his unto the end of her days.

Let her take nuts and honey and go into the bedchamber of Amnon and knead him cakes with her own hand.

Long silence.

Let her arise from her bed and go at once. How was it with her that she turned the intentions of God awry, spending the hours of darkness in waking, and lying in sleep through the best of the day?

She grieved for those flaws in her that were an offense to her father. It was indeed an unwholesome habit to lie abed until noon. As for visiting Amnon, she would certainly do so before night. But she could not go at once, for she had promised to break the noonday bread in the house of her brother Absalom.

Absalom could wait.

What difference could it make to Amnon whether she came in the morning or the evening? Was she a servant in her father's house that he should——

Let her lower her voice. No, better, let her hold her tongue. If she thought that——the rest of the sentence was lost. The King had slammed Tamar's door.

Amnon gave himself up to feverish expectation. The sound of their voices—muffled now, but still contending—inflamed his desire. His pulse hastened at the thought that her cool arrogance was being broken, that she was going down before another's will. When the voices ceased, he lay shivering and staring at the ceiling, with the coverlet drawn to his chin.

How long he lay shuddering under the coverlet he did not know. Time was shut out from him by the drawn curtains. He lay in twilight, and there were moments when it seemed to him that this twilight was, for him, everlasting, that God would smite him in his bed, would never permit him to cross the threshold and step back into the world. He was on the point of going forth into the hall to prove that it was not so when he heard her knock.

He saw at once that she had not come alone. A young man, half-hidden by the door, stood behind her on the other side of the threshold; and he wondered whether the dim twilight had stretched out longer than he had dreamed, giving her time to summon Absalom. But it was not Absalom, it was only Jonadab.

"I have brought my brother's armor-bearer up to look in upon him," Tamar said. "He has been kind enough to carry the burning brazier up the stairs, and it seemed to me that Amnon would find pleasure in the sight of his face."

The armor-bearer came in behind her and set the brazier in the center of the room, some six paces from the foot of the bed.

"I am glad that he has come," said Amnon, "for I would have him lie before my door, so that I may enjoy the company of my sister undisturbed."

The armor-bearer flashed a knowing glance at the King's son, and then swiftly, discreetly, lowered his eyelids. "Let Amnon eat his cakes in peace," he said. "I will wait at the threshold." And he was gone, closing the door behind him, shutting out the current of fresh air and the line of light.

Tamar began to move about in the musky darkness, clearing a table and laying her kneading board upon it, measuring out the honey, the almonds, and the flour. She had tied a napkin around her waist to serve as an apron. It hung, white and impenetrable, over the diaphanous folds of her vari-colored garment. Now and then she lifted it to wipe her fingers upon it, and whenever she did so Amnon's breath came faster. While she worked, she kept up a constant chatter: the day was fine; perhaps later he would care to lie in the garden; she found him less ailing than she had feared. . . . A bowl slipped from her hand, was shattered on the floor, sent up a cloud of flour. And he knew that she was afraid.

After that, there was no more talk. He sat with his back propped against the heaped cushions, feeling a bitter exultation in her fright. She knew— her knowledge gave her eyes a feverish intentness and made her movements uncertain. The little cakes were cut and laid on the pan, but fear had made them formless—the crescent moons looked like worms, the triangles were awry. She set the pan on the brazier and cried out softly because she had burned herself. For me, for fright at my desire she has burned herself, he thought. . . . And, turning his face against a cushion, he smiled.

She knelt above the brazier, waiting for the cakes to brown. Whenever she reached forward to test the crisping of the dough, her full breasts swayed. Once, twice, three times, her whole body was shaken by a long, uneven sigh. Weakly, pitifully, she put off the moment. The bedchamber was filled with the smell of burning cake.

"My sister is permitting the cakes to burn," he said.

She wrapped her hand in the napkin and lifted the pan and set it on the floor. The red glow of the embers lighted up her long throat, her fixed and suffering eyes.

"Let her bring the cakes now and give me to eat."

"They are very hot."

"Nevertheless, let her bring them." His voice was hard and compulsive, such a voice as he had heard through the door.

She gathered up the napkin which she wore as an apron and dropped the cakes into it one by one. Like a child that comes to be beaten, she walked slowly, with her head turned to one side, toward his bed. She bent over him, and it seemed to him that he breathed the perfume of her body above the smell of the burnt dough. She dropped the corners of her apron, let the cakes scatter upon the coverlet, and took one step backward. But he caught hold of her hand—her moist, hot hand—and held it fast.

"Come lie with me, my sister," he said.

She continued to draw backward, so that the weight of her body dragged upon his hand. "No, my brother," she said, "do not force me. Do not commit such a folly."

Without releasing his hold upon her, he pulled himself to a kneeling position and leaned against her. The swelling, living warmth of her breasts was against his face.

She began to whimper. "Whither shall I carry my shame?" she said. "And as for you—you will be brought low in the sight of all Israel."

He closed both his arms around her. Now she began to twist and turn, and the rippling, agonized contortions of her body multiplied his desire. This haughty one, he thought, this soft-stepping sister of the exalted Absalom, she is in my hands like a caught dove. . . .

"No, now," she said in a supplicating voice, "if you will have me, speak to the King and ask him to give me to you as a bride. Surely the King will not withhold me from you. . . ."

Liar, he thought. You know that I know how it is with you, how you would no more take me in marriage than you would take a toad. Liar, liar, liar. . . . And he thrust her down upon the bed and smothered her cries with his mouth and knew her in rage and lust, saying to himself, I have bruised her mouth, I have subdued her body and enjoyed it, I have destroyed her virginity, I have shamed and broken her utterly. . . .

Afterward, she neither moved nor spoke. She lay as he had left her, staring up at the ceiling. The thing was done—that which he had brooded upon these many moons was finished in a few moments—and there was nothing left but emptiness. He lay back against the pillows, waiting for the emptiness to be filled. By what? By the wrath of God. By retribution. By death. Death, and this offending body of his shut up to decay among creeping creatures in the darkness of the burial cave. Death, now, tonight, tomorrow. . . .

He looked at this piece of ravaged flesh that had betrayed him into the charnel house, and he hated her with a hate far greater than the love wherewith he had loved her. "Arise, be gone," he said.

She arose and covered herself with her disordered garment. "Not so, my brother," she said, weeping, "for this great wrong which you do to me when you put me forth is worse than the other. How can I go forth and show myself?"

She came forward, holding out her hands as if to touch him. She was horrible to him, she was bottomless evil, she was the grave, and he shrieked the name of Jonadab in his fright.

Jonadab opened the door and entered.

"Put this woman out from me," said Amnon, "and bolt the door."

While Jonadab stood gaping at them both, she gathered up a handful of ashes from the floor beneath the brazier and strewed them upon her head. And she rent her garment of many colors; and she laid her hand on her head and went her way, crying aloud as she went.

◆§ VI §◆

THE YOUNG MEN of Jerusalem who were in the habit of gathering in Absalom's house said among themselves that the son of Maacah was showing an unbelievable degree of self-restraint in his anguish. If they had whispered "Murder" to each other when it was spread abroad that Tamar —the untouchable one, the darling of their feasts—had run through the streets to seek shelter in her brother's house, no doubt they had been hasty and overwrought. Absalom chose to seek lawful retribution through regal justice; nor was there any among them who would raise his voice to disapprove.

They could not doubt the strength of his grief. The house that harbored Tamar could not have been more somber if a corpse had lain within. The door was bolted, and the windows were sealed against the street. Those of the good companions who dared to advance upon that house went around to the back entrance and were greeted only by a servant, who spoke in a hushed voice. The master was prostrate. He would be grateful for such expressions of sympathy as they had brought—the jar of honey, the flowers for the poor lady, the tame bird and the bright embroidery thread to help her to beguile her empty hours. But neither his lord nor his lady would come forth from their chambers. How could they show their faces to the sun? They were waiting for word from the King of Israel.

It seemed strange to the young men of Jerusalem—though not one of them mentioned it—that those who dwelt here should look to their father. In the good days they had shown a gallant independence of the son of Jesse. His name had always called up a shrugging of shoulders among the comrades. They had found him wanting on almost every score: his domestic policy was conservative; his foreign policy was shortsighted; his court was dull. It was his express intention to set a sick dog upon the throne of Israel. He entered into alliance with Tyre and Sidon, but never reached a cordial hand southward to the wealth and culture of Egypt. He mounted his army on mules because he had a superstitious loathing for horses. And he treated constantly with the doddering elders of the tribes, as though the children of God were still herdsmen and farmers concerned with their cousins and their aunts rather than the citizens of one solidly united land. At the choice and merry feasts, they had made many a jest at David's expense. Why, then, should the son of Maacah suddenly behave as though his father were the sole fountainhead of justice in Israel? Why should he wait for three days, closed up in this house, hoping vainly that the King would right the wrong?

If they had asked these questions of Absalom, he could not have answered. The event itself had left him incapable of action, incapable of consecutive thought, incapable of anything save long, uncontrollable sighs.

A strange, dazed weakness was upon him, and he kept thinking, It is as if I had lost a great deal of blood. . . . And it seemed to him that he was bleeding indeed from his whole body. Those antennae, he thought, those blind antennae which went out between us from the day when we lay in the same cradle—it is those that have been cut away; I bleed away my strength in an unseen blood which is the essence of blood. . . . He knew then that the pulsing emanations had ceased to go out between them when he had seen the bruises of Amnon's kisses upon her face. He pitied her, he would serve her, he would keep her in his house for the rest of her days. But he no longer loved her.

To love her no more, never again to love her . . . He knew with amazement that to be cut off from her was to be utterly alone. He had a hundred friends, a thousand followers, but Jahveh had given him only one companion. As for the women—it occurred to him now that he had never given an hour's thought to any of the women. Beside her dark and burning beauty, their charms had seemed pallid, cold. No, he thought, neither man nor woman. . . . He started up then from his bed, knowing to his wonderment that there was still one living creature to whom his heart went out—the aging King of Israel. And he called his servant to him and bade him go down to the palace and say to the King of Israel that his son Absalom had tarried these three days, waiting for a sight of his father's face.

When the messenger had departed, he thought of what he had done and was astonished at his own behavior. Why had he run like a child to his father? Could David restore her virginity or call back again the severed emanations of love? And why, above all, had he worded his message to the King in so urgent and pleading a fashion? Why had he, who had held himself aloof since childhood, come crawling at last to his father's knees? He walked back and forth in his bedchamber, pondering these matters. Before he had found a single reply, his servant returned, bearing the answer: "To my son Absalom: May Jahveh walk beside him. Why did he not come to me before? It was I who tarried for a word from him, afraid lest I should force an unwelcome voice upon him in the hour of his affliction. Let him come when he will, by day or by night. I am his, and I wait upon him. David, King of Judah and Israel."

He laid the tablet aside and went into the dim hall. The door of Tamar's chamber was standing partly open. She was sitting on the edge of her bed, dressed in a long robe of white linen. Her chin was raised, and she was whistling softly, mournfully, to the tame bird that someone had sent her yesterday. She flushed, and he knew that she was confused that he had caught her whistling to a bird—she should have been weeping, she had no right to whistle in her shame. She bit her lips and lowered her eyelids. Her face took on a mask of grieving. Ah, God, look how it is with her, he thought. She has grown furtive with me, she has grown sly. . . .

"I am going to our father," he said.

"Wherefore?" Her voice was doleful, and he wondered whether she would transmute all language into lamentation for the remainder of her days.

"Why, to speak with him concerning this—this matter——"

"Yes, but wherefore?"

He could not say, he did not know. "Wherefore? Why should my sister ask wherefore? To lay the business before him, to——to ask him what he will do. Surely he will give us justice and punish the offender," he said.

⊷§ VII §∾

Absalom did not go by chariot to his father's house. He who had always moved through the streets of Jerusalem like a shooting star, bright and accompanied by low cries of admiration, went now on foot in a drab and simple garment, his heavy hair bound in by cords. He chose the hottest hour of the day, when the streets were most likely to be empty. Even so, certain pairs of eyes looked long upon him before withdrawing in pity and embarrassment. "Poor soul!" the daughters of smiths and weavers said.

He scarcely noticed them. A troubling thought had come into his mind. How would it be, he kept asking himself, if I should encounter Amnon in my father's common room? What violence or what utter impotence would come upon me if we two should meet? . . .

But when he drew near to the palace, he saw that he need not have tormented himself. The King was standing at the gate, and had plainly been standing there for some time; his arm was marked from leaning against the brazen grillwork, and sweat stood on his cheeks and brow.

"I have come forth to meet my son Absalom," he said, looking directly and gravely into the young man's eyes.

"But my father has tarried overlong in the heat of the day——"

"I would have tarried far longer for Absalom's sake. Come, let us sit in the coolness of the common room. The women and the children are in the upper chambers. As for Amnon——" He paused after the name as though he had labored to say it. "As for Amnon," he said again, energetically, "he has gone forth on a pilgrimage to the ruins of the tabernacle at Shiloh."

They seated themselves in two low chairs in the shadow of a pillar, not close enough to touch, but face to face. The crimson of the King's robe was darkened here and there by sweat. His eyes, usually keen and clear, were rimmed with red, perhaps because he had been standing in the glare of the sun, perhaps because he had wept. He is growing old, thought Absalom, and for the first time he felt no contempt at the thought. He is growing old, and he stood long at the gate. . . .

The King sighed and pulled the wet folds of his sleeve loose from his arm. "Absalom has come to me concerning the sin against his sister, is it not so?" he said.

It seemed strange that his father should have used the words "the sin." He himself had called it "Amnon's sin," had linked it inseparably to the person of the sinner, until the sinner and the sin were one. The sin against Tamar—these were the words of one remote, who grieved, perhaps, but did not suffer. "I have come to my father to speak of the evil thing that Amnon has put upon my sister," he said.

The aging face, beautiful with its folds of honey-colored flesh, bent forward. But speech was futile, more futile even than weeping. There was nothing to be said.

"What shall we say to each other, Absalom?"

"Nothing. Nothing, my father and my lord."

"No, now, my son came up to me with some request. . . ."

Turn back the days, thought Absalom. Blot from time forever the moment when I saw the bruises on her face. . . .

"Would to God that it were possible to restore her," said the King, laying his hand upon Absalom's knee. "Believe me, I know how it is to cry out in protest against that which is and should not be. But what is done is with God and cannot be undone. Nevertheless, if my son has a request to make of me——"

"What is there left save vengeance upon him who sinned against her?" Absalom said.

"Upon him who sinned against her. . . ." The voice was meditative. "And who is it who has sinned against her? Amnon? Amnon alone? But it was I that begot Amnon, against the will of Jahveh. In idleness, one night in the wilderness, I shrugged my shoulders in the face of God and took Amnon's mother. Is it not true, then, that I also have sinned against your sister, inasmuch as I have begotten this dark fruit?"

A ripple of the old bitter laughter stirred in the young man's throat. He smiled a one-sided smile. And Jesse also, and all those who poured out their seed from generation to generation, lusting and mating to beget a dog. . . . "No, now, my father," he said.

The lips above the dappled beard moved subtly, kindly. "Absalom mocks me in his heart. He thinks upon my father and my father's father, and so back unto the beginnings of the world. Then let us ponder upon other sins, nearer at hand. Wherefore did Amnon reach out his hand and take Tamar? Why should he yearn after the daughter of Maacah?"

"Let my father ask Amnon," he said, stung by the thought of that yearning. "I do not know."

"But I know," said David. "I know what it is to be a wretch among the glorious."

"But my brother Amnon has been from the hour of his birth heir to Judah and Israel——"

"A wretch, nevertheless. Sick among the whole. Ugly among the beautiful. Alone, utterly alone. He crept among you, striving to attain the mean man's virtues—strict piety and humility. Is it a great wonder that he rose up at last to commit one mighty sin, to strike down what was high and forbidden, to take it for his own, even though the price should be his death?"

His death, thought Absalom. On the evening of the Feast of the First Fruits, I promised her his death. . . . "Every sin has its root," he said, staring at the floor. "Were I to kill him, that also would have its root. If we forgive all sins because we know their roots, then surely no sin would go unforgiven."

"No, now, who speaks of forgiving? I have not forgiven him, nor am I such a fool as to tell myself that Absalom will excuse his brother's deed and think of it no more. I say only this: Let Absalom apportion his wrath justly. Let him lay a great measure of it at the foot of the King of Israel, who begot a wretch and permitted him to grow up like a wretch and refused out of fright or tenderness to see how it was between him and Tamar, who brought neither the one nor the other of them to the marriage bed, who waited and waited and left it all in the lap of God. . . ." His voice broke. His hands went up and covered his face, and Absalom knew that he wept.

The son of Maacah also bowed his head, but not to weep. It was borne in upon him that, in the uncompromising light which his father had cast upon sin, he also was a sinner. Night after night he had urged her against marriage, with bodiless emanations, with jests and shrugs, with long glances. "Yet even though many may have shared in the sin, Amnon is not sinless," he said.

"Amnon has taken the full weight of his sin upon him. He has gone in sackcloth and ashes to pray at the ruined sanctuary of Shiloh. He has said to me, 'Cast me forth into the wilderness from whence I came, for I am not such a one as should hold Israel in my hand.'"

Fierce, golden, out of the wreckage of the event, rose the one burning longing that had survived in Absalom—the hunger for the throne. "Will my father cast him out, then?" he said.

"He has cast himself out. When he has prayed at Shiloh, he will go up to Gilgal, and he will go from Gilgal to Ramah, to pray at Samuel's grave. Only the God of Hosts knows when he will come again to Jerusalem. . . ." He drew his hand across his cheeks, wiping away the vestiges of his tears. "Now what will Absalom have of me? Shall I send murderers after his brother to cut him down at some altar while he prays? Will this restore the virginity of Tamar and set the heart of Absalom at peace? Vengeance was, is, and forever shall be in the hand of the Lord. The son of Noi—God help her, for she is not only shamed, she is sick also and can scarcely drag herself up from her bed—the son of Noi is already punished, and his punishment shall follow after him unto the end of his days."

And the throne of Israel, Absalom asked in his heart, what of the throne of Israel? . . .

Quietly, meditatively, David said: "God shall judge between Amnon and Absalom. Only let Absalom hold his hand, lest he also should go down before the Lord."

He has made a covenant with me, the young man thought. He has said to me, "Restrain your just wrath, and I will give you the throne." . . .

"Is there any other matter that Absalom would lay before me?"

"No, my father and my lord."

"Then let him go to his house and take off his garment of mourning. Let him come to me again, whole and beautiful, that I may rejoice in the son that God has left to me. For it is futile to speak further of these matters and futile to weep. Let him come up and break bread with me tomorrow night."

Absalom rose and lifted the King's hand and kissed it. "I will come to my father tomorrow," he said. •

❧ VIII ❧

For two years Amnon wandered back and forth over the face of the land. Now and again he came into Jerusalem to rest between one pilgrimage and another—a ghostly presence, turned lean by fasting and burned almost black by the sun. While he dwelt in the palace, the son of Jesse extended to him such courtesies as were the rightful portion of the heir to the throne. But as soon as he had departed northward to pray at Jacob's ford by the river Jordan, or southward to seek through the endless whiteness of the desert for the Mountain of God, the King beckoned Absalom to take his brother's place. And it was plain to Israel and to the world that David's heart was with Absalom.

During these two years, Tamar dwelt in her brother's house—or rather, she dwelt in that little chamber whose white rugs and crimson curtains he had bought for her in the good days, long ago. Dutifully, at the end of every feast, some visitor would go up to chat with her, to inquire after her health, to whistle to the bird that sat in a bronze cage upon her window sill. But such visitors stayed for shorter and shorter periods, because there was less and less to say. Life had become for her a matter of birds, embroidery, and food. She was no longer even fair. She ate to fill up the empty hours, and she had grown fat. Her cheek was like a mushroom—cold, hard, white.

As for Absalom, during these years he was more often in his father's house than in his own. He brought with him to the King's palace some of the brilliance that Israel had learned to link with his name. There was looser and livelier talk at the table; younger lutists sang the King's praise; the lamb was garnished with herbs, and the bread was strewn with sesame. With the help of Ahitophel, who loved the young man dearly, certain more significant changes also were made: More of the subtle faces out of Egypt appeared at the King's feasts; the officers of the host began to ride before the ranks on splendid steeds instead of mules; and it was made plain to the elders of Ephraim and Benjamin that they must not ask too much or stay too long.

The King himself was transformed by the gracious flow of life around him. He sat up far later than was his wont, taking part in the witty talk and asking for yet another song. Sometimes he would take the lute into his own hand and lift up his voice, still resonant and strong. And it was not out of courtesy to the throne that he was hailed of one accord as first among the lutists of the land. Twice or thrice his son Absalom offered him a garland, and he took it and set it upon his head. Now that he had drawn youth and beauty to his dwelling-place, it became evident that he himself was something more than comely: his pied locks flowed rich and full beneath the leaves; his skin, clear and honey-colored, glowed in the light of the lamps; and even the youngest and fairest of the women sought after his glance. He gave more of his leisure to merriment and less to meditation. Whenever some piece of wearisome business was finished, he would say, "Where is my son Absalom?"

He had come to dote on the young man—that was plain. His eyes grew dreaming and effulgent when they fixed themselves upon that dark and vital face; the judgment of older, wiser men went down before that wit, that voice; but Israel, who yearned after Absalom as a maid yearns after her lover, could not fear that the King had misplaced his trust. Where under the firmament could one find a more dutiful son? Was he not at the King's table four nights out of every seven? Had he not married the bride of his father's choosing—a princess out of Syria? Had he not disciplined his heart so that he could sit at the same board with Amnon? And if he had not permitted Israel to forget that matter completely, if he had caused the court to gasp by naming his little daughter with his sister Tamar's name, who could blame him? It was not an easy thing to go up a stairway night after night to pay one's respects to a ghost. . . .

The sin of Amnon and the sorrow of Tamar were never again mentioned between Absalom and the King of Israel. The covenant of silence was so strong upon David that he could not bring himself to call his granddaughter by her name; he referred to her always as "the little one."

Nor was there any talk as to who would sit after him upon the throne of Judah and Israel. Perhaps it was his desire to be delivered from such heavy considerations that made him so eager for gay company. He wished in the tabernacle of his heart that Amnon would find himself utterly at home one day among the priests of Ramah or Gilgal, that he would turn his back upon the kingship and devote himself to God. Whenever the unwelcome thought of the succession forced itself upon him, he took comfort in the possibility of such a solution. Surely the Lord would find a way to put the comely and beloved one upon the throne. . . .

And then, at the end of the two blessed years, Amnon came home. It was plain that he had undergone some transformation. He was erect and vigorous; there was a smoldering fervor in his eyes. He told whoever would listen that while he had sojourned by the holy springs of Kadesh, a Presence had appeared to him among the brown rocks and spoken to him with the voice of the waters. A Presence had assured him that his grievous sin was to be lifted from him at last. And lo, when he had bathed, his heart was lightened. The Lord of Hosts had seen the measure of his tears and had called it enough. He would be counted as a sinner no more.

What was the King of Israel to do? It was obvious that Amnon had not the slightest intention of departing. He went into the bazaars to purchase new curtains and rugs for that upper chamber in which he had sinned and suffered. He arrayed himself in crimson garments and anointed his scanty beard and hair. He began to ask far-reaching questions concerning his father's policy in Egypt, in Syria, in Phoenicia. "In a little while," he told David, "I will take a bride of your choosing, so that I may raise up seed to the security of Israel."

For seven days thereafter, the King spread no feasts. He walked alone —when Amnon would permit him to walk alone—through the corridors and the gardens; he went early to bed, and could not sleep. Much as he yearned after the son of Maacah, he did not call him into his presence. Again and again he strove to reconstruct in his remembrance that single conversation which he had held with the comely one concerning Amnon and Tamar. I made no promises concerning the throne, he told himself. I remember well that I left the matter in the lap of God. . . . Nevertheless, deep anxiety came upon him whenever he thought of coming face to face with Absalom.

It was the son of Maacah himself who broke the tension. He came unbidden, blithe and easy, bringing a newly slain lamb from his estate at Baal-hazor. This little gift, he said, might increase the good cheer of the home-coming. He trusted that he would be permitted to sit with his family and eat a little of the lamb tonight. And how was it with Amnon? He held his long, brown hand out to his brother. How greatly the eldest son of the King had profited by his pilgrimages—he was the very image of radiant health. . . .

On that evening and many evenings thereafter, the son of Maacah seated himself at his father's left hand. He never dreamed to succeed me, the King of Israel thought. If he had harbored so much as the shadow of a hope, he could not bear this turn of chance with such graciousness. . . . His face was cheerful, candid, innocent even of the one-sided smile. He set them all to laughing with a series of tasteful jests. The King waited fearfully for the young man's good intentions to falter. But moons waxed and waned, and there was no flaw in the general tranquillity. By the time of the Feast of the Sheep Shearing, David had ceased to wait for the old hate to flash out again. Plainly, the House of David was at peace.

The King had other matters to distract him. A dispute concerning the ownership of a certain sanctuary had arisen between the Benjamites and the Ephraimites. The elders of both tribes were in Jerusalem to lay the matter before him; they pulled him this way and that, presenting endless arguments, relating miracles and signs. He was closeted for hours at a time with Hushai and Ahitophel, Nathan, Abiathar, and Gad. Amnon showed a dutiful interest in the proceedings, but Absalom refused to concern himself. A squabble among old fools, he called it openly. For his part, he would not remain in Jerusalem to follow the testimony. He meant to celebrate the Feast of the Sheep Shearing among his flocks at Baal-hazor.

Five days before the feast, in the first flush of the morning, before the King had risen, the son of Maacah came up to his father's chamber and sat upon the edge of the bed. David had never seen him so buoyant. "My lord and my father," he said, "a thought has come into my mind——" And it was apparently so delightful a thought that he could not sit still, but clasped his hands around his knees and swayed back and forth.

"What thought, my son?"

"Come up with me, my father, and celebrate the Shearing in my house at Baal-hazor. Come and bring your servants and all your court and all your sons and all your wives, that we may make merry together."

The King wondered somewhat that Absalom should have forgotten that nothing—not even the Feast of the Sheep Shearing—could interrupt the negotiations between the elders of Ephraim and Benjamin. But then, the young man had taken that matter lightly from the beginning.

"I beg you to come up," the son of Maacah said, laying his hand upon his father's knee. "I have already consulted Adonijah and Meribaal, and they have agreed to abide with me at least for three days, and Bath-sheba has promised me that I may take the little Solomon. What is a Sheep Shearing in the city, where there are no flocks and no shepherds, where a couple of lily-fingered priests lead out an ancient ewe and a worn-out ram? Say that you will come, my father, to see proper sheep properly blessed at Baal-hazor."

David smiled, but shook his head. He could not bring himself to confess outright that he was forced to remain in Jerusalem for so trivial a matter as a quarrel between two groups of elders. "No, my son," he said, "if all of us go up, surely we will be a burden to you. Take the young men up if you will, but I will not bring a crowd of courtiers to dwell in your house, to be fed at your cost."

495

"My father, I entreat you to come. . . ."

"My son, your entreaty is sweet, and I bless you for it, but I must turn it aside for your sake."

The young man crouched over, resting his elbows on his knees and his chin in his hands, and pouted like a child. "Then, my father," he said at last, "if you will not come, let my brother Amnon at least be with us."

"Why should he go with you?" The question had been driven from him against his will by an onslaught of fear.

Absalom stared full into his father's face with wide, wounded eyes. That my father should harbor suspicion against me after all I have borne and sacrificed, his look said. . . .

"No, now, would you really have him at the feast?" said David quickly. "He too will carry friends and servants with him, and will make himself a burden. Absalom has already been too kind. Nevertheless, if my son wishes his brother to come up——"

The voice was sorrowful, reproachful, and dignified. "I would not have asked for him if I had not desired his presence, my father and my lord."

"I know, I know. Surely, then, he will come up to you. I will carry your request to him this very morning. Go up to Baal-hazor and prepare for your feast," David said.

❧ IX ❧

THE ELDEST SON of the King of Israel had suffered so long and so intensely through fear that he could no longer afford to give himself up to it. For him, the slow, cold hours of terror were more to be dreaded than the black violence of dissolution. The Presence that had spoken to him at the springs of Kadesh with the voice of the living waters had promised him that the burden of fear as well as the burden of sin would be lifted from his heart. Now, whenever the forerunners of fright—the clammy hands, the swift and uneven pulse—afflicted him, he told himself, God is with me. All that is necessary is to refuse to be afraid. . . . With this formula he had succeeded in holding off terror many times since his return; nor did he permit the familiar surge to sweep over him when his father told him that he was to go up to Baal-hazor. This, he said to himself, is only another indication of Absalom's forgiveness and God's extraordinary grace. . . .

But his palms did grow moist twice on the day of the journey. Early in the morning, when he bade his mother farewell at the gate, he felt the shadow of fear, though he could not call himself actually afraid. The blue hollows around Noi's eyes were darker than he had ever seen them before; her cheek was damp and fragile and seemed to collapse under his kiss. Her days were plainly numbered. One never departed from her without thinking, Only God in heaven knows whether her eyes will still be open to behold me when I come again. . . .

496

He felt the foreshadowings of fear for the second time in the early afternoon when he drew rein and beheld Absalom's house from the top of a near-by hill. It was one of those low, sprawling structures, half raw wood and half stone, which can scarcely be distinguished from the rocky slopes upon which they stand. Vines and lichen had fastened upon it; it had a greenish, earthy look. And while he gazed down upon it, he felt that the reins had grown slippery in his hands. His palms were moist—ominously moist—as they had been in the black days before he was granted a reprieve by the angel of God.

But as he drew closer to the house, his spirits were revived by the songs of the shearers. They were ancient songs, so familiar that whosoever heard them or sang them seemed to be making them himself. With these homely tunes in his ears, he gave his horse to one of Absalom's grooms and walked slowly toward the house, through the crowds of shearers and the flocks of bleating sheep. The shearers, dark, lithe, and naked to the waist, kept lunging after the frightened and recalcitrant beasts. He stopped to watch one of them catch and throw down a lamb; the beast bleated and struggled and then, under the sinewy hands, grew still. Something—was it a recollection or a prevision?—sent a cold shock along his spine. He shrugged and went forward, looking neither left nor right and lifting up his voice in the shearers' song.

Close to the house, in the shade of a splendid terebinth, Meribaal and Adonijah sat on a couch that had been carried out from the common room. Adonijah rose at once on seeing his eldest brother, and held out a bowl of dates stuffed with pistachio nuts. "And this," he said, "is only a foretaste. There is such food within as I never beheld before." The little Solomon darted out of the house and ran past them, shouting over his shoulder to Amnon, "Absalom has been expecting you this last hour." He was a charming lad, not tall, but well made and graceful, with his father's golden skin and his mother's soft brown hair. He had grown somewhat affected with being praised too much. Knowing that all the shearers would pause in their work to chuckle at his antics, he leaped into a great pile of shorn fleece and jumped up and down. "Then I should go in and greet my brother," Amnon said.

But Absalom came forth before he could enter—Absalom dressed in the garb of a shepherd, his long, brown legs bare below the hem of his tunic, and a garland of grass and small scarlet lilies on his head.

"So you have come at last," he said, turning his brother about and leading him back to the couch beneath the terebinth. "Sit down, sit down and watch the shearers. My common room is in confusion; my servants are not yet finished preparing the table."

They sat together for an hour in the shade of the terebinth, sometimes joining in the chorus of the shearers, sometimes making the empty, bantering conversation that cloaks the embarrassment of kinsmen who have nothing to say to one another. Solomon, glowing and breathless after a race with a ram, flung himself down on the grass beside the couch. He asked a question concerning one of the songs, and Adonijah and Meribaal fell to interpreting and arguing—a lengthy business, so dull that Absalom yawned in their faces. "Come," he said, closing his brown fingers around Amnon's wrist, "let us escape from this nest of scholarship and piety. Let my brother Amnon walk with me to the back of the house, for I must look to the spits."

Amnon told himself that he had no cause for fright, and yet he could not reason himself out of the knowledge that he was terrified. The dark face under the garland of grass and lilies, moving beside him through patches of shadow and patches of light, seemed unusually immobile and preoccupied. Some twenty paces from the back entrance to the house, three spits had been set up. Before these spits knelt four brawny servingmen, naked to their waists. Their arms and thighs, red from the heat, were heavily ridged with muscle. Wherefore, thought Amnon, does my brother Absalom keep wrestlers to be his bondsmen? . . . He started then, because something soft and slippery had given way beneath his feet. He looked down and saw that he had trodden upon the strewn entrails of the lambs. Bluish, brownish, reddish masses lay on the ground before him. He swallowed and put his hand to his lips. And even as he did so, his brother said to the servants, in a strangely incisive voice, "Behold my brother Amnon, he that is to sit upon the throne of Israel."

It was a delusion born of groundless fear, Amnon thought; but he believed that all four of these bondsmen stared boldly into his face. Their eyes, strangely pale in their scorched faces, dwelt too long upon him. This and the cold trail left upon the side of his foot by the entrails made it impossible for him to smile. But in a moment the bondsmen bowed their heads and made obeisance before him. "Our master's house is honored," they said together.

Absalom looked at Amnon and shrugged. "Well," he said, giving one of the servants a good-natured shove, "see to it that you do not burn the meat."

When they returned to the couch beneath the terebinth, they saw that evening was drawing on. The carnival spirit of the shearers had begun to flag. They were no longer singing. They went about their business grimly, showing exasperation at the struggles of the last unshorn lambs. Conversation, too, had flagged among the watchers. Absalom excused himself and went into the house; the roast meat had been carried in, and he wished to supervise the carving. As for Amnon, he could think of one thing only— the mark that the trodden entrails had left upon his foot. All meat had grown distasteful to him. God help me, he thought, I will surely offend him through his food, for I will not be able to eat. . . .

By the time the servant came to call them in to the feast, he had begun to shiver. He was the last to rise from the couch, the last to pass beneath the weather-darkened lintel. Because of Meribaal's lameness, the procession to the table was halting and slow. Solomon ran ahead of the others and found a place for himself at the board; Adonijah came after him, supporting Meribaal on his arm; and Amnon came to the table last. The room was dim; no torches had been lighted as yet. The four bondsmen who had knelt before the spits were standing in the four corners, their powerful arms folded over their red and hairy chests. Near one of the windows Absalom stood, draining off a large bowlful of wine.

"Come, my brothers, sit and be merry," he said.

But there was some confusion over the business of being seated. There was a disparity between the number of places and the number of guests. Surely, Amnon told himself, there was nothing ominous in that; to lay an extra place in the confusion of a festival was a common error. Yet he was filled with consternation to see that the empty seat should be at the foot of the table, directly opposite his own.

Now that all of them were seated, an uneasy silence settled upon them. The lamb, thinly sliced and powdered with dry herbs, lay before Absalom, ready to be served; but the son of Maacah continued to sip his wine. Amnon, like the others, took up his bowl and drank. The wine seemed harsh and sour to him, and he set it aside with shaking hands.

"No, now," said the little Solomon in a sulky voice, "I am starving. Give me at least a piece of sesame bread."

He reached out in the direction of the bread, but Absalom, who sat between him and Amnon, stayed his hand.

"Wait a little, wait a little," said the comely one, "there is another guest. We have but one sister, and it is only meet that we should wait for her to take her place among us before we break bread."

Amnon opened his mouth to say that sister's name. But terror had numbed his tongue. Terror had told him that the Presence at the springs of Kadesh was a divine double-dealer sent to deceive him by a malevolent God. The white garments of a woman fluttered in the doorway. She stopped upon the threshold and then walked slowly toward the empty chair.

Tamar? Tamar? Could it be she? Bloated and ponderous, she moved toward the table. Her eyes—the fixed eyes of a sleepwalker—were very black in her pale face. While the others looked on in utter silence, she sank into her chair. She rested her elbows on the cloth and supported her chin upon her fat, clenched hands. Amnon started up from his seat, jarring the table and spilling the wine.

"No, now, sit, my brother," said Absalom.

"Let me go forth." The words came blurred out of his mouth.

"Sit, my brother," Absalom said again. And he closed his hard brown fingers upon Amnon's wrist and dragged him downward, smiling all the while. "Sit, and I will have a torch brought in." He turned and called over his shoulder to one of the servants, "Bring a torch and hold it above the head of my brother Amnon, so that my sister Tamar may see."

It seemed to Amnon that the room was ablaze with torches. Adonijah had sprung to his feet. The little Solomon was crying out in terror. Meribaal leaned upon the table with both hands and strove convulsively to pull his crippled body out of the chair. But *she* sat still as a stone, staring into Amnon's face. He shrieked then, and tried to pull himself free, for he had seen death in her blank, unswerving look. It was no longer Absalom who held him. Two of the terrible bondsmen were standing above him, forcing him back into his chair. The third was behind him, bearing the light. And the fourth—the fourth . . . He screamed again just as the fourth thrust a dagger into his side.

"Ah, God!" he said, with the taste of blood in his mouth.

"I take this blood upon my hands," said the voice of Absalom. "It was for my sister Tamar's sake."

But Amnon scarcely heard him. Amnon sank down against the table, smiling, because there was no more weakness, no more terror. There was only silence, only death.

⋑ X ⋐

STRIVE as he would, the King of Israel could not summon up the proper measure of sorrow over the death of that timorous and unlovely one whom he had begotten in the wilderness. If the story of the violence at Baal-hazor had come to him ungarbled, if one had fallen at his feet and said, "Behold, your eldest son is slain," he might have been stricken by fierce grief. But the bearer of the tidings was an ignorant bondsman of Adonijah's, who had fled from among the shearers at the first cry of "Murder!" Absalom had slain all the King's sons, the servant said. Adonijah, Amnon, Solomon— all of them were dead. And when Jonadab arrived at the palace with a sane account, the King was not able to hide his relief. An unholy spasm in his chest had shaken him almost to laughter. "What? Only one of them? Only Amnon?" he had said.

Thereafter he could not deceive himself. I did not love him, he said in his heart. All his days I strove to love him, but what I felt for him was always pity, never love. . . . And, knowing this, he experienced an aching bruise of pathos more painful than the clean cut of loss. For three days and nights after the burial, he sat in his bedchamber quietly weeping. Slow and effortless tears coursed down his cheeks; his hands lay open and helpless upon his knees. He remembered how he had carried the little Amnon down to Gath on his shoulder and how he had covered the child's legs against the cold. He remembered the albino donkey and the scarlet coat, the hushed hour when he had held the child in his lap in the brown house of Abinadab. "I did whatsoever I could," he said aloud in the empty chamber. "I earnestly strove to love him. . . ." And the servants said among themselves that the King could not have grieved more bitterly if the slain one had been Absalom or Solomon.

The sight of Noi's affliction came like a second blow upon the bruise. Not that she had made any outcry when they brought her the tidings and led her into the chamber where Amnon's body lay. On both occasions she had simply stood staring, without uttering a word. Then, after long gazing, she had lifted up her hands very slowly and bent her head forward a little, as though she meant to clasp her brow. But before the gesture was completed, she had let her arms fall to her sides, and the coming-down of her hands—white, almost translucent—was the most wounding sight that the King of Israel had ever seen. The gesture renounced everything, even grief, as useless. With the same impassive face, she walked behind the body to the burial cave. When she returned to the palace, she took to her bed. That same night, Abishai came up from the camp of God to dwell in the King's house, that he might watch beside her. He and the gentle Haggith divided the vigil between them, Haggith sitting by the bed from dawn until dusk and Abishai keeping watch by night. On those few occasions when David brought himself to go into her chamber, she spoke as though there had been no murder, no burial. She had been worrying, she said, over a certain vat of olives that had not been put into the press. Let them be looked to, lest they be covered with mold. No, she was not in pain. Let no one think that she was dying. She would be long at dying, she said, rolling her head from side to side, too long, too long. . . .

If it had been possible for the King to return to his old mode of existence when the period of mourning was past, the ache of pity and remorse might have grown less within him. But that life to which he had given himself for more than two years—the eager talk, the sweet songs, the young faces gathered around the festive board—that life was at an end. Its creator had fled to the court of his mother's father in the desert kingdom of Geshur; his boon companions kept to their houses; and the common room of the palace seemed long and chill and empty now. Neither Bath-sheba nor the little Solomon was at hand to offer solace. The lad had been gravely shaken by the violence at Baal-hazor, and his mother had taken him off to the orchards to rest. The King wandered restlessly about, impatient with business and burdened by leisure. In every corner of the house and at every hour of the day he was forever encountering a vision of Maacah's son. Blithe, insouciant, crowned with a garland of almond blossoms—that image would be present when he awakened, sitting at the foot of his bed. And at dusk he would expect to see it standing before the spring or lying upon a bench and smiling at the stars.

Perhaps it was the persistence of the presence that kept him from the performance of a duty for which all Israel waited: he could not bring himself to issue an edict of banishment against the slayer of his eldest son. To issue such an edict seemed to him pointless in any case. Absalom was gone—gone into the white, impenetrable stretches of the desert, gone to an alien life, the more tormenting for its mystery. Nor had he left any of his household behind him. Tamar had ridden out with him on the night of the slaying, and his Syrian bride and the little one had departed into Geshur three days before. He had planned the business well. Not one of the guilty servants had been left behind.

The general silence the household maintained in regard to the son of Maacah was broken only twice—once by Joab and once by Ahitophel. The captain of the host, dining one night alone with his uncle, led the conversation circuitously to the matter of certain poisons, used frequently in Egypt and available in Israel, which did their work slowly, causing the symptoms of ordinary sickness, so that whosoever died of them seemed to have died a natural death. "Such brews," said the son of Zeruiah, raising his luminous eyes to David's face, "were surely within the reach of your son Absalom, but he is such a one as could do nothing in deceit. In his sight it was better to cast away the crown than to put a lie between his father and himself. . . ." And some three or four days thereafter, one evening when the King and the priest Abiathar and the counselor Ahitophel were sitting together in the garden, the talk happened upon the laws that had governed the children of Israel during the years of their wanderings in the wilderness. "One thing is certain," said the old counselor, "God gave a man more freedom to avenge his wrongs in those days than the courts and councils will vouchsafe him now. The ancient law did not put the name of murderer upon any man who slew to defend his women or himself. To cut down the seducer of a wife or a sister—that was just vengeance and entirely acceptable in the sight of the Lord. . . ."

Now that Joab and Ahitophel had made it plain to him that he would have their support if he chose to call the wanderer home, the King put aside all thought of issuing an edict of banishment. Someday—not, certainly, while Noi still lived, but someday—he would send into the kingdom of Geshur after Absalom. And having made this decision, he was no longer haunted by the omnipresent vision. But the palace seemed the more empty since the vision had departed. In idleness broken only by insignificant business, in silence broken only by the talk of old men and the moans of the dying Noi, he waited for the return of Bath-sheba and the little Solomon.

Their coming was delayed for a day. On the morning when they had planned to take leave of the orchards, the sky over Israel was darkened by clouds—such clouds, said the people, as had never before hung over the land. They came eastward, blown in from the mysterious and evil reaches of the sea. They were at once gray and purplish, and had churning edges, pale and feathery, like foam. They piled up one upon another until the whole firmament was overcast, save for one ragged greenish vent at the very center of the arch, through which a livid, whitish ray escaped to shine athwart the dark masses below. Hollow thunder rumbled through the high houses of the capital. Lightning slit the bellies of the clouds. Rain fell, and the strength of the wind was multiplied. Those who had been tarrying in the streets and the gardens fled into their houses, and none too soon, for it was no ordinary rain that Jahveh was hurling out of the heavens. It fell in round, hard crystals, the size of the eggs of birds. It rattled against the roofs and the walls; it bruised the heads of those who had not sought shelter early enough. How long these cold and ruinous crystals continued to fall, it was difficult to say, for the time during which they clattered against the earth was drawn out by fright and wonderment. They continued to lie about on the streets and the window sills until the clouds departed, pressed toward the east by a slackening wind. Then they melted away under the eyes of the beholders in the rays of the returning sun.

David had meant to spend the evening of that day with the beloved, and now that the storm had kept her from him he wanted nothing but solitude. The weather was cool and radiant after the downpour; the scent of wet earth and bruised herbs floated in to him while he broke the evening bread; and it seemed to him that it would be pleasant to walk awhile in the garden alone. He made his excuses to the poor remnants of his household by saying that he was curious to learn whether the plants had been injured.

"I fear the herbs are badly bruised, my lord," said Haggith.

Meribaal sighed. "I am concerned for the wheat and the millet," he said. "If such stones fell upon the fields, it will go hard with the crops this year."

And indeed when the King came into his garden, he saw ruin all about him; the vines and bushes were bent and broken, the ground was strewn with petals, and almost every green shoot in the bed of herbs was lying over on its side. He was particularly concerned for a certain magnificent red lily that he had received as a gift from one of the Syrian lords. Yesterday at noon he had noticed that the first bud upon it was ready to break, and he had meant to pluck the full-blown scarlet flower tonight for the beloved. He stopped before the stalk in disproportionate dismay. The broad leaves had been tattered by the hail; the lithe green stem was broken; the bright bud lay on the ground at his feet. He lifted it up and stared at it, and as he stared he felt the old ache, the soreness of pity and regret. Wherefore, he asked himself, does the Lord our God show such inconstancy of purpose? Why has He seen fit to bring a scarlet lily into bud only to cast stones from heaven upon it, so that it never blooms, but rots unfulfilled in the mud? . . .

He sat down on the bench before the spring, with the lily in his hand. And Amnon, he asked himself, why did God create Amnon? What profit was there in his life, since he lived all his days in terror and came in the end to violent death? And Noi? Why did the Lord bring Noi living out of her mother's womb to be seduced and rejected, to nurse other women's children, to see her sole son slain, and to die slowly, in cruel pain, with green bile oozing from between her lips? Indeed, why has God put forth His hand and created man at all, seeing that even the fairest and the most fortunate must become putrefying flesh at last? . . . He laid the broken flower upon the earth, and rose, and went from the ruined garden into the common room.

Only Meribaal had lingered at the table. He was working diligently over a block of wood in the light of a single lamp; he had taken it into his head to carve a model of a Phoenician ship to give to the little Solomon. As the King entered, he looked up and smiled.

Wherefore should you smile? David thought. Why has God made you?

Are you not robbed of the right to sit upon the throne of Israel, and also lamed in both your feet? . . . But the smile was winsome, and the cloud of pale-brown hair was luminous in the lamplight, so that the King was moved to tenderness and drew near and laid his hand upon the young man's head. "How goes it with the ship, my son?" he said.

"Alas, not well enough, my father and my lord. It is not nearly finished, and tomorrow the little one comes home."

Yes, thought David, stroking the warm, silken hair. Tomorrow both of them come home, the little one and the beloved. . . . And the very thought of her return brought peace upon him. He remained in the common room for the rest of the evening, watching Meribaal carve the prow of the ship and drinking a soothing mixture of herb tea and wine until drowsiness came upon him and he was ready for sleep.

❧ XI ❧

ON THE FOLLOWING DAY, Bath-sheba and Solomon returned from the orchards a little before the hour of the evening bread. When the King lifted the beloved down from the wagon, she laughed and slipped out of his embrace. He must not kiss her, she said; the dust of the journey was upon her. Until sunset, she was to be seen only briefly, hurrying from room to room, absorbed in the business of return. She bathed; she unpacked the clothes that she had taken up to the orchards; she had a talk with Haggith and another with the steward; she rose from the table before the sweet had been served and went to pay her respects to the dying. Meanwhile, her lord contented himself with Solomon. They talked almost exclusively of the wonders of the hailstorm, and Solomon told his father how he had found a fledgling bird thrown from its nest by the violence of the wind.

Bath-sheba came downstairs at last, grave and abstracted after her visit to Noi. She wore a simple yellow garment, girdled in blue. Neither the years nor the bearing of children had left any perceptible mark upon her; she was still girlish, slender, delicately fair. She crossed the room, unhurried now and bearing herself with dignity, holding out both her hands to her lord. "Come, beloved," she said, "let us sit together in the garden."

They usually settled themselves on the bench beside the spring, but tonight he turned away from that spot, unwilling to see what a day of heat had done to the scarlet lily. He laid his arm about her waist and drew her toward another bench, set in the feathery shadow of a palm tree. She seated herself, and for a while he stood above her, happy to have her remain within the range of his vision at last. Her days in the orchard had brought a faint rosiness to her cheeks and the tip of her chin. He sought eagerly after the self-surrendering look that she was wont to give him after they had been separated from each other, but this evening the look was less satisfying than he had hoped; something came between him and the ultimate revelation. Very likely she is still brooding over Noi, he thought. He lay down at full length on the bench, resting his head upon her knees.

He had waited long for the moment when he could tell her how the broken stem of a scarlet lily had conjured up in him certain almost intolerable thoughts concerning the meaninglessness of life and the purposelessness of God. But he could not find the words wherewith to begin, and it was she who broke the hush.

"How is it that my uncle Ahitophel was not with us at the board tonight?" she said.

He was surprised that she should feel any concern over the absence of her uncle. She had always shown a certain coolness toward him. In the years when she had been the wife of the abstemious Hittite, Ahitophel had seldom shown his face in her common room. He was awkward because of his shortsightedness, and unsociable because of his awkwardness. He seldom paid visits, and his niece had taken his uneasiness for pride.

"No, now," he said, laughing, "it never came into my mind that Bathsheba would wish to be greeted by her uncle. Otherwise, I would have asked him to dine with me tonight rather than with the captain of the host."

"Does he dine often with the captain of the host?"

He laughed again. "Truly, beloved, I do not ask him where he dines. If you wish, I will summon him for tomorrow night."

She smiled and shook her head. "No," she said. "Why should you summon him? I was only thinking that a fast bond is growing up between those two. . . ."

"So be it. If they fall into the habit of dining with each other, then we two can more frequently break our bread together in peace."

As he spoke, he lifted her hand and laid it across his lips. It was as pliant as the hand of a child and redolent only of its own perfume—a fresh fragrance, like the scent f cream. He breathed deeply and was stirred. There is nothing, he told himself, to detain us from going up the stairway together even now before the sun is set. . . . Yet it seemed to him that his delight would be marred by a sense of incompleteness if he did not first communicate to her that conviction of utter futility which had weighed so heavily upon him last night.

"There was a lily," he said, lifting her hand and holding it against his chest, "there was a scarlet lily out of Syria ready to come into blossom by the spring. I meant to pluck it and set it in your hand, but it was broken in its bud by the stones out of heaven. And it seemed to me a strange thing that the Lord should strike down that which He has made while it is yet in the bud. . . ."

She gazed down at him with grave, pitying eyes, and nodded. "My lord yearns after his son Amnon," she said, "and thinks how he was cut down also before his days could come to flower."

She had seen his heart, and he pressed her fingers in gratefulness.

"But what profit is there in mourning for Amnon?" she said. "It is with Amnon now as it was with our first little one. I have thought often how my lord said then that there was no profit in weeping, that we will go to our dead in due time, but that they will come to us no more. It is true indeed that Jahveh has dealt harshly with the seed of David. Two are in the burial cave, and one is fled into a strange land. Yet there is at least this comfort in the hour of affliction—my lord looks yet upon the living faces of Adonijah and Solomon."

The whole speech had been uttered with the utmost tenderness, and in the voice that was for him the most blessed sound on earth. Nevertheless, he felt a growing displeasure while he listened. It was not only that she had turned aside from his sense of chaotic meaninglessness; it was also that she had been more harsh than the Lord in her dealings with Absalom. She had spoken of the young man's sojourn in Geshur as though she believed he would never return. In naming only his two younger brothers, she had reckoned him among the dead. How is it possible, he thought, that she who loves me should be less merciful to my seed than Joab or Ahitophel? . . . He released her hand. "Does my beloved believe that Absalom will tarry in Geshur for the rest of his days?" he said.

"Surely, unless he is sent for, he will not come again."

"And if I should send for him?"

She gave the matter solemn consideration, still looking straight into his eyes. "The blood of his brother is upon his hands. . . ."

"That is true. And yet it is possible that one murderer might send into Geshur after another. . . ."

She flushed to the roots of her hair and turned aside. Then, after a long silence, she said, "But who is higher than the King? The King sits in judgment over all the people, and above the King, to judge the King, sits God. God said to the King through Nathan's mouth, 'I will do such-and-such to you, inasmuch as you have broken my commandments.' And behold, it is done. Our little one is dead, and Amnon is murdered, and the sword of strife has torn the House of David in twain. As the Lord is just with the King, so let the King be just with the people. David shed blood and thereby forfeited two of his children. Since Absalom shed blood, it is only just that he should lose the throne."

He was assailed by a painful bewilderment. No, now, he said in his heart, how can the King be just in such a world? For when I justly secured my eldest son, a weakling and a sinner, upon the throne, then I was unjust to Tamar and Absalom and Israel. How shall I justly exile one who rightly avenged the rape of his sister whom he loved? And if I raise Adonijah in his place, am I not again unjust, inasmuch as Adonijah is plainly not such a one as should wear the crown? . . . And he said aloud in a shaken voice, "What is just?"

She lifted his hand and held it against her breast. "I also know," she said, "that the matter is dark and confused. Indeed, I have long since ceased to ask myself such high questions as 'What is just?' Now I say to myself only 'What will cause the least pain?' or 'What is safe?' "

Ah, God, he thought, sensing the yielding warmth of her breasts, what profit is there in lying here for another hour in a vain effort to make plain to her these black thoughts which I myself cannot understand? It would be better to rise now and lead her up the stairs. All living beings are strangers, and there is but one way in which two can become one. . . .

"Being a woman," she said, "I yearn most after a quiet household in which the children are safe and the daily bread is broken in peace. If the son of Maacah were again amongst us—I am a fool, I know—but if my lord were to call Absalom back from Geshur, I could not rest. Comely he is, and on many occasions I too have been charmed by his loveliness. But he is a child of the desert, wild and strange, and I am afraid. Were he again in Jerusalem—it is a woman's fear and very childish, yet I cannot withhold it from David—I would rise out of my bed every hour to look upon Adonijah and Meribaal and Solomon, to make certain that their sleep was not such sleep as Absalom meted out to Amnon at Baal-hazor."

He withdrew his hand from hers again and stared sternly at the fronds of the palm tree. He was affronted for Absalom's sake. "Let Bath-sheba remember why it was that the son of Maacah lifted his hand against his brother. It was to avenge the rape of his sister, and not to snatch the crown."

"And yet . . ." The voice was meditative and gentle. "And yet he waited two full years to avenge the wrong against Tamar, and lifted up his hand only when David made it clear that it was Amnon who would sit upon the throne. . . ."

He could not gainsay it, and yet he rejected it. He rose from the bench and walked a few paces from her, looking down at the shattered stalks and blades at his feet. "The garden has been ruined by the hailstorm," he said.

He had the feeling that she was smiling behind him, but there was nothing but grave regret in her reply. "The overseer of the orchards was greatly troubled when we left him. He had little hope for the millet and the wheat."

He turned upon her with an urgency that was not completely innocent of anger. "Why do we tarry here in useless talk? It is more than a moon since we have been together."

She rose, meek as a dove, and laid her arms about his neck. "Yes, why should we tarry?" she said.

⤳ XII ⤪

Almost every night when Abishai came, bearing a lamp with him, into the chamber where Noi lay dying, she would raise herself on her elbows and protest that she did not require a light. At first it seemed to Abishai and the gentle Haggith that even a mild glow must be painful to her weakening eyes. But later it became clear to them that her wandering mind had carried her back to her childhood in the wilderness, where oil was a very precious commodity, bought at the cost of many skins of sour wine or many bushels of fleece. "No, now," she would say, gazing sternly at the flame, "in a single night we burn up that which I could have woven into good cloth. . . ." But suddenly, seeing Haggith's face bending above her, she would recall that this queenly daughter of Hebron had borne no part in the harsh life of the wilderness. She would smile then and lay her wasted hand upon her friend's cheek. "I am a fool," she would say, shaking her head. "The King of Israel has oil and can afford a light."

Long since, she had put away all desire to live. To live was to suffer pain, and her pain was incessant and terrible. She saw it in her mind's eye as a great black beast gnawing with insatiable hunger at something red between her ribs and her back. As soon as she learned that whatever she ate served only to feed the beast, she took nothing but a few mouthfuls of herb tea at the hours of the morning and the evening bread. In spite of her torments, she enjoyed the moments when she sipped the tea; they had for her the freshness and delight of a child's holidays. And her longing for release was transformed at the last into a longing for tea, for she had told herself that she would seize the bowl and drink her fill the moment she became certain of the imminence of death.

There were hours, there were whole days, when she completely lost her sense of time. When Abishai raised her and held her against him to ease her in a fit of retching, it seemed to her that he was lifting her up and bearing her into a long-gone night. "I must take care," she thought, "or I will lose the unborn child." . . . When he went from the room to bring her a clean napkin, she fancied that he had run up to the chamber in the loft room to fetch a lamb's tail. "Ah," she said, seeing him return with nothing but a piece of white cloth, "it is not there, it is gone." Her husband came now and then to ask foolish questions concerning her health, but she could never be certain, when she heard his step in the hall, as to what form he would take when he stood at the foot of her bed. Sometimes he was a slender young bandit, with great sorrowing eyes and flowing red hair. Sometimes he wore gold chains and crimson cloth, and his beard flowed feathery and pied across his breast. "No, now," she said, "I must go from you, seeing that you have grown so rich and old." . . . She was quieter and more lucid when Haggith was by her; Haggith could catch the interweaving years and hold them still. To Haggith she would utter maxims and exhortations in an austere, authoritative voice. "Never lay salt upon a kid until it is well roasted," she would say, staring up into the serene face. "Salt toughens the meat. Red dots on an infant's flesh are nothing—any fool knows that they come with the heat of the sun."

There came a morning when she descended again, like a tired bird, out of chaos, into a place and an hour. It was sunrise; this was the King's palace; she lay dying against heaped pillows; and, for the moment at least, the beast within her gnawed no more. Cool, opalescent blueness shone beyond the windows, and a green curve of palm fronds swayed silvery between the earth and the sky. Why have I made so much of dying? she asked herself. Really, it is a very simple matter. It is necessary to die, and one dies. . . . She knew by the faint shadow which lay across her coverlet that it was Abishai who was with her. She knew also that he was not the round and rosy youth who had stood beside her on the hearth at Hebron; he was hard and leathery now with many years and many battles; his hair and beard were dry and grizzled; he was still foolish, still tender, but he was old. And that, too, she thought, smiling, men make too much of that. We struggle and mourn over the years, as though we brought forth each of them out of our bodies in bitter labor; and all the while it is time that bears us, and we need only lie quietly, sucking out life from time's breast. How needlessly we suffer, how stupid we are. . . .

She turned her head slowly against the pillow. "Abishai," she said.

"My lady Noi. . . ."

She knew by the sound of his voice that he had been weeping. Poor soul, she thought, holding out her hand to him, he has been crying all night long because I must die. . . . "It is as it should be," she said. "There is no reason to weep. We are, and then we are no more. Believe me, my beloved friend, it is as simple as blowing out a lamp or closing a door."

He bowed his head upon the coverlet and sobbed aloud.

No, now, she thought, he must stop this weeping. He will forget to fetch my morning tea. . . . She laid her hand upon his big, round head, and the warmth of his hair was wonderfully gratifying. "Let my friend come and sit upon the bed beside me and hold me against him, for I am very cold," she said.

She feared that the beast of pain would be wakened by her moving about, but Abishai lifted her so gently that there was not the slightest stirring within her. He held her in the warm curve of his arm. How good this is, she thought. How fortunate I am that my friend is with me in this hour. . . . "Behold, I am satisfied, I am completely happy," she said. "We suffer in this world only because we ask for too much."

"My lady Noi never asked for anything. She gave of herself to the world and took nothing in return," he told her, weeping.

"No, now, my friend, you are mistaken. I took nothing—I asked for little—but in the tabernacle of my heart I wanted much—I wanted the Star of Bethlehem, the King of Israel, the very jewel of the world. . . ." Then suddenly the thought broke upon her that this plump and hairy one had loved her from the hour when he first set eyes upon her, had loved her still, unmindful of the waning of her poor measure of loveliness, through all the years. Ah, God, she thought, so many years, as many years as I have loved the son of Jesse. Surely then I must not go forth without offering him some return for such love. . . .

She was very tired, and the beast had begun again to stir within her. She would have wished to discharge this ultimate obligation briefly by raising her lips to his, but she knew that her breath was heavy with the ravages within her. Then I must tell him a kindly lie, she thought. I must make him a gallant speech, and quickly, quickly, before the teeth of the monster have caught me and robbed me of speech. . . . She groped across what seemed to her a great distance, and found his hand, and lifted it to her lips. "I had a goodly comforter," she said. "I had so goodly a comforter that there were days when I—let my friend believe me, there were days when I thought—when I said to myself, 'If it had been Abishai, if it had only been Abishai who had come to collect the tribute in my brothers' house in the wilderness.'"

He bent and kissed her mouth, in spite of the heaviness of her breath. They kissed quietly, like children, and were not ashamed when they raised their eyes and saw that Haggith was at the door.

"My darling," said Haggith, "I have brought your tea. But if it pleases you to wait a little, I will carry it down to the servants and bid them keep it warm."

"No, no, I will take it now." She held out her hands to receive it. It was warm, it was sweet, and once she had begun to drink, she could not take the bowl from her lips. She drank all of it, and sank back against the pillows. But the beast was to be reckoned with. The beast sprang forward, black and horrible, ready to fasten its teeth into its torn prey.

She cried out in a loud voice then, more in amazement than in pain. She was being drawn slowly backward, beyond the reach of the monster, beyond Abishai's face and Haggith's face, beyond the bed, the room, the world. . . .

"What is it? What is it, my mother and my sister?" cried Haggith, weeping.

"Nothing, it is nothing," she said, and patted Haggith's hand, and died.

⇜ XIII ⇝

ISRAEL had reason to remember the day when crystals of ice had fallen out of the purplish clouds. Within two moons, many of the farmers of Benjamin, Ephraim, and Judah knew themselves to be ruined. Where they were wont to reap twenty ears of grain, they reaped the single ear that had survived the storm—and that ear was lean and blasted. The great families who owned tracts of land with vines and orchards complained that no profits could be laid aside. Grapes, olives, figs, and pomegranates would keep their savings from shrinking too perceptibly; still, it would be impossible to add new heads to their herds or to build new wings to their houses now. But those sons of Jahveh—and they numbered into the tens of thousands—who had nothing but their grainfields to sustain them were in desperate case. Many of them lived from hand to mouth. They bartered their produce, and since they had no wheat, they were without all the necessities which wheat had bought for them in the past—oil, cloth, wine, meat. The public storehouses in the great cities were immediately thrown open. In Jerusalem, Hebron, Gilgal, Jericho, and Beth-shan, the children of God stood in long queues, like beggars, before the doors, each waiting to receive his cake of raisins, his little measure of oil, his portion of the waning stores of barley, millet, and wheat.

The herdsmen also suffered. The green veil of meadow which the Lord had seen fit to throw over the rocky face of the wilderness had always been precarious; the stones from heaven had left it more meager than ever; and within three moons it was eaten away by the kine, the goats, and the sheep. For a while, the breadless cities were glutted with meat, for it was better to kill and sell than to let the beasts die lean for want of grass. Then the meat became strong, dark, unwholesome. Even the hungry began to look upon it with dubious eyes.

The King of Israel did what he could to relieve the general distress. In addition to drawing heavily upon the public treasuries, he took a third of his wealth and sent it far and wide to be given in exchange for grain. But all his efforts were fruitless. The Syrian crop was small at best; Phoenicia raised next to nothing, depending as she did upon Philistia for bread; and Philistia herself was more impoverished than Israel. Hailstones as large as a child's fist had fallen in Gaza and Askelon. And if the sons of Jahveh had reaped only a twentieth of their usual harvest, a bare fiftieth had been left to the sons of Dagon and Astarte. After long negotiations, arrangements were made to procure a thousand bushels of wheat out of Egypt, and two caravans set out from Goshen to deliver the grain to Hebron, whence it was to be distributed throughout the land. But the starving tribes of the south fell upon the caravans in the stretches of the southern desert. Some of the grain was lost in the sand during the skirmish, much of it was pounded into flour in Caleb, and the rest was sold secretly and at an outrageous price to anyone who had the proper amount of gold.

Within a few moons after the harvest, meat and cheese disappeared altogether from the market stalls in the cities. Nuts and honey were still procurable, but at such a cost that only the rich could buy; a bowl of goat's milk, thin and bluish, was considered a delicacy; a partridge caught in the hills was worth a turquoise, and a large hare could bring three rings of gold. In Jerusalem, the booths offered the same gaudy and sickening display morning after morning—pomegranates, grapes, melons, dates; and the greater part of the population was reduced to a diet of fruit and wine. And then a change came upon the children of Jahveh. Their skin turned dry, and their bellies became bloated. They could no longer think of anything but their hungering bodies. In the market place they plucked away the folds of their garments to show their shrinking arms and bony chests, and they talked of the looseness of their bowels and the color of their vomit incessantly and without the slightest shame.

Long after everything but fruit and wine had disappeared from the bazaars of Jerusalem, the members of the King's household might have continued to nourish themselves on cheese and bread and meat. But the King threw them all into consternation by announcing that whatever was produced upon his estates would henceforth go to swell the public treas-uries. "While the children of God eat fruit, I will eat fruit. And if the day comes when they must eat roots and grass, then I also will eat roots and grass," he said.

His determination to take unto himself no more than the common man's little share rose not only out of a desire to be just but also from an upsurge of gratefulness. From the moment when he had heard of the failure of the crops, he had waited for the sons of Jahveh to lay the blame at his door. Whenever he left the palace, he set out in fear, telling himself, Today one of them will cry aloud, "Behold the murderer of Uriah, who has brought ruin upon the land." . . . But the hungry days dragged on, and no such accusation was made; those whom he met in the streets offered him the usual obeisance; those who stood at the foot of the altar gazed at him with sorrowful and gentle eyes. And he knew that they spared him out of love.

Thereafter, he was obsessed by the thought of the people. He would sit for hours on a bench in his garden, covertly studying the workmen who had been called in to reinforce the wall. He was startled at the discovery that the old bondsman who had been sweeping the common room for these last ten years was blind in one eye. He would find himself staring in the midst of the sacrificial ritual at some starved young mother who was pressing her flabby breast against the mouth of her emaciated child. He made attempts to speak to Bath-sheba and Abiathar and Joab concerning these things, but he could utter only such obvious generalities as "Israel is the people," or "It is terrible, it is inconceivable, hundreds of thousands of men and women and children are lying down this night without having broken bread."

And yet, as the famine persisted and their case grew worse, he found it more and more difficult to pity them. That ugliness which had manifested itself at first only in their bodies began to show in their natures also; it was as if the lack of bread had turned back the centuries and transformed them all into the dark, aggressive monsters that had ranged in legendary days over the wilderness. Reason deserted them. They knew very well that a certain portion of even this miserable crop must be laid aside for next year's planting—there must be seed if millet and barley and wheat were not to pass forever from the face of the earth. Yet in Hebron and Gilgal the multitude attacked the storehouses, leaving the dead bodies of the overseers among the emptied sacks.

They fell, too, into retrogressive ways of appeasing angry divinity. Necromancers flourished. Obscene and Canaanitish rites of fertility were practiced in those grottoes which had once been sacred to heathen gods. Jahveh appeared again in the guise of the bull and the snake—He became such a one as might delight in a street strewn with the entrails of pigeons, in a dead infant sealed up in a jar, in a bowl filled with human blood. It was said that the charred body of an infant had been buried under one of the black stones at Gilgal and that a field in Judah had brought forth grain out of season because it had been watered with a virgin's blood.

No, it was not easy to pity and love them. And yet, in these many moons of exigency, not one had lifted up his voice to speak of the grave in the Ammonite plain. Even the prophet Nathan, who came often now to the court and enjoyed marked indications of favor from Bath-sheba, showed no signs of bringing that matter to light again.

But in spite of the fact that the prophet Nathan indicated only the best intentions toward the King, the son of Jesse could scarcely endure the sight of the old man's face. Since the days of the siege of Rabbah, David had hated him with a hot hate; Bath-sheba had not been able to mitigate that hate in the slightest, and the activities of the prophet during the time of the famine had increased it threefold. In the streets, on the high place before the ark, in the common room of the palace, he preached God's demand for a sacrifice. The filth of weeks had accumulated upon him— while God was angry, he could not bathe, he said. He spoke of the slaying of Jephthah's daughter and of the fact that the eldest son of every family in Israel was once dedicated as a blood sacrifice to the Lord. And the King was furious at his own inability to forbid the old man to speak to the multitude.

"Whenever the prophet opens his mouth," he said to Bath-sheba, "evil comes out of it. They are fleshly enough without him, thinking always of their hungering bodies and their dung and their vomit. But he is working them into such a state that they will be satisfied only by some unthinkable spectacle of agony and blood."

Those grave eyes, whose innermost depths he could seldom reach of late, were fixed upon him in mild reproach. "I could wish," she said, "that my lord the King might teach himself to hide whatever wrath he may feel against the prophet. The man is ignorant, I know, and filled with coarse and dark imaginings. But his hold upon the people is as a band of iron, and, knowing this, I have dealt graciously with him, lest he should turn his heart against my lord. Since the death of our first little one, Nathan has said nothing but good concerning David and all his house. And that is fortunate—for who can say what might come of it if he should raise his voice against us now?"

He made no answer. All that she said was prudent and just; and yet, whenever he thought of it thereafter, he was burdened by a sense of uneasiness that sometimes mounted to distress. In her relationship to him she was blameless, loyal, tender; but he was disquieted and puzzled by her relationship to the rest of the world. She was equally gracious to Hushai and Nathan, and she indicated equal dislike for Joab and Ahitophel. If it could be said that she had any friends among women, Michal and Abigail were her companions. To Noi, she had been courteous and remote; to Haggith, she showed a positive coolness. Now that he paused to consider, it became plain to him that she had never cared for any of the children save her own. Tamar and Absalom had disturbed her; she had spoken of them as one might speak of some rare, exotic flower which one suspects of exuding a poisonous dew. Meribaal and Adonijah she neither blamed nor praised. She listened with obvious forbearance to their long conversations; and sometimes, when she and David were in bed, she would bury her head in the pillow and burst into a fit of laughter, remembering some utterly naïve thing that one or the other of them had said. Twice or thrice, in the feverish days of the famine, it occurred to the King that her cordiality toward Nathan might not have arisen entirely out of fear. She knew that the prophet swayed the people. Could it have entered her mind that he would be an excellent partisan? And to what purpose? Surely she could not be dreaming of setting both Absalom and Adonijah aside to make room for the little Solomon upon the throne.

Such thoughts, he assured himself, were the groundless imaginings of a man who had become lightheaded on a diet of wine and fruit. Two or three times he spoke in her presence of the return of Absalom, and her air was reassuring—she neither flushed nor paled, and she offered no more arguments. She too had grown very thin and languid with the protracted fasting. Her body—slight, precious, spare—at once tormented and delighted him. He was shamed and baffled—he loved it too much, and he could not love it enough. His sleep was light, and he would waken often and sit brooding above her. Her cheek, pressed against the pillow, her lips, fallen open like a child's, the soft, unintelligible sounds that sometimes issued from her throat—all these conjured up in him a weakening tenderness.

One evening toward the end of the winter rains, the peace of his common room was disturbed by the unexpected arrival of the prophet. Nathan had been preaching to the multitude on the high place, had been interrupted by a downpour in the midst of a sermon, and had stopped at the palace on his way to his own house. The long chamber was almost empty. Haggith and Hushai sat talking quietly near a window; the young men had gone to an upper room to pore over an ancient inscription given to them by Abiathar; and Bath-sheba was in an upper chamber with Solomon. Haggith, who had taken a quiet delight in seeing her lord discomfited ever since the day of Noi's death, arose at the approach of the unwelcome visitor and went from the room.

"Tell my lady Bath-sheba that Nathan is with us," said David to Hushai.

The old counselor went slowly up the stairs, leaving the King and the prophet alone.

David approached the couch on which the prophet had settled himself and sat down beside him. The dank, unwholesome smell of filthy garments and accumulated sweat that always emanated from Nathan's person had been increased by the rain. Let her come down soon, thought the King of Israel, before my disgust reveals itself in my face. . . . Then he turned to the prophet and asked in a false and sprightly voice, "What matters did you make plain to the people tonight?"

"Tonight," said the prophet, looking sternly into David's face, "I preached concerning the ungodliness of the House of Kish."

It was a subject so remote from the present crisis that the King of Israel could not refrain from asking, "Wherefore?"

"Wherefore? Surely the understanding of the King is not less than the understanding of the multitude."

His inability to follow the fanatical course of the man's thoughts betrayed him into the role of a pupil; and the prophet, leaning close and speaking in a strident voice, instructed him as though he were a child.

"There is a famine in the land. The famine is a punishment from the Lord. But who is it that our God punishes? Is it the people? No; since the first days of David's reign, the people have been mindful of Jahveh and all His commandments."

The prophet fell silent, and David was obliged to make himself childish and ridiculous by asking, "What then?"

"If it is not the people, then can it be the King? The people have pondered that. The priests in all parts of the land have pondered it. I have pondered it myself. And we have all arrived at the same conclusion: it is not the King of Israel. Though the King has sinned, he has atoned, and he has bought his forgiveness at a bitter price. Two of his sons are dead and one dwells apart from him among the tents of Geshur."

Nathan had spoken of the King's misfortunes and the King's penance with such evident relish that David itched to strike him across the face. Let her come soon, he thought again. . . . And a second time he said, "What then?"

"My brothers the priests of Gibeon in Benjamin—it is they who have found the cause. Saul is the sinner who has brought this evil upon us. When he quarreled with Samuel over Agag the Amalekite, then he incurred the anger of the Lord. That anger was suspended until the time when the crops grew green this year. Then it was hurled upon us in the form of cold stones out of heaven."

The King of Israel was hard put to it to discipline his face into the proper seriousness. "Surely," he said to the prophet, "the Lion of Benjamin suffered enough to appease the wrath of the Lord." Then he fell silent, hearing Bath-sheba's light step upon the stair.

She came up to them smiling, and held out both her hands to the prophet. "How is it," she said in a voice at once chiding and tender, "that my lord has not offered a little heated wine to this man of God, seeing that he is drenched to the skin and bitter cold?"

"We have forgotten wine in our concern with higher matters," said the prophet, kissing her hand. "We have been speaking together of Jahveh's anger against the House of Kish. Be gracious and permit us to follow the business to its end, and then there will be time for wine." He kept his hold on her hand and drew her down beside him on the couch, and the King was sick at heart to see the attentive look that she turned upon the man.

"What is there to say of the House of Kish?" asked David coldly. "The House of Kish is ashes and dust."

"Nevertheless, the seed of Jonathan flourishes in the King's palace," Nathan said. "Meribaal eats at the King's table as though he were a beloved son who might some day sit upon the throne of Israel. The Lord and the people thirst after vengeance upon the House of Kish, and Jonathan's son is daily before their eyes. . . ."

David clenched his hands at his sides. "We will not speak of this," he said.

Bath-sheba, poised and circumspect even before the thought of the blood sacrifice of Meribaal, lifted a restraining hand. Her lips parted upon an unspoken warning.

"We will not speak of this," he said again, fixing his eyes upon her. "Whosoever speaks of this, be he man or woman, will see my face no more."

He turned then and departed from them without another word. On the stair, he heard her voice breaking the charged silence. She will not rise and follow me, he thought. She is shrewd, she is coolheaded, she is calling now to the steward of the house, telling him to open a new wineskin. And she will sit for another hour or so with my mortal enemy, chatting and sipping heated wine. . . .

∽§ XIV §∾

It seemed to the King of Israel that no winter had ever been so bleak or so long as the winter of that year. Perhaps it was only that he suffered more, having less warmth in his vitals and less flesh upon his bones. But, with the rest of Israel, he came to believe that God had sent a scourge of rain together with the scourge of famine. A dampness too pervading for the braziers to dispel hung upon the common room; mold gathered on the figs and raisins in the store chambers; and whenever he looked from the windows, he saw a landscape crossed by gray, diagonal lines of rain.

These days he looked out of the windows less and less. Morning, noon, and evening, in ever-increasing numbers, the sons and daughters of Jerusalem stood at the great brazen gate, pressing against the grillwork, thrusting their emaciated arms through the openings, lifting their faces above the metal scrolls and leaves—hideous faces, faces of the living dead, all gaping mouths, wide nostrils, and staring eyes. And they were not only starved—they were evil. Whenever he beheld them, he wondered which of them had disemboweled a pigeon and wound its entrails around a twig for the greater glory of God, which had led a virgin daughter into a barren field to be raped by a priest of Baal, which had strangled a newborn child and buried it under a cornerstone.

He sensed their uncleanness in their arrogance—a strange mixture of boldness and fright. They advanced and retreated and advanced again, like beasts that have tasted flesh and will die if they must for the sake of tasting more. Every day they drew a little closer to the moment when they would call for a blood sacrifice and name a name. It was known throughout Jerusalem that Meribaal was their quarry—from the beginning they had made that plain by growing more excited when he appeared at one of the windows or passed an open door. But their fear was still a leash upon their desire; they had brought themselves only to the point of uttering vituperation against the House of Kish. "How little the people change," David thought. "These are the same stupid and brutal jests that were howled in the streets of Beth-shan long ago, when the corpses of my brother and my lord hung at the feet of Astarte." But, for all his scorn, he feared them. He drew the curtains and shut the doors and lived in dank, airless semi-dark. He sent futile messages into Syria and the land of Goshen, begging for wheat. He slept only fitfully, and he rose often from his bed to pray for guidance.

"Hear me, O God," he said, always in a whisper, lest the beloved sleeper should wake, "I have sinned, I have sinned grievously all my days, and now that time has depleted my strength for sinning, now that passion is transformed in me into a baffled tenderness, I grieve for my sins with all that is left of my heart. From the moment when I was conceived, I have been heavy with transgression. Like all the sons and daughters of men, in the closed darkness of the body that bore me, I knew myself and only myself. I nourished my flesh upon the blood of another; and I came into the light of the sun loving myself with an overweening love. Out of self-love, I sinned against my father and my mother, my brothers and my sisters. You, who see all things, saw how it was with me then, how I snatched from our poverty all that was best and took it unto myself, how I thought that those who were gathered together beneath Jesse's roof had no purpose in this world save to love me and find me fair.

"It is said that the years of our youth are blessed years. If I was blessed in Ephes-Dammim and in Gibeah, I knew it not. One fire within me burned away all the green delights: I longed for greatness, and whatsoever came into my hand was nothing to me, inasmuch as I desired to possess the world. I turned my back upon the hills of Judah and called them dung. I yearned after Benjamin and carried like an ulcer in my bowels the knowledge that I was a Judahite. Out of my longing for greatness, I held my tongue when it was said that I had laid Goliath low. Out of my longing for greatness, I was wily and devious in my dealings with Saul, who loved me. Out of my longing for greatness, I took the King's daughter when I loved her not. My desire to lift myself up was such that I broke Israel in twain, and sold myself to the uncircumcised, and marched up with the ranks of Philistia against the host of God, and stood idle among the burned pillars of Ziklag while the beloved was being torn by the brazen spikes that I had held in the palm of my hand. In Gibeah and in the wilderness I sinned in order to be mighty, to possess Israel. Behold, I am mighty, the land is in my hand, and what is Israel to me this night?

"All that I yearned after in the days of my youth You gave to me freely in the years of my ripeness. Surely, I said in my heart, surely I am finished now with sinning. Surely I will be righteous henceforth and sin no more. But love, released at long last from myself and from the contemplation of glory—love, buried unfulfilled in the Gibean garden—love, wasted and cheated in the wilderness, surged up and demanded its just due of me at last. Out of passion, I took my neighbor's wife and slew my neighbor. Out of passion, I lay at the side of the beloved while the one true wife, whom I took in idleness and married at Your commandment, went forth without so much as a word from me into the everlasting dark. Self-love, longing for greatness, passion—these have driven me into transgression. Now that I look with distaste upon my gaunt and aging body, now that my greatness is a burden upon me, now that my virility is less than my yearning, I earnestly repent, O Lord.

"Yet, even though I no longer put forth my hand to do evil, I am not finished with sinning. In my declining years, a sin of weakness has come upon me—I do not know what name to put upon it—tenderness, an old man's blind and doting love. Out of Your bounty, O God, I was given five children, yes, and a foster child, the son of the first beloved. They came to me late, and I loved them beyond reason. I said in my foolish heart, There is no evil in them. I rejoiced in them and found them all whole and pure and fair. And behold how it is with them now, what I have done to them out of too much love. This night two of them dwell in the desert among the black tents of Geshur, one ravaged and shamed, the other with the mark of Cain upon his brow. A third, slain by his brother, is sealed up forever in the darkness of the burial cave. A fourth sleeps an uneasy sleep, knowing that the people are gathered before the gate calling for his blood. There were six, and out of six only two have been saved from violence. And all this was brought about because of my weakness. Had I not been so tender with Tamar that I could not force marriage upon her, had I not refused to see the lust in the face of Amnon, had I not closed my eyes against the thirst after vengeance that was in Absalom, then the House of David would be at peace this night. Had I sent the son of Jonathan back to the lands of his people, to dwell in his own house and see to the fields of his fathers, who would have thought to ask that he be given to God? Rape, murder, blood sacrifice—these are the fruits of my blindness, my doting love.

"Lord God of Hosts, now that the winter of my life is upon me, I am weary with striving and sick unto death with sinning. Believe me, I have but one desire left—I hunger and thirst after righteousness. I beg You then, let me live out these last few years in decency and peace. Behold, the people are gathered before my house; they are evil with starvation; they lust after blood. It is not out of self-love, not out of longing for greatness, not out of passion, no, not even out of doting that I cannot render the last of the House of Kish into their hands to be torn apart. It is that I can no longer put forth my hand to do evil, even to preserve what remains of my greatness, even to save what is dear to me. It is only that I would deal justly now, with clean hands and a pure heart. But I have grown old in the ways of sin, and I am as a child in matters of righteousness. Therefore, do not depart from me, stand between me and the evil which is at the gate, O my God."

Since the day when the people had first gathered before the gate, David could not rest until he had visited Meribaal's bed. Seven of Joab's strongest guardsmen had been stationed before the room. At first they had been startled to see the King of Israel moving toward them down the corridor with a lamp in his hand; but now that the arrival of the regal apparition had become a matter of course, they merely bowed and opened the chamber door. They had learned also to close the door after he had entered. It was plain that no one was to look upon the King when he stood beside the young man's bed.

He remained there long, shuttering the lamp with his curved fingers so that the full glow of it would not fall upon the sleeper's face. In these days of fear, Meribaal had come to bear a much more marked resemblance to his father. His face had whitened and sharpened; a blue vein beat in the hollow of his temple; and there were webby shadows around his eyes. Save for the poor, twisted feet that were discernible beneath the coverlet, the King of Israel might well have thought that he was beholding the dead beloved. Forgive me, he would say in his heart, that for your father's sake I loved you with too strong a love. Forgive me that I did not restore the lands of Kish to you and send you forth to plow them, but kept you, out of baffled tenderness for *him*, like a young child, forever at my knees. Now it is too late—I cannot send you forth—they would fall upon you on the way and take your blood. Forgive me, then, for all the evil I have brought upon you and upon your house, and for all the evil that is yet to come. Believe me, if they take your blood, they will take it only after they have taken mine. This I will do; God help me, I can do no more than this. . . .

There came a morning when he could no longer wait. The hour of violence was at hand, and he must rouse himself. After a night of much meditation and little sleep, he came early into the common room and went to the shrouded window to look out upon the street. They were all there pressing against the gate; the sons and daughters of Jerusalem had been gathered there since the first gray light. And as he peered through the space between the wall and the curtain, ashamed that a king should have come so low as to spy upon his own people, he saw a single hand thrust itself through a brazen scroll and fumble with the latch. He stepped back from the window, strode with all the fury of an embattled warrior across the long chamber, unfastened the bolts, and flung wide the door. He saw now that they had actually unlatched the gate; it had been pushed inward only very slightly, but it was now a breach in the untouchable wall between his house and death. As soon as they saw him standing before them, terrible in his rage, they retreated. He stood glaring at them long enough to deceive them into the belief that there was no fear in him. Then he turned and slammed the door, so violently that all the pillars shook. "They will have blood," he said to his steward. "They will have blood, these rotten dogs, and I will give them blood. Send down now to the encampment and say to the captain of the host that there is a matter which I would discuss with him at the hour of the evening bread."

XV

THERE WAS a rule in the King's house that no grave matter should be carried to the table. That night there was no departure from the custom. The company ate the meatless stew, the nuts, the pomegranates, and the dates as though no multitude waited beyond the muffled windows; the son of Zeruiah bore himself as though he had been called up for a pleasant visit; and Meribaal chatted as though no hollow voices were calling his name. It was true that the servants were somewhat nervous; the steward's voice faltered once or twice, and one of the maidservants had plainly been weeping. But these lapses were covered by the endless conversation that flowed from the captain of the host. Lean, lank, looking more than ever like an old jackal, he regaled them with the raw and colorful tales of the encampment, constantly skirting the forbidden, and walking perilously on the thin line between humor and ribaldry. When they rose from the table, all of them were weak with laughter. The King of Israel, leading his guest up the stairway to the privacy and quiet of the royal bedchamber, felt breathless and shaken. He paused in the hall to take up a lighted lamp. The room was dark as night, even though the sun had just set; every curtain was drawn against the milling, murmuring crowd. One after another, he kindled the lamps on the little tables, on the clothes chests, in the niches of the wall. But the brightness seemed spurious and feverish; it was spoiled by the knowledge that beyond the shrouded window hung a pale and lucid sky.

He went very slowly about the business of settling the captain in a comfortable chair, pouring the wine, and seating himself on the edge of the bed. Surely his nephew saw the extent of the people's arrogance; surely he would offer his aid unasked; surely he would say in a moment, "Let me bring up a thousand out of the camp of God to shoot a few arrows into their insolent faces." But the son of Zeruiah sat paring his fingernails and said nothing.

"Well, then?" said the King of Israel.

"Well, then?" Joab said.

"You see how it is with us, how we are besieged in our own house——"

The captain looked the King full in the face. "Has my lord called me up to ask me to loose the host upon the sons and daughters of Jerusalem?"

"Even so."

Joab pulled at his lean fingers until the knuckles cracked. "The King is the King. Whatsoever he asks, even though it be utter folly, it will be done," he said.

"Folly? Wherein would it be folly?"

"Is David prepared to put all those who dwell within the gates of the city to the sword?"

"No, now, a few volleys of arrows will shatter their insolence. A few volleys of arrows——"

The son of Zeruiah shook his head. "Believe me, my dear uncle, you are mistaken. A hundred volleys would not suffice. Unless the son of Jesse is willing to make war against all the children of Jerusalem and, after them, against the farmers and the herdsmen and the priests and the townsmen of Judah and Israel, let him put this matter out of his thoughts. I love my uncle, and when I tell the host to draw their bows against the people, then I write the warrant for his death."

In the long silence that came between them, they heard the angry murmuring at the gate. And the King of Israel lay back upon the bed, thinking in his heart: Has it truly come to this? These walls and the garden wall beyond them—are they indeed all that stands between us and violence? Will it come so soon then, tomorrow or the day after tomorrow? It is unthinkable, it is impossible; we live, we breathe, we laughed around the board tonight. . . .

"What shall I do?" he said.

"Do? In God's name, give them blood. No, now, do not rail at me. It is not I, it is Bath-sheba's minion, it is Nathan, who stirred them up to howl after human sacrifice. There was a time when my lord the King might have seen that the ranting hypocrite was strangled on his way home in the dark of the moon. But my lord would not touch a hair upon his sacred head, my lord would have above all things, even above the safety of his children and his throne, clean hands and a pure heart. What shall you do? Give them blood."

There had been much in the tirade to stir up wrath, but the King had no strength left for rage. "Nevertheless, I cannot give the young man into their hands," he said. "I have sworn before God that they will take his blood only after they have taken mine."

The captain of the host rose and stood above the bed. "No, now, who spoke of the young man? Why should David render up the son of Jonathan when there are others who will serve as well? Seven others—believe me, I can name you seven. Give these dogs seven in exchange for one, and they will go their ways rejoicing. If it is the House of Kish that has brought famine upon us, how is it that they dwell in Benjamin in peace—the seven tall sons whom Saul himself begot upon Rizpah the concubine?"

The King of Israel raised himself upon his elbows. The children of Rizpah were nothing to him; he had seen them only twice or thrice. Seven tall, faceless beings moved across his remembrance, and his heart cried out, What are they to me? I know them not. . . .

"It would be a simple matter," said the voice of the tempter, "to outwit the prophet. My uncle need only walk into his garden this night and say to the people, 'Behold, I will give you sons in place of a son's son. Where

521

Nathan has taught you to ask for one, I will be more openhanded yet. I will send into Benjamin and bring you seven."

He barely heard the words. He lay back upon the bed and remembered the common room of Saul's house in Gibeah, curtained against the fierce light of a day long past. The Lion of Benjamin had laid violent hands upon his lutist. His lutist lay on the floor before him, half-strangled and weeping. And Rizpah the concubine came forward, so that her fragrant, opulent body stood between the madman and his prey. For my sake, thought David, she was called bitch and whore. She sheltered me in the folds of her garment and I swore to the God of Covenants that I would set her children on the high seats of cities, and call her my mother. . . .

"Only speak of it to no one until it is a finished matter," the son of Zeruiah said. "Above all, make no mention of it to Bath-sheba, for she will carry it to Nathan, inasmuch as they are boon companions and would rise up together to defend the sons of Rizpah, who in no wise stand between Solomon and the throne."

He saw the black implication, but he thrust it from him. Another time, he thought, another time I will make him eat them one by one, the words that he has said this night to poison my heart against my beloved. . . .

"Come, now, let the King my lord rise up from his bed and tell the people that he will give them the sons of Saul and Rizpah to be a blood sacrifice."

God of Hosts, he thought, why, when I hunger and thirst after righteousness, do You hold out to my lips only another cup of evil, more foul than those I have drained before? Rizpah has lived long and suffered much. She stood between me and the claws of the Lion, and behold how I have repaid her. I marched toward Gilboa with the uncircumcised; when the arrows of the heathen pierced the flesh of her lord, I was not at his side. And when she found a little quiet in Abner's house, he was slain at the hands of my kin—even this serpent who whispers to me now. Then shall I take her seven sons also and give them to the people to be torn apart? . . .
"I cannot do such a thing as this," he said.

The son of Zeruiah shrugged and sauntered over to the window. He laid his hand upon the curtain and plucked it aside, only a little. It was enough —anything was enough—to stir up the multitude below. "Meribaal!" they shouted. "Bring out Meribaal, that we may give him to God."

"How is it," said David, "that the Lord should so ring me round with evil that wheresoever I turn, I wound and kill and sow the seeds of sorrow upon the face of the earth?"

"How is it," said Joab, "that the Star of Bethlehem should be transformed under my eyes into a weak and canting fool?"

There was no anger in the King; he remembered too well how many times he had cast the name of "pig" and "dog" into his nephew's face. He has changed less than I in the crucible of the years, he thought, and it is small wonder that he finds me indecisive and overpious, now that I am growing old. . . .

"Will you give them Meribaal?" Joab said.

"No. Come away from the window. Let the curtain alone."

"In God's name, then, give them the sons of Rizpah."

"If I were to behold the sons of Rizpah rent apart, I would tear out my eyes."

"Why should you behold it? Scatter gold among these dogs that are gathered before the gate and bid them depart into Benjamin and take the sons of Saul from the houses in which they dwell. Look, now, I myself will send two thousand of the host along with the multitude into Gibeah, to see that the thing is accomplished there. Let the sons of Saul be taken in Benjamin and hung upon the high place in Gibeah, where the priests of Nob were slain. Thus we cut off the heads of two serpents with a single stroke—we gratify the people and we avenge Saul's sin against the priests of Nob."

"Saul's sin? It was I who betrayed those innocents into the hands of Saul."

"The sin lies where the people believe it lies. Come, now, arise and send up the people to give the sons of Rizpah to God."

"Speak of it no more. I cannot do it. I have done enough. I stand to my knees in the blood which I have already shed. I can shed no more."

"Then you will die."

"Then I will die. To be dead is to be at peace."

The son of Zeruiah walked across the room and sat down close to the King upon the bed. "Come, now," he said, laying his hand gently upon David's knee, "let us speak no more of such improbable occurrences as the King's death at the hands of the sons and daughters of Jerusalem. It is blood of the House of Kish that the multitude would pour out before the Lord. And it will take days—a week, two weeks—before Nathan can turn their wrath aside from Saul and fix it upon the household of the King of Israel. He will find it necessary first to remind them diligently of that which they—and he—have so far chosen to forget: that Bath-sheba was once the wife of Uriah the Hittite, who fell without succor from his fellow warriors in a sally against the Ammonites. . . ."

He paused, and in the ensuing silence David again heard the voices of the multitude.

"The prophet is all-powerful with them now," Joab said. "He has taught them to cry out after Meribaal, and he can likewise teach them to cry out against Bath-sheba and Solomon. Unless my lord gluts them with blood, Nathan will use their blood lust against David's house. Do not deceive yourself. Bath-sheba is vulnerable—both she and the lad Solomon. You they will not touch, for you are anointed with holy oil and the crown is upon your brow. But once they have called her adulteress, there is nothing to save her, nor is there anything to save one whom they consider an ill-begotten child."

The King rose from the bed and leaned his head against the wall and covered his face. "Lord God of Hosts," he said, "how have You dealt with

Your servant that You have brought him to this pass? You have so hemmed me in with evil that whatsoever I do, whether I put forth my hand to the right or to the left, I bring down death upon an unoffending head. They have said in the tabernacles and the high places that You have created man so that he may observe Your laws and fulfill Your purposes. But what are Your laws and Your purposes? That the sprout should be smitten by stones out of heaven, that the multitude should grow foul with starvation, that whatsoever is sound should become corrupt, that good should be rewarded with evil, that violence should prevail. No, now, there is but one law upon the earth—Your irrevocable law that all which lives must putrefy, that the end of everything is dissolution—this and this only is the purpose of the Lord."

"The King could find a better time to inquire into the nature and the purposes of God," the son of Zeruiah said. "While he spends himself and the hours in answerless questioning and in futile lamentations, he puts in jeopardy all that he has—his wife, his sons, his crown. Let him go to the window and tell the children of Jerusalem that he will give them Rizpah's seven. Let him say a few words, and he is strong again—the unassailable lord over Judah and Israel."

"Let the day perish wherein they anointed my head and made me king over Judah and Israel——"

"My uncle has a wife, whom he loves. . . ."

"Love, love—what has a righteous man to do with love? To love one is to do violence to another—not Uriah only, but Noi also, yes, and Michal and Abigail and Haggith—all these I have broken and cast aside because I have a wife whom I love. Would God I had died in the hills of Judah before my blood had begun to stir in my veins!"

"Nevertheless, David lived and sowed his seed and begot children, nor do these young men yearn, like their father, after death. Surely it is a man's duty that he should look to his children. . . ."

"How can a man look to his children? To have many children is to sit by helpless while the strong among them devour the weak. To lay up wealth for one's children is to make certain that only one of them will survive to anoint his father's grave."

"Have you forgotten that the people are at the gate, my lord?"

"No, I have not forgotten. But I cannot render the sons of Rizpah into the hands of the multitude."

Joab crossed the room and took David's hand and raised it to his breast. "I see how it is with my uncle," he said. "My uncle is as he was long ago before the burned city of Ziklag, when he was too distressed to rise up and save himself. Let me save him, then. Let the blood of the sons of Rizpah be charged to me. My uncle has told me a hundred times that I am bloody. And he is right—there are so many sins to my account that it is a small matter if I step a little deeper into blood. I say now before God that I do this thing at my own will and against the express command of the son of Jesse. But when I stand before them at the window, I must say that it is done in David's name. Otherwise——"

"No, now, my nephew can no longer hide my deeds from myself," said David. "Inasmuch as it is done for my sake, the evil is upon my head."

◆§ XVI §◆

It was a matter for wonderment among the children of Jerusalem that the King of Israel should wish to journey up to Gibeah where the seven sons of Saul and Rizpah hung in the heat of the sun. Surely the Lord required no such penance from him. The son of Jesse had wrought God's vengeance upon the House of Kish, and it was plain that God was satisfied. Seven days after the sacrificial slaying in Benjamin, a caravan laden with grain had come up out of Egypt. In the hills and plains of Israel, an early cessation of the winter rains had permitted an early planting; fresh and green and so thick that one could scarcely thrust a needle between blade and blade, the grain stretched down to the margins of the western sea. The Lord had blessed the flocks and herds also and made them fruitful. The wilderness was clothed again in a veil of tender green, whereof innumerable calves and kids and lambs might eat their fill. The forests of Benjamin and Ephraim were alive with partridges, and the roofs of the cities were visited by multitudes of doves. It was as if the tide of life, withheld for a year from the face of the earth, had surged back again with redoubled strength.

Only the high place in Gibeah had no part in this green resurrection. The soil had been poor and sour since the beginning of time; and the few weeds which had once grown there had not flourished since the day when Abner and Paltiel had dug the graves of the priests of Nob. Now, according to the tales that were being told from Beersheba to Dan, the last trace of grass had been trodden away by Rizpah's pacing feet, and the soil had been made barren forever with the salt of Rizpah's tears. For when the bodies of the seven had been hung before Jahveh on the high place in Gibeah, Rizpah had taken sackcloth and spread it upon a rock and seated herself upon it and watched over the bodies of her children, suffering neither the birds of the heavens to rest upon them by day nor the beasts of the field to harry them by night. For two moons, while the barley harvest grew green in the fields of Israel, she had dwelt alone with corruption, guarding her dead. Many had seen her from the roof tops of Saul's city, and a few Benjamites had advanced as far as the foot of the high place to bring her such poor nourishment as they had by them. Time and sorrow had transformed her into a lean hag, they said; her bony arms were forever striking out at the flapping ravens; her voice was hoarse with screaming at the beasts of prey. And now that the wrath of God had begun to pass from the land, they began to sicken at the thought of the old woman among the unburied corpses. "In God's name, let them be hidden decently away," they said. "They have become an ulcer upon the face of Benjamin." But the priests of Gibeon had decreed that there should be no burial until the flesh had completely fallen away; and no man dared to defy the priests, save only the King of Israel.

The son of Jesse came into the city of Gibeah attended by a small train; but he made it plain that he would go up to the high place alone. He tarried at the inn from noon until dusk, and no man save the innkeeper knew that the city was honored by his presence. At the hour of the evening bread, when none save the beggars and the outcasts lingered in the streets, he came forth like any pilgrim, his face muffled in a hood of black goat's-hair cloth, and made his way across the city which had seemed so vast to him in his youth. Time and the magnificence of Jerusalem had shrunken it to a pitiful image of the city that existed in his remembrance.

But I am not here to remember and to dream, he told himself as he hastened toward the high place. Why I am here, I scarcely know. Afterward, the children of Israel will say that I went up to decree that the bodies of the sons of Saul should be buried in the Gibean garden, but that will be merely a shadow of the truth. I could have commanded their burial from my house in Jerusalem, but to dispense mercy at a distance is not enough. I must meet her face to face in the presence of her dead. . . .

By the time he had come to the foot of the road that wound upward to the limestone promontory, evening had settled upon the world. The sunset had been brilliant—crimson, orange, golden—but now all the fires of heaven were quenched save only a line of yellow light on the rim of the west. As he climbed among the rocks and the lichen, he raised his eyes to the firmament; it was blessedly empty of carrion creatures; nothing marred the cool, lucid blue. There were moments when it seemed to him that the wind brought down the smell of corruption. Then he paused and girded himself to bear the sights and the scents above. God forbid, he thought, that I should show disgust in the presence of her dead. . . .

But he was stricken motionless at the top of the path when he beheld the high place. The earth was as gray as ashes and strewn with stones. The solitary tamarisk was vividly green in the dusk, and the bodies that hung from its branches looked long, soft, and white. The seven broken necks were turned awry; the seven heads were bent sideward and downward; the foliage thrust itself against the open hands and the dangling feet. And though the wind was at its highest, the air was unbearable. He gagged, and covered his face against the stench.

When his eyes first settled upon Rizpah, he did not take her for a living thing. She sat on a rock at the edge of the precipice, so still and dark against the pale sky that he took her for a jagged shaft of stone. Then she stirred and became—unbelievably—human and a woman; the head bent down in utter exhaustion, the knees spread wide, the long, lean arms hanging between the thighs. Her feet were bare and scarcely distinguishable from the ashen soil; her trailing hands were like the claws of a bird. Her face, darkened with filth and the fury of the sun, was half-covered with the folds of her black mourning hood. Her eyes were closed, but her head kept jerking upward, striving against sleep.

He walked forward until he stood some ten paces from her. It is not Rizpah, he said in his heart. Nothing—not time, not the death of the beloved, not murder, not blood sacrifice—could work so hideous a change as this. . . . She started wildly, and her small, bloodshot eyes, eyes of a sun-blinded bird, stared vacantly into his face.

"Get hence, get hence, get hence out of this charnel house," she said, rocking back and forth and pressing her hands to her brow. It was her voice—cracked and hoarsened, as ravaged as her face, but her voice, nevertheless.

"Rizpah," he said.

"What should a pilgrim do upon the high place of Gibeah? The priests of Benjamin have cursed it, and God has abandoned it. Turn and look what fruit the Lord has hung upon His holy tamarisk. They have been dead these two long moons, and the air is foul with their corruption."

He stepped backward and turned his head toward the tree.

"Move, move, move from the spot where you stand," she said. "For you stand upon the skull of Ahimelech, who was the high priest of Nob."

She knows me then, he thought. She arraigns me for the blood of the sons of Jahveh whom Doeg slew in the high place. . . . And he held out his hands to her and repeated her name. But no glimmer of recognition stirred in the red eyes, and he knew that he also had been completely transformed by the years, that there was not so much as a shadow left of that comely lutist who had made music in the King's garden more than thirty years ago. How should she know me? he asked himself. When she last beheld me, I was as the sun climbing through the midmorning. Now the noon of my glory is long past and the arc of my days sweeps downward, close to the night. . . .

"Ahimelech was a kindly man," she said, "and very skillful in the making of salves out of herbs. When my eldest was covered with a rash from head to foot, it was the high priest of Nob who made him whole. We smeared the salve upon his skin, and in the morning his flesh was cool and white as snow."

And even as she pointed toward the bloated body upon the branches, the sky was filled with the sound of flapping wings. Black against the luminous blue, the ravens descended, so close that their yellow beaks and scarlet mouths were visible in the fading light. She shrieked and gathered up stones and hurled them at the black ravagers. She ran forward and cursed the creatures and struck at them with her bony fists. He ran to her aid, into the stench of the decay, close to the loose hands and the dangling feet, with the flutter of the evil pinions in his eyes. Together they struggled against the ravens, and, when the ravens departed, they stood beneath the tamarisk, face to face.

He laid his hand upon her shoulder. "Rizpah," he said, "is it possible that you know me not?"

She sighed and drew her hand across her face. "Are you a kinsman out of Ephraim?" she asked him. "Do you come from the land where I dwelt when I was a child? Are you the son of my mother's sister? Do you know the house of my father? It was a stone house in a valley, and there was a stream before the door."

Ah, God, he thought, is this what You have done to a child out of Ephraim, who bathed her feet in a stream that flowed before her father's doorway, who ran about with her brothers and sisters when the fields grew dry after the winter rains? . . .

"I am the lutist," he said. "I am the Bethlehemite who played before your lord."

For less than a breathing-space her look was focused upon him. Then her eyes wandered, and she began to whimper. "Go hence and do not trouble me with such matters," she said, thrusting her hand beneath her hood and scratching her head. "It is enough that I must deal with ravens and foxes. I am old and weary, and no man should ask me to remember. How can I remember everything, seeing that there was so much, and all of it so long ago?"

She turned pettishly from him and walked in the direction of the edge of the promontory, toward the rock on which she had sat before the coming of the birds of prey. He came up behind her and laid his hand on her. "Look upon me, in God's name, look upon me and know me," he said. "I am David, the son of Jesse, the King of Israel."

"No, now, I would not wound you for all the world, inasmuch as you have lifted up your hand against the ravens for the sake of my dead. But if I am to speak truly, I must tell you this: he was a far more manly man than you—the King of Israel. If he were to stand behind you now——" She laughed a short, malicious laugh and pointed over his shoulder.

"Rizpah," he said, "I am David, King of Israel, who set the priests of Benjamin upon the children of Saul. The blood of your seven sons is upon my head."

"No, no." She came forward and laid her hand gently upon his breast. "It is not so. The pilgrim is gracious, the pilgrim is kind—for has he not fought at my side against the ravens? Out of all Israel, is he not the only one who has come up to watch with me in this place? It was the priests of Benjamin who hanged them up before the people, hanged them up and kicked the stones from beneath their feet, so that they writhed and turned blue, all seven. . . . There were a hundred faces gathered around the tamarisk that day. How should I forget a single one? The pilgrim's face was not among those faces. . . ."

"Nevertheless, believe me, it was I——"

Shyly, tentatively, her filthy and emaciated hand stroked his breast. "Would you know who it was that did the deed?" she said in a whisper. "I have told no other, but I will tell the pilgrim if he will swear to keep it locked forever behind his lips. Bend down, bend down now, and I will say it in your ear."

He bent and felt her hot breath against his neck.

"God," she said softly. "It was God who did the deed."

"No, now——"

"I tell you, it was God," she said, stepping back and fixing her burning eyes upon him. "The Lord of Hosts, Jahveh, even He. Evil and cruel He was before time began. He sat in the empty firmament and made the world, so that He might have a goodly place on which to vent His cruelty. He made the waters and the reefs beneath them so that the ships might be broken, so that they who go forth in ships might be swallowed up by the sea. He made the fish, big and little, so that the strong fish might devour the weak. He made the sparrow to be torn by the eagle, and the lamb to be torn by the lion. Earthquakes He made to sunder the fields, and molten fire to rend the mountains apart. All this He did, and this was much, but He was not satisfied, He must have more. Out of untroubled dust, He made man also. And of all His works, man is the highest, for no other thing can suffer so keenly or send up such cries for the delight of the Lord. And I—above all other creatures I am pleasing in His sight, inasmuch as He has tormented me most. For He raised me out of a valley in Ephraim and set me close to the throne and bound me flesh and spirit to the most valiant man in Israel. And lo, while I lifted up my voice in thanksgiving, He laughed and drove the Lion of Benjamin mad, and hounded him to the mountaintop, sore beset by arrows, and caused him to fall upon his sword. Then, being a fool, I bowed myself to His will, and I said unto Him: 'My beloved is gone, and I grow old. Yet have You left me a friend and a hearth and a familiar shoulder whereon to rest my head in the empty nights.' But He led the old man forth from his warm bed and murdered him before the gates, nor was I by him to lift up his head and hold it upon my knees. Surely, surely it should have been enough—even a lion in the wilderness, having eaten two, will turn aside, sated with blood. But the hunger of our Lord is never satisfied. Seven in a single day—behold them hanged upon His tree. While they were alive I tarried with each for the space of a moon, and they called me 'old mother' and set their children upon my knees. In their houses the curds and the wine are still upon the table, for they came and dragged the young men forth at the hour of the morning bread. The wives have taken their broods and fled into Moab lest the little ones also should be dashed against stones. And I—— Laugh, Evil One, laugh Your fill and fall silent, for I am as the trodden grape—there is not one drop of stuff for Your laughter left within me. Destroyer, Tormentor, Devourer, I tell You this —I know You, and You are evil and cruel. But I am not fearful of Your punishments. What can You do to me now?"

She had flung up her gaunt arms and was shaking her fists against the sky. He looked at the colorless firmament beyond her, and what he saw was more terrible even than the Malignant One whom she had seated upon the throne of heaven. He at least saw the agony that He had called into being, He at least heard the cries. But the pale Presence whose featureless face loomed before the King of Israel saw nothing and heard nothing. Infinitely remote, He stared blankly over the world which He had created. It was broken by earthquakes, divided by tidal waves, worn away by unceasing winds—and He did not see. From every hill and valley shrieks and prayers and moans went up, thousands and tens of thousands within the single hour, so multitudinous that they shook the very vault of heaven— and He did not hear. The wicked trampled upon the faces of the just, the weak were consumed by the pitiless strong, the child died in its cradle, the valiant were slain in the hour of their glory, the beautiful were torn upon the wheels of chariots, the crops were shattered by stones out of heaven, the scarlet lily was broken in the bud—but He neither laughed nor wept. And, feeling the unseeing eyes of God upon him, the son of Jesse turned cold.

Suddenly she darted past him, shrieking, for the air was filled with the sound of wings. Almost blindly now, since the last pale cast of light was fading from the firmament, they ran to the tamarisk and strove together against the birds of prey. This assault was longer and more violent than the first; it seemed to him that the whole darkening arch of the sky was filled with flapping pinions and open beaks; and twice, when he reeled backward, he lurched against the dangling feet of the dead.

"Pilgrim," she said at last, finding his hand in the darkness, "come and sit upon the stone and rest, for they are gone."

All that night he watched with her against the beasts of the fields and the birds of the heavens, and went forth with her many times to drive the fox and the raven away from her dead. Early in the morning he went down to the inn and wakened Abishai and Gad and Abiathar, and bade them come up with him to the high place. Together with these three, he climbed into the boughs of the tamarisk and cut down the bodies of the seven. Nor did he depart out of Gibeah until the sons of Saul had been buried in their father's garden, close to the cave which the Lion of Benjamin had prepared to receive the body of his beloved.

⚜ XVII ⚜

In the weeks after the burial of the seven sons of Saul, the captain of the host was greatly troubled for his lord. The man who came riding back from Gibeah was in no wise the man who had set out from the gates of Jerusalem. His hair and beard were whiter; his garments were thrown carelessly upon his body; his eyes looked large in his impassive face. The change was so marked that even the multitude said among themselves that within a matter of four days the King of Israel had grown old.

It was not outside the bounds of possibility that the son of Jesse, sitting out a whole night with the corrupted dead, had inhaled a fatal pestilence. Because of this foreboding, the captain of the host took every possible occasion to touch his lord, to clasp his arm or to embrace him. But there was no fever in the King; in fact, he was troublingly cold to the touch. Whatever illness had taken hold on him was not of the flesh, but of the spirit. Nor would he disburden himself in talk. Joab had no key to the mystery save an incomprehensible sentence that the King had spoken to Abishai on the way back to Jerusalem: "Let no man worship any more at the altar on the high place of Gibeah," he had said, "for the God who dwells in that place is a God who neither hears nor sees."

Slowly the son of Zeruiah was relieved of the fear that his uncle was about to depart from the earth, but he continued to be nagged by the other fears which had risen in its wake—fears for the succession, fears of the civil wars that might break out when the King of Israel was laid in his grave. The rightful inheritor of the crown was in Geshur—and who could say what Bedouin armies he might bring down upon the capital if he were to learn that his father was no more? The second son was an amiable youth, but unfit to reign. As for the third son, he was far too young to reach out and take the land unto himself, but his mother was a powerful woman, subtle and politic, and had plainly shown that she was not without hope of setting the fruit of her womb upon the throne. Hushai and Nathan stood with Bath-sheba against Absalom. Adonijah and Meribaal joined with Ahitophel and all Jerusalem in wishing to see the comely one again at his father's knees. Night after night, the son of Zeruiah turned these matters over in his thoughts; and evening after evening, in his high house in Jerusalem or in his tent in the encampment, he discussed the succession with the counselor Ahitophel.

The time was ripe for Absalom's return—that much at least was clear. That David desired such an event no sane man could doubt; otherwise he would have long since pronounced the edict of banishment. The young man was not in exile—he merely tarried with his mother and her father in a friendly land; there was no bloodguiltiness upon him—he had done no more than any honorable man would have done in his place. As for the aging King, who had once grown young again in the company of the youth of Jerusalem—surely, if for no other reason, the son of Maacah must be summoned home for his sake. Absalom alone could break the apathy that had settled upon him. Absalom alone could draw him from the upper chambers, where he sat all day, gazing at Bath-sheba and listening to Hushai praise the budding wisdom of the young Solomon.

Only a graceful device was needed to effect the young man's return. The captain considered a dozen possibilities and finally came upon a plan that delighted his heart. It was colorful, it was public, it would admit of no interference either from Bath-sheba or from the meddlesome Nathan. And half his pleasure in it was derived from the fact that he had borrowed it from the prophet. It would never have entered his head if he had not fallen to remembering that afternoon when Nathan had taken it upon himself to reprove the King of Israel publicly. A great assembly in the palace—a request for the King's judgment upon some entirely extraneous matter—an irrevocable sentence fallen from David's lips. . . . "Wᴏᴅ-

derful, wonderful!" he said aloud, to the amazement of his armor-bearer.
And he could barely contain himself until the hour when Ahitophel came
down to his tent to break the evening bread.

"Listen, now," he said, bending across the board and staring into the
old counselor's shortsighted eyes. "The barley harvest has been prodigious,
is it not so? What would be more fitting than that our lord should show
his gratefulness to God for such a crop, and offer up a sacrifice before the
ark, and spread a great feast in his palace on the same night? Mention it
to him tomorrow, and let me know his answer at once, for at this same
feast I will secure his explicit permission for the return of your darling,
even Absalom."

"How so?"

"I will send tomorrow to Tekoa after a woman of my acquaintance who
dwells in the place—a very subtle woman, clever and smooth of speech.
I will instruct her, and on the day of the feast she will come into the
King's house and throw herself upon her face before all the people, and
address herself to our lord——"

"Is she also then a friend of Absalom?"

"No, she knows him not, she never saw his face. She will speak to the
King of Israel concerning her two sons. Now ask me not whether she
has two sons—she has no issue whatsoever and was never married; to speak
the truth, I think she was once a whore. Before all the assembly she will
say to David that she had two sons, and that one of them rose up and
slew the other. This she will say after the manner of Nathan, who knew a
rich man with a flock and a poor man with a single ewe. . . ."

"What is this concerning Nathan? If I am to be of service to the captain,
surely I must at least understand——"

"Forget Nathan and let the matter lie. This woman of Tekoa will say
that one of her two sons rose up and killed the other, and that the
murderer is in danger of death or exile for bloodguiltiness, and that the
King of Israel alone can judge whether this one remaining son of hers is to
be taken from her. And David, who is sick of blood, will say to her, 'The
young man is forgiven.' And if the child of the woman of Tekoa is delivered of bloodguiltiness, the precedent is such that Absalom also is forgiven."

"Yet surely," said Ahitophel, "the son of Jesse will see that the words
have been put into the woman's mouth, and will know in his heart that it
was either you or I who put them there."

"What then? No, now, if you are afraid, I will tell the woman to say to
David that it was I who sent her to him for Absalom's sake. I will have
her say it, and loudly, before the whole multitude. For there will not be
one among them, save only Nathan and Bath-sheba, who will not lift up
his voice to plead the cause of the comely one. Israel will thank me, and
the son of Jesse himself will thank me, for he has long yearned after
Absalom. Only mention to him tomorrow that he should show thankful

ness to God for the barley harvest, and all that I have foretold will surely come to pass."

And the son of Zeruiah was in no wise mistaken. At the feast of thanksgiving held on the first day of the barley harvest, the woman of Tekoa pleaded in a mellifluous voice the cause of her nonexistent son before the throne. Nathan and Bath-sheba listened in consternation. The assembled company listened with growing insight and gratification. David, still abstracted and white in the face, listened gravely to her first two sentences and then began to struggle against an irrepressible smile. Twice he looked across the woman's head at Joab, and once he focused his glance upon the blushing Ahitophel. But it was not until he had passed solemn judgment in favor of forgiveness that he asked the woman to tell him who had sent her, and led her on with kindly questions to name his nephew's name.

Then the King said to Joab: "Behold now, I have given my judgment, and the thing is done. Go, therefore, and bring back the young man Absalom."

And that same night the captain of the host set out for the land of Geshur, to bring the comely one home.

XVIII

On THE SECOND DAY following the festival of thanksgiving, the King of Israel retired to his own chamber immediately after the evening bread. The members of his household smiled in satisfaction when they saw him arise and depart, for they knew that he was renewed by his periods of solitary meditation, and since his return from the high place in Gibeah, he had shown a troubling unwillingness to spend a single hour alone. "If Ahitophel or Abishai or Abiathar should come to us later in the evening, do not fail to send after me," he told them, turning on the stair. "It is only that I would stretch out upon the bed for a little, to ponder and to rest."

He settled himself against the pillows without laying aside his crimson robe. The room was cool and airy; the curtains were borne inward through broad shafts of sunlight by the wind of God. In the neighboring chamber, Hushai and Bath-sheba were reviewing the lessons of the day with the young Solomon. With perhaps a shade too much self-satisfaction, the lad was naming the genealogies of the kings who sat on the thrones of Moab, Edom, and the principalities of Syria. It occurred to the son of Jesse that for the past two moons it had been his custom to spend this part of the evening in the boy's room, along with Bath-sheba and Hushai the counselor. He thought of rising and going in to hear at least the end of the lesson, but almost at once he put that thought aside. How is it with me, he asked himself, that suddenly I am capable of enjoying solitude? . . . And he knew that this change had come upon him because the son of Zeruiah had made possible the return of Absalom.

Not that the restoration of the young man to his father's house could in any way change the chaotic nature of the world or erase from the King's mind the blank Presence, the eyeless God. Nevertheless, as a man builds his garden and somehow keeps it green in spite of the white encroachment of the desert, so he would build a life for himself and maintain it in serene disregard of the blind stare of the Lord. And he began to think of the day of the home-coming—what dishes he would order for the feast, whether it would be better to leave the entire evening free for talk or to summon a certain celebrated lutist out of Manasseh. He thought also of certain changes that he would like to make in the common room of the palace. It seemed to him that its solemnity could easily be lessened with a little help from the gardener—tomorrow he would order that thirty tall plants be taken up and potted in green jars and set against the pillars and the walls. He was trying to visualize the effect of this arrangement when he saw that Bath-sheba was standing at the half-opened door.

"I would not trouble my lord for all the world," she said. "If he desires to sleep, let him only say as much, and I will go and let him sleep."

"No, now, I have been lying here broad awake, thinking of——" He paused, knowing that for these two days no word had passed between them concerning Absalom. "I have been lying here broad awake, and thinking that I could not answer all the questions which Hushai and my beloved have been putting to my son Solomon."

"The lesson seemed very long, inasmuch as David was not with us tonight."

There was not the slightest reproof in her voice, and yet he felt himself reproved. "It is better," he said, "that I should sometimes absent myself. You also—you should not sit every evening in his room, marveling at his cleverness. For, even though he bears himself with the meekness of a dove, yet he is possessed of the natural measure of love which every boy feels for himself. And we will puff up his pride, we two, if we feed him upon praise as regularly as we feed him upon bread."

She made no answer, and he saw with amazement that she was close to weeping.

"Beloved," he said, holding out his hand to her, "if I seem severe in this matter, it is only that I remember my own childhood too well, and I would not have the lad——"

"Grow into such a one as his father?" She made a faint attempt to smile. "Surely that would be no great fault in him—not, at least, in my sight."

He laughed and shook his head.

"My lord withheld himself from us this night because he wished to be alone. I will go down now to the common room and leave him in peace."

For the first time, he sensed a scarcely perceptible desire to have her go from him. He wished to wander about the room, to open the clothes chest and take out his lute, perhaps to fashion such a song as might be suitable for the return of Absalom. But his tenderness for her was multiplied threefold by the very knowledge that he could wish her out of his sight. "No, why should you depart?" he said. "Come and sit upon the bed."

She came slowly, as though she had sensed his unwillingness to have her by him, and seated herself on the rich green coverlet close to his feet. He waited, and waited vainly, for her touch; she neither bent forward to offer him a kiss nor laid her hand upon his knee. The sunlight, still golden and flecked with motes of dust, fell upon her smooth hair, her milky cheek, the graceful folds of white linen around her breasts. She folded her hands in her lap and sighed.

"What is my beloved thinking?" he said.

"Nothing. Only that it is a blessed life that we have had together, we two. . . ."

"Does Bath-sheba consider that life a finished thing, inasmuch as she speaks of it as passed?"

"May my lord the King live for a thousand years! If one thing passes, there are yet other things to be. . . ."

"What, then, has passed?"

"Nothing. Truly, my lord, nothing at all."

Nevertheless, he was profoundly troubled. He knew her subtlety and her awareness; on innumerable occasions she had penetrated into the innermost recesses of his mind; and it was possible that she had sensed his first withdrawal into a world in which she had no part. And truly, he thought, when I wished her to go from me I deceived myself, for there is nothing on earth more dear to me than her presence. . . . He raised himself on his elbow and reached out his hand. "Surely Bath-sheba has not dreamed so idle a dream as that I could ever cease to love her?" he said.

"Not yet," she told him, laying her passive hand in his. "Not yet, my lord. When I spoke of the blessed life we have shared together, I did not speak of all the happy days and nights we have known from the hour when I came to the roof of David's house and laid my head upon his breast. I was thinking only of these last few years, when we have lived in serenity and without magnificence, even as a farmer and his wife might live in a brown house among the quiet hills. . . ."

"No, now," he said, pressing her fingers, "I would have thought that it was a dull and burdensome life for a woman who is still young and exceedingly fair. To sit evening after evening in an upper chamber, between an old man and a young lad——"

"Between my lord and my son. What more should I desire? These two, and these only, are my world." The bright tears, long withheld, spilled swiftly, easily over her cheeks. "It is not," she said, "that I can believe my lord will desert the two of us utterly. I am certain that he will come up now and again to spend an idle hour with Bath-sheba and Solomon. He will vouchsafe them a little of his company, even when he makes merry again below, with young men and young women and wine and the music of the lute. We will wait for him, and he will come up to us one or two evenings in seven, as he did in those other days when the common room was crowded with the friends of Absalom."

That she looked with displeasure upon the return of the wanderer he had always known; but he had never guessed that she saw in it a cutting-away of much that had served to make them one. Nor were her forebodings entirely without cause; he had indeed forgotten their blessed and peaceful hours in his desire to put music and laughter and younger faces between himself and the blank stare of God. When the heir is returned to Jerusalem, he thought, she may truly be consigned to loneliness. How was it with her that other time when I made carnival among the friends of Absalom? Now that I pause to remember it, she often arose early from the table, to leave us and to sit in an upper chamber, beside a sleeping boy. It is true that I never ceased to love her, but it is true also that I loved her least when I fancied myself young because I sat among the gallant and the beautiful and played upon my lute. . . .

"Hushai the counselor—he will henceforth be my chief companion," she said.

The speech exasperated him; it was too childishly doleful; it called up the thought that she had no one to blame but herself if she lived in solitude. "No, now," he said, "that is foolish. There is no reason for you to sit alone with the lad—he is no longer a child. Let Solomon spend his evenings henceforth in the company of Meribaal and Adonijah. As for Bath-sheba—whomsoever I call up to my house, whether it be the captain of the host or the ambassador out of Sidon or the friends of Absalom, her place is in the common room at my side."

She flushed and bit her underlip. "Wheresover the King of Israel commands me to sit, there must I sit," she said.

"Who has commanded? I have made a request, and lo, it is transformed into a command. Such is Bath-sheba's way—to raise an anthill to the height of a mountain. It is enough to drive a man——"

He fell silent, appalled by the animosity in his own voice. Ah, God, he thought, has it come to this with us, that we should quarrel upon this bed where we have lain together? . . .

"Let my lord speak his mind to the end."

"I have said enough. I have said far too much. Say that I am old and sick with burdens that have been too great for me to bear. All that I have been so foolish as to say this night—consider it unsaid. Come now, and lie beside me, and think upon this matter no more."

She rose and walked round to the side of the bed and settled herself in the crook of his arm, her head against his shoulder, her silky hair beneath his lips. He caressed her, and knew with astonishment that he was taking no pleasure in the touch. It is not out of love, but out of obedience, that she is lying against me, he thought. . . . He raised her chin and looked into her face. "Then the heart of my beloved is still hardened against me?" he said.

She closed her eyes and shook her head.

"Then wherefore does Bath-sheba——"

"If David would hear the truth, I am afraid."

"Afraid? Wherefore?"

She clung to him and shivered against him like a sick child. "How should I tell my lord? I have told him before, and he has forgotten. If I tell him again, he will either laugh or rail at me. . . ."

"No, now, in God's name, let there be nothing that cannot be said between us. Tell me, now and forever, what is in your heart."

"As my lord was fearful for Meribaal when the people stood at the gate, so now am I fearful for my lord. The son of Maacah is wild and strange. The mark of Cain was upon him when he rode forth from the city, nor will these many moons which he has spent among his Bedouin kinsmen have sobered him—the fire of the desert is in his blood. Amnon stood in his path, and he cut Amnon down. So long as my lord lives and holds Judah and Israel in his hand, he also is in Absalom's path. Perhaps it is childishness, perhaps these are only shadows with which I strive, but I am sore afraid of Absalom."

He did not answer at once. He stared at the ceiling, trying to conjure up a vision of the comely one. So many moons had passed since he last set eyes upon his son that the image would not take shape at first; he saw only the gleam of white teeth in a smiling mouth, a pair of straight black eyebrows, a brown forehead overshadowed by a mass of black ringlets. Then suddenly the whole countenance appeared before him, and his heart stood still. Perhaps because terror had passed from her shivering body into his, perhaps because he had seen on the high place of Gibeah the evil underlying the world, he knew that the face of Absalom was a baleful face. Exotically, malevolently beautiful, rich with the deep, deceitful dyes of the Sodom apple and the scorpion, it flashed for a moment upon him and was gone. And he knew that he had seen that face as Amnon must have seen it in the common room at Baal-hazor when it exulted before his dying eyes.

"Surely," he said in a shaken voice, "there is no such evil in him——"

"David is the King. If my lord believes him innocent, he will call him home."

"No, not yet. Let him tarry awhile in the city before I call him home. Let him dwell in his own house and ponder his transgressions—the time of waiting may serve to cool his blood. Meanwhile my beloved may learn not to fear him. She may see him for what he is—a child of the desert, but a dutiful son to David and to Israel. Let him tarry for six or seven moons, and then I will spread him a feast, and my beloved will come down willingly from the upper chamber to sit at my side."

She pressed her mouth against his cheek. "My lord is more than gracious to his foolish servant. Now, let us indeed forget the matter," she said.

BOOK ELEVEN

BOOK ELEVEN

BOOK ELEVEN

❧ I ❧

To WAIT, to do nothing, to sit still—this, said the multitude, was the policy of the King of Israel. It was for this that they maintained him in a magnificent palace, waited upon by menservants and maidservants, watched over by guardsmen, clothed in scarlet and purple and gold, and fed upon the fat of the land. It was for this that they paid for the keep of a splendid host, encamped on the untroubled borders, living in luxury and idleness among the peaceful populace of the Canaanite and Philistine cities. Since the insolence of the Ammonites had been quenched in blood on the red plains before Rabbah, there had been no war in Israel. Since the time—four years gone—when Jahveh had sent a famine upon His sons and daughters, the Lord had not lifted up His hand to do either great good or great evil in His chosen land. There were no national events save the holy days, no political events save the King's councils, which were held on the evenings of the new moon. And it was said of these councils that only septuagenarians were permitted to attend them—old men who always found themselves in agreement concerning everything, inasmuch as they had but one purpose among them—to wait, to do nothing, to sit still.

Yet for the King of Israel these years were years of swift and disquieting change. Faces that had surrounded him since his youth were withdrawing from him now—into obscurity, into retirement, into the grave. Abigail arose one night from a particularly hearty supper, tottered at the foot of the stairway, and fell dead. Ahitophel begged to be released from the duties of chief counselor; he was weary, he was growing old. After a long and pathetic struggle, the high priest Abiathar was forced to admit that he had grown too feeble to stand for hours in the sun during the high festivals; let his cousin Zadok stand before the ark in his place. Michal also had gone forth from the King's house. Why should she linger, seeing that Abigail, the only sharer of her long, dull afternoons and evenings, had left her alone? Meribaal had taken a wife at last; that same pale and undistinguished niece of Hushai's who had caught Adonijah's fancy had found that her heart was really with the lame and gentle one; and Michal had gone into Benjamin to dwell henceforth with her brother's son and his bride. These changes and others—the deaths of servants, the departure of overseers, the retirement of scribes—had come so rapidly and in such numbers that the King of Israel sometimes found himself on the point of asking for a man who had been counted for many moons among the dead.

The table in the common room was far too long for the little group that gathered around it now. Bath-sheba and Solomon, Haggith and Adonijah —these were the only members of the King's family who still dwelt within the walls of his house. Hushai the counselor, Zadok and Abiathar, the two sons of Zeruiah—these were the only habitual guests. Sometimes, but with less and less frequency, the great doors would be flung open and a multitude of unfamiliar or half-familiar dignitaries would assemble to welcome a visiting potentate. Sometimes, but far less often than the King would have desired, the stagnant silence would be stirred by the presence of Absalom.

For the King of Israel had welcomed his eldest son at last, but not with wine and the music of the lute—that, like most of men's hopes, had been a dream. The gallant and the beautiful had never returned to trouble the peace of the beloved; the lute had lain these many years in the clothes chest, wrapped in linen swathings. For two years the son of Maacah had tarried, now in Jerusalem and now at Baal-hazor, waiting for his father to call him home. For two years the King of Israel had temporized, yielding always to the remembrance of that evening when he had conjured up the face of Absalom and had seen it as evil. The young man had suffered humiliation and loneliness; even Joab had turned his back upon him; no man close to the King had cared to share the years of his shame, save only the aging Ahitophel.

Twice Absalom had sent up to the captain of the host, begging for an interview. Twice he had been told that the son of Zeruiah had no desires save the desires of David and therefore could not come. Then one hot summer night, when the weight of his boredom was intolerable, he took his servants into a barley field which David had given to Joab, and commanded the men to set the grain afire. A wind came up, and the blaze was visible for miles. "The son of Zeruiah will come to me now," he said. Then Joab arose from his bed and came to Absalom in the field and asked him, "Wherefore have your servants set my field afire?" And Absalom answered him, saying: "I sent to you twice, pleading with you to come hither, that I might send you up to intercede for me with the King, my father and my lord. Wherefore have you brought me out of Geshur? It were far better for me if I tarried there still. Let me behold the King's face, and if there is any iniquity in me, let him kill me." And the son of Zeruiah carried the tale of the burned barley to the King, who shrugged and sighed, and said, "Go to him and tell him to come up and break the evening bread with us tonight."

So, after a manner, the King and the heir apparent had been reconciled. Not that there were any words of penitence and forgiveness between them. The evening of the home-coming—and all other evenings on which the young man broke bread with his father—left much to be desired. All conversation that passed between them seemed spurious, a veil of insincere words spread over the disturbing fact that all essential things had been left unsaid. The company which assembled on such nights in the King's common room was not conducive to self-confidence on Absalom's part. Bath-sheba was condescending and remote; Solomon was accustomed to dominating the talk at the table and showed no inclination to give place to his eldest brother; and the best that could be said for Haggith and Adonijah was that they resented the newcomer less than they resented Bath-sheba's gifted son. Joab was wary and sullen—he wished to stand with the King, and none save the God of Hosts Himself could be certain where the King stood. Abishai was crestfallen and silent. Abiathar was positively senile, and his cousin Zadok—dark, supercilious, and saturnine —could stoop to discuss nothing but the finer points of dogma and ritual. Sometimes the evening would pass in complete boredom; sometimes the hot rages buried beneath the formality would dart out like tongues of fire. Solomon would utter a piece of wisdom which Absalom would immediately reduce to foolishness; Bath-sheba would make a disparaging comment concerning Ahitophel, and Haggith would defend him as though he were her blood brother; Zadok would let fall some mocking remark regarding Nathan, and Joab would say: "What else can you expect? He is a priest. All priests are fools or knaves." After a while the son of Maacah ceased to take part in the conversation. He wandered around the room or walked by himself in the garden. Then one evening he asked the King's permission to bring a friend to supper. He could no longer bear the ordeal alone.

This friend of Absalom's, whose name was Amasa, was a grave and quiet son of Ishmael, a wanderer who had spent most of his forty years in strange lands. He had served the kings of Moab and Edom; and Absalom had found him in the court of Geshur, charged with the discipline of the Bedouin King's young recruits. Why he had followed the son of Maacah into Israel it was difficult to say. The ranks of Jahveh, unbroken these many years by war, were seldom opened now to give place to a newcomer; and Amasa the Ishmaelite lived on Absalom's bounty in a modest house bestowed upon him by Ahitophel.

During the first hours of the evening, it seemed to David that Amasa might be a felicitous addition to the somber company. There was a melancholy charm about him; although his flesh was burned to a reddish brown and his hair had receded from his furrowed forehead, his eyes were large and expressive, and he had the look of one who had been unusually comely in his youth. He entertained them all with tales of the outlandish doings of Edomites and Moabites—even the young Solomon held his tongue. In the course of the conversation it developed that there was some blood tie between him and the King's nephew; his father had been a cousin to the Ishmaelite who had married Zeruiah. But before the evening was half over, the captain of the host showed a marked animosity toward the visitor—picked flaws in his tales, and made light of those battles in which he had borne a part. At first Amasa expostulated with the captain very mildly; then he fell silent and fixed a sorrowful gaze upon his tormentor; and at last he went to walk in the King's garden with Absalom. Nor did he return to the common room until it was time to make his farewells.

"Why," said the son of Jesse to the captain when the others had departed, "why have you belittled the friend of my son and affronted him, so that he will show his face in my house no more?"

"Why does the King invite traitors to sit at his board? Surely David sees that if Absalom should rise up against his father, this same Amasa will be captain of Absalom's host."

"How is it that the son of Zeruiah, who loved the son of Maacah and went up to Geshur to fetch him home, has become his accuser and his enemy?"

"No, now," said Joab, moving toward the door, "I fetched him home that he might be taken to the arms of his father and his lord, and not that the poison of the King's indifference should rankle in his blood these two years. If he is a traitor——"

"Do not call him a traitor before me!"

"Let the King of Israel cease to shout into my face. If he is a traitor, it was not I who made him so. Let the son of Jesse look into his own heart." And, so saying, he departed.

It was not the first time that the King had heard his son accused of treason. It was common knowledge that the young man spent most of his time before the city gate, engaged in questionable activities. Because the son of Jesse had come of late to distrust his own judgment, justice was meted out very slowly; David would sit for days considering a single case, and many a traveler who had come to the capital to ask for justice would tarry for weeks and be forced at last to return home without satisfaction. The comely one had been commiserating with all those Israelites who suffered from the King's delays. Whenever a traveler in search of justice arrived at the gate, Absalom would accost him and ask him whence he came and what was the nature of his cause. He would listen attentively until the end, and then he would sigh and shake his head. "See," he would say, "your cause is good and right, but the King has appointed no man to hear you, and it will be many moons before he hears you himself. Oh, that I were made a judge in this land! Then any man who had a suit might come to me, and I would give him justice!" He was all things to all men. He agreed heartily with the farmer out of Judah who complained that the crops of the southern tribes rotted in the storehouse or were sold at a wretched price. He regretted with the Kenite captain that there was no longer room for his tribesmen in the ranks of Israel. He told the elder out of Caleb that he would find but a cold welcome at the King's court, inasmuch as only the haughty sons of Ephraim and Benjamin were dear to the King's heart. And when any man drew close to the son of Maacah, to fall down and do obeisance before him, he put forth his hand and lifted the suppliant up. "Not so, my brother," he would say, and he would salute the stranger with a kiss.

Hushai and Zadok had taken it upon themselves to speak of these matters to the King. Bath-sheba had confined herself to making certain implications concerning Ahitophel: his age and weariness did not prevent him from making long journeys into Judah and Caleb and the land of the Kenites; he was still vigorous enough to ride through the streets in Absalom's chariot and to sit late at Absalom's board night after night. One of the elders out of Judah made an oblique reference to the extraordinary enthusiasm which the youth of his tribe had shown during a visit from Absalom. From the north and the south, out of the mouths of ambassadors and wandering priests and the leaders of caravans, came tales of young men barred from the ranks of the host, living in dullness and obscurity, banded together by their common disgust with the long reign of the waning Star of Bethlehem. "Will the old man live forever?" they said. And their hearts were after Absalom.

Yet the King of Israel did not lift up his hand to do either good or evil in his own house or in the land. When, on the evening of the new moon, some counselor, more audacious than his fellows, would raise his voice to speak of the matter, the King would bid him hold his tongue. Perhaps, he thought, there is treason. Ahitophel no longer shows his face in the palace; the wife and child of Absalom still tarry in Geshur; Amasa lives on my son's bounty; and my son has a baleful, beautiful, treacherous face. Yet if I smite those that I suspect of treason, I may well shed the blood of the innocent; and even if I smite only the guilty, how shall I smite them all? Shall I send the host of God north and south to put every young man who is weary of me to the edge of the sword? The world is black and rotten to the core, and whatsoever a man does is doomed to be evil in such a world. Therefore it is best to wait, to do nothing, to sit still. . . .

❧ II ❧

Stand watch for us yet this one night," said Absalom to the steward of his house. "Sit at the garden gate, and throw a great stone into the pool before the window if any man should so much as linger at the garden wall. Watch well for my sake and for your own, for you will not go without your reward in the good days that are to come."

"And if Amasa the Ishmaelite should come?" said the steward, folding the napkins and laying them upon the board.

The son of Maacah smiled and shook his head. "Amasa will not come.

He is not in Jerusalem. He will tarry behind in Hebron until the deed is done."

The steward stepped back and surveyed the table. He had been told to deck it as for a festal occasion, and he was proud of the pyramids of figs and grapes, the vase filled with fresh green oak leaves, the copper plates and bowls which his lord had brought back from Geshur, newly polished and gleaming in the light of the setting sun.

"Now take yourself off to the garden gate," said Absalom, "and admit no man save Ahitophel."

And now that he was alone, he walked round and round the table, lightly, swiftly. He lifted his arms and stretched them toward the ceiling. This is the day, he thought, this is the hour. . . . And then, because he was a son of the desert and therefore superstitious, he reproached himself for exulting over an unfinished matter and thereby tempting the wrath of God. A thousand stones may yet be hurled in my path, he told himself. Ahitophel may return out of Hebron with evil news. At the last moment, the hearts of the Judahites may have turned cold. The men of the King's bodyguard may have been sent to fall upon the old counselor on the highway. For all I know, he may at this moment be lying at the King's feet, telling the whole tale from beginning to end in order to save himself. . . .

But even as he let these thoughts flow through his mind to forestall evil, he lay down on a couch and stretched and yawned and smiled. He knew that Judah was in the palm of his hand. He knew that the King knew nothing. And he knew that he could as easily doubt himself as he could doubt Ahitophel.

The old man had his own reasons for sedition—if it could be called sedition to unseat an incapable king and place his rightful heir upon the throne. In spite of his early loyalties to the House of Kish, Ahitophel had come to Jerusalem with only one purpose: to serve the House of Jesse well. But he had no sooner established himself than he found himself shut out—a woman had come between him and his lord. A quiet niece of his, so undistinguished that the family had seen fit to marry her to a Hittite, had been lifted out of her obscurity and set at the side of the King of Israel. Slowly, carefully, with sidewise disparaging looks and casual insinuations and little smiles, she had avenged herself upon the uncle who had held himself aloof from her and her Hittite husband, the man who had failed to visit her in her somber palace. It was Hushai whom she chose to be the teacher of her child and the other children. Ahitophel had the barren title of chief counselor, but Hushai had Bath-sheba's favor.

It was impossible to make open war against her. All that she did she did with subtle urbanity. How gently she had dealt with him when he came to the palace to ask for release from those negligible duties which her malice had left to him! How she had commiserated with him over his palsied hands and his weak eyes! How lyrically she had spoken of the pleasures of retirement—the blessed quietness of the little towns of Benjamin! But even after the King had granted him the relief that he did not desire, he tarried in the capital, waiting, hoping to be called back. It had been this period of waiting—this and the sacrifice of the last survivors of his beloved House of Kish—that had finally driven him to conspire with Absalom.

"Ahitophel is the oak and I am the vine," the son of Maacah had told him over and over. "Let Ahitophel live for a hundred years, for if he should perish, I would be trampled into the earth."

"Let the son of Maacah set his heart at peace. There are more years left in me than Bath-sheba cares to think. The Lord will let me live until I have seen Absalom seated upon his father's throne."

And it was the old counselor who had drawn together into one outcry the desultory complaints which had been raised against the son of Jesse in the scattered towns of Israel. It was Ahitophel who had ridden east and west, north and south, to nourish grievances and foment rebellion. He and he alone had thought of pointing out to the Judahites that their grain rotted in the storehouses because the King of Israel chose to feed his army upon Philistine wheat; he and he alone had taught young men to assemble in caves and forests and curtained rooms, whispering together of the days when old men would no longer direct all the King's business and hold all the captaincies in the ranks of God. It was he who had led the son of Maacah down to show him to the Calebites and the Kenites; it was he who had sent men to say at every shrine and in every market, "The young man Absalom—he is such a one as should reign over Israel and Judah." From the first hour to this hour of consummation, when everything was in readiness and waited only for the signal—the beacon fire on the hilltop, the blast of the trumpet, the unfurling of the standard in Hebron—the conspiracy had been the handiwork of Ahitophel.

The son of Maacah rose and went to the window. His guest was late, but he remained serene. And it was only a few minutes until the steward coughed discreetly and stirred the foliage near the gate; it was his manner of informing the master of the house that the awaited one had come.

Ahitophel came up the garden path and lifted his shaking hand in greeting. His garments were festal garments, white crossed by deep, rich bands of blue; his meager, wispy hair and beard had been washed and anointed; to behold him was to know that he had found Hebron panting after the hour. "God is with the son of Maacah," he said, crossing the threshold and embracing his host. "Nothing is needful now save that we go down into Hebron and take the ripe fruit in our hands." His slight, dry body trembled with excitement; his shortsighted eyes were filled with tears.

"How shall I ever reward the labors of my friend? How shall I find words to tell him——"

"Come now and feed me well, for I have not broken bread these last six hours."

It was fortunate that the steward of the house was not by to behold them. They set aside his vase of oak leaves so that it might not stand between their faces; they toppled the pyramid of grapes and figs; they did not see the polished plates on which they laid their cakes of bread and their slices of meat. They ate swiftly, like men who are engaged in a prospering enterprise. They talked incessantly, caring not in the least that their mouths were full. Everything was well, everything was in readiness—the elders of Judah and Caleb and the land of the Kenites would assemble within three days in Hebron to await the arrival of their new lord. The moment he showed his face within the gates of the city, the trumpet would sound and all the children of Hebron would run forth into the streets, shouting, "God save Absalom, King over Judah and Israel!" And within the same hour, as soon as beacon fires could be lighted on a hundred hills, the same shout would go up in a hundred cities, and all the discontented youth of the land would march down to swell the ranks of that very creditable host which was already gathered in the hills above Hebron.

"And the elders of Judah—have they named the day to Ahitophel?"

"They have accepted the day which we thought best—the Feast of the First Fruits."

"Good, good, that is very good—that leaves but seven days of waiting before we two set out together. Now tell me, shall I go forth without a word to the son of Jesse, or shall I beg his leave to go down?"

"I have been pondering that matter," Ahitophel said, "and it seems to me that you will incur greater danger if you depart without a word. Go up to him and tell him that you have promised God to make a sacrifice in Hebron, the city of your birth. He will not think of it a second time, save to regret that you will be absent from his table for the Feast of the First Fruits."

The young man stared at his plate. Even at such a moment, when he was ready to sound the trumpet of rebellion across the length and breadth of the land, he felt an inward ache at any remembrance of the King's tenderness. There was a time, he said in his heart, when we made a great occasion of the feast at home. I remember well how he came to the board in his splendid robes and took the knife in his fine long hands and carved the meat. It is true that once he gave my brother Amnon a corselet of bronze to mark the occasion, and that my gift was a lesser one—a belt of tooled leather such as they make in his native town of Bethlehem. But it was a fair belt, with curious leaves and scrolls upon it. Where is it now? Have I lost it? I have not worn it these many years. . . .

"Amasa has bidden me say to Absalom that his host numbers four thousand and grows from hour to hour."

"No, now, truly?"

"Four thousand at the least, and five hundred are expected to ride in out of Caleb this very night."

"Inasmuch as we are speaking of my father——" He blushed, knowing that they had ceased to speak of his father some moments since. "Inasmuch as we are speaking of my father," he said, taking an oak leaf from the vase and tearing it apart, "I trust that Ahitophel will not cling stubbornly to that decision which he revealed to me when the two of us last broke bread."

The old counselor sighed and rested his cheek upon his hand. "What can I say to Absalom? He has asked me to consider the matter these three days. Well, I have considered it. I have also laid it before Amasa and before the elders of Judah in Hebron. They know as well as I that there is no peace while two kings are alive in a single land. While Saul and David both drew breath, Israel was an armed camp, and no man knew at what hour his fields might be trampled by marching feet."

"But they were vigorous men—the Star of Bethlehem and the Lion of Benjamin. And he who sits upon the throne this day in Jerusalem—he is no longer concerned with the matters of the world. His hands are loosened so that he cannot hold that which he has—how then should he take back that which is wrested from him? I hold with Ahitophel that the sons of David must be slain. Their hearts and the hearts of their mothers are after the throne. But an old man who is exceedingly weary, whose face is already turned away from the earth——"

"What, then, would the son of Maacah have us do with the son of Jesse?"

Absalom shrugged and covered his face with his hands. "Nothing. Give him Mahanaim, where the host of Ishbaal dwelt in other days. Leave him alone with his woman and his lute. . . ."

"No, now, he is not so depleted as Absalom thinks. He will grow strong on the bitter meat of exile. He is as changeable as the moon—I have seen him wane and wax before."

"I cannot set my seal upon the order for his death."

"I cannot leave an ulcer in the flesh of Israel."

For the space of a heartbeat their eyes blazed. Then the young man reached across the board and laid his hand gently upon the old man's hand.

"Consider it yet a little longer, Ahitophel. There is no need to settle it tonight. Lay it by, and we will speak of it again when we have established ourselves in Hebron."

"I have been considering it since I first thought that the son of Maacah might sit upon his father's throne."

"Nevertheless, consider it a little longer," Absalom said.

⇜§ III §⇝

THE CAPTAIN OF THE HOST presented himself very early at the door of the palace on the day of the feast. His brother stood behind him on the threshold, dressed in a particularly ridiculous festal garment of sky-blue linen and looking more than ever like a plump infant who had miraculously grown big and old. No one had asked them to come up to the King's palace; it had been Abishai who had thought that the King might be in need of company during the procession to the high place. For how could he put from his mind the thought of happier feast days, when Tamar had walked before him with a basket of flowers, when Amnon had toiled along at his right with a load of pomegranates, and Absalom had walked buoyantly at his left with a splendid sheaf of wheat? Now one tarried forever with her mother in Geshur, and one was dead, and the third had chosen this day of all days to go down into Hebron.

The door creaked on its hinges and swung back upon the long, dim, almost empty vista of the common room. No, now, are half of them still abed? Joab asked himself. Then he counted heads—at the table, near the window, beside the pillars—and knew that the King's entire household was before his eyes, and grieved to find it so small.

Close to one of the columns near the door, Bath-sheba was kneeling in front of Solomon. She could not offer more than a nod to the visitors because there were pins between her lips; she was busy making some change in the hem of her son's robe—furiously busy, although the procession would not set out until an hour before noon. Seeing her in morning disarray, with the puffiness of sleep still upon her face, the son of Zeruiah wondered again how it was that his lord found her so fair. She is a Benjamite matron, he thought, like a thousand others. . . . And he turned his glance upon Solomon. That fourteen-year-old shoot of the House of Jesse was rubbing his back against the pillar and casting imploring glances in the direction of the ceiling. God teach me patience with women, said his eyes. He was slender, but so soft and pale of arm and throat and face that there was something vaguely womanish in his slenderness. His face was like his mother's, delicate and clear, with milky cheeks and straight brown brows. But his mouth was troubling; it was overripe, and it still retained a childish pout. "I would gladly escape and fling myself into the arms of my uncles," he said in a drawling voice. "But I am driven against a pillar and hemmed in with pins. I cannot move."

"God walk with the sons of Zeruiah," said Haggith, rising from the couch where she had been sitting with Adonijah. "Have you broken your fast? Can I bring you a little curds and bread?" She was dressed in a garment of pleated white linen, and her graying hair was bound into a coronet above her placid brow. She gave her hand first to Joab and then to Abishai. Behold, her serene countenance informed the world, I am not such a one as is ruffled by early risings, or by uneven hems in garments. . . .

"God walk with Haggith. She is very gracious, but we have broken our fast an hour since," Joab said.

Adonijah had already risen from the couch and was advancing toward them, his hands outstretched, his mild face made doubly pleasant by a cordial smile. "You have come up to walk with us to the high place," he said, passing his arm through Abishai's, "and that was more than kind, seeing that my father will remember other feast days, when he had a longer train than that which follows him now."

The captain looked down the length of the room in search of the King of Israel. Two servants were standing near the table, laying pomegranates in a wicker basket; a third was washing clusters of grapes in a brazen basin, and a serving-maid was making garlands out of almond blossoms and wheat. The old counselor Hushai was eating curds. But the King of Israel was nowhere to be seen.

"The King will be with us in an hour or so," Haggith said. "According to the word of his armor-bearer, he scarcely closed his eyes last night, and we did not have the heart to rouse him up at the break of day."

"Take a little fruit and curds," Adonijah said, drawing both his visitors toward the table. "We will not sit at the board again until we have returned from the high place."

The captain suddenly became aware that Adonijah, unlike his younger brother, who was still squirming against the pillar, was attired in simple white linen. It was almost as if he wished to proclaim to the sons and daughters of Jerusalem: "I have put aside any thought of drawing your eyes upon me. I have an elder brother, and while he lives, I will not bear myself like a fool who fancies that one day he will be King of Israel." And yet, thought the son of Zeruiah, permitting the young man to cut him a slice of melon, I would be far more at ease for Israel's sake if he, rather than the son of the desert or the chattering little parakeet, were to sit after his father upon the throne. . . .

Bath-sheba rose from her knees at last. "There, now," she said, "it is perfect. Come out of the shadow of the pillar, my son, so that we may see."

Solomon stepped into a patch of sun and preened himself. Abishai and Adonijah nodded in his direction, but neither of them could bring himself to utter a commending word. As for Haggith, she had been staring at the empty doorway, and she continued to stare at it with insulting placidity. The old counselor Hushai, diverted from his bowl of curds by the length of the silence, started up from his chair. "Beautiful—my lady Bath-sheba has made him beautiful," he said quickly.

"Let Hushai find another word," said Solomon. "The word 'beautiful' is proper only when one refers to a maid."

Suddenly it became plain to all of them that in their zeal to be prepared for the festival in good time, they had risen too early and made too much haste. The young men—and they alone of all the King's household were to accompany their father to the high place—were washed and anointed and clothed to perfection. The morning meal had been eaten. The last pomegranate had been laid in the wicker basket, and the last garland had been put aside complete. Now they found themselves with two dull hours on their hands. What was there to do but stroll up and down the room in uncomfortable finery, growing more ill-tempered by the moment? Hushai and Haggith had a difference over the arrangement of the pomegranates. Adonijah informed Solomon that it would be well if he did not spoil all the garlands in the process of seeking out the best one for himself. Bath-sheba said with some asperity that if the maidservant had made the garlands well, they would not have fallen apart. The maid took umbrage. The garlands, she said, had been made to be worn on the head and not to be tossed about. Her insolence was such that it roused even the dreaming Hushai, who bade her honor her mistress and hold her tongue. The captain of the host, annoyed by the general ill-humor, took himself off to a shadowy corner where he could wait in peace for the King.

It was almost noon when the son of Jesse entered the common room. Seeing him in the full light of the early summer sun, Joab wondered how so worn and withdrawn a spirit could present so convincing an aspect of vigor and authority. Within the last three or four years, the King's beard and hair had gone entirely white; but that luxuriant whiteness only lent additional dignity to his spare and solemn face. He wore a long, trailing garment of yellow cloth, ornamented with diagonal stripes of white and gold; his right arm was almost covered by six broad golden bracelets, and a circlet of gold shone upon his head.

He came forward and embraced the sons of Zeruiah. He looked at the young Solomon, opened his mouth to utter praise, thought better of it, and turned to the table to take up one of the wicker baskets. "Since my armor-bearer has decked me out in gold and yellow, I may as well complete his intention and carry wheat," he said. "Adonijah will bear grapes. Solomon will carry flowers." He paused and set his basket of grain back on the table, for the steward had come in from the garden, plainly in a state of consternation.

"My lord——" said the steward.

"Well, then, what is it? We are in haste, we must meet the priests, we——"

"My lord, there is a runner in the garden. He comes with strange news out of Judah. Will you walk to the spring and speak with him, my lord?"

After the King's departure, an awed silence fell upon the little company. The captain of the host turned slowly in the direction of the doorway. He could see only a maze of sunlit hedges; he could hear only low, indistinguishable talk and the trickling of the spring. But suddenly he knew with absolute certainty what tidings the messenger had brought out of Judah—Absalom had revolted in Hebron. Without a word, he crossed the threshold, thinking that it was not good for his lord to be alone.

He waited on the path until the voices in the garden had ceased, and then waited yet a little longer, so that the King might have time to compose himself. Then he walked to the spring and looked about him. The grass was bent to one side—here the bringer of evil news had fallen on his face. But the bench was empty, and, in all the green expanse of the garden, he could see no sign of the runner or the steward or the King of Israel.

Near the brazen gate, there was another bench beneath a palm tree. He hastened toward it and saw, through an opening in the hedges, the ceremonial robe of yellow and gold. The King was alone, standing with his face to the tree. He was resting his forehead against the trunk, and his hands hung loose and open at his sides. "Is it the captain of the host?" he said, without stirring.

"Even he, my lord."

"Absalom has unfurled his standard in Hebron. It is so, I must teach myself that it is so. Absalom has stirred up Judah and Caleb and the Kenites against me. He could not wait for the day of my death—my son Absalom."

The captain stared at the motionless figure leaning against the palm tree. Caleb, Judah, the Kenites, he thought. Five thousand warriors at the least will be upon us. We must lose no time, we must man the walls. . . .

"I knew there was much that he could not forgive me. But I never dreamed he would ride armed against me out of the south. . . ."

"In God's name, rouse yourself! Where is the runner? Where is the steward of the house?"

The King did not move. "I have sent them both forth," he said. "They are gone to carry the tidings to the priests on the high place. Ah, God, who would have thought that he would choose to do it on the day of the feast? Go in now and say to my household that they must lay aside their ceremonial garments and put on sackcloth. I will come in to them in a little while. Only, for the moment, let no man come near me. Go in and leave me alone."

Five thousand at least, thought Joab, and Amasa the Ishmaelite at the head of the host, and everything well conducted according to the plans of Ahitophel. . . . And suddenly the sight of the flaccid, motionless back prodded him into fury. "What am I that my lord should send me in to comfort wailing women?" he shouted. "Am I not the captain of his host? I will not depart from David save to carry the commands of David to the ranks. If the son of Maacah can muster five thousand against us, yet have we six thousand, armed and ready to meet him in the plains below Jerusalem, waiting only for the King's word. Cease now to stand like an ailing child, leaning against a tree and bemoaning yourself. Turn and tell me, shall we go out to meet the rebels, or tarry in the city and let them dash themselves to pieces against the walls?"

Very slowly he lifted up his head and turned from the palm tree. The heart of the son of Zeruiah stood still within him when he beheld the King's face. It was gray and sagging above the folds of the gaudy garment. The mouth was open, and the eyes were dazed.

"Go in and rest," said Joab. "Lay it in my hands. I will do all that is needful. For the moment it is nothing—it is a matter of manning the walls."

"No, now, wait a little. . . ." David sat on the bench and bowed his face upon his hands. "It is in no wise my desire that the city should be defended. Any man who defends the city and sheds the blood of the children of Jerusalem does it against my will. If they will have the city, let them take the city; I give it freely into their hands. . . ."

"Surely the son of Jesse knows not whereof he speaks. Surely tomorrow he will awaken and say to himself, Yesterday I was mad."

"Today, tomorrow, and forever, I will not defend Jerusalem. I would swear it before God, but I have ceased to take oaths before Him. He hears, but He does not hearken. He looks upon us, but He does not see. Let Joab lay this to his heart: I will not remain. I will flee northward out of Jerusalem and leave it to Absalom."

"In God's name, wherefore?"

"How shall I make my reasons plain to Joab, who looks upon the world with the indifferent eyes of the unseeing God? I cannot shed the blood of the sons and daughters of Jerusalem, nor of the young man Absalom, nor of those that stand with me, nor of those that have come up against me. If there is blood to be shed, let it be my own. For it has come to this pass with me—I do not expect the captain of the host to understand it—it has come to this pass with me now, that it is easier for me to accept evil than to inflict it. Therefore I will go forth, and if they take me upon the road, then they will take me, and if they slay me, then I will be slain. . . ."

Joab was stricken wordless. He stood above the King and stared down upon his bent white head.

"There is also the city," said the son of Jesse. "It is a fair city, with gardens and palaces. I have labored to build it these many years, and it is as though it were the work of my own hands. Look across the length of Israel and see how few are the cities and how vast are the barren regions of brush and shale and dust. Jahveh cares nothing for Jerusalem—it is as an anthill to the Lord our God—but I have builded it, and it is mine, and I have come to love it well. In the end it will be devoured by unceasing winds and buried under shifting sands. But I would not have it destroyed before its time. Therefore, let it stand. . . ."

"No, now, surely my uncle has gone mad. Is there so little blood left in him that he will lie down before this dog of the desert and say to him, 'Come and trample upon my face'?"

"Is he indeed a dog?" said David. "Is he so evil in that he reached for the crown? Perhaps it is I that am evil in that I should have made way for him long ago. I am old, and the people are weary of the sight of me. I have grown slack, and the meaning of things is no longer clear to me. It is possible that Israel will be blessed when he sits upon the throne. . . ."

"God of Hosts!" said the son of Zeruiah. "Surely You have made a mockery of me all my days, that You should have bound me to serve a coward and a fool!"

The King of Israel dropped his hands and lifted up his face. It was as expressionless as the face of a corpse, as unreachable as an image carved out of stone. "I will set forth tomorrow before dawn," he said, holding out his hand to the captain. "It is possible that we will not meet again. Therefore, farewell."

"Farewell?" And he knew again that he could no more depart from the son of Jesse than he could depart from his own body. "My lord is as the heart in my breast," he said, seizing the cold hand and pressing it against his lips. "How then should I bid him farewell? He is a madman and a fool to go forth out of his city. But if he goes, I will go with him. For I have followed him since the days of my childhood, nor will I cease from following after him to the hour of my death."

⚜️ IV ⚜️

THE KING and all his household were prepared to go from the palace before the sun had fully risen. It was his intention to depart unseen out of a sleeping city. For why should I show myself to them in the hour of my affliction? he asked himself. It is possible that I will weep, and I would not have them behold my tears. . . . So he rose very early and did not permit himself to linger over the bed, or over the table where he had broken bread these many years, or over the tall pillars rising out of the milky mist, or over any object that he had loved. With an ample hood of black goat's-hair cloth in which to muffle his face, he crossed the threshold of his house, and walked past the spring, the blooming iris stalks, the green hedges, and the towering palms. He paused at the gate and held it open for those of his household who were departing with him—Haggith and Adonijah, Bath-sheba and Solomon, the steward of his house, twelve menservants and twelve maidservants, three scribes, a keeper of accounts, a smith, and a carpenter. Then, without glancing back upon the garden, he stepped into the hushed, unpeopled street.

Look, now, he thought, walking between Adonijah and the steward, I am bearing myself well. If I have not yet wept, surely I will not weep. I have gone out calmly, as though I were setting forth on but a little journey and would come again tomorrow night. So if any eyes should behold me, they will behold an old man who bore himself not too well in the days of his splendor, but walks in his defeat like the King over Judah and Israel. And when we meet the sons of Zeruiah and the guardsmen and the host on the Hill of Olive Trees, they will know that they are not following after a fool. . . .

On the way to the bazaars, he spoke quietly and casually to Adonijah and the steward concerning the country through which they were to pass and the supplies which were to be brought up behind them. He would far rather have walked in silence, but he was fearful that his thoughts might turn upon the comely one. Some hours since, in the stillness of deep night, he had awakened of a sudden and felt his heart melt within his breast; he had drawn the coverlet over his head and wept for that loss which swallowed up every other loss—the loss of Absalom. For by his very act of rebellion the son of Maacah had shed forever the balefulness that had brooded over him since his return from Geshur. So, David had told himself, there was no other evil in him save only the desire to take the crown. His malevolence was such malevolence as dwelt within me when

I sat at Saul's knees in Gibeah and yearned to hold Judah and Israel in my hand. He is less sinister than I was when I marched up with the ranks of Philistia toward the mountains of Gilboa—far less sinister, inasmuch as those he brings up against me are all sons of Jahveh, nor has he rendered his land into the hands of the uncircumcised. . . . And this thought had so moved him that he wept upon the pillow and pressed his mouth against it.

He would think of it later, he told himself. Some night in the wilderness, he would go apart from the others while they slept, and lie down in the shadow of a stone to ponder upon it and to weep. But now he was drawing near to the street of the merchants; in another moment he must turn a corner and walk among the stalls; the tradesmen, the earliest risers among the sons of Jerusalem, would be laying out their wares and would stop to stare after the fleeing King of Israel.

"Listen," said Adonijah, laying his hand upon his father's arm.

He stood still and heard a murmur of multitudinous voices rising from the unseen streets and alleys of the market place. And as he rounded the corner, he beheld them—all the children of Jerusalem, men and women and little ones, darkening the doorways and the pavements, sitting in the openings of windows, standing upon roofs and stalls. What, now, he thought, leaning upon Adonijah, have they come forth to mock me? . . . But they were clothed in sackcloth, and every soul among them had strewn ashes upon his head. Slowly, dumbly, the multitude divided to make way for him to pass, and he saw that all of them—bondservants and tradesmen and sons and daughters of high houses—wept bitterly to see him depart. Shy, tender hands reached out and touched his robe, his arm, his shoulder. A child took a length of scarlet cloth and spread it for him to walk upon. A slave seized his hand and wept upon it, and a grave matron fell in the dust before him and kissed his feet.

Then all the children of Jerusalem, whom he had thought weary of his reign, began to bemoan themselves to see him depart. "He builded the city," they said. "He broke the yoke of Philistia in the Valley of Rephaim." —"He lifted up Israel above Moab and Edom, and he shattered the insolence of the Ammonites."—"His judgments were righteous, and his heel was not upon the neck of the poor."—"He was splendid in the ranks of God, and he rode forth like an angel into battle."—"He made war only that he might establish peace."—"Whosoever was born in the term of his reign has had no portion but glory."—"How then will it be with us when we behold his face no more?"

He had scarcely issued out of the midst of them when he beheld another multitude—plumed ranks with burnished corselets and swords—filling up the narrow street that ran between the houses of the poor. He knew by their crests and their banners that they were men out of Gath and Cherethites and Palethites. They are about to depart into their homelands now, he thought, and it is very gracious—seeing that they have not served long in the host of Jahveh—that they should rise up early to bid the fleeing King farewell. . . . One of them, a tall and lordly son of Dagon mounted on a splendid horse, dismounted and walked toward the King of Israel. The bearded face beneath the plumed helmet was open, cordial, fair. "My lord," said the steward in David's ear, "this is Ittai of Gath who comes to greet the King. He it was who brought a goodly company of six hundred of the children of Gath into my lord's host not two moons ago."

The Philistine captain halted halfway between David and his ranks and shouted a command. "Turn," he said in those accents that were dear to David for the sake of Achish. "Turn, and march toward the Hill of Olives before our lord the King of Israel."

Then the King came and laid his hand upon the hand of Ittai of Gath, and said to him: "Surely the son of Dagon does not think to follow after us. Wherefore should you depart with us? For you are aliens, and you came to us only yesterday, and I cannot require you to go up and down the land with me, seeing that I am in flight. Return to your own country then, and take all these your brothers with you, and may mercy and peace be upon you for the remainder of your days."

And Ittai of Gath lifted the King's hand and kissed it and answered him, saying: "As God lives, and as my lord the King lives, surely in whatever place the King shall dwell, there also will his servants be. Whether our portion be glory or shame, whether we live with him or die with him, yet we will not cease from following after the King our lord." So David said to Ittai: "Follow me, then, if you will. Tell the ranks to pass over the brook Kidron when they have come to the margins of the city, for when we depart out of Jerusalem, we will go by way of the wilderness."

And Ittai of Gath led the march from the city and passed over the brook, and all his host went over with him—they and the other mercenaries, the Cherethites and the Pelethites. And the people came up behind at a distance, weeping and holding out their hands to their lord. Nor did the multitude turn back from David until he had gone out of the gates of the city and passed, together with all his household, to the other side of the brook.

There, in the Vale of Kidron, between the city and the Hill of Olive Trees, the son of Jesse found that he must sit and rest. The tenderness of the people and the freehandedness of Ittai had unmanned him utterly, so that he had feared to cross the brook and could not trust his footing on the steppingstones. And he covered his head with the mourning hood, and sank upon a hillock, and wept freely, no longer caring how red and swollen his eyes might be when he showed himself to Joab and the host.

After a little, he felt a hand upon his shoulder and saw that Adonijah was standing at his side. "Much as I regret to trouble my father," the young man said, "I must ask him to look toward the city, for a procession of priests has issued out of the gates and is drawing close to speak with my lord."

He saw them through the mist of his tears—the train of old priests and young Levites, their long robes trailing over the grass. First came Abiathar, picking an old man's unsteady way across the brook. Zadok followed after him, erect and self-confident, clad in the vestments of the high priest of Jerusalem. Then, on a low car drawn by two white oxen and attended by twenty young men in voluminous garments of white linen, came the ark of God. As the wagon drew closer to David, jolting over the little hillocks and the stones, he saw the pale box of timeworn acacia wood before which he had danced in the day of his glory.

Why was it, he asked himself, that I loved the ark of God with a boundless love? This box of acacia wood which approaches me now across the sunlit vale has nothing to do with any God that I have ever known— neither the Indulgent One who loves whom He chooses to love, nor the Other Jahveh who visited me in the days when I parted from Jonathan, nor the Stern Avenger who would not be moved to spare the little one, nor the Featureless One who has sat these last three years in the empty arch of Heaven. . . . And yet, as the procession drew closer and he beheld the rippling edges of the wood, he felt some vestige of the old yearning. It went with Moses, he said in his heart, and with the forlorn company of men and women and little ones when they wandered, as I must wander now, in the wilderness. . . . And he rose up and stood before it, not because God dwelt within it, but because multitudes had loved it and had changed it into a thing of wonder and beauty with the constancy of their love.

He leaned upon Adonijah's arm and remembered the voices of the people saying that he had lifted up Israel and fought with valor and judged with righteousness and brought the children of Jahveh an age of gold. If God is merciless, he said in his heart, time at least is merciful. As they have taken this box of acacia wood and made it holy, so also they may deal with me when I am no more. Out of a vain and weak and iniquitous man, those who are yet unborn may create a hero. Who can say what holy emanations may yet go out to lift up the hearts of the faithful from the bones within my burial cave? . . .

He walked forth then to meet Zadok and Abiathar, and bowed down in the grass before the ark of God.

"We have come with the ark," said Abiathar, raising him up, "to journey into the wilderness with the King our lord."

But he did not wish the ark to depart out of Jerusalem. In that tabernacle where I set it in the day of my glory, he thought, there let it abide. For I builded the city, and I brought the ark out of Philistia to be a beating heart within the city, nor will I carry the heart away with me, out of the reach of the multitude who have wept for me in the hour of my affliction. . . .

"No, now," he told the priests, "carry back the ark to the city. If God has any mercy to show unto me, He will bring me back and let me behold the ark again, together with Jerusalem in which it dwells. But if He takes no delight in me, then I am in His hands, and whatever He does,

He does, whether the ark is with me in the wilderness or with the children of Jerusalem."

The priests pleaded with him, pointing out that if he left them in Jerusalem, he left them in Absalom's hands. But he brought forward several excellent reasons for their staying behind: a procession of priests would retard his flight; any harm that might befall the ark on the long journey would be a loss not only to David but to all Israel; Zadok and Abiathar and their sons—stalwart and loyal men—might well serve the son of Jesse by sending him word of what came to pass after the ranks of Absalom had marched into the capital. Their lord was utterly right, the priests said at last; they would return to Jerusalem and offer up a solemn sacrifice for him on the high place. But before the little procession turned and retraced its way across the Vale of Kidron, the King drew close to the cart and touched the silky, age-old wood and laid his lips upon the unintelligible signs.

It was bright morning when David began his ascent of the Hill of Olive Trees. He covered his head and went up weeping, because he suddenly knew that once he had passed the crest of the hill, he would no longer be able to turn back and behold Jerusalem. And all the people that were with him covered every man his head, and the whole company went up, weeping as they went. The sons of Zeruiah had not yet brought the host of God to the meeting-place. Only a single figure stood on the summit of the hill—an old man whose features were indistinguishable because of the brightness behind him. When he beheld the exiles toiling up the slope, he came forward, and the King saw that he was Hushai the counselor, come in a mourner's garment and with earth upon his head to share the wanderings of his lord. And Hushai fell upon David's neck and embraced him, saying: "Let me come with you into exile and sit at your knees to offer you counsel, for Ahitophel is with Absalom, and we two shall strive together against the counsels of Ahitophel."

But David put him gently aside and said to him: "I will say unto you the same words that I said but a little while since to the priests and the Levites: If you follow after me, you will retard my flight. But if you return to the city and say unto Absalom, 'I will be your servant, O King, even as I have been your father's servant, in times past,' then you will defeat for me the counsels of Ahitophel. Zadok and Abiathar the priests will also abide within the walls, and whatsoever you will hear in my house, you can tell unto them, and they will send their sons to bring your words to me. Thus, even though I dwell in the wilderness, I will have knowledge of all that comes to pass in Jerusalem. Until I have word from you, I will tarry in Benjamin, at the fords of the Jordan. Go and do this for me, and no man will serve me better than Hushai the counselor."

So Hushai kissed David on both his cheeks, and stopped also to bless the young Solomon. Then he went down to the city, to dwell in the palace and wait for the coming of Absalom.

After his friend had departed from him, the son of Jesse sat upon a moss-covered log and stared down at the city which he had built. Between the houses—all luminous gray and golden under the sun—were patches of garden; he could distinguish the silvery shimmer of olive trees, the soft gray-green of figs, the bold, sharp green of palms. "If it should come to pass that I die in the wilderness," he said to Ittai, who was standing by, "let the son of Dagon see to it that my bones are carried back to the city and buried within the walls." And Ittai answered him, saying: "Surely, surely. But this will not come to pass. We will bring the King of Israel living into Jerusalem. We will lead him over strewn palm leaves back to his home."

So the King of Israel turned his back upon Jerusalem, and bade his steward bring up fruit and skins of goats' milk, so that all who were with him might eat and drink and be strengthened. And even as he ate, he saw the host of God approaching on the other side of the hill, and he rose up and went down to meet them between the trunks of the olives, nor did he turn back to look upon the city any more.

It was a settled matter that the host and the King's household should proceed through the territory of Benjamin toward the town of Bahurim, where they would pause that night to sleep. To this same town—a place of sleepy markets and dusty streets—the Star of Bethlehem had come long ago to meet Saul's daughter, when she had left her husband Paltiel for his sake. Hereabouts also lay the farmlands that were the portion of Meribaal; and, somewhat northward, the sons of Saul and Rizpah had planted a barren hill with vines whose fruit they had not lived to see. And, even though he was mounted now upon a donkey, the King grew exceedingly weary in his passage through Benjamin. All the sorrows which he had brought upon Saul's house weighed heavily upon him, so that he could not bring himself to converse with Abishai, who rode at his side. As I mourn now over the faithlessness of Absalom, he thought, so in the Gibean days Saul must have mourned over the faithlessness of Jonathan, who turned aside from his father and laid his love in my hands. . . . The day waxed very hot; all through the afternoon he rode across open farmland, with only a few scattered places of shade. And he asked himself, How is it that Benjamin does not send a host against me in the hour of my feebleness, seeing that the House of Kish, which I deserted and betrayed and ground into the dust, was once the glory of Benjamin? . . .

But the low hills and green valleys of Benjamin were open, empty, still. Between Jerusalem and Bahurim, the exiles had only two encounters, and the first of these was as balm upon the sore spirit of the King of Israel. Ziba, the overseer of Meribaal's estates, came forth to meet him with two saddled donkeys, and upon them two hundred loaves of bread and a hundred clusters of raisins and five baskets of summer fruits and a skin of wine. And Ziba said: "The donkeys are for the King's sons to ride upon, and the bread and the summer fruit are for the young men to eat, and the wine is for such as grow faint in the wilderness." These were the gifts of Meribaal, who, being lame in both his feet, knew that he would be a burden to the King if he followed after him. And David took a pomegranate and ate it; for it seemed to him that not only Meribaal but Jonathan also had sent him a gift of fruit in the hour of his affliction.

But the second encounter—it took place before the low brown gates of the town of Bahurim—did much to shatter the peace which Meribaal's devotion had established within David's breast. An old man—one Shimei of the House of Kish—ran forth cursing from the gates of the city, and mounted a ridge of shale that hung above the roadway, and stood against the red of the sunset, glaring down upon the exiles and cursing the King of Israel.

"Begone, begone from the city, you man of blood, you dog out of Judah!" Shimei said. "Jahveh has returned upon your head all the blood of the House of Saul, in whose stead you reigned. Behold, you are caught in the toils of your own iniquity, because you are a man of blood." And he bent and clawed up dust and shale from the ridge, and threw it down upon David and his host.

Then Abishai said: "Why should this dead dog curse my lord the King? Let me go up to him and take off his head."

But the King of Israel would not be moved from his knowledge that it was better to accept evil than to inflict it. He only drew the folds of his mourning hood closer to protect his face from the sharp bits of shale. "Who shall say who has put it into his head to curse me?" he said to Abishai. "Perhaps God Himself has put it into his head. Then wherefore should you stop his mouth? And wherefore indeed should he refrain from cursing me? If my own son, who came forth out of my bowels, rises up to seek after my life, then why should this Benjamite, a stranger, cease from cursing me? Let him alone, and let him curse his fill."

The old man followed them to the very gates of the city, clenching his fists against the blood-red sky, hurling imprecations at the House of Jesse, spitting upon the travelers from the ridge, and casting stones. And Joab, who had come first to the walls of Bahurim, rode back and said to the King that if all the men of Bahurim were as this squealing pig upon the ridge, it would be far better for the company to tarry in the fields for the night.

So they turned from Bahurim and moved into the meadows beyond the town and set up an encampment among the weeds. And all who had come up with David were worn with the journey and lay down to sleep as soon as they had broken bread. But the King of Israel neither drowsed nor slumbered. He found a hillock and laid his head upon it; and so long as the light lasted he presented to all those that were with him a calm and stedfast countenance. But when night came upon them, he turned his face against the grass and wept for Absalom.

◄§ V §►

"WHEN we are come into Jerusalem," Ahitophel had said a dozen times to the son of Maacah, "you must show yourself to the people in the role of the King of Israel. In all respects, from the smallest to the greatest, you must take your father's place."

The young man had heard this counsel so often that he knew the words by heart. And yet he had somehow failed to grasp their meaning. When he dismounted before the gate of the palace, he was appalled by the discovery that he could not escape from a literal observance of the admonition; he must cross the threshold of his father's house, he must dwell henceforth in the rooms and corridors which the son of Jesse had built and called his own.

When he first entered the common room and saw the empty board in the pale effulgence of the dusk, he was so discomfited as to consider the possibility of retreating from the house. "Look, now," he said, laying his hand upon Ahitophel's sleeve, "is it truly needful that I tarry in this desolate pile of stones when, not half an hour's distance beyond it, I have a much more comfortable dwelling-place?"

The old man smiled and shook his head. "You saw how it was with the people of the city, my lord. They drew their curtains against us when we rode through the streets. Their hearts are with David, and, so long as no man dwells within his palace, they will look for the hour of his return."

"No, now," said Absalom, laughing uneasily, "it was no more than a jest. I did not truly mean to take flight."

But in the hour of his triumph a heavy torpor had settled upon him. It was Ahitophel who summoned the servants and bade them spread a feast; it was he who sent ten young men of the bodyguard to search the palace lest some fierce partisan of David should be lurking in one of the rooms.

"We will lay the table for fifteen," said the counselor. "My lord, and Amasa, and twelve captains over thousands—is Absalom mindful of the fact that there are now twelve thousand in his host? And when we have eaten, we will hold a council, inasmuch as we must decide without delay when we will move northward. To my mind, it would be best to set out tomorrow at dawn."

One of the ten young men returned from the upper rooms and announced that the house was utterly empty. "I have been in the bedchamber of the son of Jesse," he said blithely, "and let me relate to you what I beheld. Lying on a clothes chest are all the regal ornaments—the collars, the bracelets, even the crown. It is as if the son of Jesse had thrown them all down in a heap, saying, 'Take them, for they are less to me than a handful of common stones.'"

"My lord," said Ahitophel, "inasmuch as David has left the ornaments, go up now and put them on, for they are your own."

"Later. I am weary. Let me rest."

"How is it that so young and vigorous a king should be too weary to take up his crown and set it upon his head? I will call your armor-bearer and tell him to come up to you——"

"No. Leave me in peace. Since it is plain to me that you will plague me until I have gone up, I will go. But let me go alone."

When he came into the dusky bedchamber, he found it difficult to breathe. David had plainly departed from the room in haste, forgetting to draw the curtains, and all the oppressive heat of a summer day was stored in the walls. Across the bed lay a splendid garment—yellow, with rich diagonal stripes of gold and white. Were I to enter the common room arrayed in it, the young man thought, I would dazzle the eyes of the company. . . . But when he held it against him, he was seized by a strange revulsion. Its folds gave off a scent that had clung about his father of late —the scent of the herb tea which David was wont to drink, morning and evening, to dispel an inward cold. God of Hosts, thought Absalom, will they require that I sleep in this chamber? I will not close my eyes tonight. . . .

He went to the clothes chest and began to sort out the ornaments. Collars, rings, bracelets—he laid them all in separate heaps. He found the golden circlet and set it upon his head. On the other side of the room, near a window which opened on clusters of palm leaves and a pale-green sky, stood another clothes chest with a great brazen basin upon it. The basin was filled with water which held upon its surface the color of the sky and the darkened image of a palm frond. He leaned over the water and beheld his face floating upon it—dim, shadowy, beautiful, the black locks flowing back into darkness, the mouth parted, the circlet gleaming upon the brow. He bent closer, smiling at his reflection. Comely, very comely, he said to himself. When was there so comely a king in Israel, so comely a murderer, so comely a parricide? . . .

No, no, he thought, I cannot permit them to kill him. I cannot let them ride forth tomorrow to take him in the wilderness. Somehow I must find a means to make them tarry until he has found refuge behind the walls of Mahanaim. Otherwise, how could I sleep upon this bed which is hollowed by the weight of his body? Otherwise, how should I wear this crown which has been shaped to the curve of his brow? . . .

"My lord the King," said a voice from the doorway.

He started and told himself, It is not my father of whom my armor-bearer speaks. It is I; I am the King of Israel. . . .

"My lord the King, here is a man who would have a word with you."

He wheeled round and saw, behind his armor-bearer, the tall, spare form of Hushai, his father's chief counselor. "Hushai? How is it that Hushai has tarried in Jerusalem?"

Hushai walked round the armor-bearer and held out both his hands to Absalom. "Long live the King!" he said, and bowed himself down at the young man's feet.

The son of Maacah waved his armor-bearer away from the door. He stood silent for some moments, frowning and staring down at the bowed white head. He could find no suitable name by which to refer to David. To say "the King of Israel" was impossible, nor could he force the words "my father" from his lips. To say "the son of Jesse" seemed an evasion and an affectation, and there was something unbearably pathetic in the phrase "the Star of Bethlehem." At last he bent and raised Hushai up. "Is this your kindness to your friend?" he said. "How is it that you did not follow your friend into the wilderness?"

And Hushai said to Absalom: "No, now, he whom Jahveh has chosen and the multitude and all the warriors of the land have chosen, his will I be and with him will I abide. Whom else should I serve? If I have served the father, shall I not serve the son? As I was in David's presence, even so will I be in the presence of Absalom."

Whatever further reproaches came into the young man's thoughts died without finding voice. For, he told himself, it is not my place to berate him—I who stand in my father's bedchamber, with his crown upon my head. . . . And he turned and went to a clothes chest and opened it. "Come, then," he said, "and show me which of these robes have not yet been worn. There is to be a feast below, and a council after it, and I cannot sit at table in these dusty garments that have been upon my back since dawn."

They knelt together then before the clothes chest. Most of the garments which lay toward the top of the chest had, according to Hushai, been worn on one occasion or another by the King of Israel. But near the bottom there was a splendid robe of pleated white linen embroidered with squares of blue and violet, and this, the old counselor vowed, he had never seen before. The son of Maacah put it on, and Hushai gathered it in at the waist with pins, and covered his rough handiwork with a broad violet girdle which he found in another chest. By this time they were chatting together with complete ease and amity. And, before they descended to the common room together, Absalom had invited Hushai to sit at the feast and had asked him expressly to raise his voice in the council that was to be held that night.

❧ VI ❧

It could not be said of the son of Maacah that he was a winebibber. From his early childhood, when he had learned to take his little cupful with his father, he had shown himself to be a tasteful and temperate drinker. He seldom drank more than two bowlfuls in the course of a council, and one bowlful was all that he required with bread and meat. Yet it could not be said of him either that he had never been drunken, for twice his servants had seen him flushed and wild and unsteady on his feet. On that day when his sister had come to him with her garment rent, he had emptied a tall cruet between dusk and moonrise, and he had consumed enough wine to unman two strong warriors while he supervised the preparations for that supper at which his brother Amnon was slain. Much to the distress of Ahitophel, who had never seen him otherwise than abstemious, he took to deep drinking on the evening of his arrival in Jerusalem.

564

He had set out to drink more than usual for certain very trivial reasons: The accursed pins that Hushai had seen fit to put into his garment were chafing his flesh, and his head had begun to ache because of the pressure of the circlet against his brow. He found it difficult to hold conversation with his captains over thousands—his witty sallies fell blunt before the stolid faces of Judahites, Kenites, and Calebites. Whenever he raised his eyes from his plate, he was oppressed by the length and the somberness of the room—gray pillars whose capitals were lost against a shadowy ceiling, high windows curtained against the silent, hostile multitude that had congregated outside. "This house is hideous!" he shouted to Ahitophel across the wondering faces of his captains. "There is but one way to mend it—tear it down and build another in its place."

He had no sooner uttered the words than he regretted them. Not because they had sown consternation among the captains—he cared no more for the captains than for a flock of sheep. But it was a sorry business—or so at least it seemed in the fumes of his fourth bowlful of wine—that he should have spoken of pulling down the stones which the son of Jesse had set up with so much pride and eagerness in the days of his prime. "I was mistaken concerning the house," he said in the uncomfortable silence. "It is a good house, even if it is somewhat oversolemn. A few plants brought in from the garden, a few lengths of bright cloth, will set it to rights."

Yet the ache within him would not cease; he no longer heard what was being said to his left and to his right; he rejected the pastry and the fruit. Gazing at the vista of shadows and columns that stretched out before him, he wished himself in Geshur, among his grandfather's black tents and shaggy herds; he yearned after his little daughter and wondered how it was with his Syrian wife. When she comes to me in Jerusalem, he thought, we will go up to the high place and implore the God of Hosts to give us a son. The moon-god Sin gave us three boys, one after the other, but what was the good of it, seeing that all of them were born dead? . . . The flames of the lamps swelled and blurred before his eyes, and he wiped his cheeks furtively, afraid that he had begun to weep. He saw by Ahitophel's admonishing glance that he had remained silent too long, and he turned earnestly to the Judahite captain who sat at his right. "I will build me a tall pillar in the King's dale in Jerusalem," he said. "I have but one daughter, called Tamar. God has given me no sons, so I will raise up a pillar to commemorate my name." And he grew even more desolate because the Judahite offered him no condolences, but stared into his face with amazed eyes.

I am drunken, I am exceedingly drunken, he thought, filling his bowl for the sixth time. Surely Ahitophel will see how it is with me and send them all forth and let me lie down upon my bed. . . . He leaned over the board and made certain signs to Amasa, who sat at the far end of the table conversing with Hushai and a valiant Calebite. The signs were intended to indicate to Amasa that he should tell Ahitophel that the King of Israel was drunken and could not give proper attention to matters of state. But

565

though Amasa bent far forward and strove earnestly to understand, he was forced in the end to shrug his shoulders and shake his head. No, now, thought Absalom, if I cannot make myself plain to Amasa who dwelt with me among the black tents of Geshur, who then will understand? . . . And he lifted his bowl and drank off a long, blinding draught, so that he seemed to be transported away from the table, away from the world. . . .

He was wakened out of his drowse by the clatter of dishes. The servants had begun to clear the table, and many of the guests had left their seats. "Are they departing, then?" he said aloud, and saw that he had addressed his question to Ahitophel, who had come round the board and was standing at his side. "If they are departing, it is well. I am very weary. I will bid them farewell and go up to sleep."

"No, now," the old counselor said softly, "they are merely stretching their legs while the servants carry away the leavings of the feast. In a moment they will come again to the table to hold council with the King my lord."

Through the blur of wine, Absalom could see Ahitophel's face—the wispy beard, the bald forehead, the red, shortsighted eyes. He speaks to me softly to soothe me, he thought. He believes that he can cajole me and direct me in my drunkenness. . . . "Look, now," he said aloud, drawing away from the old man's touch, "we will hold council tomorrow. Wherefore this haste? I am in no great haste for anything but sleep."

"My lord," said Ahitophel in a patient voice, "I also am weary and would gladly put the matter off, but it cannot wait. Come, now, rise and walk about the room a little. It is only that you have journeyed long and eaten heavily——"

"It is neither of these. I am drunken with wine."

"That too will pass. Furthermore, it is not necessary that the King should trouble himself. I will say whatever is needful. Nothing is required of the King save that he should nod his head."

Absalom rose from his chair so suddenly that the counselor started backward in fright. If he dreams that he can drag the council this way and that and accomplish whatsoever he chooses, the son of Maacah thought, then I will show him. I am not so drunken as he thinks. . . .

And yet when he turned his back upon the counselor and found his way into the middle of the room, it became plain to him that he could not walk any considerable distance alone. As soon as he came to a pillar, he leaned back against it and stood staring down at two gray paving stones. They were joined together by a dark, uneven line which seemed particularly loathsome to him. I will never forget that line, he thought; it is engraved forever upon my memory; I will surely vomit if I stare at it much longer. . . . Then Amasa came and linked arms with him and drew him back to the table.

"Here is my lord the King. Let us begin," Amasa said.

The son of Maacah scarcely heard the long introductory speech that issued from the lips of the melancholy Ishmaelite. Amasa made no pretence to eloquence; he spoke in a low, almost sorrowful voice, looking down at the lamp that had been set before him and now and then letting his chin drop to his chest. He murmured that there were some twelve thousand sons of Jahveh gathered beneath the banners of Absalom, that more than threescore towns and cities and villages had offered their allegiance, that there were six hundred horses, eleven hundred mules, and an undetermined number of camels which the sons of Caleb had been so obliging as to bring up out of the south. . . . And the son of Maacah, lulled into drowsiness by the monotonous flow of his voice, rested his arm against the table and his cheek against his arm, and thought with disgust that the board smelled of wine.

When the captain had seated himself and the congratulatory whispers had died away, an uncomfortable silence settled upon the room. What are they waiting for? Absalom asked himself. . . . The silence persisted, and he saw that he must bestir himself. He straightened and found his voice. "God walk with Amasa. He has spoken exceedingly well," he said. "Now let us hear from Ahitophel."

He had thought that the old counselor sat at some distance from him; he was surprised to see him rising out of the chair at his right hand. Ah, God, he thought, shielding his eyes from the glow of the lamps, why have I called upon him? He will lift up his voice and urge them to pursue my father. . . .

He could not bring himself to raise his head and look upon the speaker's face; he could see nothing but the old man's hand, white and palsied, tapping lightly against the board. It is a loathsome hand, he thought, cold and spotted like a toad. Is it possible that I have kissed it? And he wiped his lips.

"Hearken, my lord the King," said Ahitophel. "Hearken also, Amasa, captain of the host, and all you gallant warriors who have led up thousands to follow after the banners of the King our lord. In the days when I served the House of Kish—may the peace of God be upon their bones!—I had many an occasion to see the fruits of victory rot in the hands of the victorious while they said to one another, 'Now which way shall we turn? Have we not accomplished enough? Is it not better to wait, to consider, to reinforce our ranks?' Had the Lion of Benjamin not wasted his triumphs at the council table, Philistia would never have marched up to Gilboa and Israel would never have been torn in twain. This, then, is the counsel which I offer to Absalom: Let us take the twelve thousand men whom God has given us, and arise and pursue after David this very night. Thus we will come upon him while he is weary and weakhanded, and his host will be panic-stricken, and all the people that are with him will flee. Of all who are exiles in the wilderness, we will smite David only. We will bring back the rest unharmed, so that no son of Jahveh can find anything but mercy and loving-kindness in Absalom. Only let my lord the King accept the counsel of his servant, and tomorrow he will be the sole king in Israel."

The son of Maacah lifted up his head and saw that every one of his captains waited only for his word to be up and away. They are in league with Ahitophel against me, he said in his heart. While I tarried by the pillar, they whispered together, saying, "He would not have his father slain this night, but he is drunken and cannot raise his hand." . . . Then, at the far end of the table, another rose up, very tall and spare and old. "Behold, I also am a counselor," said Hushai. "Have I not come to serve Absalom even as I served his father before him? Let me say a word then before the King my lord."

Another speech, thought Absalom, will at least add a little time to the sleep which my father sleeps this night in the wilderness. . . .

Ahitophel turned and laid his hand upon Absalom's arm. "No, now," he whispered, "there is no time——"

But Absalom thrust his hand aside. "We will hear Hushai, my father's chief counselor," he said.

For the first time that night, those who sat around the council table were given a taste of courtly eloquence. David's chief counselor—lordly to behold with the glow of the lamps on his white hair and his meager, expressive face—spoke to them in the language of the sweet singers and the prophets, dazzling them with a shower of comparisons and parables. It was true, he said, gesturing with his delicate fingers, that the son of Jesse had but a few warriors with him. But the host of David was bereaved and filled to overflowing with bitterness. The host of David was as a bear who has been robbed of her whelps in the field, as a she-bear who falls upon her tormentors to tear them apart. Who, then, could believe that such a host would resort to flight? If the son of Jesse had not fled from the Philistines, the Ammonites, the Edomites, the Moabites, why should he turn and run now, when nothing was to be gained by flight, when cowardice, like valor, could have no end but death? Surely Absalom at least knew his father to be a man of war. As for this matter of panic, the wise counselor Ahitophel—all honor to him—had said some moments since that panic would surely descend upon David's host. Had it never entered his mind that panic might fall upon the ranks of Absalom?

"No, now," said Ahitophel, starting out of his chair. "Why should twelve thousand look upon six thousand and flee?"

Hushai smiled. "Ahitophel thinks to find the son of Jesse sleeping in the open fields," he said. "But when he comes into the wilderness, he will search the face of the land for him in vain. Behold, I tell you that even now he is hidden in some pit or cave or stretch of brush, and he will fall upon the host of Absalom suddenly in the black of the night, and there will be slaughter among the people that follow Absalom. Then panic will descend upon us, and even he whose heart is as the heart of the lion will utterly melt; for those who are with us know that David is a mighty man, and they will think him mightier still when they feel the edge of his sword in the dark, and they will turn and flee. Therefore I earnestly entreat the King my lord not to accept the counsel of Ahitophel.

Let us tarry in Jerusalem instead until we have gathered a host whose numbers are as the grains of sand beside the sea. Let us wait until we have brought all the men of Jahveh from Dan unto Beersheba to serve beneath the standard of Absalom. Then we will light upon David as the dew falls upon the ground, and of all the men that are with him we will not leave so much as one to be a thorn in Absalom's side. Furthermore, if the son of Jesse can be got into a city, then shall all Israel bring ropes to that city, and we shall draw it into the river until there is not one small stone of it left behind. Such is my counsel. Now let the King choose between it and the counsel of Ahitophel."

Then Absalom and all the men of war that were with him at the council table said as in a single voice, "The counsel of Hushai is better than the counsel of Ahitophel."

It was about the third hour of the evening when they rose from the board. Absalom turned from Ahitophel and leaned upon Amasa, who led him to an upper chamber and loosed his garments and laid him upon a bed. Hushai went from the palace to the high place, where he recounted all that had come to pass before Abiathar and Zadok, that they might send their sons with tidings to David in the wilderness. Then he returned to the King's house and lay down to sleep. But Ahitophel went forth from the house of David and returned to it no more. That same night he journeyed to his native town of Gilo, and set his house in order, and made a testament unto his sons. And, after he had prayed a little and made his peace with God, he went up into his loft room and fastened a rope to a beam and hanged himself.

⇜§ VII §⇝

MAHANAIM, that crumbling fortress town east of the Jordan, had harbored a royal household once before. Here, more than twenty years ago, Ishbaal had filled his empty hours with eating and gardening and wrestling matches, until that day when the sons of Rimmon smothered him in his bed. Here Abner and Rizpah also had made a garden. Both of them had departed into Sheol now, leaving neither sons nor daughters, but it was possible that some of the vines that wandered over the brown bricks of Mahanaim had been planted by their hands.

It was a drowsy town, mellow and aimless; its very name was a sleepy murmur upon the lips. The fields and orchards beyond it yielded a sufficiency of grain and fruit; the meadowland along the river nourished sleek flocks and herds; and the men of Ishbaal had brought the vine into the midst of the city, so that a man had only to thrust his hand forth from his window to take the wherewithal for his raisins and his wine. The bees, drunken with plenty, reeled over the meadows and the orchards with a continuous, slumbrous sound. Honey stood in the comb for the taking, and golden drops of honey oozed from the wax as slowly as the hours.

It was, thought the son of Zeruiah in the first days of his sojourn there, such a town as would tempt the exiled King of Israel to fall into that same daze which had brought him to such a sorry pass in Jerusalem. When the ranks of David entered the brown gates, it was made plain that the host would be cared for. A storehouse had been set aside for them, and the sons and daughters of Mahanaim had already begun to fill it when the King of Ammon anticipated their generosity by sending up a month's supply of oil and wine and flour. Two wealthy elders of the land of Gilead —Barzillai of Rogelim and Machir of Lo-debar—brought beds and basins and earthen vessels, wheat and barley and parched grain, beans and pulse and lentils, honey and butter and cheese of the herd. "These are for David and for the people that are with him," they said. "For the people are hungry and thirsty and weary after their sojourn in the wilderness, and it is only fitting that they should eat and drink and rest."

The captain of the host was glad that Machir at least departed along with the donkeys that had carried his bounty. But Barzillai tarried in Mahanaim, and for three full days the son of Jesse did nothing but talk with his guest in his little garden. God of Hosts, thought the son of Zeruiah, passing the two of them on his way to the encampment, while they sit, the host of Absalom has grown to thirty thousand, and we are but six thousand behind crumbling walls. . . . And on the evening of the third day he could bear it no longer. "If my lord the King wishes to live out another moon," he said at supper, "let him bestir himself and think of the battle that is to come." The son of Jesse pushed his plate aside. "I have been thinking of it," he said. "It might be well to meet the host of Absalom in the forest of Ephraim. Let us go down and look upon that same forest tomorrow before noon."

From that moment forth, the Star of Bethlehem was all that his captain could require—a man of war, a brilliant strategist, sage in council and vigorous in his dealings with the host. That he should have chosen the forest of Ephraim as the place of battle was in itself a proof of his genius; here and only here six thousand might be able to confound thirty thousand, with the help of God. The uneven ground, the slippery, winding paths, the low, interlacing boughs of the wild olives and the terebinths, would be a salvation to those who knew them well and a snare to those who knew them not. Now he dragged the unwilling Barzillai along with him on the business of war. When he was not examining the forest, he sat at the gates of the city, reviewing his ranks and instructing his captains over hundreds and captains over thousands. The fame of his army was spread through the land, so that three thousand farmers came to him out of Gilead. And the town of Mahanaim was roused out of its long sleep and resounded with the ring of the anvil day and night.

"A great change has come upon my uncle," said the son of Zeruiah to the King of Israel one afternoon when they were wandering unattended in the forest of Ephraim.

The son of Jesse stopped beneath the boughs of a terebinth and turned a thoughtful face upon him. "Change? What change?" he said.

"Surely my lord the King remembers how it was with him not long since—how he said that he would not lift up his hand to save himself or his throne."

The King smiled. "And does the captain of the host believe that an angel of God has come to me by night and restored to my heart the desire for life and the wish for a throne? Do not deceive yourself. As I was in Jerusalem, so I am in Mahanaim. If I go out to make war in the forest, it is not for the sake of my life or for the sake of the throne."

"I have lived in the presence of David nigh unto fifty years," said Joab. "Yet I cannot say that I have known him. There is much in David that I cannot understand."

"No, now, it is a simple matter. Behold, when I came up to Mahanaim, I thought to tarry here even as Ishbaal tarried, until such a time as those about me grew weary of me and sent up a strong man to smother me also in my bed. This I said to Barzillai, who is very old and somewhat foolish, but he made me a good answer. He said to me, 'Are you not a shepherd? What of the sheep?' And I thought then—no, now, what does it matter what I thought? Let it pass. . . .'"

"Am I less than Barzillai in the eyes of my lord, that he should tell a stranger what is in his heart and straightway turn his back upon me, saying, 'Let it pass'?"

The long pale hand of David—dry and veined and withered now—reached out through the greenish light and rested gently upon Joab's hand. "It was only that it was a strange thought, and I did not wish to burden the ears of the captain of the host. Long ago, in the hills above Bethlehem, I made a mighty name for myself because I killed a young lion that came to harry my father's sheep. It was not for the sake of the lambs and the ewes that I killed the lion—it was for the glory that the slaying of a lion would bring upon my own head. But now, being utterly weary of the world and of myself, having had all things and yearning after nothing more, I still cannot lie down to sleep while the flock is left to be ravaged in the open field. I will go back to Jerusalem for the sake of the children of Jerusalem, who wept to see me depart. Before I take unto myself my everlasting rest, I will kill one lion for the sake of the sheep."

And as the weeks of waiting were drawn out to three moons, Joab saw that the Star of Bethlehem was truly willing to do far more for his flock than for himself. He dwelt in a black tent in the encampment. He seldom showed his face to Bath-sheba and the others of his household, but pored over the battle plans far into the night. He went with small bands of warriors into the forest of Ephraim and explored the face of the land until he knew every alley, every grove, every network of branches. He insisted that he would march forth with them on the day of the battle, and would not be dissuaded until they made it plain to him that he would be a charge to them in the midst of the fight. It is with him now, thought the captain of the host, as it was in the days of his glory. Even though I should die in the forest of Ephraim, yet would I die with a high heart, for I have been the first servant of the greatest warrior who ever fought in Israel. Not Saul, not Abner, not Joshua, not Barak, could be likened unto my lord. . . . And when they brought him the news that the ranks of Absalom were marching northward thirty thousand strong along the western bank of the Jordan, Joab was not afraid. "When we depart for the forest tomorrow," he said to David, "stand at the gate of the city and wish us well, for the men of Israel are bound flesh and spirit to David, and their souls will be strengthened by the sight of his face."

At sunrise Joab brought the host of David out by the gate of the city, and the King stood at the gate smiling upon them. They came forth in three divisions, because they were to be stationed at three different points in the forest—a third of them with Joab and a third with Abishai and a third with Ittai of Gath. Then the King put forth his hand and blessed them, and they made ready to depart. But even as they turned their faces toward the distant green of the forest, David called Ittai and the sons of Zeruiah back, as though he had forgotten some final command. In a loud voice, so that the host might hear, he charged the three of them, saying, "Deal gently for my sake with the young man Absalom." And they swore before the God of Hosts that they would obey the King's command.

✑ VIII ✑

IT WAS pale morning, gray and misty, when the men of David took up their stations in the woods. The plan of battle had been drawn around a certain grove which the Canaanites had cleared generations since in the center of the forest for the worship of Baal and Astarte—a place of uneven ground covered with lush, high weeds that concealed the stumps of felled trees and the remains of ancient altars. This grove, roughly triangular in shape, was bounded on all sides by the interlacing boughs of wild olives and terebinths. Joab and the flower of David's host were stationed at the northernmost point. The captain and the first three hundred of his men stood in the clearing, their banners spread to catch the eye of the advancing enemy and tempt him forth into the midst of the grove, where his cavalry might come to grief among the slippery weeds and the hidden stumps and stones. But the men of Abishai and the men of Ittai stood far to the south, on opposite points of the triangle, screened by the thick trees at the eastern and western tips of the grove, motionless, holding their shields and swords beneath their cloaks so that they would not shine in the first rays of the sun. For it had been determined in council that the men of Abishai and Ittai would not give battle until the ranks of Joab had engaged the warriors of Absalom. Then, at the sound of Joab's trumpet, they would fall upon the rebels from left and right, and smite them and drive them forth out of the glade into the winding alleys of the forest, where, with the help of God, they could be taken in small numbers and slain.

Their wait was long. The host of Absalom, which had crossed the Jordan and advanced toward the forest during the night, tarried on the western fringes until midmorning; and even when they plunged into the green shadow at last, their advance was slow. Plainly the rebels were at odds with the forest: they were coming up at a snail's pace; there were calls and curses, commands and countercommands. The men in the ranks of Ittai peered through the network of leaves and twigs, eager to catch a glimpse of Absalom. That same morning, on the march down to the forest, their captain had promised ten pieces of silver to any warrior who would bring him the son of Maacah untouched. "For," he had said, "I also have sons in Gath, and I would behold the old King's face when the eldest of his house is restored to him."

It was Amasa who was the first to break through the screen of trees at the southern border of the grove. He was mounted on a dappled horse and clothed in a scarlet tunic. On either side of him, the foremost ranks of the rebel cavalry issued into the clearing, drew rein, and looked about them. The archers of Abishai, seeing the magnificent figure of the melancholy Ishmaelite through the interlacing boughs, were hard put to it to contain themselves. As one man, they drew a long, deep breath. Afterward no man could say how it had come to pass—whether it was that long inward gasp of zeal or the will of the Lord that made the rebel captain blind to Joab's flying banners and drew his eyes to Abishai's hidden host. But from that moment there was no longer a plan of battle. Amasa, who was to have fallen upon Joab, straightway wheeled his ranks around and rushed at the men of Abishai, and the matter was given into the hand of God.

The ranks of Joab and the mercenaries under the command of Ittai surged forward in complete disorder to the aid of their comrades. They were intercepted—and their line of advance was shattered—by the innumerable and impetuous troops of Absalom. From the third hour of the morning until the sun hung hot and high above the clearing, there were confused commands, clashes between isolated groups of horsemen, aimless showers of arrows, swift assaults and retreats. Then, very slowly, the battle moved out of the confines of the grove and was drawn through the winding pathways into every part of the wood. The boughs of the terebinths and the wild olives were snapped by the passage of terrified riders. The alleys of the forest echoed with the screams of the dying; the greenish light was sifted down upon the open hands and wondering faces of the dead. And the men of David saw that God had done for them that which the plan of battle had failed to do; for the host of Absalom was divided and disorganized, fighting on unknown ground, with slippery weeds and roots beneath their feet and vines and leaves before their faces. Then their courage waxed great within them, and they called to each other among the trees, saying, "Take heart, for the day is ours!" They stood firm among the growing heaps of the slain, and the men of Absalom grew sore afraid, so that they gave way by fifties and by hundreds, and turned and took to flight. And there was a great slaughter of twenty thousand men that day in the forest of Ephraim, and the forest devoured more of the sons of Jahveh than the sword devoured.

Since the beginning of the encounter, the son of Zeruiah had twice ridden the width of the forest of Ephraim. Ten young horsemen had been with him from the start. They had made it their purpose to seek out the rebel captains; and, although they had not once caught sight of Amasa or the son of Maacah, they had slain some fifty of the flower of Absalom's host. Now, finding themselves in a secluded glade with the noise of battle far from them, they knew themselves to be greatly in need of rest.

"Let us stop and bind up our wounds," said Joab. He himself had twice been grazed by arrows, once on the shoulder and once on the knee. "Go and care for each other," he told the little crowd of solicitous youths who gathered around him as he dismounted. "I am well enough. If I am gray in the face, it is only with weariness, and you will cure that most swiftly by leaving me to myself."

He tethered his horse to the twisted trunk of an olive tree. Even though shouts and the clatter of arms still sounded in certain distant reaches of the forest, the battle was over. Those among the ranks of Absalom who had survived would soon be in full flight toward the Jordan—he knew it as certainly as a mariner knows that the day will be fine. Well done, he said to himself; and he sat down in utter weariness in the shadow of a tree.

He looked at the wounds on his knee and shoulder; they ached, but they were nothing; they were already well covered with dried blood. He was resting his head against the trunk of the wild olive when he heard footfalls behind him. A Judahite warrior, one of his own men, squat and stolid and shining with the sweat of battle, came up and stood before him. "Not fifty paces from this place I have seen a strange sight," the warrior said. "Absalom, the son of our lord the King—he is hanging in a terebinth, and his life is yet whole within him."

The captain started up and clutched the Judahite's shoulder. "What? What is this?" he said.

"The son of Maacah was riding upon his mule in flight before the men of David, and the mule went under the thick boughs of a great terebinth, and the King's son was taken up by the boughs between heaven and earth, and the mule that was under him went on."

"You saw him and smote him not? I would have given you ten pieces of silver and a fine girdle if you had told me, 'I struck him down.'"

The Judahite stared somberly into the captain's face. "Though a thousand pieces of silver should be laid in my palm," he said, "yet would I not put forth my hand against the King's son; for in our hearing the King charged you and Abishai and Ittai, saying, 'Have a care, whosoever you be, that you do not touch the young man Absalom.' Had I taken his life, the King would have known as much, for nothing is hidden from the King our lord. And as for you—you also would have set yourself against me and punished me before the host for David's sake."

He is not so stupid as he looks, thought Joab. Nevertheless . . . A quiver filled with darts hung round the Judahite's waist, and Joab thrust his hand into it and drew forth three darts and tested their sharpness against his palm.

"Inasmuch as the King our lord has charged us expressly——" said the warrior.

"No, now, I cannot tarry here in speech with you," said the captain, and he turned and went from the glade, following the trail of trodden grass that had been left by the Judahite.

God keep the mercenaries of Ittai away from the spot! he said to himself. For the sake of ten pieces of silver any one of them would take him down, so that he might yet live to murder his father in his bed. . . . But all about him the forest was empty. Even the last sounds of battle had ceased, and the place was oppressively still. Suddenly he stopped, and his heart beat violently, for he saw the tree and that which hung upon it—the fair body in its tunic of white linen writhing against the green—the chin caught in the fork of a branch, the long hair spread out among the leaves.

Because the Judahite had told him that Absalom was hanging between heaven and earth, the son of Zeruiah had expected to find him high in the midst of the tree. He saw now that the young man had been taken up by the lowest of the boughs; his toes, not more than three hand-breadths above the ground, grazed the tips of the tall grass. Then it will be a small matter to smite him while he is yet in the tree, he told himself. . . . And he drew close to the terebinth, holding the darts in his hand. Absalom's face, thrust backward by the prongs of the branch, was blue and distorted. His eyes were two watery, colorless slits beneath his swollen lids, yet the captain felt that those eyes were fastened upon him. Is it possible that he can see? he asked himself. . . . He did not pause until his face was level with the taut neck. Then, with his left arm, he clasped the young man and held him still. "Traitor, rebel, fratricide!" he said. And he thrust the darts into Absalom's heart.

Yet the son of Maacah lived, struggling and twisting. And terror seized upon Joab, so that he sprang backward. Behold what I have done, he said in his heart. I have taken the son of my lord helpless, and I have thrust at him with shaking hands, so that he suffers and will not die. For this my lord will surely hate me and utterly turn from me. . . . There was no other weapon upon him—he had left his sword beneath the olive tree. In his horror he called aloud after the ten young men who had accompanied him to the glade. They came swiftly, thinking that some evil had befallen him, then stopped and stared in consternation at the writhing body in the tree. "Smite him now," said Joab, "for he is in great anguish." And they compassed Absalom about and slew him with many wounds, with spears and swords. And because his comely face was swollen beyond recognition and his fair body was torn by twenty wounds, they did not dare to bear him back to Mahanaim to his father, but cast him into a pit in the forest and raised over him a great mound of stones.

While they labored over the monument, the son of Zeruiah sounded the trumpet to bring the host of David together. Among the first to come out of the midst of the wood was a certain Ahimaaz, the youngest of the sons of Zadok, who had come up to Mahanaim with messages for David and had tarried in the ranks of God. "Come, now," he said, lifting his dark and winsome face to Joab's, "let me bring the news to the King. I am a swift runner, and all the news that I have carried before this day has been evil news, and I desire for once to take our lord such news as will delight his heart." But the son of Zeruiah pushed the youth aside and chose from those who were gathering around the terebinth an Ethiopian slave, a servant of Ittai's, to bear the tidings to the gates. When he had instructed the slave and sent him on his way, he wandered apart from the others and sat down on a knoll with his back to the terebinth and covered his face with his hands. His body had begun to shake so violently that he did not wish any man to look upon him. For they will say among themselves that I am old and outworn, he thought, pressing his palms against his quaking jaw. . . .

Ahimaaz, the son of Zadok, came and flung himself down at his captain's feet. "Even though you have sent the Ethiopian to Mahanaim, yet let me run also," he said.

"Bear tidings another day. This day you will bear no tidings, inasmuch as the King's son is dead."

"Nevertheless, whatever has come to pass, let me run after the Ethiopian."

"Wherefore would you run, my son? I tell you, you will get no thanks for the news from the King of Israel."

"Nevertheless, I beg you——"

Why should I trouble my mind over what will befall this young fool? the son of Zeruiah thought. . . . And he shrugged and thrust at the lad with his foot. "Go then. Run," he said.

It was late afternoon before all the host of God was assembled. Their delight in the victory was clouded by the knowledge that they had left more than three thousand of their comrades among the slain. Abishai had come forth unscathed out of the engagement; but Ittai of Gath could scarcely sit upon his steed alone. He had been thrown from his saddle and trampled; his arm was mangled; there could be no cure save to lop it off, the surgeons said. During the long wait in the forest, one warrior after another walked round the great gray mound of stones. They stared at it and whispered together. "God help that man who laid the son of Maacah low!" they said. "For did the King our lord not charge all of us expressly, saying, 'Deal gently for my sake with the young man

576

Absalom'?" And their hearts were heavy when they departed out of the forest of Ephraim.

❧ IX ❧

From the first hours of the morning until late afternoon, the King of Israel sat upon the ground before the gates of Mahanaim. He had made it plain to those who remained within the city that he wanted no company. I am an old man now, he told himself, and I have waited many times—in the Valley of the Rocks, in the plains of Sharon, in Ziklag, in the high house in Jerusalem—and this at least I have learned in the passage of the years: that no man can fully share another's exigency. . . . The meadowland before the gates of the town stretched out for miles before him; far off the trees of the forest of Ephraim stood dark against the sky. The world upon which he gazed was as empty as though the race of men had departed from it, for no herdsman had led his beasts into the fields and no farmer had gone out to gather the grain.

He did not lift up his voice to God that day, but he spoke very earnestly to the dead. "Look, now, my father," he said, turning his face toward the purple hills of Moab, "at long last I have remembered the sheep." He conjured up a vision of Noi going down the hall with a lamp toward the room of a sick servant. "See, now," he told her, "should we meet in Sheol I would blush the less, inasmuch as I also have risen from my bed by night to tend the wounds of Israel." To the Lion of Benjamin he said, "They strive now in the forest of Ephraim so that all which you brought to pass at Michmash and Ephes-Dammim and Jabesh-Gilead shall not have been in vain." And to Jonathan, "Though I should die while the land is broken in twain, yet have I endeavored to mend it, nor will I cease while the breath is yet in me, believe me, beloved."

High above him, in the tower room in the right-hand pylon of the gate, a single watchman had been stationed. The King of Israel had not seen the face of the watchman; he was no more than a voice raised against the utter silence, for the city was hushed with waiting and no sound of battle could carry across the broad fields. Now and again the son of Jesse would lift up his voice and call to the watchman, "What do you see?" And all through the morning and the early afternoon the answer was "Nothing, my lord."

Nothing, nothing—the agony among the trees was so small as to be invisible in the magnitude of the earth; the dark, uneven line of the wood remained solid, imperturbable; a thousand died, and not one of the upper branches stirred. . . . And then at last, when the sun had begun to decline, the watchman called from his tower, saying to the King, "Behold, a man has come forth out of the forest land and is running across the fields alone."

"If he is alone," said David, "then he is not fleeing out of the battle.

577

Surely there are tidings in his mouth." And he rose up and stood against the gate.

In a moment the watchman called again. "Behold, there is another man, and he also is running alone."

"Then he also brings tidings."

"I think the running of the foremost is like the running of Ahimaaz, the son of Zadok."

And the King said, "He is a good man and will bring us good news."

Now, over the curve of the sunlit meadow, he also could see the first of the runners—Ahimaaz, the son of Zadok, who had outrun the Ethiopian in his zeal to tell good tidings to the King of Israel. Far off—so far that his voice was scarcely audible even in the complete silence—he stopped and made a trumpet of his hands and shouted, "All is well!" And he came and flung himself down at David's feet, and said, "Blessed be Jahveh your God, who has delivered up the men who lifted up their hands against my lord the King."

Then at least it was well with the sheep. But the heart of the son of Jesse was not lifted up within him. He stared at the bowed, glistening shoulders of the runner and said, "Is it well with the young man Absalom?"

The stripling did not raise his head. "When Joab sent me forth out of the battle, I saw a great tumult, but I knew not what it was——"

And David was sore afraid, for there was uneasiness in the lad's voice; and when the King raised him up from the earth, he turned aside and could not bring himself to look into the King's eyes. "Well, then," David said, "stand with me here against the gate until the second runner also has told us his news."

"Behold," called the voice from the watchtower, "he that comes now is an Ethiopian, a servant unto Ittai of Gath."

The second runner, black and sleek as a wild beast out of the mountains, came in long strides across the grass. For one moment he stood erect before the son of Jesse, smiling, his teeth and eyeballs white in the glistening blackness of his face. Then he flung himself, still smiling, upon the ground, and took the hem of David's robe in his hand.

"Tidings for my lord the King," he said. "Jahveh has brought vengeance this day upon all those who rose up against you."

The King said to the Ethiopian also, "Is it well with the young man Absalom?"

Then the Ethiopian answered, saying, "All the enemies of my lord the King, and all those who rise up to do him hurt, may they be as that young man is."

And the King was much moved, and went up to the watchtower above the gate, and wept as he went, saying, "O my son Absalom, my son, my son Absalom! Would I had died for you, O Absalom, my son, my son!"

Would I had died on that night when I sent them forth to bring him out of Geshur, for I have long been old and unfit to reign, and he might have reigned in my place and loved me still. . . . The watchman, departing in haste lest he should look upon the King's sorrow, brushed against him and begged forgiveness. But David neither saw nor heard; he knelt and laid his head upon the sill and wept. Far away, at the margin of the forest, the men of Jahveh issued into the plain. They will come singing over the meadows, he said to himself; they will light torches and make a great noise of rejoicing in the streets because they have taken my enemy and laid him low. To them he was the lion that came upon the flock by night. I also said amongst them, "He has torn Israel, and therefore he must be taken." But he was my little one, the child of my bowels, flesh of my flesh, blood of my blood. . . .

He heard the thud of hoofs on the dry earth below him. Ahimaaz, mounted now, was riding out toward the advancing host. He has gone to them to hush their singing, David thought; he will charge them, saying, "Put off your garlands now, for the King is in the watchtower, mourning for Absalom." And it is not right that they should be denied their songs and their garlands, inasmuch as they have fought nine thousand against thirty thousand all this day, and they have done it for my sake. If only they had brought him living out of the forest, if only I might have taken his face between my hands and kissed him upon the brow! . . . And he saw that face, vital and beautiful, the dark cheeks washed by tears of reconciliation. He knew then that it was utterly lost to him—blank, unbreathing, blind. And he covered his face with his hands and cried out again in a loud voice, "O my son Absalom, O Absalom, my son, my son."

And that day the victory was changed into mourning for all the people. Those who were within the gates and those who returned out of the battle alike whispered to each other, saying, "The King of Israel is grieving for his son." And the host of God broke ranks in the field and put aside their garlands and lowered their banners. By twos and threes, stealthily, like those who steal away from the field of defeat, they crept through the gates of the city; and no man came forth to meet them or to bless them or to give thanks unto them for their valor, nor was there any shouting in the streets.

At about the hour of moonrise, when the King was utterly worn with grieving, he heard footfalls on the stair of the watchtower. Darkness had begun to settle upon the little chamber, and David's eyes were weak with weeping, so that he stared long before he could be certain that it was the son of Zeruiah who stood before him. Now I must rise up, he told himself, and give thanks to him who has delivered me. . . . And he rose, leaning heavily upon the sill, and opened his mouth to speak graciously to the captain of the host.

But Joab stood motionless on the threshold. "This day," he said, "you have shamed the faces of all your servants who have saved your life and the lives of your sons and the lives of your wives and the lives of all those who have followed after your uncertain cause. This day you have made it plain that you hate them who love you and love them who hate you. You have shown before all Israel that the princes and the servants who fight for you are nothing in your eyes. I see now that if Absalom had lived and all we who bled for you this day had died in the forest, it would have pleased you well. Arise, then, go forth and speak comfortably to your servants, for I swear before Jahveh that if you go not forth to thank them, not one man among them will tarry with you through this night, and what comes to pass tomorrow will be worse for you than all the evil that has befallen you from the days of your youth until now."

The King rose then and took water in a basin and washed his face. Leaning upon Joab's arm, he went down and sat between the gates of the city. And it was spread about among the people that the King had come forth to give thanks to them and bless them; and they kindled torches and gathered from all parts of the city and came before him, wearing garlands and singing his praise. And he spoke fair words to them, saying that they had saved the flock. He went also among the wounded and laid hands upon them; and he found Ittai where he lay dying, and embraced him and kissed him upon the lips. All things that were fitting he did, even though he did them late. But his spirit was not with his people. His spirit had gone forth from them to stand in the forest of Ephraim, where they had buried Absalom.

❧ X ❧

THE WAR between the men of Absalom and the men of David ended when Joab sounded the trumpet and called back the host. But ten moons waxed and waned, another harvest was gathered in, battles were fought, cities were besieged, and captains were murdered in cold blood before peace, unheralded and almost imperceptible, settled upon Israel.

If the King thought to find some recompense for his private sorrows in the sense of public well-being, he was mistaken. Every plan that he conceived for expressing his devotion to his flock somehow went awry. It was impossible, for instance, for him to return at once to Jerusalem. The sons of Zeruiah, Hushai the counselor, and Barzillai of Rogelim all advised him, and rightly, that he would do well to tarry in Mahanaim until every tribe in Israel would have sent up elders to invite him home. It seemed to him in his sore and restless state that these embassies were very slow in presenting themselves; the Kenites and the Calebites did not send their representatives until twenty days had passed; and Judah, the tribe of his fathers, sent no representatives at all. He learned then to his consternation that those men of Judah who had come living out of the forest of Ephraim were still congregated in his capital; that Amasa had not raised his hand to disband them; that, although they were willing to see the son of Jesse crowned again, inasmuch as all the other Israelites seemed to desire it, they were by no means panting after the return of their lord. So, in the first weeks after his triumph, he was forced to humiliate himself by sending messengers into Jerusalem.

Zadok and Abiathar, the priests, carried the words of David into the encampment of the men of Judah. "Thus says our lord the King of Israel," they said. "'You are my brothers. You are my bone and my flesh. Why then are you the last to call me home?'" And to Amasa also they spoke for David, saying, "'Are you not my kinsman? God do so to me and more also if I do not make you the captain of my host to lead my armies continually in the place of Joab.'"

For the son of Jesse knew what had come to pass at the great terebinth in the forest of Ephraim. From slaves and foot soldiers and young heroes of the cavalry, he had drawn out—with infinite patience and agony—the whole tale: the three darts, the protracted anguish, the twenty wounds with spears and swords. He did not speak of it to Joab; he gave him the usual greetings and permitted him to sit at the council table in his usual place. But the Star of Bethlehem never again laid a hand upon his nephew, nor met him privately, nor said any word to him save a required word.

Ittai of Gath had died in Mahanaim three days after the battle. Those Philistines and Cherethites and Pelethites who had followed after David were divided into two parts and given in equal numbers to Joab and to Abishai. And the son of Zeruiah knew how it was with him—that he was a subordinate officer, no higher than his younger brother, that Amasa had been called out of the capital to lead the host, and that he would ride in the forefront of the ranks of God no more.

Meanwhile the men of Judah, eager to hide their earlier hesitation in a fine show of cordiality, sent a thousand of their number to the western bank of the Jordan, near the city of Gilgal, to welcome the King. The tribes of the north, not to be outnumbered by Judahites, likewise sent a thousand, all men of war, led by a certain Sheba, a wealthy and distinguished Benjamite. Those who had congregated by the side of the river, seeing the two splendid hosts that had come up to await the ferryboats that would bring the King and his household across the water, might well have said in their hearts, Now, surely, the last thunder of war has rolled away from the hills and plains of Israel. . . . But it was noted with some foreboding that the men of Judah and the men of Benjamin did not mingle with each other. They went so far as to exchange bitter words when they met in the bazaars and on the high places; the Ephraimites and the Benjamites spoke of fair-weather friends, and the Judahites recounted the story of Shimei the Benjamite, who had reviled his fleeing King. The Benjamites sent for this same Shimei and instructed him to kneel on the bank at the point of the crossing so that he might be the first to make obeisance and beg forgiveness. The sons of Judah said that there might well be other faces which the King of Israel would prefer to look upon at the moment of his return. The Benjamites agreed vehemently with the sons of Judah; surely it was only fitting that the King should be welcomed by one of his own. And they called up Meribaal to stand at the brink of the Jordan beside Shimei. "For the heart of our lord will be lifted up," they said, "when he beholds the son of Jonathan."

When David crossed the Jordan and came again into his own land, his heart was indeed lifted up—but not for long. He took tender leave of Barzillai, who had conducted him across the river; he bestowed a hurried pardon upon Shimei; he clasped the hand of Amasa and embraced Meri-baal, and he kissed the cheeks of all the elders who had come up to welcome him home. Since the men of Judah had the greater reason to blush before him, he went to some length to show them that they were wholly restored to his favor; he tarried long among them and promised to break bread with their elders in Gilgal that same night. But he had no sooner turned his face toward the city than a great confusion arose in the multitude. The men of Benjamin, affronted by what they considered the King's show of preference for his native tribe, had seceded from the triumphal procession. Sheba, their leader, whom David had failed to greet in the confusion of landing, rose and blew the trumpet. "We Benjamites have no portion in David, nor any inheritance in the son of Jesse," he said. And he summoned the men of Benjamin to rise up in arms against the south, saying, "Every man to his tent, O Israel!" So the men of the north departed from David, and went up to follow Sheba; and only the tribes of the south journeyed with David from Gilgal to Jerusalem.

For almost a year thereafter, no man could say to his brother, "Behold, peace is upon the land." There were no vast armies or great battles, for most of the children of the northern tribes, appalled at the prospect of Israel rent again in twain, turned their backs upon the men of Sheba and called them traitors and hotheaded fools. But the rebels made themselves secure in the fortified cities of Abel and Dan. They raided the peaceful countryside; they fell upon the herdsman and took his herd; and they waited on the highway to smite the pilgrim and to attack the caravan. So, before the son of Jesse had been given time to rejoice in his return, he was forced to call Amasa to him. "Go now," he said, "and call up the men of Judah who have returned to their fields, for we must have a host to send up against Sheba the Benjamite. Here we have only the men of the guard and a few Philistines and Cherethites and Pelethites under the command of Joab and Abishai. Therefore, get me an army in Judah and return to me within three days."

But Amasa tarried long in Judah—so long that the King of Israel sent Joab and Abishai up to battle before him, with the mercenaries and those other men of war who were encamped in the plain before Jerusalem. When the Ishmaelite came at last, bringing with him five thousand Judahites, David sent him to join forces with the sons of Zeruiah near a sacred stone in Gibeon. Then Joab, girded for war, came forth to meet Amasa, and there was a sword at his side. "Is it well with you, my brother?" said Joab, taking Amasa by the beard and drawing down his face as though to kiss him. And, even as they embraced, Joab killed Amasa beside the stone in Gibeon, as he had killed Abner at the gates of Hebron. With one blow he killed Amasa, striking him in the belly so that his bowels were shed upon the ground and he lay wallowing in his blood and died.

But the men of Jahveh did not turn back from pursuing after Sheba. "Behold," they said, "the son of Zeruiah, who was our captain in the wilderness and in Hebron and in Jerusalem—him will we follow still." And they followed him into the north, where he took the city of Dan by storm and besieged the city of Abel until those within it grew weary of war and threw the gory head of Sheba down to him from the walls.

There came a day when the last Benjamite who had fled into the hills before the ranks of Joab left the cave in which he had hidden himself and journeyed back to his own people and dwelt again in the light of the sun. There came a day when the breaches in the walls of Abel and Dan were mended, when the grass had grown thick enough to hide the graves in the forest of Ephraim. Time passed, and the elders of Judah no longer looked askance at the elders of Benjamin, but sat down side by side with them at the King's table. Moons waxed and waned, and that widow who had wept the longest ceased to weep, and looked at a young man singing in a field, and said in her heart, How would it be to live again? . . . There was a day when war ceased utterly and there was no clamor of arms nor any grieving in any part of the land. But that day came so late and so quietly that no man perceived it. Not one of the sons of God turned from his late summer tasks to say to his brother, "Behold, there is peace in Israel."

BOOK TWELVE

BOOK TWELVE

§ I §

Now DAVID was old and stricken in years; he had reigned so long that the youth of the land and those who were in the flower of their days had known no other king in Israel. Of all that came to pass in his house and in the kingdom, he said in his heart: There is no new thing upon the face of the earth. This too I have seen before. . . . When Adonijah went forth from the palace and took a high house in Jerusalem, the lights that shone in his windows on summer nights were only reflections of those lights which had glowed upon the feasts of the son of Maacah. When the young man thundered through the streets in a chariot, with twenty horsemen before him and behind him, it seemed to the King of Israel that he heard nothing more than the echo of that other splendid procession which had ridden with Absalom long ago. Nor was his spirit greatly troubled within him. In good time, he thought, when my death is upon me, I will call one or the other of the two sons whom the years have left to me, and set him upon the throne. Whatsoever I do may flower into evil; for who shall know which of these is the better man to tend the flock—the valiant or the wise? Perhaps when I am in my grave one brother will rise up in arms against the other, but I will not know it. Perhaps there will be another revolt in Israel, but there have been revolts since the beginning of time, and they have passed, and this, too, will pass. . . .

In those days he remembered often certain words that Barzillai of Rogelim had said to him on the afternoon when they had sat side by side in the ferryboat that brought the King of Israel across the river Jordan to his own land. "Come," David had said to Barzillai, "come and dwell henceforth with me in Jerusalem, and break bread at my table, and walk with me in my garden, so long as we both shall live." But Barzillai had answered the King, saying, "How many are the days of the years of my life that I should go with my lord to Jerusalem? I am this day fourscore years old. Can I discern any longer between sorrow and delight? Can I taste what I eat or what I drink? Can I hear any longer the voices of singing men and singing women? Then let your servant turn back to the eastern bank of the Jordan, that I may lie down beside the graves of my father and my mother and take unto myself in my own city my everlasting sleep."

Can I discern any longer between sorrow and delight? the son of Jesse asked himself on those rare evenings when the doors of the palace were thrown open to visitors, and the board was laden with meat and fruit and wine. . . . The days of feasting—the high holy days and the anniversaries of his great victories—were more wearisome to him now than the days of mourning. Burdened by the weight of his ceremonial robes, shivering in the chill draughts that swept across the length of the common room, he wandered up and down, encountering unfamiliar faces, holding out his hands to be kissed by unknown lips. The steward of the house had grown too old to walk beside him; another man, younger and somewhat less patient with the King's inability to remember names, walked in his place. "Behold," he would say, suppressing a yawn, "this is Bani the Gadite, he whom my lord has set over the ranks of the Cherethites and the Pelethites." And David would say to himself, What is Bani the Gadite to me, seeing that Joab is utterly divided from me and that Abishai rides in the host of God no more? . . .

For, not long since, the second son of Zeruiah had been gathered to his fathers. He who had come forth out of so many battles died in Jerusalem on a day of peace because his horse was frightened by some unseen spirit in the air and reared and hurled him against a wall. Before they could carry him back to his house, he knew that his death was upon him, and he sent his armor-bearer up to David to instruct the King concerning his burial. "Inasmuch as I have served my lord long and honorably," he said, "let my lord see fit to find me a grave in Jerusalem, within sight of those tombs wherein he and all his house will rest." And David saw that it was for Noi's sake that Abishai wished to be buried within the city, and he took his body up to Mount Zion and laid it in one of the royal caves, close to the spot where Noi slept.

Nor was the countenance of Hushai the counselor to be seen any longer among those that gathered on nights of festival to trouble the King's weakening eyes. One winter evening, while he was sitting at the King's table, the old counselor had fallen into a drowse and had died so peacefully that no man knew when his spirit arose to depart. A certain Benaiah, a squat and solid ancient with the flat face and majestic bearing of an aged lion, had taken his place. For him the King of Israel felt a degree of cordiality. But the hours which Benaiah could spend with his lord were few; like Hushai before him, he was forever engaged in conversation with Bath-sheba and Solomon.

Long since, the son of Jesse had ceased to listen attentively to the talk of those who assembled beneath his roof. Nothing that they said stirred him; they spoke constantly of events and projects which he would not live to see—an alliance with the court of Egypt, a house to be built in Jerusalem for the ark of God, an expedition to be sent up against the Syrian kings; and almost every sentence that they uttered would have been prefaced, but for politeness, with the phrase "When our lord the King is dead. . . ." There were times when he was filled with bitterness against them all. How is it, he would ask himself, that they cannot speak now and then of matters in which I bear some part? But when he tried to think what these matters might be, he smiled a wry smile. For I am concerned with nothing, he would say in his heart, save the dead and this everlasting coldness which is upon me. . . .

Sometimes he would catch a glimpse of some member of his household —Bath-sheba or Haggith, Solomon or Adonijah—standing among the assembly of strangers that filled the house on days of festival. Then a faint glow, as of old embers when the breath is blown upon them, would spread within him, and he would hasten forward, eager for anything—a touch, a word, a smile—from one of his own. But what do I seek? he would ask himself. If the house were empty and we chanced upon each other in the common room, I would yearn to be left in peace. . . . Between him and Haggith there was coldness and reserve; Noi had long since been beyond his slights, but Haggith, sustained by her own grievances, bore resentment toward him still for Noi's sake. With Adonijah he was uneasy, inasmuch as the unsettled question of the succession always hung over their talk; nor could he find much pleasure in the subtle, devious, and equivocal utterances of Solomon. Surely I should love my youngest well, he thought. Is he not the son of the true beloved? It is no great matter that he is smooth in his face and delicate in his person, that there is a little too much fragrant oil upon his pointed beard, and that his hands are not a warrior's hands. Saul was exceedingly manly, and I was somewhat less so. Israel also grows soft with the years, and perhaps it is only fitting that he who reigns after me should be yet a little softer than I. . . .

As for the beloved—seen at a distance across the crowded room, that compact form, erect, regal, and self-possessed, bore little relation to the slight young woman who had stared at him across the palm fronds in the green hush of that long-gone eventide. Bath-sheba was forever about the affairs of Judah and Israel. No tablet of clay went forth from the palace before it had passed through her hands; no matter of state was hidden from her clear, keen eyes. He no longer deceived himself by saying in his heart, "I love her" or "I love her still." He had learned to say "I loved her once" and "There was a time when I loved her, but it was long ago." Nor could he recall the day or the hour when their spirits had ceased to cleave one unto the other. Perhaps, he thought, it was when Solomon was born that we first turned a little aside; for she gave half her heart to Solomon, and I am not such a one as can thrive on half a heart. . . . So when he sought her out at all, it was to admire her as he might admire a skillful counselor—to listen while she soothed the wounded pride of some elder or drew a concession from an Egyptian ambassador or settled a quarrel between the court of Gath and the court of Tyre. It was impossible to recapture his first tenderness for her in her presence, nor could he always conjure up a vision of her young and ardent face even when he was alone.

Sometimes when the common room was crowded with visitors, he would grow weary with standing and would take himself off to the laden board, less out of hunger than out of a desire to pass the time. He would move restlessly up and down the length of the table, looking at the slices of beef and mutton, the delectable honey cakes, the clear and sparkling wines. And suddenly he would be assailed by a longing to taste such bread as he had taken hot from the hearth in Jesse's house, such water as sprang from the earth in the hills above his native town. Then all that he ate was displeasing to him, and the words of Barzillai sounded in his ears: "Can I taste what I eat or what I drink?" He would ask for water and put it aside as soon as his lips had touched it, saying that the springs of Jerusalem were flat and savorless beside the living waters of Bethlehem.

Can I hear any longer the voices of singing men and singing women? . . . So he would say to himself when the sweet singer out of Ephraim tuned his lute or the chorus of damsels from the high houses of Jerusalem lifted up their voices to praise him in an antiphonal song. Though he would find himself broad awake as soon as his head rested upon his pillow, a few strains of music were enough to lull him into a weak and shameful sleep. "No, now, I cannot sit nodding here," he would say to his steward. "Tell them that I rose up before dawn today to pray before the ark of God. Tell them anything, so long as I may leave them without wounding them. I am exceedingly weary and must go to my bed."

But as soon as he entered the dim and empty chamber with his armor-bearer, he would wish that he had remained among the warm, moving mass of living beings below. No matter how much heat had been stored in the room in the course of the day, no matter how many braziers had been set in a glowing circle around his bed, he would find himself wretchedly cold. They rubbed his body with oil; they wrapped him in woolen garments; they laid rugs of goat's-hair upon him and weighted him down with bearskins and sheepskins; and still the shivering would not cease. I have been cold since I beheld Rizpah and her dead on the high place of Gibeah, he thought. I am inwardly frozen by the chill stare of the sightless God. . . .

One night when he lay trembling beneath a mound of coverlets, his armor-bearer said to him, half in earnest and half in jest, "Why should my lord lie shivering all night, alone in his bed? Since there is no warmth in him, let him send his servants forth to find him a fair damsel, young and pleasant to look upon, to lie by him and cherish him and keep him warm."

The King raised himself a little on his elbow and stared at the foot of his bed. There, in the roseate light of the braziers, he saw a vision of a fair young maid. Almost ten years ago, desire and the force of desire had passed from him; how many years had gone by since he had beheld a girl in the naked loveliness of her youth, he did not know. And yet he had not forgotten; the damsel whom he had created out of the empty air and the glow of embers was as clear to him as a living presence; he saw the down on her slender thighs, the unblemished rounds of her hips, the pale buds at the tips of her breasts. And before she was reabsorbed into the light and shadow out of which he had fashioned her, she smiled upon him and held out her hands to him palms upward—thin hands, open and bent down at the wrists. . . .

"No, now, there is not such a one in Israel. . . ."

"Is it possible that my lord has forgotten that he is the King? Not one, but three thousand virgins in Israel would come rejoicing to tend and to cherish my lord."

He did not believe it. And yet it was a pleasing fancy; it almost soothed him into sleep. He turned and drew down the corner of the pillow and rested his cheek upon it. "Go then and find me such a one," he said.

⁕ II ⁕

ONE LATE AFTERNOON toward the beginning of the winter rains, the son of Zeruiah wandered down toward the encampment, carrying a broken corselet in his hands. The corselet had been useless to him these last three moons. The fool of an Egyptian who waited upon him had left it lying on a bench in the garden; some visitor had seen fit to sit down on it; and the metal, worn with some thirty years of daily use, had been split and dented beyond repair. At the moment it had seemed a small matter to go down to the tent of the old Kenite master craftsman who followed the ranks of God and instruct him to fashion a new corselet patterned after the old one. But so many raw and painful considerations had managed to gather around the business that he had put it off from week to week, and would have put it off forever if certain jests concerning an armorless captain had not been noised about among the host.

It was impossible, for example, for him to buy a new corselet without giving some thought to the number of days left to him upon the face of the earth. The old corselet had been the butt of innumerable witticisms among his captains. "What, has it not yet fallen apart?" they would say when he seated himself among them at the council table. "Shall we go with an empty pouch from man to man, saying, 'Throw in a coin or two for the captain's sake'?" And he had always answered, laughing, "No, now, the corselet is strong enough; the corselet will last as long as I." Then somehow, in some dark crevice of his mind, his reply had been turned roundabout. He had said in his heart, "I will last as long as the corselet." And when he had seen it lying, crushed and cracked at the shoulder seams, on a bench in his own garden, he had thought, foolishly enough, It is not long now until the hour of my death. . . .

So for weeks he had tinkered with it and plagued his armor-bearer to mend it. He was ashamed to carry it out of the house to a smithy, knowing well enough that any craftsman would look at it once and laugh in his face. "It is not that I begrudge the price of another," he kept saying in the presence of his servants. "You have seen how it is with me—I am willing to pay a king's ransom for a good sword. But this corselet has been with me since the days when I rode before the host in Ziklag. It is scarred with the blows of Philistines and Edomites and Ammonites and Moabites. It is very old. . . ."

"Yes, and exceedingly weary," the exasperated armor-bearer said.

Once he was convinced he must buy another, he found himself faced with an equally disturbing question: Should the new corselet be an exact replica of the old? There was a raised star on the left side of the bruised and battered thing—he had always gone into battle wearing the insignia of his lord, nor had any man questioned his right, even in these latter years when he came to David's house no more. But to have the same star emblazoned upon a new corselet was to be an old fool, to proclaim to all the world "Even though he has utterly turned his face from me, yet am I bound flesh and spirit to the Star of Bethlehem."

I want no star upon my armor now, he told himself, walking toward the encampment through the thin gray arrows of the rain. I will tell the Kenite to put some other thing in its place. And yet, if I were to have a star, it is very likely that no man would think to comment upon it. How many of us are left to remember the days in the wilderness when the son of Jesse was called the Star of Bethlehem? . . . And again he was at a loss as to what he would say to the Kenite, and stood musing in the street.

He was roused out of his dream by the thunder of approaching horses. That will be the son of Haggith, he told himself; that will be Adonijah riding back to his house from the fields which his father has given him in the neighborhood of Baal-hazor. . . . He stepped back against a wall, so that he might stand by and greet the rider. For though the son of Bath-sheba looks coldly upon me, he thought, the son of Haggith bids me to his board and calls me his cousin still. . . . And his heart grew a little warmer within him, nourished by one of those considerations which began with the phrase "When my lord the King is dead. . . ."

When my lord the King is dead, surely it will be the son of Haggith who will reign after him, he said to himself. The tales of a secret covenant between Bath-sheba and the son of Jesse are the vain fancies of gossips and fools. The old King is weak and sickly and withdrawn, but no man has said of him that he wanders in his mind, and only one who has lost his wits could set aside a sturdy warrior and raise up a little, priestly, niggling, white-handed fop in his stead. When my lord the King has been gathered to his fathers, Adonijah, even he who pulls on the reins of his steeds and stops in the midst of his course to greet me now, will be King of Israel. . . .

The son of Haggith stepped down from the chariot and embraced the captain of the host. "How is it, then?" he said, smiling to see the broken corselet. "Has the son of Zeruiah no armor-bearer that he should walk about carrying his own armor through the rain?"

The captain flushed and shrugged. "My armor-bearer has seen far too much of this. I dare not ask him to look upon it again," he said.

"How so?"

"These last three moons he has been trying to mend it. . . ."

The young man ran his hand, long and pale like that other hand that had plucked the lute in Gibeah, over the dented surface. "It is beyond mending. Get another, and hang this one upon the wall of some temple in Shechem or Gilgal, so that our children's children's children may look upon it and marvel when the name of Joab is a legend in the land."

The compliment was all the more nourishing to the hungry spirit of the captain of the host because it had sprung spontaneously from the young man's lips. Adonijah, plainly embarrassed by his own courtliness, continued to examine the corselet. He has grown comelier of late, the son of Zeruiah thought. He has worn away some of the flesh that was upon him by walking the fields around Baal-hazor. Now he is almost as lithe as his father was when we ranged together over the face of the wilderness. . . .

The son of Haggith shook back his soft brown hair, and raised his gray eyes to the threatening sky. "Will Joab ride with me?" he said.

"No. Inasmuch as it is growing late, and I have vowed this night to go down to the tent of the Kenite. . . ."

"In the rain?"

"Surely. What is a little rain?"

"Then let me send my chariot home and walk awhile at the captain's side."

"In the rain?" said Joab, mocking the young man's slow and musical speech; for he was moved and did not wish to show what had passed in his heart.

"Come, let us walk together. I too have wet the crown of my head before," the son of Haggith said.

They walked in uneasy silence toward the outskirts of the city. Until this day they had never found themselves alone together. Meeting at the crowded board and the council table, each of them had felt a desire to engage in private speech with the other; but now that no man was by to set a bridle upon their tongues, it was plain, at least to the captain, that such matters as might stir them to ardent talk were better left to silence until the son of Jesse had departed from this world. For surely, he thought, I cannot say to this young man, "When your father is no more, will your servant Joab, old as he is, be permitted still to lead the host?" . . . And the silence between them had become so heavy by the time they reached the city gates that Joab could only wish that Adonijah would turn and take himself home.

But the son of Haggith passed with Joab between the gray pylons and into the open field, dragging the hem of his splendid garment through the wet grass. When they were some fifty paces from the walls, when the lights of the encampment were visible against the slate-gray sky, he laid his hand upon the captain's arm. "Does my cousin know that I also am rejected of my lord the King?" he said.

"Is it possible that the Hope of Jesse's house believes this foolish talk concerning a secret covenant between Bath-sheba and David? My lord is old and overtender of Solomon, that is true. Nevertheless——"

The King's son turned his fair, rain-spattered face full upon the captain. "Would God that it were an idle tale!" he said. "But the wife of Zadok had it from her husband and told it unto the daughter of Abiathar, who brought it straightway to my mother, nor does my mother doubt it in the least."

Haggith is not such a one as to be ruffled by vain gossip, the captain thought. If she believes it, then very likely it is so. . . . He stared down at the broken corselet and knew that it would be foolish to order another, inasmuch as Solomon would send him home to the hills of Judah and choose a younger man to ride before the host. And his whole being cried out against it. To slip peaceably out of his saddle, to hang up his shield and his sword, to render up quietly that for which he had shed the blood of Abner and Amasa, to look upon the supper fires of the camp of God no more. . . . "Not while there is yet breath within me," he said.

"My captain and my cousin——"

Joab turned and looked upon Adonijah and saw a hope, a wild possibility, in the young man's eyes.

"Would that the son of Zeruiah might go up to my father and plead with him for my sake. . . ."

"That would be useless. Between me and David there has been nothing but empty talk and silence these many years. Nevertheless, there is a way——"

"What way, my captain?"

Joab's thoughts, long imprisoned in neglect and idleness, sprang through the shattered bars. He stood motionless for the space of ten heartbeats, feeling the old lightning flashes of insight darting out from him in every direction, until all the dark places had been made plain. And when he spoke again, he spoke in that hushed, conspiratorial voice that had whispered at the ear of the son of Jesse in Gibeah and in the wilderness.

"Why should we wait?" he said. "If we say in our hearts, Such-and-such we will do when the King of Israel goes down into his grave, then we will be too late. For the King your father is concerned for his flock; he will not leave the matter to be settled in civil blood; when he feels the hold of death upon him, he will anoint Solomon. Therefore I say unto the son of Haggith, Go, now, and make a pact with all those thousands who would not see a little jabbering priest upon the throne. The men of Jahveh who are with the host will follow me. And who will be left to unsheathe a sword for Solomon? Mercenaries only—a few Pelethites and Cherethites, a few men of Askelon and Gath. But we must not let the grass grow beneath our feet. It is a matter that must be settled before the coming of another moon. Before the son of Jesse pours the holy oil upon the head of Solomon, the people of Jerusalem must rise up and say as in one voice, 'God save Adonijah, our King!'"

Now that he had spoken, sick fear took hold upon him. If the son is like the father, he thought, he will draw himself up and say, "What have I to do with the son of Zeruiah and his treachery?" . . .

But the young man leaned forward and laid his hand upon the captain's shoulder.

"Consider the matter," said Joab, deeply moved and eager to escape into the dusk. "Meanwhile, I will go down to the tent of the Kenite——"

"Come and break bread in my house instead. We will open a skin of new wine. . . ."

"But I have made a vow to myself concerning the Kenite."

Adonijah took the corselet out of his hands. "Let the son of Zeruiah put the whole matter from his mind," he said. "Tomorrow I am riding forth into Ashdod, where there are horses and chariots out of Egypt to be bought at a good price. In Ashdod also is a foundry, and there I will order a splendid corselet which I will bestow upon the captain of the host. What emblem shall I tell the smithy to raise upon it?"

He stared once more at the emblazoned Star of Bethlehem, tarnished and battered and scarcely visible in the growing dark. "Tell him to fashion me an oak leaf," he said, "even such an oak leaf as Adonijah wears above his heart."

৶ III ৶

How is it?" said the King of Israel, rubbing his hands above one of the braziers in the common room. "Have they plagued me more than usual this evening? Or is it that I bear it with less grace, seeing that the winter rains have multiplied the afflictions in my bones?"

He had intended the question as a jest, but Benaiah the counselor gave it his grave attention. "If my lord considers it plaguing, then they have plagued him more than usual," he replied, rubbing his own hands for courtesy's sake and slowly nodding his leonine head. "But this at least should be plain to the King of Israel—that neither my lady Bath-sheba nor the prophet Nathan nor the high priest Zadok would come with trivial matters to disturb his rest. If they have plagued him, they have plagued him with good cause."

Come, now, thought the son of Jesse, save your weighty and thoughtful manner for my son Solomon, who is more impressed with it than I. . . .

But the counselor, too engrossed in his speech to see the flicker of annoyance in the eyes of his lord, droned on. He said, as he had said at least ten times in the course of that same evening, that Adonijah the son of Haggith had taken himself off to buy steeds and chariots in Ashdod, and that the buying of steeds and chariots was no preparation for a year of peace. Therefore—he paused long upon the word—therefore it would indeed be well——

"I know, I know," the son of Jesse said. "Therefore, it would be well for me to name Solomon my successor today and arrange to die tomorrow, before Adonijah has been given time to summon up his host."

"Far be it from me, far be it from any man in Israel, to think such a thought. May the King live to see his hundredth year. Only——"

"Only it would please Benaiah and all Israel exceedingly if the King, still stubbornly alive, would at least have the grace to behave as though he were dead."

"No one has said to my lord that he should drop the reins of the government. No one has said anything to my lord save that, for the peace of the land, it would be well for him to anoint the head of one of his sons. . . ."

"Which son?"

"The King knows that his servant, like the lady Bath-sheba and the prophet Nathan, is utterly convinced that Judah and Israel would flourish in peace if they were rendered up into the wise and gentle hands of Solomon."

Very slowly, with a malicious smile twitching the corners of his mouth, David turned his head over his shoulder. They are listening, he thought, and I will let them see that I know as much. . . . Halfway down the length of the somber room, Bath-sheba and Nathan were sitting together at the table. They had been talking eagerly all evening, but now the murmur of their voices had ceased. He flung a swift, accusing glance into their static faces and had the satisfaction of seeing them both turn aside and stare at the wall. They hear me well enough when I speak of the succession, he told himself. Yet when I ask to see again the last letter that I received from Hiram, King of Tyre, or say to them that it is time to go down and pour oil and wine upon the graves of the House of Kish, their ears are as dull as stones. . . .

"My lord——" said Benaiah.

"Your lord is weary with much useless talk and will go up to his chamber. It is late. The prophet keeps Bath-sheba long at the board. Send him home. Behold, she can scarcely contain herself, inasmuch as she has heard many things this night that must straightway be whispered into the ears of Solomon."

He left them in anger, without troubling himself to bid them good night; but on the dank and draughty stair his anger turned to remorse within him. Why have I railed at the old counselor? he asked himself. There was no cause to accuse him of wishing me dead. And she also—why should I sneer at her? What mother would not wish to see her son upon the throne? Surely it is no vice that she should go up to him when strangers have departed from the house, and sit talking upon the edge of his bed. . . . And he walked unsteadily down the dim corridor, feeling the old ache in his throat, the old film of weak and easy tears in his eyes.

There was no light in his chamber save the glow of the six braziers that his servants had set around his bed. Tonight he sensed a new sweetness in the air—a dry, elusive scent of marjoram and thyme. His armor-bearer, hidden from him now in some shadowy corner, must have found new herbs and scattered them upon the fires.

"That is a very pleasant scent," he said, sinking into a chair close to one of the braziers. "Whence came the herbs? Did the son of Jonathan send them down to me out of Benjamin?"

"No, my lord." The voice of the armor-bearer rose out of the blackness near one of the curtained windows. "They are the herbs of the village of Shunam which is in the land of Gilead."

"Send a messenger up to the Shunammites to bear them my thanks and a goodly gift. The herbs are very fresh and sweet. Perhaps they will find it in their hearts to send me more."

"There is a Shunammite in Jerusalem this night, my lord."

"Truly?" But I have talked enough this day, he thought. Come, cease this chatter now and take the weight of my robes from my body that I may rest. . . .

"The maid for whom the King sent some weeks ago, she is of the village of Shunam."

"What maid is this?"

"Why, that same maid who is to tend my lord and cherish him and give him warmth by night that he may sleep. It was she who carried down the herbs for the King."

He could not say that he had forgotten the matter. It was only that he had never thought of it as an actuality. He had created her out of the glow of embers; she was as insubstantial as a dream, nor had he ever thought that they would be such fools as to lead a mortal maid into his house one night. And now that his armor-bearer spoke to him of a living girl brought out of a specific village to lie at his side, his blood burned in his face. He was shamed in the very core of his being. It was as if he had been spied upon in his weak and childish imaginings; it was as if all Israel had seen him clasp the coverlet, gathered into the shape of a damsel, against his cold and lonely breast. "Ah, God," he said, "why have you done such a thing as this? It was a jest, I meant it not. What has such a one as I to do with a maid?"

"My lord——"

"We will speak of it no further. Go to her in the morning and give her a suitable dowry and send her back into Gilead. See also that you do it publicly, lest I become a mockery before Judah and Israel."

Suddenly he was aware of a stirring upon the bed. There, in a cloud of roseate light, sat a slight young girl. She sat upright, with her back propped against one of the great pillows. She was clad in a thin white shift, and a crescent-shaped amulet hung between her small, high breasts. Her head drooped a little to one side, borne down by the weight of her thick brown hair, so that she looked like a flower whose bloom is too heavy for the stalk it rests upon.

The King rose and stood far off from her, looking down upon her.

"No, now, my child," he said after long silence, "how is this? Have they taken you from your father and your mother and brought you down to a strange city to lie in an old man's bed? Surely no such thing is done in Israel. Believe me, I did not mean that they should use you so."

She raised her head and shook back her hair and gazed at him. Her face was a dim, pale triangle floating between red light and gray shadow —cool, parted lips, high cheekbones, a pair of large, earnest, reverent eyes. She cannot see me in the darkness, he thought in his heart. Her look is such a look as one might fix upon the face of an angel of God. . . . And he turned aside.

"Then I have not found favor in the sight of the King. He will not have me in his bed to give him the warmth of my body and to cherish him," she said, and she wept.

Even an old man, he thought, even a solitary old man dreaming in the closed darkness of his bedchamber, sows sorrow upon the face of the earth and causes the innocent to weep. He sat down on the edge of the bed and laid his hand upon her knee. The living flesh shed its warmth through the thin cloth, and there was a trembling within him—such a trembling as he had known when, after long weeks of mourning, he had laid his hand upon the lute. "Look, now, my daughter," he said, taking his hand from her quickly, "tomorrow I will send you home with fifty pieces of gold and three fields and a goodly orchard. This house is a house of many rooms, and God has so dealt with me that many of them are empty. Go and lie down in one of them and sleep, and think upon this matter no more."

"If it will not be too great a burden to the King," she said, "let him grant me this at least—that I should lie in his bed for a single night. For they have sent me forth from my father's house as to a marriage feast, with singing and with torches, and even though I should come again with a hundred fields and orchards, yet would I be shamed before my sisters, who will smile and say of me, 'Behold, they made her a fine garment and sent her down to the palace in Jerusalem, and she has been despised and turned from the King's bed and thrust through the King's door.'"

A ripple of laughter rose in his throat—perhaps because she had pleaded her cause with sturdy eloquence, bringing her little household tragedy plainly before his eyes, perhaps because her voice, warm and husky and clouded by weeping, roused up in him a delight which could be released only in stifled laughter.

"Let my lord the King hear me also." It was the voice of the armor-bearer, and David started, for he had utterly forgotten that the servant still tarried in the room. "It would indeed be a sorry business if my lord did not take the maid to his bosom for at least one night. For the people of Shunam sent her forth with lutes and cymbals, on a snow-white mule, bearing herbs and a cruet of the sweet balm of Gilead for the comfort of my lord. And they said, 'Behold, we are blessed above all the great cities, even Gilgal and Shechem, even Beth-shan and Jericho and Jerusalem.

For has not the shepherd of the flock taken from amongst us the fairest ewe lamb in all Israel, to cherish him in his latter days?' "

Is it possible, he asked himself, that I am beloved among the Shunammites? . . . And he covered his face with his hands and thought in the dark of those who had gathered in the market place on the day of his flight from Jerusalem—all the shy, tender hands held out to touch his garments, all the murmuring lips, all the wide, wet eyes. Surely, he said in his heart, since they have sent me a gift, I cannot reject it, nor can I send this little one back to her sisters, who will say to her that the King of Israel has thrust her forth through the door. For this one night I will lay me down at the side of the ewe lamb who has come to me out of the flock; nor will anyone be so base as to reproach her, inasmuch as all the world knows that I am old and weary and beyond love. . . .

"Come, then, my child," he said, "lie down beneath the coverlet for this one night, and I will lay by my garments and cover myself with a wrapper of woolen and give myself the delight of lying at your side."

He went into the darkest corner of the room to hide his nakedness from her, but he could not rid himself of the belief that no shadow was deep enough to hide his lean and withered person from her great wet, shining eyes. Of late it had been his custom to divest himself of his garments on the bed, surrounded by a circle of glowing fires. Now, in the chill and blackness, he was assailed by bitter cold. And yet, for all his wretchedness, he could not leave her to the discomfort of silence in an alien room. "What is the name of the damsel out of Shunam?" he said.

"Abishag is my name."

"And her father and her mother?"

"They are tillers of the soil in the fields beyond Shunam. Three sons they have and four daughters, and your servant is the youngest of these, being sixteen years old. It is said of your servant that, being the little one, she was too softly bred, and it is true that I can neither spin nor weave nor bake good bread. But the herbs which pleased my lord the King—I mingled them tonight with my own hands. Also, I sing the songs of Israel and the songs of Gilead, and the priests of Shunam have taught me to play skillfully upon the lute."

His throat was stirred again by the rippling laughter. Behold, he thought, she comes to me like some young warrior who would enroll in the ranks of God and presents his credentials boldly before the captain so that he will not spoil his chances for modesty's sake. . . . "What songs can you sing?" he said.

"I can sing the songs of David, even he who is exalted above all the sweet singers in Israel. Nor did they teach me these songs hastily on the night before I departed, that I might sing them before my lord in order to find favor in his sight. Since the day when I first learned what it was to ease the fullness of my heart by pouring my spirit forth from my lips, I sang the songs of David in the fields of Gilead. I know the songs of David as I know the branch that grows across the window near my bed."

"Before I send you forth tomorrow," he said, drawing the folds of the woolen wrapper around his trembling nakedness, "I will put the lute in your hands and hear you sing these songs of mine. For they were fashioned long ago, and I have not heard them sung for many years, and there are certain lines that have passed utterly out of my remembrance."

He came out of the darkness then and moved toward the bed. His armorbearer gathered up the scattered garments and departed, closing the door. No, now, the son of Jesse thought, seeing the slight curve of her thigh and shoulder beneath the coverlet, has he left us alone? Surely I cannot do this thing, surely I . . .

"While the King my lord laid by his robes," she said, "I made free to lie for a little on his side of the bed. Let him come now and lay him down in the hollow that I have made for him while it is yet warm."

Warmth—the living warmth of her body—had taken the chill from the sheets. The pillow had been dented by the weight of her head and scented with the freshness of her sun-dried hair. She laid her hand lightly upon his palm, and at her touch an inward warmth—slight, tingling, tentative, like the beginnings of a song—crept outward from the center of his being and was carried on the slow tide of his blood to the tips of his icy fingers and the soles of his numb feet. It is not desire, he said in his heart, but I would not speak truth if I said that it was innocent of the memory of desire. . . .

She turned against him and laid her head upon his shoulder, her arm across his breast. "So," she said, "on the journey down from Shunam, I told myself I would lie against the King my lord."

The vibrant music that was within him rose and swelled. Ah, God, he thought, brushing his lips across her hair, how can I turn my back upon this fair, heavy-headed flower that blooms at the edge of my grave? . . .

"Why does my lord the King hold himself apart from his servant, who has no desire beneath the sun save to cherish him and keep him warm?"

Why? Why indeed, my daughter, my ewe lamb, my companion, my beloved? It is the way of the world to say, "In such-and-such a manner, and only in such-and-such a manner, I love the fruit of my seed and the wife of my bosom and the friend of my spirit and the mother who suckled me at her breast." But when desire and the force of desire have gone forth out of the flesh forever, when the spirit hangs shivering between existence and dissolution, then at last is the matter made plain, then at last can a man say freely, "I loved them all, and the love wherewith I loved them was the same love." Wherefore, on one of these few nights that are left to me before my going forth into the dark, should I trouble my heart with laws and interdictions, saying, "This is of the spirit, therefore touch it," and, "This is of the flesh, therefore touch it not"? Seventy years I have dwelt among the sons and daughters of men, and I have loved so many that their names and their faces have grown dim in my remembrance; nor can I say of one of them "Here I loved only with the spirit," or "On that night my flesh alone went out unto the beloved." There is no love so high that it is not nourished by the sweet manna engendered in the blood. There is no love so low that it is not washed in the holy waters which pour forth abundantly from the high places of the heart. . . .

"Will my lord kiss me? In Shunam my mother and my father came every evening to our beds to kiss us before we slept."

Gladly, gladly. Kiss me and lie unto the end of my days in my bosom. Be unto me all those whom the world has changed beyond recognition or the grave has taken from my sight. Be my mother and my daughter, my friend and my sister, my wife and my beloved. Be warm bread unto my flesh and cool water unto my spirit. Be mine in all ways, inasmuch as there is no way in which you can be truly mine. . . .

She sighed and stirred against him. He held her against his breast as the shepherd holds the young lamb on a winter night. Then that music which had swelled greatly within him sank to a serene murmur; and knowing that he would never cease to hear it, he slept.

⋅⊰ IV ⊱⋅

ONCE he had satisfied himself that there was no evil in his intimacy with the little Shunammite, he ceased to care in the least how the matter might appear to the rest of the world. If he did not lead her to the table on the morning after her coming, it was only that he did not wish to expose her to sidelong glances and knowing smiles. In just such a voice as he might have used to ask for a second serving of curds, he informed the assembled household that he had taken a young damsel to his bed, a certain Abishag out of the land of Gilead, who had come very graciously from her father's house to serve the King and keep him warm. In the moment of silence that followed his announcement, he marshaled up a series of sharp answers, lordly and conclusive enough to put any objector in his proper place. But he had no occasion to use them. No one glanced secretly at his neighbor. No one smiled.

"And did my father sleep well last night?" said Solomon at last.

"Very well indeed."

"And the young damsel," said Bath-sheba, "where will she break the morning bread?"

"In my bedchamber. I have sent the steward up to her with cheese and fruit."

"If it pleases my lord, let him bring her to sit among us at noon. It is an ill reward for her kindness to the King that she should eat like a servant, apart and alone."

He could not tell whether their complaisance rose out of pleasure in his evident contentment or out of complete unconcern for him and all his activities. So long as he might eat his every meal with her henceforth, he did not care. And as the weeks passed and he was given many occasions to observe Bath-sheba's friendly bearing toward the girl, he came to the conclusion that his wife was prompted equally by charity and indifference. Nor can I complain of her coolness toward me, he told himself. Were she less indifferent, she could not be half so kind. . . .

The little Shunammite moved unscathed through the complexities of existence in the King's palace. Silence was her strength and her security; though her speech flowed swiftly enough in the upper chambers, she seldom lifted her husky, musical voice in the lower rooms. Her sole fault was that she was given to staring. She had sensed at once that it would be an impropriety to stare publicly at her lord, and she deliberately stared elsewhere—at Solomon's rings or Adonijah's girdle or Haggith's hands. But her eyes rested most often and most reverently upon that self-possessed and masterful woman whom the world knew as the true beloved of the King of Israel. She listened with wonder to Bath-sheba's penetrating conversation and observed with awe the exquisite simplicity of Bath-sheba's garments, the vital eloquence of her hands, the regal pose of her head. Sometimes, sitting in the firelit chamber with her cheek against David's knee, she would ask him endless questions concerning the beloved—where she had garnered her store of worldly wisdom, what she had worn and how she had borne herself in the days of her youth. "Would God I might have beheld her in the bloom of her loveliness," she would say, "for she is unbelievably lovely still." And in her ardor she triumphed over the years. Out of the stately companion of priests and counselors she conjured up the grave girl who had given herself to him utterly in one long look. Out of those dull and sagging cheeks, netted over with fine wrinkles, she evoked the pale rounds of flesh that had shimmered in the light of Uriah's lamps—cool as an iris, fresh and translucent as the foam on new milk.

He did not share any of Abishag's concern for the proprieties. He rejoiced in the sight of her; he did not know how long he would be blessed with seeing eyes, and he gazed in her direction whenever he chose. He had learned from his armor-bearer that she had been brought to him less for her beauty than for her understanding—her subtle, searching conversation was renowned in the land of Gilead. It was apologetically pointed out to him that her charm was marred by certain flaws, but it was from these very flaws that he drew the greatest portion of his delight. Her heavy head, weighted down by its mass of unruly hair, her eyes, excessively large and so bright that they seemed always on the verge of weeping, the soft mane of down between her shoulder blades, the rosy birthmark, shaped like a berry, under her left breast—by these tokens the image that had hovered at the foot of his bed was made flesh, and awe was transmuted into tenderness.

During the first moon of her stay in the palace, he gave her no occasion to speak of high matters. When there was a day of sun, he walked with her in the garden, talking of the ways of plants and birds, telling her such harmless tales of his wanderings in the wilderness and his sojourns in alien cities as one might recount to a child. On rainy evenings he put his lute in her hands and asked her to sing such songs of his as she and the children of Gilead had been kind enough to remember. In a secluded corner of the common room, while the household and the court went about their usual business, she sat on a cushion at his feet and sang the songs of David in a husky voice—songs of Ephes-Dammim, songs of Gibeah, songs of Ziklag and Beth-shan and Jerusalem. I have written a hundred songs in my day, he would say in his heart, and the children of Gilead have been kind enough to remember them all. . . . Hills and valleys, forests and stretches of desert, great cities and brown villages baking under the summer sun—all that had been dead to him, all that had lain sealed up in the burial cave of oblivion, came forth on the current of her living voice. Even as, in past ages, the note of the trumpet had dissolved the walls of Jericho, so her singing melted away that citadel which he had raised up against remembrance in his bitterness. And at last the beloved dead themselves—Jesse and the mother, Saul and Jonathan and Michal, Noi and Abigail, Amnon and Absalom—returned to him, and he held out his hands to welcome them, and wept.

Yet this new warmth and tenderness, which kept him serene and almost joyous when he was alone or in the company of the little Shunammite, served him ill when he found it necessary to deal with the rest of the world. Since he was capable of affection, he was vulnerable; the smallest slight was a bruise upon his heart. One evening while they sat at table, Benaiah and Bath-sheba fell to talking about some quarrel between the King of Ammon and the King of Moab. The son of Jesse was in complete ignorance of the whole matter, and the fact that they had not seen fit to lay it before him made it impossible for him to touch his meat and wine. He waited only until he was certain that he was master over his own voice and then broke rudely into their discussion. "Since when is the King of Israel kept in the dark concerning the affairs of the kings his neighbors?" he said.

Bath-sheba flushed, Benaiah stammered, and Abishag, forgetting the proprieties at the sight of his distress, sought his hand beneath the table and clasped it between both her own. There were apologies and explanations: the tension between Moab and Ammon was a relatively recent one; they had heard of it only through undependable channels, and had meant to wait for further news before intruding upon the peace of the King of Israel. . . . Yet it was plain that they had carried the matter to his son—he saw a swift exchange of glances between Bath-sheba and Solomon; and the hurt within him was so great that he rose from the board and hurried into the garden, not so much in anger as in fear that he might weep before them all.

Since the early hours of the morning, a chill, intermittent rain had been falling; but now the gray cloud banks had separated a little, and the garden was lighted by a silvery and uncertain sun. He walked through the wet, unblossoming, monotonous green of winter to the bench beneath the dripping palm tree, and sat down and rested his chin upon his hands. The garden looked vast and lonely, and he longed for the little Shunammite. And yet, he told himself, it is better that she should tarry behind in the common room. For she has some childish fancy that I am glorious, and even though it has outlived many things—the sight of my withered body and the knowledge of my numberless frailties—yet it may well perish when she beholds me weeping in a garden alone. . . . Nevertheless, his heart was lifted up when he beheld her coming toward him, burdened down with robes and shawls and balancing two big cushions upon her head.

She put one of the pillows beneath him; she wrapped his legs in a robe, covered his shoulders with a shawl, and laid the second pillow on the damp grass at his feet. "That," she said, looking down at it, "is for the King's servant to sit upon. It would be more to her liking if she might sit upon the knees of her beloved. But inasmuch as he chooses to spend the evening in the garden under the eyes of his neighbors, she must sit apart."

Perhaps, he thought, she yearns after the merriment of the common room; perhaps she takes a secret delight, unknown even to herself, in those young men who come to the palace to talk with Solomon. . . . And he would not take the hand which she laid upon his knee, but stared stubbornly over her dark, drooping head at the drenched grass.

"Wherefore does the King of Israel choose to sit in the wet garden?"

"Wherefore is the King of Israel alive and above the earth? Is it not plain that he has overstayed his time? He is an old man, useless to himself and useless to the kingdom, nor is there any son of Jahveh who will not utter a sigh of relief at the news of his death."

She sat back on her heels, her lips parted in wonderment. Her eyes could not have been wider or more unbelieving if she had seen the arch of the firmament rent apart. "Surely my lord says it to mock his servant. Surely he cannot believe so manifest a lie," she said.

"No, now, has Abishag not seen how they have taken this business of Ammon and Moab and laid it in Solomon's hands, unwilling to wait until I am dead?"

"Let me speak a word to my beloved. When I came to Jerusalem to minister to the King, I came not of my own will alone—though I willed it with all my spirit. I came also to be an emissary for every living soul in Israel, to bear all the devotion of the children of Jahveh to my lord and lay it at his feet. If David says in his heart, 'I am old and they want me not,' then I have left the better part of my task undone. The King is old, that is so indeed. The King is as a mountain that has stood for generations looking down upon the land, so that the old men say, 'I saw it on the night of my marriage,' and the young men say, 'The shadow of it was upon me when I was born.' The King is old, and his hair is white as the flower of the almond, and his flesh has grown light and delicate upon him, so that the sons and daughters of Jerusalem say to each other, 'Behold, I saw him walking in his garden, and he is more spirit now than flesh, and his eyes are so deep with understanding that I thought I looked upon an angel of God.' The years of David are dear to his people. He is an old father to them, and his frailties are sweet and to be cherished. When they speak of his death, it is only to say: 'He will live forever and return to us in our evil days. He has established an age of gold upon the earth, and he will intercede for us through ten thousand years at the throne of God.' If my lord and my beloved despises the years that have been vouchsafed him, let him despise them. But let him not put his bitterness into the mouths of the children of Israel."

He could not believe her, yet her long and breathless speech had stirred him deeply—so deeply that he did not wish to let her see his face. "Those who know me little may dream such childish dreams concerning me," he said, turning aside. "But those who dwell beneath the roof of my own house—you have seen this night how eager they are to take the kingdom from my hand."

"They are eager to lift the burdens of the state from my lord's shoulders, seeing that he has served long and is weary. . . ."

"They are eager to take that which is mine and give it to Solomon. . . ."

"They wish—and perhaps they are somewhat wiser than my lord in so wishing—to teach a fledgling bird to fly a little before that day when he must fly long and alone."

"How do they know which of my sons I wish to seat upon the throne of Israel?"

"Inasmuch as my lord has not troubled himself to tell them, they can only guess. . . ."

"My little one is as unpleasant and persistent a reasoner as Benaiah the counselor."

"But say at least," she said, laughing and flinging herself forward to embrace his knees, "that I am somewhat more pleasing to look upon."

Then, quite without reason, all bitterness left him, and he also gave himself up to laughter. He pressed his face against the top of her head and breathed the sweetness of her sun-dried hair. They sat in the garden until moonrise, laughing over nothing, even as Jesse and the mother had laughed in their bedchamber in the brown house in Bethlehem.

But that same night he went to Benaiah and asked to see all the clay tablets dealing with the quarrel between Ammon and Moab, and sat studying the matter through half the night.

"What will my lord do, now that he has read all the tablets?" she said, snatching the last one from his hand and sitting down upon his knees.

"Nothing as yet," he told her. "I will call a council tomorrow and lay the matter before both Adonijah and Solomon."

✦ V ✦

Since he knew that this council would be his last, he wished to make it solemn and memorable. He spent three days in careful preparation, arranging and rearranging the clay tablets, seeking out the most trustworthy of the scribes, tasting the several wines that the steward brought in from the storehouse, and writing the order of procedure with his own hand. In addition to himself and his two sons, only four were to be bidden—Abiathar the priest and the captain of the host, partisans of Adonijah, and Zadok and Benaiah the counselor, partisans of Solomon. During those three days he withheld himself from the few activities that he still considered pleasures. He neither walked in the garden nor lingered in idle conversation over the board; and save for the few brief hours of the night when she lay against him, he did not see the little Shunammite. "Let Abishag know," he said, kissing her forehead, "that only the needs of the flock could call me away from her side. When Solomon and Adonijah have judged the matter of the quarrel between Ammon and Moab, when I have weighed their judgments and seen which of the two young men will be the better king in Israel, then I will come to her again. Perhaps we will even go on a little journey together, for it has come into my mind to look once more upon my father's house in Bethlehem."

More to give her pleasure than for any other reason, he went to the high place on the morning of the awaited day to ask for divine guidance before the ark. Not that he harbored any belief that his prostrate person was reflected upon the eye that gazed from the remote arch of heaven; that eye had remained as unaware as it had been on the evening when it had stared indifferently upon Rizpah and the seven bodies on the sacred tamarisk. But inasmuch as he had scrupulously performed the rituals and kept the holy days and dealt openhandedly with the priests and prophets, the people called him pious; and he was certain that his piety endeared him to the little Shunammite. She had been fostered among priests; the language of the sanctuary was upon her tongue; the hushed waiting for some heavenly manifestation had widened and brightened her eyes. And far be it from me, he said to himself, to tear the warm cloak of faith from her spirit and drag her after me into the empty cold. . . . But since he could not lie outright to her, he always led their talk away from sacred matters.

For the remainder of the morning he sat at the long board, reading again those clay tablets whose contents he knew by heart. He made it impossible for the meal to be served indoors; the family ate, with as much grace as they could muster, at a table set up in the damp garden; and he himself refused all nourishment but a little curds and bread, not because he hoped to gain favor in God's sight by fasting, but because he had learned that food thickened and oppressed his thoughts. In the afternoon he sent servants down to the camp of God and up to the high place to make certain that those who had been invited would arrive at the specified hour. While his household broke the evening bread under a threatening sky, he arranged with his own hands the bowls of fruit for the guests. Then, having eaten another serving of curds and a slice of honey cake, he went up to his chamber to array himself.

The maid of Gilead had chosen him a garment of fine linen, intricately pleated and dazzlingly white; she had taken from his jewel chest only such ornaments as were light enough to lie comfortably upon his weary body and yet rich enough to proclaim his lordliness. She asked with gratifying curiosity about all that had been done in the common room—what bowls had been chosen for the fruit, where each of the guests was to sit, whether Solomon had been instructed to enter before or after the other guests had assembled around the table. While she talked, she ministered to his person with light and proficient hands. As a young priest strives to adorn the tabernacle of his Lord, so she labored to adorn him, setting every fold and pleat in place, brushing his hair and beard into a light, white mist. And when she had completed her task, she sat back on her heels and watched him walk the length of the room; she bade him sit and stand and turn for her delight. "My lord is unbelievably comely," she said, sighing with satisfaction. "Though God should give the nation ten thousand years, yet would there never be another king so comely to reign in Israel."

It had been his custom of late to go down to the common room before any of the guests had come; he was ashamed of his slow, uncertain steps, his evident confusion in the presence of visitors, his feebleness. But tonight he tarried long in his bedchamber, partly because her delight in him made him less critical of himself, partly because it was sweet to pause and look forward a little, while the high occasion—the last solemn council of his days—still hung before him untouched.

The voices of Adonijah and Joab made themselves heard at the same moment in the room below. He was glad that they had come up to the palace together; since they had been accused of joint conspiracy by half the court, they might well have chosen to belie their connection, each of them arriving alone. "My son Adonijah—he is a good lad," he said, stroking Abishag's hair. "He is open and honorable and above deceit. Nor has it displeased me in the least that he has not sought to find favor in my eyes by turning his back upon his friend the captain of the host." Solomon and Benaiah the counselor had joined in the conversation; all four of them were speaking in an uneasy fashion of inconsequential matters. Then, with commendable promptness, the priests Abiathar and Zadok arrived. "Go now," she said, "for they are all assembled." And he bent and kissed her cool, smiling lips, and walked down the long stairs.

Lamps were kindled in every part of the common room, and the faces that he beheld below him were washed in yellow light. He saw his own kingliness affirmed in their eyes. They also know, he thought, that this is the last council. . . . The steward of the house, even he who had grown weary of his lord's forgetfulness in the matter of names, said in an awed voice, "Behold the King of Judah and Israel."

He seated his guests in the foreordained order—Benaiah, Solomon, and Zadok on his left; Joab, Adonijah, and Abiathar on his right. As he took his place before the pile of clay tablets, he cast a sidelong glance at the captain of the host. It is strange, he thought, that the son of Zeruiah, who is only some five years younger than I, should remain strong and sinewy while I wither like a fallen leaf. But it is not battles and conspiracies and murders that drain the strength from a man; it is wrestling in the spirit—and the son of Zeruiah has not once striven with himself. . . .

He pushed the tablets aside, knowing that he would not need to consult them further. "We are gathered together," he said, "to decide among us the policy of Israel in regard to the quarrel between Ammon and Moab. Here is the matter, as I have drawn it out of much needless writing: The King of Moab, no longer content with the lands which his gods have given him, has raised up a strong host and looks with longing upon the southernmost fields of the Ammonites. Now the King of Ammon, unlike his grandsire, who held us many moons at the gates of Rabbah, has been a friend to us since he ascended the throne. When I tarried in Mahanaim in the days of my exile, he gave freely of the grain of his fields and the fruit of his vineyards, sustaining my uncertain cause with bread and wine. Now he has sent an ambassador to us in his exigency, saying, 'Behold, Moab is in arms at my door. It is with me now as it was with my neighbor when he languished in Mahanaim. I must hold out my hand to my neighbor and cry unto him that he help me in my distress. Send me but six or seven thousand of the men of Jahveh to stand at my borders in full array of battle, and the Moabite that persecutes me will fly before their faces, nor will one of those whom you send to me return to Israel with so much as a scratch upon his cheek.' Thus say the tablets out of Ammon, nor has any message of explanation come from the Moabites. Inasmuch as these my sons have never before lifted up their voices in extraordinary council, it is my wish that they speak first, that I may rejoice a little in their wisdom before I depart from the world. Now let us eat of the fruit and drink of the wine while they ponder. And when a little time is past, we will hear judgment, first from Adonijah, inasmuch as he is the elder, and then from Solomon."

He had not made so long a speech in many years, and he found that his hand trembled when he reached toward his bowl. Solomon went down to the scribe at the end of the table, took a stylus and a tablet from him, and began to write diligently. Adonijah walked toward a pillar at the far end of the room. There, resting his forehead against the stone, he fell into an attitude of profound thought. A light and pleasant conversation concerning the history of Moab rose among the others. The King listened, nodded, smiled. It is the last council, he told himself, and they wish it to be a merry one. . . . And he permitted himself to laugh even at the bitter witticisms of the captain of the host.

Adonijah was the first of the two to return to his place at the council table. It was plain that he had struggled mightily with the question: his soft brown hair, moistened by sweat, clung to his cheeks and brow; his lips were parted; and David could not look upon him without feeling a forbidden, partisan tenderness. Solomon returned with measured steps, biting at the end of his stylus and studying the clay tablet in his hand. He nodded gravely to his father, smoothed his small, pointed beard, assumed a look of serene attention, and seated himself.

"Arise, now, my son Adonijah, and give judgment between Ammon and Moab," said the King of Israel.

The young man rose and fixed his gray, candid eyes upon his father's face. "Were the business in my hands," he said, "I would assuredly send seven thousand to the succor of the Ammonites. For is not the King of Ammon a friend and a brother unto my father? Has he not slept beneath the roof of this house and sent splendid gifts and gracious messages? Has he not stood with my lord in the time of his affliction? How then can my father give back indifference for loving-kindness? It is probable also that matters will come to pass even as the King of Ammon has said. Seeing the ranks of God assembled upon the border, the King of Moab may well turn and flee. Then will my father lay up praise for himself among all the peoples of the world, for they will say, 'Behold, now as always, the Lamb of Judah has established peace among the nations.' For these two reasons, then—because it is a hard thing to turn coldly away from a friend, and because it is well to take a little risk in order to avert the shedding of much blood—I would bid the captain of the host take seven thousand, nay, ten thousand, and march straightway into the country of the Ammonites."

The King of Israel smiled upon the son of Haggith. He had spoken simply and directly, out of his honorable heart. Then, before the smile could fade or stiffen on his lips, David turned to his left and said, "Now let us hear the words of Solomon."

The son of the beloved did not lift up his face to his father. His eyes, scarcely visible beneath their heavy lids, were fixed upon the tablet that lay on the board between his wine cup and his bowl of fruit. "My brother Adonijah," he said, "shows a commendable disinclination to shed blood. It is unfortunate, however, that, in his solicitude for the comfort of the heathen, he has lost sight of the security of Israel. He has said that the King of Ammon is our friend and our brother. He may be right; I do not know. But the father of this same King, who held us for seven moons before the city of Rabbah, *he* was not our friend and brother, nor can we be certain whose blood will flow in the veins of the next King of Ammon —the blood of the violent Hanum who made mock of our ambassadors or the blood of the mild Shobi who has seen fit to curry favor with the King of Israel. I entreat the members of this distinguished assembly to consider with me for a moment the state of the land. We are strong, but we are girt round with heathen. Philistia, weak but still capable of recovery, lies between us and the western sea. To the east lie Moab and Ammon and Edom; to the north the fierce, implacable lords of Syria; to the south the hordes that come out of the desert and are as numberless as the grains of sand. It is a sweet and gracious thing to say on a high occasion, 'Come, let all the nations join hands and dwell in everlasting peace.' But should the nations that are at our borders indeed join hands, then would we be in a sorry case, then would we be hemmed in and ringed about, held from the highways, barred from the seacoast, squeezed and pressed upon until we could no longer draw breath. Let us not, then, permit ourselves to grow foolish with tenderness for the children of strange gods. If the King of Moab falls upon the King of Ammon, let us hold our hands and rejoice, even as the deer rejoices when a lion falls upon a bear in the wilderness."

During the three days of happy anticipation that had preceded this council, it had not once occurred to David that after he had made his decision, it would still be necessary for him to listen to endless and unenlightening arguments. For him, the event was at an end; he had made his choice; and he could not say that he felt either exhilaration or relief. He took up a cluster of raisins and stared at it mournfully while those other counselors, who would not see that they had been called only to listen, droned on. Benaiah and Zadok rose to sustain and elaborate the arguments introduced by Solomon. Abiathar, who had long since pledged his support to the son of Haggith, delivered himself of a long, abstract, and tenuous disquisition upon the state of chaos that was bound to descend upon the world as soon as the nations ceased to be governed by brotherly love and depended upon selfish policy alone. As for the son of Zeruiah, inasmuch as he could not justify the words of Adonijah, he said nothing. When the King asked him to rise and speak, he only sighed and shook his head.

It is not that I have decided for Solomon, the King of Israel thought. It is that I have seen the world as it is. Of these two sons that the years have left to me, I cleave with the stronger love to Adonijah, nor has he ever been so dear to me as at this moment, when I say of him, "Let him never wear the crown." Honor, simplicity, tenderness for all the sons of man who dwell upon the face of the earth—these would be blessed attributes in one who was to reign over a kingdom of angels. In such a kingdom, the remembrance of a happy evening might disperse the sentinels who stand at the borders; in such a kingdom, a grateful heart might turn back the marching hosts. But behold Israel as it is and as I must leave it—ringed round with heathen and divided within itself. When the south and the north contend against each other, when the elders strive against the governors, when the priests accuse the prophets and the prophets accuse the King, how can I lay the land in the hands of a valiant and honorable child? He will never see the world as it is. His eyes will be fixed forever on a vision of the world as he wishes it to be. And while he dreams, the lions will fall upon the flock, and he will look in wonder upon the slaughter, saying, "How is it possible? Lord, Lord, what have You done to these Your little ones?" Therefore I will raise up the son of the beloved. Because he is wily and suspicious, because his subtlety has robbed him of his innocence, because he is too wise for visions and too cold for love, his heart will not stand in the way of his judgment. Inasmuch as there is no virtue in him save only wisdom, he will be a strong king over a corrupt and divided nation in an evil world. . . .

So the King of Israel thought, gazing sorrowfully at his cluster of raisins and waiting for his guests to make an end of useless talk and depart. And at last Benaiah said, "What is the decision of my lord the King?"

He had almost forgotten the matter of Ammon and Moab. Now he started and dropped the raisins and rubbed his aching eyes. "Surely that is plain. We will send no help to our good friend the King of the Ammonites, who succored us in the hour of our affliction," he said.

When they had gone forth from the palace, David took a lamp and mounted the stairs and knocked lightly upon Bath-sheba's door.

"Solomon?" she said in a hushed and eager voice.

"No. It is only I."

He opened the door and stood on the threshold. It was very late, but her chamber was still bright with lamps. She sat in a chair near the window, still clothed, still alert, plainly waiting to hear from the lips of her son all that had come to pass below. At the sight of her lord she flushed and folded her hands primly upon her knee.

"No, now," he said, smiling, "I will not stay. I will not keep you from your usual midnight tryst with Solomon. I have come only to tell you that my mind is at peace concerning the succession. Publish it not to the others—let Benaiah and Zadok and Nathan wait until the day when I lay me down to die—but the fruit of your womb, even he whom we called into being in the first years of the love that was between us, it is he whom I have chosen to raise up over Judah and Israel."

✑§ VI ß✑

THE SEASON of the winter rains was brief that year. The children of Jahveh rejoiced in rich and early crops, and the King of Israel rejoiced in the warmth of the sun. He was no longer content to experience that heat as it came to him in the garden, sifted through leaves and commingled with shade; he yearned now to know its full-bodied opulence, to lie half-naked, with nothing between him and the burning arc of the firmament, all day long. So he bade his steward prepare a couch on the roof—a couch padded with quilted linen and heaped with cushions, a broad couch, so that the maid out of Shunam might lie at his side. "I will lie here," he told her, "from morning until eventide. For the sun gives strength to all things, even to the aged eagle and the blasted tree and the vine that no longer bears fruit. Me also it may restore a little, so that I may find strength to go down with my beloved to my father's house in Bethlehem."

During the first day that they spent together on the roof, they quarreled with each other. She drove him into a sulky silence by insisting that he must be shielded by a canopy and by forbidding him to drink cold wine. She spent the morning in making him a fine awning of yellow and violet linen; she was childishly proud of her handiwork, and grew angry with him because he would not say that it was fair. He repented and tried to make friends with her, but she was not ready to excuse him. He sulked again, and drank three cups of chilly wine for spite. "It is plain to me," she said, weeping, "that you do not love me. If you loved me in the least, you would not strive in every possible manner to hasten away from me and from the world." So they wasted the hours of the morning and the hours of the afternoon, and it was evening before they were reconciled.

Most of the second day also was marred for them because they strove too eagerly to be tender with each other. Both of them knew that the time which they could share was very brief; both of them felt bruised and remorseful over the lost yesterday; each of them was on the point of admitting to the other that he had been happier in the garden and would prefer to return to the roof no more. But toward evening they began to recall the excitement with which they had talked of the days that they were to spend on the roof together, and by dusk they were tense with the determination to enjoy themselves there at any cost. "I am so enamored of this place," he said at the hour when the wind of God began to blow, "that I cannot bring myself to go inside. Run down, then, and fetch coverlets, so that we may spend the night together under the stars."

Yet the serene pleasure that they had known in each other's company still eluded them. Strive as they would, they could not grasp it, not even when they lay side by side on the broad couch, watching the stars appear, large and liquid, in the pale, opalescent, inverted bowl of heaven. He was annoyed with her because she had not thought to bring a certain bearskin rug which she always laid across his feet; instead of making mention of the matter, he let it rankle within him; and when she chose to speak on a forbidden subject—when she said to him that it was a blessed thing to lie in the presence of God's stars with him who knew the Lord of Hosts better than any other man in Israel—he gave vent to the sour temper that had been muffled all day beneath precarious folds of tenderness.

"Yes," he said in a malicious voice, "I know God. I have sought Him all the years of my life—I have pursued Him even to the very edge of the firmament. And behold, there He has vanished from my sight. I have known Him so well that He has ceased to be."

He waited for the suspended breath, the shocked protest. But her head lay motionless upon his shoulder, and her hand, closed around his, did not stir. "Then is God truly nothing to my lord and my beloved?" she said.

He would gladly have retreated, but he could not bring himself to put her off with sophistry or to silence her with a lie. "Nothing," he said. "A blind eye staring out of the emptiness of heaven. A deaf and pitiless ear turned upon the lamentations of the world."

She drew the coverlet more closely around him and embraced him. "Tell me," she said.

"Tell you? What is there to tell you?"

"Tell me how it was that the Lord became blind and deaf and nothing unto him who loved Him with the greatest love and served Him best?"

"How is it possible," he said, pressing his mouth against the warmth of her forehead, "how is it possible to speak of such matters to a pure and righteous child?"

"Let me say a word or two to my dearly beloved. There was a time when I stood in the field behind my father's house in Shunam and called in a loud voice upon the name of God, and heard no answer, and said to myself, 'Behold, He is in no place, neither in the earth nor in the heavens. He is not, He was not, nor will He ever be.' This I said because my foot had trodden upon a nursling fawn, dead in the field, with flies and beetles gathered black upon its eyes." She shuddered to remember it and clung to him still more urgently. "What horrors has my beloved looked upon in the seventy years of his life?" she said. "What has he seen that he should believe that God neither sees nor hears?"

A nursling fawn, dead in the field, he thought. A red lily, broken in the bud by stones out of heaven. For many years, since that evening when I walked alone in the garden after the storm, I have borne this ulcer of meaninglessness at the core of my spirit. I spoke of it once to the beloved, but she would not listen, and since that hour I have wandered as a stranger among men, inasmuch as I had no brother in anguish. And now when my little one says to me, "Tell me," how shall I hold my peace? . . .

"What have I seen?" he said. "Evil—profitless evil—chaos and darkness and the cries of the children of men rising up everlastingly out of every corner of the world. I have seen the valiant man wasted by madness. I have seen the fairest and most honorable creature that ever walked beneath the sun torn by the wheels of chariots and left to rot upon a temple wall. I have heard the blameless infant scream out his life. I have seen an old and righteous shepherd, who loved his sheep and his brown house and the soil of his native land, languish out his days in a foreign court and come to rest in an alien grave. I have seen the lustful ravage the innocent and the strong murder the weak. I have seen a whole life's love poured out upon an unanswering heart. I have seen three thousand dead on one field of battle, staring at the empty sky with empty eyes. I have seen seven guiltless sons of a high house hung upon the boughs of a sacred tamarisk, and their mother shouting blasphemies into the face of God. These things I have seen, being mortal and therefore cursed with seeing eyes. But He who made them—He is not afflicted with sight—He stares upon it all and sees it not."

He knew suddenly that she was no longer beside him. She was sitting at the foot of the couch, drawing the folds of the wind-turned coverlet over his legs and looking upon him with large, untroubled, radiant eyes.

"Let not my lord believe that my ears have been closed because I have looked to the coverlet," she said. "Believe me, I have heard every word that issued from his lips. My lord has waited many moons to tell me that the world is evil. Is it possible that he thought I did not know there was evil in the world—how the lamb eats the tips of the blooming grasses before the seed can be scattered, how man slays the lamb and eats of its blood and its body, and being strengthened, rises up to devour his own brother with the spear and the sword? The womb is a dark and bloody place wherein the child nourishes itself on the flesh of its mother. To be conceived, to be arrayed in flesh, to issue forth as a living thing, is to make a covenant with evil and to accept a portion in decay. Had my lord rejected that covenant—had he shut himself away from all evil—he would not be that which he is, a king among men. To shut oneself away from evil in the world is to sicken in the presence of life and to stand in terror before the face of death."

No, now, he thought in amazement, has she unfolded this hard and bloody doctrine among the shepherds and the tillers of the soil in Gilead? Has she dared to say to the priests of Shunam that whosoever clothes himself in flesh has made a covenant with evil and is a cold and cowardly hypocrite unless he keeps his bond with sin and death?

"Has Abishag said these things in the midst of her people?"

"Many times, my lord."

"How is it that they have not cast her forth from the high places and hurled stones at her?"

"Wherefore? For saying that the beast eats the seed and the man eats the beast and the sons of men devour each other? The people of Gilead are poor shepherds who carve the lamb while the warmth of life is still upon it, and hang the skin upon two posts before the door of the house, so that in their goings-out and their comings-in their faces are spattered with blood. With their own hands they slay the thief who creeps upon the flock, nor have they any magistrate to wield the sword for them, saying, 'I do this not in my own person, but for the people and in the name of God.' They weave their winding-sheets upon their own looms, and they wash the bodies of their own dead, nor ever render them up to servants, saying, 'I am too delicate to wash this corpse. Wash it for me, and lay it in the grave.' If I have said to my people that life is a covenant with evil and decay, I have told them nothing that they do not know."

"And what of me?" he said, strangely moved. "Will the daughter of Shunam wash me also when my spirit has departed?"

She bent and embraced his legs and laid her face against his knees. "When my lord has gone to his everlasting sleep," she said, "I will surely wash his body and prepare it for the burial cave. Why should I leave to a servant that which is dearer to me than myself?"

"But you must leave it to the earth," he said, stroking her cheek with the back of his hand.

"The earth has a claim upon it and takes it hospitably to her breast. I will give up my love only to such as will receive him with love."

She rose then and kissed his eyelids and walked about a little on the roof, holding up her arms to the coolness of the evening wind and staring at the stars.

"Will you leave me only half answered?" he said. "I have said to you that the world is evil, and you have said, 'Even so.' But I have said also that God is blind to the evil which is in the world, and you have answered me not."

She came and stood at the foot of the couch, smiling upon him. "Even as my lord and my beloved says, so it is. God sees us not. I have never spoken of it before the priests of Shunam, but I have known it long. God is utterly remote—beyond hearing and beyond sight." She bent and took his hands and pulled him to his feet. "Come," she said. "Come with me to the edge of the roof and look upon the bright, blind stars."

Night had come down upon them while they talked together. The stars and a virgin crescent stood apart from the world and from each other —golden, isolated points of light against a vast expanse of deep, impenetrable blue. She rested her elbow on the parapet and stared upward, leaning her cheek against her hand. "He does not see," she said. "Is it so hard a thing to my lord and my beloved that the eye of God does not hold a reflection of his face? Has he never thought in his heart that perhaps this also is a part in the heritage of evil that we take upon us in the womb —this vain and childish desire that God should look upon us, should see and rejoice, should see and be moved to mortal anger, should see and shed human tears? What are we that God should look upon us? Why do we stand forever shrieking into the vast sky, 'I am everything, let the Lord behold me,' when it is plain that we are nothing? That He does not see us is a small matter, once we have delivered ourselves of the burden of our pride and our selfishness. All that is needful is that we should see God."

He had heard much holy wisdom in his day; he had listened to the austere pronouncements of Samuel, the fierce ravings of Nathan, and the obscure and tenuous discussions of Zadok and Abiathar and Gad. Yet it seemed to him now that he had never heard so sure a revelation as that which issued out of her profound and reverent simplicity.

"Is it so hard a thing to my beloved," she said again, "that God does not behold him? Is his covenant with sin and death still so strong, even in these his latter days, that he cannot content himself with seeing God?"

And suddenly he knew that he no longer bore resentment against that Unseeing Eye which gazed out of the firmament. For the first time in his days, he who had been everything—shepherd and king, sweet singer and lover, warrior and seeker after the face of the Lord—knew that he was nothing in the boundlessness of space and the endlessness of time, and was content to be nothing, was infinitely lifted up in his heart to know that he was nothing. "Behold," he said, turning and smiling upon her, "I see that God sees me not, and I am resigned. But I am flesh, and will be flesh until my mind is extinguished in the everlasting dark, and while I am flesh, how can I see God?"

"It is no mystery. My lord already understands it. He sees, but he does not know that he sees. The covenant which he made with sin and death in the beginning has been fulfilled—every term thereof has been utterly fulfilled, save only the last. He has known the exigencies of the flesh and has put them from him one by one. He is no longer bound to the earth by passion or by yearning after greatness. He is delivered even from himself, for he has said, 'I am nothing. Let me look upon the Lord.' And now no trace of his mortality remains to veil his sight save only his tenderness for his little one. As he clung to the breast of his mother when they brought him forth into the light of day and laid him at her side, so he clings now to his beloved at the time of his going-forth. Tenderness is yet whole within him, and he cannot see the face of God through the blur of his tears. But I tell him that in the end this also will surely pass. Only let him not hasten to cast it from him. Let him wait patiently, for my sake and for his own. For of all the bonds of the flesh, this is the lightest and the sweetest, nor would it be a heavy sin in him if he were to hold it to him even unto the final hour. . . ."

He turned and drew her to him and embraced her. In the faint light of the crescent, he could see nothing but the earnest shining of her eyes. "I am in no haste, my beloved. Believe me, I am with you even unto the last," he said.

✠ VII ✠

WHEN he made it known in the palace that he meant to journey to Bethlehem, the consternation was as great as if he had announced an intention to ride into the southernmost stretches of the desert to look for the legendary Mount of God. Solomon and Benaiah the counselor told him that he would find the raw life of a village intolerable after the luxury of the capital; Bath-sheba pointed out that he ought to spend every available moment instructing the young son whom he had chosen to sit after him upon the throne; Nathan visited him twice and managed to say on both occasions that to depart out of Jerusalem was to tempt Adonijah to raise the standard of revolt; and the physician whom they chose to consult as to the wisdom of his making such a journey sighed deeply and shook his head. It was a matter of the King's heart, the surgeon said. He was by no means satisfied with the King's heart. Anyone who put his ear against the King's chest could hear the signal of danger—a kind of murmurous, fluttering sound. No, he could not say that he was satisfied at all. . . .

But the son of Jesse was eminently satisfied. The sound which they heard, and the strange, disintegrating, inward movement that begot the sound, were far less painful to him than the slow beats that had pushed the sluggish blood through his body in the days when he had suffered from the cold. Now it was as if his heart, swollen with the warm wine of life, stirred and trembled out of an access of wonder and thanksgiving and tenderness. Wave after wave of melting warmth passed over him; the green hedges, the streams of water in the garden, the moving shapes among the gray pillars in the common room, the heavy, drooping head of his little one—all these seemed on the point of dissolving into mist, all these shimmered and lost their edges before his eyes. The physician might say what he wished, but the son of Jesse was content.

His longing to go down to Bethlehem had been intensified of late by his aching affection for the little Shunammite—he wished to be alone with her, he wished to take her beyond the reach of other men's eyes. It had become plain to him that she was no longer insignificant in the sight of the children of Jerusalem. She was the King's favorite and therefore desirable; young men stood behind her now when she sang to him in the common room; tall captains, riding past the garden wall, reined in their steeds to salute her from the street. When I am dead, he thought, she will take a husband. Another man, young and ardent, will reap what I could not reap. She will pause only now and then in her spinning and her weaving to remember me, and even that recollection will pass from her once she has held a child against her breast. . . . And so long as she was in the midst of the court, he was troubled and could not refrain from staring at every youth who crossed the threshold.

Perhaps it was this sorrowful apprehension that prompted him to send heralds before him to all the villages between Jerusalem and Bethlehem. The King and the daughter of Shunam, said the heralds, would be journeying this way on such-and-such a day, to look upon the town where the son of Jesse had lived as a child. They would be gratified if the children of Judah would not come forth from their houses to greet them. It was their desire to travel like simple folk making a visit to cousins in the south. The King was old and sick and had little strength to spare, and a considerate withdrawal would be far more acceptable to him in his weariness than any number of dances and antiphonal songs.

They traveled in a big, lumbering cart drawn by two peaceable donkeys and driven by a bondsman out of Egypt, who could not constrain them inasmuch as he barely understood the Israelite tongue. When they had loaded the cart with the pillows and coverlets, the baskets of bread and fruit, the skins of curds and wine, that were necessary for their journey, they found that they had left scarcely enough room for themselves. They sat at close quarters, crowded but very cheerful—the little Shunammite perched upon a pile of cushions, the King upon a folded coverlet, his arm across her knees. The air was light and delectable, the landscape bright with the fresh, abundant green of millet, barley, and wheat. Although the children of Judah had obediently withdrawn into their houses, they had been unable to refrain from leaving tokens of their devotion behind them: the road was scattered with the yellow, pungent blossoms of the mustard flower; fine clusters of raisins had been tied to the lower limbs of trees; and every wayside stone bore a cruet of ointment for their feet, a nosegay of fragrant almond blossoms for Abishag, or a garland of summer flowers for the King of Israel.

Even though they journeyed through stretches of land that he had known in his childhood, he thought of nothing but the present moment— the fragrance of her hair and the scent of the pomegranates in one of the

617

baskets, the soothing creak and rumble of the cartwheels, the long vistas of field and meadowland, blurred now and again by the waves of warmth that rose from his tremulous and exultant heart. But when they came within sight of Bethlehem—a low mound of dull brown houses seen through the green of wild olives—he experienced a nameless sense of depression. He began to ask himself why he had come, what he had hoped to gain by his journey, whether it was possible, after so many crowded years, to recapture the past.

It was midafternoon when he left the cart at the lowly gate of the city and walked, leaning heavily upon her, into the shadow of the walls. All the fervor of high adventure had departed from him. He turned aside from the cistern where he had meant to stop for a deep draught of the waters of Bethlehem. He lifted up his eyes only once to the houses on either side of the gate; then he bowed his head and stared at the dusty paving stones. Not one of the children of Bethlehem walked in the street. They had left the town to him and to the past, even as he had desired. And that past which he had journeyed so many miles to seek yielded up to him only heavy remembrances, unfulfilled yearnings, futile regrets.

To this same gate the elders of the city had come to delight in grave talk and the coolness of the wind of God. He could see them still, their misty beards and hair stirring in the breeze, their heads tilted to one side while they listened to the son of Jesse singing his latest glorious song. Their voices sounded again in the oppressive quiet of the place: "Such songs have not been sung in the land of Judah before. Go now and make a name for Bethlehem in Israel." And I, he thought, a Bethlehemite, have held the land in the hollow of my hand, but they knew it not. They said of me, "He is a bandit in the wilderness," and, so saying, went down to their graves, even as I must soon go down to mine. . . .

Suddenly the brown streets were filled with a host of forgotten beings. Faces which he had not seen these fifty years crowded upon him in be-wildering haste and multiplicity—old shepherds who had served his father, matrons who had visited his mother, boys who had chased errant goats with him and his brothers, fair daughters of Bethlehem going to the cistern with vessels balanced on their heads. And he stopped in the midst of the street and leaned upon the little Shunammite. "How is it possible," he said aloud, "that all those whom I knew in my childhood should have departed utterly out of my memory until now? They were my people, but I have gone forth and forgotten them, nor is there any way to reclaim them, inasmuch as not one among fifty still draws his breath."

"Come," she said in an urgent voice, "my lord is too weary to stand in the street. Let us go to his father's house, where he may rest."

"Only let my little one hear me for a moment. Beyond this same garden wall there was a fig tree once, and its lowest bough was thrust over the top of the wall, above the street. When I was a child, it seemed to me that

618

the bough was very high, and I said in my heart, I will grow tall and lift up my hand and touch the bough. And I grew tall, but I forgot the fig tree. Now it is no more—they have cut it down, and I touched it not. . . ."

She caught his gesturing hand and kissed it. "What can I tell my beloved to comfort him? I will find another fig tree and touch it in his name," she said.

He walked the rest of the way to Jesse's house in silence. Other images rose up to encounter him—the austere Samuel in conversation with the village priest, the fat Zeruiah moving laboriously down the street with the little Abishai in her wake, a lithe young woman whom he had loved for a week or so coming on some forgotten errand to his father's door. His father's door—it stood open before him. The room, low and brown and woundingly bare, was lighted by the pitiless brightness of the afternoon sun. It had stood empty nigh onto fifty years, but some kindly neighbor had swept and scrubbed it in preparation for the royal visitor. The smell of damp wood and clay clung to it; it had been left naked, stripped of even the thin veilings of cobwebs and dust. The table and the long benches remained; three bowls, cracked and ancient, stood on the shelf; a little rug of goat's-hair, gray and moist with recent washing, lay between the table and the door. Some unknown hand had striven against the bleakness—a few embers burned on the hearth, and the worn, wet wood of the board was strewn with almond flowers.

At the sight of the room he started back from the threshold, pressing his hands over the fierce struggles of his protesting heart. "Here, here——" he said, and could say no more, because the breath was driven out of him by pain and grief over all that was irretrievably lost.

"My lord must rest, my beloved must sit and rest awhile," said the little Shunammite. She led him to the bench beside the table; and while he leaned upon the board and wept against the rough, moist wood, she went to the door and closed out the bright cruelty of the sun.

He wept for the forfeited mornings when he had sat among his brothers at this same table, breaking the bread that came hot from the hearth. He wept for the lost evenings, for his father's voice recounting the tales of Barak and Jephthah, for his mother's withered hand resting upon the loom, for the moments of solitary exaltation under the moonlit boughs of the fig tree. He wept for all the departed sounds—the ring of Jesse's hammer, the clack of his mother's spinning whorl, the muffled laughter that had risen behind the door of the chamber where the two old lovers slept. And he yearned after his dead with so strong a yearning that he could not hold his peace, but called upon them aloud and held out his shaking hands.

The little Shunammite hovered anxiously above him. She was hard put to it to remain silent, yet she permitted him to weep in peace and did not speak to him so long as there were tears within him. It was late afternoon and the sun had withdrawn from the window before she touched his arm.

619

"Shall I go down now and bring up food from the cart? Will my beloved eat the evening meal in his father's house?" she said.

"No, no, let us arise and go forth. I had thought to light a lamp and break bread in the company of those who have departed. But it was a dream—it is impossible for the living, yes, and for the dying also, to break bread with the dead."

"But David will surely eat——"

"Let us go up into the hills and break bread beneath the sky. I know a place, a grotto with a spring. We will eat there, even as I ate in the days when I watched my father's sheep."

He rose with a show of energy and eagerness, and tried to smile. I can comfort her, he thought, by saying that a long and cheerful evening still lies before us. . . . But whatever he had meant to say remained unsaid. He could not speak—he needed all his strength to move, so violent was the agitation within his chest. That which had been a murmur and a fluttering had turned to a wild knocking now, so hard, so swift, that he could scarcely draw his breath. He flung his arm over her shoulders and crossed the threshold, ashamed that he should rest his whole weight against her slender body, but utterly unable to support himself. It will be well with me when I am sitting in the cart, he thought, looking with disbelief upon the distorted and darkened street. A little air, a few more steps, and this knocking will subside, this purplish mist will melt away. . . . But with every step the thumping grew louder. He gasped, and swayed against her side. It was she who made it known to him that he had come to the cart and need only climb up and lie down—so thick was the darkness that had gathered before his eyes.

With the driver's help, he managed to drag himself up among the shawls and coverlets and baskets of fruit. She supported his head upon her knees and stroked his face and kissed him. She begged him to rest and poured a trickle of wine between his lips. But he would not abandon his intention of going up to the grotto. If I am to die, he thought, let me die in the hills, with the sound of living waters in my ears. . . . And he told her in a stern, gasping voice to see that the driver followed the little path that began not ten paces beyond the gate. "Do not turn from it until we have come to a grotto where there is a granite wall, with vines, and with water gushing forth from the rock," he said. Then he closed his eyes and loosed his hold upon her hand and gave himself up to the wild buffeting, the pain, the helplessness, and the dark. . . .

There is no happiness on earth so sweet as this, he thought, rising to the surface of the roaring blackness. There is no happiness so sweet as the cessation of pain. It is enough to lie still and know that my heart has grown quiet again within me, to hear the liquid music of the spring and feel the wind of God moving across my face. . . . He sighed and turned his head and felt her cool flesh beneath his cheek. It is her knee, he thought, she has pillowed my head upon her knee. Am I not blessed above all the sons of men in that I have a quiet heart and a little one to cherish me and to say to me, "How is it now with my lord and my beloved? . . ."

"It has passed—the pain has utterly passed from me," he said, and opened his eyes.

The shadow that lay before his eyes now was not the purplish shadow of gathering blindness; it was the wholly good and acceptable shadow of eventide. Somewhere beyond the ridge of granite that stood behind him, the red sun was going down. Small, pinkish clouds, driven like sheep before the wind of God, moved across the sky. The land, rolling in low hills to the right and to the left, was already folded in semidarkness; the green of the wild olives and the terebinths was muted; the rocky projections of granite and sandstone were darkened to one even cast of grayish brown. But if he raised his head a little and looked over his own supine body toward the lower slopes, he could see a flock of sheep grazing in an open glade, and their wool was softly effulgent—reddened by the last slanting rays of the sun. The same rosy tint lay upon the two shepherds who wandered among them, upon the topmost leaves of the highest terebinths, and upon the trickles of water that ran between the rocks. Blessed is the eventide, he said in his heart. Blessed is the glow of the eventide, shining upon all the sheep and shepherds and streams and wind-turned treetops in the world. . . .

"Is my lord and my beloved warm? I have sent the bondsman out to gather twigs so that we may have a little fire. The shepherds on the lower slope have promised to give us a burning brand."

"I am warm," he said. "I have not been so warm as this for many moons. Nevertheless, it will be pleasant to break the evening bread before a fire."

She bent and kissed him lightly on the lips. The touch of her mouth begot in him again that subtle, tingling music which he had known on the evening when they brought her to him. He raised his hand and stroked her cheek and found that it was wet. She wept for me, he thought. She wept, believing that I had gone down to death without taking leave of her, yes, and without a sight of the face of God. . . . He wished to reassure her, and raised himself, and asked that pillows be put behind him so that he might sit and watch the flock in the glade below. And while she settled him against the heaped cushions, the vibrant music grew within him. The splash and ripple of the spring, the sound of the wind-stirred leaves, the coming and going of her breath—all these became a part of one broad, endless antiphonal song, rising, swelling, opening out above him, encompassing new voices lifted up from the sands of the desert, from the snow-tipped mountains of Lebanon, from the unknown countries beyond Edom and Moab, from the legendary islands in the western sea. Behold, he thought in wonderment, if my heart had ceased to beat while I lay in the churning darkness, the music would not have lessened—some other heart, still closed away in the secrecy of the womb, would have begun to beat in its place. That moth which floats past us now on sun-tinged wings cannot live beyond the passing of another day; but the white, fibrous

621

hammocks hung upon the twigs are already stirring—a thousand moths will break forth tomorrow into the new eventide. . . .

And while he gazed at the muted green and brown of the land and the rosy arch of the firmament, it seemed to him that all barriers fell away, that the hills bowed down, that it was given to him to see even unto the very margins of the earth. And every part of the earth, every plain and mountain and valley, was clothed in a glimmering veil of life. The green shoots of life trembled against the sky; the frail tendrils of life crept over blasted trees and unbreathing stones; life moved on soft, animal feet through the fragrant grass and soared on beating wings into the upper air and darted on radiant rainbow fins through the hidden depths of the sea. Innumerable infants reached out after nourishment and tenderness, and drew the white wine of life from their mothers' breasts. Countless children ran through the twilight, playing the immemorial games that had been played in fields and shadowy alleys since the beginning of time. Young men rose up by the thousands in an endless search after the beloved; young women put sprigs of almond blossom in their hair and stood on lighted thresholds, gazing with shining eyes into the dark. Flesh merged with flesh in shuddering ecstasy and begot life in blood and blackness. Young mothers held up their arms to receive the newborn. In Bethlehem and in a thousand other cities, women kindled lamps and laid the board and lifted up their voices to call the shepherds home. The dying watched the first star appear in the square of the window, and turned to the wall, and slept the everlasting sleep. And the living closed the eyes of the dead and went and stood at the door, and heard the voice of life still singing unabated, singing now and forever unto the end of the world. . . . Behold, he said in his heart—and the thought brought peace and wonder with it—behold, when I am no more, when she has washed my body and prepared it for burial, she will go forth to receive her due portion of love. . . .

"I would say a word or two to my little one," he said.

"Let my lord wait a while, inasmuch as he is tired——"

"After I have spoken I will rest. . . . When I have taken unto myself the everlasting sleep, mourn for me only so long as it is meet to mourn for a father or for a beloved brother. And when the due time of mourning is past, arise, and dry your tears, and reach out your hands and take your portion in the world."

"What portion have I in the world after my lord has departed from me? How should I rise up and dry my tears when I——"

"Only listen, for I am very short of breath. Let Abishag walk among the sons of men arrayed in purple and scarlet, so that her beauty, which has delighted my fading eyes, shall delight the eyes of all Israel. Let her take a husband and know him in love, so that it may not be said of me, 'He laved his flesh in a living spring and left it dry.' No, now, I beg you, do not weep. Only listen a little, and then we will say no more concerning this matter; we will have our fire and eat our fruit and bread. It is my desire that the daughter of Shunam should bring forth children. If she has one son, let her name him for her father. If she has a second, let her name him for the father of her husband and her lord. If there is a third, and she still remembers me with tenderness, let her name him with my name. And when he is tall and reaches up his hand to touch a fig tree, let her say in her heart, This he does in David's name, for David's sake."

There was no time for her to answer. The bondsman and the young shepherd were coming up the slope together, bearing twigs and a brand for the making of a fire. He kissed her swiftly, covertly, and pushed her lightly from him. "Go now and spread our feast, that we may be merry together," he said.

ᦡᦉ VIII ᦃᦀ

NOW THAT he had come again to Jerusalem and laid him down upon his bed, he longed for quietness. Some awesome change had come upon his person—he knew as much by the faces of those who had gathered to greet him at the garden gate, by the fact that neither Benaiah nor Bath-sheba permitted themselves to make mention of the matter of the succession, by his steward's discreet suggestion that he should walk very slowly up the stairs. Even when they had assured themselves that he was comfortably settled in his bedchamber, propped against pillows and covered with warm coverlets, their minds were not at peace; they continued to come up and stand in shamefaced helplessness on his threshold. And yet, for all their solicitude, they did not give him the silence that he most desired. Evening after evening, the sounds of laughter and eager talk rose to him from the common room. His palace—burdensomely silent in those days when he had longed to see it crowded with visitors—was never empty now. All the youth and wit and beauty of Jerusalem had gathered there to warm themselves in the light of the rising sun. While I tarried in Bethlehem, he thought, Bath-sheba broke her covenant. She could not hold her tongue, and those to whom she whispered—they also could not hold their tongues. Now it is known that the son of the beloved will sit upon the throne, and the hearts of Judah and Israel are after Solomon. . . .

If they thought he resented the noise of the feasting because it broke his rest, they were mistaken; his weariness was such that he could have slept in the midst of a battle. It was only that their voices drowned out that subtle music which had sounded in his ears ever since his awakening in the grotto above Bethlehem. Since the hour when he had beheld the web of life spread over all the hills and valleys of the world, his eyes had been dimmed by a light, perpetual mist. "But I have been given a recompense," he said to his little one. "Though I can no longer see your face with the same clarity, I hear your every breath. All night long, even in my sleep, I hear the beating of your heart."

There were times when he would start out of his listening and dreaming, driven into complete wakefulness by the knocking in his chest. How is it with me? he would ask himself then. Death may come upon me while I sleep, and I have not yet publicly set the son of the beloved upon the throne. Tomorrow I will surely rise and put the crown upon his head. . . . But on the morrow there was always some other matter to distract him—Hiram, King of Tyre, would have sent him a long, tender, philosophical epistle, which Abishag must read again and again; Haggith and Adonijah would have come to bring him a jar of ointment for his eyes; Meribaal would have journeyed down from Benjamin to show his benefactor the first fruit of his seed, a fair, pale infant with Jonathan's eyes and Jonathan's cloudy hair. So the days went by—scarcely to be distinguished one from the other, save for the growing look of urgency in Bath-sheba's eyes—and the thing remained undone.

Twice or thrice he was assailed by a sudden and unreasonable desire to behold the son of Zeruiah. All those among the living who had been bound to him by strong ties came and stood at his threshold or sat daily at the foot of his bed, save only the captain of the host. How is it with him? the son of Jesse thought. What did he say when they told him that I came home from Bethlehem a dying man? . . . And he no longer looked upon his nephew with that cold loathing which had obsessed him since the day of the slaughter in the forest of Ephraim. Once, falling into a drowse in the warmth of the late afternoon, he dreamed that the son of Zeruiah, clad in a battered breastplate and carrying a broken sword, stood at the foot of his bed. Even as he lifted up his arms to embrace the presence, it withdrew from him. "Come, now," he said, starting up and weeping aloud, "let us be reconciled." But when the clear images of the dream had given place to the dim room veiled in the everlasting mist, he knew that he and Joab could never be reconciled. For to leave him alive in Israel after my going forth, he thought, is to leave a lion in the midst of the fold. I have done much evil all my days, but this at least may be said of me—that I knew evil, even when I had done it with my own hands. As for the son of Zeruiah, he sees no difference between evil and good. Since his childhood, he has known that God sees us not, but it will never be given to him to know that we should strive to see God. . . . Nevertheless, he yearned after the captain of the host and asked that a certain girdle which Joab had given him should be laid within reach of his hands.

There came a morning when he wakened to find his little one weeping bitterly against him. Solomon and Bath-sheba were whispering somewhere in the umbral reaches of the room; the high priest Zadok was chanting an incantation; the cold finger of the physician was pressed hard upon his wrist. "What is it now?" he said in a voice as blurred as his sight. And before they could answer, he knew that the terrible knocking had come upon him again, that he had been tossed about on the violent tides of pain and darkness in his sleep. He withdrew his hand from the touch of the physician. It was strangely numb, but he managed to bring it down upon Abishag's warm hair. "Do not grieve," he said to the maid out of

Shunam. "I am with you yet for a little while." Then he raised himself on his elbows and said to his wife and his son: "I will surely attend tomorrow to this business of the succession. Set your hearts at rest. It is not yet too late."

He permitted them to tarry in the room and to minister to him. What is it to me if they are less skillful than Abishag? he thought, lifting his head so that Solomon might straighten his pillows, opening his lips so that he might sip from the bowl of wine in Bath-sheba's hand. It is a comfort to them to make these gestures. They will say among themselves, "At least we did such-and-such for him while he was yet with us," and this will set their spirits at peace when I am dead. . . . But he was glad in his heart when they kissed him and departed from him. Lifted up yet once more and moved to weak tears by the sweetness of rest after pain, he wished to be alone with his beloved, to cling to her arm with his numb fingers, to listen again to the subtle, unabating music of the world. . . .

All that day the streets of Jerusalem sent up a multiplicity of sounds. It was as if the preparations for some high event were being accomplished in the city: doors creaked on their hinges; a thousand hurrying feet passed over the paving stones; snatches of carnival music floated by; a host of horsemen rode across the glowing afternoon, drowning out the quieter sounds with the magnificence of clattering hoofs and clanking swords. Surely, he thought, all this blithe agitation is not to be heard on an ordinary day. . . . His curiosity grew keener with the hours. But since he had seen that it grieved Abishag to hear the thickness of his speech, he forced himself to wait until he was certain that he could form the words with some precision before he said to her: "What comes to pass? Is there a festival below?"

"It is the birthday of your son Adonijah," she said. "When I went down at noontide to fetch the broth for my beloved, I heard the steward of the house say to my lady Bath-sheba that the son of Haggith had gone to the holy stone of Zoheleth, which is near the high place, to slay oxen and fatlings for the delight of the Lord of Hosts. Joab the son of Zeruiah and Abiathar the priest have gone with him. They will make a feast after the sacrifice and eat of it, together with their comrades, in the eventide."

And raise the standard of revolt also, he thought. For why should he, the elder and the more valiant of the two, sit by and watch another take the crown? Tonight at sunset one will rise up at the board and shout, "God save Adonijah our King!" even as in Hebron long ago one lifted up his voice and cried aloud, "God save King Absalom!" . . .

"My lady Bath-sheba is burdened down this day with many anxieties," said the little Shunammite. "She is troubled for her lord, and for the kingdom, and for her son Solomon. She——"

"Listen," he said, lifting his heavy hand to his lips. "Listen, they are holding council below."

A confused babble of voices rose and subsided. Only two continued to speak—Solomon and the prophet Nathan were contending with each other.

625

"Let me go up to him with your mother," the prophet Nathan said. And the carefully modulated voice of Solomon replied: "As I have said these twenty times, it would be better for my mother to go up to him alone. Follow her later, if you will. But she will find far more favor in his sight if she breaks the matter to him privately at first, as from the heart."

"As from the heart," said the King of Israel. "Come, now, my little one, and make me comely if you can. Comb my hair and beard and set my crown upon my head, for my wife will come to me in a moment, to speak to me as from the heart."

And even as the maid out of Gilead ministered to him, smoothing his beard and draping his shoulders with an embroidered shawl, his door was opened and the beloved came and stood at the foot of his bed.

In spite of the wounding knowledge that she and her son and the prophet had been referring to him with the detached, undignified "he" in the common room, he found himself smiling wryly at her consummate self-control, her peerless queenliness. She was dressed in a white robe—a robe equally appropriate to a funeral or a coronation. He knew that if he served her as she hoped to be served, she would bind her waist with a scarlet girdle. Her eloquent hands were clasped between her breasts; her lips were parted; she had the air of a frightened young woman who at the first foreshadowing of danger runs to the arms of her lover. "My lord and my husband——" she said, panting, and she bowed over the bed so that her forehead touched his feet.

"Arise now and tell me whatsoever you require." His speech was blurred and uncertain. God forbid, he thought, that she should think me moved to tears. . . .

"My lord, you swore by Jahveh to your handmaid, saying, 'Assuredly your son Solomon shall reign in my place.' And now, behold, Adonijah reigns. He has slain oxen and fatlings and sheep in abundance, and has called up all his comrades and Abiathar and Joab also to feast with him, but he has not called Benaiah or Zadok or Nathan or your son Solomon. Before this day is spent, one will rise up at the board and salute the son of Haggith and call him King. Meanwhile the eyes of all Israel are upon David, waiting for him to make known whom he has chosen to sit after him on the throne. For unless he lifts up his voice within the hour, it will come to pass that I and my son Solomon will be hunted down as sinners when David is gone to sleep with his fathers. It will come to pass that even our lives——"

And now the prophet Nathan, breathless and staff in hand as though he had just come in from the street, crossed the threshold and bowed his head upon the coverlet. "My lord," said the prophet, "tell me, have you said, 'Adonijah shall reign after me and sit upon my throne'? For the son of Haggith has gone down this day, and slain oxen and fatlings and sheep in abundance, and has called all his fellows and the captains of the host and Abiathar the priest and the son of Zeruiah, and behold, they are eating

626

and drinking before him and saying, 'Long live Adonijah the King!' But me, even me your servant, they have not called to the feast. Neither have they called your servants Zadok and Benaiah, nor your son Solomon. Is this thing done by my lord the King? Has he indeed chosen his son Adonijah to sit after him on the throne?"

Suddenly he was too weary to find further amusement in the tawdry comedy. They shame me, he thought. They make a mockery of my dignity in the sight of the little Shunammite. Long since, Bath-sheba has whispered to the prophet Nathan that which I told her in confidence, and were my voice less thick in my throat, I would tell them that I know as much. . . .

"Let my lord the King only enlighten his servant——"

"Go now and leave me with Bath-sheba," David said.

The prophet flushed and stammered and withdrew, closing the door. The maid out of Gilead walked quietly to a far window and turned her back to the room. For the last time, the son of Jesse thought, I am left face to face with the beloved. . . . And he gazed steadily upon the white-clad, regal figure that stood at his feet. All that he might have said—words of reproach, words of reconciliation, words of tenderness—he left unsaid because he could not trust his heavy tongue. He bent forward and strove to tell her all things in such a glance as they had once exchanged over the fronds of the palm tree in the charged hush of the green eventide. Whether she saw or did not see, he could not tell—her eyes were vague spots of darkness; her face was a pale blur against the pale wall.

"I swear to you by Jahveh, the God of Israel, that Solomon your son will assuredly reign after me," he said. "I will accomplish the matter this day, so that my house and my kingdom may be at peace."

She bowed and did obeisance, with her brow against his knees. Through the folds of the coverlet, he felt her hands pressing upon him. He let his numb fingers fall upon her cheek, and found it wet with tears. "Would God that my lord the King might live forever!" she said. And she kissed his lips and went from him weeping aloud, as from the heart.

And now he did all things that were needful for the kingdom and for his house. He sent the little Shunammite to bring Zadok and Nathan and Benaiah to him. Though he was very tired, he did not spare himself; though he found it necessary to repeat his words many times because of his halting tongue, he gave them explicit directions concerning the crowning of Solomon. "Take the men of the guard and the Cherethites and the Pelethites," he said, "and form a procession at the gates of my house, and seat my son Solomon upon my own mule, and lead him to the high place with pipes and cymbals and antiphonal songs. And when the procession is come to the high place, then let Zadok the priest and Nathan the prophet take the holy oil from before the ark of God and anoint him King over Israel. Let Benaiah blow the trumpet and shout in a loud voice before the sons and daughters of Jerusalem, 'Long live King Solomon!' And when he is anointed and crowned with this crown which I give into your hands, then bring him back to the palace and seat him upon the throne. Go forth now and do these things without delay, for I have chosen him to reign in my stead, and I have made him a shepherd over Judah and Israel."

Now that the others were gone out from him, he called his little one back from the window and drew her down beside him on the bed. They sat comfortably together against the heaped pillows, holding each other's hands, watching the room grow mellow with the setting of the sun and listening to the ebb and flow of festal sounds. Far off, borne in on the wind from that part of the city where the stone of Zoheleth stood, they could hear voices raised in a drinking song. "They are making very merry at Adonijah's feast," she said. But that far, faint music was soon lost in the swelling tide of other sounds—the shouted commands of the captain of the guard, the measured tread of the Cherethites and the Pelethites, the voices of singing men and singing women, the clash of cymbals, the clatter of hoofs, the clanking of shields and swords. Then suddenly the whole city, every street and alley thereof, reverberated with the noise of running feet. "Listen!" he said, holding up his trembling hand. "Listen, the sons and daughters of Jerusalem are running forth from their houses to look upon the face of their new king."

He closed his eyes and waited while the tide of sound ebbed swiftly from him, moving in great waves toward the high place to break upon another man, another King in Israel. He heard the blast of the ram's-horn, the murmur of expectation, the thunder of ten thousand voices shouting "Long live King Solomon!" For the space of one heartbeat, it seemed to him that he must weep. Then he turned toward the little Shunammite and kissed her. "I am nothing," he said. "Let me look upon the Lord."

⇜§ IX §⇝

ALL THROUGH THE NIGHT he had kept an unwilling vigil. His sleep had been broken constantly by talk and laughter in the palace, by shouts and the glare of moving torches in the streets. He could not remember a time when he had been so wretched, and he said as much—often and in a scarcely distinguishable whisper—to the little Shunammite. Now he knew at last what the prophets meant when they spoke of the flesh as a burden. "My body," he said, "has become an intolerable heaviness." His tongue, his hand, his eyes, refused to obey him; to draw his breath was to call down upon himself wave after wave of disintegrating pain; and, however he turned against the pillows, he could find no relief.

He had comforted himself with the thought that some measure of peace would descend upon him when the carnival expired. But when the last torch was stifled and the last shouting voice was stilled, he was shaken into wakefulness by the wild knocking of his heart. Twice I have been delivered alive out of the seething dark, he had told himself, but the third time I will not rise again. . . . And, knowing that there was yet a lion to be taken from the midst of the fold, he had raised himself upon his bed and called in a loud voice after Solomon.

Truly it is a pity, he had thought, seeing the young man standing in his nightshirt at the foot of the bed, it is a great pity to rouse him up, to put a hard duty upon him while he is yet warm with the glow of his festival, while he yawns and rubs his eyes like a tired child. . . . Nevertheless, with the help of Abishag, he made his last testament, saying: "I am going the way of all the earth. Be strong therefore and show yourself a man and keep the charges of Jahveh your God, to walk in His ways and keep His statutes and His commandments and His ordinances and His testimonies, that you may prosper in all that you do and find blessedness wherever you turn yourself. . . . I have yet one duty to set upon you for the sake of the security of Israel. You know what Joab the son of Zeruiah did unto me, and unto the two captains of the host, Abner and Amasa, how he slew them, and shed the blood of war in peace, and put the blood of war upon his girdle that was about his loins, and in his shoes that were on his feet. Do therefore unto him according to your wisdom, and let not his hoar head go down to Sheol in peace. . . ."

And even when he had made an end of this and all lesser matters, when the new King of Israel had crossed the threshold and walked with conscious dignity into the dark hall, he found it necessary to strive against the buffeting tides, to hold them off yet a little longer; for his command concerning the captain of the host had distressed his little one, and he could not go forth unjustified in her sight. "See now," he said, clinging to her hand, "inasmuch as I am a King in Israel, I cannot follow the dictates of my own heart. Were I a herdsman in Bethlehem, I would call him to me and we would be reconciled. For is he not my kinsman and my companion, has he not served me with utter devotion since the hour when he first looked upon my face? But he who takes the flock in his hands cannot spare that which he loves if it runs ravening amongst the sheep. Not I, not David of Bethlehem, but he who is King over Israel and Judah, must rise up in the last hour to say, 'He is evil and will beget evil. Therefore he must die.'"

Thereafter he had been given no time to behold love and comprehension in her face, no time for seeking after the Lord. In sickness and in shuddering, in helplessness and wretchedness, he had consigned himself to the turmoil and the blackness and the pain, knowing well that it would be the last. . . .

But now—was he not blessed above every man in Israel?—now it was given to him to waken once more, and to waken in the charged and tremulous beginnings of the dawn. Beyond the window, beyond the dim, stirring fronds of the palm trees, the sky was arrayed in veil after veil of glimmering, expanding light. The birds lifted up their voices in shrill, exultant song; the sound of living waters rose from the spring in the garden; he turned his head slowly and heard the beating of her heart.

"Arise, my little one, my beloved," he said. "Come and sit at my feet, that I may see your face."

She came and sat between him and the pearly window. Her head drooped to one side, like a bloom that is too heavy for the stalk it rests upon; her features were scarcely discernible to his fainting sight, but he could still see the shining of her eyes. And mortal tenderness smote him yet once again, so that his heart made sweet, discordant music in him, like a stricken lute. "I have loved Abishag with all the love that was within me," he said.

"Even so I have loved my lord."

And now it seemed to him that if he suffered at all—suspended as he was on vibrant tides of music, borne up as he was on quivering veils of light—he suffered not from bodily pain, but from the intensity of his love. Ah, God, he thought in wonderment, I have loved so many of the sons and daughters of men, and so many have gone forth before me, that it cannot be a great matter to rise up and follow after. . . . And he gasped and raised himself upon his elbows, for they were with him in the room— all who had journeyed out before him, all the beloved dead.

"Have you forgiven the long exile and the unhallowed graves in the land of Moab?" he said aloud. They came toward him through the shining swaths of mist—his mother and his father, holding out their withered arms to him and saying, "Are you not the flower of our latter years? Are you not our little one, our blameless child?" And he lifted up his voice and asked absolution at the hands of the Lion of Benjamin, an aging warrior in a scarlet cloak, his leathery cheeks wet with tears and his feet stained with the wine of Jabesh-Gilead. And Saul said unto him, "Set your heart at peace concerning me, my son David. Are we not both outworn kings who have done what we could? Have we not both taken our hearts from our breasts and given them to the flock?" Then, from the midst of all the voices of life that sang through the strengthening dawn, a single voice rose clear and piercing above the others. "Is it the song of a bird?" he said. But he knew that it was an inward sound—sound of a single pipe, one high tone, wild and shatteringly sweet, lifted above the clanging as of a monstrous cymbal in his heart. And the mists parted, rent by the sound, and he beheld Jonathan. "Dearly beloved," Jonathan said, "arise and come to me. While we two were yet in the flesh, we yearned to touch and could not. But for those who put off the flesh, there are no interdictions against love." And Noi and Michal came also and beckoned him forth, and he loved them greatly, inasmuch as it was no longer required of him that he should love them after the manner of the flesh; and they took his hands and smiled upon him and were satisfied. And Achish came also, and Abner, and Amnon and Absalom—all of them came and laid hands upon him, yes, even that infant who had been the first fruit of the womb of the beloved. And as the rising sun broke like a hosanna of trumpets upon the room, all those whom he had loved—the dead and the living alike—became as incorporeal as light and were merged before his amazed eyes into One. And he said aloud, in wonderment, "Behold, they are not many, but only One Everlasting and Changeless Beloved. From the first hour when I reached out my hand to touch my mother's breast until now when I take my last leave of my little one, I have sought only after God. For to love, to yearn to lose oneself utterly in any mortal beloved, is to strive darkly, imperfectly, in spite of all the exigencies of the flesh and the world, to become a part of that Everlasting Being from whom we issued forth and unto whom we go at last. All these, the dead and the living, all these and I myself, were divided from the Eternal and the Changeless only for a little while. Behold, the sweet bond of mortal tenderness is loosed, the heaviness of the flesh drops from me, the world falls away, the hills and valleys are lost to me in veils of living light. A moment, only a moment, and I will be merged forever in the Lord with those whom I have loved. Why should I tarry? Into Your hands I render up my spirit, O my God."